THE REUNION

A JON SUMMERS NOVEL

★ JEFFREY THRALL ★

Design and distribution by Bublish, Inc.

ISBN: 9781647045852 (paperback)

DEDICATION

To my father Meade, my stepfather Roy, and my father-in-law George. All have been a great influence on me throughout my life. I dedicate this story to them, and to all who have served their country during times of war and hardship. Their actions have defined the terms sacrifice, honor, and courage.

ACKNOWLEDGMENTS

I would like to thank my wife Marilyn for her patience and help putting this project on paper. God bless her, she is a saint for putting up with me for forty-seven years. Thanks to my mother Ann, father-in-law George, daughter-in-law Tracy, son Michael, sister-in-law Kathy, niece Katie, Barb, and Michelle for all their help and input with editing.

A special thanks to my son, ET3 Jon Thrall of the U.S.S. Shreveport for his help in editing and research for the project. Thank you, your shipmates, and the marines you carry for all you sacrificed for us after September 11, 2001, on your tours to Afghanistan and Iraq. We owe you more than you will ever know.

CHARACTERS

Military

Captain Jonathon Summers: Naval Intelligence; Navy Reserves
Admiral W. C. Putnam: Naval Intelligence
Colonel George Ellison: Naval Intelligence
General Sam Michalowski: Retiring Chairman of the Joint Chiefs
Admiral Richard Kingston: Commander of the *Nimitz* battle group
Lieutenant Commander Stephen Williams: Kingston's senior aide
Lieutenant Andrea Handcock: Kingston's junior aide
Captain Judy Demmer: Michalowski's aide
Lieutenant Colonel Charles Naylor: 75th Rangers
General Ben Goodman: Incoming Chairman of the Joint Chiefs
Admiral John Cummings: Chief of Naval Operations
Commander Robert Grant – Captain of *USS Kamehameha*
Lieutenant Commander Tim DeCook – SEAL Team 5
Allen Wiedenkeller: Senior Chief, SEAL Team 5
Captain Tom Brothers: Captain of the *USS Nimitz*
Sergeant George Reardon: 75th Rangers
Captain Tiffany Rice: Marine officer in charge of security on *Nimitz*

Law Enforcement

Jaime Franco: Captain of Police, Davao, Philippines
Sergeant Ron Hapke: Lakeview Police Department
Glenn Grey: Senior FBI Agent
Mark Wells: Senior NCIS Agent

Washington

Norman Jeffers: Secretary of Defense

Other Characters

Nancy Summers: Jon Summers's wife
Sean Summers: Summers's oldest son
Justin Summers: Summers's middle son
Stephen Summers: Summers's youngest son
Ray Summers: World War II vet and patriarch of the Summers Family
Louise Summers: Ray's wife
Julie Romero-Summers: Jon's sister
Howard Quinn: Nancy Summers's father
Emily Quinn: Nancy Summers's mother
Bill Gateway: Longtime friend of the Summers's family
Becky O'Keefe: Gateway's daughter
Sarah O'Keefe: Becky's daughter
Kevin Gateway: Gateway's son
Josh Ericson: Retired SEAL and restaurant owner
General Roberto Mangoba: Philippine Army Intelligence
Captain Jorge Sanchez: Mangoba's aide
Sam Donavon: Veteran
Don Smith: Veteran
Catherine Smith: Don's wife
Sandy Monroe: News reporter
Shinpachi Osaka: Businessman/terrorist
Emil Montoya: Moro separatist
Patrick O'Keefe: Terrorist
Suzanne Rolle: Terrorist
Toshio Akiyama: Businessman/terrorist
Gerald Wilson: Mercenary
Hans Boerst: Mercenary
James Holiday: Mercenary
Benny Montoya: Moro separatist/terrorist

WORLD WAR II

Zamboanga Peninsula
Mindanao, Philippines
August 15, 1945
0530 Hours

The temperature was into the seventies and the humidity was close to unbearable even though the sun just started over the horizon. It was unusually peaceful this morning and the only things moving were the birds starting to feed along the beach. The palms rustled in the slight breeze coming off the ocean, offering no relief from what promised to be another sweltering day in the jungles of the Philippines. Just beyond the tree line, in the first of a series of palm groves, the rows of green tents began.

The encampment nearest the beach belonged to company A, first battalion, 162nd Regimental Combat Team, 41st Infantry Division, United States Army. They landed on a beach the previous March, not far from where most of them now slept. First Lieutenant Raymond Summers, freshly relieved from his duties as officer of the day, made his way back through the small green city of tents. He headed towards the beach and the last group of tents in a double row. His home away from home. He walked to the last tent overlooking the beach. The flaps were all open and inside you could see two cots. One cot contained a sleeping soldier, the other was empty. Summers quietly entered the tent, walking over to the empty cot. Next to the cot was a makeshift field desk containing pens, pencils, paper, and other items used by both the tent's occupants. He took off his WEB belt removing his Colt 1911 from the holster. He put it in the waistband of his pants near the small of his back. He threw the WEB belt on the cot. He stripped off his uniform shirt and threw it on the cot next to the belt. He opened a footlocker and pulled out a clean tee shirt. He fumbled through some items on the top of the desk until he found a pencil and a large pad containing drawings. He left the tent as quietly as he entered.

He walked down onto the beach, stopping when he reached several large palm trees. He looked out onto the ocean. The sun rising on the horizon made a sparkling trail across the water and up onto the beach. He took a deep breath of salt air, stretching as he looked up and down the beach. He was the only one out besides the feeding birds. He sat down, leaning against one of the trees, making himself comfortable. Once he was settled, he opened the notebook to the first empty page and began to draw. He drew quickly and effortlessly, outlining the shading as he went. He would look up occasionally, covering his eyes from the glare off the water. The gulls and other sea birds danced up and down the beach, paying no attention to him while he drew. The lapping of the waves on the shore and the noise of the birds would normally have covered the sound of anyone approaching, but these were tenuous times. Even the birds scattered when the stick snapped in the sand.

Summers immediately dropped his pad and pencil and rolled to his left. With his right hand, he reached behind his back and pulled the pistol from his waistband. He came out of his roll, bringing the weapon up aiming at the movement and potential target in front of him.

"Jesus H. Christ, Summers!!" gasped Captain Bill Gateway tripping himself trying to stop. He was Summers's tent mate and commanding officer. After catching his breath, he continued, "You're crazy, you know that? You could have killed me with that thing. Never point a loaded weapon at your own men, you asshole!"

Gateway fell into the sand next to Summers. Summers looked at his friend laughing.

"Bill, you know better than to sneak up on someone while you're in a war zone. I may be an asshole, but at least I'll be alive."

Ray lowered the pistol and placed it back in his waistband. He picked up his pencil and paper and sat down next to his friend, starting to sketch again.

"You must have a short memory, Captain," he said quietly, glancing at the man.

Gateway, still half asleep and in shock, looked puzzled. "What are you talking about?"

"They're still pulling Japs out of caves just a few miles up the coast and small units are surrendering every day."

Gateway was still visibly shaken. "You could have killed me you asshole! You're nuts! Do you know that? You're nuts! We're in a secure rear area. Why are you carrying that thing like we're at the front?"

Ray smiled at his friend. "You're just upset because you got caught. Come on, Bill. You didn't get shot."

"Christ, Ray, you scared the shit out of me!"

Gateway knew that his senior platoon leader was correct. Even though they were in a *secure area* there had been Japanese soldiers still surrendering while they crawled out of their hiding places all over the Philippines. There was trouble with the local black market stealing from American installations as well. In several cases, American service men were hurt trying to stop the thefts.

"Damn," said Gateway, "how'd you get so fast with that thing?"

Summers continued to draw. "It's called staying alive, boss. You've done your share of that. As I recall, you've got a bunch of medals that say you're good at that."

"Yeah, Ray, but I'm not that fast, my friend. You have a talent of staying one step ahead of the bad guys. You've proved that better than any other officer in the battalion. You should think about staying in the army when the war is over, which, with any luck, will be soon."

Summers smiled at his friend. "Unlike you, my friend, I plan to get away from this madness, finish college, get married, and raise a family."

"Ray, you're one hell of a soldier. Why would you give up all this adventure to go back to the states and teach a bunch of kids who will never understand or care what we did here? You'll be throwing away a bright career. Men want to follow you. They'll go wherever you want them to and will do whatever you tell them to do. It's a gift most of us in this profession would kill for."

"Bill," Summer's voice turned serious, "you may think this line of work is adventurous, but I don't. It becomes too easy to kill and after a while, you forget who the enemy is. Teaching kids how to live seems a lot more adventurous than leading them to their death. It's a whole lot more positive anyway. I think I can pass on a career with the army."

Gateway shook his head. "I still think you're making the biggest mistake of your life. Even if you stay in the reserves after the war, you'll do well. Take your time and at least think about it. You'll have plenty of time to decide before they let you out. What are you drawing now?"

Summers was famous in the battalion for his sketches. He kept a collection of all his drawings in notebooks like the one he was currently using. He managed to keep a pictorial record of his entire time overseas from when he had first joined the division in New Guinea. He sketched each soldier he served with and captured every major incident that occurred since his arrival with A company. Every detail showed in the drawing from the reflections off the waves, to the feeding birds on the beach. Gateway could imagine the colors that would go with the real thing. It made him feel so peaceful, he almost forgot why they were there.

Gateway grinned as he looked at his friend.

"So, Ray, you going to teach art when you get back to the world? You have a real talent for it."

Summers gave Gateway an irritated look. Gateway knew Summers was planning on teaching history and considered his art to be a hobby. Summers finally smiled, standing up, and shaking his head.

"You know, boss," Summers laughed, "if I didn't know better, I'd say the army is paying you to give me grief. Well, you'll have to follow me to the tent and wake me up to continue this abuse. I'm bushed."

Gateway stood and both started walking back towards the tent. Gateway put his arm around his friend's shoulder.

"You're right, buddy," Gateway said, "Old Uncle Sam is paying me a whole bunch extra to keep you in this man's army. Sleep deprivation is supposed to be part of the treatment, but after seeing how you handle a firearm in your current state, I think I'll let you sleep. I'll even go so far as to promise not to wake you unless the war ends, or MacArthur comes to visit."

Both men walked back to the tent laughing, disappearing into their tent while the rest of the camp started to stir. All around the encampment, the birds continued to play, and the waves lapped up onto the beach. All was quiet and peaceful. Too bad neither man knew what was going to take place that day. It would change the future of both men and their families for years to come.

CHAPTER 1

THE GOOD LIFE

The rented Buick pulled into the long driveway leading to the large two-story house. The driveway went up a slight incline where it split. One direction took you up the side of the house and a large four-car garage. The other way took you around passed the front door and then circling back to the gate. The driver, an older man, pulled the car up by the front door. He turned the car off and got out. He was about five feet, nine inches tall with a medium build. He was fit for his age and alert blue eyes flashed along with a beaming smile. He was bald with trimmed gray hair around the sides. He covered this with a baseball cap turning to look at his wife while she got out the passenger side.

"Ray," said Louise Summers, "you can be so thoughtless at times. How do you expect anyone to get past you parked like this?"

Ray looked at his wife, smiling, "I don't think Bill will mind and I can always come out and move it."

Louise shook her head in disgust. Ray met Louise Andrews in the winter of 1950, while teaching in the Rochester City School District. She came to his school to pick up some work for a neighbor. He was immediately taken with her assertive manner and straightforward way of dealing with people. Ray's reputation of being the most eligible bachelor in the district changed after meeting Louise. He spent most of his time asking her out and being rejected. Being an optimist, the more she rejected him, the harder he tried. He mailed her cards, sent flowers and candy, and even started banking at the bank where she worked as a teller. He finally discovered from one of her friends she thought him too old because of the eleven years difference in their ages. Ever persistent, he changed his tact and eventually won her over. They were married in June of 1951 and immediately set up housekeeping in his modest apartment. Ray was surprised to find her father was the president of his new bank and how quickly her family accepted him. She didn't change much in all the years they were together. She was still strong willed, which meant they disagreed on most things, except that they were in love with one another. Her red hair was now silver and there were a few wrinkles in her face, but they were still far and few between. He loved every minute of their time together.

Louise walked over to join her husband. She was giving him her best *you behave yourself* look.

"Now, don't get carried away with Bill talking about the war and…"

The front door opened and General William Gateway, United States Army, retired came running out to meet them. He threw his arms around Louise, giving her a big hug and kiss. He then gave Ray a big hug, "Damn, it's good to see you guys. Welcome to L.A."

Gateway walked them towards the front door continuing to talk, "So, when did you get into town?"

"Just now," said Ray, "from San Diego. We flew in there the day before yesterday."

"What's in San Diego?" asked Gateway.

"Jonny was finishing up his two weeks summer camp for the reserves. We were able to spend some time with him before he flew out this morning," said Louise.

"It's good to hear Jon stayed in after all these years and the garbage he's put up with," said Bill holding the door for his guests. "What is he now, a lieutenant commander?"

"No," replied Ray, "he's a full commander. We had a chance to talk to his commanding officer. He put Jon in for promotion to captain and said it looks good. Jon will probably leave once that takes place though. He's tired of the politics of it all. Since he left the navy and went into the reserves, they've really made it miserable for him."

"True," answered Gateway, "but Jon intimidates the living daylights out of them. Ever since he won the medal in Nam, most regular navy guys squirm the minute he walks into the room. He doesn't have to do or say anything, he…"

"I just love your house!" said Louise changing the subject. They weren't even past the foyer and the two of them were already talking about the military.

She was also happy to change the subject because her oldest son was the topic. She, like most mothers, was very protective of her children and they could continue this discussion when she wasn't around to hear it.

"Sorry, Louise," said her husband, "we should have waited until we had you settled at the pool. Louise gets a little sensitive regarding this subject, Bill. Jon's a big boy and deals with his own problems, but women have to worry."

"Sorry, Louise," echoed Bill, "When Mary was alive, she was the same when it came to Becky."

Louise ignored the two of them as she stepped into the foyer, "Ray says you've done some remodeling. What did you change?"

The two men looked at each other not replying to Louise's question.

Louise smiled asking, "Is the bathroom still in the same place or have you moved that?"

"No, it's in the same place, down the hall and to the left."

Louise did an about face and walked towards the bathroom. As she did, she passed a very pleasant looking Hispanic woman who nodded. She approached Gateway, smiling, and held out her hand to Ray.

"Mr. Summers, my name is Angelique, and I'm the housekeeper for General Gateway and his daughter. Rebecca asked me to make sure that you and Mrs. Summers got anything that you needed after your long trip."

"Angie," Gateway tried to sound hurt, "these are my guests, not Becky's. I think I'm old enough to take care of them. You and Becky don't have to butt in…"

Angie was a short woman in her late thirties with a slender build and jet-black hair. Her dark brown eyes flashed in amusement while she and the general began to fence.

"Old enough," she said, "to know better. I could hear you ranting about soldiers and war all the way in the kitchen. Mr. Summers, I must apologize for the general's manners. He hasn't even asked if you wished to have something to eat or drink before he drags you off to talk."

She smiled at Gateway as if to say, *your turn.*

Gateway could do nothing but laugh.

"Ray, this young lady is our housekeeper, cook, maid, and babysitter. Call her Angie, but don't get too friendly because she's meaner than old Sergeant Major Cappon ever dreamed of being."

Ray smiled as he shook Angie's hand.

"Very pleased to meet you, Angie, and please call me Ray. If you call me Mr. Summers, I'll keep looking over my shoulder for my father, God bless him."

Angie laughed. "Okay, but only if you don't believe the part about me being mean."

"Oh, don't worry about that," whispered Ray loud enough for all of them to hear. "Bill's always been jealous because Sergeant Major Cappon and I got along."

They both laughed, Gateway put on his best pout.

"Looks like you're already out numbered, Bill," said Louise reentering the room.

"Hi, Angie, I'm Louise Summers," she said as she walked over and took Angie's hand, "I've heard so much about you from Bill's letters."

The two women smiled at each other as they shook hands.

"I've heard so much about you, too," replied Angie giving the older woman a polite hug. "I'm happy to finally meet the two of you. Can I get you anything?"

Louise shook her head. "Not for me, but why don't you and I go get some iced tea for these two old warriors and get to know one another."

"Loui…" started Bill before he was cut off.

"Don't even think of trying to dictate to me, Bill Gateway!" interrupted Louise winking at Angie, "If you and Ray want to talk about the good old days when people were trying to shoot you both, that's up to you. But Angie and I will not be subjected to that. You never know, we might try to shoot you ourselves."

Both women smiled, turning towards the hallway. The men chuckled.

"You might try, Louise. You might try," said Bill smiling in rebuttal.

Louise looked over her shoulder.

"Try! Ask Ray about the last time we went to the state fair."

Gateway gave Ray a puzzled look. Ray shrugged.

"General, Sir, I got my clock cleaned. All these years of marriage and I never knew her father taught her to shoot."

They both laughed, Gateway motioning for them to sit.

"Damn, it's good to see you buddy. Let's talk about this reunion I wrote you about."

Mindanao, Philippines
August 16, 1994
0230 Hours

The old Chevrolet moved quickly along the paved highway out of Davao. Inside were four men. No one spoke as the youngest, only eighteen years old, expertly drove the vehicle through the many curves they encountered. They had the road to themselves at this hour, so he was driving faster than he normally would. The man sitting next to him was staring straight ahead and didn't seem to be bothered by the speed. The two men in back weren't as calm about their colleagues driving but said nothing. When they approached a crossroads, the man in the front passenger seat motioned for the driver to turn right. The driver slowed slightly, then turned sharply onto the dirt road. Because of the road conditions, the driver was forced to slow down to a more comfortable pace for his back seat passengers.

After driving about five miles, the driver again turned right and almost immediately came to a closed gate. Next to the gate was a small building. As the old Chevy pulled up to the gate, several high intensity floodlights came on, illuminating the entire area. Before any of the men could get their eyes focused, armed men surrounded the car. The first thing they noticed was none were Filipino. All appeared to be Caucasian and were armed with assault rifles. One of the men approached the driver's door motioning for him to roll down his window.

The driver complied saying to the sentry in Filipino, "Mr. Montoya is here for his appointment with Mr. Osaka."

The sentry looked at all four men in the Chevy before replying in English, "Mr. Osaka is expecting you, gentlemen. I'm sorry, but we will have to search all of you and the car before you enter the compound.

The man's voice was polite and even. The men in the car didn't hesitate to comply with the directions that followed. They were asked to get out of the vehicle and were led towards the building stopping just short of the door. Five more men carrying rifles joined them, three of these appeared to be Filipino. Each man was quickly, but thoroughly, searched for weapons. While this was being done several of the guards were searching the car for weapons and explosives. When the search was completed, they were allowed to get back in the Chevy.

The guard spoke again. "I apologize for the inconvenience, gentlemen, but this is procedure for anyone entering the compound. Thank you for your cooperation."

The man in the front passenger's seat was impressed with how they were treated. These men were obviously professionals. There was no doubt in his mind if any of them resisted in any way they all would disappear very quickly and quietly. The gate was now open, so the driver was motioned through.

The car moved slowly through the gate, never going over twenty miles per hour the remainder of the trip. The road curved back and forth through the heavy jungle. It was well maintained with a large shoulder on either side. After five minutes, the car came around a corner and the jungle disappeared. They could see an open field in the moonlight ahead of them and beyond that was a large, well-lit house. The driver was able to speed up moving into the clearing. The house maintained a well-lighted perimeter standing in the middle of the field. It was a huge two-story structure with an outside covered porch all the way around both levels. There were large picture windows allowing quick glimpses of well-furnished rooms. The car pulled up in front of the main entrance of the house. There were wide stairways leading to the second-floor porch located on either side of the main door.

The car came to a stop and was met by three men. Two of the men carried rifles, like the men at the main gate. The third man was unarmed and came down the steps to meet the Chevy. While the men in the car stepped out, the third man, an Oriental, stepped forward, bowed slightly addressing the man from the front passenger seat in perfect English.

"Mr. Montoya. Mr. Osaka is expecting you, sir. Would you and your associates please follow me?"

Emil Montoya looked around at his surroundings before complying. He thought he knew the island well having lived here all his thirty years. In all that time, he had no idea this plantation existed. He could make out several other buildings nearby, guessing them to be for storage, housing the men he saw, or even generating all the power being used. He heard no generators but knew they were there because there was no electric power this far away from any of the large cities. Montoya turned and followed the man up the steps to the porch and inside the house. His three companions were right behind him.

Inside the house they were ushered through a huge entrance hall and into a large meeting room. There was a long oval shaped table with twenty heavily padded chairs around it. Beyond that there were several sofas near a large, screened television. The television was turned on to CNN International and a story was running regarding rioting on the east bank. Three men, whom had been watching the piece, stood the minute the visitors walked into the room. A slender Japanese man in his early fifties hit the mute button on the remote but didn't turn off the television. He walked forward stopping in front of the table. The two men with him, both Caucasians, stood exactly one step behind him.

The man who met the car spoke, "Mr. Emil Montoya, I would like to present Mr. Shinpachi Osaka of Tokyo."

The man bowed and took a step back. Montoya thought it to be one of the most graceful movements he had ever seen.

"Welcome to my home, Mr. Montoya," said Osaka. "I hope your visit will prove to be profitable."

Montoya knew little about Osaka except he was very wealthy and liked to support groups promoting the overthrow of the current government. Montoya suspected this support came at a high price, but he was willing to listen.

"I would like to introduce you to my associates. Mr. Ishimoto, you have already met." He motioned to the man who met the car, who again bowed. "He is one of my closest and most trusted advisors. This tall gentleman is Captain Gerald Wilson, my pilot and communications liaison."

A tall man stepped forward and shook Montoya's hand saying hello with a deep southern drawl. The man was an American and the handshake was firm. He was big, but not fat or overly muscular. He towered over Montoya and his three companions.

"And this is Patrick O'Keefe, my Head of Security."

A good-looking man with long wavy blond hair stepped forward taking Montoya's hand in a firm and energetic handshake. He smiled a big toothy smile and said in a heavy Irish accent, "Hi there. How are you today, gentlemen?"

Montoya, not sure what to do, bowed slightly saying, "It is an honor to meet you all. I don't wish to sound rude, Mr. Osaka, but this is an odd time for a meeting. Most of us would normally be sleeping."

Osaka smiled. "But it's a safe time to meet. The business proposition I have for you will be beneficial to your cause, but only if it's kept secret. I find this time of day to be very advantageous to keeping secrets. Gentlemen, please have a seat so we can talk."

Osaka motioned towards the table. Montoya nodded to his associates, and they all took the seats closest to them. Montoya sat next to the young driver and the two men who had been passengers in the back of the car sat to his left. Osaka sat at the far end of the table with his lieutenants sitting on either side of him. Ishimoto stood directly behind him. Osaka was dressed in a business suit, which Montoya guessed to be Japanese formality. The room was air conditioned, so he didn't appear uncomfortable.

Osaka smiled at his guests. "May I offer you some tea or other refreshment?"

"No, thank you," responded Montoya. "We would like to hear this business proposition you spoke of and get back home. My associates wish to remain anonymous currently because of security reasons. I hope this won't offend you, but it's a necessity we've come to live with."

"I quite understand," said Osaka, "but unnecessary here. The young man who drove you here is your nephew, Benjamin, or Benny, as he likes to be called."

All four of his guests stiffened uncomfortably.

"The gentleman to your immediate left is Raul Argento who is here representing your biggest financial backer, the Moro National Liberation Front. His brother is one of the leaders of that organization. The Manila government suspects he's involved with that organization also but hasn't been able to link him officially. The man next to him is Ernesto Eduardo, a bookkeeper for Mr. Argento."

There was silence as the four Filipinos looked at each other with both alarm and amazement. Osaka smiled at their uneasiness.

"Don't be alarmed gentlemen," he said. "If nothing else, this shows you how efficient my organization can be."

Argento spoke, his voice showing impatience. "What's this business? Let's get it over with so we can move on!"

Osaka looked at Argento passively and spoke in a quiet, even tone. "I would like to propose a quiet merger of your organization and mine. I am very sympathetic with your goals and would like to help you achieve them. You are always struggling with the Manila government politically and are out gunned and poorly trained."

Montoya was the only one of the four men who was listening to what was said. He noticed Argento still seemed irritated with the fact their security was compromised, and the bookkeeper was simply scared. The young driver was bored and would do what he was told.

"I am willing to finance training for your freedom fighters and provide your organization with arms superior to that of the current government. You see how well my organization works. I am willing to make it available to you for intelligence purposes, as well as tactical support. To win your freedom you must be daring, well equipped, and well-motivated. Mr. Montoya, that's why I contacted you. Your organization is small, but you are the most aggressive of the separatist groups. With this merger, I feel we can benefit all concerned and have a profound effect on the negotiations currently underway between Manila and the MNLF."

There was a moment of silence while Montoya looked at his host. He was intrigued by the proposal, while the others' attitudes hadn't changed.

"You mentioned tactical and intelligence support," asked Montoya cautiously. "Are you saying you would pick targets, or you would allow us to pick targets?"

"My people may make recommendations, but the final decision on what you call targets would be up to you. If you pick a target, we will help gather intelligence and help to plan your mission. If specialized weapons or equipment would be needed, we would provide it."

"Give me an example of a target you would recommend."

Osaka was silent for a second watching the four men in front of him. He nodded to O'Keefe.

O'Keefe leaned forward. "Next year is the fiftieth anniversary of the end of World War II. There are plans to have reunions here in the Philippines of units on both sides of that war. If hostages were to be taken and the current government embarrassed so concessions can be made with the negotiations, th…"

"No!" shouted Argento. "We are not terrorists. We are freedom fighters. This type of operation would hurt our cause and we will not be part of it."

O'Keefe glared at the man. "Mr. Argento, I'm just giving you an example of the type of operation you could do if you accept our offer of support. I…"

Argento cut O'Keefe off with a wave of his hand looking at Osaka, speaking with a raised voice. "And what do we have to give you in return for this support you want to give us?"

Osaka leaned forward speaking quietly. "My hope is to help you not only reach your goal politically, but to help your people economically as well. My organization represents many industries in an excellent position to invest in your country and your people with money and jobs. All you have to do is listen to the rest of our proposal and let your conscience decide what's best for your cause."

Argento rose to his feet shaking with anger. "You couldn't conquer us by force fifty years ago and won't do it now economically. I won't sit here and be part of this."

"I wish to hear the full proposal before I make that judgement for myself, Raul," said Montoya.

"Emil, think carefully about what you say and do here. You come back with me, or your little band will lose all support of the MNLF."

Montoya stood facing the other Filipino. "My friend, all I want to do is listen to the full offer and then make the decision together. I don't think that's too unreasonable."

Argento stared at his colleague. "You don't want to take this path. If you do, you're not my friend, or that of the MNLF. Are you coming with me or not?"

Montoya stared back at Argento.

"You're not my superior and this isn't your decision to make. I'll listen to the proposition and then decide what's best for my people and those they represent. If you can't accept that, then we don't need the support of the MNLF."

Montoya turned, sitting back down in his seat. Argento looked at Eduardo and motioned for him to get up. He immediately responded. He then looked at Benny and repeated the motion. The young man refused to comply saying, "I'll stay with Uncle Emil."

"We'll deal with you both," threatened Argento. "You can make your own way back; we're taking the car!"

"Gentlemen," smiled Osaka, "I will arrange for Mr. Montoya and his nephew to get back after we're done. Feel free to leave or stay, it's your decision to make. I humbly apologize for having wasted your time."

Osaka bowed slightly as he bid Argento and Eduardo farewell. He glanced at Ishimoto and smiled as he bowed again. Ishimoto led the two men out, followed by O'Keefe. Osaka continued, "I apologize to you for causing this problem between you and your associates. This was not my intention. I only wanted to help a cause I'm sympathetic to."

"I must apologize for the rudeness of my countrymen," Montoya interrupted. "I'm ashamed they brought up history long forgotten. Please don't feel all Filipinos are like him."

"Of course not, my friend," smiled Osaka. "Let me explain my proposal to you in more detail."

As Osaka and Montoya continued their meeting uninterrupted, Argento and Eduardo followed Ishimoto out to the waiting car. Ishimoto walked to the car, opening the front passenger door for Argento, who started to move past him. As he did Ishimoto quickly and quietly reached out, grabbed Argento by the chin and back of his head, twisting the head in one smooth motion, breaking his neck, killing him instantly. Eduardo watched this in horror, but before he could scream, O'Keefe struck him in the throat, crushing his windpipe. He fell to the ground with a slight gurgling sound and a few gasps for air. Several men ran up, looking to O'Keefe who told them to load the two bodies into the back of the car. He then got into the driver's seat.

Ishimoto looked at O'Keefe, who was smiling. "You enjoy this don't you?"

"They were a threat and needed to die. Besides, I didn't like them."

Ishimoto shook his head. "It's to be an accident?"

O'Keefe nodded. The car started and drove off towards the gate. Inside Osaka was pouring tea into a ceremonial cup to celebrate his new partnership.

Beverly Hills, California
August 15, 1994
1530 Hours

The red Mercedes convertible pulled into the Gateway driveway and slowed as it came up the incline. The driver looked at the Buick sitting near the front door of the house. She then continued to the garage. Stopping in front of the first garage door, she exited the Mercedes, and stretched. It was the end of a long day for Dr. Rebecca O'Keefe, and she was ready to take a relaxing swim in the pool. She looked at her watch. The Summers's made good time this morning and would be spending the night. She needed to get a quick swim in and then help Angie in the kitchen. She hadn't seen Ray and Louise Summers in sixteen years and didn't remember much about them except they were nice to her and her brother at a time when she needed an adult who was sympathetic.

Rebecca, or Becky as she preferred to be called, reached into the car, and pulled out her bag. She guessed they would be at the pool. She walked through the gate of the high stockade fence and headed around the garage towards the pool. Dr. Rebecca O'Keefe, MD was a well-respected general practitioner who maintained an office in downtown Los Angeles. She spent a great deal of her time working in the emergency room of St. Margaret Mary's Hospital treating people in their street clinic. Her reputation was that of an honest and tough lady. As a professional, she was always calm, quiet, detached, and in control.

Becky O'Keefe, the person, was completely different. She was always a forceful person, as well as a bit of a rebel. With her father a professional soldier and very much a part of the *establishment,* she actively protested the war in Vietnam. Her sympathies were with the counterculture of the time, putting her at odds with the rest of the family. She married Patrick O'Keefe, an Irish national, because her father didn't like him. She found him exciting to be around and enjoyed being the rebel of the family, taking his side against her father. O'Keefe was in the country raising money from Irish Americans to support the IRA in their fight against the British. Becky would argue with her parents that Patty was continuing what the American's started two hundred years before. Her father argued that he was nothing more than a cruel and violent thug who was using her to make himself look respectable. The day she told Patrick she was pregnant with their child he proved her father right. O'Keefe became so enraged that he beat her within an inch of her life. He broke her jaw, nose, shoulder, right arm, and several ribs. She suffered from a severe concussion and her face was bruised and swollen for days. She spent almost two weeks in the hospital and was fortunate not to lose the baby. O'Keefe was arrested for assault and spent several days in jail before being bailed out by friends. He never showed for his trial.

Her daughter Sarah was born healthy and normal, Becky's life changed forever. She continued to be outspoken and a bit of a rebel. She finished college and medical school. She volunteered for any program where she would be in contact with the poor, especially women abused by their husbands.

Becky came around the back of the garage finding no one at the pool. She walked towards the back door and could hear people laughing. She opened the door to the kitchen and was struck by a blast of cool air from the air conditioning. The laughter was much louder, and Becky could tell that it was all female. She entered the kitchen to find Angie, her daughter Sarah, Angie's daughter Crystal, and Louise Summers.

Louise looked to be in her fifties when Becky knew her to be at least ten years older. Her short silver hair came down around her face and she sported a slender build. Her light complexion complemented her hair, and her smile was the friendliest of anyone Becky knew. Becky put her bag down on a chair by the door and walked around the table giving Louise a hug.

"It's so good to see you after all these years," she said. "You look well."

Becky was at a loss for words. She felt the emotion starting to well up inside her. Tears started to form around her eyes and Louise reached out and lightly brushed them away.

"I'm afraid we were having a laugh at your expense," Louise said. "I was telling everyone how you and Jonny used to fight when the families got together. How are you, dear?"

Louise held Becky by both shoulders looking at her. Becky was dressed in a comfortable pantsuit and white blouse. Her dark brown hair was cut close to her head and shoulders and accented her eyes. She was slender and trim at forty-three years old. Both women were about the same height and build and embraced each other for a few moments.

"Louise, I never did get a chance to thank you for all you did to help Mom when I was in the hospital," said Becky. "I feel foolish thanking you after all these years."

"Nonsense, child, that's what friendship's all about. Mary was there more than once for me. Besides," Louise looked at Sarah, "that trip to the hospital was worth it."

Sarah blushed.

"Yeah, it was," replied Becky looking at her daughter. "It sure was worth it."

Angie smiled at her friend. "We knew you lived a colorful life, but you never said you had such interesting friends."

Becky looked at her friend nervously. "What do you mean?"

"Louise was telling us what a brat you were when you were a kid," said Sarah.

"I was that" Becky breathed a sigh of relief. "I would regularly beat Jon up and had a crush on Matt and used to torment Julie."

"Matt?" asked Angie, Sarah, and Crystal all in unison.

Louise laughed as she answered the question. "Matt is my middle child. He's the one that inherited his father's good looks and way with women. A real heart breaker."

"Sure was," interrupted Becky. "I was four years older and out of high school and was crushed when he wouldn't have anything to do with me. Julie is the youngest Summers and as pretty as her mother."

"Far prettier," said Louise modestly.

"And Jon," asked Becky, "is he still being beaten up?"

"You were the only one who ever got away with that," replied Louise.

There was a moment of silence as the two women looked at each other and smiled.

"It really is good to have you here, Louise," said Becky.

"Your mother would be proud," was Louise's only reply.

Pentagon
Washington, D.C.
August 15, 1994
2130 Hours

Commander Jonathan Summers walked up to the security checkpoint, surrendering the briefcase he was carrying to the MP on duty. He was wearing his white, short sleeve uniform and was looking sharp for the upcoming meeting. He carried his hat under his left arm and the rows of campaign ribbons above his breast pocket were evident to the soldiers at the checkpoint. The most senior man at the checkpoint was a young sergeant who asked for the officer's identification card. As he took it, he glanced at the neat rows of decorations. There were quite a few ribbons and badges indicating this officer was no armchair commander. He was drawn to the Naval Special Warfare Trident and blue and white ribbon on top of the other ribbons. The sergeant looked at the ID card and handed it back to the officer. He then checked a clipboard sitting on the table next to him, finding the officer's name at the bottom.

"Thank you for being patient, Commander," the sergeant said handing back the briefcase. "You're the last appointment for the Joint Chiefs tonight, Sir, and they're running late. Do you know the way, or would you like an escort?"

Summers smiled. "No, thank you, Sergeant. I'm all set."

"Very well, Sir," the sergeant saluted smartly.

Jon returned the salute and started to walk past the checkpoint but stopped abruptly. "I'm sorry, Sergeant, but do they have any snack machines down here?"

"Sir?" the army sergeant gave the officer a puzzled look.

"I haven't eaten since breakfast. Are there any snack machines down here?"

"Sorry, Sir, nothing at all," the sergeant looked genuinely disappointed.

"Why is it that generals and admirals never think of common folk needing to eat? Oh well. Thanks anyway, Sarge."

The sergeant smiled watching the officer walk down the hall. He picked up the telephone on the desk and punched in a number.

Jon walked past several dark offices with closed doors. Most of the offices in this area of the building closed at five o'clock. He turned another corner and came to a large door with two marine guards behind a desk. Both looked too young to be responsible for such a sensitive area.

"Commander Summers," said the marine closest to Jon, "the Chiefs are running late this evening and will be with you in a few minutes."

Jon showed the first marine his identification card while the second marine made another quick check of his briefcase. The inspection was no where near as thorough as the one done by the army, or they knew he hadn't had time to secretly find any weapons to hide in the case. He knew the latter was true because of the video surveillance throughout the building. Jon took back his identification and the briefcase. He moved through the door when one of the marines pushed a button that released the catch. Inside was a large waiting room with several desks, some couches, chairs, and tables. All the desks were empty but one. A young, female air force lieutenant sitting behind the desk was smiling as he entered. She got out of her chair and walked around the desk to meet him.

"Commander Summers, I'm Lieutenant Demmer. I'm one of General Michalowski's aides."

Jon returned the smile. "It's a pleasure to meet you, Lieutenant."

"I'm terribly sorry the Chiefs are running late. I'm afraid you'll miss your flight home this evening. I've taken the liberty of rebooking your flights for the morning and planning for a hotel room for you, Sir. I apologize for the delay, but it's unavoidable and necessary the Chiefs see you tonight."

"May I make a call, Lieutenant? My wife was going to pick me up. I'd like to warn her off if I could."

Demmer smiled. "Certainly, sir. You can use the phone over there."

Demmer returned to her desk. Jon picked up the telephone, dialing his home phone number. The telephone rang twice before someone answered.

"Hello?" said the voice of his sixteen-year-old son, Sean.

"Hi, Sean, it's Dad."

"Dad, where are you? Mom ran out to the store for a minute. She'll be pissed your home early. She wanted to surprise you with something."

"Well," laughed Jon, "she's going to be even more pissed because I'm not getting home until tomorrow."

"Jesus, Dad…"

"Sean!!"

"Sorry, Dad," Sean's voice got quiet. "I get carried away. I mean it, I'm sorry."

Jon smiled at his son's reaction. "I know, son. Look, tell Mom I'm still in Washington and that I'll call her tonight from the hotel, okay?"

"Sure, Dad. I'll tell her."

"Thanks. I've got to go, buddy. Love ya."

"Love ya, Dad."

Jon smiled again as the telephone went dead. He got up from the desk walking over to a couch located across from the desk Demmer was working at. He smiled at the young woman, who smiled back.

"Thanks for the use of the phone, Lieutenant."

Demmer nodded, looking the visitor over. He didn't look all that special, just another naval officer. He stood just under six feet tall with medium build. He looked to be in his forties with graying hair. He was bald on top with neatly trimmed hair around the sides and back. He wore gold wire rimmed glasses over twinkling blue eyes. He looked fit but was by no means a body builder. Just an average looking guy.

She smiled at Summers, who was leaning back with his eyes closed. "Can I get you anything, Commander?"

The sailor looked over at her smiling. "No, thank you, Lieutenant. The fact I don't have to spend another minute on a plane tonight was enough. Just point me to the hotel and somewhere I can get dinner and you'll have my eternal gratitude. That won't get you much, not even coffee, but I'll be happy."

Demmer laughed. "If you change your mind, Sir, let me know."

The door opened and an army officer walked out. He walked over to Jon, who stood up, "Commander, I'm Lieutenant Colonel Charles Naylor. The Chiefs are just about ready to have a look at your report. They've asked me to again apologize for making you miss your flight home and asked me to see if there is anything I can do for you?"

Demmer noticed that Naylor's eye fell on the four rows of ribbons above the left pocket on Summers's uniform. He became visibly uneasy looking back into Summers's eyes. Demmer wondered what he saw that changed his demeanor. Naylor was not a man to be easily rattled. She thought it looked as if he were afraid of the naval officer. Summers held out his hand.

"Please call me, Jon," Summers smiled at the soldier. "I'm at the end of my summer tour and headed back to the civilian world. It'll take weeks to get used to that and will drive my wife nuts."

Naylor looked more at ease as he let go of Summers's hand. "OK, Jon. Sorry we're holding you up this evening."

"Nothing can be done about that. Lieutenant Demmer has been good to me."

Demmer blushed.

"I'm all set though," continued Jon, "and I do appreciate everyone's trying to keep me happy."

Both men laughed and the last of the tension Naylor felt seemed to disappear. Naylor looked the opposite of Summers. He stood six feet two inches and could have easily passed as a movie star with his good looks. His full head of neatly trimmed brown hair gave him the look of an action hero.

The door behind them opened and two officers came out of the meeting room used by the Joint Chiefs. Both were naval officers dressed much the same as Summers. The officer in the lead bore the rank of rear admiral on his shoulder boards. Above his left breast pocket were five neat rows of decorations and above that, a set of pilot's wings. The man behind him was a lieutenant commander and a pilot. He followed a full step behind his superior and carried both his hat and a briefcase. The admiral was six feet tall with a full head of dark brown hair that was graying around the temples. He was starting to show a bit of a bulge around the middle from lack of exercise and too much rich food. He was a good-looking man with the smile of a politician. The officer behind him was at least three inches shorter, slender with thinning light brown hair. The telephone on Demmer's desk rang. She said "Yes, Sir," several times then put her finger on the receiver rest to disconnect the line. She then pushed another button on the telephone and waited for a second. She said something softly and hung up.

While Demmer was on the telephone the admiral spotted the two officers and locked eyes with Summers. His smile changed from that of the politically correct to one of the overly smug. He changed direction and walked over to the officers.

"Summers," said the admiral, "how are the reserves?"

The tone wasn't meant to be friendly by any means.

Summers's smile didn't change, and his blue eyes never wavered. Demmer came around the desk and was standing, holding a folder, between Summers and Naylor. Both Demmer and Naylor were standing at attention while Summers seemed much more relaxed. The door Summers entered through opened, and a marine guard and a sailor walked up behind the admiral and his aide coming to attention as well.

"Admiral Kingston," answered Summers, his tone neutral, "how are you, Sir?"

"Exceptionally well, Summers. I'm off to command my first battle group. Pity you'll never know what that's like. Nothing like it in the world, but that's the real navy as opposed the reserves. Oh, that's right, you were never part of the real navy running around in jungles and such. Never what you would call a true sailor."

It was obvious to all in the room that Admiral Richard Kingston didn't care for Summers. Kingston's smile was meant to agitate Summers. It wasn't working.

"True, Sir, but I have spent my share of time at sea."

"But not as a true sailor. You can't drive a ship, or a sub and you don't fly. You're more a support sailor. It fits you moved to the reserves. Even at the academy, you were more like an enlisted man than an officer."

"I guess old habits are hard to break, Sir. Good luck with your new command."

Kingston was starting to get irritated because he wasn't getting the reaction he wanted. The smile disappeared.

"Thank you, Summers. Do you know my aide, Commander Stephen Williams?"

Summers nodded, "Commander Williams, nice to meet you."

"So, when do you retire, Summers? Commander's not bad for a reservist. Shows you worked hard over the years."

Demmer stepped forward saying, "Sir, here are your orders. Seaman Jones is here to take you and Commander Williams to your hotel."

Kingston smiled again, "Thank you, Miss Demmer."

Demmer flushed at the remark. Summers knew Kingston had deliberately left out her rank. She calmed down when Naylor's hand touched her arm. Summers's smile and attitude didn't change during the entire conversation.

"It was good to see you again, Admiral," Summers said dismissingly, "and it was nice meeting you, Commander Williams."

Williams wouldn't look at Summers and didn't answer.

"Give me a call when you retire and hang that medal up," said Kingston turning to leave, "you should get a proper farewell, you know."

"You're on my list to invite, Sir."

Kingston didn't turn at the last remark, he followed the sailor out the door. Demmer and Naylor could see the back of his neck flush red against the white uniform. Williams did turn, but never looked directly at Summers. As the door behind them closed the smile disappeared from Summers's face and he let out a deep breath.

"What a fucking asshole!" said Demmer.

The remark caught everyone by surprise. Naylor stiffened, his face expressionless, and looking at Summers. The marine guard covered a smile, stifling a laugh. They all turned to look at Summers's face. There was a moment of silence as they waited for a reaction from the naval officer.

He smiled, looking at the young lady. For the first time he noticed her pretty face and pleasant eyes. She was blushing because of the comment and was looking down, ashamed. "You know, Lieutenant, you're right. I don't often agree with the air force, but you are right. Now, please tell me that I'm booked into a different hotel than he is?"

Demmer continued to look down. "Sorry, Sir."

Summers looked at Naylor and they both laughed. So did the marine, though he tried to hide it.

There was a noise from the door behind them. They all turned to see General Goodman in the doorway. He was also stifling a laugh. It was finally time for Jon to go in.

★ CHAPTER 2 ★

REFLECTIONS

Summers finished the last of his dinner. It had been a longer day than expected. He was sitting alone in the booth trying to put everything in perspective. All he really wanted to do was sleep, but knew he better get something to eat, or he would pay dearly in the middle of the night. The hotel lounge was open late, so he decided he would stop after checking into his room. The lounge was crowded, mostly with people there for cocktails. It was large and dimly lit with a long bar across from the entrance. The bar was lined with stools and there were booths along the walls. In the center of the room were square tables covered with white tablecloths, flowers, and candles. Soft music played over the speakers in the ceiling. Given the atmosphere and the events of the day, dinner allowed him the time to reflect.

Jon's day started in San Diego when he left his parents standing in the airport, boarding a flight to Dulles. He was heading home to Rochester, New York, but had to report to the Pentagon to turn over some dispatches and deliver a report he authored regarding intelligence gathering. With the meeting with the joint chiefs almost upset by his encounter with Kingston, he forced himself to keep his perspective. Richard Kingston graduated a year ahead of him from the naval academy. They were at odds since he entered as a plebe and their relationship deteriorated from there. Kingston cut a dashing figure all through his years at the academy and through flight training at Pensacola, Florida. He came from a wealthy Virginia family, bred for politics. His family decided early on to send him into the military hoping for bigger things. He was intelligent, ruthless, and would trade his own mother for another promotion. His record was spotless, making a deliberate rise through the ranks since graduating in 1975.

Summers first met Kingston in the fall of 1972 having just reported for his first year at Annapolis. He missed his *plebe summer* because of wounds he received in Vietnam while an enlisted man. He joined the navy following graduation from high school. After completing basic training at Great Lakes, he volunteered for duty as a SEAL. He completed SEAL training just prior to his deployment to Southeast Asia, being assigned to a unit carrying out operations in the Mekong Delta. Summers and his squad were ordered to accompany some boats to evacuate an army company from an isolated position along the river. During the evacuation, the North Vietnamese attacked and in the firefight that ensued, the enemy was driven back, but at a cost.

Summers was wounded in the battle and brought to the aide station near death. The army commander was so impressed by the reports of the sailor who swam out to the burning boats to bring wounded back and then organized the resistance around the aide station that he recommended Jon for the Purple Heart and the Medal of Honor. The navy decided that even though the United States was withdrawing from Vietnam, they still needed to have heroes for the folks back home.

Summers was awarded the Medal of Honor by President Nixon. When asked what his plans were for the future, Jon joked he thought the naval academy would be the ideal place for him to get a college education. Before Jon was ready to leave the hospital, he received his appointment to the academy.

Because he was an enlisted man entering an officer's world, plus the fact he missed *plebe summer*, he became an immediate target. Most found him to be an unwilling target, and some soon found the tables reversed. Second year Midshipman Kingston was the first to find out it was not good practice to throw a blanket over someone and beat them with socks filled with tennis balls. The blanket made it over Jon's head, but it was Kingston who ended up in the hospital for a week. The official version was they had been playing touch football. Word spread among the midshipmen that Jon was not to be trifled with. Over the next four years, he gained a reputation as the protector of the underdog. Kingston never forgave Jon and was constantly trying to get him in trouble or humiliate him any way he could. He never managed to succeed. For the most part, Jon ignored Kingston and all his attempts. Jon managed to graduate the top half of his class in the spring of 1976. After graduation, Jon married his high school sweetheart, Nancy Quinn, in the naval academy chapel. He was sent back to the teams as an ensign.

Because of his history, Jon found himself a favorite of the navy hierarchy. He was sent to counter terrorism school and learned several languages including Vietnamese, Japanese, and Filipino. He was stationed in the Philippines. While at Subic Bay in the summer of 1978, he was assigned to a highly classified mission. He was sent back into the jungles of Vietnam to bring back a small group of American POWs who were still being held. The team consisted of SEALs and Vietnamese refugees who were trained for this type of mission. They hit the camp and found five American service men in various states of health. During the extraction, they got into a firefight and the team leader was killed. Jon assumed command. When the team got to their extraction point, they watched the helicopter and supporting fighters turn around and head back out to sea.

With a vengeful Vietnamese Army after them and only the delta to hide in, Jon moved his men into the swamps and spent the next week using all his escape and evasion skills. The team leader and three other men were killed during the mission. Five more men, including Jon, were wounded, so moving through the jungle was slow. After a week of hiding, they stole a large boat and sailed down the river and into the South China Sea. The boat was outfitted with an old diesel engine and got them out of Vietnamese waters where they used what was left of their radio batteries to call for help. Within an hour, a frigate picked them up and they were off to the Philippines and the hospital.

In the debriefing there was much confusion about the recalled extraction. Jon's boss maintained a verbal order came from above. Admiral Randall C. Mantell, who ordered the mission, denied any such order was given and disciplined the officer, implying poor judgment on his part. Jon defended his commanding officer, implying that a junior aide to Admiral Mantell passed the order on. The admiral defended his aide, Lieutenant J.G. Richard

Kingston, and dismissed all the evidence presented in the case. The matter was buried because of the highly secret nature of the mission. Jon immediately put in for a transfer from the teams. He figured that as a SEAL he was too easy a target for the navy bureaucracy and safer duty would suit his wife and new baby boy much better. Jon was awarded the Navy Cross and a second Purple Heart for his actions on the mission. No one ever talked to the media about the rescue.

Jon transferred to naval intelligence and finished his active-duty tour there. While finishing up his time with the navy he obtained a teaching degree. When he left active duty in 1981, he moved back to Rochester and got a job as a science teacher at his old high school. Since Desert Storm he was working on a program to increase the amount of human intelligence that the Pentagon was getting. In the age of the satellite and computer, most intelligence was electronic in nature. It could give you numbers and locations of troops and equipment, but could tell you little about training, morale, or attitude of your enemy. This was the report he took into the joint chiefs earlier in the evening.

The meeting was a different type of meeting. As tired as he was, the impression was the joint chiefs already looked at and approved his report. The main topic of conversation seemed to be Jon and his career. They asked about his civilian responsibilities and seemed to be genuinely pleased he was now a vice-principal at his school. Goodman especially seemed to take some glee in relating the recent encounter with Kingston in the outer office. After about thirty minutes General Michalowski quieted everyone down and made a brief statement directly to the naval officer. Everyone in the room, including Naylor and Demmer, fell silent as the general spoke.

"Commander," he started, "your report on human intelligence sources isn't the real reason I wanted to see you today. I have watched your career over the years, and I wanted to say *thank you* for helping me so many years ago."

"I don't understand, Sir," was Jon's confused reply.

Michalowski smiled. "I was shot down over South Vietnam in 1968 by the Viet Cong and was captured by a sadistic little bastard named Li. I spent the next ten years being moved about and living in cages hanging in the jungle. At one point, Li had eight American prisoners working in his poppy fields. One tried to escape in 1975 after we were told that the Americans left Vietnam. Li took great pleasure in executing him. His name was Johnson.

What a waste. Over the next three years, we were moved all over the delta. Two more of my fellow prisoners died before the camp was attacked by a small band of soldiers sent to rescue us in the summer of 1978.

"As you know, the rescue was not without incident. The team commander was killed, and a young ensign took command. He got us out a week later and put his career on the line defending his commanding officer who was being accused of something he didn't do. What hurt most is the fact that because of my position in this little fairy tale, I have never been able to repay you for what you did. I..."

The general stopped, the emotion of the moment overwhelming him. Tears began rolling down his cheeks. Jon remembered feeling confused. Fear of a bad memory being resurrected, astonishment because this took him completely by surprise, sympathy because of the tears he saw in the general's eyes, and embarrassment because of the way others were looking at him. Jon was only able to sit there in shock and look back.

"Commander," said Michalowski regaining his composure, "you'll have to pardon me, I still have some pretty strong emotions about this time of my life."

He stopped again, allowing Jon a chance to react. "Sir, I was doing my job and my best to keep us all alive. I don't deserve your thanks because you sacrificed so much more for all of us while you were a POW. No, Sir. I should be thanking you for your example and your courage."

The general again regained his composure. "I can accept that and would probably agree with you, but you have to understand the situation. When the extraction failed both my comrades and I gave up and expected to die there in the delta. Most of your men were angry and would probably have died with us had you not taken control. Even wounded, you convinced us there was hope of escape. If you ever doubted that fact for yourself, you never let any of us know it. I was convinced you were crazy to try and sail that junk into the South China Sea, but you made that work."

"That was the entire team making that work, Sir."

"No, it was you. As I recall, you didn't give any of us a choice."

Goodman took up the conversation at this point. "Commander, you did one hell of a job on that mission and have never been able to really voice your concerns about the botched extraction. Your defense of your CO was commendable, but I don't agree with how you went about it. Because of the sensitivity of the mission, there was no way you were going to win. All you did was to allow the person who gave that order the opportunity to cover his tracks and ruin your career in the process."

Jon remembered these words stinging like a Band-Aid being ripped off an arm. He couldn't believe what Goodman said and at the same time realized he was correct. If he and his commanding officer hadn't made an issue, the navy probably wouldn't have sided with Mantell and Kingston. POWs had been brought home and someone tried to stop that from happening. There would have been a very discreet investigation, and someone would have been retired without another word being said. Instead, they forced the navy to decide to keep the operation a secret for political reasons.

"Don't look so hurt, Commander," continued Goodman. "You were right to suspect who you did, and he would have been weeded out of the service too…"

"Ben, please!!" said Michalowski. "Commander, I agree with General Goodman's assessment, but unfortunately there's nothing to be done about it now. I can do something else that is long overdue and that's making sure you're taken care of properly. I've asked Admiral Cummings to investigate your file and make recommendations. He did this favor for me because I'm announcing my retirement in a week. So, my time to complete this little personal mission is limited. Admiral, if you will do the honors."

Jon remembered feeling uncomfortable at this point. Cummings opened a folder, looking around the room. He made a show of smiling and clearing his throat.

"I won't bore everyone with the dates the decorations were awarded or list the engagements that were fought but will read the collective list I compiled. During your career of twenty-four years, you have been awarded the Medal of Honor, th…"

"Recommended by an army officer, I might add!" interrupted a chuckling Goodman.

Cummings feigned an irritated look, "the Navy Cross, the Distinguished Service Medal, the Silver Star, the Navy and Marine Corps Medal, the Bronze Star, the Purple Heart, the Navy Achievement Medal, the Presidential Unit Citation Ribbon, the Navy Unit Commendation Ribbon, Good Conduct Medal, the Navy Reserve Meritorious Service Medal, the Vietnam Service Medal, the Navy Overseas Service Ribbon, the Naval Reserve Medal, the

Republic of Vietnam Service Medal, the Republic of Vietnam Presidential Unit Citation, the United Nations Service Medal, the Inter-American Defense Board Medal, and the Kuwait Liberation Medal from both Kuwait and Saudi Arabia. You graduated from the United States Naval Academy. You have served as a SEAL and with Naval Intelligence."

Cummings looked at his colleagues and snarled, "No comments!!"

There were smiles and a stifled laugh or two, but no one spoke. He continued. "After looking at your record, Commander, I have to say that even I was surprised. Even after going into the reserves, you have served with a great deal of distinction and honor. You never complained once about what hand you personally were dealt in the way of assignments, and you completed one hell of a job during both Desert Shield and Desert Storm. I'm very proud to recommend that you receive the Combat Action Ribbon, which has been overlooked on three occasions. In addition, I am pleased to award you the Navy/Marine Corps Commendation Medal by the direction of the Secretary of the Navy and promote you to the rank of Captain upon the recommendation of your commanding officer. Congratulations, Captain Summers."

Jon was in shock. He could only sit in the chair and look back at everyone. Everyone stood, walking over to congratulate him. Goodman and Cummings seemed especially happy about their part in the proceeding. Goodman shared his agreement with Jon's assessment of Kingston. He even jokingly offered Jon a transfer to the army. At least Jon decided to take it as a joke.

The last person who walked over to congratulate Jon was Michalowski. He was obviously still coming to grips with some emotions, his walk wasn't as confident as before. The general took Jon's hand in both of his and just held it for a few seconds.

"Jon," he started, "I'm sorry for surprising you like this because I wanted to do something where your family could be present. The nature of the issue forbids them even knowing what took place. I feel like this is a rotten way for this to happen, but it's richly deserved. You're an excellent officer and I hope what Kingston said isn't true?

Jon looked puzzled. "I don't understand, Sir."

"Everyone in this room heard him talk to you about retiring," continued Michalowski, "I hope that's just wishful thinking on his part. You're not thinking of leaving the service, are you?"

Jon laughed. "If I was, Sir, the minute Dick Kingston made an issue of it, I changed my mind. I wouldn't let him have the satisfaction."

The general released Jon's hand and a serious look came over his face.

"I have dreams about the years I spent as a POW, or should I call them nightmares. There are nights I don't get any sleep at all. I have very vivid memories of those years and especially of the rescue. You really did an amazing thing, even if you don't realize it. Not many people could have turned what was sure to be a disaster into a victory. You kept us alive for a week in enemy territory and then got us out with minimum losses. The fact I'm here today is because of you. You need to know that even if the world can't know what took place that summer, you helped not just us, but the entire process. Apparently, the Vietnamese really didn't know of our existence and after the mission they became very cooperative in the search for others like me. Thank you doesn't seem to cover it."

"Sir, I don't have the words. I did what I had to do to save my men and my mission."

The emotions that Michalowski had submerged in the depths of his being came to the surface again as he hugged Jon. The meeting ended and Jon was shuttled to the hotel.

Jon smiled coming back to the present. He decided to go to the lounge instead of the restaurant in hopes of avoiding Kingston or Williams, who he figured wouldn't be caught dead there. The food was good, but he decided not to stay for a drink because he was tired.

The waitress came with the check, and he paid her immediately. Out of curiosity, he looked around to see what else was going on while he waited for his change. He saw mostly couples and businessmen scattered at tables throughout the room. There was a table of five marines near the door who seemed very drunk. They looked young; Jon guessed them to be on their first assignment out of basic infantry school. They were in uniform with their dark blue pants and green shirts. He saw nothing more than one stripe on any of the sleeves. They were by far the loudest group in the room, but still, things were quiet. He continued to look about the room and saw nothing else of interest. As the waitress returned, he noticed a middle-aged oriental man rise from his booth, putting some papers in a briefcase. He was talking to another man at the table, his back to Jon. Jon raised an eyebrow, turning to smile at the waitress.

"Thanks," he said as he took his change. The marines near the door laughed loudly and the waitress seemed annoyed.

"Sorry," said the waitress. "I don't mean to look pissed, but this is the third night this week those guys have been in here."

"You don't have to apologize to me. Drunks are drunks no matter what they're wearing."

"I meant because you're in the same branch of the army an' all. I figured you might get mad at me for being pissed."

Jon smiled. "They're marines and I don't think the army would claim them, or me for that matter. I'm just an ol' sailor here for the food. Trust me when I say, I won't take offense. Like I said, drunks are drunks."

Jon handed her a five-dollar tip for an eight-dollar meal.

"Gee, thanks," said the girl. "You don't have to do this, you know."

"I know," replied Jon, "but you look like you've had the same kind of day I've had and..."

"Hey, look at the Jap!" interrupted Jon's sentence.

The noise of chairs being pushed back, and loud voices came from the direction of the marines. Jon turned to see the five service men surrounding the middle-aged oriental man. He was a small man, with dark hair and glasses. He wore his hair combed back and was dressed in a business suit. He carried his briefcase in front of him with both hands hanging onto the handle. The five marines towered over him while he circled looking up at them.

"What have we here?" said a marine directly in front of the smaller man. "I think you ought to buy us all a drink for what your people did to the marines in Okinawa."

The other marines all voiced agreement.

"I don't understand. What marines in Okin..."

The marine pushed the smaller man back into two of the other marines who grabbed him under each arm, causing him to drop his briefcase.

"Don't play stupid with us, Tojo. You know what we're talking about. You bastards are always thinking that you can tell us what to do in territory we took from you fair and square. You're buying us all drinks to make up for wrongly accusing those guys of rape and putting them in prison. Jack, get his wallet!"

One of the other marines started to reach inside the suit coat pocket when the man tried to kick him. The marine easily dodged the kick, which hit his buddy, knocking him backwards. The marine fell back into a young lady who was entering the lounge with a garment bag. The woman was pushed into a table but didn't fall. She moved away quickly. The first marine regained his balance, starting to move back towards the man who was now being held by his companions.

"You son of a bitch!"

His hand was balled up into a fist and his arm started to cock back to strike his foe in the face. As the arm started forward it was grabbed from behind and he was easily thrown sideways, falling into two of his comrades. When this took place, the oriental man was able to break loose from his captors, moving off towards the bar. The marines regrouped, turning to go after their former captive. They found their way blocked by a man in a naval officer's uniform.

All five hesitated for a second.

"Gentlemen, I think it's time to go home and sober up," Jon said calmly looking into the eyes of each man.

The first marine took a step forward.

"Son," the tone of Jon's voice became hard, "you don't want to do this tonight."

"Get out of the way, Navy," the man's voice was loud, uneven, and his speech slurred. "You're the one who's not wanting part of this. You know who you're fucking with? You're fucking with the United States Marine Corps and we're going to kick his ass."

Jon's voice remained quiet, and he maintained eye contact.

"I don't think the gentleman wants your company tonight. Now just go home an…"

"Look Swabbie, don't fuck with me. I…"

"That's Swabbie, Sir," was the quick reply taking the marine by surprise. "That's Swabbie, Sir." Jon repeated. "That's what marines normally address an officer as, Sir."

"Marines don't answer to Swabbie officers, asshole!" The young marine was really drunk.

"Ed," said one of his buddies, "this isn't worth getting busted for, man. Look at the ribbons on this guy. Let's get out of here."

"Fuck you, you chicken shit. This guy's nothing, and besides, I want my drink the chink owes me."

His other three friends agreed, making him feel braver and a bit more aggressive.

"I believe the term you're looking for is Japanese. He's Japanese, not Chinese," said Jon.

"What?"

"There you go again being disrespectful. That's 'What, Sir?' You forgot the sir."

"Fuck you!!!" the young marine didn't move forward or back. He turned quickly to look at his friends who all nodded encouragement.

"Son, you've been asked to leave and have decided not to. That's not smart and most marines I know are smart."

"Fuck you, asshole!"

"The marines I know are also proud of the fact that they don't need to go five on one to get the best of someone. You guys need to back off, cool off, and..."

"I said fuck you, Navy!! Shut the fuck up!!"

Jon's eyes were steady on the young marine, his voice got even quieter. "That's sir. A simple three letter word spelled S. I. R, sir."

"You fucking..." the young marine came at Jon and never even felt himself hitting the floor with Jon's hand at his throat. The other four Marines were grabbed by the Washington D.C. police officers who came rushing through the door. The marine on the floor choked for breath while Jon dragged him to his feet. Two police officers took the marine from Jon moving him against the wall where they handcuffed him and did a pat down search for weapons. One of the officers found a knife in the man's back pocket and turned to hand it to his sergeant standing behind him. When he did this the young marine pushed himself off the wall at the officer. Both police officers caught the young man pushing him to the floor. The marine struggled for a few seconds before calming down. The sergeant looked down at the young man shaking his head. He smiled at Jon, walking off to talk to the bartender. The police officer who found the knife got back to his feet and looked over his shoulder at the other four marines, who were being led out in handcuffs. He smiled.

"Sorry about the marine coming after you, Commander," he said to Jon.

"You don't have to apologize for him, officer," answered Jon. "I'm more concerned about that oriental gentleman over there they were picking on before I intervened."

Both men looked over to the middle-aged man who had been the butt of the marines' harassment. He was talking to another police officer.

"I guess I'm apologizing because I'm a marine myself, Commander. I've done some stupid things on liberty, but nothing like this."

"Once a marine, always a marine!" Jon said to the officer who laughed shaking his head. "I didn't take offense, Officer. No harm, no foul."

The police officer looked at the decorations above Jon's right pocket. He noticed the Naval Special Warfare Trident above the ribbons and straightened up. The smile turned into a grin and then a laugh. The sergeant came over and looked at the younger officer.

"Sarge, this idiot on the floor looks to be fresh out of basic infantry school. He gets himself all drunked up tonight and starts to take a swing at the Commander, here."

The sergeant looked a little confused as he replied, "Yeah, so?"

"Sarge, the Commander is a SEAL. The poor asshole never had a chance sober, much less drunk. As a matter of fact, if he had been sober, he would hopefully have had the common sense to salute and keep his mouth shut."

Both men laughed as the marine was lifted to his feet and led out of the lounge.

"Will you be pressing charges, Sir?" asked the sergeant laughing as the younger officer trotted off to help his comrades.

"No, Sir, I'm more concerned about that gentleman over there," Jon said.

"He's filing a complaint," the sergeant managed to stop laughing, "but he's going to stay with the bartender until we get these guys secured and the other witnesses interviewed. Hey, Commander, it's been a pleasure."

The sergeant extended his hand to Jon who shook it. He left after the other officers.

Jon looked at the oriental man with the bartender. He judged him to be a successful Japanese businessman. His suit looked to cost five hundred dollars and the Rolex watch he was wearing probably cost just as much. He walked over to where the two men were talking.

When he reached them, he bowed to the smaller man, saying in perfect Japanese, "I apologize for the actions of my countrymen, sir. Please don't judge us all by the actions of a few. We really are a friendly people."

The businessman was taken back he was addressed in his own language. The bartender looked as surprised.

Jon continued, "May I have the honor of buying you some refreshment to help make up for this terrible incident?"

The businessman bowed in return, replying, "I'm surprised to find someone here that speaks Japanese as well as you do. I am pleased to accept both your assistance and apology. My name is Toshio Akiyama. If you hadn't intervened, I think I might have been injured by those soldiers."

Jon tried not to smile. "My name is Jon Summers and it's my honor to meet you."

"Where did you learn to speak Japanese so well? You almost sound like a native."

"I learned several oriental languages early in my career with the navy. I don't get a chance to practice, so it's a pleasure for me to be able to do this."

"You are quite brave, Jon. Five against one aren't good odds. Are you hurt?"

Jon guessed all this polite conversation was covering something, because for all his composure, this man seemed nervous. He suspected that Mr. Toshio Akiyama knew the five young men were marines and that he was wearing the insignia of the Navy SEALs. While he looked over Jon's uniform, the man's eyes gave him away when they showed some recognition and approval of what the ribbons and badges stood for. Jon glanced at the table where the businessman came from. The other man was gone.

Jon ignored the comment asking, "Are you hurt, my friend?"

"No, thank you for asking, but I will take you up on your offer for refreshment."

"What may I get for you?"

"Normally, I would ask for tea, but I have developed a taste for American Bourbon."

Jon turned to the bartender who was looking very bored with the conversation. The man immediately came alert.

"Yes, sir, can I help with something?"

"Can you get us two glasses of bourbon, please?" Jon asked the man.

The bartender nodded and started to walk off when Toshio added in English, "No ice, please?"

"Make that two with no ice," Jon smiled at the bartender. He watched the man walk down the bar. He walked past the young lady who had been knocked into the table by the marine. She was looking directly at Jon with a big smile. He nodded to her in recognition. The young lady politely nodded back.

Jon turned his attention back to Toshio. "I hope this incident won't keep you from visiting more of my country?"

"No, I am here quite often and like much about your country. This won't affect how I do business here."

"What business are you in?"

Jon saw a second of hesitation in Toshio. "I am in the information business. I have been here to deal with your military regarding some new information systems that are becoming available to them. I was meeting with one of your fellow naval officers before this unfortunate incident took place. What do you do for the navy?"

"I'm what one of my naval academy classmates calls a support sailor. I can't drive a ship or a sub, so that makes me support."

The drinks came and Jon handed Toshio his. The bartender went back to his job. Jon raised his glass. "To new friendships and forgiveness."

"To you, my friend, for being there to help."

Both men downed the liquid in their glasses and looked at each other smiling. One of the police officers reentered the lounge, looking around. When he spotted Toshio, he waved and walked over to where the two men were standing.

"Mr. Akiyama," said the policeman, "we're ready for you, sir. If you can come with me, we'll get the paperwork out of the way."

"Thank you, officer," said the businessman stepping away from the bar. Jon followed suit, extending his hand to the smaller man. They shook hands.

"Take care of yourself, my friend," said Jon. "Thank you for being understanding about what took place."

"I am pressing charges, so I guess I'm not being that understanding." They both laughed. "Thank you again for having the courage to intervene. Not many people in either of our countries would have done that. It speaks highly of you."

"You would have done the same," Jon replied, although he suspected that Toshio would not.

They each bowed and Toshio turned to follow the policeman out of the lounge. Jon stood for a minute watching the businessman walk away. He didn't know what was wrong with Toshio, but something was out of place. He didn't appear to be the type of man to be afraid of much, including five marines, but the act of a mild-mannered businessman was for some reason. Jon shook the thought out of his mind and turned to look at the young lady who was still sitting at the bar. She had put the clothes bag over the stool next to her and was now sipping a glass of wine. Jon walked down the bar, taking a seat next to the woman.

"So, sailor, you're a bourbon man."

Jon turned looking into the pretty blue eyes. "No, Lieutenant Demmer, I'm a Labatt's Blue man, but I do enjoy an occasional shot of bourbon."

"Can I get you something, Commander?" asked the bartender. "The manager says it's on the house for doing what you did."

Jon leaned on the bar. "Labatt if you have one? Also, something for the lady, what'll you have, Lieutenant?"

The bartender looked at the woman next to Jon as she replied smiling, "I'll have another white wine, please."

The bartender smiled, quickly getting the drinks. He then went off to check on other customers.

"I was warned that sailors get into a lot of bar fights. General Thomlinson is going to be pissed about this."

The young woman leaned close to Jon as she talked so no one else could hear. Jon smelled her perfume, White Shoulders, and it reminded him of home."

"Why are you here, Lieutenant?"

She patted the clothing bag next to her. "Compliments of General Michalowski. He wanted you going home as a captain instead of a commander."

"So, he sent you down?"

"No, I volunteered because it's my night off and I'm meeting some friends. The general was pretty drained after the meeting."

"I know how he feels. Say thanks to him for me."

Demmer giggled. "I should thank you for the show, and please call me Judy."

Jon took a sip of this beer and looked over to the young lady next to him. "Judy, its Jon and I wonder if you can do me a favor."

Judy giggled. "For another glass of wine, I'd do most anything. God, that sounds indecent."

Jon smiled back.

Beverly Hills, California
August 15, 1994
2330 Hours

The night was hot; too hot to sleep. Ray never got used to air conditioning and left Louise sound asleep in their room. The other problem was he and Bill consumed more than their fair share of alcohol while talking about the upcoming reunion. All the talk allowed memories long buried, to resurface, causing the nightmare to return. He felt the need to stay awake to keep the nightmares away and wanted more to drink to numb his body from the emotions running so close to the surface. He sat in the lounge chair next to the pool, looking up at the stars. The night was not only hot, but clear with an excellent view of the night sky.

"Uncle Ray?"

The voice was soft, but still startled him, making him jump. He turned to find Becky and Sarah, standing behind him. They had been out to a movie. Sarah was as pretty as her mother. She was about two inches taller with long, curly, dark brown hair that came to the middle of her back. She had a little bigger build than her mother. Ray guessed Becky was going crazy with all the boy friends. Becky was all of five feet three inches tall with short, dark brown hair and a slender build. At forty-three, she was still an attractive woman. Ray secretly hoped she had her share of suitors, so Bill would be going crazy.

"Is everything all right?" There was a tenderness and concern in her voice that reminded Ray of her mother.

Ray smiled. "I'm fine kiddo, just couldn't sleep."

"Is that all?"

"No, your dad and I had a bit too much to drink. That's not helping matters any."

Becky laughed as she turned to her daughter. "You go to bed, sweetheart. I'm going to stay and talk to Uncle Ray for a few minutes."

"Sure thing, Mom."

She gave her mother a kiss on the cheek and then walked over to Ray, bent down kissing him on the cheek as well.

"Good night, Uncle Ray. Sleep well."

She turned, walking away disappearing into the house.

"Well," started Becky as she sat down next to Ray, "why can't we sleep. Can't be the liquor because that usually puts all of us to sleep. Maybe the excitement?"

Ray smiled and thought back to days when he would not have believed they would live to see their children or grandchildren. Bill had Becky and Kevin and three grandchildren. He and Louise had Jon, Matthew, and Julie and seven grandchildren. Life had certainly changed in fifty years.

"You're probably right, doctor. At my age too much excitement can cause sleeplessness and irritability."

"You and dad still planning the big reunion?"

Ray's facial expression changed unintentionally when he answered, "Yeah, we are. I don't think many will be able to go back to the Philippines though. Between the cost and health problems, most of the guys who are still alive won't be able to make it. It's a lot of work to get a few people together."

Becky took Ray's hand squeezing it tight. "What's wrong, Uncle Ray? It's not like you to be this down on something."

"You a psychiatrist now, doctor?" replied Ray. "I must have missed that part of your schooling."

Ray tried to sound indignant but couldn't. The woman sitting next to him was like family and he couldn't hide things from her. Her intuition about people was excellent, and he knew it would be impossible to keep anything from her. This probably served her well as a doctor.

"Uncle Ray, you and daddy are the driving force behind this reunion and getting people to go. Daddy talked to me, and we've agreed to help pay for anyone who can't afford it. Six days of going to the places where you spent some of the most extraordinary times of your lives fifty years ago and seeing how things have changed since then. Meet some of the people you shared those experiences with and have a chance to honor the men who didn't come back."

Ray shook his head smiling. "Honey, did you write your father's speech?"

Becky laughed. "No, but he's recited it so much, I have it memorized. Come on Uncle Ray, I want to help. If you're mad at daddy, I promise I won't tell. He can be an asshole at times. I know I can help. All I need to know is what's wrong."

Ray looked into Becky's eyes and saw compassion and the need to heal all hurt and injustice wherever it was. He hadn't told anyone except his wife and his oldest son what he decided to tell Becky. He knew that part of it was the alcohol talking, but he also knew from experience talking about it would be therapeutic.

"Becky, honey," he started handing her a beer from a cooler hidden next to his chair, "I hope you drink beer because you're gonna need it before I'm done."

He pulled a second beer out for himself. Becky took a pull from hers.

"I didn't know you drank beer."

Becky smiled. "I'm an army brat. It was beer or whiskey, so I learned to drink both."

Ray shook his head. "You're right about your dad being stubborn and pig headed, but he's also one of the finest human beings I've had the privilege to know in my life."

"I believe I called him an asshole, Uncle Ray. Say, you know, I've never heard you swear. Why is that?"

"Back in 1941 when I made corporal, I was standing there cussing up a storm when my Sergeant came up an..."

Ray waved his empty hand back and forth as he drank some of his beer. He continued, "Different story. You're getting me sidetracked, Becky. Anyway, your dad and I served in the 41st Infantry together in World War II and we saw lots of action. You heard of the good old days?"

"Yeah?"

"These weren't those if you know what I mean. We saw some heavy combat and we both killed our share of people to stay alive. We were both good at it. Damn, I'm starting to sound like an old, war mongering fool."

"No! Please don't stop. Dad doesn't talk about this time of his life much." said Becky. "He talks mostly about the times when he wasn't directly involved with any fighting. I'm really interested to know what it was like."

Ray looked at the woman next to him, he sipped from his beer. He thought carefully about what he was going to say next.

"You had the right idea about war in general when you were involved in the protests during the Vietnam War. It's a bad thing and there are no real winners when a conflict gets to the stages it did in those days. You need to understand, though, that there's a time and place for it. When you have a Hitler or someone like him, you must make a stand and do what needs to be done. The alternative could be worse than war itself. War isn't the flag waving and other garbage that you hear about. Its death and destruction, plain and simple. Don't get me wrong, you must believe what you're fighting for is right and worth dying for. You need to know when talking will get you the same results and when there's no other alternative. As one of my grandsons says, *Dying is a bad thing.*

"You asked me why I couldn't sleep. It's the damn nightmares! Haven't had them in years. Tonight your dad and I start talking about the *glory days,* and Bam! Nightmares came back! Last time I had them was when Jonny was in Vietnam. Before that, it was for three years after I was back from Japan. I don't mean occasionally, either. Every single night, the same nightmares just kept repeating."

Ray put his beer down and then put his head in his hands, rubbing his eyes. Becky put her hand on the old man's shoulder and stroked his back.

"Uncle Ray, this sounds similar to what some Vietnam vets go through wh…"

"You're damn right it is!" Ray snapped. "This isn't something just the Vietnam vets have. Anyone who's been in war goes through this again and again. Jonny had them too, after he got back both times."

"Both times?" asked Becky innocently. "I didn't think he saw any combat in the Gulf War?"

Ray ignored the question and continued. "Let me tell you what I dream about when I go through this garbage. I remember starting with a platoon of over fifty men and pulling back at the end of the campaign with only eighteen guys. I saw men shot, knifed, blown up and die of disease. I watched a six-foot two baseball hero shoot himself in the foot, so he didn't have to go into combat with the rest of us because he was scared. I watched the rest of my platoon go into combat just as scared and not question why I was sending them there. They were the reason I did the things I did back then, and I think your dad felt the same."

Becky gave him a curious look. "I don't understand, Uncle Ray. Did you and daddy do something wrong?"

Becky saw tears in Ray's eyes as he continued. "Nothing that anyone else didn't do to stay alive. You see, Becky, the guys we were leading would do anything to help each other out. I saw men who were the mildest mannered people back here turn into highly effective killers. We had to stay alive against an enemy that was just as deadly as we were. I had a little guy, an Italian named Gaetano, who carried the platoon's BAR and all the ammo. The thing weighs a ton. I felt sorry for him because of his size. When we got this big baseball star assigned to the platoon, I assigned him to the BAR, figuring because of his size and strength, it would be a breeze for him. Gaetano was crushed. It was like I had physically beaten the man to the ground. He reported to sick call for three days in a row and was miserable. I tried talking to him about why I made that decision, but he would just walk away. Then, just before his first patrol, the baseball hero shoots himself in the foot, so I gave the BAR back to Gaetano. He hugged me and told me that I was a military genius, and he would do me proud. The man was deadly with that weapon. I didn't consider him a killer, but damn, was he good with that rifle. I guess we all got a little crazy back then."

"But if you did it to keep your men alive, you can't blame yourself. In war, you're fighting your enemy and I would think that you would fight to win. It doesn't make sense to do otherwise."

Ray, still teary eyed, looked at Becky and his face became very cold. "Honey, in war, you're fighting other human beings that are just as terrified about what's taking place as you are. They believe in what they are fighting for, as you do, and they believe they will win, as you do. The problem comes when people sacrifice themselves for these beliefs in large numbers. Sometimes because they really do believe and other times because the only thing they know how to do is follow someone who does believe. Killing the *enemy* becomes all too easy in an atmosphere like that. You point your weapon, you fire, and sometimes you watch the other man die and sometimes you don't. You do it because you believe the other guy is trying to do the same thing to you. You do it because you believe the other guy believes in something evil. You do it to erase that evil from the earth and you get so used to it that killing becomes almost second nature. You watch your men get wounded and killed by these *evil* people and you force yourself to make decisions you normally wouldn't think about making. I ordered men into situations they never returned from or at the very least never came back the same. On one day, I ordered at least a dozen artillery and mortar barrages. I did it to keep my men from being killed by what I thought were superior Japanese forces. They gave me the Bronze Star. I was decorated by Douglas MacArthur himself, because the operation was such a success. They estimated over three hundred Japanese were killed by those barrages I ordered. I got a medal for killing over three hundred people to capture a road."

Becky put her hand on the older man's shoulder. "Uncle Ray, you can't let that keep you from seeing the whole picture."

"Honey, I don't. Please don't think that I haven't thought this through. I've had fifty years to run this period of my life through my mind over and over. If I were faced with the same decisions today, I would make them all over again. I wouldn't hesitate for a second to do the same thing to keep my people from harm. I still believe what we were doing was right and just. It's the horror of it all that keeps me awake at night. It's the fact the same circumstances could be allowed to happen again, because we, as a species, can't learn from our mistakes. That's what scares me. It's the fact I can sit here with you and casually tell you I would have no problem taking a human life to protect what I think is right because it's so easy to do. That scares me more than anything else because I think at times, that's how society approaches its problems. Kill it, bury it, and once it's gone, forget about it. I spent a year stationed in Japan after they surrendered and found out why they fought the way they did. They believed in what they were doing and thought it to be right for the betterment of their people. They are a very hospitable people, very gracious in defeat. I just remember the bodies of men from both sides and at times it keeps me awake."

"Well, at least we didn't commit the atrocities that the Germans and the Japanese did. It was a much cleaner war than Vietnam."

Ray's look turned cold. "Let me tell you a story that only the United States Army and two other people know about. The only reason Louise and Jon were even told about it is because I was drunk like I am now. We had our problems the same as they did in Vietnam. We didn't have the mass killings of civilians by American troops where I was, but there certainly were other issues that can be looked on as suspicious."

Becky again looked puzzled. "I don't understand."

"I was leading a patrol and we were in heavy jungle. Like most operations, there were other patrols out from other companies, and we knew their approximate locations so we wouldn't run into one another. It had been quiet for a few days, and we'd been sent out to see what the Japanese were up to. I was to report back to your father. As we moved through the bush, we heard some heavy small weapons fire some distance away. We reported this by radio and were ordered to proceed in the direction of the fire. After the initial flurry of fire, we only heard sporadic fire for about ten minutes. We were moving slowly because we didn't want to walk into a trap. I received word from your dad that the patrol from the other company hadn't checked in and they thought they could be in trouble. They were sending a second patrol to the area where they were last heard from. They wanted us to go as well. As we approached the area, we smelled smoke, so we radioed in and started towards the source of the smoke. As we approached the area, we could hear voices, so we spread out into a skirmish line. We came upon a clearing and found a small Japanese encampment. The Japanese were getting ready to cook their dinner which consisted of whatever they could scavenge and GI rump roast."

Becky's expression was half horror and half confusion. "I don't understand, Uncle Ray. They were eating roast?"

Ray held her gaze. "They had wiped out the other patrol and dragged the bodies back to their camp. They had pulled down the pants of the dead GI's and cut steaks for themselves. There they were cooking them when we came upon the clearing. They were starving and had resorted to cannibalism to survive."

Becky's hand quickly covered her mouth while she looked away.

"The man next to me got sick to his stomach," said Ray. "He spent most of the day throwing up but was still able to attack when I gave the order."

"What did you do?"

"None of them went home, my dear."

"What do you mean?"

"What do you think I mean?"

"You killed them all?"

There was a second of silence before Ray answered. "Yeah, to a man. We fired so many rounds you couldn't tell they were human beings. This incident's haunted me ever since."

"They were wrong to do that. That's barbaric, to eat human flesh. They deserved to die."

"That's a pretty condemning statement for a young lady who protested for peace against an unpopular war. Don't think I'm criticizing you. I'm not. You should have seen the look of horror on your face when you just heard about my nightmare. It's easy to condemn when you're not there. What if the tables were reversed and it was American troops that were starving? Would we revert to cannibalism to survive?"

Becky stared blankly at the older man.

Ray continued. "I'd like to think not, either. The problem is, I've had fifty years to think about this incident and I still have more questions than I do answers. Do you think this was an atrocity, a war crime?"

Becky was still looking blankly at Ray.

"Do you, young lady?!?"

She nodded.

"What's more of an atrocity? Starving Japanese soldiers eating the flesh of dead Americans or American soldiers killing the Japanese for doing it by shooting them so full of holes you couldn't recognize they were once men."

Becky could only shake her head.

"Yeah, kiddo, I know. I'm still wrestling with that one myself. Understand I'm not feeling sorry for what happened and I'm not making any excuses, either. Chances are good, faced with the same incident today, I'd make the same decision all over again. The only thing I really decided was that the real atrocity is war itself. It forces people to make decisions they will have nightmares about for the rest of their lives."

"Oh, my god!" Becky was finally able to speak. "Oh my god."

Ray took a sip of his beer before speaking to the young woman. "Becky, you're a doctor so I don't expect you to understand what takes place out there. You're dedicated to healing and the saving of lives. Back in the Philippines we were dedicated to staying alive and to accomplish that, we did whatever we had to. In most cases, for us to do that, other men had to die. The Japanese did the same, as did the Filipinos. Like with you, the reaching out to the sick is second nature. For us, it was killing the enemy. We were exceptionally good at it, your father and I."

"I'm sorry, Uncle Ray. I had no idea."

"Don't be sorry darling, we did it for a greater good. I do believe that, even though right now it may not sound it. If we hadn't gone and did what we did, the alternatives wouldn't be acceptable to any rational human being. Be there when we need you and your dad, and I are happy to have had to go through it all. Look, I'm finally tired, how about you?"

Becky nodded. Ray reached over putting his arm around her and helped her get up. They walked back to the house together. It was Becky's turn for a sleepless night.

City of Davao
Mindanao, Philippines
August 16, 1994
0925 Hours

The vehicle was fully involved in flames when the fire trucks pulled up next to the old warehouse near the docks. Two police cars pulled up behind the fire trucks. A crowd was already watching the burning vehicle and the police set about moving them back so their counterparts in the fire department could do their job. The firemen were hosing down what was left of the car as additional fire and police units appeared. An older police captain arrived and took control of the officers working the crowd, as well as the officers there to investigate the vehicle fire. The captain grabbed one of his officers by the arm and motioning to the crowd. Within minutes, additional police units arrived, and the crowd was moved back. The firemen quickly put the fire out but continued to hose down the hot metal from the vehicle to cool it and keep the fire from rekindling.

The captain noticed the firemen pull two bodies out of the vehicle. He decided not to go over and look. In the thirty years he had been a police-man, he had seen more than his share of burned bodies and didn't feel like ruining an otherwise good day. A crew from the morgue, did a preliminary examination of the bodies, placing them in the plastic body bags. It was a grisly job the captain knew he couldn't do. The coroner walked over to the policeman giving him a quick report before leaving the scene.

The honking of a horn made the captain turn. He could see a car slowly pushing through the crowd to get to the scene. When it got closer, he could see it was a military staff car. That's all he needed was the army trying to tell him how to do his job. He served in the army as a young man and, aside from the experience it gave him for his career as a policeman, he had little use for it. The car made it through the crowd coming to a stop. A young officer got out of the back and immediately went after one of his policemen assigned to crowd control. *Arrogant bastard!* All the policeman could tell him would be speculation and rumor. He looked carefully at the wreckage of the car. It looked as if there had been an explosion of some sort from inside the vehicle. Not a large explosion, but enough to burn the entire car.

"Good morning, Captain."

The captain jumped, startled, being brought back to reality. Standing next to him was General Roberto Santos Mangoba. He oversaw intelligence for the army chief of staff. There was an intelligent look about him and compassion in the eyes behind the gold wire rimmed glasses. The captain knew his reputation of being a tough military commander who was fair with his troops and ruthless to his enemies.

"I'm sorry, General," said the policeman, "you startled me."

"I apologize, Captain. It was rude of me to come up on you from behind while you're working."

The captain smiled. He was being polite, unusual for a military commander assigned to this area. The policeman decided to use the straightforward approach with the general.

"Is the general interested in our little mishap here today?"

Mangoba smiled. "Yes, I am, Captain. The car is registered to Raul Argento of Zamboanga City. He has suspected ties with the MNLF and was seen leaving that city last evening with three other people."

"Really?" the policeman was surprised the general just gave him that information. "We haven't even received that information yet."

"We've been looking for the car all night, ever since it left Zamboanga. It looks to have been a small internal explosion. Do you speculate they were carrying a bomb?"

The captain looked at the general. "Why is the chief of army intelligence and Manila so interested in this case?"

Mangoba didn't hesitate. "Manila sent me to Mindanao to reach out to the MNLF regarding a truce. I am trying to reach the brother of the man who owns this car, and he was our best lead, as you police would say. I won't interfere with your investigation, Captain. I'm only on a search for information and I feel there is more to this than meets the eye. I'm also prepared to cooperate with you in any way I can."

The captain thought for a minute, assessing the man standing next to him. He was dressed in a casual shirt and pants. He knew if he was being offered help from this man, it was a sincere offer and not just leverage for information. Mangoba's reputation for honesty preceded him.

"All right, there was a small explosion in the passenger compartment, but I believe it was set intentionally to cover up the fact that the occupants of the car were already dead."

"How do you know that?"

"Right now, it's all speculation, really. The coroner feels that one of the bodies found in the vehicle had a broken neck more consistent with being attacked from behind than from an explosion. I'll have more facts after the two bodies are examined more carefully. Right now, my instincts are telling me we're dealing with murder instead of an act of terrorism."

The general was silent.

"I have great respect for instinct. It's served me well on many occasions and I have learned to trust the instincts of those around me. Captain, after you get more facts, I would appreciate a call. I offer all the resources available to me to help you solve this mystery. I think we have a new twist to our ongoing differences with the MNLF and I'm not sure I like it. Thank you for your insights."

Mangoba shook the captain's hand and walked back to his car. The captain watched as the car drove away.

CHAPTER 3

A NORMAL LIFE

**Rochester International Airport
Rochester, New York
August 16, 1994
1020 Hours**

The red Chevrolet minivan raced into the short-term parking lot. It jerked to a stop by the wooden arm that kept cars from entering without getting a ticket. The window came down and sixteen-year-old Sean Summers stuck his head and shoulders out. The van lurched forward and again jerked to a stop. Sean looked around in bewilderment.

"Mom," he said to Nancy Summers, "where the hell do you get the ticket from."

A calm voice from the front passenger seat spoke softly.

"Huh?" responded Sean. "Oh, sorry."

Sean reached out to the metal box the wooden arm was attached to, pushing a large red button. The box immediately spit out a ticket. Sean grabbed the ticket, and the arm went up. Looking pleased with himself, Sean urged the van forward before he was back inside the window. Sean drove the van into the ramp garage that served as short-term parking and started to pull into a space next to the walkway to the airport. His mother pointed out this was a handicapped parking spot. The van jerked to yet another stop, then jerked back out of the spot, lunging forward to the first available parking spot. While Sean put the gear selector into park, his mother reached across the front of the van removing the keys from the ignition.

"Jeez, Mom, I'm not that bad a driver," Sean said with a disgusted tone.

His mother smiled, opening her door. "I know dear, I just want to give your father the choice of who is going to drive. It's not dignified to see a naval officer in dress whites prying a teenager away from the steering wheel of a car."

There were giggles from Sean's two brothers, Justin, and Stephen, who were exiting by the sliding side door. Sean glared at them and Stephen, the youngest stuck out his tongue in return. Justin glared back in defiance closing the door. The two younger boys started to run towards the terminal but were checked by their mother's voice calling their names. They waited impatiently while their mother and older brother caught up.

"Stay together, boys. The airport is probably crowded, and I don't want you getting lost."

The two younger boys acted like they didn't hear their mother but stayed close while they crossed the covered roadway to the passenger pickup area. Sean was the only one who objected.

"Aw, Mom, I'm sixteen years old. I think I can find my way around the airport without getting lost. I'm not like Steve and Justin who'll run off without looking where you are. Come on, Mom, I..."

"Sean Raymond," said Nancy, "that's enough!"

Sean decided to quietly withdraw. His mother had used his middle name and that meant that if he were to continue the argument, not only would there be punishment from mom, but dad would be brought in on this as well. He didn't want any part of that today. His father always found it difficult *reentering the normal life of the civilian world,* as his mother liked to phrase it. Stephen again stuck his tongue out at his brother from the safety of his mother's arm. Sean didn't know what else to do so he stuck his tongue out in return. Justin just giggled.

They entered the baggage claim area of the terminal and Nancy walked the children to the nearest monitor to check the arrival time of Jon's flight. It was on time and was arriving in the west terminal. She walked the boys over to the escalator and they started up to the second level. Stephen was racing up the escalator on his own while Justin was facing backwards. This drove Nancy crazy, and she quickly was after her two younger children. Sean stood quietly behind his mother, grateful that his brothers monopolized her attention.

Reaching the second level, they moved passed the ticket counters. Nancy walked the boys by several fast-food restaurants allowing Stephen and Justin to disagree about where to eat lunch. Again, Sean stayed out of the discussion. He was thinking that a good report to Dad about his behavior at the airport might get him a chance to drive home.

Nancy talked the two younger boys away from the restaurants, telling them they could go through the security checkpoint to meet their father. They made it through the security checkpoint without incident to the disappointment of Stephen, who wanted to see bad guys being dragged away. As they moved away from the checkpoint Nancy breathed a sigh of relief. She sat all three down in a row of chairs while she walked over to a monitor and again checked the arrival time of Jon's flight. It should be landing at that very moment. Thank God!

She ushered the boys to the designated gate to await the plane's arrival and turned them loose in the boarding area. Stephen and Justin immediately went to the window where they could see the planes take-off and land. It was a busy day so they would be amused for a while. She sat in a chair and Sean sat down next to her. He was a handsome boy with strawberry blond hair, blue eyes, and a slender build. He was very athletic, being on the cross country, basketball, and track teams. His grades were better than hers in high school, but they were still nothing to brag about. He reminded Nancy a lot of her husband when he was sixteen. Sean's brothers were similar in their features, although each had their own unique personalities. Sean would be people oriented. He was going to be a survivor and would do well in anything he decided to do. Justin possessed all the family's artistic talent. He could sing, act, and play piano, guitar, and trumpet. He was quiet with a good sense of humor and a very subtle way with his peers. Stephen looked to be the scholar of the three. He had a thirst for knowledge that could not be quenched and had the grades to prove it. He also was blessed with an endless amount of energy. The other two boys were like their father, thriving on late hours and then sleep in. Stephen was usually the first one up and would sleep when he was tired. She looked at him as her Energizer Bunny. He just kept going and going.

Sean smiled at his mother. "You think dad will let me drive home?"

She reached and put her hand on his. "Your dad can be difficult after returning from summer camp. I'm guessing he'll also be tired. I'll speak to him about it."

Sean leaned over and gave his mother a hug. As he did, he looked down the terminal. He recognized the man walking towards them in the white uniform of the United States Navy. When Sean and his mother separated from their embrace, he motioned for her to follow his gaze.

"Do you know him, Sean?" Nancy asked.

"Yeah, he's Tommy McAvoy, the navy recruiter assigned to our school. I met him through Bobby during lunch a couple of weeks ago."

"You haven't enlisted yet, have you?" Nancy asked looking at her son with surprise. Kids tended to grow up on their parents when they least suspected it. The fact that her son was old enough to meet and talk to a navy recruiter was a big shock for her. She didn't feel that old. She was a little worried though. Bobby Sherman, Sean's best friend, had already enlisted and she was worried that her son might rush to do the same.

Sean stood up so the man could see him. There was immediate recognition. He waved and smiled. The sailor moved towards them, and Nancy did a quick evaluation. He was tall with light brown hair, slender build, and light complexion. He had several ribbons over his right pocket and showed the rank of petty officer second class. His walk was confident. Nancy guessed he had been in the service about six years, maybe a little more. He carried a large manila envelope sealed with tape. Nancy knew it to be the type of envelope used to carry written orders.

"Summers!" said the sailor walking up to them. He slapped Sean on the shoulder. "What are you doing here?"

"We're here to pick up my dad. What are you doing here?"

The sailor turned to Nancy holding out his hand. "I'm Tom McAvoy, Mrs. Summers. I'm the Navy recruiter assigned to your son's school."

Nancy smiled back. "It's nice to meet you, Tom. Have you signed him up, yet?"

Nancy looked towards Sean smiling. McAvoy looked concerned for a second, and then smiled, realizing the boy's mother was joking.

He shook his head. "No, Ma'am. I'm going to wait until he makes Eagle Scout and then go after him. He's worth more then."

"Please take him now. Let Uncle Sam teach him to drive."

Both adults laughed.

"So, why are you here, Tommy?" asked Sean. "Are you flying out somewhere?"

"Nah," replied the sailor, "I got a call at home to rush to Buffalo this morning and pick up a priority message from Washington and deliver it to some captain here at the airport. Apparently, this guy's important enough to get something from the Joint Chiefs. He's just another ship jockey to me."

"You don't care for officers?" asked Nancy with a smile.

"It's not that, Ma'am," replied McAvoy, "I don't have any use for officers who think they're important. I'm going to guess this guy thinks he's important. Not a real line officer. They're the real good ones. Why do you ask?"

Sean started to say something, but Nancy stopped him with a hand on his arm. She smiled at the sailor while looking at her oldest son out of the corner of her eye. He looked a little confused.

"No special reason. My husband has spent some time in the reserves, and I think he might agree with your assessment of a good many officers."

McAvoy returned her smile. "My guess, Ma'am, is this guy is the old seadog type. Full of stories of the good old days and knows nothing of the new Navy."

Just then, Stephen came running up to them. His energy was contagious, and Nancy felt herself getting excited.

Mommy," he said, "Daddy's plane is pulling up at the ramp over there. He's home! He's home!"

"Settle, Stephen," said Nancy gently to her youngest, "go back with your brother and see if you can see your father in one of the windows."

Stephen dashed off to join Justin at the window. Nancy knew that this would keep both boys busy until Jon walked off the plane.

"Do you have a name for this mystery captain?"

"No, Ma'am, I don't. I was told to be here in uniform, meet the United flight from Washington, and he would make himself known to me. I hate this cloak and dagger stuff."

Nancy felt a little better. Jon was only a commander and probably wouldn't make captain with the enemies he'd made over the years.

"United Airlines Flight 2230 from Washington D.C. now arriving at gate number 15 in Concourse A", the PA system blared.

Nancy, Sean, and McAvoy moved to the center of the terminal so they could see who was coming out the walkway. The passengers began to slowly file out of the gate. McAvoy looked worried standing near Sean. Sean was talking away and Nancy knew the sailor wasn't hearing a thing the boy was saying. She gently tapped Sean on the shoulder and motioned for him to go round up his brothers. He gave her a disappointed look but went off to do as asked.

"Don't look so serious," she said to the young sailor.

McAvoy relaxed a bit. "Sure, Ma'am, I'm just a little worried about meeting this guy. You never know what to expect from some officer who's visiting a reserve town. What branch of the service is your husband in? Sean never told me that his dad was in the reserves."

"He's one of those guys who have been in a while. He's an officer in the navy reserves. He finally made commander during the Gulf War. With any luck this will be my last year to deal with *summer camp*, if you know what I mean."

McAvoy laughed. "Yes, Ma'am I do. He must be the one reserve officer I haven't met. I know most of the guys well, except for a few who never do duty at the reserve center.

"That's him all right. He gets sent all over for his weekends. For his two weeks he's usually sent to Norfolk, San Francisco, or San Diego. Spends a lot of the time traveling."

"Well, Ma'am," said McAvoy, "someone has to do all that traveling for the navy. Sounds like a nice reserve gig though. Most of those reserve guys end up spending their two weeks on some second-rate bucket that used to pass as a ship. I don't envy them too much."

Nancy looked at the man smiling, "It's a nice gig if you get to go along. San Diego was nice duty for a wife, of course that was before Jon went to the reserves."

"Did your husband go to OCS or go through ROTC Ma'am?" asked McAvoy.

"Graduated from Annapolis," Nancy replied with a straight face. She caught the sailor's uneasy expression. She tried not to look too smug. She guessed this young man was trying to recruit her oldest son and she was enjoying this little game. It would get more intense when Jon came off the plane. He wasn't a captain, but a full commander still carried some weight with an enlisted man.

The passengers began to file out of the walkway between the plane and the boarding lounge. Justin and Stephen were both bouncing up and down looking for their father. Nancy always enjoyed watching people meet their loved ones after they'd been away. She watched as a family met who appeared to be a grandmother. The children squealed with delight as they hugged her and the young mother and father both threw their arms around the older woman. She watched the businessmen who were always in a hurry race around the happy scene. She heard Stephen shout, "Daddy!" and looked in the direction of the walkway entrance. Jon was reaching to pick up Stephen and his other arm was around Justin as he moved into the concourse. Sean moved forward, a big smile on his face. Nancy looked at the sailor standing next to her seeing all the color drain from his face. She smiled. The young man was learning a little humility but never knew her husband to have this effect on any sailor. She looked back at Jon, suddenly realizing why. On Jon's shoulder boards were four wide stripes, indicating the rank of captain. *Damn him!* He'd been promoted and hadn't told a soul. That meant he would stay in the reserves at least another two years. Sean reached his father and took the briefcase he was carrying. Jon set Stephen back down after receiving a gigantic hug from his youngest son. Jon reached his wife and threw his arms around her giving her a deeply passionate kiss. When he finished, he looked at the young sailor standing next to his wife.

"Petty Officer...," Jon stepped back, cocked his head, reading the name tag on the sailor's uniform, "McAvoy, is it? I have to assume you're here for me or has the navy reinstated the practice of using press gangs for recruiting new enlisted personnel?"

"Sir," replied the confused sailor.

"I see by your badge," Jon pointed to the emblem of the United States Navy that appeared on a badge McAvoy wore on his right pocket identifying him as a recruiter, "that you're with the recruiting detail here and press gangs are what used to be a recruiting tool. You know, where they used to go and kidnap people to serve on a ship."

McAvoy nodded but couldn't take his eyes off the rows of ribbons and insignias above the left pocket.

"So, McAvoy," said Summers, "is that envelope for me?"

"Huh?" McAvoy was jolted back to reality. "Aye, Sir. It is."

Before he could answer, a man in a pilot's uniform approached the small group and cleared his throat to get their attention.

"Excuse me," he said, "but does this young man belong to you?"

He motioned to Justin and both of his parents shifted nervously.

"Yes, he does," replied Nancy. "Is there a problem?"

The pilot laughed. "No, Ma'am, we saw him watching us while we were doing our shut down of the aircraft. The young man looked so interested we felt he might like a tour of the aircraft."

Justin's eyes were filled with excitement.

Nancy breathed a sigh of relief. "I'm sure he would be delighted. May his brothers come along?"

The smile on the pilot never wavered. "Absolutely, Ma'am."

"Honey," Nancy said turning to her husband, "I'll go with the boys, and you can do business with Petty Officer McAvoy."

Nancy stepped over to the young sailor and extended her hand. He took it. As they shook hands she said, "It was nice meeting you, Tom. Don't let him push you around or intimidate you. He didn't even call me to tell me he was promoted so I think a mutiny is in order."

She winked at the young man and again at her husband. McAvoy smiled weakly responding, "It was nice meeting you, too, Ma'am."

Sean waved to the young recruiter and yelled back as he was following his brothers toward the entrance to the walkway. "See you in school, Tom!!"

McAvoy weakly waved back at the teenager. "Sure thing, kid."

McAvoy didn't look at the officer standing next to him right away. Instead he watched the three children and their mother as they followed the pilot into the walkway.

"Let's have a seat over here out of the way," said the officer motioning to a row of empty seats.

McAvoy followed him. Summers held out his hand for the envelope. It took a second for the sailor to realize what the officer wanted, but he quickly responded when the older man pointed to the item in his hands. Jon opened the envelope taking out several sheets of paper and began to read. A smile began to cross his face when he finished reading the first page and moved onto the second. When he finished the third and last page, he returned all three sheets of paper to the envelope and turned back to the young sailor.

"McAvoy," he started, "did they expect a return message?"

McAvoy was startled by the directness of the question. "Yes, sir, my orders were to return to Buffalo with any return message you have."

Summers was silent for a second, "Are you stationed out of Buffalo or here in Rochester?"

"Out of the Lakeview Recruiting Office, sir."

"And they want you to travel all the way back to Buffalo for a message?" the officer's voice showed no emotion at all regarding the question.

"Yes, sir."

"Do you have any other business in Buffalo?"

"No, Sir."

Summers was silent for a few seconds and then pulled a pen out of his briefcase and looked at the young petty officer next to him. "What's the phone number there?"

Without thinking, McAvoy rattled off the telephone number of the recruiting office in Buffalo.

"And who is your commanding officer there?"

"Ensign Pulcino, Sir."

Summers again reached into his briefcase and this time came out with a cell phone. He extended the antenna and pushed the power button. He then quickly pushed the number, hit send, and waited. After about thirty seconds, Summers said, "Ensign Pulcino, please."

"I'm sorry, Sir. He's in a meeting right now. May I take a message?" replied a polite female voice.

"This is Captain Summers. He had a message forwarded to me this morning. Would you please interrupt him and ask him to come to the telephone?"

There was silence for a few seconds before the voice responded, "I'm not sure I can interrupt him, Sir. Is there a problem I can assist you with?"

Summers smiled and winked at McAvoy, "Yes, there is a problem, but unless you are a higher rank than Ensign Pulcino, you can't help me. Is he in the building?"

"Yes, Sir, but he..."

"Then, please find him and get him to the telephone immediately," Summers voice remained even throughout the entire conversation, but there was no question about his authority.

There was silence again for a few seconds. "Ensign Pulcino. Can I..."

"Mr. Pulcino, this is Captain Summers."

"Yes, Sir! Can I help you, Sir?"

"Yes, you can Mr. Pulcino. I do appreciate all you and your people have done to get me the message today, but I have to say we are going to have to come up with a better system than this."

"I don't understand, sir. Is there a problem with McAvoy?"

"No, Petty Officer McAvoy has done an excellent job. The problem is there may be more such messages and we have to come up with a better way to deal with them."

"Sir?"

"We can't have McAvoy or anyone else from either Rochester or Buffalo running back and forth just to deliver messages to me, can we? It's a waste of your time and the navy's money, do you agree?"

"Yes, sir!"

"Now, McAvoy is a signalman so unless you have a problem, I would like to keep him as my contact."

"No problem, sir."

"Okay, then, let me give you my return message. Just te..."

"But, sir," interrupted the voice on the other end of the telephone, "this isn't a secure line, and your message is going to..."

"I'm very aware who my message is going to, Mr. Pulcino!" Jon's voice remained even. "The message you need to send is simply the word *yes*! Nothing more and nothing less, do you understand?"

"Yes, sir. No problem. sir!"

"Very well, I'll be in touch with you in regard to the details regarding my using one of your people within the week and Mr. Pulcino?"

"Yes, sir?"

"I appreciate the help you and your section has given me. Please pass on a well done to all hands."

"Yes, sir! Thank you, sir!"

Summers smiled as he put down the cell phone and looked at the young sailor next to him.

"So, McAvoy," Jon said to the young man, "are you a good signalman?"

"I'm an excellent signalman, sir," replied the sailor smiling at the officer.

"Do you mind working on the fringes of naval intelligence?"

"Not at all, sir!"

"Then welcome aboard, McAvoy, you are now in the company of thieves, and I think I should warn you sometimes the hours aren't fun."

"Sir," said McAvoy, "I enjoy my recruiting job, but I am a sailor, too. This gig's good for some family stability, but it gets real boring at times. Maybe working with you will break up some of the monotony."

Jon laughed. "Don't hold your breath as far as excitement. You'll grow old and gray before you see a lot of excitement in this business. It does keep you busy though. What's your first name McAvoy?"

"It's Thomas, sir. I go by Tom."

"Well, Tom," Jon smiled taking McAvoy's hand and shaking it, "you'll be contacted sometime this week and the navy will let you know how to proceed with any message traffic that needs to get to me. I have a new assignment as of yesterday according to this message and I really don't know what to expect."

McAvoy took a good look at the officer sitting next to him for the first time. He carried himself with confidence and his manner made him comfortable. There was no question he was in control, but he didn't talk down to you or belittle you like many people in authority did. He wasn't a real imposing figure, but Tom guessed he knew his business and judging by the ribbons, proved it on more than one occasion. He also felt he'd seen this man somewhere before.

"Sir," Tom asked, "you look familiar. Have we met at the reserve center before?"

Jon smiled again, "No, Tom, we haven't. Until now, usually the only contact I've had with the reserve center has been to call in and keep them advised of where the navy is sending me next. You've probably seen me at Lakeview High School, I'm a vice-principal there."

Tom thought for a minute and then nodded. He saw Summers when he was doing recruiting during the lunch periods in the cafeteria. Jon was one of the people who regularly did lunch duty for at least one period during the day. Lakeview High School was one of several secondary schools in the suburb of Lakeview. The community sat on the shore of Lake Ontario and was the largest community in the county, next to the City of Rochester.

"Tom," Jon was scribbling something down in a small notebook, "if you need to reach me, call me at any of these numbers. If all else fails, use the pager number. You might as well, the wife and kids do. I can't find anywhere to hide in peace anymore. I'm not hard to reach."

"Aye, aye, sir," responded McAvoy.

Jon reached out and shook McAvoy's hand again.

"I appreciate everything you did today, Tom. I look forward to serving with you."

Tom smiled, "Not a problem, sir. Is there anything else you need me to do right now?"

"No," Jon shook his head, "get out of here."

"Thank you, sir. I think I will. I'll check in at the office and see what else needs to be done today."

The two men said goodbye and then the enlisted man walked down the passage towards the main terminal leaving the officer sitting alone in the seat. Summers felt much better about many things, the most important of which was he was home after an extended summer tour. He visibly cringed. Sean would want to drive home.

Beverly Hills, California
August 16, 1994
0620 Hours

Becky walked down the stairs looking at her watch. She knew at this hour there was no one up to bother her while she did her morning exercises in the pool house. She learned a long time ago she felt and worked better if she stayed fit. Keeping fit was the one thing in her daily schedule she did religiously. She purchased a treadmill, a rowing machine, and a universal gym and set up in the pool house. She got up every morning at six and did stretching exercises in her bedroom followed by a half-hour work out on one or more of the machines. She finished up her morning by swimming laps in the pool for half an hour before showering and going to work. This, she felt, helped give her energy to get through the day.

She approached the door to the kitchen, hearing voices. Ray and her father were huddled together at the large table on the screened porch. Papers were strewn about, and they were deep in discussion about something. She smelled coffee, noticing a cup sitting next to each man. Opening the French doors to the porch, both men looked up, smiling.

"You gentlemen don't believe in sleep?" she asked.

"Doctor," replied Ray, "haven't you read that the older you get, the less sleep you need."

"I thought I taught you to dress better when company was here," was her father's comment.

Becky blushed. She hadn't even thought about what she was wearing. She had on a gaudy, multicolored, nylon, one-piece swimsuit that was low cut at the neck. Becky's build was small, but this suit showed everything. It was tight around her crotch and buttocks and a good portion of both her cheeks showed. While her breasts weren't large, the cut about the neck showed a generous amount of cleavage. Becky wore the suit at home when she exercised and swam because it was comfortable. She hadn't thought their guests would be up at this hour.

"You know, Ray," said her father, "we tried awful hard to get Rebecca and Jonathan together. He should see her in this suit and see what he missed."

Becky's embarrassment turned to anger. She said, "Just what I need to start the day, a couple of dirty old men with nothing better to do than comment about my wardrobe and love life."

Becky guessed her father knew he crossed the line, and his daughter was holding her temper. He laughed at what she said but decided to ease the tension. "You're right about that kiddo, we men just don't know when to appreciate a good woman."

Seeing his friend was floundering, Ray decided he would lighten things up. "You can come around me dressed like that any time you want, young lady. I can't speak for this old fart because he's your father, but I sure as hell don't mind. The really neat thing is I'm safe."

Becky's anger started to fade, "Safe, because of your age?"

"Naw, safe because Louise would make life very painful for me if I did anything but look. I think she would qualify as a doctor of some kind."

Becky laughed. "Okay, okay. Just let me swim my laps and enjoy the rest of my day off. Louise and I are going shopping to spend all of your money, Ray."

Ray smiled and shrugged. "So, what's new?"

Becky met her father's gaze returning his smile. The anger she felt a moment earlier was gone. She knew he hadn't approved of her choice of a husband, and he always liked Jon. She was sure that Jon was a fine man, but she only remembered the brat of a kid that used to follow her around when the families would get together. She guessed him to be a macho warrior type like the rest of the men her father always tried to fix her up with. Conveniently, he was married and lived on the other side of the country, so she didn't have to worry about finding out. Bill stood and put his arms around his daughter, giving her a hug.

"Sorry, pumpkin. I always seem to say the wrong thing when it comes to the men in your life. Will you accept an apology from an old fool?"

"No offense taken, Daddy," replied Becky. "Besides, I haven't done well in that area, so I can't complain if you get critical. Just don't get too critical."

"Say, old fool," said Ray, "why don't you bring Becky and the rest of the family to the reunion in April? It would be good for all of you to get away. Let them see where you started."

Becky cringed visibly. "Thanks, but no thanks, Uncle Ray. The last thing I want to do is sit around with a bunch of old soldiers and literally listen to war stories. Besides, I've been in a good number of the major cities in this country and am not interested in shopping malls."

"The reunion is in the Philippines, remember. Shopping might be just a bit different than going to the mall. I think it would be good for you guys to travel as a family and just site see. You wouldn't have to be with us old soldiers unless you wanted to be. Otherwise, you could do what you wanted. So, what do you think? Sound good?"

Becky looked first at her father and then at Ray. She hadn't expected the response she got and was intrigued by the offer. She certainly had enough vacation time, and she knew she could get Sarah out of school.

"Dad, do you think Kevin would take his family, too?"

"Why, Becky?" answered her father. "What do you have in mind?"

Becky was silent for a second before she answered. The twinkle in her eyes told both men Ray hit on something. Bill felt like hugging his old friend. His family hadn't done anything like this since Mary passed away. Kevin was his oldest child and currently was the President and Chief Executive Officer of Webber Media, the family business. Mary's father inherited the business and built it into an empire. Mary's brother had done well with the company too, but Kevin had a flair for the business and did better than all of them. Becky and Kevin's wife, Kathy, enjoyed a strained relationship so he was surprised at his daughter's suggestion. Maybe they all did need a vacation.

"Daddy," Becky looked at her father, "give Kevin a call and see if he and the old ball and chain want to go on vacation. Lord knows, he needs one!"

Gateway looked at his friend and smiled. Ray returned the smile saying, "That's settled! General William Gateway and family will be traveling to the Philippines in March."

Grand Philippine Hotel
Mindanao, Philippines
August 23, 1994
1400 Hours

O'Keefe sat comfortably at the table, sipping his beer. He wished the man he was waiting for would deliver the information. He wasn't a patient man and the longer he sat, the harder it was going to be for him to be pleasant with the messenger. He enjoyed the climate in the Philippines compared to his native Ireland. While this time of year was warmer than he would like, he didn't always feel chilled to the bone in the winter. He also enjoyed the job he was doing. He acted as bodyguard and advisor to Osaka. While Osaka showed all the appearances of being a businessman, he in fact spearheaded a coalition from the Japanese underworld moving into other countries. O'Keefe brought his experience from the Irish Republican Army to Osaka's staff. He helped problems disappear. He brought a little terror into the lives of those who opposed Osaka. He got paid well for doing the same work he did with the IRA.

He was enjoying his work for Osaka almost too much. Most of the time, he posed as a tourist or businessman, like he was now, living first class all the time. Here, he was posing as an English businessman who purchased native products from all over the Far East. He was dressed in a lightweight tan suit with a white shirt and no tie. His shoes were Italian, and he carried a fine leather briefcase. The suit was cut so the nine-millimeter semi-automatic handgun he carried couldn't be seen. The briefcase and the papers in it were for show, but today carried money to pay for services that hopefully were soon to be rendered.

The hotel restaurant wasn't busy, even though the food was excellent. Currently there were mostly tourists trying to escape the summer heat in the hotel's air conditioning. Patty watched them as they came and went. He felt out of place being alone and looking the part of a businessman. He was waiting to meet someone with information for the next phase of Osaka's plan. Osaka was much more patient than he because he would have already used the military hardware they were stock piling to leave the entire island in chaos. Osaka's plan was much more detailed. He told his staff they would be in control of the island within the next year and a half. He figured he could wait that long for his boss to complete his project.

O'Keefe took another sip of his beer while he watched several hotel employees walk into the restaurant. There were two men and a woman, all three dressed in the blue uniforms of the hotel. The woman stopped at a table near the entrance, talking to the people seated there. The young lady intrigued Patty. She was tall for an oriental. He admired her slender build, medium complexion, and jet-black hair. He found her extremely attractive and was imagining what it would be like to be with her. He shook his head; it had been a while. The woman moved to another table and was talking to the people there, as well. Her movements were graceful and very subtle. He turned back to his beer, finding himself very distracted. Damn, he wished this contact would get here so he could finish this business and get out.

"Hello," the voice behind him was pleasant and warm, "how has the service been, sir?"

O'Keefe turned to find the woman standing next to him, smiling. He found her beautiful and was so distracted he couldn't answer.

"I'm Suzanne Rolle, the hotel assistant manager. I hope you've found everything to your liking, sir."

"Yes, I have."

Her facial expression changed slightly, but she continued smiling. Her eyes seemed to be studying him.

"Are you a guest here at the hotel or are you just enjoying our restaurant?"

O'Keefe was so busy smiling back he almost missed that she gave him the password. He forced himself back to business.

"No, I'm just visiting your fine restaurant ma'am. Would you like to have a seat?"

The smile now seemed more businesslike than friendly.

"Yes, thank you."

She sat down next to him, "So, you're English?"

He smiled, "Good lord, no, Irish!"

"Sorry, I didn't mean to offend you."

O'Keefe maintained his smile, "Not a problem, I thought you were going to be a man. So what do you have for me?"

"The money first," her voice took on a cold tone.

Patty held eye contact with her, reaching into his briefcase, and pulling out an envelope. Her eyes were dark and held his gaze without blinking. She was cool as well as beautiful, that excited him.

"Please count the money. It's in American dollars, as you requested. I've also been instructed to offer a bonus if your information is as good as you say."

"And you are?" The question was direct, and the tone indicated Suzanne was not just making conversation.

O'Keefe smiled, sliding the envelope over to her. He left it sitting on the table and withdrew his hand. The two of them continued watching each other. Suzanne made no attempt to reach for the envelope.

"Name's Patrick Sean O'Keefe ma'am, but most people call me Pat or Patty. Other acquaintances call me by other names. I hope you'll call me Pat."

O'Keefe held out his hand and smiled. By most standards, O'Keefe was quite handsome. He had a full head of blond hair, blue eyes, and a light complexion. He gained weight over the years, but all things considered, remained in rather good shape for someone forty-five years old. His quick wit and Irish accent made him extremely popular with the ladies wherever he went.

Suzanne took his hand and shook it and the hint of a smile appeared on her face. After releasing her grip, she pulled the envelope to her and counted the money. She looked back up at O'Keefe, "Well, Pat, it's a pleasure to meet you and to do business with Mr. Osaka. Does he send you to charm all the female contacts he uses?"

O'Keefe laughed, "We didn't know the contact was a lady, but if we did, I would have been here either way. May I buy you dinner?"

Suzanne smiled. "No, but you will be my guest for an early dinner. I've had nothing to eat all day."

She raised her arm and a waiter rushed over. She quietly gave him some directions. When she returned her attention to her guest, she reached into the inside pocket of the blazer she was wearing and pulled out an envelope handing it to Patty.

"I believe you've paid for this," she said.

O'Keefe smiled, opening the envelope.

"That's the current reservation list for the reunion scheduled here in March. It lists American, Filipino, and Japanese guests currently scheduled. When the time comes, I'll make sure Mr. Osaka has all of the security information and everything else he needs."

"You do excellent work," O'Keefe responded. "I'm sure tha..."

His sudden stop made her nervous.

"What's wrong? Everything should be in order..."

O'Keefe smiled and looked up at Suzanne. His finger rested on a name on the list. It read *General William Gateway and family...Total - 5.*

"Nothing's wrong darlin'. Nothing's wrong at all."

★ CHAPTER 4 ★

HIGHER EDUCATION

Lakeview High School
Rochester, New York
September 21, 1994
1035 Hours

John Regis Haughout walked swiftly down the hall. The halls were empty except for the occasional student or staff member. Each would smile and give him an enthusiastic, *good morning, Mr. Haughout*, as he hustled past. He would smile wishing them well while moving on. John was proud of the job he did as athletic director and vice principal at Lakeview. He was a big man, surprising many he oversaw athletics at the school. Right now, none of that mattered because he was a man on a mission.

He entered the eleventh and twelfth grade office running into Beth Pacella, the twelfth-grade vice-principal, and her secretary Ginny Smith. Kathy Henderson, Summers's secretary, came out of his office, smiling and closing the door behind her.

"Hi Reggie," said Beth, "what's up?

"I need to see Jon!" he said moving passed Beth and her secretary.

"He's got a student in with him right now," replied Kathy staying between the door and the visitor. "I don't think he'll want to be disturbed unless it's an emergency."

Reggie knew better than to lock horns with Henderson.

"Kathy," he said as calmly as he could, "I have to see Jon. It is an emergency."

The secretary looked at him with a discerning eye before picking up the telephone on her desk and pushing several buttons. There was a moment of silence before she said, "Mr. Summers? Mr. Haughout is here to see you and says it's an emergency."

Before Kathy could hang up the phone, the door opened, and Summers stepped out. Behind him, you could see the conference room attached to his office. There were two young men with their heads bowed sitting across from each other at the table. Reggie guessed they were caught doing something they weren't supposed to and looked very remorseful. Summers was good with student management and discipline. Most of the students at Lakeview knew you didn't want to end up in Mr. Summers's office for doing something wrong. Reggie was well liked by the students, but he wasn't sure they respected him. When they were really in trouble, they all went to Mr. Summers because they knew him to be fair and open minded.

"What's up, Reggie?"

"Willie Katz is in the building," Reggie took a breath and could see the two students sit straight up. "He and three of his friends are in the cafeteria right now trying to create a disturbance. Sue is on her way there with security to throw them out of the building. Jon, I think there's going to be trouble."

The smile on Summers's face disappeared. Sue was Susan Olivia Singleton, the principal of Lakeview High School. Willie was a student who was suspended the previous year for putting another student in the hospital. Singleton was famous for either getting her problem students suspended long term or transferred to one of the other three high schools in the district. Katz was suspended long term, threatening to make trouble for the school. Jon knew Willie's two full time jobs were burglary and dealing drugs. He suspected Singleton would be quickly in over her head when she went to confront him.

"Were the police called?" Jon asked stepping back into his office. Reggie shook his head and took a handkerchief out of his back pocket, wiping his forehead nervously.

Jon glanced at the students sitting at the table. Both their heads dropped, and they nervously shifted in their chairs.

"Kathy, you or Ginny get on the line to 911 and get the police here as quick as they can. Give them Willie's name and tell them he's been known to carry weapons. Then, get these two to 'in-school'. If they give you any trouble, call me."

Jon grabbed the small portable radio off his desk. There were identical radios behind both secretaries' desks. Jon turned the squelch knob until he could hear static and then turned it back until the static stopped. Beth had stepped into her office, coming back out with her radio. Jon looked at Reggie who shrugged his shoulders. "I forgot mine."

Beth looked at Jon rolling her eyes. They took off toward the main hall, rushing past the library. As they approached the main commons area by the student cafeteria, they could hear shouting.

They heard Tommy Rybak, the senior security officer, call on his radio, "Tom to office. Get LPD here now!"

Ginny responded immediately. "Twelfth grade office to Tommy. I already called them. They're on the way!"

"Call them back," Rybak's voice was calm, but you could hear a great deal of yelling in the background, "tell them to step it up!"

Jon was worried pushing his way through the crowd of students. Rybak was formerly Lt. Thomas Rybak of the Town of Lakeview Police Department. He was an individual who didn't panic easily. Jon didn't know what to expect but continued to push through the crowd.

Reaching the center of the crowd, Summers could see Singleton and the school's fourth vice-principal, Mary Bruno, standing on the far side of the room with Rybak and two other security officers. Singleton wasn't an individual who dealt well with confrontation. When something happened in the school, she reacted emotionally. She was now engaged in an argument with Katz in front of the entire student body.

"Mr. Katz, you, and your friends aren't welcome here! All of you will accompany security to my office immediately! Do you understand!?!"

Katz was laughing, responding, "Fuck you, bitch! I ain't going nowhere with you! Bite me!"

Singleton was beet red. She was a woman in her early fifties who spent a lot of time keeping up her tan. Her anger deepened her color that was further emphasized by her blond hair. She wore a navy-blue pantsuit, a white blouse, and heels. She stepped forward saying, "I will not have you talk to me in that manner, and I expect to have my requests obeyed immediately!"

This time everyone laughed as Willie stepped forward, "Shit, bitch, you ain't in charge here, I am! Get out of my face!"

Jon forced his way to the edge of the crowd.

"Mr. Katz, I will not tolerate this insubordination. You will comply or I will have security forcibly remove you from the building! You are not in charge here!"

The statement caught everyone off guard and all three of the security officers looked at each other in disbelief. Before they could react, Willie took another step forward punching Singleton in the face, knocking her to the floor. As all three security officers moved forward, Willie and his three friends began to spread out, allowing their leader to step behind them. Each of them immediately began to pull out a weapon of some kind. The young man closest to Jon pulled out a small baseball bat and stepped towards the security officer nearest him. The aggressor just beyond him reached into the waistband of his jeans and Jon could see a small caliber pistol.

Before the first student could take a second step towards the security officer, Jon grabbed the hand holding the bat, pulling it back, and at the same time kicking the young man's legs out from underneath him. He seemed to fly up and then immediately down, landing flat on his back knocking the wind out of him. This distracted the young man with the gun, who was able to get it out and was starting to raise it. He swung the weapon towards the movement, but Jon grabbed the boy's hand, and using his own momentum, pulled the boy's arm behind him while forcing him down towards the floor. The young man pulled the trigger, and nothing happened. Someone shouted, *he's got a gun*, but the movement all seemed to freeze when he found himself inches off the floor on his knees and his arm pinned behind his back. To his right, he could see his friend lying on his back groaning, the small baseball bat next to the crowd where it had landed. He looked up over his shoulder at the man holding his arm behind his back. There was no expression on the man's face. No anger or fear like he had seen in the others just before Willie hit the lady principal. He looked into the blue eyes behind the glasses. They were cold and expressionless. There was something else. He looked around as much as he could. There was no sound or movement anywhere. Everyone was standing still, frozen, and all were looking right at the two of them.

"I don't know who you are, son, but I will not have anyone bringing a firearm into my school. I will not have any of my students getting hurt so you can prove your manhood."

The tone had been quiet and even. At the same time he was saying the words, Jon applied enough pressure to the young man's arm, causing him to let go of the gun.

"I'm glad you decided to cooperate. Now I want you to lie flat on your stomach and put your hands on your head."

The young man did as he was told and was lowered to the floor where Jon let go of his arm. The young man slowly moved both of his arms above his head as he turned to look at Jon again. For the first time, everyone could see the handgun Jon took away from the intruder. Some of the crowd started to move towards the exits while the rest stayed transfixed at the scene in front of them. Jon held the Ruger 9mm pistol in his left hand, the barrel by his wrist. The young man could now see why his weapon hadn't fired. When he pulled the trigger, the hammer came down on the fleshy part of Jon's hand between his thumb and pointer finger. The young man watched as Jon reached over and pulled the hammer of the pistol back. As he removed his hand, blood spewed from the puncture wound on the hand. Sirens and the sound of screeching tires could be heard from outside. Jon's eyes never left the young man on the floor and his expression never changed. For the first time in his life, the young man felt what it was like to be truly afraid, he wet his pants.

In what seemed to be one swift motion, Jon released the magazine and removed the slide, rendering the weapon useless. More bystanders in the crowd started to move towards the exits. He handed the pistol over to Rybak. Jon turned his attention to the two remaining intruders, Katz being the closest and holding a knife. Behind him, Jon heard the police as they cleared the crowd. Willie's eyes were fixed on the blood coming from Jon's left hand. There was a lot of commotion from the Commons area entrance as several police officers entered. Jon didn't look at them but kept his gaze on the two young men. To Jon's right, Marie Bruno and a security officer were helping Singleton to her feet. She was holding her nose in her hands and Jon could make out traces of blood. They quickly moved her towards the police officers. Jon heard weapons being pulled out of leather holsters.

"He's got a knife! Watch it, he's got a knife!" Jon recognized the voice of Sgt. Ron Hapke. Jon could see out of the corner of his eye that Hapke was the only officer pointing his weapon.

"Drop the knife, Katz!!" ordered Hapke. Willie just stood there, still looking at Jon's bleeding hand for a second and then looked up at the policeman pointing the gun at him. Willie was instantly nervous looking between the pistol and the crowd around him, searching for a way to escape.

"I said drop the knife, asshole! You put the knife down on the floor, now!!"

Willie stared directly at the police officers for a second with a sorrowful, lost look.

Jon watched Willie's expression change from fear to anger. His posture went from that of a cowering animal to that of a dangerous, cornered one. Jon glanced over his shoulder at the four policemen who were now standing behind him. Hapke was still the only one pointing his weapon at Willie. Hapke's eyes were filled with excitement. Jon knew how the adrenaline was pumping through the police officer and turned back to look at Willie. The young man was going to stand his ground and quite probably try to take on at least one of the police officers. For that error in judgment Jon knew that Willie would pay with his life. Not in his school and not in front of half of the student body. Jon looked Willie in the eye stepping into the line of fire.

"Hey, Summers. Get out of the line of fire!" shouted Hapke. Jon ignored him and stood with his back to the policeman. Hapke moved to his right to get a clear shot and Jon moved with him, never looking back. He moved again, this time to the left, and Jon stayed in his line of fire.

"Come on, Summers, you're blocking my shot. Don't let this asshole get away with this," said Hapke. He wasn't shouting any more, but his tone was less than friendly.

"Summers, get out of the way and let the professionals handle this!"

Jon smiled at the last statement. "I am letting the professionals deal with this. No one, Hapke, and I mean no one is going to be hurt more than they already have been today. Willie!!"

The young man jumped when his name was called but kept Jon between himself and the police. He didn't look as angry as he had a moment before and was back to looking around the crowd.

"Willie, look at me!" said Jon.

"Katz, you drop that knife, or I'll fucking shoot your ass!" said Hapke from behind him. Willie looked at him and his eyes started to harden again.

"Willie, look at me, not at him," Jon said. "I'm the one you have to worry about. I'm closer than he is."

Willie looked startled; his gaze shifted from the policeman to the vice-principal. Fear returned to his eyes as they darted about the room frantically. Jon understood the fear was not of him or the police, but of being in a situation you lost control of. It was time to give a gentle push.

"Look at me, Willie," said Jon. "Remember this is my school and we both know what will happen if you don't do as you're told."

"You ain't sending me with the cops. I ain't going!" replied Willie.

"Summers, get out of my line of fire!!!" shouted Hapke.

Jon didn't give Willie a chance to react to what the policeman said. "Willie don't worry about Sgt. Hapke. Remember, the person you need to watch is me. I'm the guy who will take that knife away before you can use it. Now, why don't you put that thing down and you and I can talk."

Willie smiled looking at the vice-principal. "Fuck you, Mr. Summers. You ain't in charge of me no more. That bitch Singleton threw me out of here, so you can't tell me what to do any more."

Jon sensed a change in the crowd and smiled back at the young man in front of him. "I'll say it again, Willie. Put the knife down and let's talk. This isn't a situation you can win. You're smarter than to let yourself be suckered into a confrontation with the police."

Jon watched his eyes. There was still a smile on his face, but his eyes were telling Jon he was about to achieve his goal. He took a step forward towards the two young men. Willie was upset and not really in a rational state of mind, but was still calling him *Mister,* so Jon decided to accept little victories.

"Don't step no closer, Mr. Summers! Don't come no closer or I'll cut you. I'll cut you good, too. You ever been cut, Mr. Summers? You know how that feels? You don't wanna find out, so back up!"

Jon's smile broadened. "Been there, done that."

Willie looked puzzled, "What?"

"I said, Willie, been there, done that. That means I've been cut before and not in the kitchen or with a little knife like you've got."

Jon took a step closer, and Willie looked more concerned. The young man behind Willie looked ready to panic, taking a step closer to his friend.

Willie looked around the crowd, they were being pushed back. Behind Summers he could see several more policemen arrive. Several others moved to his two friends who had been lying on the floor. They were quietly handcuffing the two young men and moving them off to the side. The other officers were working their way around the crowd slowly and methodically. Willie looked at the vice-principal as Jon took another step closer to him.

"I told you to stay back, Mr. Summers and I meant it," Willie held out the knife in his hand out to threaten Jon.

"I want you to put the knife down on the floor and kick it away from you and you need to do it now. Lieutenant Ferland and his officers are patient, but they won't wait much longer before doing something. When they do, someone's going to get hurt," Jon didn't have to look to know that Steve Ferland, the police department's second platoon lieutenant, had arrived. He could tell by the way the officers were now reacting to the incident, there had been a shift in command.

"You are!" shouted the young man.

"Maybe," replied Jon, "but I guarantee both you and your friend here probably will be. There's nothing for you to gain here, Willie. You don't need to leave here both hurt and under arrest. You're a smart young man, do the right thing and put the knife down."

Jon exchanged stares with both young men. The fear in Willie's eyes was gone and he seemed to be reflecting on his options. The other young man looked nervously about the cafeteria, "Willie, come on man, do something! I don't wanna get my ass kicked. What are we gonna do, man?"

Willie tossed his knife to the floor. It slid to a stop in front of Jon's feet. "We're gonna do what Mr. Summers says and at least walk out of here. Put your knife down."

The young man gave Willie a puzzled look.

"Do it man," said Willie, "and don't get stupid on me."

The second young man dropped his knife by his feet and kicked it over next to Willie's. Three police officers cautiously moved in starting to frisk and handcuff both teenagers. As Hapke rushed forward, still carrying his pistol, he pulled Katz away from the officer who was cuffing him. Willie winced as the handcuffs were tightened a little too much.

"You're mine, you son of a bitch!! No one to protect you an…," Hapke's loud oratory was interrupted by Summers who pushed his way in between the two of them. The policeman looked surprised and let go of Willie stepping back out of reflex. The two men stared at each other for a second.

Jon spoke first. "Put the gun away, Sergeant. You don't need it now."

"Fuck you, Summers," replied the policeman angrily as he looked up at the vice-principal. "You assholes in the schools coddle these shitheads and then call us when you can't handle them anymore. He's a piece of shit and deserves to be treated that way and now he's in my custody and I'll make sure he gets what's coming to him. You stay the fuck out of my way, or I'll make you sorry you were ever born. Do you understand?"

Jon looked down at the policeman and then glanced over at Ferland, who was walking up. Jon nodded to Ferland, who responded with a quiet hello.

"Sergeant," Jon said looking back at Hapke. "I don't really care about your opinion of me or the school system, but I will not have you flashing a drawn weapon in a room crowded with kids. If you want to push this point, I assure you it's a battle I'll win and that's not the way I would prefer to deal with this."

The sergeant looked nervously at his commanding officer, who nodded in agreement. His face flushed while he put his pistol back in its holster.

Jon's expression didn't change, "Thank you, Sergeant. I'll be down to sign the complaints on these four for trespass as soon as I get this hand taken care of."

Jon raised his hand so the sergeant could see it. It wasn't bleeding as bad as it had been. The police officer paled looking at the injured hand. The man's commanding officer turned his head to hide his smile.

"You could have been shot with that stunt you pulled," Hapke said. "You were trying to keep me from doing my job and I don't appreciate people who aren't cops doin' shit like that. You don't know what it's like…"

Hapke noticed his lieutenant stiffen and immediately knew he'd made a mistake. He observed Summers's entire manner become threatening. Suddenly, he caught himself stepping back.

"I don't understand what, Sergeant?" interrupted the vice-principal stepping forward to compensate for the policeman's backward motion. Jon's voice got quiet. "I don't know what it feels like to be shot. I've been shot before, Sergeant, and by people who were actually trying to kill me. It's no big deal. They shoot you, it hurts, you bleed a lot, and if you're lucky enough, you live. Or is it that I don't understand what it's like to do your job day after day, not be appreciated for doing it well, and constantly take abuse from the public that you serve. Is that it, sergeant?!?"

The policeman stood there turning red with anger. He stopped backing up and both of his fists were clenched tight. He looked ready to attack the man opposite him.

"I've been there more than once myself," continued Jon. "I guess the thing I don't understand is how cops think they're the only ones who have those feelings about their occupation. Don't be stupid!"

Jon could see Hapke was about to take a swing at him when Ferland spoke, "Sgt. Hapke, you have prisoners to deal with. Get them where they belong, and I'll be along in a few minutes."

The younger police officer turned and glared at his superior for a second then came back to reality. His face was still flushed, but he was managing to regain his control. He stepped back from the civilian saying, "Some other time, Summers. We'll see how good you are."

Hapke turned leaving with the officers who were escorting the last of the four prisoners. Hapke's eyes never left Summers until he was out of the room. For the first time since he started the confrontation with the four young men, Jon looked around the room and felt himself relax. Teachers and other school staff were moving students on about their business. Jon knew no one in the building would get much of anything else accomplished today because of this incident. He noticed one of the history teachers, Debbie Bush, headed towards him with what appeared to be a towel.

"You OK, here?" she asked handing him the towel. "You put on quite a show, there Mr. S. Better clean up that hand before you meet the Dragon Lady, although she won't be doing much talking today with that fat lip and broken nose of hers."

Jon smiled at the way Debbie referred to Singleton, wrapping the towel around the wound.

"I'll call Nancy and warn her about what to expect when you get home. Now go get that looked at by the nurse. Stupid, grabbing a gun like that. She gets paid to look at silly injuries when kids get careless."

Debbie turned, disappearing around the corner.

"Nice, supportive staff, Summers," said Ferland with a smile.

"She's a good kid."

"I'm sure she is. She's also smart. She was right about the gun. You should have let us handle that."

"And have Hapke shoot the poor kid in front of the entire school? No thanks."

"Well, that would have solved two problems."

Jon looked at his friend, "What do you mean?"

"First, you wouldn't be standing here bleeding and second, I would finally get rid of that asshole. Now, I have to go tell him how I saved his life from the big mean teacher who was about to rip his heart out. You were going to rip his heart out, weren't you? Isn't that what SEALs do?"

Jon laughed shaking his head.

"No, you ignorant grunt, that draws too much attention. But I would love to choke him, just a little bit."

"You're too willing, and besides, he's not really that bad a guy. You really pushed his buttons today."

"He's a certified loon, Steve. Did you see his eyes? There was absolutely no control on his part until you talked to him."

"Jon, don't judge him until you know what it's like…"

"Not you, too?" Jon said indignantly.

"I didn't mean it that way and you know it," Ferland defended himself. "All I'm saying is the man is good at his job, and I wouldn't expect him to judge you the same way. You just don't like each other."

Jon smiled. "That, my friend, is true. I guess he probably thinks I'm crazy."

"You are my friend. You're just a lot more controlled than he is. Now, let's go find the nurse and get that hand looked at so you can sign a statement."

Davao University
Mindanao, Philippines
September 22, 1994
0115 Hours

The night hid their movement between the buildings. They were a small group moving silently on their errand of death. They reached one of the largest buildings on the campus and all huddled around the door leading to the basement. While one of them worked on the locked door, the other members of the team kept a lookout. Suddenly the door swung open and one by one they moved into the building. Once inside, the door was secured behind them and they moved to where they could turn on a dim flashlight. They were all wearing casual clothes and carrying small duffel bags. They looked like many of the young students on campus. Filipinos valued their education, one of the many things they adopted from years of being governed by the United States.

Once the light was turned on, they opened their duffels, taking out black coveralls, and putting them on over their clothes. Next out of the duffels came the Heckler and Koch sub-machine guns. Each put their own weapon together, including the noise suppressor, and loaded it. Additionally, each carried five spare clips for the sub-machine gun, a silenced pistol, and a knife. Once they all were ready, black ski masks were donned, and they started on their journey upstairs.

The third man in the single file line slowly working its way up the fire stairs was the group's leader. He was the only person who knew the real reason for their presence on the campus. The team was told they were here to show the government in Manila they could strike anywhere and escape safely. While this and scaring the entire population of the southern Philippines were nice bonuses, the main target was one of the rising lieutenants of the local MNLF organization. Only the team leader knew his identity and where he would be at a given time. This was meant to send a message to the MNLF to not interfere in the operations of this powerful new organization emerging in the separatist movement.

The organization was dubbed the Mindanao Freedom Alliance or MFA. The only thing the government officially said about this new threat was it was a very militant and violent spin off of the MNLF. The MNLF denied having anything to do with this new group and even sent messengers to Manila offering assistance in stopping the group. Both sides were frustrated with the surprising firepower this new organization mustered in such a short period of time. There were a few small, well-planned raids on barrios and local police stations. There were even some assassinations of local politicians in rural areas. This would be their boldest strike to date, and they hoped it would send fear throughout the island.

The team snaked their way up the fire stairs of the high-rise dormitory. The point man was a landing ahead of the rest of the team and the rear guard remained a landing behind them. When they reached the fifth floor of the building, they stopped, and the team leader checked to make sure everyone was ready. While he gave final instructions, there was a noise from the other side of the fire door. The team instinctively hugged the wall. The fire door opened, and a young Filipino woman walked through the doorway. The team leader grabbed her quickly, putting his hand over her mouth so she could not scream. The girl struggled, but her small size and weight offered her little help against the large male holding her. A female member of the team drew her knife, stabbing the young woman several times in the chest. Muffled screams escaped so the woman cut the girl's throat. All noise stopped. The team leader said nothing, putting the now limp body on the floor next to the doorway. The female team member was smiling while looking into the dead, lifeless eyes of her victim.

The team moved through the door. Their plan was simple. They broke up into pairs, each assigned specific rooms on the floor to hit quickly and quietly. The odd member of the team was assigned to secure the hallway so they could safely escape. They moved down the hallway, checking the doors. The team leader and his female partner found their first door unlocked.

They pushed the door open, entering with lightning speed taking the occupants in the common area by surprise. One of the coeds stood, catching the burst from the female terrorist's sub machine gun in the chest. She fell backwards into two males. The female terrorist continued firing while her partner kicked in the door of the first of two bedrooms. When the door flew open, the team leader could see the man he was looking for on top of a young woman in the closest bed. Both were naked and in the heat of passion. The man started up, a look of sheer terror on his face. The young woman had her eyes closed and her head back having no idea what was about to happen. The team leader fired his weapon and continued to fire until the entire clip was empty. Rounds hit the male and female, shaking both bodies violently. The man fell on top of the woman, bullets continuing to strike his body. When the clip was empty, he ejected it from his weapon and put in a fresh one, immediately putting a live round in the chamber. He pulled out his pistol, walking over to the bodies firing two rounds into their heads. The male body shuttered at the impact. He quickly checked for a pulse, finding none.

Before leaving the room, he pulled an envelope from his coverall pocket and dropped it on the floor next to the bed.

He exited the bedroom and entered the second, finding it to be empty. As he came back into the common area, his partner was using her pistol to finish off any survivors. The terrorists entered each of their assigned suites killing anyone who might have been unfortunate enough to be there. The silencers on their weapons were the best money could buy and afforded their victims little warning. Twice, students had run from the rooms looking to escape only to be cut down by the terrorist watching the hallway. Most were caught in their beds because of the hour, never having a chance. One poor soul even came off the elevator only to be shot.

The whole mission took less than ten minutes to complete. They disappeared down the fire stairs, moving swiftly back to the basement. Stripping out of their coveralls and disassembling their weapons, everything went back into the duffels. They exited the building the same way they came in. Once outside, they separated into the same pairs. The terrorist who stood security in the hallway went with the team leader and his partner. Each group went to a different pickup point, and no one pair knew the location of the others for security reasons.

The team leader and his two companions reached the main entrance to the university where they were met by a cab. When they reached a hotel near the Davao Airport, they exited the cab without their duffels and casually walked to the elevator. They went to a room on the third floor, entering and locking the door behind them. Within fifteen minutes, the other two pairs arrived in similar fashion taking rooms on either side of the first. Almost immediately, the two male members of the first group left dressed like they were going out on the town. They went down to the lobby, one hailing a cab while the other got into a waiting car.

The team leader, Benny Montoya, looked at his Uncle Emil in the front seat and smiled.

"How'd it go?" asked Montoya.

"It went as planned, Uncle," said the young man. "Watch the news on the TV. We'll be remembered for this."

"The entire floor?"

"Yes," answered Benny, "but was it necessary? They were all students, mostly women."

"I know. You need to understand that if we are to discredit our brothers in the MNLF, we must do things that aren't to our liking. They're still too strong and by making it look as if they did this while trying to eliminate a disloyal soldier, they'll start to lose the support they have, and we can shift it to our benefit. How'd the woman work out?"

The smile disappeared from Benny's face. "She's deadly, Uncle Emil. A real cool professional, never wavered from the mission and knew just what to do."

His uncle now smiled, "Like you, this was her first mission. Osaka's people have taken an interest in her for some reason and sent her on this mission to see what she could do. Good, I'm glad she did well. While I'm calling Osaka's security people, you sit back and relax. You've earned it."

Montoya picked a cell phone from its cradle next to him and punched in a number.

"This is Montoya."

Benny could only hear one side of the conversation.

"Yes, the mission went exactly as planned. Your subject performed well. She was perceived to be a professional."

There was silence as Emil listened.

"Very good, I'll see you then."

Emil pushed the end button.

Several miles away, Rolle got into the rear of the limousine as O'Keefe hung up the cell phone located on the rear deck behind him. Patty smiled while she closed the partition between the passenger compartment and the driver. She wore a black halter-top evening dress and smelled of perfume.

"Where to, Sir?" asked the driver over the intercom.

Patty smiled at Suzanne.

"You heard the man, where to?"

Suzanne reached across O'Keefe to push the intercom button. As she did, her low-cut dress opened, exposing her to O'Keefe. She looked at him, smiling, "To my house and please take the long way."

"Yes, Ma'am."

She never went back to her seat but moved over to sit on O'Keefe's lap. She undid the shoulder strap allowing the dress to fall. She then put her arms around his neck.

"You know," she said as the dress fell, "the adrenaline rush turned me on."

They both disappeared to the floor of the limousine as it drove slowly through the streets of Davao.

★ CHAPTER 5 ★

THE DAY-TO-DAY GRIND

Davao University
Mindanao, Philippines
October 15, 1994
0815 Hours

The rain came down in torrents, pounding against the windows at the end of the hallway. Franco stood silently looking at the bloodstained carpeting outside several rooms. Near the dark discoloration on the carpet were taped outlines where each victim fell. It was hard for him to visualize the people responsible for this carnage. He watched one of the detective teams while they looked around for clues. The police department initially sealed off the entire floor, spending hours going over every square millimeter looking for evidence.

Jaime heard one of the detective's shouting with delight from the room next to him. He walked in and saw both men on their hands and knees looking under the couch in the center of the room. When they saw him enter, they both jumped up looking nervously at their boss.

"Sorry, Sir," said the shorter of the two, "we bet about what we would find when we moved the couch and I won. I didn't mean to disturb you."

Jaime smiled at the two young men. "And what did you find?"

Both detectives looked nervous. "We found money, sir, coins from the sides of the cushions."

Franco remained silent for several seconds. "What would that tell you about the investigation to this point?"

The young man thought before answering. "I would say, sir, these were not caught in the initial sweep for evidence on the morning of the shootings."

He looked so proud of himself.

"And what else can you conclude?"

There was a long silence as the two detectives stopped smiling, thinking. The taller of the two men suddenly spoke, "Sir, would you like me to call the forensics lab to do another search of the crime scene?"

Jaime smiled saying nothing. He picked up the phone to make a call.

"Yeah, what do you want?" answered a very uninterested voice.

Jaime's smile grew. "This is Captain Franco. Is your lieutenant there?"

There was an immediate change in tone. "Yes, sir, but he is in a meeting currently, briefing the commissioner and someone from Manila. Should I have him call you back, or can someone else help you?"

Jaime's voice remained even. "Interrupt him and have him come to the phone immediately."

"But, sir, I…"

"Interrupt him or I'll page the Commissioner and interrupt him that way."

"Yes, Sir!" and the line went silent.

Franco waited quietly, while the call was transferred. He could hear someone taking a deep breath before speaking.

"Captain Franco, this is Lieu…"

"Lieutenant, don't say anything, just listen and do exactly as I request."

His statement was met with silence.

"Two of your investigators have found more evidence in one of the rooms. It's not much, but it shows that the initial search of the crime scene was most likely done very quickly and not anywhere near thorough enough. You get a forensic team down here to assist these two officers in doing another search of the scene. This is to be done immediately, do you understand?"

Without a moment's hesitation. "Yes, Sir, but…"

Jaime's voice grew louder. "Lieutenant, be careful here. I am looking at sloppy police work on a major case and you're briefing the Commissioner telling him what a good job you and your people are doing. I would advise you to tell the Commissioner that you are sorry about wasting his time and get back to work solving this crime. Am I making myself clear, Lieutenant?"

"Yes, Sir!" the voice on the other end replied shakily.

"Get those people started and I'll speak to you later."

"They're al...," the voice on the other end was cut off by Jaime hanging up. The two detectives looked at each other and then at their Captain. Most people that worked with Jaime were afraid of him because of the expectations he put on subordinates. He demanded, and usually received, the highest level of performance from all officers under his command. When he found what he considered substandard performance, they were drilled until the performance reached his expectations. Most of his people didn't see it as an expectation/performance issue, they just thought of him as a son of a bitch. He didn't mind because the job still got done correctly.

Looking at the investigators he said, "I commend the two of you. There'll be quite a few of your colleagues arriving shortly. Make sure they're as thorough as you've been, and we just might solve this crime. Keep up the good work, gentlemen."

They knew instinctively they were dismissed. Jaime walked towards the fire exit. The door was propped open and there was dried blood with a taped outline on the landing of the fire stairs. Looking at the outline, his thoughts drifted back to the night of the crime.

He'd been at home with his wife. It wasn't often he was able to spend an evening at home with his family and they'd enjoyed the opportunity. His telephone rang, and he was told there was a terrorist attack at the university. He found an orderly crime scene considering the magnitude of what happened. The media was kept out and all the other residents were sequestered in another building to be questioned. The police supervisors on the scene did an excellent job of containment, making everyone else's job easier.

The first responding officers didn't know the size of the scene until they checked the entire floor. As more help arrived, the crime scene was expanded and wounded removed. In all his years, Jaime had seen nothing like this. People were indiscriminately killed for no apparent reason. They found thirty-seven bodies, most executed in their beds. Eight students managed to survive the attack, but two died in the hospital.

The current theory was this was a MNLF hit gone bad, because of a note found by one of the bodies. Jaime didn't agree with this theory. The fact most of the killings appeared to be done execution style led him to believe this wasn't an operation targeting one individual. The note was sent to a military lab in Manila to be analyzed and he was optimistic it would yield something useful. He was sure additional searches would produce more clues. He felt this brutal atrocity was meant to send a message to the MNLF and to weaken the confidence of the population of Mindanao in the Manila government's ability to protect them. This wasn't the way the MNLF operated. They would have just made the individual in question disappear, never to be seen again. Mass murder wasn't their style.

The sound of people getting off the elevator interrupted Franco's thoughts. He looked down the hall and saw the two young detectives meet the first of the forensic team. They all immediately set to work with an occasional glance in his direction. He strolled back down the hallway. There was another flurry of activity at the elevators. The Commissioner rushed off, followed by the Lieutenant in charge of the forensic team. General Mangoba brought up the rear. The Commissioner and the policeman were dressed in business suits, looking uncomfortable in the heat. The General was dressed in military fatigues. The Commissioner and the Lieutenant didn't look happy.

"Captain Franco," said the Commissioner, "this is highly irregular to call the Lieutenant out of a briefing like this. This better be worth our while."

While the commissioner was a good man, he was still a bureaucrat and couldn't see all the dimensions of the case. Jaime took a breath before he answered.

"Mr. Commissioner, I apologize for disturbing your briefing, but it is most important I talk to the lieutenant, if you will excuse me for a moment."

The commissioner's face flushed, just as the lieutenant's went pale. Jaime motioned for the other policeman to follow him. The older policeman put his arm around the younger one's shoulder, speaking quietly.

Mangoba smiled watching the Commissioner shake his head.

"I apologize for Captain Franco," said the commissioner as he unclenched his fists. "He can be rather difficult at times. I don't think this trip was necessary, and I apologize."

"Don't apologize, Commissioner," said Mangoba. "I'm aware of Captain Franco's reputation and you couldn't have a better man working on this investigation. If anyone can solve this, he can. Come, lets you and I get a briefing from the captain to see what's prompted this new visit to this sad place."

Mangoba motioned for the commissioner to precede him. The commissioner reluctantly complied.

First Ranger Battalion Headquarters
Fort Benning, Georgia
October 15, 1994
1600 Hours

Charlie Naylor looked at his watch as his operations officer mapped out the details of the next day's training exercise for his company commanders and their senior NCO's. He liked his operations officer, even though he was a bit long winded. He looked over the gathered crowd of soldiers noticing some were near sleep as the officer droned on. Naylor observed one group of soldiers who appeared to be more attentive than the rest, taking special note of the NCO keeping his people on task. Naylor wrote down two quick notes. The first he gave to his aide to deliver to the commander of Echo Company. The note requested that the commander and his staff report to his office after the briefing. He also made a note to himself to talk to Captain Carmichael about his presentation style. The second note he put into his pocket.

Naylor was assigned to the First Ranger Battalion as its new commanding officer. Since being here he realized several things. First, because of never serving in combat, both the soldiers serving under him and the officers he served under looked upon him with suspicion. It would be unusual for someone of his rank and years of service to take command of a battle-ready unit without combat experience. He understood this and could only counter by saying whenever there was a war to be fought, the United Sates Army assigned him other duty. He always volunteered for combat, and that reflected in his record. He was a skilled tactician and staff officer with a unique ability for communicating. This, more than anything else, kept him from getting a combat command.

The second thing he realized was he was a good leader and people liked working for him. He quickly discovered if he used his skills as a communicator, he could bring his subordinates around to his way of thinking. He would need their allegiance if he ever expected to lead this battalion into combat. The fact his staff came to trust him was helping when he met with each of the companies in the battalion

The third and last thing he found was the men serving under you were willing to do most anything if you were wallowing in the mud with them. Every day he went through the same training as his men, providing his schedule would allow. The fact he was not married made it easier for him to spend more time in the field than his counterparts with families. The men seemed to enjoy seeing their new commanding officer running the obstacle course or working on his hand-to-hand combat skills next to them.

Being in command of a combat ready battalion of Rangers was far different from his life as senior aide to General Goodman at the Pentagon. It was an abrupt change from the life in Washington D.C. Maintaining a busy social schedule while posted there was easy, but here at Fort Benning he was barely able to catch the 11 o'clock news. He would miss the nightlife but knew this would pay off for him career wise in the long run.

He found his mind wandering as Carmichael continued to talk. Bringing himself back to reality he listened to the other officer.

"…and Echo Company will drop in here at this LZ. The terrain will be working against a high-level drop, but it is quite adequate for the low level drop we have planned. Echo Company will secure the objective from the southeast and will hold until relieved by Baker and Foxtrot Companies. The Third Ranger Battalion and elements of the Fifth Mechanized Infantry Brigade will provide resistance. Our intel is coming from two A-Teams that have been infiltrated into the area over the last twenty-four hours. Based on the information supplied by these teams we should be successful in landing enough troops to secure the objective using the LZ's we've selected and get them back out safely. Are there any questions?"

Captain Carmichael looked out over his audience and saw no hands raised. He glanced over at Naylor, "Sir?"

Naylor shook his head in response to his operations officer's offer to address his troops. He knew he probably should, but there were other things on his mind. Carmichael didn't miss a beat turning back to face the assembled men.

"Gentlemen, reveille will be at 0330 and we'll start our part of this operation at 0430. Good luck, gentlemen! Dismissed!"

Naylor stood nodding to Carmichael walking towards the door. All the assembled men rose coming to attention. He walked down the hallway and entered a door labeled *Battalion Commander*. In the outer office were several clerks busy working. They started to rise as he opened the door. He motioned for them to stay in their seats, walking past them, and into his office.

He went to his desk. The office was clean and neat. His office in Washington was always cluttered with reports and studies. The telephone rang constantly, and the interruptions were endless. Things here at Fort Benning seemed to run more efficiently. His mission here was much more defined than it was in Washington. Here his mission was to have the battalion ready to move into combat on a moment's notice. His staff made sure that would take place as quickly and effortlessly as possible. It didn't take them long to find out that their new commanding officer spent long hours in the field and in turn long hours at night catching up on paperwork. Because of this schedule, his staff added two runners to headquarters to rush urgent items to the colonel as needed. They also learned to put a package of nightly *homework* together for him. He surprised them by completing everything on time or ahead of schedule.

On top of his desk, Naylor found two items needing to be signed and returned to his administrative staff for processing. He quickly read through both and signed each. He placed them in the out basket and called his secretary on the intercom.

"Colonel Naylor, Captain Klintworth and his staff are here to see you as ordered."

"Thank you, Florence," he replied. "Send them in and then you can go home. I'm done for the day. Did you need to process either of these items you left?"

"No, Sir. I'll take care of both tomorrow."

The door opened and Captain Richard Klintworth and eight officers and sergeants entered.

"You have a good evening, Florence."

"You, too, Colonel."

The phone went dead, and Naylor turned his attention to the soldiers standing at attention in front of his desk. They stood in two rows, looking straight ahead.

"As you were, gentlemen."

Immediately the men stood at ease. Some shifted nervously, others looked concerned thinking they might be in trouble. The sergeant who kept his peers on task during the briefing seemed bored. Older than the rest of the men, he looked to be in his mid-thirties and a career soldier. He stood six feet tall, with short-cropped hair, big shoulders, and a pair of dark eyes that looked right through you.

"Captain Klintworth," asked Naylor, "I assume you and your men are ready for this mission tomorrow?"

"Yes, Sir," replied the officer. "We'll kick ass tomorrow, Sir!"

Naylor's expression was serious. The officer looked confident standing at parade rest.

"Captain, you will kick ass tomorrow because I will be with your company."

"Yes, Sir!" replied Klintworth.

"Now," continued Naylor, "you and your staff will ignore the fact I'm with you. I'm along to see what I can pick up from your people because I've been sitting at a desk in Washington too long. I am to be considered one of your troopers for this mission. Am I clear?"

"Yes, Sir!"

Naylor noticed the men standing in the formation reacted to his statement except the one sergeant. His facial expression remained unchanged, and he looked more bored than ever.

"Captain," asked Naylor, "do you or any of your staff have a problem with me accompanying you on this exercise?"

Klintworth looked genuinely hurt by the question, while some of the other men showed fear in their eyes. The one sergeant's eyes and face remained unchanged.

"Absolutely not, Sir!" responded Klintworth, fumbling for words for the first time. "It would be an honor to have you accompany us on this exercise tomorrow. I don't understand how you get…"

Naylor stood up, raising his hand to stop the captain. The entire group stiffened. If there had been room, Charlie was sure several of them would have taken a step back. He didn't like intimidation as a leadership technique but could appreciate how easily it could be used. Only the one sergeant remained unaffected. Naylor looked directly at the sergeant, who very deliberately returned his gaze. The man was not intimidated in the least and

Naylor was intrigued by the man's casual behavior regarding him. Charlie decided that the direct approach would be the best.

"Sergeant," Naylor said casually pointing at the man, "I'd be interested in hearing your perspective on this. What do you think?"

The sergeant straightened up, coming to attention. Klintworth leaned forward glaring at the noncom. The facial expression of the soldier still didn't change.

"Sir," began the soldier, "if the Colonel is interested in learning what we do, and how we do it, then he has come to the right company. If he is coming to evaluate us as soldiers then he should be up front with us, Sir."

Klintworth went red with rage, but worked at maintaining a calm voice, "Sergeant Rear…"

"Captain," Naylor broke in, "the sergeant can speak for himself."

There was a pause. The captain, caught off guard, composed himself. He turned, looking straight forward, and took a deep breath. He wasn't sure what his first sergeant was up to but trusted the man.

"Sorry, sir, it won't happen again," said the company commander.

Naylor transferred his gaze from the young officer to the NCO.

"What's your name, sergeant?"

"First Sergeant George Reardon, Jr., Sir!" answered the soldier without hesitation.

Naylor smiled. "Sgt. Reardon, would you like to explain your comments?"

"Sir, if the Colonel is serious about learning, this company is the best to be with during any exercise. We are good at what we do and any one of us would be happy to assist you with your education. I don't mean that in a disrespectful way, Sir, but we take what we do very seriously. With respect, Sir, if all you want to do is evaluate us, you don't have to get in our way to do that."

Klintworth's facial expression went from that of a stone cold professional, to one of a little boy who knew he was about to be scolded. Naylor smiled.

"I assure you, sergeant, any evaluation I do is strictly secondary. I have been assigned to a desk in Washington for the past six years and feel my soldiering skills might just be a little rough. Just because some say it's like riding a bike, I don't want to have to remember on the battlefield. Is that an acceptable answer to your concern?"

Reardon smiled for the first time.

"Yes, Sir, your answer is more than acceptable."

"I'm glad we've resolved that issue. Captain Klintworth," Naylor turned to the junior officer, "if you would assign me to one of your platoons for tomorrow's exercise, I would appreciate it. You can leave a message at my quarters as to the assignment and all of the particulars."

"Yes, Sir!"

"You and your men may be dismissed, Captain. Have a pleasant evening."

"Yes, sir! Thank you, sir!"

The men in front of him started out the door. Reardon continued to smile at Naylor while being pushed out by his company commander. There was no doubt in Naylor's mind whose platoon and squad he was going to be assigned to in the morning. He shook his head wondering if he would be good enough to keep up with these kids. Naylor knew if he continued to dwell on this he would fail and that wasn't acceptable. He quickly looked over the work on his desk before he walked to the door. As he turned out the office lights, he decided a good meal and a good night's sleep was just what he needed.

177 Pinecreek Drive
Rochester, New York
October 15, 1994
1900 Hours

The garage door opened as the black Chevrolet Blazer eased into the driveway, then into the garage. It was the end of a long day for Summers. It started routinely at 5:30 a.m. with a glass of juice and quick run on the treadmill. After thirty minutes of running and listening to the news, Jon grabbed a quick shower, dressed, woke up Sean so he could get ready for school, and found time to grab a simple breakfast. As he was leaving the house at 6:45 a.m., Sean was getting ready to walk to school while Nancy, Justin, and Stephen were just getting up. Sean went to Robert Kennedy High School, which was within walking distance. He started school at the same time Jon did, at 7:25. Justin went to Robert Kennedy Middle School, which started an hour later. He also walked to school. Stephen went to the Alcott Elementary School catching his bus at 8:30 a.m. This was a half-hour after Nancy needed to be in her classroom at the Irish Hill Elementary School where she taught kindergarten. Nancy's parents put Stephen on the bus every day. This was easy for them to do since Howard and Emily Quinn lived in the in-law apartment attached to the house.

Jon pushed the button to close the garage door and checked his watch. He shook his head in disbelief realizing he'd just put in another twelve-hour day. He got out, grabbing his briefcase as he went. He glanced at the garage door to make sure it closed and walked into the combination entranceway and mudroom. This room was small, but still big enough to contain a full-size washer and dryer, as well as a small coat closet. Jon was shocked back to reality when young Stephen met him. The boy was full of questions about his day, filled with the endless energy he was famous for.

"You know you missed dinner, Dad?" Stephen's comment was more a statement than a question. "Moms really pissed at you!"

"Stephen Michael!!!" Nancy shouted from the kitchen.

Jon knelt next to his son, "Any chance of reprieve?"

The boy gave his father a puzzled look. "Any chance of what?"

"Do you think she'll give me another chance?"

The boy became profoundly serious, motioning for his father to move closer. When his father complied, the boy whispered, "If you're real nice to her, I think you'll be O.K. Just tell her she's pretty and she'll probably forget you're late."

Jon looked into his son's eyes and smiled. "Do you really think that'll work, son?"

"Sure, Dad," replied the boy in a voice louder than before, "it works all the time for me. Mom can't stay mad at you when you tell her the truth."

Jon's laughter surprised his son. He didn't know what he said, but his father liked it.

"I'm gonna trust you, son," said his father, "but if I get my butt kicked, you're going to owe me big time."

"Aww, Dad," the boy's response was immediate, "that's not fair. Mom always kicks your butt."

Both the boy and his father laughed heartily until they looked up to find Nancy standing in the entranceway. They stopped laughing for a moment, looked at each other, and immediately started laughing again. Nancy was standing with her mother, Emily, and both were smiling. It wasn't unusual for Jon's in-laws to be in at this time of day. They often ate dinner together, although lately Jon seemed to be tardy for these meals.

"Out of the mouths of babes," said Emily walking over to her grandson and placing her arm on his shoulder. "Let's go find your grandfather, young man and see what kind of trouble he's getting into in the workshop."

"Aww, Grandma," replied the nine-year-old with a sour look on his face.

"Well, what would you say if your grandmother talked him into playing a game of pool?"

The boy's look showed he was giving this some serious thought. "I don't know Grandma. I'll go along with you, but I don't think you'll get him to do it."

With that Emily ushered the boy towards the basement stairs. She smiled and winked at her son-in-law as she passed him.

Jon and Nancy chuckled watching them disappear down the stairs. Nancy walked over to her husband, kissing him on the cheek. "How was your day, besides long?"

Jon returned her kiss, giving her a gentle hug as she put her arms around him. He leaned back smiling.

"Not bad, just a typical day at Lakeview High. The crew took their usual lunch and I got to use my family counseling 101 skills for a mom and dad who can't understand why their All-American son dresses like Count Dracula and is in trouble for threatening to kill Miss Zuckerman and rape her cold, dead body."

Nancy laughed. "Was Zuckerman sober when this took place? Damn, she was old when you and I went to school at Lakeview. You would think she'd retire after all this time and do us all a favor. Besides, you're being redundant when you're using the adjectives cold and dead to describe her."

Jon laughed hugging his wife again. "The kid only told her to go fuck herself. That makes more sense considering whom we're talking about. The old lady has an active imagination for someone her age. The kid's as honest as the day is long. He's even a pretty good student, but mom and dad are in denial about this issue big time and plan on suing everyone. Man, I wish these people would come up with something original."

Nancy hugged her husband. "You work too hard for people who don't care. You don't have to put so much into everything you do."

Jon kissed her on the forehead. Stephen was right about her being upset over his being late.

"If this were a kid in your classroom," he countered leaning back to look into her eyes, "would you deal with this halfheartedly, or would you dig in and fight for all you're worth?"

Nancy pushed away from him, not letting go of his arms, but enough to show that she was upset. She looked into his alert blue eyes and deliberated for a moment before responding. "That's not a fair question. I deal with kindergartners and for the most part the parents are supportive about what we're doing with their kids. When they get to middle and high school both the kids and the parents seem to get more mercenary. You're also dealing with an unfriendly administration that won't back anyone about anything. Look at what she did to you after you saved her life from that punk with the gun."

Jon's smile disappeared. "She did what she thought she had, too. You may not agree w…"

"Not agree!!" responded Nancy with a touch of anger in her voice. "She had a letter placed in your file that stated that you had completely mishandled the entire situation. She listened to that idiot cop Hapke instead of you and everyone else who works for her. That fat piece of you-know-what just agrees with her and everyone else is scared for their job, so nothing's said. You go along with it because you always go along. You did the same thing in the navy and ended up leaving. You could have been an admiral by now. Damn, I get so frustrated because of your loyalties and this chain of command bullshit. You need to get out of that school and into one where you'll be appreciated. You deserve it. Go see Pete Schiller and see what he says!"

Jon shook his head in frustration, "Peter's going to tell me to be patient and talk to me about being tolerant of other people's management styles. We both know that he'll be 200% correct in what he'll be saying. Susan knows her stuff and does an excellent job when it comes to procedures, laws, student and parent rights, and school organization. We disagree on how to handle some of the day-to-day stuff, but we agree on so much more. Besides, both Pete and the school board agreed that the way I handled the incident with the gun was more than appropriate. They'll take care of whatever Susan placed in my personnel file."

Jon could tell by the expression on Nancy's face what he said placated her. This topic was a reoccurring argument between them. Jon didn't want to see the evening ruined, so decided to take the advice of a very wise man.

"You know, Stephen's right," he said, the smile returning to his face. "You are pretty, even when you're pissed at me."

The frown on Nancy's face started to disappear and was replaced with a big smile, "You old smoothie. You have to rely on advice from your nine-year-old son to get you out of trouble."

"Hey, Babe," he replied, "whatever works is fine by me. And besides, if that kid's nine, he's going on twenty-five. I think he's been hanging around Sean too much."

Nancy finally laughed.

"By the way," asked Jon, "where are Sean and Justin?'

Nancy took her husband by the arm and led him into the kitchen. She took his briefcase and set it down next to the island in the center of the room. Then she put her arms around Jon's neck and kissed him gently on the lips.

"I gather this means they're not home?" he said quietly when the kiss ended.

"Both Sean and Justin are at scouts tonight," she explained with a smile. "Sean had to be there early to work on his eagle project with one of the scout masters, so Justin went in at the same time. You must pick them up at 8:30, so you best sit and eat. We're having your favorite, cold meatloaf and mashed potatoes with salad."

Jon laughed at his wife, putting his hands around her waist, and giving her a big hug. "You know, kid, you're so good to me, I just might have to take you with me to boy scouts and work on a merit badge in the parking lot while we're waiting."

Nancy laughed and jokingly slapped her husband on the chest, "None of that, Jon Summers, you earned that merit badge a long time ago. I don't think the scout leaders want all those young men achieving that badge just yet."

They both laughed and Jon poured two glasses of wine.

880 Country Lane
Murrell's Inlet, South Carolina
October 15, 1994
1900 Hours

The phone rang and Ray grabbed the extension in the kitchen before his wife could turn from the stove and pick it up. Louise looked perturbed but said nothing in response to her husband's smile.

"Hello," he said, "Summers's residence."

"Summers's residence, how the hell are you?" said Bill Gateway.

"Hey buddy, how're you doing?"

"Not bad at all," responded the retired general. "I've got some great news about the reunion."

Ray's manner became excited. "Tell me what you have."

"Well, I've got some familiar names signed on to be in Davao come March. You remember Donnie Smith, don't you?"

"Sure, he was the company clerk for both of us. Damn smart kid. Smart, gutsy, and one hell of a typist. What's he doing now?"

"You won't believe this, Ray. The guy's a retired minister. He moved up high in the Methodist Church. National position, I believe."

Ray laughed, "I don't know why you're surprised. The kid was sharp as a tack. Who else did you get?"

"The only other name that looked familiar was your old buddy, Sam Donavan. He's a retired banker from somewhere down south."

"I'll be glad to see him. We went through a lot during that campaign. Where down south? Somewhere near here?"

"Nah, don't think so. The return address is Arkansas. I know how you southern boys stick together. I'll have to put the two of you in separate rooms."

"Having to put up with you is the reason that we stuck together. Anyone else coming you know of?"

"No," answered Gateway, "anyone else interested can't make the trip because of medical issues. Several will be sending video tapes to be played."

Ray asked, "So, bottom line, how many signed up for the reunion at this point?"

There was silence on the other end.

"That bad?" commented Ray.

"No, not really," replied his friend. "Currently we have over a hundred and seventy people from all the divisions involved and 22 from the 41st alone. Not bad, considering. Is Louise still holding out on us?"

Now Ray was the silent one. He'd asked his wife at least a dozen times to make this trip with him and she refused each time. She made it clear she wasn't going on a trip to remember a war that cost her several friends and almost cost her a brother. She understood why her husband and his friends needed to make the trip, but she couldn't join them.

Ray finally sighed. "No, no change there, how about your family?"

"Good news on my end," replied Bill. "It looks like the entire family will be going. It's exciting to have all of them coming. Kevin's taking some time off and even his socially prominent wife agreed to come along. She's worried she may have to rough it, but I think she's a lot tougher than she lets on. So, how's your family?"

"Doing well, Bill. Jon and Julie are still up in Rochester with their families and doing fine. Jon's three boys are getting huge. Matt's down here in Myrtle Beach running computers for some company. I'll tell you I'm glad I don't have his girls. They're gonna be real heartbreakers."

"Speaking of heartbreakers, how's Julie doing?"

Ray hesitated for a second before he responded about his youngest child. Julie Summers-Romero was recently widowed. Her husband was a City of Rochester police officer who was killed in an automobile accident in the line of duty. Ray was glad there hadn't been any long period of suffering for his son-in-law. He had been a good husband and father.

"She's doing well, Bill," he finally responded. "The teaching keeps her busy and Jon and Nancy are close by to help when she needs it. She'll be OK."

"Glad to hear that, Ray. She needs anything you give me a call right away. Look buddy, I have to go, but I'll be out your way in two weeks regarding the reunion, so I'll see you then. I'll keep you updated on any more news. Hey, love to Louise and my best to the rest of the family."

"Same to you, Bill. Love to the family."

The line went dead, so Ray hung up. He looked up at his wife. Louise smiled asking, "Everything okay with the reunion?"

Ray smiled. "Going great so far. Bill says that there's over a hundred seventy people signed up. I can't wait to see them. Say, did I ever tell you about my old company clerk, Donnie Smith?"

Louise shook her head.

"Well, he's going to be there and so is Sam Donavon."

"Did you think to ask about Becky or Kevin?" asked his wife.

Louise's question was met with silence and a puzzled look. She knew better than to ask, but ask she had. And she received the answer she expected. This reunion had become all-consuming for both men and she knew it would come off without a hitch. She shook her head.

"You know," she said, "when he's here in two weeks, I expect that both of you will give me a full report on how his family is doing. Now, get out of my kitchen so I can get this baking done."

Base Camp Freedom
Mindanao, Philippines
October 16, 1994
0800 Hours

The portable radio squawked an indiscernible message in the ear of the man in charge of the detail by the main gate. He unclipped the lapel mic from his tactical vest speaking into it. He turned to the others on the detail motioning for them to open the heavy wood gate. They looked to be professional soldiers. None were Filipino.

The compound was large, with approximately twenty-five miles of high perimeter fence. The soldiers didn't clear all the trees and brush away from the perimeter, to maintain the secrecy of the base. Motion sensors were strategically placed in the jungle around the camp to alert the guards to any uninvited guests. Perimeter patrols were kept busy with local wildlife frequently setting these sensors off. The sensors, patrols, and the use of night vision equipment were well worth the price of secrecy. The layout of the compound made it look like a rubber plantation from the air. The entrances to the underground bunkers scattered throughout the complex were disguised as tool sheds.

The double gates were pushed open by the guards while their supervisor stood alert, watching the road. They were all business, not letting anything distract them. The noise of the vehicles could be heard from down the road. The roadway was made of gravel but was well maintained. It was wide enough to accommodate the largest military vehicle. After several seconds, a Toyota Land Cruiser came around the corner, followed by another, then a third, and finally a fourth. The four vehicles kept a steady pace until they reached the main gate. They slowed so the guards could see inside. The guard in charge nodded at the driver of the first vehicle and motioned for him to proceed on. After all four SUVs moved slowly through, the guards quickly closed the gate under the watchful eye of their supervisor.

The vehicles wound their way through the complex, stopping at the largest of the buildings. All through the complex they observed soldiers dressed like the ones at the front gate. They all carried weapons. When the Land Cruisers came to a halt in front of the building, several men came out of the large double doorway. All were dressed in jungle BDU's and carried side arms. Two of the men rushed forward, opening the door of the second SUV. They stepped back, coming to attention. Shinpachi Osaka stepped out of the vehicle looking around at the men who surrounded him. A tall slender man with gray hair came forward and bowed slightly, shaking Osaka's hand.

"Mr. Osaka," the man spoke with a thick German accent, "how nice it is to have you visit our little encampment."

"Colonel Boerst," replied Osaka, "how nice to see you again. You, of course, remember my associate, Mr. Ishimoto?"

Colonel Hans Boerst, late of the East German Army looked at Ishimoto, bowing his head slightly. "Of course. So good to see you again. Mr. Osaka, I believe you will be pleased with the progress we've made. We've recruited enough of the local population so we will be going into this operation with the force the size of a reinforced regiment. Approximately four battalions of infantry, tanks, artillery, and air support."

"Total number of people, Colonel?" asked a man with an Irish accent walking up behind Osaka.

Boerst looked at the man but didn't answer. He looked at Osaka for clarification.

"Colonel," Osaka smiled as he spoke, "please meet Mr. Patrick O'Keefe, formerly of the Irish Republican Army. He oversees my personal security force. He'll be assisting Mr. Montoya with the planning and execution of the initial phase of our plan. Please feel free to answer the question."

Boerst bowed slightly in Osaka's direction.

"Just over 4,500 men. Most of these are in the infantry battalions being disbursed throughout the island. The other units will be working out of this camp for the time being. Mr. Montoya and his team are currently in the field training. Would you like me to summon him to come here to meet with you?"

Osaka shook his head.

"No, Colonel, I will talk to him as I tour the facility. Please have your associates cooperate with my people and give them any information they request. Mr. Wilson will need access to your aircraft and Mr. O'Keefe to the weapons stores and other supplies while you give me a tour around the base."

"Yes, sir," replied Boerst again bowing slightly.

Osaka turned, nodding to his associates. He then spoke directly to O'Keefe.

"As you look through the stores, please look for someplace to accommodate our guests when they arrive. We'll also need room for any unwanted visitors that may follow. Our contacts who are in place will be able to warn us in advance of any attempted rescue. But we'll still need somewhere to keep them."

O'Keefe bowed and smiled.

"It'll be my pleasure, sir. I would guess accommodations for approximately one hundred and fifty should be sufficient. If there's nothing available, I'll make sure something is constructed between now and their arrival."

"That would be quite excellent, Mr. O'Keefe," replied his boss.

Osaka nodded, turning back to Boerst.

"One last question, Colonel, while we are still here together. My associates are concerned about controlling our local recruits. Having them spread out over the island must make that difficult?"

Boerst smiled and nodded. "Of the 4,500 troops that will be ready, half are already on our payroll. By that, I mean I've been able to recruit the best soldiers for hire from Europe, Asia, Africa, and South America. The money you are paying them ensures their loyalty to our cause and in turn they will keep our recruits in line. These soldiers will act as our little army's officers and non-commissioned officers. Once the operation is underway, I don't think there'll be any problems in controlling these peasants."

Osaka looked at Boerst wondering if he used those words intentionally. He thought it funny a man who was the product of an Eastern Bloc country would use the word peasant to describe anyone. That was a term that he expected someone from Western Europe, or even Japan, to use. The thought passed as Osaka gave the word for his people to go about their business. Osaka and Boerst returned to one of the Land Cruisers and headed west from the headquarters building. They drove about five minutes before they stopped in front of a large grove of trees. The sound of men singing cadence rose from the grove. Boerst opened the door of the SUV and exited, followed by Osaka. Several men jogged out of the trees, one being Montoya. Montoya and Osaka walked away from the Land Cruisers leaving Boerst by the vehicle. Montoya talked quickly while Osaka nodded repeatedly. The meeting lasted half an hour. Finally, they turned around walking back to the vehicle where they shook hands and Osaka got in the Land Cruiser followed by Boerst. After watching Montoya jog back into the grove, they continued the tour.

While Osaka and Boerst toured the facility, Wilson inspected a series of hidden enclosures housing over thirty helicopters to be used by Osaka's mercenaries for transportation and gun ship support. Most of the aircraft were Bell 'Huey' UH-1 utility and transport helicopters. Even though these were older aircraft, each was in excellent condition. In addition to the Hueys there were several Bell Textron OH-58 Kiowa attack helicopters. While Wilson was busy with the aircraft, O'Keefe was kept busy checking all the other supplies and vehicles. He quickly went through the storage areas for food and clothing. O'Keefe guessed there was enough food and military clothing to keep the force Boerst described comfortable for some time. When he got to the weapons bunkers, his pace slowed. He inspected inventories, checked storage methods, and visually checked some weapons. Everything he saw could be purchased on the open weapons market, but the quantities led him to believe Osaka made some under the table deals. There were large numbers of assault rifles, pistols, sub-machine guns, anti-tank missiles, and shoulder held anti-aircraft missiles. He found enough ammunition to fight a medium size war. There were Vietnam era jeeps and trucks designated for transportation duties during the upcoming operation. All were in the best condition, with mechanics keeping them like new. Next, he inspected the armored personnel carriers and armored cars. These were Vietnam vintage vehicles. The tanks Osaka obtained were mostly older M-60 main battle tanks. These were also Vietnam vintage, but like all the other vehicles, they were in like new condition. The purchase that amazed O'Keefe was the four M1A1 Abrams main battle tanks. These would stop anything the Philippine Army put in the field.

Happy with what he saw, O'Keefe rejoined the other members of Osaka's party at the headquarters building. They all gave positive reports about their observations. A few more questions were asked of Boerst, who answered them without reservation. Osaka, happy with the answers, motioned for his party to board their vehicles. The Japanese businessman departed happy. The vehicles left the same way they arrived. The large gate was opened, and the four Toyota Land Cruisers left the compound, disappearing around the bend. The gate was closed, and all was again quiet.

CHAPTER 6

OUT IN THE REAL WORLD

Lakeview High School
Rochester, New York
November 12, 1994
1020 HOURS

Summers sat in his office looking over a student's file as the telephone rang. He let it ring several times before he picked it up.

"Summers."

"Your sister's here to see you if you have a minute and you wanted to be reminded that Mrs. Bush and Mrs. Edgerton have you speaking to those combined English and Social Studies classes in fifteen minutes." said Henderson.

"Shit!" Summers said under his breath.

"Excuse me, Mr. Summers?" chuckled his secretary.

"Sorry, Kathy. Only on a day when there aren't enough hours to accomplish all the work that's backed up."

"Sounds like a normal day around here," replied Henderson.

"Send Julie in and where am I supposed to meet the combined class from hell?"

"That would be in the auditorium. Should I tell them you'll be late as usual, or on time?"

The door to the office opened and Julie walked in smiling at her older brother. Jon nodded, motioning for her to sit. "Yes, I'll be on time. Just make sure that my new body armor is ready."

Henderson laughed hanging up the phone. Julie was a music teacher at Kennedy Middle and High schools, where Sean and Justin attended. She was a pretty woman reminding Jon a lot of their mother. Her build was small with petite features. The shoulder length, natural blond hair accented her bright blue eyes perfectly. Jon felt her eyes were his sister's best feature and the fact she tended to wear too much make-up around them started more than one argument between the siblings. Jon was protective of his younger sister, especially since her husband had been killed.

"So, how's the hotshot vice-principal today?" asked Julie, "You don't seem happy to see me?"

"It's not you, kid," answered her brother, "I need to speak to some of Peggy and Debbie's students about Vietnam in about fifteen minutes. As you can see, I'm less than enthusiastic about it."

Julie reached out and took her brother's hand.

"Sorry, Jonny. I know how you feel about that part of your life. How about when you're done, I take you out to lunch?"

Summers smiled at his sister, grateful for her compassion. "Thanks, but I can't today. I have a double lunch shift because of some issues here at school. How about I take you to dinner?"

Julie returned her brother's smile. "You, me, Nancy, and all the kids? What fun?"

Jon laughed and shook his head, "Naw, just Nancy, you, and me. We'll leave the kids home with the in-laws. I'll tell you a secret, Howard and Emily were already buying pizza tonight for the boys. We'll pay Sean to watch his cousins and you'll be all set. See that wasn't hard to arrange. Say, why are you here at Lakeview slumming instead of at Kennedy with the other elitists?"

Julie laughed again; Jon knew he always made her feel relaxed.

"I had a meeting with the secondary music teachers this morning," she said. "It was your school's turn to host. I must say though, donuts went out of vogue years ago. Most places that know what's good for you serve bagels now. You guys on this side of town must really get with it if you expect to keep up with the rest of the world."

Jon looked over his glasses at his sister and smiled mockingly. "Most of the rest of the world is starving and would kill for a donut, besides who says they're out of vogue. We don't try to keep up here at Lakeview, we set the trends for the rest of the district to follow. Kennedy is always playing catch-up."

Julie picked up a pencil from Jon's desk and jokingly threw it at her brother, "Ron Hapke was right. You are an asshole."

Julie grinned at her brother knowing she just pushed one of his buttons. She knew the two men didn't care for each other, especially since Hapke dated her a year after Hector passed away.

Jon's expression didn't change, but his tone hardened. "You still seeing him, or can your older and wiser brother breathe a little easier now? I really should introduce Sgt. Dickhead to dad, but I don't want to have to bail the old man out of jail."

"You're right about that," Julie laughed.

Jon knew Hapke wouldn't be the type of person that their father would approve of her seeing. If the old man suspected the relationship went as far as Jon thought it had, he would have to be bailed out of jail. Ray was old school. He wouldn't approve of his daughter seeing a married man, especially one with the reputation Hapke had. It had taken Hector quite some time to win Ray's approval to marry his baby, but in the end, they became extremely close. Ray took Hector's death hard and refused to talk about it to anyone in the family. Jon always suspected Ray and Hector had more in common with one another than anyone knew. Julie didn't believe Jon when he told her the two men shared something more besides their love for her. She thought it crazy since they were from two vastly different worlds.

"You know, let's not tell dad about the good sergeant, Jon. We'll save us both a lot of cash and the old man some aggravation." said Julie noticing her brother's mood was suddenly serious, "You don't have to worry about Ron, he's harmless."

The look on Jon's face scared his sister. "Sis, he's not harmless. He's an extremely dangerous man. He's not all there upstairs. I don't know exactly what's wrong with him, but I do know he likes hurting people. His eyes are, oh, how do I put this? I guess, crazy."

"You don't like a person because his eyes are crazy? Come on, Jon…"

Jon smiled at his little sister saying, "Sorry, Sis. You brought it up. Not me. The guy and I don't get along. What can I say?"

Julie leaned over and hugged her brother.

"Apology accepted. You know? It's nice to have someone who cares."

She hugged him again, kissing him on the cheek. She looked at her watch. "The girls are going to kill you if you're late."

Jon picked up the radio from his desk. They laughed as they left the office.

**Town of Princesa
Mindanao, Philippines
November 12, 1993
2320 Hours**

Twelve-year-old Ramon Franco looked out the window of the small house he shared with his parents and seven brothers and sisters. He was the oldest and it fell to him to help his mother watch his siblings while his father was away. His father was one of the local policemen assigned to this provincial town and had been sent to the City of Zamboanga to be trained on some new procedures being instituted by the Philippine Constabulary, the country's national police force.

Ramon looked out the window watching what appeared to be soldiers sitting outside the bar across the street. Over the last day he noticed many these men, all dressed in military style camouflage, enter town. They seemed to congregate in small groups around town, mostly near public places such as restaurants, bars, and the movie theater. Ramon felt uneasy. He wasn't sure what the problem was, but they seemed like trouble. Maybe it was because they didn't carry the same weapons the local police and soldiers did. He'd seen a variety of rifles and sub-machine guns being carried. While some of the rifles were the American made M-16s like the Philippine Army carried, many more were not. The other thing that bothered him was the fact the men outside the bar seemed to be on edge. One man seemed especially nervous, pacing back and forth at front of the door.

Ramon watched an Army officer come out of the bar with his arm around one of the girls who worked there. He staggered slightly, leaning on the girl, moving passed the uniformed men. The officer said something to the men, who laughed. He wheeled around to face them. The men stood. The soldier slowly pushed the girl away as he took one step forward, pointing at the young man who had been pacing. One of the men raised his rifle and fired. The bullet hit the officer in the chest, throwing him backward. The girl screamed, covering her mouth with both hands in horror. The door to the bar opened and two men, one of them another Army officer, came running out in response to the gunfire. Both were shot several times by the uniformed men now moving aggressively in several directions. Both victims fell, lifelessly propping the door to the bar open. Several men moved quickly to enter the bar, stepping on the bodies as they did. Within seconds you could hear gunfire coming from inside, accompanied by shouts of anger and screams of fear. The girl continued to scream stepping backwards. Before she moved far, one of the men raised a sub-machine gun firing a burst, hitting the girl. He fired a second burst killing her before she hit the ground. She came to rest in the middle of the street.

Sporadic gunfire could be heard erupting throughout the town. The men who hadn't entered the bar were now standing with their rifles at the ready. They looked nervously up and down the street. Ramon's mother came up behind him and pulled him away from the window.

One of the men standing near the bar across the street caught the movement in the window out of the corner of his eye and turned raising his rifle. He opened fire, knocking the glass out of the window, and spraying it across the room. Large chunks of the wood covering the exterior of the house flew off as the bullets hit their mark. When no one shot back, the man stopped firing. He trained his rifle down the street, but nervously kept watch on the house.

Lakeview High School
Rochester, New York
November 12, 1994
1045 Hours

Jon walked into the auditorium followed by Julie. In the front of the room Mrs. Bush and Mrs. Edgerton stood talking to a group of students, who were all sitting in the front of the center section. Edgerton was speaking to the class but stopped when she saw Jon enter.

Jon reached the front saying, "Sorry I'm late ladies and gentlemen, but as some of you have discovered during your time here at Lakeview, I have other duties that sometimes keep me away from gatherings of this sort."

There was laughter and whistles. Summers noticed Julie found a seat behind the last row of students and positioned herself so she could see her brother clearly. Bush and Edgerton combined their classes for the next two periods to allow for a discussion on the Vietnam War. They invited staff members who served in the military during the war to take part in the discussion. This year Jon was the only staff member available. After the discussion, students were required to write a term paper on the war using what they learned from the discussion combined with independent research.

"As we discussed over the past several weeks, this is going to be an open discussion and we expect all of you to act accordingly," said Edgerton.

There was a loud round of applause accompanied by more whistles. Jon stepped forward, which brought more applause and shouts from the audience. Edgerton raised her hand to quiet the crowd down.

"The rules of the discussion are simple," resumed Edgerton. "Mr. Summers will tell us some background about his experiences during the Vietnam conflict and you guys may raise your hands to make comments or ask questions. Any questions?"

There was more laughter.

"Then without any further ado, I yield the floor to Mr. Summers."

Edgerton stepped back to make more room for Jon as the students continued to clap and cheer. Jon smiled and raised his hand to bring the crowd back under control.

"Hey, Mr. Summers, is it true that you were a SEAL?" shouted one student.

Jon kept his hand raised as the audience responded to the outburst with laughter.

"No, Jim, I'm not a seal. A seal is a marine mammal and I know that for a fact because I used to be a biology teacher."

There was a roar of laughter from the assembly, but again the room quieted quickly when Jon raised his hand. It was going to be a long two hours.

Ramon and his family moved quickly through the streets heading towards the small police station in the center of town. They could hear gunfire erupt here and there so they tried to stay under cover as they moved. They left their home through the rear door just before the front of the house was sprayed with bullets. They could hear screams still coming from the bar across the street.

They turned onto the street where the police station was located, heard an explosion, seeing flame and debris fly across the street. Ramon knew the explosion came from the police station. He grabbed his mother by the arm, forcing her to follow him into an alley. Once they were safe, Ramon went back to the street, looking around the corner. He could see the police station was on fire. Another group of the men were surrounding some local policemen, whom they made kneel. One of the men took a pistol and placed it to the head of the policeman in front of him. He fired the gun and the policeman slumped forward. Ramon jumped back in shock. There was a second gunshot, followed by a third, and then a fourth. He slowly looked around the corner again. All the policemen were lying on the ground. The entire scene was well lit because of the fire. Ramon could see everything, even with the slow-moving smoke rolling across the street.

The man who shot the policemen was young but in command of the other men. He turned giving orders and half his men left heading north. As the men left, he ordered the others to destroy the police cars parked nearby. They raised their weapons and opened fire on the vehicles. The noise made Ramon jump back again and flatten himself against the building. He slowly peeked around the corner and down the street. Ramon could see the windows and tires of the cars shot out.

Ramon heard explosions back towards his home, followed by heavy gunfire. A pillar of fire and heavy black smoke rose above the rooftops. Ramon guessed a vehicle exploded. There were government troops stationed to the south of the town where the firefight appeared to be taking place. The volume of gunfire increased. Ramon hoped the troops were here to rid the town of these ruthless murderers. More explosions were followed by increased gunfire, this time from the east. More flames could be seen, but this time they appeared to be coming from buildings because the smoke was white or grayish.

Screams drew Ramon's attention back towards the front of the police station. He saw a group of the intruders bring the town's mayor, his family, and the local priest to the man who just killed the policemen. The mayor's wife and family were screaming as they were dragged in front of him and thrown to the ground. The mayor and the priest were each being held by two men. The mayor seemed to be struggling with his captors, the priest was not.

"Who are you?!?" screamed the mayor at the top of his lungs.

The rebel leader spoke quietly. Ramon strained to hear what was being said but couldn't make anything out.

The mayor responded by trying to lunge at the man only to find that he was too well restrained. He then tried to kick the rebel leader yelling, "You're a pig! You're filth and they'll kill you all!"

The response from the young man was instantaneous and final. He shot the mayor, killing him. The mayor's wife and children, crying, crawled over to where the body landed. The priest tried to move towards the mayor's killer but was being held too tight. The rebel leader pointed his pistol at the priest, but nothing happened. The struggling priest suddenly broke free, rushing over to the mayor's family. His two captors moved to restrain their charge, but their leader grabbed a sub-machine gun motioning- them to stay back. The mayor's wife, seeing the movement, jumped up between her family and their attacker. She was screaming as she moved towards the man pointing the gun. The rebel leader fired the weapon, hitting his target and knocking her backwards into the priest. The priest and one of the children looked to be hurt.

The rebel leader spoke to one of his companions. The man raised his rifle, firing one round into the body of the mayor's wife. The body flinched with the impact of the bullet. The rebel leader laughed, ordering his comrades to follow him down the street, directly towards the alley where Ramon and his family were hiding. Ramon watched as the rebel leader exchanged the sub-machine gun for a bottle of Coca-Cola. Ramon quickly left the entrance of the alley and moved back to where his family was hiding.

Lakeview High School
Rochester, New York
November 12, 1994
1230 Hours

Summers walked into his office followed by Tom McAvoy. He smiled at Henderson as he passed her desk.

"So, what has the afternoon got in store for me? Please tell me that I'm going to be happy?"

Henderson followed him into his office with her steno notebook. McAvoy held the door for the secretary. She wasn't smiling, which Jon took as a bad omen. Jon motioned for McAvoy to take a seat in the chair next to his desk, turning his attention to his secretary.

"You're not going to be happy," Henderson said looking at the pad. She spent the next five minutes running down his phone messages and afternoon schedule. Summers would comment after each item and Henderson would take more notes if needed. When she was done, she gave the visitor a discerning look and left.

"What do you have, Tom?" asked Summers turning to the sailor.

The young petty officer opened the black brief case taking out several folders. He handed them to Summers and sat back without saying a word. Jon placed them on his desk and opened the first one. It contained an update on an issue he had been following and he read through it quickly. When he finished, he looked up saying, "I don't have an answer to this one at the moment but call me in the morning and I'll have something ready then."

"Yes, Sir," answered the sailor.

Jon opened the other folder and began to read through the several pages of documents.

"Damn!" he exclaimed.

"Sir?" asked the petty officer looking concerned.

"My appeal about the last set of orders you brought me was denied. Looks like I'll be spending Christmas in Hawaii on active duty."

"I can think of worse places to spend Christmas, Sir."

Summers shook his head, looking the papers over again.

"Well, I'd rather spend the holidays here at home than off playing sailor for ten days. At least the admiral is letting me take my family along. Even better, he's offering to pay for it because of the short notice of the call-up."

"That's generous, Sir. Usually they don't do that."

"Means they want something, Tom. Well, I guess tonight I better convince my wife not to divorce me."

"I know the feeling, Sir, I have to deal with the same thing."

Jon laughed asking, "Anything else, Tom?"

"Yes, Sir," replied the recruiter as he reached into the briefcase and pulled out a single sheet of paper. "This came just before I left the office to come here. The sender is requesting a reply regarding your inquiries she has been making."

Jon's smile disappeared as he read through the document. He quickly grabbed a legal pad and was writing his response. He looked at the document again, shook his head in disbelief. He finished writing, tore off the paper, then folded it in half as he handed it to McAvoy.

"Tom," said Jon, "get this out to Lt. Demmer immediately, top priority, with a copy to Admiral Cummings. If you get any questions regarding this message, you contact me immediately."

McAvoy took the piece of paper, opened it, and read it through quickly. When he had finished, he said, "Aye, aye, Sir."

Jon handed all the documents back to McAvoy. As the petty officer placed the items back into the briefcase he asked, "Sir, will the captain be at home this evening if I have any questions or further communication on the last issue?"

Jon smiled. "No, the Captain plans to be out getting drunk, and maybe even getting lucky later tonight if I play my cards right. Why don't you go back to your office and send the message? Then you get out of there and take some time off yourself so they can't find you, to find me. Any questions on that, Petty Officer?"

McAvoy shook his head laughing. "None at all, Sir."

Jon laughed and stood up.

"Thanks, Tom. I appreciate your taking time to deliver these."

"No problem, Sir," responded the sailor, "and I should be the one thanking you. This assignment has helped my career."

Jon smiled again. "Call me tomorrow. I'm sure there will be more correspondence on the last issue."

Both men walked out of Jon's office.

Town of Princesa
Mindanao, Philippines
November 13, 1994
0045 Hours

Ramon and his family remained behind the barrels in the alley. He could hear the soldiers approaching. The first soldier moved slowly past the alley without a glance. Ramon breathed a little easier. He shifted, accidentally striking one of the fifty-five-gallon drums, causing the top to fall, and making a loud bang. The second soldier stopped, rifle at the ready, when one of the other soldiers called to him. The rebel leader appeared, and the two men spoke briefly. Ramon heard the leader speculate it was a cat or dog. The rebel in the alley questioned his boss but was ordered to move on. The soldier shrugged and moved off. Ramon watched quietly as several more soldiers followed.

The gunfire continued to be heavy, occasionally accented by explosions. Ramon told his mother what he witnessed, so she was anxious to see if she could help the priest. After moving to the end of the alley, Ramon carefully looked up and down the street. Seeing no soldiers, he motioned for his mother and family to follow him. As they entered the street, they kept close to the buildings, moving away from the soldiers. They came adjacent to where the bodies were laying, still using the buildings for cover. Ramon was grabbed from behind, causing him to jump. He recovered quickly seeing the person who grabbed him was an old man his father knew.

Ramon wasn't sure how old the man was, but he was known throughout town for his stories about the resistance to the Japanese during World War II. Ramon always considered him a crazy old man but was happy to see him none the less.

"Boy," he said to Ramon, "you and your mother were smart to get out of your home. These pigs are sure to go there because of your father's position. Get your family into my house, they won't look for you there."

The old man smiled at the boy.

"Go now, get your family inside where it's safe."

Ramon hesitated and pointed to the soldier's victims still laying in the street only meters away. "But what about them?"

The old man put his hand on Ramon's shoulder. "I didn't say we weren't going to help but putting your family in the safety of my home comes first. Now, get them inside and then come back here to help me."

Ramon nodded and started to turn around when the old man grabbed his arm again. "Have your mother keep the door open because we'll be moving fast."

Ramon nodded again moving his family into the nearby house. When he returned the old man pointed to the body of the mayor's wife saying, "I've been watching, and the mayor and his wife are dead. The priest and the children are still alive, although some appear to be hurt. I've heard some of the children crying and seen the priest move."

Ramon nodded.

"We'll move out there quickly and will bring back anyone who's still alive. If we take two trips, we'll bring back the most seriously wounded on the second trip. Understand?"

"Yes."

The old man put his hand on the boy's shoulder asking, "You scared?"

Ramon nodded.

"Good. Now, when I give the word, you stay with me and do as I say. Keep your eyes open and let me know if you see any soldiers. Ready?"

When Ramon nodded, the old man grabbed him by the arm pulling him along. They moved quickly into the street. It only took a few seconds to reach the bodies. The mayor's wife lay on top of the pile, her light blue dress covered with a dark red stain. The old man grabbed the lifeless arm and seemed to throw the body into the street. Ramon quickly bent down and found himself looking into the open eyes of the priest.

"Ramon," said the priest, "get out of here quickly before they decide to shoot you, too."

"Father," answered the old man before Ramon could say anything, "they're gone for now and probably won't be back. We must get both you and the children to safety."

The priest didn't argue, rolling over showing he was shielding the children. Ramon could now see three children. The oldest, a girl his age had been struck by a bullet in the thigh and couldn't walk. The priest had also been hit in the leg. The youngest of the children, a boy of about six years, was crying, but unhurt. The old man quieted the boy, speaking softly, instructing the two younger children to stay close to him and Ramon. Both nodded. Before Ramon knew what was happening the old man was helping the priest to his feet. The priest put his left arm over the old man's shoulder and the two of them started to slowly move towards the building. Ramon never thought about what he was doing, but he followed suit with the wounded girl. Before they were halfway to the house, he saw his mother running out to meet them. She grabbed both younger children.

Within seconds they were safely inside the house. Ramon was met by an ancient woman who directed him to place the girl on a bed in a room in the back. After setting the girl down on the bed he was pushed out of the room. He returned to the main room where he found the priest on the floor with the old woman leaning over him. The old man, Fidel, was stationed at the door. He was looking up and down the street acting as a lookout. When he convinced himself it was clear he closed the door, calling Ramon's younger brother over to keep watch. When the boy took his place, the old man moved to the side of the woman who was tending the priest. Fidel called Ramon to help him move the priest to another room. The two of them lifted the holy man from the floor, following the old woman to a room, placing him gently on a bed. The woman immediately continued to work on the wounds, cutting away the clothing that covered the injured area. Ramon and his companion quietly exited the room.

"Fidel, I need you to go for the doctor." Came the demand from the room they just left.

"Mother," answered the old man evenly, "I believe the doctor will be extremely busy this morning. It would need to be a real emergency...."

"These people have been shot! Don't you think that's an emergency?

The old man shrugged his shoulders and turned to Ramon. "Do you think you can find your way to the doctors in all this confusion?"

"Yes!" answered the boy, his voice confident.

"Go quickly and stay to the alleys. It sounds like most of the fighting is still to the south, but I'm sure that there are more rebels about."

Ramon accepted a pat on the shoulder from the old man and quickly left the house by the rear exit before his mother could object.

Jimmy's Restaurant
Rochester, New York
November 12, 1994
2130 Hours

Laughter came from the table where four women and one man had been sitting for several hours. They had eaten dinner and stayed for several rounds of drinks. They were not a rowdy group but were enjoying themselves. Jimmy's was located at the center of the mall, right next to the food court.

Nancy excused herself from the table to go to the ladies' room. Debbie and Peggy joined her, leaving Jon and Julie.

"You know, Nancy," said Debbie standing in front of the mirror. "I figured Jon would be furious with us for putting him on the spot today. He's being really good tonight, although I do believe he is more than a little drunk."

"Yeah," said Peggy jumping into the conversation, "he hasn't said a thing about how we nailed him about the Medal of Honor."

All three women laughed as they finished up and started to head back to the table.

"He's had a different attitude about the time he's spent in the service since he's been back from his active duty this summer," said Nancy. "Something happened during this tour that made him more at peace with it. A year ago, he would have been beside himself about you guys doing something like this. He would've brooded for weeks, but today he's buying you dinner and drinks."

"And we said we were going to take him out," said Peggy. "I guess we're still going to owe him one."

Jon and Julie were sitting next to each other at the table where there was a fresh round of drinks for everyone. Jon was holding his beer, trying to explain something to his sister. Nancy sat down on the other side of her husband, while Debbie and Peggy sat across from them.

"Jon was just telling me what he has planned for revenge on the three of us while you all were out powdering your nose," said Julie with a laugh.

"This ought to be good," Nancy said as she took a sip of her wine, "of course he'll have to remember it tomorrow after he sobers up."

They all laughed. Debbie asked, "So, what is this great revenge going to be?"

Taking a sip of beer, he took his time before responding.

"Well ladies, you are both now blessed with your master's degree in school administration and can be called upon to fill in various vacancies when vice-principals are away on vacation or at conferences. Having considerable influence on who gets these choice assignments, I think it can be arranged for you ladies to fill in when Susan and Marie go away in a couple of weeks."

Both women stopped sipping their drinks, almost choking on them.

"That means working with Reggie!" exclaimed Debbie, coughing.

"Come on, Jon," said Peggy, "even you wouldn't do that to us, would you?"

There was a big grin on Jon's face.

"What's wrong ladies, not happy with the assignment?"

"You really wouldn't do that to us, I mean, he's OK an' all, but he's always out of the building. We'd end up doing his work as well," pleaded Debbie.

"I'd do it to you in a heartbeat. You know the old saying, *don't get mad — get even*. Sounds even to me. Yep, this ought to do nicely."

"But what about Julie?" asked Peggy.

"She's family so she gets the ultimate revenge," said Jon. "She has to eat my cooking for the next year every time she comes over."

Julie's face had a disgusted look on it.

"That doesn't sound too bad, Julie," said Peggy. "Do you want to switch fates here with me?"

"At least Reggie Haughout is funny and a gentleman," replied Julie. "That's more than I can say for this guy's cooking. He'll probably be feeding me recycled MRE's."

They laughed.

"You are such an ass," said Nancy to her husband taking his hand and squeezing it.

"You are one hundred percent correct, Madam," said Jon raising her hand to his lips and gently kissing it. "And, with any luck, tonight I'm going to be a lucky ass."

They laughed again.

"So why are you being so generous and buying everyone dinner?" asked Nancy. "You're not the cheapskate your father is, but I think we all want to know why you're so insistent when the girls planned on buying all along."

The other three women looked nervous as they waited for the answer. They had planned on surprising Jon with dinner knowing how reluctant he was to talk about his experiences in Vietnam. When the waitress had brought the bill for dinner, Jon very quietly, but forcefully insisted on paying. Nancy knew about the plan from the start and decided it was time to get to the bottom of this.

It was obvious Jon was drunk because the smile never left his face. He took a final swig of his beer, finishing it.

"Why Nancy Quinn Summers," he started to slur his c's and s's, "you don't trust me?"

Nancy looked into her husband's eyes and saw the twinkle. The smile was still there.

"You're right," she said. "I don't trust you! What's up?"

"Well, babe," started Jon, "I heard back from the Pentagon about those orders regarding me being away on assignment over Christmas."

"Damn!" Nancy's face showed her disappointment. "You have to go and be away over the holidays, right? God damn Navy!! Who heard the appeal?"

"General Goodman."

"General Ben Goodman, Chairman of the Joint Chiefs of Staff?" questioned Debbie.

Jon nodded.

"Damn, Summers," said Debbie, "You really do travel in some different circles in your other life."

Everyone smiled at the comment except Nancy, who was visibly upset.

"Away from home again over the holidays. I expected as much when I first saw the orders, but I don't have to like it," said Nancy barely in control of her emotions. "I thought we were all through with this bullshit, when do you have to leave?"

"We leave the day before school lets out for Christmas break."

Nancy looked puzzled. Something Jon said didn't sound right, but she was so upset she couldn't figure out what. She repeated what he said again in her mind. It was Julie who figured it out. "Wait a minute Jonny, you said the word 'we'. What did you mean?"

"Well," Jon took his time, "I knew that General Goodman and Admiral Cummings wouldn't approve my appeal not to go at all, so I requested my family be allowed to accompany me on this assignment because of the time of year. Both approved my request and the travel orders for Captain Jon Summers and family to report to the United States Naval Base at Pearl Harbor arrived today with their answer to my appeal."

Nancy didn't answer. She had been so upset over the fact that Jon had to be away over the Christmas holiday, that she hadn't been prepared for this announcement.

It was Peggy who spoke first. "Now wait just one minute. You're telling us that you knew this guy Goodman and this Cummings fellow," she turned to look at Debbie, "I assume that he's someone else of importance?"

Debbie nodded, "Chief of Naval Operations."

"Right," snorted Peggy, "anyway, you knew that they were going to tell you no about *not* sending you away from home over Christmas, so you asked them if you could take your family?"

"Yes," Jon kept his answer simple.

"And they said *yes* to this and are going to *pay* for this to take place?" said Peggy a little dumbfounded.

"Yes," answered Jon as matter-of-factly as he could, "they have something that they need done and they want me to do it."

"And you wrote an appeal to the Chairman of the Joint Chiefs of Staff and the Chief of Naval Operations in Washington, D.C.?" continued Peggy, her face giving away her disbelief.

"No, I called them from my office at school using my AT&T card."

"Right," scoffed Peggy finally," and I talked to the Pope the other day."

Jon just smiled at the teacher sitting across the table from him. "And how is His Eminence these days, Peg?"

Julie was laughing softly as she sat next to her brother. Peggy looked at her asking, "He's serious, isn't he?"

Julie nodded.

"Summers," asked Debbie, "you got room in your house for a couple of older daughters?"

Nancy finally allowed everything to sink in as she took Jon's arm in hers saying, "Christmas in Hawaii?"

"Only if you want to, Hon," answered Jon with a smile. "You can always say *no*."

"Screw you, Captain Summers," she said as she returned the smile, "do the kids have to come?"

Jon smiled back at her, "If your parents want to watch them, that's fine with me, but remember the Navy has dibs on me for part of the time we're there."

Nancy's expression changed quickly. "My parents! We're supposed to spend the holiday with my parents."

"They live under the same roof, Nancy. We'll see them before and after Christmas. Besides, they plan on being with your aunt for Christmas Eve and Christmas Day, remember?"

She put her head on his shoulder, "I guess, we have a little time to work out the details."

Jon looked around the table. All four of the ladies had finished their drinks and were getting ready to leave. He looked at his watch. It was late and he had to be up early in the morning. He stood up, putting on his coat. Jon pulled Nancy's chair back, allowing her to get out and then did the same for Julie. He followed the four women out the front door and into the parking lot. He picked Nancy up at home and brought her to the restaurant so she could drive the two of them home. Julie, Debbie, and Peggy all came in Julie's car, which was parked next to Jon's Blazer. They talked and joked as they walked across the lot.

As they approached the vehicles, a pick-up truck drove past them and honked its horn. Jon immediately recognized the driver of the pick-up as Ron Hapke and swore under his breath.

"Jon, don't you dare make a scene!" ordered his sister.

"Don't worry," responded Nancy before her husband could open his mouth, "we're going straight home."

The pick-up stopped in the middle of the traffic lane and Hapke and the passenger got out. Hapke was not tall, standing five feet nine inches. He was in his mid-thirties with pleasant facial features and a full head of styled brown hair. He was known to have many girlfriends, even though he was married. The man with him was a giant in comparison. He stood over six foot. Hapke said something to his companion as they approached and got a laugh in response. It was obvious they, too, had been drinking.

"Hey, Julie," shouted Hapke. "You and your friends want to go back in with us for a couple of drinks and maybe a late dinner?"

"Hi, Ron," responded Julie with a smile, "nice to see you. You haven't called in over a week."

"Business, Babe. Business. You know Bill Larson. I think I introduced you to him at the PBA dinner last month."

Julie reached out and took the man's hand, shaking it. "So nice to meet you again, Sergeant Larson."

Julie glanced over to her brother to make sure that he was behaving himself. There was a bored look on his face, and he was doing his best to ignore the whole meeting. Nancy moved in close to him, holding on to his arm as if to support him. Her two friends moved between Julie and her brother. She didn't know if this was intentional but was grateful to them for doing it.

"So, you guys gonna be able to join us for the evening?" asked Hapke again as he reached out and took Julie's hand from his friend. "We'd like all four of you to stay. Your friends are pretty."

"No, thanks, Ron. We all have to be at work tomorrow. Besides these other three ladies are married."

Hapke smiled at the ladies. "So, we'll be gentlemen if that's an issue. We wouldn't want to keep Summers here up. We'll even make sure that you ladies get home safely. That seems to be more than Summers can do."

Nancy grabbed hard into Jon's arm. He could feel her fingernails through his jacket. Debbie and Peggy both moved closer to him and looked back and forth between Jon and the off-duty policeman. Jon's expression remained the same, he even looked a little amused. Nancy relaxed her grip.

"Don't mind me being here, Sergeant," said Jon lightly. "If these ladies want to go with you and your friend, that's their business. Honey, I'll leave the door unlocked. Make sure you check on the kids when you come home."

Jon bent over slightly kissing Nancy on the forehead. All four of the women looked at Jon trying not to laugh. He gently took Nancy's arm guiding her a step away from him, towards the two off-duty policemen.

"Summers," Hapke chided, "you wouldn't know what to do with that good looking wife of yours. You think you're such hot shit dealing with those kids. Maybe these girls need to go out with some real men to see what they're missing."

Nancy moved back to Jon and took hold of his arm. Debbie and Peggy instinctively moved closer to him as well. All three looked irritated. Julie was still close to Hapke. He was holding her arm.

"Ron," she said softly, "let it go. We don't need a confrontation here."

"Your brother's an asshole and I think someone needs to tell him," said Hapke with a raised voice. "What's worse, I think he's a spineless asshole."

Jon didn't respond to the remarks or even act like he heard them. He leaned onto his wife's shoulder and whispered something in her ear to which she laughed and nodded.

"If you want to insult me, do it to my face, asshole!" said Hapke loudly.

Jon ignored the other man and looked at his sister and her two friends. "Ladies, we'll be headin' home. If you need a ride, we'll be happy to get you where you need to go. So nice to see you again, sergeant."

Jon guided his wife to the driver's door of the Blazer and was about to open it when Hapke moved closer and shouted, "I was talking to you, asshole! Don't walk away from me when I'm talking to you. You said something to her about me. Why don't you say it to my face, or aren't you man enough?"

Jon noticed their little crowd had attracted the attention of mall security when one of the small red pickup trucks they used began to circle. He continued to ignore Hapke as he started to reach for the door handle.

"Summers!" shouted Hapke as he took another step forward dragging Julie.

It was Julie that broke the silence with a raised voice. "Ron, stop this! Ron, let go of my arm and stop this!!!"

Hapke stopped and looked at Julie but didn't let go.

"Ron," she said more softly, "Jon is doing what I made him promise to do."

"Which is what?" responded the man indignantly.

"Not create a scene with you and go right home. Now, please let me go, you're hurting my arm."

Nancy sensed Jon stiffen but saw no change in his expression.

"You're goin' out with me tonight," said Hapke. "You're going out with me and he's going to tell me what he said to her about me now or I'll make him tell me."

"Ron, I don't want to go out with you when you're like this. And I won't go out with you again if you don't let this go now," said Julie as forcefully as she could. "You're drunk and I don't want to be part of this."

Hapke pushed Julie away from him hard, slamming her into the front of Jon's Blazer. His complexion reddened, and he raised his hand as if to hit Julie while she struggled to raise herself off the vehicle.

"Screw you, you bitch!" he shouted and then turned to face, Jon. "Now I'm gonna kick your brother's ass!"

As the confrontation started to become physical, Hapke didn't see the red security truck stop behind him. The security officer, a young man in his early twenties, jumped out of the vehicle, quickly moving forward. He slid between the two men, putting out both of his arms with his hands up in a motion to get Hapke to stop. Before the security officer could say anything, the off-duty police officer grabbed his arm and threw him into Julie. On impact, they both fell to the pavement and Hapke immediately kicked the security officer several times as hard as he could. The security officer instinctively curled himself around Julie to protect her. Hapke's friend grabbed him pulling him back from the confrontation.

A second red security truck pulled up and two security officers piled out. Several more came running out of the main mall entrance. One of the security officers was an older man with sergeant's chevrons on his white shirt. He was breathing hard, but immediately took control.

With the situation unraveling before her, Nancy witnessed a change in her husband's attitude. When Julie was knocked into the car, Jon instinctively moved in front of Nancy to protect her. He took a step forward but didn't leave her side because of the arrival of the first security officer. What terrified her was the change in demeanor when the young security guard was attacked. Jon's whole being seemed to come alert and focus on the threat in front of him. The light, carefree twinkle in his eyes present when they had left the restaurant was replaced by the cold and calculated gaze of the professional soldier. When Hapke's friend pulled him back, Jon moved to a more defensive position allowing him to protect both Julie and the security officer. She smiled as she saw Jon's body relax when the additional security personnel began to arrive. Only an exceptionally stupid move on the part of the off-duty police officer would escalate this situation further.

"You, asshole!" shouted Hapke as he broke loose from his friend's grip, "I'm going to kick your fucking ass!"

Hapke stopped short when he made eye contact with Jon. The blue eyes that stared back at him were cold and threatening. No, menacing. The body language told him it would be a mistake to attack. As relaxed as the man in front of him looked, Hapke knew it would be a mistake to attack. He'd dealt with enough violent suspects in his career to know he was going to need a lot more help to win this fight.

"You don't want to fight with me, Hapke," responded Jon in a quiet tone making the hair on the back of the policeman's neck stand up. "I'm not worth your time or trouble. Take some advice, there's a time to fight and a time to listen and this is one of those times to listen."

Hapke stood his ground, but didn't move forward towards Jon. He was agitated shaking his fist in Jon's direction. "You son-of-a-bitch!! You can't talk down to me like that."

"Look, Hapke," Jon's voice became cold, "I'm not talking down to you and could care less about what you want to do to me. You need to take a couple of deep breaths, calm down, and look around. This is a fight you're not going to win. As a matter of fact, you won't even place. Why don't you just turn around, get back in your truck, and go home to sober up."

Jon stopped for a second and looked at the sergeant from mall security. "He can do that, can't he?"

"I would prefer that, yes," replied the sergeant as he nodded. "I know where to reach him about this later if I have to."

"You can't do anything to me," blurted out the off-duty policeman as he took a step backwards. "Remember you have to work with the cops in this town. You come after me and they'll stop cooperating with you guys."

The sergeant looked perturbed about the man's response. "Do what you feel that you have to, Mr. Hapke. Just remember that this whole incident was videotaped."

Hapke looked to where the security supervisor was pointing. A video camera could be seen on top of a pole on the roof above the carousel. It was pointed directly at them. Jon smiled, guessing there was another security guard at the console inside the mall cursing, because he had to tape the incident instead of being outside with his friends. He didn't realize that at this moment his job was the most important.

"Now," continued the sergeant, "unless you would like to be taken away by your friends tonight, I would do just what this gentleman has recommended and leave."

"Fuck your video tape."

Sirens could be heard in the distance. Hapke quickly turned his attention back to Jon. "One of these days, Summers, I'm going to thump your ass."

Jon's gaze remained steady. "Hapke, be careful what you wish for. You just might get surprised. Remember what I said about talking? It's usually a better way to deal with issues like this, son. Go home and sober up."

Hapke was moving towards his truck more quickly as the sirens were getting louder. "You're mine, asshole!!"

Jon's eyes were narrow and cold as he answered. "Trust me, son, I'm not your type."

Hapke and his companion quickly entered his truck. The engine roared to life, and it jumped forward, squealing the tires as it raced out of the parking lot.

Jon turned to help the security guard up off the ground. The young man brushed off his clothes, while Jon helped his sister get to her feet.

"Thanks for jumping in," Jon said. "I know the ladies appreciated it. You okay, or did our intoxicated constable get one where it counts?"

"I'm fine, sir."

"You did good, Tommy," said the sergeant walking over. "Thank you, too, sir, for stepping in when you did. Knowing Ron Hapke as I do, I think he would have pursued this if you hadn't stepped in between them. Would you mind giving the police a statement?"

Two police cars stopped next to the security trucks. One of the other security guards spoke to the officer in the first car. The sirens stopped within seconds.

"No problem, Sergeant," said Jon. "I assume that you'll need statements from each of the ladies as well?"

"Yes, I would, sir," replied the security guard. "Would you be able to ask them if they would do that?"

"I would be happy to," replied Jon with a smile.

With a nod and a smile, the security supervisor moved off. Jon walked to where the ladies were helping brush off Julie's dress. All four of the women smiled at him as he approached.

"Our hero," said Peggy in an attempt to lighten the mood."

"You know," said Debbie, "I really think that Neanderthal was serious. He actually planned on hurting someone tonight.

"He was serious all right," said Jon, "but he was too drunk to make the right decision. He was the only one being carried away from here tonight, no one else."

They were surprised by the coldness of Jon's tone, as well as his change in demeanor. They had never seen it before. There was a sudden soberness about the man they had missed during the confrontation. They realized the look in Hapke's eyes was more fear than anger.

**Town of Princesa
Mindanao, Philippines
November 13, 1994
0430 Hours**

Ramon crawled for most of his journey to the doctor's home. The rebel soldiers were in control of most of the town and were shooting at anything that moved. Ramon wisely stayed to the side streets during his passage through the heart of Princesa, arriving at the doctor's home unnoticed.

He approached cautiously, peering through one of the windows. Seeing rebel soldiers holding rifles on the doctor and his family, he remained quiet. The doctor was attending to a bullet wound to the arm of one of the intruders. While he sat behind a bush, he listened as the battle grew more intense.

When the doctor completed treating the wounded soldier, the rebels left, locking the doctor and his family in their home. Ramon watched them move away from the battle. He could see other groups of rebels moving off into the night as well. When all looked clear he moved to the door, unlocked it, and entered. The doctor was surprised to see the boy.

Ramon related to the physician what took place near his home, as well as by the police station. The doctor didn't seem the least bit surprised.

"You know, young man," started the doctor, "these soldiers aren't from any of the existing factions of separatists. They're much more violent. They're well equipped and financed. I've treated members of two separate groups, and they have different backgrounds. The first group appeared to be mercenaries. This last group was local but talked of foreign money backing their operations.

All this talk was going right over Ramon's head. "Doctor, the wounded by the police station, you have to come."

The doctor thought for a second.

"No, Ramon, I can't go. If things are as bad as you say, then there are going to be many in town who'll need my services. I'll have to set up my hospital here, where all my equipment and supplies are. You make your way back. Tell old Fidel to bring those wounded here. He'll know what to do. Have him bring his wife and mother, they're experienced with this sort of care. You be careful. We'll need your help in cleaning this up when it's over."

The boy acknowledged the doctor with a nod and started for the door.

"Wait," said the doctor suddenly, "from the sounds of the battle outside it won't be long before the government troops start to enter town. You take special care to stay away from the fighting."

Ramon nodded. He'd decided that after all the trouble he'd encountered trying to get to the doctor's home that he would stay to back lots. He also decided that the fastest way back to his family was as the crow flies, so he moved silently over the fences and through the alleyways that were between the rows of houses. He was making better time on the return trip. He was about halfway back when there was the sudden sound of gunfire. He dropped to the ground as several bullets whizzed over his head. Ramon stayed on the ground while gunfire erupted all around him. When the shooting finally subsided, he slowly rose to his feet moving forward. He moved about ten feet when rebel soldiers climbed over the fence next to him, surprising him. One of the men fell on him, knocking him to the ground. The soldier pinned him there.

"Benny," the man shouted, "Look what we have here!"

Benny Montoya looked down at the struggling teenager. "Leave him and let's move before the government troops find us."

"Let him go?" protested the soldier. He kept his knee on Ramon's back.

Ramon suddenly recognized the man they called Benny, as the rebel leader who had been at the end of the alley.

"With all that's happened here tonight the boy can recognize us," said the rebel harshly. "Should I kill him and catch up?"

The rebel soldiers stood. They looked at each other and one shrugged his shoulders, starting to raise his rifle. There was a deafening noise that was accompanied by a bright flash. Ramon could hear bullets whizzing over his head followed by screams. The boy instinctively covered his head at the first sound of the explosion. This protected him from the falling dirt, wood, and other debris. He remained in this position until everything was still. He slowly raised his head just enough to look around. He saw all the men that had been standing over him a moment earlier were now on the ground. There was no movement, and he could see blood on their clothing and skin. He heard one of them moan but decided to stay where he was.

He heard voices approaching from where the fence used to be. He realized for the first time how lucky he was to have been lying on the ground at the time of the explosion. He sat up slowly as the first of the government soldiers moved cautiously to where he sat.

177 Pinecreek Drive
Rochester, New York
November 13, 1994
0245 Hours

Everything around Summers appeared hazy. He could see smoke. Thick smoke. Swirling across the water and along the shoreline in front of him. He was swimming towards the shore but couldn't make anything out through the haze. He could see flashes of light that appeared to be coming from the shoreline and could make out what looked to be shadows moving about, but there was nothing definable. He could hear explosions and gunfire all around him. He turned and looked behind him and could see boats burning. He could hear the screams of dying men. He could now see that he was pulling men strapped together behind him. All were wounded. He could feel himself gasping for breath. Trying to fill his lungs, but not being able to. His body felt heavy. He wanted to sink in the water, but his mind kept telling him to stay afloat. To swim. He heard an explosion from behind him and turned to see one of the boats turn into a million pieces of burning debris that fell all around him.

Suddenly he found himself dragging the men onto shore, being helped by other men dressed in combat fatigues. They dragged the wounded into a bunker where he found rows of bandaged men on pallets. Many looked familiar. Moans of agony and screams for help filled the air. He felt pity, but before he could react, he found himself fighting for his life. He held a rifle in his hands and was firing at men in front of him. The compound was covered in the same thick smoke that was on the water moments earlier. He could smell the gunpowder and could hear the bullets flying over his head. Suddenly, he was in pain. He could see blood running down the leg of his trousers. He looked again, seeing hundreds of men running toward him in slow motion, firing their weapons as they came. He continued to fire his M-16, hitting every man he aimed at. They weren't hard to hit because they were moving so slow. As quickly as they fell, more men replaced them. He continued to fire, never having to reload his weapon. They were suddenly running around him. He was fighting hand to hand. All around him were the screams of the wounded and the dying. He would shoot them, strike out at them with the butt of his rifle or fist. Suddenly, there was a bright light and a deafening roar.

Jon found himself sitting straight up in bed. He was wearing a pair of flannel boxers and a tee shirt saying *Property of the United Sates Naval Academy*. He was covered in sweat and the tee shirt was soaked. He felt where the pain was moments before and then looking at his hand. No blood. He was OK. He was shaking uncontrollably, and his breathing was fast. He knew he had been dreaming and the nightmares returned. He felt a hand on his shoulder and turned to find Nancy sitting up in bed with him.

"It's okay, honey," she said rubbing his back. "You're home and you're fine. You just had that nightmare again. Take it easy."

The softness of her voice and the gentleness of her touch were helping him regain control. At the very least, bringing his breathing back to normal.

"Where were you?" she asked softly.

Jon didn't answer her. He was still shaking even though his breathing leveled, and his eyes still looked glazed over. Nancy continued to speak to him softly rubbing his arms and shoulders. She had seen this several times since they married and knew it wouldn't last much longer. Jon's eyes slowly began to clear and the shaking subsided.

"You back in Vietnam?" she asked brushing her hand across his forehead.

Jon shook his head. "The battle was Vietnam, but it wasn't Vietnam."

Nancy looked puzzled.

"Everything was hazy, and smoke covered," Jon explained. "Just like the battle in Vietnam, but it looked like one of the areas where we used to drill when we were stationed in the Philippines. I don't know, but I think that's where I was. Damned scary either way."

Jon shook his head as Nancy continued to rub his shoulders. He stopped shaking and now seemed to be back in total control. He put his arms around his wife and hugged her.

"Thanks, Babe," he said. "Let's get some sleep."

Nancy smiled at her husband and hugged him back. They both lay back down and in a matter of minutes were asleep in each other's arms.

CHAPTER 7

THE BUILD-UP

177 Pinecreek Drive
Rochester, New York
November 13, 1994
1840 Hours

The news started off with a story about several members of congress under investigation for accepting illegal campaign contributions. The second story was equally generic. A labor leader charged with the murder of the president of an opposing local. By the time the first set of commercials came, Jon was helping Nancy clear the table. Though he usually watched the news religiously, he was finding tonight's broadcast boring because he'd read about both stories in the newspaper. He was always on a quest for information, a habit he developed working for naval intelligence.

When the commercials ended Jon glanced up from what he was doing to listen to the anchor lead into the next story. Jon reached for the remote, turning up the volume.

"In the Philippines today, rebel forces attacked the provincial Town of Princesa, on the southernmost island of Mindanao. Sandy Monroe reports."

The television switched from the New York studio to a paved highway flanked on either side by heavy jungle. There was a wide shoulder on the highway packed with civilian and military vehicles. Soldiers were spread out amongst the vehicles, cautiously watching the jungle, their weapons at the ready. Ahead of the stalled column was a pillar of black smoke.

"The Town of Princesa was viciously attacked during the nighttime hours," said a husky female voice, "and relief for the stricken town has been agonizingly slow in arriving. Columns of Philippine Army troops and National Police reinforcements have been delayed because of a carefully planned rebel campaign of ambushes using rockets and land mines. Three Philippine soldiers were killed and six more wounded in this column when the armored personnel carrier they were riding was attacked and destroyed by an anti-tank rocket fired from the jungle. It's been slow going on all roads into the provincial town. An even bigger shock awaited relief forces when they finally reached the town."

The scene changed to the Town of Princesa. Video showed burned buildings still smoldering. Covered bodies lay in the street in front of a simple church, which displayed fresh bullet holes. People were congregating in front of the church looking down at the dead. The video that followed moved through the town pausing on scenes of destruction, the wounded, and the suffering.

"What awaited us in Princesa was even more horrible than the ambushes on the roads into the provincial trading center. The mayor, his wife, and the entire police force were executed while the citizens of this quiet hamlet watched helplessly. All were unarmed, gunned down in the middle of the street as the police station burned. The local garrison of the Philippine Army suffered an undisclosed number of casualties while retaking the town. There was no estimate of rebel casualties, although there are unconfirmed reports several were killed and wounded. Police and Army officials have been closed mouthed as they search for those responsible for this atrocity.

"Security in the area is tight as government troops have moved in to take control of the district. Roadblocks and sweeps through the area have resulted in several minor skirmishes since last night's attack. The exact number of civilian casualties is currently unknown. Neither side is commenting."

The scene shifted again to show a few officials talking to some of the town's people. Two of these officials were high-ranking military officers, both of whom had well-armed subordinates standing nearby. The officials moved away from the camera as it approached.

"Officials refused comment at the scene, but one government source in Manila stated the Moro National Liberation Front, or MNLF, has denied any involvement in this attack. This group is one of the largest and best organized of the separatist groups currently opposed to the Manila Government.

Residents have expressed fear this vicious attack on a seemingly peaceful town is the handiwork of a new, and very militant faction that recently claimed responsibility for the attack on a college dormitory in the City of Davao."

The picture again changed to show the female reporter in front of the church. Her long, light brown hair was tied back with several strands blowing in the wind.

"While no one here is talking about a response to this attack, the posture of the government clearly seems to say that they plan to deal with this decisively. Residents appear to be angry both with the rebels for the attack and at the Manila government for not protecting them. The feeling here in Princesa is this won't be the last incident until there is some type of cease-fire between the government and the rebels. We'll keep watching these developments as they unfold."

Jon turned off the television. He stood silently for a moment, absorbing what he just saw. Nancy walked over to him, taking the serving dish he was holding.

"Honey, we're washing the dishes, not trying to catch flies with our mouth," she joked. "What did you see that was so important?"

"I'm not sure," he answered. "Did you recognize that Filipino general?"

"No, should I have?" she responded.

Jon smiled. "Do you remember Robbie Mangoba?"

Nancy returned the smile remembering the dashing, young Filipino officer from Manila. She chuckled.

"Always knew he would make general, best dancer in that God forsaken place. Man, I don't miss those long overseas deployments."

They both laughed and Jon kissed her on the forehead.

"What was so important about the news broadcast?"

Jon turned serious. "The Philippines has a first-class military infrastructure and the last I heard Robbie was pretty high up. He was there to investigate who screwed up in that province and how the attack could happen. Those soldiers in the convoys were scared stiff. Whatever group is responsible for this attack, they're well financed and have more than their share of guts."

Nancy asked, "What did you mean when you said that those soldiers looked scared? They looked cautious to me, but that must be part of the job. These rebels can't be that good, can they?"

"What it means is this faction of rebels is bold enough to attack a provincial trading center according to the news. That alone is enough to scare me. They are well organized and well financed enough to mount an operation of this magnitude or are so incredibly stupid that they don't mind pissing off the local military commanders. Judging by the looks on the faces of the soldiers I'll go with the well-financed theory. Right now, these rebels appear to have enough of a reputation for the regular army to worry."

Nancy shook her head closing the dishwasher. "Sorry I asked. Okay, sailor, the dishes are done, and the kids are busy with Mom and Dad. So how about you take me out for some ice cream?"

Jon looked at his wife. He held out his arm, which she took, and the two of them walked off to get their coats.

Philippine Army Intelligence Headquarters
Mindanao, Philippines
November 15, 1994
0900 Hours

Franco pulled his unmarked car to a stop at the gate of the military base. A young soldier stepped smartly out of the guard shack located between the two lanes of traffic. Franco looked at the soldier with his impeccable uniform from his helmet all the way down to his highly polished boots, trying not to show his amusement.

"May I help you, sir?" asked the young sentry.

Jaime handed the man his police identification. "I have an appointment with General Mangoba. He told me to enter the base through this gate."

The soldier took the identification wallet, turning on his heel, and walking into the guard shack as smartly as he came out. Franco looked around. He could see at least three armored vehicles within seconds of the gate. There were also dozens of well-armed soldiers should someone be foolhardy enough to try and force their way onto the installation. These soldiers were not dressed for show, like the ones in the guard shack. He smiled to himself; the army was taking no chances.

Movement in the guard shack brought him back. The soldier handed him his identification saying, "Sorry for the delay, Captain. We had to locate the general. If you follow the jeep, it will take you directly to him."

Jaime took back his identification, smiling at the young soldier. The corner of the young man's mouth started up into a grin before he caught himself. Jaime thought these young soldiers took themselves entirely too seriously. A jeep pulled up on the other side of the guard shack. The sentry came to attention and waved him through.

The jeep led him through the winding streets that laced back and forth across the installation. Office buildings and barracks lined both sides. Armed men and armored vehicles were evident throughout the base. The security level was high.

He'd heard about the attack on Princesa and, like many of the people on the island, was concerned, especially since he had family there. As a policeman he learned to deal with facts, not the stories circulated around the streets, and hoped to learn a few while on this visit to the general. Based on what he was seeing he guessed the attack was serious. At least the military was serious about it. The MNLF and the other separatist groups had been fighting for decades to set up their own government on the island. He found through his law enforcement experience many of the splinter groups were more dangerous than the parent. This new group, if nothing else, enjoyed the attention of the Philippine military. The jeep pulled up next to a one-story brick building. Franco was directed by the soldiers to park his car near the door. A soldier, dressed in tropical khakis came out to meet him. The rank insignia of captain was on his collar and the gold braid on his right shoulder distinguished him as a general's aide.

"Captain Franco," said the soldier, "General Mangoba wishes me to express his thanks for your quick response to his request for a meeting."

Jaime took the officer's offered hand. The grip was firm.

"The pleasure is all mine, but I'm at a loss as to what he needs to see me about?"

The officer smiled politely and motioned for the policeman to follow.

"My apologies for not being able to give you more information over the phone, but this is a highly classified matter, and we couldn't be sure your communications weren't being monitored.

Jaime stopped, forcing the officer to look at him. "My people are loyal. You have no reason to suspect them of anything."

"My apologies," responded the army officer. "I didn't mean to imply anything. To the contrary, our backgrounds show every one of your people to be loyal to the government and fiercely loyal to you. You seem to have a way of bringing out the best in your subordinates."

Jaime looked at the soldier for a moment before deciding the man was being sincere. The policeman began moving towards the door. The officer easily moved in next to him.

"My name is Jorge Sanchez, Sir," continued the soldier. "I am the general's aide. General Mangoba speaks very highly of you and your ability to bring sanity to chaos."

Sanchez opened the door, motioning for the policeman to follow him down the main corridor.

"I think General Mangoba has an inflated opinion of me," responded Jaime. "He obviously hasn't seen my more recent work. I have two major cases open and no suspects in custody."

They turned at the end of the hallway stopping in front of a bank of elevators. Jaime gave Sanchez a puzzled look.

"We'll be going down," was the reply to the unasked question. "There are several floors below this one. There is a need for a high level of security, and this is the most secure building on the island."

Jaime guessed Mangoba stepped on some toes taking over this facility, but if the local military command allowed it then Mangoba carried more authority than anyone realized. The elevator door opened, and Sanchez pushed the button labeled "Sub Level Two". The doors closed and it was only seconds before the elevator stopped.

A security checkpoint manned by two armed soldiers greeted them. There was no attempt to stop the two men. They walked down a short corridor and through a set of heavy wood doors. They entered a large room filled with desks, soldiers, and sailors busy with their assigned tasks. On the far side of the room Mangoba looked upset as he talked to several officers. It was obvious to Franco the general saw them.

The policeman followed Sanchez into a private office, closing the door. It was Spartan in the way it was furnished. There was an old metal desk with a swivel chair, an old metal table and several folding chairs. On the table was a twelve-cup coffee maker with a full urn of dark coffee. Sanchez looked at the coffee and then at his guest motioning towards the pot.

Jaime nodded. "Please, that would be nice."

Sanchez found two cups, filling them.

"One of the few things I have continued to do since I was in the army is drink too much coffee." said Franco taking a sip. "Mmmmmm, good coffee. So, Captain, can you tell me why I was summoned today?"

Sanchez slowly turned looking out the door window. He sipped his coffee.

"I am not the one to tell you, Sir. General Mangoba will be with us momentarily. I know you will find the reason interesting."

Sanchez looked up as Mangoba walked through the door with a broad smile on his face.

"Thank you for coming so quickly," said Mangoba. "I'm glad you're here because we have much to discuss. I have information for you I believe to be important to the car fire and university murders."

Jaime was intrigued, but before he could ask the general what he meant the man continued, "I also desperately need your help. I'm sure you have questions, and I'll answer all of them soon, but first if you would please come with me. I have something I would like to show you."

Before Jaime could respond he was ushered out. Mangoba was in the lead, followed by the policeman, and then Sanchez. They went through a single door leading into a narrow corridor. There were several doors on either side of the hall. Mangoba entered the first door, holding it open for the other two men. The room was larger than Jaime expected. There were several soldiers sitting behind desks along the wall watching TV monitors and typing on computer keyboards. When Mangoba sat down in one of the chairs he motioned for Jaime to sit next to him. Sanchez stood behind his commanding officer.

"Look at the man on the monitor," said the general, "do you recognize him?"

The policeman was quiet as he looked intently at the young man on the screen. He was lying on a cot. He was dressed in a khaki short sleeved shirt, blue jeans, and on his feet, he had a pair of paper slippers. The young man appeared to be reading a magazine, occasionally looking around the small room in which he was confined.

"I don't recognize him, General," said the old policeman, "but I'm going to guess he has something to do with my unsolved cases."

Mangoba smiled at Jaime, "You're correct. Does the name Emil Montoya mean anything to you?"

There was a moment of silence as the policeman seemed to be sifting through the vast storehouse of information he kept in his head. He looked cautiously at the general.

"He's one of the men you feel left Zamboanga with Argento and Edwardo just before they were killed. This isn't that man."

"This arrogant, young whelp," said Mangoba "is Montoya's nephew, Benjamin. The same information that places Montoya in the car with Argento and Edwardo places Benny in the driver's seat. I also have information he was part of the raid on the dormitory at the University of Davao. He was captured by one of the first Army units to arrive at the Princesa massacre."

Franco looked into the eyes of the soldier sitting next to him. He saw frustration. He looked back at the monitor and saw the arrogance and defiance in the young man's face.

"What can you prove?" asked the policeman.

"Not enough to put him on trial for anything but his involvement in the Princesa raid," was the reply. "We have witnesses that can testify to the fact he executed the police officers and public officials in the town. We have a witness, a twelve-year-old boy. Quite a brave young man. The boy's name is Ramon Franco. Is he any relation?"

The policeman's expression remained unchanged. "He's, my grandson."

Mangoba smiled. "He's safe and very much the hero. You should be proud of him."

Franco nodded.

"We know Benny is guilty of the other two crimes. We have other prisoners who have implicated him but no hard proof. That's why I've asked you here today. You have a reputation for getting information from suspects who don't want to talk. I could have my people do it, but with their methods, he would admit to being part of the Japanese invasion in 1941."

Jaime smiled. "So, you would like me to speak to him for you?"

"Not just for me," answered Mangoba, "but also for you. If you can get anything out of him, then both of us will win. I will get my insurgents and you will clear two outstanding cases."

Jaime was quiet. No one interrupted as he stared at the monitor and stroked his chin. At one point the young man lying on the cot looked up and glared at the camera. The policeman allowed a slight smile. He turned to the general's aide.

"Captain," asked the policeman, "I assume aside from being the general's aide you've been educated in the proper way to interrogate a prisoner?"

Mangoba's gaze landed on Franco. He saw a gleam in the older man's eye he'd never seen before.

"General, I'll need to borrow your aide here and make sure you're recording everything that we do," said the policemen. "What I have in mind is a long shot but may give us some leverage with this bandit."

Mangoba nodded as the older man walked out, Sanchez following behind him.

The door opened and Benny tried to act as if he didn't hear the two men enter. He continued to read the magazine, shifting on the cot so he didn't have to look at them. He recognized the younger man as the army officer who interrogated him previously. Benny felt good this interrogation would be no different than the previous ones. They weren't successful thus far and he was confident this time would be no different. They got physical the last time, leaving bruises where they hit him. He guessed they were getting frustrated.

The other man was older, maybe in his late fifties or early sixties. He was wearing a police uniform. Benny wasn't impressed. These people were stupid and unimaginative. He smiled to himself. This man was what he imagined all policemen looked like.

"Sit up, boy!" ordered Sanchez grabbing the magazine away from the young man lying on the cot. Benny got up quickly as the army officer moved forward to push him back down. He was surprised when he got to his feet and wasn't met with a fist or open hand. He stood there for several seconds before realizing the old man stopped the army officer. His confusion was visible. He looked at the two men, not knowing what to do next.

"Sit, sit, young man," said the old man. "Make yourself comfortable. We're not here to hurt you."

The puzzled look left Benny's face as he looked at the army officer. There was hatred in his eyes. He didn't know what their plan was, but was determined to foil it, no matter what. He looked back at the older man. The man made a polite gesture for him to sit, which he did. He sat on the edge of the cot. *Why not be comfortable while frustrating these two bureaucrats.* He returned the old man's smile.

"Young man," said the policeman pulling the only chair in the room over opposite Benny. "I am Captain Jaime Franco of the Davao Police Department."

Benny didn't realize his whole body stiffened when he heard the introduction. The man wasn't who he thought he was and that temporarily threw off his concentration. He quickly cast a nervous glance at the army officer. He too looked irritated with the old man.

"I have some questions for you if you don't' mind," Jaime continued. "Can I get you something to drink?"

There was a moment of silence. Benny didn't know how to respond. He looked at the army officer whose expression still reflected irritation with the old man. Benny hated Sanchez as much as the army officer obviously hated him. He thought he saw a way to pit his foes against each other.

"Could I have a Coke?" Benny asked grinning. Rage consumed Sanchez's face. The officer started to object, but the old man raised his hand stifling the outburst.

"Captain Sanchez," said the policeman in a quiet, but even tone, "would you please get our guest a soda. Please leave the door open in case I need to get something else. Thank you."

Franco never looked at the soldier as he spoke. Sanchez, irritated at being ordered about by a civilian, opened the door with a key he was holding in his hand. There were no door handles on the inside for security reasons. As he left the room Sanchez propped the door open with an airport style floor ashtray. He glared at the two men one last time before he marched down the hallway.

Benny listened to the soldier's footsteps carefully as they disappeared. He looked at the old man sitting across from him and decided he really wasn't a very smart policeman. Benny guessed him to be no match for a younger man such as himself, especially since he'd just completed months of intensive physical training. Now that Sanchez was gone, he decided this would be his chance to escape. When he heard the door at the end of the hallway close, he lunged at the old policeman. Benny prided himself on his speed and agility, guessing he could quickly overpower the old man. He would use the confusion that would follow to make his way to the outer hallway, up the elevators, and hopefully, off the base. He never hit the old man. *Everything became a blur! He couldn't breathe!* His momentum carried him passed the policeman, onto the floor. He tried to focus, but all he could think about was how he was going to get his next breath. It felt like a vice closed on his throat. He couldn't get it to release. His mouth was open, he tried to gasp for breath, but the only sounds to be heard were the low guttural sounds of his vain attempts to bring oxygen to his lungs. He kept telling his body to fight, but it needed oxygen. Slowly he began to lose consciousness. He thought that he heard a soft, gentle voice telling him to sleep.

City of Pagadian
Mindanao, Philippines
November 15, 1994
1500 Hours

It was a busy afternoon in the city of just over 100,000 people. A gentle breeze blew in, moving the palms along the shoreline. People moved freely in and out of the shops lining the business district. Women carrying their groceries and men going about their daily routine walked through the busy traffic clogging the roads. Bicycles rushed about, making their way between the cars and small trucks.

No one noticed the woman park the small van in front of the bank. Her movements were casual and drew no one's attention. After parking, she adjusted the mirror, checked her make-up, and brushed the hair out of her eyes. A young man passed on his way to enter the bank. He looked at the woman, smiling at her. She returned the smile, watching him enter the bank. The woman again checked her side mirror and got out when the traffic allowed. She walked away from the van at a leisurely pace, not looking back. She smiled, occasionally nodding to the other pedestrians who would greet her.

She walked a little over a block when a taxi slowed alongside her. She got in. The taxi immediately jerked forward moving through traffic at a good pace. Inside the vehicle the woman joined the driver and another passenger, a man. When they were several miles away from the van, she nodded to the other passenger. He told the driver to drop them off around the next corner. The driver did as he was told, bringing the cab to a stop out of sight from the street. Before the cabby could collect his fare, the male passenger produced a small, silenced pistol, firing one round into the man's temple. The driver slumped over in the front seat, lifeless.

The two passengers took all the driver's money to make the killing look like a robbery. They then disappeared into the crowded streets as if they didn't even exist.

The people of Pagadian went about their business, paying no attention to the van parked in front of the bank. Even the police officers patrolling this sector of the city ignored the vehicle.

It was business as usual as the young man who smiled at the van's driver exited the bank. He walked on, lost in thought. He was completely surprised by the explosion. The sound was deafening. He was knocked to the ground, not knowing what hit him. Lying motionless on the street he was pelted by falling debris. Whatever was hitting him was small. He could feel it cutting into the exposed skin on his arms. He couldn't differentiate any sounds except the ringing from the explosion. He managed to cover his ears because they hurt from the magnitude of the sound.

After what seemed an eternity, objects stopped hitting him. He remained on the ground for several minutes, still covered up, his eyes closed. He then slowly opened his eyes trying to remember where he was. From where he was lying on the sidewalk, he could see parts of brick and metal all over the ground. He could also make out the sparkle from millions of shards of glass. Smoke rolled along the ground past where he lay. He moved his head slightly and could see a woman sitting in the roadway several feet away, dressed in what was once a white dress. The dress was covered with blood from her head and face. She appeared to be screaming, but he couldn't hear her.

He decided he needed to sit up. He moved, feeling pain. Once he was sitting, he looked around. Where the van had been, a crater now existed. The front of the bank was gone, as were the fronts of the buildings on either side. Vehicles were strewn about the street, some in pieces, some burning, and the rest just motionless. Debris was scattered everywhere. Bricks, metal, glass, even furniture littered the street. Mixed in with the debris were the bodies. Some were moving like him, while others just lay there, motionless. Most were covered in blood, dirt, and soot. Thick, black smoke poured from the burning vehicles, while lighter colored smoke came from where the buildings once stood.

The smells from the scene finally hit him because his senses started to clear. He could smell the burning gas and oil from the vehicles as it mixed with the odor of wood burning. There was also another smell he didn't recognize. He thought he knew what it might be, but quickly put it out of his mind. He was starting to hear faint sounds, even though his ears continued to ring. He could now tell that the woman a few feet from him was screaming for help. He thought that he could hear sirens in the distance but couldn't be sure.

He decided he needed to move and tried to stand. The pain in his back was so intense he couldn't. He did a quick self-inventory of his injuries. He could see blood covered his blue shirt but assumed most of it came from the many small cuts on his arms. He guessed that occurred when he covered his head. He could find no wounds on the front of his torso or on his legs. He couldn't see if there were any injuries to his head. He felt no pain there. His back was what hurt. Where the debris struck him. He couldn't even reach behind him to feel if the injury was bleeding without passing out from the pain. He could see police and fire personnel moving through the injured and decided to wait for help.

U.S.S. *Kamehameha*
Pearl Harbor, Hawaii
November 20, 1994
0900 Hours

Commander Robert Grant stood on the bridge of the *Kamehameha* waiting for his visitors to arrive. He wasn't looking forward to this meeting, and even less to the upcoming operation. He assumed command of the *Kamehameha* less than six months earlier and was being assigned to the *Nimitz* Battle Group under the command of Admiral Dick Kingston. Grant hated the politics the navy involved its commanders in and knew with Kingston everything was political, no matter what the orders. The admiral had been two classes ahead of him at the academy and on an upward spiral even then. Connections made a difference in the military if your family controlled the right members of Congress. Grant didn't like Kingston, not many people did, but knew he ran a tight ship and was a good sailor.

He looked out over his boat with pride. She was not one of the new fast attack subs, but she was well maintained. Her officers and crew were first rate and knew their jobs. It showed. The *Kamehameha* was a *Benjamin Franklin* class submarine and was originally commissioned in the mid 1960's as a ballistic missile submarine. In the past several years, the *Kamehameha* and her sister boat, the *James K. Polk*, underwent modifications and were reclassified as attack submarines. Missile silos were removed and replaced with berthing, storage, and exercise areas. Aft of the sail was a large cylinder looking to the average person to be an extra fuel tank. This was in fact a dry lock shelter allowing the *Kamehameha* to support SEAL and other Special Forces operations. The main purpose for the modifications was to enhance the United States Navy's Special Warfare capabilities. Grant had yet to see a SEAL on board his boat but knew that would only be a matter of time.

Grant was proud of the fact he had risen to command the 425-foot submarine. She displaced 8,250 tons submerged and could travel at a top speed of 20 plus knots, about 23 miles per hour. She carried MK-48 torpedoes and, though she was one of the last two boats in her class in active service, she still had a sting that she could carry to any enemy. Grant watched the crew scurry about the ship. There were 12 officers and 107 enlisted men under his command, and he felt like a proud parent watching how well they worked together.

Grant graduated from the United Sates Naval Academy and went right into submarine school. He didn't graduate at the top of his class, but because he was a bright, hardworking, energetic man, he caught some good breaks. His first assignment had been aboard another *Benjamin Franklin* class submarine as its engineering officer. He then spent time on shore as a supply officer. This was followed by two more sea assignments one on a *Los Angeles* class attack submarine and the other on an *Ohio* class ballistic missile submarine. His last assignment had been four years in research where he worked with experimental submarines. His current command seemed to be as intriguing as the last one. Submariners by trade worked in stealth to do their job. His current assignment required him to be even stealthier to deliver his deadly cargo to hostile shores and get them out undetected. He hoped he would be up to the challenge.

The sound of voices near the gangway caused him to look down the sail. Two men dressed in camouflage fatigues were in the process of boarding.

Grant guessed these men to be the SEAL officers he was to meet with Kingston. The officer of the deck was pointing to a hatch on the side of the sail. Both men disappeared from Grant's view just as the growler phone next to him buzzed.

"Captain!"

"Sir," said an upbeat voice. "Lieutenant Commander DeCook and Senior Chief Wiedenkeller from SEAL Team Five are here."

"Give them my compliments, Mr. Krause," replied Grant to his executive officer, "and please escort them to the wardroom and make sure that it's secured for this meeting. I'll be along with the admiral as soon as he arrives."

"Yes, Sir, Skipper." replied Krause smartly. "I'll make sure that there's coffee and something to eat, Sir. We wouldn't want you in trouble the first time you meet the new boss."

Grant smiled at the officer's attempt to cheer him up. He hadn't been looking forward to meeting with Kingston. He'd spoken to several of the other ship captains he knew assigned to the battle group and wasn't encouraged. None were happy with the assignment of Kingston as their boss. All agreed that he was an excellent officer when it came down to getting the job done. The problem was he'd developed a reputation as a *career killer* for those who didn't perform to his standards. The word was out that he was campaigning for the job of Chief of Naval Operation after this assignment. What made Grant nervous was the description of the man hadn't changed from the naval academy midshipman he remembered. He felt confident as he looked about the boat. She really looked good. The crew had outdone themselves getting her ready for this meeting. Grant's upbeat mood was short lived when a black staff car pulled down the pier.

The car came to a stop near the gangway. A chief petty officer stepped out. He took a second to straighten his khaki uniform and then opened the back door of the car. Grant recognized the man who got out of the car as Admiral Kingston. The khaki uniform was tailored, and everything was in place. After stepping out of the car, he returned the driver's salute and waited for the other occupants. The first officer was male. He, too, was dressed in a tailored uniform, but didn't have the dignified look of his boss. He was shorter than the admiral and had a much smaller built. Grant wondered if Kingston purposely chose an aide that looked the opposite of him, just to project a better self-image. The second officer was female and, like her male counterpart, looked the part of an admiral's aide. She was about the same height as the male aide but didn't have the plain look of the first officer. Grant thought she looked quite attractive, though women in uniform never really caught his attention.

Grant made eye contact with Kingston. He could tell the admiral looked disturbed about something. He sighed deeply, turning to go down the ladder from the bridge to the hatch that led to the deck. Grant went out of the hatch onto the main deck of the boat just as the admiral and his party reached the officer of the deck.

The admiral saluted the flag and then the OOD, who smartly returned his salute. Even Grant was impressed by how sharp the young man looked. Grant noticed that Kingston didn't asked permission to board the boat, as was custom. He was irritated further when both admiral's aides followed suit. His eyes met Kingston's for the second time. He could tell he was being challenged.

"Welcome aboard, Admiral," Grant said hiding any trace of his irritability.

"The boat looks sharp, Grant," replied the admiral as he took Grant's outstretched hand. "You are to be commended. It's been a long time since the academy. You look as if submarines have been good to you."

Grant was cautious, the admiral's tone was polite, but not necessarily friendly. "Thank you, Sir. I enjoy the duty. If you will follow me, Sir, the wardroom is this way."

The admiral and his party followed Grant as he led them past the control room. Grant decided that he had to be polite. "Been on a submarine before, Sir?"

"Don't like submarines, Commander. Nothing personal. I prefer the surface. Again, my compliments, Grant. The boat looks to be in excellent shape. How's the crew?"

Grant breathed a little easier. "Eager bunch of kids, Sir. I've only been with them through some sea trials, so I haven't really had an opportunity to evaluate them at sea. They're hard workers though. Always busy."

"Are the Special Warfare people here, yet?" asked the admiral.

Grant sensed the shift in mood. "Yes, Sir. The SEALs arrived just prior to you, Sir. They're waiting in the wardroom for us. It's one more deck down, Sir."

As they continued down the ladder, the admiral spoke. "I'll be straight forward about this, Grant. I don't like Special Ops people. I find them to be unconventional and, in most cases, not fit to wear the uniform of the United States Navy. I tolerate their presence because I must, and I don't see their value to the upcoming operation. I understand your job is to take them into their objective, drop them off, and then pick them up when they're done and that's all I want you to do. You work for me on this trip, and you'll do your job as I tell you. Not the way Special Ops wants. Understood?"

They reached the second deck.

"Understood, Sir!" replied Grant. "The wardroom is over here."

Kingston put his hand on Grant's shoulder. "Not quite like the academy, heh, Grant? At least we all know who's in command of this operation."

Grant flushed as he led them into the wardroom. He'd hoped that the admiral wouldn't bring up the academy and the problems the two of them experienced there. Grant decided to ignore the comment.

When they entered the wardroom the two individuals who preceded them stood, coming to attention. Both men looked to be in their thirties, clean shaven, with short, cropped hair.

"Gentlemen, please be seated," said Kingston jumping right in. "I have a meeting with CINCPAC in an hour, so I'll make this briefing short. I know Commander Grant. He's the captain of this boat."

When Kingston stopped talking, the SEAL officer spoke.

"Sir, I'm Lieutenant Commander Tim DeCook and this is Senior Chief Allen Wiedenkeller, SEAL Team Five.

Grant glanced at Kingston. It was obvious to even the most inexperienced seaman the admiral took an immediate dislike to both men. He said nothing in response as he walked past them taking a seat.

"All of you, please, be seated," said Kingston. "I want to get this over with and get onto more important issues."

The others found a seat around the table except for Chief Wiedenkeller who stood behind DeCook. Grant caught Wiedenkeller's eye and nodded towards the empty chair next to him. Wiedenkeller smiled, as if to say thank you, but shook his head.

"The two officers with me are my aides," continued Kingston, "and you will obey all orders from them as if they've come from me. This is Lieutenant Commander Stephen Williams and Lieutenant Andrea Handcock. I will be sending most of my orders and directives through these two officers and won't tolerate anyone challenging them. Are there any questions?"

"No, Sir," was the response in unison from everyone gathered around the table.

"Now," continued the admiral, "this war game we're going to participate in is against reserve and national guard troops. Part-time soldiers and sailors, who are no match for professionals. There'll be no excuses for failure, gentlemen."

Grant remembered why he never liked Kingston. Arrogance hung on every word. He glanced at the other officers around the table. The two aides both were smiling. Grant decided he didn't like them either. They were enjoying this. DeCook and Wiedenkeller were doing their best to ignore the admiral's attitude.

"I have worked out a plan with my staff that should prove to be successful against these part-timers. I expect you'll review it and then get back to Commander Grant."

They all looked at Kingston for a second as Lieutenant Handcock handed out sealed, manila envelopes to both officers.

"Commander Grant will be in overall command of this portion of the operation and you, Commander DeCook will report to him. No other chain of command will be acceptable."

Grant noticed DeCook's face flush. His mood calmed, though, when Wiedenkeller placed his hand on his commanding officer's shoulder. Kingston seemed irritated by this but continued.

"Gentlemen, I don't care for Spec Ops in any branch of the service, but especially in the navy. Sailors should sail their ships, not run around shooting up Third World countries. You don't even dress like sailors. Do your job, stay out of my way, and you won't have any problems. Understood, DeCook?"

DeCook remained calm. "Yes, Sir."

Kingston looked even more irritated when the response from the SEAL was so simple. He continued, "I'll leave you with these orders. Commander Grant, you will coordinate all the activities pertaining to this aspect of the operation. I don't expect there to be too much trouble because of the caliber of troops you'll be facing. DeCook, you'll get all your orders regarding this operation through Commander Grant. Commander Williams will be your contact at my headquarters, Grant."

There was a brief silence before Kingston rose from the table. Everyone stood, coming to attention. Kingston left the room followed by his two aides and Grant, who looked back apologetically. The admiral moved quickly up the ladder and stepped out onto the deck of the *Kamehameha*. Both of his aides moved quickly passed him as he turned to speak to Grant.

"Grant," he said, "you keep those cowboys under control during this operation. You have a good record thus far in your career, but I know from the academy how you tend to side with Special Operation types. I'll not tolerate it here. Any questions about the assignment?"

Grant took a deep breath. "One comment, Sir. Don't you think you're underestimating the caliber of the troops we will be facing? Reserves and guard troops did quite well during Desert Storm."

The calm response from his superior surprised Grant after the display below.

"Entirely true, Commander, but be assured we've looked at the leadership currently here in the islands that would be in command during the exercise. I see no surprises. They're good officers and I'm sure their troops are well trained, but they're weekend warriors, none the less. They play soldier once a month and then go back to their civilian jobs the rest of the time. Don't worry about them. Everything has been factored in. They just don't have the depth to stop us."

Grant still wasn't convinced but decided not to press the point. Kingston was smiling, knowing he wasn't going to be questioned further.

"Just keep those SEALs under control," said Kingston. "Remember what I said about your career."

"Yes, Sir. Point taken."

Kingston rejoined his aides. Kingston saluted the flag and walked across the gangway without asking the officer of the deck permission to leave the boat. Both of his aides followed suit. Grant found it curious that Handcock went before Commander Williams. Williams could just be acting as any officer and gentlemen should, but Grant doubted it. More than likely, there was something between.... He shook his head to clear the thought.

Grant went back in the hatch and down the ladder. As he reentered the wardroom, both DeCook and Wiedenkeller stood up with a look of apprehension.

"Gentlemen," Grant said, "the man was an ass at the academy and is still an ass today."

DeCook breathed a sigh of relief as Wiedenkeller smiled broadly.

"Coffee?" asked Grant.

Both men moved forward, taking the cups offered them. DeCook broke the silence.

"I was afraid it was just me who thought he was an asshole. Man, he has a low opinion of the people who work for him. Commander, how well do you know him?"

"Mostly from the academy. Only by reputation since. He was a bully then and appears to have gotten worse as he moved through the ranks. Family has money and is well connected. I'm sure that's what protected him when he was a junior officer. Once he got rank, the word is not many people are willing to cross him for fear of having their career torpedoed. He seems to have a lot of pull in political circles."

"Just what we need leading us into this operation," said DeCook, "someone with a political agenda. I assume he's looking to go higher than just rear admiral?"

"He's currently campaigning for Chief of Naval Operations and making no secret about it," replied Grant. "My guess is his family has a political career lined up for him after that. He's the type and has the contacts to walk into the political arena without any problems."

Grant looked at Wiedenkeller who was listening intently. He sat next to DeCook, slowly sipping his coffee.

"Chief," he asked, "nothing to add to the conversation?'

"I wasn't asked, Sir. Not all officers want input from the enlisted side of the fence."

"Not the case with me, Chief," said Grant. "I learned a long time ago to listen to your men because they're the ones that are going to get you through the tough times. I'd like to hear your impression."

"I agree with both of you, Sirs, as to your impression of the admiral," replied Wiedenkeller without hesitation. "What makes matters worse in my eyes is that he's the type of commander who will sacrifice his people if it forwards his career. That makes him dangerous to me and the people who work for me. I'll be interested to see what he does on this exercise. It also worries me that he has this hatred of Spec Ops and particularly SEALs. I wonder where that came from."

Grant put down his coffee and looked at both men. "I can answer that question for you, Chief."

"Sir?" Wiedenkeller looked puzzle.

"The guy must be jealous of all the recent press on the teams," said DeCook.

"No, Commander," replied Grant, "hatred of another man, a professional rivalry."

It was DeCook's turn to look confused. Wiedenkeller shifted in his chair leaning closer with curiosity.

"It goes back to our academy days. Kingston was two years ahead of me and a real terror to underclassmen. He was always in our face and pulling borderline stunts on us. There was this guy one year ahead of me who Kingston always seemed to have a conflict with. The guy was always sticking up for us and always going back after Kingston. This guy, his name was Summers, had been a SEAL in Vietnam and received an appointment to the academy for an act of heroism."

"I worked with a Summers during Desert Storm," said DeCook. "A Commander in the Reserves, an Intelligence type, as I recall. Nice guy and seemed to know his stuff."

"He's the same man, Sir," replied Wiedenkeller. "Was a decorated SEAL in Vietnam and was awarded the Medal of Honor. Went to Annapolis by presidential appointment after getting out of the hospital. Went back to the teams for a while, then into Intelligence."

"No shit!" exclaimed DeCook. "I just figured him to be an OCS guy like myself. Learn something every day."

"No shit is right, Commander," continued Grant. "When he arrived at the academy, Kingston and a bunch of his cohorts jumped him for no apparent reason and Summers kicked the shit out of the whole bunch. The academy played down the fact he was in Vietnam and the only thing that was really out there was the fact he was an enlisted man and received an appointment to go to Annapolis."

"Must have really pissed the admiral off," Wiedenkeller grinned.

"Judging by the ego I saw today, so did the beating," added DeCook.

"You're both right," said Grant chuckling, "the admiral spent some time in the hospital because of that. He was also upset when they wouldn't even consider pressing charges against Summers. He could never understand the self-defense issue."

They all laughed.

"Anyway," continued Grant, "that's why the admiral doesn't like SEALs. Too bad, I hear Summers is going to retire from the reserves. I know I'll miss him. I saw him this past summer in San Diego."

Wiedenkeller looked at DeCook. "Sir, if I may, I recommend we use the admiral's recommendation and go through Commander Grant for our orders. Our guys will try to kill the admiral if he cops the same attitude with them, he did with us today. I'm not sure how those rangers we're going to be working with will react to him either."

"Rangers?" questioned Grant.

DeCook looked at him and smiled weakly. "We just got the word; this is a joint operation between us and the army. Sorry you haven't heard. Just happened."

Grant smiled back. "Then we better get busy. I'll stock up on seasick meds for the Army."

First Ranger Battalion Headquarters
Fort Benning, Georgia
November 20, 1994
1800 Hours

Klintworth entered the office as Naylor was cleaning his desk. The colonel looked tired. He spent more time in the field than any battalion commander Klintworth ever worked for. Usually that meant the office work would back up, but not the case here. The extra runners Naylor assigned to headquarters were earning their pay.

"Klintworth," Naylor sounded upbeat. "I have some good news and some bad news."

"Sir?"

"I need you to select a group of your men for a war game that's to take place just before the Christmas holiday. Select twenty officers and men not scheduled for leave, to take part in a joint exercise with a SEAL team. Sorry, I don't have much more information, but the orders just arrived from headquarters. You know the drill, more information to follow."

"Sir," Klintworth asked, "will I be asking for volunteers or selecting my own crew?"

Naylor looked at the junior officer. "Select your own crew, Captain. Pick people scheduled to be on base during the entire holiday season. Also, tell these people that the DOD will transport family to the exercise site due to the timing of the game."

"Will that be wise, Sir?" Klintworth didn't like being negative with his boss. "Some of these locations can be pretty remote. Wives don't tend towards the Christmas spirit when there isn't' much around to do."

"Then they shouldn't have a problem with Honolulu, should they?"

Klintworth stopped cold. "Sir?"

"The exercise is in Hawaii and the DOD has authorized the families to go along and wait for our people in Honolulu. I can't guarantee the accommodations, but it beats Fort Benning."

A smile came to Klintworth's face. "You're serious, aren't you, Sir?"

Naylor returned his subordinate's smile.

"Sir," Klintworth came back quickly, "I'll have a list of troopers to you within the hour, along with a list of dependents. There are enough people who have volunteered for holiday duty that have just wives so we can keep the cost down for DOD. I also have an old friend who is stationed in the islands who may be able to help us with accommodations."

"Excellent, Captain," replied Naylor, "let me know in the morning where we stand and who will be assigned to the exercise. I don't have to let division know until noon. Carry on, Captain."

Klintworth came to attention and saluted, "Yes, Sir!

Naylor weakly returned his salute. The younger man wheeled around and disappeared from the office as quickly as he had appeared. He looked about the office noticing the time on the small digital clock. He shook his head and looked at his calendar for tomorrow's schedule. It looked light except for his noon meeting at division headquarters.

Naylor smiled and headed for the door. He would worry about tomorrow's schedule tomorrow. For the first time since he had arrived at Fort Benning, he had a date.

880 Country Lane
Murrell's Inlet, South Carolina
November 20, 1994
1930 Hours

Ray picked up the telephone and pushed speed dial. It took several seconds for the number to connect. It rang twice before it was answered.

"Hello?" said the familiar voice of Bill Gateway.

"Bill?" said Ray. "How are you doing, buddy?"

"Ray! Good to hear your voice," replied his old friend. "We're doing well. How about you guys?"

"Not too bad, I guess. I've been fighting the flu or something the last week or so, but other than that, perfect. How is the reunion shaping up?" asked Ray.

"Looking good, buddy," replied Gateway. "Still about one hundred seventy people from all the units. From our company, right now, there's Donnie Smith and Sam Donavan. With you and me, that makes four. Most of the rest I've talked to can't travel because of health reasons. How about you?"

"Same thing here, Bill, "replied his friend. "It's a bitch getting old, isn't it?"

"Sorry to hear that, but I have to say we're looking good right now. We have plenty of people signed up and I've arranged to tour some of the areas where we fought. Not just from our unit, but some of the other divisions as well. I'm going to be kept busy out here for a while and won't be getting down to see you for a couple weeks."

"Probably best with me feeling under the weather." replied Ray.

"Well, you get better, and we'll see you soon." chimed Gateway.

"Sounds good, Bill. Give my love to the family and I'll be talking to you soon."

"Love to Louise."

They both hung up, not knowing it would be the last time the two friends would talk.

CHAPTER 8

LOSSES AND GAINS

Summers Cabin
Adirondack State Park, New York
November 24, 1994
1430 Hours

Ray sat at his favorite spot on the porch. It looked out over the lake from the top of the small hill where the cabin stood. He was lost in thought. A light snow from the night before, covered the ground and the trees. He didn't notice the grandchildren running and playing near the cabin. The family got together at least once a year at the cabin in the summer, but he insisted on another trip this Thanksgiving. Jon, Matt, Julie, and their families all came up without question. The kids seemed to be enjoying the snow and cool weather.

Ray was brought out of his daydream by the sound of his three children coming out onto the porch. He'd requested the private meeting, and since it was unusual for him to include them in major decisions regarding the family, they all knew it would be important. Julie came up to her father smiling and carrying a cup of coffee. He took the steaming mug from his daughter, who then leaned down and gave him a hug.

"You wanted to see us, Daddy?" She asked kissing him on the cheek.

He motioned for them to sit down. All were dressed in boots, jeans, and warm coats. The temperature was in the mid-thirties, but that was still cold enough to need to keep warm when you weren't moving.

"I want to thank you and your families for honoring my request to get together here for Thanksgiving," he started. "I know this is a bit unusual, but I think I have a valid reason for the request. I don't want to prolong the conversation, so I'll get right to the point."

"How long do you have, Dad?" asked Matt looking a bit uncomfortable.

The statement took the older man by surprise. He hesitated. Julie looked confused, then frightened, then hurt. She obviously hadn't known, but the looks on the faces of his two sons told him that they both knew.

"Two weeks to a month," he answered Matt's question.

"Daddy, what's Matt talking about?" asked Julie. "I don't understand. What does he mean how long do you have?"

Ray felt heartbroken watching the fear in his daughter's eyes. He didn't consider himself a coward, but this was a meeting he hoped he would never have. He watched his daughter's face as the realization of what they were talking about sunk in. Tears started down her face. She stood and raised her hand to hit her older brother. Jon moved quickly between the two and took the slap intended for Matt.

"You bastard," she said trying to reach around Jon to get at Matt. "How dare you! How dare you not tell me! You son-of-a-..."

Julie buried her head in Jon's shoulder and began to weep. Jon gently stroked his sister's hair. "Don't blame Matt, Jules. We both found out by accident and were told not to tell anyone. We wanted to, but also knew Dad wanted to tell us all together."

"So how did you find out?" asked Ray relieved the tough part was over. He looked at Matt who was genuinely hurt at his sister's reaction.

"We walked in on Mom at a weak moment. We found her crying in the kitchen and she told us both but made us swear not to tell anyone. She said you would do it in your own way and insisted we honor that. Dad, it's been the toughest thing I've ever had to do. Sorry, Jules. We really wanted to let you know. I feel like such an ass.

Julie hugged Jon, kissing him on the cheek.

"Sorry I hit you."

She let go of Jon and went over to Matt hugging him.

"Sorry, Matt. I should have known better than to think you would intentionally keep something like this from me. I'm so sorry."

The tears came again, and she hugged her brother. She went over to her father, tears flowing freely down her face. Ray produced a red bandana out of his coat pocket attempting to dry the tears.

"I'm sorry, Angel," he said. "There's no easy way to tell you about this. I've been diagnosed with cancer. I wanted to meet here while I still could because this is the place where it's most comfortable for me to deal with it. It's one of those fast-moving bugs and the doctors say there's no chance to deal with it using chemo or radiation. I decided that I'm going to deal with this on my own terms. No life support or anything else. I don't want to prolong this for your mother or any of you. I've already signed the papers, but I need to talk to all of you about how we tell the kids and what I need each of you to do for your mother."

They talked for over an hour, each willing to do what their father asked. There were more tears for all of them while they worked through the more difficult issues. When they were done, Ray seemed to be more at peace than any of his children could remember. Even Julie, who took the news the hardest, managed to smile. Each of them took some responsibility for helping their mother through the upcoming ordeal.

When they all rose to discuss these decisions with their own families, Ray asked Jon to stay for a minute more.

"I have something special to ask of you, Jon," said his father. "I know you'll understand more than your brother and sister. It's something that's important to me."

"What is it, Dad? You know I'll do anything you need me to," replied his oldest son.

There was a tear in his father's eye as Jon watched him struggle for the words.

"You know about the reunion coming up in March?"

Osaka Pineapple Plantation
Mindanao, Philippines
November 30, 1994
1030 Hours

Osaka sat in the bright sitting room looking out over the ocean far below. He could see the swells with their white capped tops moving in towards the shore below the cliffs. He'd purchased the plantation years before when he and his colleagues began planning this operation. He even harvested enough pineapple to post an annual profit so as not to draw attention to the real reason for being in the Philippines. The location was specific because of where the plantation was along the coast. The cliffs were a bonus and served their purposes extremely well. The heavy jungle in this area of the Mindanao coast helped cover the smuggling of arms and mercenaries into the country. It would help them in this new phase as well.

Osaka was pleased because his superiors were pleased. The organization he worked for put up millions of dollars to finance this operation and they were now starting to see their objectives achieved. The military portion of the operation was to start with the coming of the New Year. They were working diligently on the political phase of the project which was ahead of schedule. He'd made a full report to his superiors in Japan the evening before. They were concerned about the Philippine and Japanese governments finding out about the operation before they could put it in motion. Osaka assured them that the guise of a separatist takeover of the island was the perfect cover. No one would realize an outside interest was controlling the take over until it was too late, if at all.

Osaka smiled, enjoying the sunlight streaming in the large picture windows. He was a person who required the sunshine to recharge himself emotionally. He smiled to himself thinking about the upcoming operation. If successful, it would propel him up the organization.

He was brought out of his daydream by the sound of Ishimoto bringing in morning tea. His friend and servant bowed slightly, placing a tray on the table.

"Thank you, Ishi," said Osaka. "When do our guests arrive?"

"Most of them are just arriving, but Toshio is here to see you before the full meeting as you requested."

Osaka noticed Ishimoto brought an extra teacup on the tray. "Show him in, my friend."

Ishimoto bowed slightly, walking out of the room. Osaka smiled, pouring tea for both he and his arriving associate. There were no illusions about the relationship between him and his servant. The same went for any of the other people he was associated with on this operation. The organization they worked for demanded loyalty. Anything less meant a shortened life expectancy. Ishimoto was not only a friend, servant, and bodyguard to Osaka; he was there to insure his loyalty to their superiors in Japan.

Toshio entered the room and walked over to Osaka. Osaka rose, bowing slightly.

"Toshio, my friend. How was your trip?"

"Very nice," replied Toshio returning the bow. "It's good to see you. You look, well."

Osaka smiled. Toshio Akiyama was another member of the organization about which he knew little except he was exceptionally good at gathering information. He also knew the greeting was genuine, not superficial like so many others he dealt with. Toshio was assigned to the operation by their superiors. Osaka could only assume he was a watch dog from the home office. He liked the man but treated him with a great deal of caution and respect.

"Please, sit down, Toshio," said Osaka motioning to a chair. "Ishimoto has brought us some tea. Would you care for some?"

"Yes, please. I understand you have some questions regarding the upcoming operation?"

"Yes," he said, "I do have a few questions after talking to Tokyo last night."

"Whatever I can do to answer them, my friend."

"There are concerns when this operation starts the United States will try to intervene," said Osaka. "Are there any assurances they will not?"

Toshio put down his teacup. "No, my friend, there are no assurances. One can never completely predict how a foreign government will react when their nationals are a target of terrorism."

Osaka shifted uneasily. Toshio smiled. "Make no mistake, that is exactly what the United Sates will call our operation. But that's also the strength of your plan. They will not deal with terrorists and have a history of not responding when a friendly nation is in control of the situation. Politically, there'll be a great deal of pressure on Manila, but it's highly unlikely they'll commit their military to any action here in the Philippines."

Osaka nodded. "I understand all of this, but our friends in Tokyo are looking for some guarantees their investment will pay off. The last thing we need is the American military marching in to save the world again."

"Please believe me, I mean no disrespect when I say if they want guarantees they should go shopping for a car. What we're involved in is a gamble. The government in Manila is predictable, as are the Americans. The problem with America is you never know what will send them on a crusade. Right now, their government is busy trying to help Bosnia solve their problems. The Middle East is still a major concern with Iraq intact after the Gulf War. Believe me when I say, it is highly unlikely they will commit themselves to another country having internal problems.

"To put it in perspective, there's not the interest in the Philippines on the part of Washington there once was. With their major military bases gone, there's no real need to support the Manila government in a fight against separatists. The support they give will be in aid, nothing more."

Osaka looked at Toshio's eyes. He believed what he was saying. "So, your advice to me would be what?"

Toshio was silent while he thought.

"Make sure all of our people understand no one can know our real purpose."

Osaka smiled. "That shouldn't be a problem since only about six people really know what this operation is about."

"You'll have to watch the Filipinos carefully. If they get the idea you're not supporting a separate Muslim state on Mindanao, you'll have to deal with them quickly and decisively."

"Mr. Montoya is the only one to be concerned about, and he's not that intelligent."

Toshio looked at the man sitting across from him. He looked relaxed. Toshio sensed the statement was meant to be factual, not an insult.

"I'd agree with your assessment of Mr. Montoya," replied Toshio, "but don't underestimate what would happen if he discovered we have our own reasons for wanting a separate country on this island. There's a history here that can't be ignored. The Philippine people, and especially the Moros, have always managed to resist whoever was in power over this country. I don't mean to lecture, but it's a point none of us can afford to forget."

Osaka nodded. "Your point isn't wasted. Tokyo was quick to say the same thing last night. That's a factor we have a good deal of control over and not a big worry to me. I am more concerned about the unpredictability of the Americans."

Toshio responded quickly. "I share your concern and unpredictable is an excellent term to describe them. As I said earlier, this operation is a gamble, but with their other commitments in the world, I don't see any active involvement by the United Sates. Our assets in Hawaii are in place and reliable. If the American military makes any move to intervene, we'll know in advance and be able to respond accordingly."

"How reliable is your source in Hawaii?"

Toshio was reluctant to answer, hesitating a second.

"My source is extremely well placed. He has the potential of becoming even more valuable in the future. If the Americans decide to use a military option for any reason during our operation, we'll have plenty of notice. I find most Americans have a price and will sell their allegiance to the highest bidder. There are few with the honor and integrity to be trusted in a business deal of this type. I've only met one in their military I would worry about and he's in their reserves."

The sound of the door opening made both men become quiet. Ishimoto walked in, bowing. "Mr. Osaka, the others have arrived. Shall I show them in?"

Osaka looked at his colleague who nodded. "Yes, please, Ishimoto."

Ishimoto bowed, leaving. Osaka looked at Toshio smiling. "This meeting should be interesting. Our new colleague seems eager to get started. It'll be interesting to see how the Manila government responds to this threat."

Osaka was interrupted by the rest of the planning group entering. He motioned for them to take a seat, joining him and Toshio.

"Good morning, gentlemen. First, I would like to introduce a new member to our little group. Gentlemen, this is Lieutenant Commander James Holiday, formerly of the Royal Navy. He will be heading up a new phase of our little operation that will support Mr. Montoya and Col. Boerst directly."

Montoya jumped in. "No disrespect to Mr. Holiday, but why do we need another person at this level of the operation? Don't we have too many of us involved in planning?"

Montoya was always suspicious of people involved in the operation who weren't Filipino. The fact Osaka hadn't used more Philippine nationals of Muslim decent made Montoya question many of the aspects of the operation. This didn't surprise Osaka. He anticipated it.

"Emil," responded Osaka. "Commander Holiday has a skill none of us have and is also an integral part of the plan. Don't concern yourself with the security aspect of the operation. We have compartmentalized ourselves in such a way each of you knows your own aspect of the overall operation, but no more than that."

"I apologize, Mr. Osaka," said Montoya. "I didn't mean to speak out of turn."

"You weren't speaking out of turn, my friend. If you have concerns, they must be on the table and be addressed for this operation to succeed. Now, before we go any further, let's have our reports. Gerry, will you start us off?"

Osaka looked at his pilot who smiled and leaned back in his chair. Wilson talked slowly; his southern drawl very pronounced. He spoke to the number of aircraft and pilots to fly them. All the helicopters were in good shape with few maintenance issues. His only concern was supplies and ammunition. He was followed by O'Keefe and then Boerst, each giving similar reports about their part in the operation. Each managed to compliment Montoya and his people for all their help and cooperation. Montoya absorbed the praise, looking pleased with himself.

Osaka next looked to Montoya.

"Emil, my friend, you're next."

"I have little new to report. The training is going well, and I am pleased with the support your people are giving mine in the field. I am concerned we have several men missing after the Princesa raid we haven't been able to account for. One of them is my nephew, Benjamin."

"I am sorry to hear that, Emil. I didn't know," said Osaka, not telling the entire truth. "Toshio, what have you heard?"

"There have been no reports of the government troops taking prisoners. They're quick to boast about that, but just in case, I will inquire again. There were reports of a half dozen of our people being killed, but that's all."

"Those figures are correct, Sir," added Boerst. "We have accounted for the rest of our people. Benny was one of our unit commanders and it was his unit that took the most casualties. They were involved in the heaviest fighting. Knowing Benny, he was out in front of his people."

"Toshio, would you please make those inquiries as soon as possible?" Osaka looked at his colleague who nodded in response. "Emil, my sympathies are with you and the rest of your family. Hopefully, we will be able to find something out for you."

"People make sacrifices," said Montoya, "and Benny knew what was expected for us to win a free Muslim state. He was willing to make that sacrifice if needed. I would just like to know if he or any of the other missing men are still alive."

"We'll find out if it's at all possible, Mr. Montoya," said Toshio.

"Thank you very much," replied Montoya. "I'm in a position where I'm not able to get much information. I really do appreciate your kindness."

"Any time, my friend," said Osaka. "Do you have anything else to report?"

"No, as I said there's not much new for me to report. All is going well and moving on schedule. I'll look for places to safely store supplies and ammunition and, hopefully, will have them ready before the jump-off time for the operation."

"Very good, Emil," said Osaka. "Please keep Toshio advised about your progress. We can't afford to lose any supplies at this stage of the operation. Now, about our newcomer, this is Lieutenant Commander James Holiday. His naval experience was with the British Royal Navy, which he left eighteen months ago."

"Gawd!!" exclaimed O'Keefe. "Just what we need is one of Her Majesties' officers."

Osaka looked irritated for the first time. Before he could say anything to chastise his Irish security chief, Holiday spoke, "Mr. O'Keefe, don't be concerned with me. Her Majesty, her admirals, and I had a slight disagreement about how my job should be done. I'm no longer in her service and am in business for myself. If it makes you feel any better, some of the best sailors I've served with were Irish."

"It helps some, Mr. Holiday," replied O'Keefe with a grin. "What would your specialty have been in the Queen's service?"

Holiday returned O'Keefe smile. "I was in the submarine service."

O'Keefe turned to face Osaka. "My compliments to you, sir, and my apologies for speaking out of turn."

Osaka smiled and bowed slightly.

"I guess that explains why we don't have any extra helicopters," said Wilson.

"I don't understand," said Montoya. "Why do we need a submarine expert if we don't have a submarine?"

All the eyes in the room were on him for several seconds before it sank in. Suddenly he began to laugh out loud. Everyone in the room joined in.

Philippine Army Intelligence Headquarters
Mindanao, Philippines
November 30, 1994
1100 Hours

Franco now drove his car through the main gate of the base without even being stopped. He was in and out of the base so much the regular sentries knew him by sight and waved him through. Jaime drove to the building where Mangoba worked. He took the elevator to the sub-level being hustled through the checkpoint. As he entered the main office he ran into Sanchez.

"Jaime," said the officer sounding rushed, "the general is in a meeting and then will be on a plane to Manila. I doubt he'll have the time to see you."

"I'm not here to see either you or him," responded the old policeman. "I need to see our young friend to ask him some more questions."

Sanchez looked surprised.

"An interview with the prisoner hasn't been scheduled," said Sanchez cautiously. "I'm not sure the general would approve of an unscheduled interview."

"Why is he going to Manila, Jorge?" asked the policeman.

"Jaime, he's a general and he has to report to his superiors just as you do. I don't know why he's going and if I did, my guess is I couldn't tell you."

"Look," said the older man, "bear with me here. I was up most of the night trying to figure out what this kid's been telling us the last two weeks."

"He's a tough kid. Each answer he's given us has been something different. Nothing makes any sense. He's been very well trained and briefed on how to deal with interrogation. Face it, Jaime, we've run up against a wall."

Jaime shook his head. "No, no, my friend. This young man has been telling us the truth the whole time. We haven't been asking the correct questions.

"I don't understand," said the soldier. "You're telling me that all of the information we have is correct?"

"Yes, now listen to me completely before you interrupt. When we asked him who was behind these attacks, what was his answer?"

"The Japanese," answered Sanchez, looking confused.

"Who did he say was responsible for the military training these rebels received?"

"The Germans and Americans."

"When we asked about where they learned terrorist techniques, who did he say taught them?"

"He said an Irishman taught them. Jaime, the man is talking gibberish. He makes no sense."

"What were the two things we felt he was telling the truth about?"

"Jaime," Sanchez started to protest. "We don't have time to..."

"Jorge," Jaime interrupted, "answer the question."

Sanchez let out a loud sigh. "He described the girl we think is a suspect from the Pagadian bombing as being involved in some of the training. She was also on the raid on the dorm here in Davao. The other thing he described is his uncle's involvement in these incidents as one of the conspirators."

"Good," said Jaime. "Now put all of that information together and what does it tell you?"

"That he is smarter than us, or at least thinks he is by telling us stories."

"But what if they're not stories? What if everything he's told us is the truth?"

Jaime was surprised he was being so patient.

Jorge cautiously answered. "It would mean we have something larger going on than just Moro separatists launching a terrorist campaign."

It took a second for what he just said to sink in and another for him to react. He motioned for a sergeant standing nearby to come over to him.

"I may regret this, but if you think it's worth a try, I'll let you question him on my authority," said Jorge, looking at the older man. "Sergeant, would you please have the prisoner escorted to the interrogation room immediately."

"Yes, Sir!" replied the noncommissioned officer smartly.

"I hope you're right about this, Jaime. I'm sticking my neck way out on a policeman's hunch."

"You won't be sorry," replied the policeman. "I've spent the better part of my life learning to interrogate and read people and I don't feel I could be this wrong. The kid is telling the truth and we've given him credit for being tougher and smarter than he really is. We're making this too complicated. I promise you I'll take full responsibility for this. I need to retire anyway. I've been here so much the last two weeks my boss thinks I work here."

Sanchez laughed.

"Look, Jorge," said Franco, "make sure the entire interview is being taped from start to finish. We'll need that later."

"Sure thing," responded the soldier. "We would tape it as a matter of policy."

The sergeant came back and waved to Jorge. The officer still wasn't convinced this was the right thing to do. He waved the sergeant over and took a pad of paper off the desk, quickly writing a note. He gave it to the sergeant along with directions on where to deliver it.

The older man looked at the young officer. "Are you ready to do this?"

"I am now," replied Sanchez. "I've learned it's a good practice in the army to cover all your bases before moving forward. The local military commander wants to take young Montoya and put him on public trial. If I screw up here, that's just what might happen."

"Don't worry. I have a feeling about this, and I think we'll be just fine."

Both men walked to the door leading to where the prisoner was being held.

Like most of the other rooms in the building, there wasn't much furniture. There was a table and several chairs in the room. In each of the four corners of the room, a video camera was mounted by the ceiling.

Benny sat in the chair on the far side of the room. When he saw Jaime walk in the door, he visibly stiffened. Ever since their first meeting, Benny was cautious around the old policeman. The fact he could be rendered unconscious by someone this man's age left an impression on him.

"Good morning, Benny," started Jaime. "How are you feeling today?"

"They told me I wouldn't have to answer any more questions today," growled the young man. "I don't want to talk to you especially."

"That's too bad," said Jaime as he sat down across the table from the terrorist. "You see, I need to straighten a few things out in my mind so I can move onto other matters. It might even get me out of your life for a while."

Benny looked at the policeman skeptically.

"I must apologize, Benny," continued the policeman, "I'm the one who's insisted on talking to you today. I didn't realize the army told you they didn't need to talk with you anymore."

"I didn't say they didn't need to talk to me anymore. I said they were going to leave me alone today."

"Sorry," responded the older man, "They didn't tell me when I insisted to see you. They did argue, but the fact this is such a pressing investigation puts us all under a lot of pressure. I need to talk to you about your previous statements to us."

"Why don't you people just leave me alone?" Benny fired back angrily. "I've told you the truth and no one believes me. Why should I talk to you anymore?"

"You're right, Benny," said Jaime, "and that's why I'm here today. I couldn't sleep last night and spent most of my time going over your answers to all our questions. I decided you've been telling us the truth the whole time."

"Why the sudden change of mind?" asked the prisoner.

Jaime leaned back in his chair looking at the young man across from him. "Sometimes we are so intent on finding out something, we listen for the answers we want or expect to hear. When that happens, we don't hear or see the truth when it is placed on the table right in front of us."

"So, now you believe what I'm telling you?"

"Let's say I don't think you've been lying to us, but I'm still not making much sense out of what you've told us. I've come here today with some different questions to ask you."

Benny looked at the policeman. He looked away when the older man met his gaze, shuffling his feet back and forth underneath the table. He looked down and acted as if he weren't going to respond.

"You know, Benny," said Jaime. "I'm going to ask the questions anyway. Since you've cooperated with us so far, it would be counter-productive to stop now."

The young man looked up at Jaime and glared. "What can you do to me if I don't?"

Jaime smiled. "I'm sure I can talk the army into releasing you to my custody and have you taken back to Princesa to stand trial for the murder of the mayor, his wife, the policemen, the soldiers, and the other civilians that died. Problem is, I doubt that you would make it to trial. There are enough people that would want to see you dead it would probably end with you being killed before going to trial."

Benny continued to glare at the policeman.

"My guess is your own people will want you dead."

This last statement seemed to hit home, and Jaime saw the reaction he'd been waiting for. He decided to move ahead with the questioning.

"So, how did you get involved in this whole business?" asked Jaime, knowing what the answer would be.

"I already answered that question for you!" countered Benny quickly.

"I know," said Jaime patiently, "but I'm trying to put a sequence of events together in my mind. Please answer the question."

Benny let out a frustrated sigh and answered, "My uncle and several other people were asked to go to a meeting with a man just north of here. At the meeting, this guy offered to support our cause to try and make Mindanao a Muslim state. The other two didn't want to hear the guy out, so they left my uncle and me there. My uncle and I have been working on this ever since."

Jaime smiled as he asked the first of his new questions. "Benny, who were the other two men who went to this meeting with you?"

Benny folded his arms.

"Benny, you've already been arrested for how many counts of murder, as well as treason? The more you help me, the more I will be able to help you."

Benny relaxed his arms. "Raul Argento and Ernesto Edwardo. They left in the same car we came in. I haven't seen them since."

"Did you know they were both murdered the next morning in Davao?" Jaime asked.

Benny sat straight up stuttering as he spoke.

"Y…, you can't pin that on me! They were alive the last time I saw them when they left the meeting."

"Take it easy, Benny," said Jaime, "no one said they thought you were responsible. I just asked if you knew they were killed."

Benny settled down. "Look, I didn't know about them. Honest, I didn't. I'd guess my uncle doesn't even know. After the meeting, we've been on the go."

"Let's go back to the meeting. Who was it with?"

"My uncle made the meeting with a businessman; I think he was a businessman, anyway."

"What do you know about him?"

Benny took a second to think about his answer. "I think he was Japanese. I'm not sure, but I think he's Japanese. He was well dressed and had people all around him. I remember Mr. Argento was really upset with the deal he was proposing. Mr. Edwardo was simply scared."

"Benny, do you remember his name?"

"Oh, yes. It's Mr. Osaka."

There was silence for a few moments.

"Benny, this is important. Do you know his first name?"

"No, I just know him as Mr. Osaka."

"OK, Benny, did anyone leave with Argento and Edwardo? This is important, too."

Benny took a few moments to think.

"I think the Irishman and Mr. Osaka's servant left with them. I don't remember the Irishman coming back."

"Irishman?" questioned Jaime. "The same Irishman you said helped teach some of the techniques for the assault on the dorm and making bombs?"

"Yes, he is," said Benny sounding amazed, "you do believe me after all."

"Yes, Benny, I believe you. Do you know the Irishman's name?"

"It's O'Toole, O'Keefe, or O'Rourke. Something like that. He didn't spend time with us like some of the other instructors did. He spent most of his spare time with the woman who was with us on the dorm raid. As a matter of fact, he brought her into the operation."

Franco talked to the prisoner for over an hour. The answers kept Sanchez and the soldiers monitoring the interview busy. By the time he stood to leave the interview room, Jaime felt he was well on his way to solving several crimes. Two soldiers entered and escorted Benny back to his cell.

"I knew you would get to the bottom of this. Now we must find out how far this has gone," said a familiar voice.

"Hello, General Mangoba. What do you think of the information now? You know this is bigger than the boy understands. Whoever engineered this whole thing has done a good job of keeping important information out of the hands of everyone but their top people. Benny was obviously one of the leaders in the Princesa and Davao dorm raids. He knows very little, and we wouldn't have the name of the Japanese businessman who appears to be behind the whole thing if he hadn't gone to the meeting with is uncle."

"So you're telling me you think this is a bigger problem than just some Muslim separatists?" asked Mangoba. "You'll have to do more than just be able to talk about it to the people in Manila when you go with me."

"Then I'll need some information on all the names Benny gave us. I see the businessman, I believe he called him Osaka, as the biggest key. Then the Irishman, he gave several names for him. It should give us something if we can get those names pinned down. I assume the names of the military instructors who helped train these separatists should be easy to track down since those names are more complete."

Mangoba laughed and looked at the policeman.

Jaime smiled saying, "Robbie, you asked for my help and that's what I'm doing. This'll get worse before it gets better, and you know it."

"True," said Mangoba, "but I'm not the one you'll have to convince. We need to convince the people in Manila this is more than just a minor terrorist campaign that will fizzle out in a month or two. They need to understand there is someone out there raising and training an army for their own purposes."

Osaka Pineapple Plantation
Mindanao, Philippines
November 30, 1994
1230 Hours

The meeting finished and everyone was leaving. Osaka thanked each of them, seeing them to the door. Osaka asked Toshio and O'Keefe to stay behind. After the others were gone, Ishimoto wheeled in a cart with roast turkey, various breads, and salads. Each man helped himself to some of the food and took their seats.

"Patrick," said Osaka, "I wanted to talk to you about several things before you went back to Davao."

"I'm sorry about my comments to the Brit today, sir," said O'Keefe. "My way of testing someone I've been trained all my life to distrust and hate. I still don't trust him, sir, but that's because of my background. I can't apologize for that."

"No need, Patrick," said Osaka. "I know you will conduct yourself appropriately with Commander Holiday. I'm concerned, though, about how you might react if your ex-wife ends up among the hostages.

O'Keefe seemed unfazed by the questions taking a bite from his sandwich. Osaka waited patiently.

"Mr. Osaka," said O'Keefe, after swallowing, "I won't sit here and lie to you by saying I had no idea my ex-father-in-law would be there. I have a score to settle with him and went as far as checking the guest list to make sure he was attending. I assume, because you asked the question, my ex-wife is planning on attending as well."

Osaka and Toshio smiled. Toshio answered, "Both Mrs. O'Keefe and daughter Sarah will be attending."

O'Keefe stopped eating, looking back at the two men. For the first time since being employed by Osaka the Irishman was speechless.

"I can see you didn't expect your daughter at this reunion," said Osaka with a chuckle. "You must forgive me, my friend; it's not often I can have a laugh at your expense. As you might guess the question is even more important now. How will you react?"

O'Keefe's expression changed from one of shock to all business. He set the sandwich down on the plate, looking at his employer.

"When you hired me, you did so because I have a reputation for getting the job done, no matter what. I think you've been happy with my work so far, or at least there have been no complaints."

"True, I feel your work is the best I've seen," replied Osaka.

"Then let me assure you I'll follow through with everything you've contracted me for, and more. A person in my business doesn't get too many chances to do what you've asked of me. If we're successful with what we're planning, I'll be able to retire from this business if I want, but even more importantly I'll be able to write my own ticket. Who knows, maybe even go into business for myself and have a dozen Commander Holidays working for me. I assure you gentlemen; you can trust me when it comes to this. It'll just be a bonus to see my family after all these years."

Osaka said, "I thought that would be your answer. You do as you see fit, Patrick. Get your revenge if it works out. You've earned it as a bonus for what you've done so far."

"Thank you, sir, and I promise to be discrete with whatever I decide to do with the old general."

"Mr. O'Keefe," said Toshio, "can you think of anything special I should be on the lookout for on the list of hostages?"

"What's their ultimate purpose?" asked O'Keefe. "Political leverage, ransom, or is there some other goal I don't know about? You gentlemen are exceptionally good at your job as well. There are many aspects of your plan I can only guess about, but I would have to say judging by what I know, you would be interested in the political end."

Toshio looked at Osaka. "Very good, Mr. O'Keefe. Most of our inner circle wouldn't have been able to deduce that on their own. I'm impressed."

"Patrick was selected for this job because he is more than a good terrorist," Osaka said. "Unlike most of his counterparts, he understands the politics of the profession better than most professional political analysts. That's why he left Ireland. He knew what needed to be done and what price had to be paid. No one, but he, was willing to follow through."

O'Keefe looked at his employer, smiled, and bowed. Osaka returned the bow.

"Patrick, another issue. Can this new friend of yours be trusted?"

O'Keefe smiled. "At the moment, yes."

"At the moment?" questioned Toshio.

"Yes, at the moment," countered O'Keefe. "She's new to this business and one of the best natural killers I've ever seen. Currently, our relationship is enough to keep her in line, but as I know all too well, relationships don't always last. If she makes it through this operation, we'll have to look at how she's done and if any adjustments need to be made."

Osaka was quiet for a moment, "Good. Keep me advised of her progress."

O'Keefe rose from his chair. "Gentlemen, if there are no more questions, I have a family reunion to plan for."

Osaka rose, both men bowing slightly before O'Keefe turned, walking away. When he left the room, Toshio said, "A very dangerous man."

"You don't like him, Toshio?" asked Osaka.

"I didn't say that. Just making an observation. I'm glad he's working for us."

"So am I," Osaka remarked. "So am I."

Beverly Hills
Los Angeles, California
December 1, 1994
1800 Hours

Becky raced into the kitchen from the hallway as the telephone rang for the second time. Her hands were full between her medical bag and the bags of groceries she was carrying.

"Angie? Sarah? Can someone get the phone?" she yelled.

The telephone continued to ring while she fumbled with the items in her hands. As she raised the bags over the counter, the bottom of one caught the edge, ripping open, and spilling the contents all over the floor. Becky placed the remaining bags down reaching for the telephone with her free hand.

"Damn! Huh, hello?" she said somewhat embarrassed.

"Is William Gateway there please?" asked a tired voice.

Becky reached down to pick up the spilled groceries. As she did her medical bag opened, emptying some of its contents.

"Shit! I mean, damn it!" She exclaimed wanting to just throw her hands in the air.

"Sounds like you're having a bad day," said the voice sounding sympathetic. "I'm glad I'm not in your house right now."

"Look," said Becky her tone frustrated, "I'm really sorry, but it hasn't been a particularly good day. I'm sorry my father isn't here right now; is there a message I could give him when he returns?"

There was a moment of silence. "Becky, its Jon Summers."

Becky's tone immediately changed, "Jon, I'm really sorry. I was bringing in the groceries when one of the bags broke open. Here I sit trying to answer the phone and pick up the mess and I drop everything else on the floor. I really do apologize for my outburst."

Jon's tone changed as well. He sounded more cheerful and less nervous, "Well, it's good to hear someone else has had a day like mine. How are you doing, Becky?"

Becky laughed. "You know Jon, I haven't seen or talked to you in years and for some reason I have to say it's really good to hear your voice."

"I was thinking the same thing," was the reply, "and you don't sound bad for an affluent, hippy flower child."

"Ahhhh," the laughter got a little louder, "I see we haven't changed much mister; you still work for the war mongering Pentagon as a part-time spook."

"You know I always liked James Bond."

They both laughed again, it suddenly got quiet.

Becky broke the silence, "Hey Jon, Dad told me about Uncle Ray. I'm sorry to hear he's so sick. How is he?"

Again there was silence. "That's the reason I'm calling your father, Dad passed away this afternoon."

"Oh Jon, I'm so sorry," replied Becky, a tear starting to form. "I really mean it, I'm sorry. Uncle Ray was special to me. Both he and Aunt Louise stood by me when I really needed the support. Is there anything I can do?"

"You've already done it Becky," said Jon sounding exhausted. "I mean by answering the phone instead of your father."

"I think I can understand, he can be rather intimidating at times."

"The general doesn't bother me; I find him to be somewhat of a big teddy bear."

Becky decided she needed to lighten the conversation, "Sure, be the big tough war hero and don't be scared of the general."

Becky was sure she could almost hear the smile in Jon's voice. "You know for a flower child so full of peace and love, you really can be damned obnoxious. What I meant was I'm glad it was you answering the phone because I needed to hear a friendly voice. Maybe it's because, oh hell, I don't know, it's just damned good to hear your voice. Our dads were close so I guess I knew this call would be tough to make. You just made it a whole lot easier, that's all."

"Hey Jon, don't worry about it. I'm glad you got me instead of him too. I've always found you comfortable to talk to. No matter what you and I did you always managed to make me feel at ease around you. You were always there to listen."

Jon laughed. "As I remember, and correct me if I'm wrong, we argued about everything and agreed about nothing. Somewhere in between I remember the two of us throwing a lot of things at each other. I guess being a target was to be my lot in life."

"Maybe that's why I was always so comfortable around you." it was Becky's turn to laugh, "There was never any illusion about what our relationship was. It's always nice to know where you stand with a guy."

Jon continued to laugh, "Look Becky, I'm serious, I'm really glad you answered the phone. Our relationship was always honest if nothing else. Not many people can say that when it comes to friends. For some reason I'm really feeling better talking to you."

"I'm really flattered, Jon," she replied. "I can't tell you how much that means to me. Look, I'll let Dad know, but he's going to want more details."

"No details yet," Jon said, "Mom and Matt are still at the funeral home making the arrangements. I'll give you another call when I have more information, but at this point it doesn't look like there will be any formal funeral service. I'm just guessing, but I think Mom will be going with a memorial service."

"Are you going down to be with your mom?"

"Julie and I are flying out tomorrow. Nancy and the kids are staying here because of school and the fact there will be no funeral down there. Nancy and her parents will be watching Julie's kids while we're away."

There was another awkward silence.

"Look," said Becky quietly, "tell your mom if she needs anything to call me. Lord knows she's always been there for me."

"I'll pass it along Becky, I know she'll appreciate it. You take care of yourself."

"You, too."

As Becky was about to hang up the phone Jon's voice was there again. It no longer sounded tired but sounded softer and friendlier. "Hey Becky?"

"Yeah Jon?" the change in tone made her smile.

"Thanks."

There was nothing more to be said. Jon hung up before Becky could respond. She smiled picturing the young man she'd known years before. The sound of her father coming in the door caught her wiping a tear from her eye.

Osaka Pineapple Plantation
Mindanao, Philippines
December 16, 1994
1400 Hours

It hadn't been an easy job building the pier for the submarine so it couldn't be seen from the sea or air. Because the jungle came right down the cliffs to the water's edge along the coastline in this area the camouflage was the easy part. Building it so no one noticed the construction was harder. It required a great deal of slow painstaking work on the part of several hundred workers imported specifically for the project.

Osaka walked along the dock followed by Ishimoto and Wilson. He was talking to O'Keefe on his cell phone.

"All I know is the army has at least one prisoner, maybe more, from the Princesa raid," said O'Keefe over the cell. "I don't know for sure where they are, but my best guess is here in Davao. There's no way we can find out where they may be holding any prisoners."

"Any word on the dead? I mean as to the identification of the dead."

"No, Sir, nothing," replied O'Keefe. "The general running this investigation seems to be a shrewd one. Fella by the name of Mangoba. Seems to keep most of what he's gathered out of the regular channels."

"Roberto Mangoba has that reputation," said Osaka. "Keep clear of him. He's smart enough to figure this entire thing out and ruin our operation. You might even put him on your list of people to be eliminated."

"Already on it, Sir. Both he and a police captain named Franco are on my list, but they've dropped out of sight. Franco oversees the dorm investigation. Shame, too. Would have liked to upset the apple cart even more by killing a general."

"Don't underestimate this one, Patrick," cautioned Osaka. "He's smart and has been a target before. If he suspects you're after him he'll be more dangerous than anyone you've targeted. The police captain is also no push over. He has a reputation of being extremely thorough."

"Not to worry, Sir. Both are whereabouts unknown right now, so we'll move onto those we know are available."

Osaka smiled at the Irishman's humor. He really liked this man, even though they were from two different worlds. He was a good employee, loyal to the person who employed him. Money was not the driving force for O'Keefe, although Osaka knew it was helpful. O'Keefe enjoyed both style and character. Both qualities made him keep the commitments he made with people. That made him an honorable man, and one Osaka enjoyed having around him. Even Toshio conceded this.

"Patrick," said Osaka, "use care in approaching either of these men. We can't afford to have our foes alerted at this stage of the operation."

"I'm always careful, Sir," replied the Irishman. "I won't do anything if it'll put the operation in jeopardy. I'll keep you advised if I find anything out further on the other issue."

"Thank you, Patrick," said Osaka as he waved to Toshio, Holiday, and Boerst coming down the gangway from the submarine. "Take care of yourself, my friend."

"I'll call you with an update tomorrow, Sir," said O'Keefe. The connection went dead.

Osaka met the rest of his staff near the gangway.

"Well, Commander Holiday," he asked, "you are now in command of our one ship Navy. What do you think?"

A big smile crossed the face of the former Royal Navy submariner. "A newly modified Japanese Yushio class boat, my compliments Osaka, my guess is this is the boat the Japanese government listed as missing during maneuvers over a year ago."

Osaka bowed slightly. Toshio looked irritated, as usual, with the sailor's comment.

"Your people have done well with the new systems that were added," continued Holiday. "She'll be the quietest diesel boat at sea."

"How soon will you be able to start your part of the operation, Commander?" asked Osaka politely.

"The crew has to be trained," answered Holiday without hesitation, "and getting the sea trials out of the way, I would say we could start operations just after the first of the year."

"That soon?" commented Osaka surprised.

"Your people have made running this boat as simple as you can. Also the crew you've gotten to operate her is first rate. Along with your own people you have some very experienced and capable submariners. We'll do what you need done and deal with anything the Philippine Navy sends against us."

Osaka looked at Boerst, "Colonel, do you have anything to add?"

"Nein," replied the German. "I'm also impressed and as Commander Holiday pointed out to Herr Toshio and me, the submarine can be used to transport troops if needed."

Osaka nodded to the military man's response.

"I will leave the two of you to your planning. Toshio, will you please come with me, Patrick has called, and I have some news to share."

Highland Cemetery
Rochester, New York
December 17, 1994
1400 Hours

The wind blew flakes of snow across the cemetery. It was cold, but not the bitter cold that could come this time of year. Captain Jonathan Summers, United States Navy, and his wife stood in front of his father's grave. Jon was in his winter blue uniform and wore his long, blue overcoat, whose shoulder boards indicated his rank with four gold stripes. His white cap stayed on in the wind, the scrambled eggs on the brim standing out in the gloomy day. Nancy seemed to be dressed warmer than her husband. She was wearing a pair of heavy dress slacks and a heavy down ski jacket with its hood pulled up around her ears.

Jon stood in silence, his hands clasp in front of him, looking at his father's head stone. There was no official funeral. This was because Ray passed away in South Carolina, where he resided, but mostly because he wanted things simple. He requested his remains be cremated and buried in his hometown of Rochester. Jon and Nancy arranged for a memorial service, which they just left. They were now on their way to the airport to catch a flight for Washington D.C. Jon was to meet with Admiral Cummings before catching a military flight to Hawaii. Nancy was pleased the navy was allowing her children and herself the opportunity to go along and spend the holidays with him. She knew he wouldn't be with them on Christmas, but at least she would be able to enjoy his company some of the time.

"Honey?" Nancy said quietly to her husband.

"Huh? Oh, sorry babe, I was thinking about something Dad asked me to do before he died."

"We need to go if we're going to make the flight on time," she responded as sensitively as she could. She knew this wasn't easy for her husband because of the bond he shared with his father.

"You're right," said Jon taking a step back from the grave in front of him. He put his arm around his wife's shoulder.

Nancy looked at her husband. There were many things in their life together she never questioned. One of them was this relationship. She looked back at the gravestone and then broke quietly away from her husband, taking several steps forward. She reached into her jacket and pulled out a single red, long stemmed rose she had been protecting from the cold. She reached down, placing it on top of the gravestone. Then, she took several steps back to where Jon was standing.

"You okay, babe?" asked Jon gently.

She nodded *yes*, a tear in her eye. They both put their arms around each other's shoulders and walked quietly back to the waiting van.

CHAPTER 9

THE WAR GAME

Kaena Point
Oahu, Hawaii
December 22, 1994
0230 Hours

The corporal drove the Humvee down the road, ignoring the officer sitting next to him. He wasn't happy to be playing soldier just a few days before Christmas. His entire unit was activated as OPFOR troops for this major war game and were the bad guys against the Navy and Marine units participating. That, coupled with the timing of the operation was upsetting to the citizen soldiers. They didn't mind being called on to protect their country in time of need, but they certainly weren't happy with the recent call-up to be sent out as targets for the regular military to shoot at.

The soldier was especially upset when he was assigned as the driver for this officer. His lieutenant told him the officer was commanding all the guard and reserve forces involved in the operation. He was from New York State! Their own senior officers weren't available for the exercise! The Pentagon sent a replacement all the way from New York to help the United Sates Navy kick the butts of some reservists and guardsmen in Hawaii! He was even less thrilled when he found out that the man was a naval officer. What business did a naval officer from New York have commanding ground forces assigned to protect the Hawaiian Islands? He was convinced this war game was rigged.

"Sir?" asked the corporal no longer able to contain himself. "Why did they send you here for this exercise? No disrespect, sir, but couldn't they have sent someone like an army general or something?"

The officer was leaning back in his seat with is eyes closed. He turned slightly, looking at the man next to him. It was too dark to see the man's expression, but the corporal could feel his presence.

"Does the fact I'm a sailor present a problem for you corporal?" was the simple, yet direct reply.

"Permission to speak candidly, Sir?" asked the corporal.

"Go ahead trooper."

"Well, Sir," said the soldier turning off the main highway onto a dirt road. "I figure the Pentagon wants to shake up the fleet out here in the Pacific, so they come up with this war game close to the holidays. I guess I resent having to be called up to be their targets for this little game when I could be home with my family. We've been told we're playing the bad guys on this exercise. We're to get our ass kicked. At least that's the word we got from your Admiral Kingston to our Deputy Battalion Commander."

"Corporal," said the officer quietly sitting up, "I think you need to stay with me when I speak to the Echo Company commander. You should consider yourself an aide. Take notes for me and let me know how the men feel about things."

"You mean spy on my friends, Sir?" came the indignant reply.

"No," the officer responded. "I mean doing what you just did. Tell me how you and the men feel about what's going on. If you're not getting the truth about why this exercise was called, then neither are your officers. You've just been appointed to the staff of the man in charge of a renegade army whose sole mission in life is to give Admiral Richard Kingston heartburn."

The corporal smiled to himself. He always thought the army was crazy, now he was sure of it. Here he was days before the Christmas holiday, running around playing soldier, and working for a sailor he was convinced was a nut case. The officer was quiet when they pulled up to a group of darkened tents on a knoll above the beach.

When the Humvee stopped, the officer exited, heading to the command tent. The corporal followed him as fast as he could. He decided maybe keeping his mouth shut would be a better idea. The sentry at the entrance snapped to attention when the officer breezed by. The corporal, only steps behind, saw the guard's stunned look at the officer's appearance. The corporal just shrugged. He entered the tent, seeing soldiers scramble to their feet, and come to attention.

"As you were people," said the sailor stopping in front of a group of soldiers. "Who's in command of this area?"

A young captain stepped forward. "I am, Sir."

"How long have you been in the National Guard, Captain?"

"Six years, Sir."

"Desert Storm?"

"Yes, Sir, but no combat experience. We were held in reserve securing the Bahrain area."

"Anybody here have any combat experience?"

About a third of the people in the tent raised their hands.

"Good, we're going to need to fall back on your experience before this exercise is done. My name is Summers. Captain Jonathon Summers, United States Naval Reserves. Don't be deceived people. I'm not here to help you get your ass kicked by the navy and marines as seems to be the rumor."

The captain flashed an angry look at the corporal. Summers smiled.

"I'll keep this simple because we don't have much time. You people have been told you're to lose this exercise. Am I correct in my information?"

"Yes, Sir!" responded about half of the people in the tent in unison.

"And who gave those orders?" asked Summers.

There was a second of hesitation before the captain answered.

"There were no official orders, Sir. Admiral Kingston told all of us in a briefing he expected us to give his task force a good fight, but in the end, we were to lose in a professional and dignified manner."

"Captain," asked Summers emotionless, "what do you do in civilian life?"

"Sir?"

"What is your occupation, Captain? How do you earn a living and support your family?"

"I'm an accountant, Sir."

"Do you consider yourself a good accountant?"

"Yes, Sir. I work for the best firm in the islands."

"If the president of a rival firm were to say to you your firm was to put up a good fight for a client, but in the end his company was going to get the client, what would be your reaction?"

"We'd be pissed as hell, Sir," came the response, "and we'd fight that much harder to get the client."

"Good man!" replied Summers, "now listen to me people and listen well. If a foreign power were to send troops here to Hawaii, they very possibly may come by submarine or parachute as we are preparing to defend for in this exercise. It may not be a large force, but a small, highly trained force…"

"Like the SEALs or the rangers, Sir?" interrupted one young soldier.

Summers smiled hearing the enthusiasm. "Yes, soldier, just like the troops you're facing in this exercise. Look people, you've received instruction on what to look for and I would start looking now. They're not going to wait until the time Admiral Kingston set for the start of the exercise. They'll be moving now so make sure all your people are alert and on target with their calls. With these troops we're up against we won't get a second chance."

"But, Sir," said the captain, "the exercise doesn't officially start until 0330. Why should they be moving early?"

"Because that's what I would do. Admiral Kingston is a man who expects everyone, including his enemy, to fight the way he lays it out in his battle plan."

"It sounds like you've done this before, Sir?" asked the guard officer.

"I have, Captain," came the reply. "I'm here because I know how special ops troops fight. Like you, I'm a weekend warrior, but before that I was in the teams for a time."

"You're a SEAL, Sir?" asked an astonished radio operator.

Summers smiled. "I was once. Now it seems those higher than you and I want to see how much I remember. Look, everyone, get to your assignments now. Keep radio traffic to a minimum and keep your eyes open. Captain!"

"Sir!" responded the young officer.

"Quickly show me your positions and I need to know where you placed the other set of tents."

There was a flurry of activity as everyone moved out to get their jobs done. The corporal stayed two steps behind the naval officer and was rethinking he just might enjoy this assignment if everything went right.

Kingston looked out the porthole of his cabin. He could see the running lights of one of the escort ships about a half mile away. He was looking forward to returning to Pearl Harbor and celebrating Christmas ashore. After reviewing the reports on the reserve and National Guard units involved in the exercise, he was optimistic about an early resolution to the war game. He planned some time alone with someone special and was impatient to finish this last piece of business. He looked at himself in the mirror, everything on his uniform was in its proper place.

There was a knock at the door.

"Come!"

The door opened and Commander Williams entered the cabin. He carried several folders.

"Close the hatch behind you, Stephen." said the admiral flatly.

"Latest reports on the exercise sir, we're ready to start our attack on schedule."

"What's in the folders?" asked the admiral.

"The top folder contains the flash message from CINCPAC stating that there are hostages being held and authorizing a rescue mission. It's signaling the start of the exercise at 0330."

"Very well, what else is there?" said the admiral looking bored.

"The second one was the intelligence report on who the OPFOR commander might be. There's currently nothing specific. There are no possible prospects currently here in the islands except for the National Guard major you spoke to the other day. The best guess is they're importing someone from the mainland to command the operation opposite you. No flag reserve or guard officers have been ordered to the islands."

"You're sure about that, Stephen?" asked the admiral.

"Absolutely, Sir," replied the aide. "None have arrived in Hawaii per Seventh Fleet Intelligence. I called them myself to make sure. Also no military personnel over the rank of colonel have arrived in the last seventy-two hours having any ground combat experience. It's like they don't have any specific leadership. We don't know who, or where for that matter, their command and control is even located."

"We must be missing something, Stephen," said Kingston, "it would be nice to know who one is about to destroy. Call Seventh Fleet back. Check and see if they have any further information on the exercise. Sometimes they make you ask the obvious. Damn, I hate being in the dark."

"Yes, Sir," replied the aide. "I'll contact them immediately and see if our friends in the army have heard anything. They're as much in the dark as we are on this one, Sir."

"Have they said anything unusual indicating what's going on?"

"Nothing except the units involved have spent the last three days in the field preparing. My contact found that to be a bit unusual."

The admiral sighed sitting down at his desk. "Very well, Stephen. Send in Hancock to take care of some signal traffic and give Captain Brothers my compliments. He's to commence the exercise as planned."

Williams came to attention. "Aye, aye, Sir."

He left closing the door behind him. Kingston sat at his desk looking into space. He was disturbed they'd received no information on the OPFOR commander. He liked to know who his opposite number was. It certainly made the planning of an operation much easier. They planned an assault by SEALs and Marine recon. The SEALs were using submarine insertion and the Marines were being parachuted in by helicopter. He ordered an amphibious assault to extract both special operations units and the hostages. Everything was planned to the minute.

There was another knock at the door. "Come!"

The hatch opened and Handcock walked into the stateroom, coming to attention in front of the admiral. She carried a steno notebook in her hand and wore a pair of wire rimmed glasses making her look more like a secretary than an aide. He met her right after being promoted to admiral. While Williams handled most of the daily business, Handcock dealt with all Kingston's signal traffic and social scheduling. With Mrs. Kingston in southern California, Handcock played an even more important role as companion for the admiral.

"Commander Williams said you had some signals to send, Sir!" said Handcock in a formal tone.

"No, Andrea," said Kingston smiling. "I didn't want to go the day without seeing you alone."

Handcock returned the smile replying, "This is dangerous on-board ship, Admiral, and you know it. If they suspect we're seeing each other, the navy will end both of our careers."

Kingston answered, "No danger of that. You're here to take some signal traffic. Make up some routine traffic and send it at a convenient time. Have a seat, Andrea."

She sat down in one of the two armchairs across from the desk.

"It's not like I'm dragging you to bed," continued Kingston, "although that sounds better than invading the north shore of Oahu."

Handcock laughed while pretending to write something down on the steno pad.

U.S.S. Kamehameha
Kauai Channel
December 22, 1994
0247 Hours

"Sir, there's incoming flash traffic," said the signal officer.

Grant tried to look as if he hadn't expected the signal from the flag ship. He wasn't happy with the plan the SEALs and Rangers came up with. They decided to jump off early to ensure their part of the exercise was a surprise. He didn't share their enthusiasm in disobeying Kingston's timetable.

The signal officer handed him the teletype copy of the message just as Bob Krause said, "Message has been verified, Captain."

Grant smiled. "Bring her to periscope depth, boys. We have some cargo to deliver."

He couldn't keep from laughing thinking of the old-World War II movie where submarine captain, Edmond O'Brian delivered frogman James Garner to a Japanese held island. He didn't consider Tim DeCook or Al Wiedenkeller the James Garner type, but that ranger colonel could pass for a Hollywood leading man.

"Periscope depth, aye." repeated the planesman.

Grant smiled again. He didn't feel like Edmond O'Brian. He looked quickly around the control room. His people were doing what they were trained to do. He was pleased they would be done with their part of the operation in a few hours. There was one extra person in the control room not normally with them. The navy sent along an officer to act as an umpire. While Grant understood the purpose of the officer's presence, he still resented it. It was like having a spy from SUBCOMPAC on board reporting everything they did wrong back to his commanding officer. He decided he would ignore the man's presence and carry on with business as usual.

"Skipper, we're at periscope depth," said the Chief of the Boat.

"Thank you, Chief," said Grant moving around to look at the gages by the planesman. "Officer of the Deck, up scope."

"Aye, Sir. Up scope," replied Krause.

The periscope began to rise, and Grant moved towards the center of the control room. When he got to the periscope, he waited for it to finish rising. He put his eyes up to it, moving around the mast until he found what he was looking for.

"Negative radar emissions from the coast, Skipper," said one of the nearby sailors.

"Damn!" said Grant. "XO, come take a look at this."

Krause took over Grant's position. Krause chuckled for a second before allowing Grant back at the periscope.

"As much as I hate to say it, Skipper," said Krause. "Admiral Kingston may have been right about these National Guard troops. That command center is lit up like a Christmas tree."

There was a chuckle from most of the men in the control room.

"If they're all like this," continued Krause, "We'll finish up this exercise and be back in port by Christmas Eve, ready to celebrate."

Grant smiled but didn't want to sound over optimistic. "XO, who's supposed to have the defense of this section of the coastline?"

Krause reached down and picked up a clip board from the Officer of the Deck's watch station. He leafed through the papers on the clipboard until he found what he was looking for.

"Elements of the 52nd Division of the Hawaiian National Guard. Makes you feel all secure, doesn't it, Skipper?" answered Krause.

"That it does, Mr. Krause," replied the submarine commander. "That it does. Chief of the Boat, get me Mr. DeCook on the line!"

"Aye, aye, Sir!"

Grant grinned. "This is almost too easy, Bob. These National Guardsmen must be really pissed at Kingston to light the target up that way. Most of them are young and inexperienced, but this borders on the ridiculous."

"There is another scenario, Sir," replied his second in command.

"A trap?" asked Grant thinking out loud.

"Yes, Sir," said Krause, brainstorming. "Not that I think it's likely. I'm not the expert."

Grant went back to the scope and increased the magnification. This took him to where he could see men moving about the tents and in some cases, he could see sentries posted in the darker areas.

"Skipper," said the chief, "Mr. DeCook on the horn, Sir."

Grant picked up a handset attached to the rail around the periscopes. "Mr. DeCook!"

"Yes, Sir, Skipper," came the reply.

"Are you seeing what we're looking at?" asked Grant.

"Yes, Sir, the pictures coming in good." said DeCook of the video he was watching on one of the submarine's television monitors.

"It looks like they're rushing to get ready for the exercise. A lot of activity right now, but I bet they settle right down the minute we get closer to zero hour."

"You don't think it's a trap, Commander?" asked Grant. "I don't want to get blasted right out of the gate."

"It's a possibility, Sir, but not very probable." came the reply. "They'd have to know our tactics and think like we do to spring something like that. I've studied the units we're going up against and they don't have that kind of depth in their personnel. They've put in a lot of training hours the last week or so, but there's been no movement of any Special Forces troops to help them train. Watch them, Sir. The closer we get to 0330, the quieter they'll get. My guess is even the lights will go out. Just like the real army. They just don't expect us to fight dirty. There are rules of engagement of course. The problem is that SEALs don't know how to read according to our beloved exercise commander, so…"

Grant laughed out loud looking about the control room. "You're call, Commander; take your people out when you're ready."

"Aye, aye, Sir!" came the reply. "We'll be on our way now, Sir."

"Very well, Commander," said Grant, "good luck and have a nice swim."

"Thank you, Sir!" the intercom went dead.

Grant shook his head, "I don't know who I feel sorrier for."

"Sir?" questioned Krause.

"I mean the poor guys on shore who don't know what their about to have unleashed on them or the poor rangers who probably haven't been told these are shark infested waters," Grant grinned making the statement. "Chief of the Boat, sound General quarters and let's deliver our cargo!"

"Aye, aye, Sir!"

The alarm sounded.

Kaena Point
Oahu, Hawaii
December 22, 1994
0255 Hours

The two men huddled into the quickly dug bunker housing their observation post. They were hidden in a stand of palm trees about halfway up the rise. It was located two hundred yards from the bogus command post. Both men thought this a waste of time. They received training over the last several days on night vision equipment they were issued and what to look for out to sea. They concentrated on the beach and ocean below them.

They both jumped when their sergeant came up behind them. His squad was assigned along the ridge to observation posts overlooking this section of the coast. Each was like the one they were in. They were two-man positions concealed in hastily built bunkers made to blend in with the palm filled hillside. Each bunker was connected to their company command post by field telephone.

"Sarge," said the older of the two soldiers, "is all of this really necessary?"

The sergeant looked at the National Guardsmen. He pushed the helmet down over the young soldier's eyes, "You guys pay attention tonight and watch close. You treat them SEALs as if they're the enemy. The new CO made a good case a little while ago about us not being the bad guys in this exercise. You just pretend they're foreign terrorists coming to the islands to create another Pearl Harbor."

"What happened at Pearl Harbor, Sarge?" asked the other soldier, who was busy looking through one of the scopes.

"Don't play stupid, soldier," said the sergeant jokingly, "you know what I'm talking about."

"Naw, Sarge," replied the young man seriously. "What happened at Pearl Harbor? The navy have an accident or something?"

The sergeant reached across the bunker and hit the young man in the back of his Kevlar helmet.

"Hey, Sarge," complained the young man. "I thought I saw something."

The sergeant looked at the young man saying, "You heard of World War II, knot head."

"Yeah, Sarge, I heard of it," answered the soldier. "But that was a long time ago."

"Pay attention to what you're doin'!" said the sergeant. "What'd you think you saw?"

The soldier got back on his telescope. "Thought I saw somethin' moving through the water about eleven o'clock."

"Let me take a look," said his partner, "where abouts?"

The soldier moved to the second scope set up in the bunker and looked out in the same direction as his friend. He gasped in disbelief.

"What is it soldier?" asked the sergeant.

"It's a periscope, isn't' it?" exclaimed the older soldier, astonished.

"Sure as hell looks like it," responded the younger soldier.

The NCO pushed his way into the bunker tapping the older of the two on the shoulder. "Let me have a look, son."

The young man moved out of the way. The sergeant took off his helmet and squinted as he looked through the scope.

"Damn!" exclaimed the sergeant after looking for several seconds. "Call it in, boy. Call it in."

The young man reached the field telephone picking up the receiver with one hand while turning the hand crank of the old piece of equipment with the other. There were a few seconds of silence then there was a buzzing noise on the other end of the field telephone. A pleasant female voice answered.

"Yes."

"Echo six," said the young soldier, "this is Beachcomber two, two, four. We have a contact at our location. It's a periscope about a mile and a half out."

"Beachcomber two, two, four, can you get me a better bearing and we'll start help on the way."

"Sarge, they want a better bearing," said the young man looking at his sergeant, "and they're sending help."

The sergeant smiled. "You come back over here and keep an eye on this thing. Give me the receiver, I'll talk to them."

The soldier handed the sergeant the handset, switching places.

"Echo six, this is Beachcomber two, two, six. I'm on scene with two, two, four and can verified the contact. Current location of the contact from this position is bearing one, seven, three, moving east to west at approximately three to five knots. She's about a mile and a half to two miles out."

"Copy that Beachcomber two, two, six. Echo six is requesting that you stay with two, two, four while we see if two, two, three or two, two, five can also see the contact."

"Roger that Echo six," said the sergeant looking out of the bunker towards the lights from the tents at the top of the rise to their west, "Echo six you might want to have the lights extinguished at the position to our immediate west. They're exposing themselves needlessly."

"Roger your last, two, two, six. They'll be off before the exercise starts. Standby while we call the other OP's."

The sergeant shook his head. If this were the real thing, they would be giving away an important position costing a few of them their lives. He hoped Echo six knew what he was doing.

Echo Six
Kaena Point
December 22, 1994
0253 Hours

Major Michael Norton, United States Army, drew the assignment of being the judge around Echo Company on Kaena Point. There were three other judges working with him and they were all in agreement with the troops.

This was a stupid time of year to plan a war game. He was in the tent when the OPFOR commander gave his pep talk. He witnessed the change in the attitude of the troops assembled there and hoped it would make a difference. These National Guard troops were facing a far superior force and he hoped they were up to the challenge.

He decided to walk Captain Summers to his vehicle and the two of them were talking about some general topics when a soldier came running up to them.

"Sir," said the excited soldier, "we have a contact. One of the observation posts spotted a periscope."

"Lead the way, son," said Summers following the young man, "do we have a direction of travel?"

"I believe so, sir, but I'm not sure what it is. The captain's talking to them now."

Norton swung in next to Summers as they made their way back to the tent. Summer's driver, an excited little National Guard corporal, followed several steps behind them, steno pad and pen in his hand.

"What's the big deal about a periscope sighting, sir?" Norton remarked. "The operation doesn't start until 0330. Why would they start early? Kingston is a stickler on being punctual for everything. He wouldn't tolerate one of his units starting early."

"True, Major," replied Summers, "but Dick Kingston won't watch his special ops troops because he doesn't respect them. He tends to rely on the more conventional troops and tactics to overwhelm his opponent. If I were the SEAL commander, I would jump off early and hit my objective early in the exercise when they're not expecting an attack. That's what they'll do, and we'll be ready for them. Admiral Kingston won't say anything to them if they succeed and they know it."

"If they don't?"

"Then Dick Kingston can knock Special Ops around for a while and they won't be able to do anything about it."

Norton smiled entering the tent with the naval officer. Like many of the reserve and guard people he was surprised by the assignment of the naval officer to command OPFOR troops in the exercise. It seemed to have been a closely guarded secret and he was beginning to see why. There was a method to what Summers was doing. He was applying unconventional tactics to a conventional game. While he still thought the OPFOR troops were out gunned, he now thought they would at least wake up the regular troops involved in the exercise.

When they entered the tent soldiers started to rise. Summers said nothing but motioned for them to carry on while moving quickly through the maze of personnel and equipment. The young company commander was on the field telephone. He handed Summers a piece of paper. Summers looked at it and then moved over to a map laid across the table next to where communications was set up. Summers looked at the paper again and then spent a minute looking at the map. He put his finger on the map and moved it from left to right smiling. He tapped his finger on the map several times as the younger officer placed the field telephone back on its cradle.

"That was Beachcomber two, two, three, Sir," said the younger man. "They confirmed the sighting that two, two, four made. The squad leader also confirmed the sighting. Right where you said they would be. They don't appear to be trying to hide either."

"That's because they don't know we're looking for them. The captain of the sub feels safe because the exercise hasn't officially started yet. He might even be bold enough to try and stay at periscope depth through their entire portion of the operation. If they do that, you know what to do."

"Yes, sir!" said the National Guard officer smiling.

"They'll probably land here," said Summers tapping the map again. "You know how to deal with that as well. Just as we discussed, Captain. You should be able to get the entire team."

The young officer smiled. "Yes, Sir! Nice and easy, don't rush, and tighten the noose when they're all in. The hard part will be keeping the lid on the troops."

"Captain," Summers said knowingly, "that's always been the problem in any army. I have faith that you and your people will do what you need to do. Get the job done, Captain. We can all celebrate when it's over."

"Yes, Sir!' said the captain smartly. "What about Echo Forward, Sir? Any change in plans?"

"None, Captain. You have your instructions."

"Yes, Sir!"

Norton turned to say something to Summers only to see him walking out of the tent followed by his driver. He looked at the soldiers moving quietly about their duties. The attitude was different than it had been when he joined the unit earlier in the day. He was glad this was just a game otherwise it would be a hell of a fight.

U.S.S. Nimitz
Kauai Channel
December 22, 1994
0325 Hours

Captain Tom Brothers had been in the United Sates Navy twenty years and wasn't a fan of practicing for war, even though he knew it was necessary. He knew Admiral Kingston wouldn't be easy to deal with but was confident he would hold his own knowing how the admiral reacted to most situations. The admiral himself was not the problem in Brothers' mind as much as his two aides. He didn't trust them and knew he would have to be discrete when dealing with the admiral.

"Admiral on the bridge!" said the officer of the deck loudly.

Kingston walked onto the bridge followed by Williams and Handcock. Brothers almost laughed because the spacing between them was perfect, as was everything else about them.

"Good morning, Admiral," said Brothers. "How are you this morning?"

Kingston didn't look at the ships commanding officer as he walked across the bridge, taking a seat in the captain's chair on the starboard side. He finally smiled at the man.

"Are we ready to commence Operation Whirlwind, Captain Brothers?" asked Kingston smugly. "Any delays I should know about?

Brothers took a deep breath deciding this was going to be a long cruise.

"No, Sir, no delays. We're ready to start the operation on time."

"Then I recommend we do so," Kingston said looking into the dark night.

Brothers looked at the two aides standing on either side of the admiral. Williams ignored everyone looking out the window like the admiral. Handcock occasionally glanced around giving a glare of disapproval if she caught someone watching them. Brothers sighed, again thinking this was going to be a long cruise.

"Officer of the Deck!"

"Sir," responded the lieutenant standing the watch.

"Take the ship to general quarters and inform all ships in the battle group Operation Whirlwind is under way."

"Aye, aye, Sir!"

Nimitz Battle Group
Kauai Channel
December 22, 1994
0330 Hours

The *Nimitz* Battle Group came to life in a matter of seconds when the message to commence the operation was communicated to all ships. Throughout the battle group alarms sounded and sleeping sailors rushed to get into their clothes and get to their assigned battle stations. Hatches were dogged and secured, and each bridge received word that all stations were manned and ready. The battle group was a mixed group of ships of the line and amphibious transports. *Nimitz* served as the battle group's flag ship. There to protect her were the *Ticonderoga* class cruiser *Lake Erie* and the cruiser *California*. There to support these larger ships in the anti-submarine warfare function were the *Arleigh Burke* class destroyers *John S. McCain* and *Russell*, the *Spruance* class destroyers *Ingersoll* and *Fletcher*, and the *Oliver Hazard Perry* class frigates *Ford*, *Jarrett*, and *Simpson*. Carrying the marine assault force was the *Wasp* class amphibious assault ship *Essex*, the *Austin* class amphibious transports *Juneau* and *Ogden*, and the LSDs (Dock Landing Ship) *Anchorage* and *Rushmore*. Along with the surface contingent of the task force was the *Los Angeles* class attack submarine *Columbia* and the *Sturgeon* class attack submarine *Hawkbill*. All totaled, a little over fifteen thousand men and women readied to test themselves against less than half of their number on shore.

On the flight decks of *Nimitz* and *Essex* aircraft were being readied for the start of the assault to rescue fictitious hostages being held on the north shore of Oahu. Dummy missile and rocket loads were placed on the F-18 Hornet fighters and the Cobra helicopter gunships preparing to lead the assault on the island. Sailors moved with determination to make sure all was ready for the aircraft to jump off on time. The pilots in the ready rooms were receiving their last-minute instructions regarding their targets and expectations of resistance. In the troop carriers, marines were checking and rechecking their equipment. On *Essex*, crews were readying six Sea Knight helicopters to carry the marine recon rescue force. They would be going in with an escort of Cobra gunships and the first wave of Hornets.

The first target of the jets would be the lone radar installation detected on the tip of Kaena Point, on the northwest end of Oahu. They would be simulating a HARM antiradar missile launch and, following the destruction of the radar site, would cover the landing of the marine recon unit. Once the marines landed, the F-14's would take on the expected assault from the OPFOR F-15's while Harriers from *Essex* would support the amphibious assault linking up with the recon unit and the SEALs to extract them and the hostages. The war game was expected to last for the next two days, the approximate time it would take to complete an operation of this type.

The task force started to turn to starboard. This turn into the wind by the ships was monitored by the lone radar installation on Kaena Point. Everyone knew the game was starting.

OPFOR Command
Kaena Point
December 22, 1994
0335 Hours

Summers walked into his headquarters finding everyone busy monitoring the movement of the battle group. His driver followed him.

"What do they have you doing, Corporal?" asked Summers.

There was a moment of silence. "Nothing, Sir. Just waiting for you."

"Good!" responded the officer. "You stay with me son and cover my six."

"Sir?"

"Watch my back, run errands, take notes, or anything else that needs to be done. No one sits in my command, son. There's always something needing to be done."

"Yes, Sir!" replied the corporal.

The site they were using was once the home of a wealthy industrialist. The military obtained a temporary lease for using the compound. They turned it into a comfortable headquarters complex. Downstairs they set up a complex communications system relying both on radio and telephone communications. A series of runners, set up like the pony express with relay stations, also operated out of the first floor. The runners were picked for their knowledge of Oahu and assigned a partner and a vehicle. On the second floor were the operations, supply, and intelligence functions. This included both air and land-based operations as the OPFOR force consisted of all reserve branches and National Guard units.

Jon led the way up the stairs and into what must have been the master bedroom suite. Here was a series of tables and desks covered with maps and reams of paperwork. Soldiers looked busy updating maps and documenting troop movements. Summers walked over to a National Guard major serving as his deputy commander. The major was the officer Kingston spoke to. He shared with Summers his frustration with how the admiral treated him. The use of guerrilla tactics to fight Kingston suited him fine, even if they didn't win. The man felt being a thorn in the admiral's side, even for a short period of time, was going to be a pleasure.

"Are the others here?"

"Yes, Sir, Captain," replied the major. "They're in the other room double checking on the battle group. It turned west, probably to launch their first wave of aircraft."

"No doubt, major," replied Summers looking about the room, "Corporal, could you find me some coffee? It looks to be a long night."

"Yes, Sir!" replied the young soldier, looking at the major. The army officer motioned to the other side of the room.

"Make that two, corporal," said the major, "and get yourself one. I don't think you're going to get much sleep working for the captain."

Summers laughed as several other officers walked in from the hallway. There was an air force major, a marine major, and a navy lieutenant commander.

"Gentlemen," said Summers motioning them over to a map, "I believe Admiral Kingston is going to land part of his special ops people here where Echo Company is deployed."

"That's where they spotted the periscope?" asked the marine officer. "Lucky sighting, can we be sure that's where they'll come ashore?"

"No, major, we can't," said Summers. "Let's say it's an educated guess. I want you to send one of your armored companies to this point to support Echo. They'll also be able to move quickly if they happen to come ashore somewhere else."

The marine officer looked to where Summers was pointing on the map, "Consider it done, Sir."

Summers then looked at the air force and naval officers, "Are your people clear about what's expected of them?"

The naval officer spoke for both. "We're set, Captain. We may not win this game, but we're gonna have a hell of a good time giving the admiral worms, Sir."

Summers couldn't contain the smile anymore.

"Good. Make sure your people keep their cool and don't engage and tip our hand too early."

Both men acknowledged, "Yes, Sir."

Summers looked at the army major, "Reserves?"

"Three companies of infantry with an Air Guard unit who'll fly them where they need to deploy. Cobra gunships will cover the Huey's. We can get them anywhere along the line in less than twenty minutes."

Summers smiled confidently, "Gentlemen, let's go kick some ass!"

Kauai Channel
Oahu, Hawaii
December 22, 1994
0345 Hours

For as warm as the air was, the water was cold. Thirty men swam just below the surface, making their way slowly towards the shore. Each man was using a Draeger rebreathing system that recycled the diver's air, enriching it with oxygen. Several of the divers carried compass boards to help them navigate to their target. They swam in pairs, taking their time because of the equipment they carried.

Naylor was DeCook's swim buddy. He expected this could be difficult, and they worked hard to get ready. He was exhausted but knew he couldn't stop. He was offered the opportunity to observe from the submarine or from shore but was compelled to participate. He knew he would regret his decision later with sore muscles. He was a few years older than DeCook, but figured he was as fit. He now understood why they stressed endurance in the training they received. They would be at the beach soon and what was to follow he knew how to do. He knew he could tough it out. He kept swimming, moving onto other thoughts to distract him from his exhaustion.

Nimitz Battle Group
Kauai Channel
December 22, 1994
0348 Hours

The battle group was facing into the wind and started launching their aircraft. The first to go off were four Tomcat fighter-interceptors. Once in the air, they took position over the task force, assigned as combat air patrol to protect the ships from air attack. Next to be catapulted into the early morning skies was the first of three squadrons of Hornets. Their job was to lead the assault on the Kaena Point radar installation and escort the helicopters carrying the recon unit into their landing zone.

Kingston sat in his chair on the bridge watching each of the fighters launch into the dark sky. He could make out the silhouettes of the flight deck crew moving about as each aircraft was moved into place on the catapults and then launched. He smiled looking about the bridge. Everyone was doing their jobs. He missed this and was glad to be back at sea.

The last of the Hornets went aloft and *Essex* launched the Sea Knight helicopters filled with the marine assault force. They were accompanied by four Cobra gunship helicopters to support the air assault. After all the helicopters launched, they circled *Essex* several times waiting for word to proceed. Circling for the third time, they received the order to attack and turned east towards Kaena Point. As they made their turn, several thousand feet above them the squadron of Hornets streaked past them to clear the way.

OPFOR Command
Kaena Point
December 22, 1994
0355 Hours

Summers huddled with several others over one of the maps in the room. There was a steady hum of activity throughout the building. Telephones were ringing with ever frequent regularity and messengers were now busy. A young Air Force reservist picked up one of the field telephones near where the officers were working.

"Yankee six," said the young airman, "go ahead, radar."

Jon saw the young man looking in his direction. The airman motioned he would be with him in a minute.

"Sir," he said to Jon, "the radar station at Kaena Point has monitored the launch of fighter aircraft from the *Nimitz* and helicopters from the *Essex*. Estimating one squadron, probably F-18's, Sir. At least the operator says that's what they fly like. Also, six large helicopters escorted by four smaller ones coming in behind the jets. Possible assault force. *Essex* and several of the other ships have changed course and appear to be positioning themselves for an amphibious assault."

"Thank you, airman," said Summers turning to look at the air force liaison standing next to him.

"We're ready for them, Sir," the man said.

"I hope so," said Summers unemotionally, "because we'll lose a war of attrition with Kingston. We have to end this quickly."

"We will, Sir," said the National Guard major standing next to the air force officer, "we have a good solid plan and everyone in this command wants a piece of the admiral."

Summers returned the man's smile. "I hope so, Major.

AWACS Deltastar
Circling the Kauai Channel
December 22, 1994
0355 Hours

The AWACS slowly circled the engagement area. The radar operators noted and marked the locations of the various units currently involved in the exercise. On board were several high-ranking Army, Navy, and Air Force officers acting as judges. The communications from the electronic warfare plane to participating units remained constantly open.

An airman watching one of the radar scopes looked up at the officers as they passed his station. "Sirs, *Nimitz,* and *Essex* are launching their aircraft. The action's about to start."

The officers stopped to look at the young man's scope. They looked at the blips on the screen and then looked at each other.

"Admiral Kingston isn't using enough aircraft on his initial strike. I think he's being a touch over-confident." said the first officer with a grin.

"It's going to be interesting. I'm not sure if the strategy OPFOR's using will prevent being overwhelmed, but it'll be unique if nothing else. I talked to the reserve commanders and their plan seems a little off the wall. That might be what they need to put up a fight against Kingston."

The others laughed. "You're right there. Let's get to work."

VFA-147
Over the Kauai Channel
December 22, 1994
0400 Hours

The planes of fighter attack squadron VFA-147 flew east towards Oahu and their target. They watched their attack radar's looking for OPFOR fighters to target and destroy as they approached the coast. The only aircraft currently registering on their radar screens was Deltastar. They kept their formation tight, and all were alert for anything that might mean the OPFOR forces were responding to their assault. They looked at the intelligence reports and knew the OPFOR forces had several fighter squadrons at their disposal. They had more aircraft than *Nimitz* did, but the pilots of VFA-147 were confident they were better fliers and could handle anything the reserve forces could throw at them.

The squadron leader, a Commander from Texas, took another look at his radar and decided to call *Nimitz*. "Eagle, this is Liberty flight lead."

"Go ahead, Liberty one."

"Eagle, do we have any TEW support for this mission?"" asked the pilot checking the aircraft on both wings. He was referring to the EA-6B Prowlers that were *Nimitz's* tactical electronic warfare aircraft. These four-seater, all weather aircraft were used to detect and jam enemy radio and radar traffic during attacks. This morning's attack did not call for their use until the amphibious assault later in the day.

"Negative, Liberty one," was the response. "Liberty, you guys feeling lonely up there?"

The pilot smiled to himself. "Yes, we are. It's nice knowing the TEW boys are around just in case."

"Sorry, Liberty, they'll just slow you down. There is no radio traffic and there is still only the one radar signal. You have a green light to destroy that installation."

"Roger that, Eagle," said the pilot. "Approaching point of launch in three, two, and one. Fox three!"

Liberty one simulated the launch of a HARM air-to-surface missile. This type of missile homed in on the radar emissions of the target and proved effective during the Gulf War.

"Liberty one, this is Eagle," said the voice in the headset. "You have enemy bogies launching from Waialua in possible squadron strength. Your vector is 030 for the bogies."

The squadron leader looked at his attack radar and saw the blips representing the OPFOR aircraft on the extreme edge of his radar screen. Still out of range for the air-to-air missiles his squadron was carrying. He looked at the radar again and thought it looked like the aircraft were moving away from them. He thought this strange since the purpose of war games such as this was to help improve dog fighting skills. He couldn't understand why the reserve squadron was moving away from them.

"Eagle," he said, "this is Liberty one. Are the bogies moving away from us or am I imagining things?"

"That's affirmative, Liberty one," came the immediate reply, "the bogies appear to be circling away from you. They appear to be waiting for a second group launching on the far side of the island."

"Eagle, permission to proceed with the mission and clear the LZ for Hatchet."

"Roger that, Liberty one."

"Roger, Eagle. Liberty One to Liberty flight. Proceed to primary mission delta."

The entire flight of Hornets started a gradual decent towards the island of Oahu.

OPFOR Command
Kaena Point
December 22, 1994
0403 Hours

The entire command staff was listening to the chat between the F-18's and *Nimitz*. Even though it was practice, you could feel the tension in the room. The reserves weren't only participating in the exercise to practice, but also to gain some respect from the full-time soldiers and sailors. Jon was feeling the weight of command because they all looked to him for the right decisions. He could feel himself starting to sweat.

"Deltastar to Yankee Six," the squawk box came to life again, "your radar site on Kaena Point has been destroyed by missile fire."

The airman who had relayed the message from the radar installation earlier looked at Summers, who smiled and nodded. The airman picked up a handset next to him. "Yankee Six copies Deltastar."

Immediately the lone radar site on Kaena Point went down and all radar emissions ceased. The OPFOR troops were now blind to what the ships and planes from the battle group were doing.

"Liberty One, this is Eagle. Radar is dead, proceed with Hatchet to Check Point Oscar."

"Roger that, Eagle."

"Liberty One, bogies have made their turn and are heading towards you."

"Copy Eagle, we are picking up their radar emissions."

Everyone was intently listening to the box monitoring the communications from the battle group when a second squawk box came to life.

"Springboard lead to Tomboy." said voice with a heavy southern drawl. Everyone in the room knew the call sign of the squadron leader of the F-15's that just turned to meet the Hornets.

"Tomboy on for Springboard, over." replied a very pleasant female voice.

"Tomboy, we are approaching your ten o'clock and request a visual assist."

There was a second of silence, then a response, "Springboard, it's still a little dark for a visual. You'll have to give us a better fix than that."

"Roger that Tomboy. We'll be over you in fifteen, fourteen, …"

The box monitoring the task force came back to life, "Liberty One, the bogie flight is having some sort of difficulty and is requesting assistance."

"Ten, nine, …"

"Roger that Eagle, we still show them in bound.

"Six, Five, …"

"Hatchet to Liberty flight. ETA to check point Oscar is three."

"Two, one, over you, Tomboy."

On Springboard's last message five additional radar installations went live and immediately pinpointed the aircraft of the Liberty flight and the Hatchet assault force for just over fifty SAM batteries. These sites immediately locked onto targets and simulated firing.

Liberty One's only comment over the squawk box was, "Motherfucker!"

The entire headquarters of Yankee Six cheered. Summers smiled at the response from his troops as well as from his elation they just took the task force by surprise. He turned to his staff and nodded, but they were already on the field telephones talking to their people. For the first time, Summers was feeling optimistic.

AWACS Deltastar
Circling the Kauai Channel
December 22, 1994
0405 Hours

The operator almost jumped out of his seat when the five new radar sites went live. At almost the same time three more squadrons of aircraft appeared from behind the mountains and hills south of Waialua. They had been flying low managing to stay undetected. Within seconds another four squadrons seemed to appear from the surface of the ocean to the north of the task force.

"Holy shit!" exclaimed the operator speaking for most of his colleagues. "Where the hell did all that come from. Sirs, we're about to have a hell of a war down here."

Everyone on the AWACS immediately went to work identifying what was taking place and recording everything going on. The sudden appearance of the additional radar sites took everyone by surprise. It was obvious the SAM launches that followed took the aircraft from the battle group by surprise.

"Deltastar to Liberty flight," said the naval officer standing over the operator of a tracking radar. "Your entire flight has been destroyed by SAM fire."

"You're joking, right," was the response from one of the pilots.

"Negative, Liberty flight, it's no joke. We show all your aircraft sustained at least two hits. Please vector 090 and proceed to Check Point Sierra."

"Liberty One, to Deltastar, there must be some mistake."

"Deltastar to Liberty flight, this is not up for debate. Your squadron is out of service. Follow directions immediately and respond to Check Point Sierra."

"Roger Deltastar," the voice sounded irritated, "turning 090."

"Deltastar to Hatchet flight," the officer continued as he watched the blips on the radar screen that represented the Hornets change direction, "Hatchet Four, Hatchet Six, and Bulldog Three are the only aircraft in your flight left intact. All other aircraft should follow Liberty flight to Check Point Sierra."

"Copy that Deltastar," said one of the pilots from the flight of helicopters without argument.

The officer on the AWACS looked down at the radar operator smiling. The airman smiled back, "Do you think the battle group is in trouble, Sir?"

"Son," chuckled the officer, "you can bully your way around a lot of things, but not a well-planned trap. Someone down there knows how this admiral thinks and is going to use it against him. Let's watch and see what happens."

Nimitz Battle Group
Kauai Channel
December 22, 1994
0415 Hours

Kingston got out of the chair and walked over to where Brothers was on the phone with CIC. Brothers did not look happy and was talking softly so the others on the bridge couldn't hear him.

"What's the hold up, Captain?" said Kingston loudly. "Why are there no updates from Liberty or Hatchet? The marines should be just about ready to land."

The look the ship's captain gave him made the admiral step back. This was noticed by everyone on the bridge. Brothers made no other move but knew he just intimidated his superior. He pushed one of the several buttons on the telephone in front of him.

"Air, this is the captain," he said into the mouthpiece. "Get the rest of our aircraft up. Now! We have multiple bogies inbound. Get a Hawkeye up. Looks like we're gonna need some eyes."

After he got the response he needed, he turned to Kingston. "Admiral, apparently OPFOR has some tricks up their sleeve we didn't know about. Liberty and Hatchet just flew into a trap. All of Liberty flight has been shot down, an…"

"What?" yelled the admiral in disbelief, "That can't be right."

"And Hatchet has only two choppers left and Bulldog three. After Liberty destroyed the Kaena Point radar site, they went in to clear the way for Hatchet because the OPFOR flight responding appeared to be circling away to wait for reinforcements. What they were doing is tracking our aircraft on their long-range radar in the F-15's. When our planes got to a certain point, five new radar sites went live, and SAMs were launched. They never had a chance. Now we count eight squadrons of OPFOR aircraft inbound and we only have four Tomcats airborne to protect us."

Kingston now understood the look Brothers had given him. His plan put the captain's ship in danger. His plan for an easy victory in this game appeared to be thrown out the window.

"Captain Brothers," he said calmly, "do what you have to do to protect the ship. Would you please have all transmission piped up to the bridge so that we can monitor them."

"Yes, Sir," said Brothers, his expression softening. This was the closest thing to an apology he would get from the admiral. The telephone next to them buzzed and Brothers picked it up and put it to his ear, "Captain speaking."

There was a second while Brothers listened to who was on the other end of the phone.

"What is it?" asked Kingston looking concerned.

"Someone's jamming our radar and radio signals."

Over the Kauai Channel
December 22, 1994
0420 Hours

Leading the air assault coming in from the north were three navy reserve Prowlers. They started doing their job the minute the new shore-based radars went live. At the same time leading the air assault from Oahu were three Air National Guard Wild Weasels. These aircraft were F-4 Phantom fighters converted to electronic warfare planes and did the same job the Prowlers did. They, too, were jamming radar and communications of the task force.

Behind the Prowlers came four flights of aircraft. The first two flights were Marine Corps reserve Hornets. They were followed by two flights of naval reserve Intruders and a lone E-2C Hawkeye providing help to coordinate the attack on the battle group. As they closed on the ships, they spread out to make it tougher on the four F-14's covering the battle group. At the same time, two squadrons of air force reserve F-15's followed the Wild Weasel's out from Oahu. Behind them were two squadrons of Air National Guard A-10 Thunderbolts. Just behind the Thunderbolts was another Hawkeye to coordinate the attack with the other four squadrons coming in from the north. These planes also spread out to make interception by the F-14's as difficult as possible. Just taking off were the last of the OPFOR air power. That was one more squadron of F-15s and one squadron of F-14's. OPFOR had just committed its entire air wing.

As they approached, the sailors on *Nimitz* frantically rushed to get their planes ready for launch. Kingston sent one pair of F-14's in each direction on what everyone knew would be a suicide mission. They would not be able to stop the OPFOR planes from coming in, but they would hopefully slow them down long enough for the rest of *Nimitz's* aircraft to be launched. On board *Essex* the sailors were clearing the flight deck of helicopters so they could launch their Harriers. This would take time they didn't have. They knew they were going to have to rely on the *Nimitz* and her aircraft for cover for the initial assault by the OPFOR aircraft.

When the OPFOR F-15s and F-18s were within 80 miles of the battle group, they simulated a massive HARM launch and then rose to meet the four Tomcats. The Tomcats lasted a few minutes in the dogfight that ensued before they were told that they had been destroyed by Deltastar. The

OPFOR forces lost two aircraft in the engagement. While the dogfight took place, the Intruders and the Thunderbolts slipped by and when they were within 60 miles of the task force, simulated a massive Harpoon anti-ship missile launch.

As quickly as they appeared on the radar screens the OPFOR aircraft turned away to return to their airfields. The only plane remaining on station was the Hawkeye following the attack from Oahu. Four F-15's also remained, given the task to protect it until reinforcements arrived.

Everyone waited with anticipation to see the outcome of the attack. *Nimitz* managed to launch the remainder of their F-14's and about three quarters of her F-18's. All the senior officers in the battle group knew they were in trouble.

**Beachcomber 223
Kaena Point
December 22, 1994
0430 Hours**

The swimmers crawled up the beach in pairs looking for cover. There were a few high sand dunes to take cover behind, but the beach was exposed. DeCook was concerned about this but saw no movement on the hill in front of him. If someone saw them land, they surely would have sent out an alarm of some kind. He motioned for the first squad of men to move forward. He watched the rangers who were mixed in with his men. They all made it to the beach and were performing admirably.

The first squad reached the base of the hill taking up defensive positions to cover the rest of the men while they moved forward. The squad leader gave DeCook the all-clear signal. He motioned for the rest of the men to proceed. They rose from the sand and went over the top of the small dune. When they were about halfway to the base of the hill, there was a sudden sound of automatic weapons fire. Muzzle flashes could be seen all along the crest of the hill directed at them. The SEALs and Rangers scrambled for any cover they could find. Flares went off and lit up the entire area exposing the command. DeCook could hear heavy vehicles moving forward. This was immediately followed by the sound of artillery fire directed at the ocean behind them.

The flares kept the entire beach lit up. DeCook could see movement all over the hill, coming down towards them. He looked up and down the beach and saw infantry being led by armored vehicles coming from both directions. He knew they walked right into a trap, but how did they know where they were going to land? The SEALs and rangers fought for as long as they could, but it soon became apparent it was futile.

They surrendered to a very young Army National Guard captain who took the time to salute both Naylor and DeCook. His men collected their weapons and lined them up to march off the beach. DeCook and Naylor listened as he called in on the radio.

"Echo Six to Yankee Six, over," he said into the handset. "Assault came ashore at Beachcomber Two, Two, Three. Have captured entire assault force and moving them to the holding area."

There was several seconds of silence as the young officer appeared to be listening to someone on the other end. A big smile came over his face as he said, "Roger that, Sir, and thank you, Sir."

The young officer slapped the sergeant who was standing next to him on the back, "Sergeant, Yankee Six says, '*Well done.*' Take a couple of squads and two of the vehicles and escort these men to the holding area at Echo Six. The rest of you, get back on post in case more come in."

The captain looked up to a marine lieutenant sitting on top of an LAV-25 armored car. "Lieutenant, the boss says good shooting. Your tanks hit the sub's antennas and periscopes, putting it out of service,"

The marine officer produced a big grin. "Thanks, Cap. I'll pass it on. Say, let me help your sergeant get these boys off to detention."

The Guard captain waved at the officer and then disappeared up the hill. As the prisoners started to move forward, Naylor noticed an Army major with a Judge's arm band on.

"Major," he yelled and waved to the officer to come over to them as they started up the beach. The major trotted over to the officers marching in the column of prisoners. He slowed to a walk when he came up next to them.

"Lieutenant Colonel Charlie Naylor, First Ranger Battalion." Naylor held out his hand to the officer.

The officer shook it, smiling. "Major Mike Norton, Colonel, nice to meet you."

DeCook reached in front of Naylor holding out his hand. "Tim DeCook, United States Navy."

"Mr. DeCook," said Norton, "nice to meet you."

"So where are they taking us?" asked the SEAL. "To the encampment at the top of the rise?"

Both DeCook and Naylor were surprised when Norton laughed. "Boy, you guys fell for everything, hook, line, and sinker. I wouldn't have believed it if I hadn't seen it myself."

"What do you mean, Major?" asked Naylor impatiently.

Norton continued to smile. "The installation at the top of the rise is a decoy. They kept it lit to draw you in and it appears to have worked. The same thing seems to be happening to the task force."

DeCook, looking somewhat ashamed asked, "What are you talking about? I don't understand?"

"I'll explain when we get to where you're going," said the major.

AWACS Deltastar
Circling the Kauai Channel
December 22, 1994
0430 Hours

The crew watched as the OPFOR strike force fell back after launching their missile attack. To their east, the lone Hawkeye and its escort remained on station. The squadrons that made it off *Nimitz* were forming up to their west near the island of Kauai. The remainder of Hatchet and Bulldog flights were targeted by shore-based SAM sights and fired on. Deltastar informed all three aircraft that they were destroyed sending them to Check Point Sierra.

The radar operator looked up at the officer standing next to him. "I'm glad I'm not the one that'll have to notify the battle group about casualties, Sir."

The officer smiled. "How long until HARM impact?"

"Thirty seconds, Sir," responded the operator looking down at his screen. The two of them watched the computer projected course of the incoming missiles. Each missile selected a target, homing in on the ship's radar signal.

About fifteen seconds before impact, the *Fletcher* turned off her radar. The two missiles homing in on her immediately acquired secondary targets. In this case, it was *Nimitz*.

Nimitz Battle Group
Kauai Channel
December 22, 1994
0435 Hours

Deltastar started to notify the ships in the task force who was hit by missiles. *Nimitz* led the list of ships now operating without radar. In addition, *Lake Erie, California, McCain, Russell, Ingersoll, Simpson, Essex, Juneau, Anchorage,* and *Rushmore* all were told they had been hit by the attack. That left only the *Fletcher, Ford,* and *Jarrett* with radar still operating. Additionally, both *Essex* and *Nimitz* were told they received damage to their flight decks, stopping all flight operations on both ships.

Kingston ordered all ships in the task force to take evasive action to avoid the incoming Harpoon missile attack. The ships all turned to starboard just as the simulated attack struck. Kingston hoped this would expose the fewest ships to the incoming flight of killer projectiles. The first to be told she was hit was *Essex*. She was told she was hit by three missiles. All the other amphibious ships were also hit by at least one Harpoon. *Ogden, Anchorage,* and *Rushmore* were told they were dead in the water and sinking. *Essex* and *Juneau* were told they were on fire and heavily damaged.

Of the ships of the line, *Fletcher* and *Jarrett* were the only ones not damaged. *Russell* was told she was sinking, and the rest were told they were damaged and on fire. *Nimitz* was told that she had taken two more missiles, making any flight operations impossible. The aircraft started off after the retreating OPFOR aircraft only to be called back to protect the crippled task force.

Kingston knew he was now on the losing end of a war of attrition. He needed to manage a tactical retreat without losing any more ships. He knew he wouldn't have much time before the OPFOR planes would rearm and return to finish the job they started. He wasn't a happy man but knew he could blame only himself. He underestimated an enemy. It was a mistake he would pay for when he reported back to Pearl Harbor, but not a fatal one. He did need to straighten that National Guard major out though and would do so in short order.

A sudden call from the Fletcher put the task force in a panic. Both she and the Jarrett had picked up incoming aircraft, coming from the direction of Oahu. They estimated at least two squadrons that would be in range of the air umbrella in three minutes. It was going to be a long day.

OPFOR Command
Kaena Point
December 22, 1994
0700 Hours

The war game was winding down as the OPFOR aircraft continued to pound the battle group with missile and bomb attacks. Summers looked at the tally board his staff set up in the main situation room. His commanders managed to keep the enthusiasm the troops were now feeling in check so they could complete the exercise in an orderly manner. The change in the reserves attitude was evident. The talk of the poor timing of the exercise was gone. Every one of them looked confident and professional as they went about their assigned duties. They knew they completed the job they were sent to do. Summers was pleased, it would be a feather in his cap. He was not looking forward to the debriefing with the brass and Dick Kingston.

He sat back in his chair near the window looking out over the large grounds around his headquarters. As he sipped another cup of coffee, he looked at the tally board again. The *Nimitz* Battle Group had lost fifty-seven aircraft, including the helicopter strike force, to OPFOR's twenty-five. They sunk five ships in the battle group and damaged all but four of the remaining ships. This included damaging one of the battle group's three submarines. They also captured the entire SEAL landing force on the beach. Not bad for a day's work. The two-day war game was shortened to less than six hours. The exercise would be officially over at 0900 hours because the *good guys* didn't have anything left to fight with.

His deputy commander walked over and handed him the latest report on the movement of the battle group as it tried to pull out without further casualties. While Summers read the report over, a soldier came over to the major quietly saying something to him. The major looked disturbed.

"What is it, Major?" asked Summers. "Did we just lose the exercise?"

"No, Sir," responded the National Guard officer, "Admiral Kingston's aide is on the line for me. The private says he's very insistent. The man's a pain, Sir. He called me twice after the admiral met with us to make sure that I understood what was expected of us."

Jon smiled. "Are we still recording all communication in and out of this headquarters?"

The major looked puzzled. "Of course, Sir. That order hasn't changed."

"Then take the call, Major," said Summers as he got up and handed the report back to the officer, "and put it on the speaker so we can all hear."

The Major looked at his superior for several seconds before he broke out in a huge grin. "Private, you heard the boss. Put Commander Williams on speaker and turn up the volume."

"Yes, Sir!"

A small crowd gathered to hear the conversation. The entire room was quiet as the major nodded, giving the all-clear to turn on the speaker.

"Commander Williams," said the Major, "what can I do for you?"

"Major," came the curt reply from the box, "I think you know why I've contacted you. Admiral Kingston is very unhappy with you. I thought you understood what the admiral expected of you and your people during this exercise."

"I don't understand, Commander," said the major trying not to laugh, "I'm only following the orders I've been given."

"You were told your people were expected to put up a good fight, but that in the end we all knew who would win this exercise."

"Commander," a chuckle squeaked out this time, "I'm sorry you're not happy with the outcome, but like I said, I'm just following orders."

William's voice sounded irritated. "Damn it, Major, your orders from the admiral were to lose. I think your career in the military is about over and…"

"Commander, are you threatening one of my people?" said Summers loudly into the box.

There was silence.

"I'm waiting for an answer, Commander," Summers repeated evenly. "Are you threatening the Major?"

"Who is this?" asked Williams.

"I'm Yankee Six," Summers said with the hint of a smile on his face, "Now, answer the question."

"I…ah…how do I know who you are?""

"Sir!" said Summers raising his voice slightly.

"Excuse me?"

"You can address me as, Sir!" Summers's tone turned hard. "Now answer the question!"

"The admiral will want to talk to you, Sir. I'll ge…"

"Commander, you're avoiding the question," Summers said flatly. "That's a big mistake."

"Sir, I…"

Summers wrote something on a piece of paper, handing it to the major as he spoke. "In this exercise it's my understanding Battle Group 68 is supposed to be the *good guys* and I'm supposed to be the *bad guy*, right?"

"Sir, I…"

"Commander, at this point I'm not really interested in anything you have to say," Summers's face broke into a smile and several of the people gathered around the box laughed, "You've threatened one of my people and now you'll have to pay the consequences."

"Sir, I really think you…"

Summers pushed a button on top of the box, disconnecting the man on the other end. A cheer went up from the gathered group as he moved away from the box. The Major looked at him grinning.

"They'll be on their way in ten minutes," said the Major.

Gateway Compound
Oahu, Hawaii
December 22, 1994
0830 Hours

The limousine turned off the main highway and onto a long driveway. Nancy sat in the back with her children who were in awe of all this luxury. They were picked up in front of their hotel about an hour before and enjoyed a very pleasant drive through the city and out to the compound. As the limo drove up the driveway, Nancy thought of how the grounds and house reminded her of the set of an old detective show she used to watch on TV. The grounds were immaculate, with well-trimmed shrubbery and trees placed about the green grass. She could see a tennis court near the main house and several smaller buildings about the compound. She assumed there was a pool because Gateway told them to bring their swimming suits. She could also make out the ocean beyond the house.

When the limousine pulled up to the house it was met by an older man and a woman Nancy's age. Nancy recognized them both, though it was twenty-five years since they'd seen each other. Bill Gateway looked to be in his seventies. He had a full head of gray hair, looked fit, and was wearing one of those colorful Hawaiian shirts you always saw in the movies. The woman was slender and pretty. She was dressed in a comfortable top and shorts as well. The limo came to a stop, it was time to get out.

"Nancy," said Gateway as she got out, "it's so good to see you after all these years. Jon's been so busy you two have never been around when we visited with Ray and Louise."

He gave Nancy a gentle welcome hug and stepped back. Nancy thought about how Louise described Gateway on the telephone. She was right when she told her daughter-in-law she would like him. His smile was warm, and his pleasant manner put her immediately at ease.

"I'm so glad you were able to come and spend the day with us. You remember my daughter, Becky."

The woman took Nancy's hand. "Nancy, it's good to see you again after all these years. I see the war hero is off saving the world again."

The comment caught Nancy off guard, and it must have shown on her face.

"Sorry," said Becky, "don't mind me. Jon and I have always had this thing. I call him war hero and he calls me…oh…usually a lot of things. Anyway, I'm sorry."

Nancy smiled and was glad she wasn't the only one nervous. She put her hand on Becky's shoulder and gave her a hug. "You don't have to explain. Louise tried to and lost me somewhere around 1968. You did leave quite the impression when we met at Jon's high school graduation party."

They both laughed. Nancy turned to find her three children standing outside the limo door in height order. She almost laughed, they all looked like angels. Each was dressed in shorts and a tee shirt. All wore a baseball cap, Sean wearing his backwards.

"These are the boys," said Nancy with a sigh. "This is Sean, our oldest. He's sixteen and a sophomore."

Bill stepped forward with his hand out. To Nancy's delight, Sean stepped forward extending his hand as well.

"Sean," Bill said as he shook his hand, "nice to meet you. Good strong grip, Nancy. You and Jon have done well."

Becky rolled her eyes and looked apologetically at Nancy, "Sorry, he gets like this once in a while."

Bill gave his daughter a dirty look and then held out his hand to Justin, "And you are?"

"My name's Justin, Sir," said Justin stepping forward and taking Gateway's hand, shaking it. He let go, stepping back, saluting. Gateway stood straight returning the salute. When Justin lowered his salute, Bill followed suit. "Grandma says you're a general and I should do that when we got here."

It was Nancy's turn to look at Becky and roll her eyes. They both laughed.

"Looks like Jon has done a good job with this young man," said Bill smiling looking back at the two women. "Justin, my boy, I think you'll go far in this world. Now who is this hiding behind his big brother?"

Stephen moved behind Sean while watching the exchange between Justin and Gateway. He peeked around from behind Sean just as the man was squatting down to get a better look at him. The boy suddenly dropped the duffel he was holding and ran towards the older man, jumping up into his arms.

"Whoa," said Gateway standing and holding the boy, "a surprise attack. You're not as shy as you make out to be."

Stephen laughed and giggled as Bill swung him around. When Gateway finally put him down, he still held onto the man's hand.

"My Dad says you're really just a big teddy bear," said Stephen, looking up at the retired soldier. Gateway could do nothing but smile while the two women laughed hysterically.

"Well, Dad, I guess the secret's finally out," said Becky.

"But he said it with a great deal of respect," smiled Gateway.

They started moving towards the house. Gateway stayed back with the boys, moving them towards the pool, while Becky and Nancy walked along the lawn towards a large patio area.

"I thought you lived in California?" Nancy asked finding a seat overlooking the pool where some children were already swimming.

"We do," Becky answered, "this is my brother's place. He's taken over the family publishing business from my mother's father and my uncle. This estate has been in the family since before World War II. My brother has the entire family here for Christmas every other year or so."

"Jon never mentioned it when we've talked about Bill and your family. Louise said he had been here before. It's beautiful. I don't understand why he didn't say anything."

Becky smiled shyly, looking down at her feet. "Jon was only here once. Ray and Louise were here visiting Dad and Mom. Dad was stationed here, and Mom invited Ray and Louise to come for a visit. Jon was on his way to Vietnam at the time and had a couple of days before he shipped out."

"Still strange he didn't mention it," said Nancy looking puzzled.

Becky looked at Nancy. "Not really, Nancy. I don't think he has particularly good memories of this place."

Nancy looked concerned seeing a guilty expression on Becky's face. "I don't understand, Becky. What could've happened that was so bad he wouldn't want to remember?"

"You see, at the time, I was heavily involved in the anti-war movement."

"A lot of us were against the war," Nancy replied, watching Becky closely.

"Not like this," Becky continued. "I was active in a number of militant organizations, mostly because I knew it would drive Daddy nuts. Anyway, Jon shows up in uniform, ready to ship off to the war I was protesting, and I guess I freaked out. I said some terrible things. When I'd heard he'd been seriously wounded, it devastated me. I'd been so horrible to him I blamed myself for what happened. It's the last time I ever saw him face to face."

"Jon said you were always good friends."

"That's the part that hurts. I think I destroyed the friendship that summer. You have no idea how bad I was to him. I was hoping to see him when we heard you guys were going to be here over the holiday."

Nancy smiled putting a hand on Becky's shoulder. "I've been married to Jon now going on twenty years and you need to know he's never said anything but good things about you. I even have to admit to being jealous at times."

Becky looked surprised at the last statement, but Nancy motioned not to worry.

"You have to understand," she continued, "Jon is one of those people who is fearless. No matter how scared or unsure of himself he may be, he decides what his actions will be. He's been wounded more than once. Did you know that?"

Becky shook her head.

"He made those choices to get involved in actions where he could, and did, get hurt and has never complained about those decisions. It's like this additional tour of duty here. The Navy needed him here over Christmas, so they offered to transport us as well. He's not here on a holiday. He's here to solve a problem for the Navy. You need to know he probably would have come anyway. It's this sense of duty, I guess. I can understand it, but I sure as hell don't like it. Becky, your friendship with him has never been an issue for him. He gets busy and doesn't allow himself time is all."

Becky smiled drying a tear from her eye. She patted the hand on her shoulder saying, "Thanks, Nancy. I don't even know you and I'm spilling my woes out to you. I've always worried about Jon and from the stories I've heard from Louise you're a saint for putting up with him."

"Well, will you look at that?" Gateway interrupted as he walked onto the patio with a pitcher of lemonade. The two women followed his gaze to the pool. There they saw Sean and Sarah sitting by the pool, holding hands, and talking.

"There is a God in heaven," the old man said with a grin.

CINCPAC Headquarters
Pearl Harbor
December 24, 1994
0900 Hours

Summers entered the naval base at 0800 hours after spending the last two days debriefing with his OPFOR staff. He drove to his assigned quarters where he showered and changed into his whites. He packed the remainder of his gear hoping to join Nancy and the kids' right after this meeting.

He drove directly to the base headquarters building, going to the third floor and the office of the Commander in Chief of the Pacific Fleet. He noticed the exercise was the talk of the base. Most appeared to be shocked the task force was beaten so badly. Some were saying the OPFOR forces cheated, causing Summers to chuckle.

He was coming to grips with the talk when he entered the office. He immediately recognized Commander Williams sitting in a chair next to an attractive female officer. There were several secretaries and enlisted clerks hard at work in the outer office. The female officer looked at him showing no interest. Williams didn't look up.

"Captain Summers," said the secretary as Jon let the door close behind him, "the admirals are expecting you, Sir. One moment and I'll let them know you're here."

All the enlisted personnel came to attention when the secretary said his rank. Seconds afterward, the two officers followed suit. Jon smiled walking up to Williams. "Commander Williams, how nice to see you again. How is Admiral Kingston these days?"

Jon motioned for the enlisted personnel to carry on with their business.

"It's good to see you again, too, Sir," said Williams looking straight ahead and not sounding happy.

"You didn't answer my question, Commander," said Summers.

A puzzled look crossed Williams face.

"The Admiral is fine, Sir. I'll let him know you asked about him. We didn't know that you were in the islands, Sir."

The female officer finally glanced over at Summers. She looked from his face to the rows of ribbons on his uniform. Her facial expression did not change, but her eyes had landed on the top ribbon and were as big as saucers.

"My being here is classified, Commander, and you still haven't seen me."

"Understood, Sir."

Jon smiled and leaned over and whispered something to Williams. The reaction was immediate. Williams turned pale and his hands began shaking as he stood at attention. When Jon finished, he leaned back and looked William's square in the eye. The man immediately dropped his eyes to the floor.

"Now, I think you understand, Commander," Summers said. He turned to face the secretary, winking. Handcock blushed looking away.

The secretary turned away hiding a grin.

"Captain," she said, "the admirals are ready for you in the conference room."

Looking beyond Summers, Williams was leaving the outer office.

Summers smiled at the secretary. "Must have had a rough night."

The secretary laughed quietly, while Handcock glared at him. Jon shrugged his shoulders looking down at the secretary, who was still laughing quietly.

"You said Admirals," Summers quietly asked. "How much trouble am I in?"

"The CNO, CINCPAC, and the commander of the *Nimitz* Task Force," replied the secretary, "but I don't think you're in trouble. Second door on the right."

"Thanks," replied Jon.

He left the secretary walking to the second door on the right. He quickly checked himself to make sure he was squared away. His whites were clean, his shoes were shined, and he was ready to meet the brass. He took a deep breath, knocking on the door.

"Come," was the response from inside.

Summers took another deep breath and opened the door. He stepped inside, closing the door behind him. A quick glance around the room showed CINCPAC sitting at the far end of the long conference table. Admiral Cummings stood by one of the windows overlooking the harbor and the fleet. Admiral Kingston sat next to CINCPAC not looking happy. Summers smartly stepped to the opposite end of the conference table coming to attention.

"Captain Jonathon Summers, United States Naval Reserves, reporting as ordered, Sir!"

CINCPAC smiled at Summers. "It's good to see you again Captain, although I have to admit that right now, you're not my favorite person."

Jon kept a straight face continuing to stare straight ahead. "I understand, Sir."

"As you were, Summers," said the admiral forcing a smile, "have a seat."

"Aye, aye, Sir," replied Jon as he relaxed and moved up the opposite side of the table from Kingston. CINCPAC motioned for him to take the seat across from Dick Kingston. Jon complied and flashed a quick look at Admiral Cummings who smiled in return.

"You know everyone here I believe?" asked CINCPAC motioning to the other two admirals.

"Yes sir, I do."

"Good," said the commander of the Pacific Fleet, "let's get down to business then. Give us your impression of the exercise from where you stand, Captain."

Kingston was quiet and indifferent to this point. At the invitation for Summers to speak, he sat straight up in his chair.

"Sir, I don't think anything Captain Summers can add to what we've already discussed will enlighten us further about the exercise. Naval Intelligence wasn't much help, and we don't need to add insult to injury now."

Summers never took his eyes off the admiral sitting across from him. He showed no emotion as Kingston gave him a smug look, folding his hands in front of him.

"Dick, you got your ass kicked at Kaena Point," said an irritated Cummings, "No offense, but I want to hear what the captain has to say."

"As do I," said CINCPAC coolly, "Is there some other reason you don't want Captain Summers to speak, Richard?"

There was a long moment of silence as Kingston stared at Summers. The look of indifference was replaced by one of pure hatred. Summers gazed moved away from Kingston and towards CINCPAC.

"Sir," he said calmly, "may I speak freely?"

The admiral nodded his permission.

"Sir, it's no secret in the service that Admiral Kingston and myself are not friends," said Summers coolly. "As a matter of fact it is no secret among those who know both of us, we go out of our way to avoid each other since we left the academy. Still, I feel Admiral Kingston is a fine officer and exceptional commander. He knows his job and how to get the needed results from his people. I've never known him not to succeed on any assignment he's been given."

Kingston looked stunned by the praise he received from someone he considered an enemy. The CNO and CINCPAC both gave each other surprised looks because they knew what had just been stated was true.

"What was different this time, Captain?" asked CINCPAC.

Summers looked at both CINCPAC and the CNO. The fleet commander leaned forward over the table in anticipation of the upcoming answer, while Cummings just gave Jon a small nod of the head.

"Sir," said Summers looking at CINCPAC, "again request permission to speak candidly?"

The admiral again nodded his approval but looked irritated at the request.

"Sir, I think this entire exercise was a trap for whoever commanded the battle group right from the beginning."

Both CINCPAC and Kingston suddenly looked extremely interested in what Jon was saying. Cummings continued to look out the window.

"The timing of the exercise, to start, right at the holidays. No one wants to be involved in any type of exercise now. You don't approach it seriously because your mind is always on home."

"I don't understand where you're headed with this," said Kingston.

"It's like Valley Forge," Summers explained. "The British didn't expect the Colonials to attack when they did. Ask our people on both sides. None were happy to be there. Additionally, they picked an officer who knew Admiral Kingston, his habits, moods, and most importantly, his reactions to given situations. Someone who could anticipate what he would do before he would do it."

"And who would that have been?" asked Kingston.

It was Jon's turn to be surprised looking at the other two flag officers. The expression on their faces told him Kingston didn't know. He turned back to face Kingston.

"That would have been me, Sir," said Jon holding Kingston's gaze. He watched Kingston flush immediately. The Admiral turned and looked at both his superiors. Both men returned the look saying nothing. Kingston turned back to Summers but kept his temper.

"Since we're speaking candidly, Captain," said Kingston calmly, yet sternly, "I don't appreciate you practicing guerrilla tactics on my command. There are rules wars are fought by, and you violated most of them."

Jon felt like a teenager coming home late from a date with the way Kingston was speaking to him. Before responding, he took a deep breath. "Admiral, your rules are all well and good if your opponent will follow them.

My orders were to throw your timing off in any way I could. The point here is not that I broke the rules, but that there are organizations and even countries out there now that could give a damn about your rules."

"Nothing sheer force can't overcome, Captain. This wasn't a fair test. If I had bee…"

"Been told, Dick?" Summers was starting to allow Kingston's arrogance to get to him. He just raised his voice to a flag officer in front of two other flag officers and called him by his first name. He recovered quickly. "That was the point, Admiral. You couldn't know. You needed to walk into this blind and take the lumps as they fell. Not just for you, but for everyone else who commands a carrier battle group. We can't afford for someone to make this kind of mistake during the real thing. The days of a big conventional war are over. The Gulf proved that. There's no one out there that can meet us head-to-head and win, and they know it. They'll hit and run, like I did with you."

"You were lucky, Summers, and you're not experienced with large unit tactics."

"True, Sir," replied Summers smiling. "There was a great deal of luck involved. The sea was calm enough for the lookouts to spot the periscope of the *Kamehameha*, and that sure as hell was luck. The rest was predictability, not just on your part, but on the part of the other commanders involved in the exercise. We tell the world our tactics every time a battle group deploys to a trouble spot. You can get that information off the Internet."

"You're full of shit, Summers!" said Kingston, his voice raising.

"That's enough Richard!" said CINCPAC looking as upset as Kingston. "So what you're telling us, Jon, is the task force was meant to take a beating."

Jon turned to the fleet commander. "Yes, Sir, that's correct. Although luck played a big role in this exercise as Admiral Kingston said, I was able to control certain things to tip the scales."

"Like what?" asked CINCPAC.

"I was able to control the intel the Battle Group was getting about the exercise. If Admiral Kingston knew I was the OPFOR commander, he would have had the advantage, not me. My orders were to rock the boat in any way I could, to make this point. The rest was due to what you've trained me to do, set a trap and spring it at the most opportune time."

"You certainly proved you're able to do that when you worked for me during the Gulf War," said CINCPAC. "Your orders certainly came from above me, Jon. My bosses should be congratulated on making my day."

The last comment was obviously directed at Cummings. He showed no sign of emotion as he continued to look out the window. There were several seconds of silence before the CNO responded.

"You're right about a lot of things, gentlemen. We did keep 7th Fleet out of the loop on this one because we wanted to make the exact point the captain has discussed. He didn't know exactly what we were after, but obviously figured that out quick enough. The issue I have is he was able to drive that point home so well. This exercise was approved by all the Joint Chiefs so we could see how our people would respond and we got our asses kicked. All the Chiefs will be issuing orders based on the outcome of this exercise to review the security on all American Military installations and response tactics used by units in the field.

"The captain did his job well, almost too well. He showed us to be vulnerable where we didn't think we were and showed us we must be smarter than the other guy. The *might makes right* mentality didn't work here. All it did was increase our losses because we relied too heavily on our strength. It was used against us. It can't happen in the field. I don't think I can say it any plainer. It can't happen!"

There was no response to the CNO. Instead, he turned back from the window smiling at the three men sitting before him.

"Gentlemen, it's Christmas Eve," Cummings said pleasantly. "Let's finish this up and get out of here for the holiday."

"I'll second that," said CINCPAC.

Cummings looked at Kingston.

"Admiral, now you know you were set up from the start and I hope that helps explain the beating you took. Go and enjoy the holiday, Dick. You can deal with everything when you get back in a couple of days."

"Thank you, Sir," Kingston replied looking calmer than earlier. "After the last several days, I need a break. I won't make the same mistakes again."

"That's why we practice these things, Richard," said CINCPAC holding out his hand to Kingston. As they shook, he continued, "Call right after the holiday and we'll look at the exercise and see what we need to change. Now, if you'll give Admiral Cummings and me a minute alone with the captain here, we would appreciate it."

"Yes, Sir!" said Kingston obediently. "Merry Christmas, Sir. Merry Christmas, Admiral Cummings."

Both admirals responded to the greeting as Kingston came to attention and asked to be excused. As he left the conference room, he gave Summers a look noticed by the others. Summers let out a deep breath as the door to the conference room closed.

"I'm afraid Admiral Kingston doesn't like you much, Jon," said CINCPAC. "He can be a powerful enemy."

"Yes, Sir, I understand that. I also must admit to not helping the relationship in the past, throwing fuel on the fire so to speak."

Both CINCPAC and the CNO laughed. Cummings responded, "Just be careful around him, Captain. You know what he's capable of. If I, were you, I wouldn't provoke him? Not so much for what he can do, but what his political allies could do to you."

"Thank you for the advice, Sir. I'll try to avoid the Admiral whenever possible."

"That would be a good policy, Jon," said CINCPAC with a smile. "I want to congratulate you on a job well done and thank you for not picking the obvious fight with Richard. His attempt to subvert your people was unacceptable. He says it was Williams on his own, but there appears to be a history. Anyway thank you for keeping a lid on it."

"Yes, Sir."

"I will admit those last attacks on the task force were overkill, but on seeing why you ordered them, you certainly know how to make your point."

Jon didn't respond to the last comment.

"Good job, Captain," CINCPAC said in closing. "You'll be the talk of the fleet for some time to come."

"I'm not sure that's a good thing in this case, Sir."

Both admirals laughed again.

"Are you going right home, Captain?" asked Cummings.

"No, Sir," replied Jon smiling. "The family came with me, so I think we'll spend some time here before going home. Schools closed for the holiday and like Admiral Kingston, I could use the time off."

Both admirals wished Jon a good holiday and shook his hand, again thanking him for a job well done. Summers left the conference room. The outer office was empty except for the secretaries and enlisted personnel working there. Jon wished all of them a good holiday and walked out into the hallway and to the elevator. He was engrossed in his own thoughts so didn't notice the two people waiting for him.

"Summers!" said a familiar voice.

Summers turned to find himself facing Kingston. His face was flushed, and his movements were aggressive. Standing immediately behind him was the female officer. A quick look around told Summers there was no one else nearby.

"Summers," continued Kingston, "you need to know this isn't over. You humiliated me and I won't stand for that. Your career is just about up."

Summers could see the hate in Kingston's eyes. He held the gaze and his whole demeanor changed. Summers's body shifted involuntarily into a defensive position and calmness seemed to take over as he looked squarely at the admiral.

"Dick, you've been threatening me since the academy," said Summers coldly. "You need to know I'm a little tired of it. You like threatening careers. Go right ahead and do what you must. Just remember that when you're done, it's my turn."

Kingston's expression changed. He expected a loud response when he tried to push the junior officer's buttons. His surprise showed. He looked around seeing no one close enough to hear. He hoped for loud threats and a big scene in front of witnesses. That obviously wasn't happening.

"There was nothing personal in what I did during the exercise. You just happened to be the unlucky bastard to draw the assignment. Our history just made it easier for me to do my job. Let it go! All I want to do is enjoy my holiday and go home, but if you want a fight, you go right ahead and start one. Just remember the rules!"

"The rules?" Kingston said with a puzzled look.

Jon glanced around the admiral at the officer standing behind him. Kingston's immediate reaction was to quickly turn and look at the lieutenant, then back at Summers. There was terror in his eyes. Jon smiled.

"You wouldn't…er…I mean, you know?" Kingston showed uncharacteristic panic.

"Just leave me alone, Dick," said Summers turning and leaving the admiral and his aide standing there. Summers smiled to himself walking away. He hadn't known a thing when he had decided to use the suggestion, but he knew now. He was confident that Kingston would leave him alone unless he provoked a confrontation.

The Saigon Club
Honolulu, Hawaii
December 24, 1994
1500 Hours

The warm afternoon breeze came in off the ocean mixing the smell of the salt air with the aroma of the various oriental dishes set up along the buffet. Men and women danced to music coming from a stereo system in the corner. The Saigon Club was one of the more popular night spots for many of the servicemen and women stationed in the islands. It was also known for serving the finest oriental food in Hawaii. Joshua Ericson went to great lengths to make sure the club and his other restaurant were first class. This club catered to the younger crowd while Ericson's Tropical Breezes Restaurant was considered one of the best sea food restaurants in the United States.

Ericson was an extremely successful and well-respected businessman. He was an accomplished athlete, coach, and artist. He actively participated in foot races and coached swimming at one of the local swim clubs. He recently took up painting stills of military life. His work was well received. When people described Josh and his many activities, they saw the tall, handsome, and distinguished looking man of fifty-six years' old. What always shocked them was the fact he was confined to a wheelchair. A former SEAL, he was wounded on an operation losing the use of both legs. After being medically discharged from the navy, he invested his money wisely opening the Saigon Club. His gift for managing a nightclub and restaurant resulted in the opening of his next venture five years later. Both drew different crowds and were gold mines for their owner.

The current event was the Christmas party for SEAL Team Five. Ericson hosted the event every year, paying for it out of his own pocket. This year many of the guests included the visiting rangers and crew members of the

Kamehameha. As SEAL parties went, the ones he threw were usually quiet. There was a lot of good-natured fun, but there seldom were problems.

Josh sat at a table with an old friend. Walter Samcevic was a retired SEAL who went on to write several successful novels about the Vietnam War and SEALs. Samcevic was Ericson's team leader during his first tour of duty in Vietnam. He and Samcevic stayed in contact and after the latter's retirement from the navy managing to get together once a year. Also sitting at the table were Tim DeCook and his wife, Bob Grant and his wife, and Charlie Naylor and his guest. It was a fun group of people to be with.

They'd been swapping stories about the exercise. Both the special operations troops and the crew of the *Kamehameha* were upset about being taken out of the exercise.

"I just don't understand it," said Grant between sips of beer. "There was no radar or active sonar. How could they have known exactly where we were? I'm not looking forward to the debriefing with Kingston day after tomorrow. The man's a bastard."

"Bob Grant! That's enough," protested his wife, trying to keep her husband out of trouble.

"Sorry, honey," replied Grant sheepishly, "but it's true. He was just as bad when we went through the academy. The arrogant son..."

"Bob!"

"Sorry, honey," this time he remained subdued.

They all laughed at the submarine commander who obviously drank more than his share of the free beer.

"I've only met the man once," said Naylor, his speech slurred, "but I have to agree with your assessment. He's a first-class ass."

"And he doesn't like SEALs which makes him a second-class ass, as well," chimed in DeCook.

They all laughed but Ericson. Samcevic noticed, asking, "You don't' agree, Josh? I've met the man more than once and have never been able to bring myself to like him."

Josh smiled weakly. "I know the man better than any of you. You haven't even begun to describe him. I..."

Before the club owner could go any further, he saw a familiar face walk in the door. An attractive woman in her early forties, with brown hair and a pleasant smile. She was stopped at the door by one of the waiters. Josh waved to the waiter, who pointed him out. The woman waved starting to make her way towards him.

"I'm sorry, if you'll excuse me a minute, I'll be right back," he said wheeling himself through the crowd to meet his newest guest.

Surprisingly, he made it through the crowd faster than she did, meeting her at the far side of the dance floor.

"Josh!" said the woman throwing her arms around the man, giving him a big kiss on the mouth.

It took a few seconds for Josh to catch his breath as he returned the hug.

"Josh, you look terrific!" said Nancy. "As handsome as ever."

Josh was still catching his breath. "Damn, Nancy, when are you gonna dump Jon and come live with me. Many more hellos like that and it won't just be my legs that don't work."

"Sorry, Josh," Nancy blushed. "I was at the hotel alone when you called and couldn't wait to get here to see you. Hell, you're one of the main reasons Jon agreed to take this assignment."

"Jon left a message on my voice mail to that effect. So, where is he?" Josh asked still holding Nancy's hand. There was a special place in his heart for Nancy. When he was so gravely wounded, Jon was wounded as well. Nancy spent as much time consoling him as she did her husband. He credited both with keeping his spirits up when he needed the support. At least until he made the decision to move forward with his life. He smiled up at her.

"Since he's busy saving the world, why don't you come live with me?"

Nancy laughed hugging him again. "With pleasure, as long as you take the three children that come with the deal."

Josh laughed and held his fingers up, so they made a cross.

Nancy laughed. "I always thought you were a fair-weather suitor. Now, I'm sure. Besides, Jon would just go find SEAL Team Five and come looking for us."

It was Josh's turn to laugh. "Well in that case let's stay here and get drunk. When he comes here to get SEAL Team Five, we'll kidnap him."

Nancy laughed again. "Sounds like a plan, sailor. Where to?"

Josh motioned for her to follow him. When they reached the table all the men stood up. Nancy was quick to notice they all were a little wobbly. It brought back memories of days gone by.

"Fight hard! Party hard! Nothing changes," she said under her breath grinning.

"Easy tiger," said Josh squeezing her hand. "We all grow up at some point."

"You're wrong there," she said looking down at her friend with an understanding look. "I didn't mean any offense. I was remembering."

Josh smiled turning his attention to his other guests. As he was about to introduce Nancy, Samcevic said, "Mrs. Summers, I'm Walt Samcevic."

Nancy took the outstretched hand shaking it. "Mr. Samcevic. How nice to meet you? Please call me Nancy."

Josh smiled at his friend. "Hey, she's my girl, buddy. I saw her first."

"But I out-rank you, Josh," Walt replied smiling.

"Ahhh, team-mates to the end," said Nancy and the whole table laughed.

Josh smiled as he introduced everyone at the table. Naylor ran off to find another chair. When he returned, they sat. A waitress immediately appeared.

"What would you like to drink, Nancy?" asked Josh looking around the table to see if anyone else needed one.

"Something tropical would be nice," she replied settling in the chair. Ericson said something to the waitress, and she disappeared.

"Is your husband coming?" asked Charlie politely.

"He should be," said Nancy, "he had some business to finish up and then will track me down."

"He was in SEAL Team Five wasn't he, Ma'am?" asked DeCook.

Ericson answered. "He was in with me. He was with me when I was shot. Saved my life, as a matter of fact. Then this one stayed with me in the hospital until I could make it on my own."

"You guys were doing what?" asked Samcevic smiling.

"Live fire exercise that went bad," replied Ericson smiling at his friend.

Nancy saw Naylor shuffle uneasily in his seat. Their eyes met and he immediately looked away. She hated military secrets.

"Come on, Josh," his friend pleaded, "you lost some guys on that one. Don't give me the live fire exercise shit."

"It was an error in judgment, an accident. That's all. Not worth writing a book about."

"Nancy, what do you think?" Samcevic asked her. "I'm trying to get this old seadog to open up so we can write his story. He's quite a hero, you know."

Naylor looked back at Nancy to see her response to the question. This time, he held her gaze as she answered.

"You're right about the hero part," she said, "to be wounded like he was and to have come back and accomplish everything that he has. He's a hero to both my husband and me. As far as the rest goes, Mr. Samcevic, I lived the other side of it and don't care to do so again."

"Well put, Mrs. Summers." laughed the author, "That's probably why my wife and I are no longer together. Please call me Walt."

Nancy smiled at him and said, "Only if you call me Nancy. When you call me Mrs. Summers, I keep looking for my mother-in-law, God bless her."

Everyone at the table laughed and Naylor nodded approvingly. The talk turned back to the exercise and Nancy was surprised to hear the SEAL Team was taken prisoner. She could hear frustration in the voices of the officers at the table deciding to stay out of the conversation.

"I would really like to spend five minutes with the commander of the OPFOR units," said DeCook. "He cost me a shit load of harassment for getting captured."

"OPFOR?" asked Connie Taylor, Naylor's date. "What's that stand for?"

"Military talk for opposing force," answered Josh.

"I wouldn't be too worried about that," said Grant, "I saw the stats for the exercise, and it looks like we all got suckered in."

"What do you mean?" asked Naylor sipping a beer.

"The first wave of planes and the Marine Recon unit were ambushed and destroyed in the air."

"What! How?" asked DeCook.

"Not exactly sure, but I heard something about a decoy radar site. Anyway, they flew in and suddenly they were blown out of the sky by hidden SAM sites. Then, the OPFOR aircraft, who were hiding somewhere out of radar range, rushed in and fired a missile attack retreating before the *Nimitz* could respond."

"Hit and run?" said Ericson looking at Samcevic. "That's not a normal Air Force tactic. Especially for reserve and guard fliers. Sounds like it wasn't your normal exercise."

"Ambushes?" responded Samcevic. "It's been done before, but you're right. I don't see reserve guys using a special ops tactic on this type of exercise."

Ericson started to laugh, causing everyone to look at him.

"The funny thing is, they just kept coming like that," continued Grant confused with Ericson's reaction. "They'd come in, launch an attack, and then fall back. They never gave us a big fight anywhere. They just kept whittling away until we didn't have anything to fight with. The only ships that didn't register any damage were the other two subs."

"Damn," said DeCook, "if this had been the real thing it would have been worse than Pearl Harbor."

"Pretty good tactic, don't you think, skipper," Ericson said to Samcevic. "When you fight a war of attrition?"

"Yeah," replied the author, "Hit and run, then hit again. Never getting drawn into a big fight because you'll lose the war of numbers. Good tactic. Used to use it all the time in Nam."

It was as if a spotlight went on inside his head. Samcevic turned, looking at his friend, then at Nancy. Ericson nodded. Nancy looked back and forth at both.

"What?" she asked defensively. "What'd I do?"

She made eye contact with Ericson and suddenly understood what they were talking about. She was speechless. Jon never told her why they were being sent to Hawaii, just that there was something to do for the navy. It explained why she didn't see him for three days and why the days he was putting in were so long.

Before they could say anything to everyone, there was a commotion on the other end of the dance floor. Everyone turned to see one of the SEALs and one of the rangers wrestling. Both were big men, in their early twenties and looked to be evenly matched. Reardon and Wiedenkeller circled around the two men, keeping any unwanted interference away from them. Reardon was wearing jeans with the pant legs rolled up and a colorful tropical shirt with the buttons open. Wiedenkeller was dressed as Santa Claus. His red pants were rolled up, like Reardon's, and the fake beard down around his neck. All the dancing stopped, everyone's attention on the wrestling match. DeCook and Naylor were shouting like most of their men, except they were openly putting money on the table. Wives and girlfriends cheered as well.

Nancy leaned over and put her arms on Ericson's shoulders. "You see, Master Chief, nothing changes."

Ericson turned and looked into her deep blue eyes. "You really do miss the navy."

"Only the times like these," she said over the roar of the crowd, "the rest I left behind willingly."

They both turned their attention back to the wrestling match that moved up the ramp towards the front door. Reardon took off his shirt and was now waving it over his head. Wiedenkeller grabbed two large glasses of beer from a passing waitress and jumped in front of Reardon, stopping his movement. He handed the beer to the ranger sergeant and the two of them howled at the top of their lungs and then downed the beer. It became evident to everyone that wrestling was not the only contest going on. The crowd cheered. The two wrestlers fell over the handrail along the ramp leading from the entrance to the main floor, landing in front of the door.

When both men went to get up, they found themselves looking at a pair of polished, white shoes. Both men looked at each other and then up at the man standing in front of them. It was a naval officer dressed in his whites looking down at them. Both men looked at each other, scrambled to their feet, and snapped to attention.

"Sorry, Sir," said the SEAL, "we didn't see you there."

Both men now saw the braid on the bill of the cap and the ranger saw the eagle indicating the rank of captain.

"Shit," the ranger said to himself.

"I assume this is a friendly contest?" said Summers keeping a straight face. He knew full well what was happening.

"Yes, Sir!" replied the SEAL.

"Who's winning?" The question took both enlisted men by surprise.

"I...ahh...I guess it's pretty even so far, Sir," replied the soldier.

"Then you're not done. Carry on, gentlemen," said Summers walking by the two men. Both turned watching him in disbelief.

"Excuse me, Admiral," slurred a voice from the bottom of the ramp, "but this is a private party. Only members of SEAL Team Five are allowed past this point. And you, Sir, are not a member and are not welcome!"

Jon looked down the ramp and saw Reardon leaning against the rail for support. Wiedenkeller scrambled to get next to the sergeant to keep him quiet. The entire room went silent watching to see what the officer would do with the drunken sergeant.

"Senior Chief, it's good to see you again. I see you're dressed for the holiday," Summers said to Wiedenkeller.

"Good to see you, too, Sir," said the chief trying to hold up Reardon. "Sorry about this, Sir. He's a ranger and…"

"A ranger!" said Jon trying not to laugh. "You're a real ranger?"

Reardon pushed Wiedenkeller away trying to stand up straight. "Yes, Sir, First Sergeant George Reardon, First Ranger Battalion."

"Strange, I came here for the SEAL Team Five Christmas party. No one said anything about rangers."

Reardon waved his hand back and forth.

"You don't understand, Sir. There's a bunch of us here from the First Battalion training with SEAL Team… ahhh …"

"Five," said Wiedenkeller.

"Yeah, what he said," continued Reardon, "so we're kinda honorary SEALs, ya see. Right Al?"

Wiedenkeller was not as drunk as Reardon, he was trying to act as sober as he could. "That's correct, Sir."

"Tell you what, sergeant," said Jon waving a waitress over to them. She had several beers on the tray she was carrying, and Jon took them. He handed one to Reardon, one to Wiedenkeller, and kept one for himself. "I'll make a toast and if you drink to it, I'll let you stay at the party."

Reardon looked as if he were thinking about it. Several people started to laugh, including Wiedenkeller.

"Pardon me for askin' Sir," said Reardon, "but are you a SEAL?"

"Sergeant," said Jon speaking softly as he leaned closer to Reardon, "I'll tell you a secret."

"Sir?" Reardon leaned closer.

"A seal is a marine mammal."

"I know that Sir. Cute little things they are."

Wiedenkeller couldn't handle it anymore and started to laugh uncontrollably. Several others joined him, including Naylor.

"I did serve with SEAL Team Five though, a few years back," said Summers pointing to the Naval Special Warfare Trident on his uniform.

"Damn, Sir, you won the Medal of Honor!" said Reardon standing a little straighter.

"Don't change the subject, Sergeant. Will you drink a toast with me or are you headed for the beach?"

"Sir, it will be an honor to drink a toast with you."

Jon raised his glass and waited until most of the people in the room followed suit.

"Ladies and Gentlemen, including you, Sergeant."

There was laughter throughout the room.

"I give you the United States Army Rangers."

"The United States Army Rangers!" repeated everyone in unison. They all watched as both Jon and Reardon finished their beers. Reardon looked at Jon, "Sir, you are a gentleman, even if you are a sailor."

Jon nodded at the compliment and then turned to look at the two young servicemen who were wrestling.

"Gentlemen, I believe I asked you to carry on."

A cheer went up from everyone in the room. The two men looked at each other for a second and then picked up where they left off. Jon walked down to the bottom of the ramp where he was met by Ericson. The two men embraced, and a tear could be seen in Summers's eye.

"Master Chief, it's damn good to see you," said Jon.

"You, too, sailor," said Ericson.

"You haven't seen my wife, have you?"

"Kidnapped her, man," said Ericson, smiling, "knew you'd look for Team Five to find her."

"Say, Master Chief," said Summers standing up straight and starting to push the wheelchair, "I haven't had any real food in three days. You wouldn't have a meal a guy could have, would you?"

"She was right, things haven't changed at all. You're still mooching food." said Ericson.

"And you're still a better cook than my wife. By the way, where is she?"

Ericson pointed to the table. Jon could see Nancy talking and laughing with several of the ladies. She looked over to him and waved. He smiled waving back. When they got to the table, all the men again stood up.

Jon hugged his wife and gave her a kiss. Nancy had consumed just enough alcohol to make the kiss as passionate as she could, not caring about the people at the table.

"Where are the kids?" Jon asked between kisses.

"With the Gateways," said Nancy, her arms around her husband. "It seems that Sean has a new girlfriend."

Jon raised an eyebrow.

"Sarah O'Keefe," continued Nancy.

Jon kissed his wife, "The general must be ecstatic."

"Funny," Nancy kissed him one more time, "that's just what Becky said."

"OK kids let's not go for it right here in my restaurant. They'll close me down. Although I think the crowd might like it," said Ericson.

Jon reluctantly pushed his wife away turning to the table. He reached out and took Grant's hand, shaking it.

"Good to see you again, Bob," said Summers. "How's the new command going?"

Grant responded in kind introducing his wife to Summers. Summers next introduced himself to DeCook and his wife. When he reached Naylor, he repeated the same question he asked Grant. Everyone at the table was surprised to find out the two knew each other. Everyone, except Nancy, who already suspected good old Charlie knew something about both her husband and Ericson she did not. They were even more surprised to find out Naylor's date for the week was the niece of the Chairman of the Joint Chiefs. Ericson finally introduced Summers to Samcevic. Both men met some years before while Samcevic was still in the navy.

"So, how does it feel," asked Ericson when Jon sat down.

Jon looked at his friend for a second before answering. "I guess I don't understand the question, Josh. How do I feel about what?"

"It took the three of us a bit of time," said Josh, indicating both Walt and Nancy, "but we think we know what you've been up to while you've been here in the islands."

Jon smiled looking at his friend. Ericson always was a very cool customer when the two served together. A lot of what he learned about surviving in the military he learned from Master Chief Ericson, so he knew where this game would head if he allowed it to.

"That's a good question, Captain," asked Naylor. "We all came here to get our asses kicked by the weekend warriors. What caused the navy to bring you all the way out here over the holiday?"

Jon looked over to Ericson and then back to Naylor.

"Charlie, for god's sake call him by his first name," said Ericson.

"That's right," said Samcevic, "you take a SEAL and promote him to captain and his brain turns to shit unless you let him out to play. You spend all those years pounding guerrilla tactics into a man and they need to use them.

For as drunk as he was, Grant was the first to figure out what they were talking about.

"Oh my god! No wonder they knew where to find my boat and fire on her. I'll be damned. Used my own tactic against me."

The others at the table still looked puzzled.

"A calm ocean and a submarine running at periscope depth feeling comfortable no one on shore knows they're there." said Ericson.

"But if you know about where to look for the scope of an unfriendly sub that's maybe dropping off commandos, and you're lucky enough to spot that scope…" continued Samcevic.

"Then you not only take a free shot at the sub, but you can wipe out the commando assault force at the same time."

"Jesus Christ, you're good," finished Grant. He got hit in the shoulder by his wife for his last statement.

Naylor and DeCook looked at each other finally figuring out what everyone was talking about. They both looked at Jon and then at Ericson.

"Josh, you're telling us Jon here commanded the troops that captured us," said Charlie, still not believing what he was being told.

"Motherfucker!!" exclaimed DeCook.

Jon very nonchalantly looked over at DeCook saying, "That's exactly what the squadron commander of the first flight off the *Nimitz* said when we took the entire flight out."

There was laughter around the table.

"Dick Kingston has to be having a cow, does he know it was you that beat him?" asked Grant.

Summers nodded in response to the question.

Bob raised his glass into the air, "Merry Christmas, Captain. It was worth having my conning tower shot off."

Ericson raised his glass into the air. "To Jon: Navy SEAL and dragon slayer extraordinaire.

They all toasted Jon. Samcevic asked, "What's the dragon slayer comment about?"

Ericson looked at his friend and just smiled.

CHAPTER 10

TURNING UP THE HEAT

Celebes Sea
Philippines
December 28, 1994
0100 Hours

The inter-island freighter moved slowly through the calm sea. The first officer was standing watch on the bridge with the helmsman. With the seas this quiet he didn't anticipate any problems. There were two other men on the bridge completing the duty watch. Their cargo was a company of Philippine Army infantry.

The first officer worked on local freighters since he was twelve. At thirty-five he considered himself more than qualified to pilot the ship in and out of the reefs anywhere in the islands. This was the second load of soldiers they transported from the islands in the Sulu Archipelago up to the City of Cotabato along the Moro Gulf. He could only guess relations between the Moro separatist and the government were getting worse. He read in the papers of the bombings and assassinations taking place. If they didn't affect his world, he wasn't concerned.

He looked through the binoculars sitting next to the helmsman. He spotted the landmark he was looking for and ordered a gradual turn to starboard taking the freighter into the Moro Gulf. The helmsman turned the wheel, and you could feel the ship respond. The first officer walked out onto the wing off the wheelhouse to enjoy the night air. It was warm. There was a gentle breeze blowing through his long hair.

He was joined by one of the other seamen on watch. Looking out over the deck they saw a few soldiers standing about. Several were even seen leaning over the rail. As the two men laughed, they heard a high-pitched whine and saw something go by the ship at over forty knots. The men looked at each other in confusion and then back at the wake headed towards Basilan Island. They started for the wheelhouse when there was a deafening explosion.

U.S.S. *John Paul Jones*
East of Basilan Island
December 28, 1994
0100 Hours

U.S.S. John Paul Jones was an *Arleigh Burke* class destroyer assigned to patrol the waters around the Philippines because of the recent developments on Mindanao. She'd been on station for almost a week and the crew settled into the dull routine of a long patrol. The night was warm, and the warship moved along at a leisurely pace. She spent the last week patrolling between Borneo and Mindanao. She was monitoring shipping and air traffic going into the southern Philippines, seeing nothing out of the ordinary.

Lieutenant James Smith was the officer of the watch. He stood on the bridge, cup of coffee in hand, and looking at the navigation radar. The seas ahead of them appeared clear except for some smaller commercial ships. Most everyone on the ship was asleep, including the captain. He decided to sleep in his stateroom because Smith was one of his most experienced watch officers.

"Bridge, Sonar!" came a voice over the intercom.

"Bridge, aye!" responded Smith without even thinking.

"Lieutenant," responded the female sonar operator, "we have a submerged contact at the extreme edge of our sonar range, possible submarine, bearing 340."

Smith thought for a second, "Heading of the contact, Rosewood?"

"Appears to be heading 280, Sir. Away from us, but..."

Smith was bothered by the sonar operator's hesitation. "What is it, Rosewood?"

"I don't know, Sir. The submerged contact appears to be tracking contact Baker Three Five. Sir, if I were to guess, it looks like an attack course."

"What's Baker Three Five?"

"Bridge, CIC," came the calm voice of Chief Petty Officer Jesus Martinez. "Contact Baker Three Five is an inter-island freighter. We've been tracking her for several hours. Lieutenant, we don't show anyone's sub in the area. I recommend that we do this one by the book, Sir."

"Roger that, Chief."

"Bridge, Sonar!" Rosewood's tone changed; there was panic in it. "I have torpedoes in the water bearing 340. I repeat high speed propellers in the water. They're on course for Baker Three Five."

"What!" Smith responded. He turned looking at the boson's mate standing watch next to him. The expression on the man's face told Smith he didn't believe what he'd heard either.

"Two torpedoes headed straight for Three Five, Sir," repeated Rosewood over the intercom. "Impact in three...two...one. Sir, the first torpedo missed and is headed into shore."

"Track it!"

"Aye, Sir! Second torpedo impact in three...two...one."

There were several seconds of silence.

"Rosewood?" said Smith.

"Sir, the second appears to have hit the target."

"Confirmed!" said Martinez joining in the conversation. "Contact Baker Three Five has been hit and is sinking."

Smith looked at the boson's mate next to him. "Sound General Quarters."

"Aye, Sir!"

The officer of the deck picked up the telephone next to him and pushed the first button. The alarm for battle stations sounded.

"This better be good, Mr. Smith," growled the captain.

"Yes, sir, it is," Smith said looking in horror at the glow that started to show on the horizon.

Submarine *Kyushu*
Off Basilan Island
December 28, 1994
0100 Hours

The torpedoes were on their way to the target. Both torpedoes were running dead on until the target started to change course. Holiday knew instantly the first torpedo would miss.

"Damn!" he said out loud.

"Target's turning, Sir," said his sonar operator, "first torpedoes going to miss. Second torpedo still running hot, straight, and on target."

Holiday didn't say anything to the sailor, he was doing his job. They were a good crew. Willing to learn. He would be happier if there was more time to get them ready to go into combat.

He wasn't worried about tonight though. The target was an unarmed merchantman carrying troops. Osaka's agents watched the soldiers load over the last two days. The cargo was a full company of two hundred and fifty men plus their supplies. The submarine was in no danger. Holiday knew the United States Navy was in the area. The only traffic they found on their scopes was commercial and fishing traffic.

There was a sudden flash of light in the periscope. Holiday could see flames shooting into the air, as well as burning oil on the water. The small freighter appeared to have listed to port and was going down fast.

"She's going down," said Holiday. There was a cheer from the men in the control room. He raised his hand and the cheering stopped, but a definite air of jubilation remained.

"This is the first of many gentlemen," he said looking through the periscope. "Sonar, is there another target close by?"

"No, Sir," said the sonar man, "Just fishing...."

The sudden silence made Holiday look at the sonar man. The sailor was looking down at the scope in front of him.

"What is it?"

The sonar man looked puzzled. "I have a warship approaching at twenty knots and her sonar has gone active. My guess is it's the American destroyer that's supposed to be closer to Borneo. She's headed right for us, Sir."

"Damn!" said Holiday thinking quickly. "Change course to three five five, all ahead full."

"Aye, Sir!" came the reply.

Holiday sighed, "Time to get out of here, the neighborhood's about to get crowded."

U.S.S. *John Paul Jones*
Celebes Sea
December 28, 1994
0900 Hours

Commander Andy Halsted stood on the wing off the bridge watching the boats look for survivors. He held out little hope of finding anyone else alive, but knew they had to look. He was still having problems believing what his crew was telling him. No world powers with submarines in the area would condone an attack on the ship of another country without some type of provocation.

When he reached the bridge most of his crew were already at their battle stations. Sonar tracked the sub until it disappeared around the far side of Basilan Island. The freighter hadn't put out a distress call, so he ordered communications to put one out. *U.S.S. Doyle* responded immediately, being only one hundred miles away. She sent her three helicopters in advance of her own arrival. Several fishing and commercial vessels also responded to the *Jones'* call for assistance. The Philippine Navy sent coastal patrol boats, but they didn't arrive until after dawn. So far, the rescue ships only found thirty-three survivors. The Philippine Navy reported there was a crew of twenty and two hundred fifty passengers. The launch from the *Jones* picked up the first officer from the stricken freighter, and based on his testimony, they knew what the cargo was. Several of the survivors, including the first officer, were able to tell them they saw the first torpedo miss the freighter. The big question was whose submarine fired it.

Smith, Martinez, and Rosewood came out on the wing and stood at attention behind the captain. He continued to watch the gruesome task going on off the port side of the ship.

Smith cleared his throat. "Sir, we're reporting as ordered."

"As you were," said Halsted without looking at them. He continued to look out at the boats searching the debris floating all around them.

"You did an exceptional job this morning. I'm putting all of you in for a commendation. If you waited to get more data, we wouldn't even have the survivors we do. The sharks have been terrible on this one. They're still striking at bodies as we try to recover them. Terrible thing!"

All three remained silent as their commanding officer turned around to face them.

"In about an hour," he said, "a helicopter carrying some Filipino officials will land on deck and will be allowed to question all of you who were on watch at the time. CINCPAC has approved this, and I want all personnel involved to give them our full cooperation."

"Yes, Sir!" they said in unison.

"In case you haven't heard," continued Halsted, "this freighter was carrying a full army company. It was being redeployed to Mindanao because of the recent trouble there. These people are real interested in what we know, and the brass wants us to cooperate because they're allies. Understood!"

"Aye, aye, Sir!" they replied in unison again.

"Chief," said Halsted looking at Martinez, "I want the entire crew working in CIC at the time ready when they arrive. They may not talk to all of them, but they need to be available."

"Aye, Sir!" replied the chief.

"Lieutenant, the same goes for the watch on duty on the bridge with you."

"Aye, aye, Sir!" said Smith.

"Rosewood, can you pinpoint the area where you lost contact with the first torpedo?"

"Yes, Sir!" replied the sonar operator.

"Are you sure, Petty Officer?"

"Yes, Sir," replied Rosewood squinting her eyes in the bright sun light. "It died right about where I expected it would. It had the sound and range of a Mark 46, Sir. I thought that a bit unusual."

Halsted raised his eyebrows. "Have you mentioned this to anyone?"

"No, Sir," she responded apprehensively.

Halsted thought for a second. "Rosewood don't lie about that if you're asked, just don't volunteer information unless I tell you to."

"Aye, Sir!" replied the young sailor.

"Get everyone ready and yourselves cleaned up. It won't be long, and our guests will be here. Dismissed!"

Halsted returned his attention to the launch just off their port side. They were hauling a relatively intact body on board.

"What a waste," he said to himself shaking his head.

U.S.S. *John Paul Jones*
Off Basilan Island
December 30, 1994
1535 Hours

The afternoon heat radiated off the steel deck of the ship. Halsted sat in the captain's chair on the bridge looking out over the bow. Since the sinking of the freighter, his ship was assigned to assist the Philippine military recover the torpedo that missed the ship. They were currently patrolling back and forth, protecting the Philippine Naval vessels recovering the projectile. Both the Philippine government and the United States Navy were worried whoever sank the freighter would return to recover the torpedo that missed. Halsted didn't mind this duty because it kept his crew on their toes.

Lieutenant Smith was again the officer of the watch. Halsted was pleased with the way the young officer handled the incident two days before. The officer was one of the best he'd seen in the last couple of years.

The telephone next to Halsted buzzed.

"Captain."

"Skipper, we have a helo inbound. It's got a Filipino general's aide on board."

"Did he say what he wants, Chief?"

"No, Sir," replied the sailor, "but I got the impression this wasn't going to be a social call. Very businesslike. Sounds like an intel type."

"More questions. Just what we need," replied Halsted, not sounding pleased.

"Sounds like it, Sir. Should I have my people ready for another interrogation?"

Halsted sighed. "You better, Chief, but they talk to no one until I tell you."

"Aye, Sir!" responded Martinez. "They should be ready to land in about ten minutes, Sir."

"Thank you, Chief."

He thought for a minute, then looked over his shoulder.

"Mr. Smith, there's a chopper coming in with some Filipino officials. Make sure that the flight deck is ready to receive them."

"Aye, aye, Sir," replied the young officer. He picked up the hand set off the wall behind him.

"Captain," said Smith replacing the handset, "it's not a Filipino helo. It's one of the *Doyle's*. They picked up the officer from one of the Filipino ships and are five minutes out. He'll be with us for a while."

"Thank you, Mr. Smith," replied Halsted. "Have an officer meet our guest and escort him to the wardroom. I'll be in communications for a few minutes, and then I'll be in the wardroom."

"Aye, aye, Sir!"

Halsted got up from his chair leaving the bridge. He went down a ladder stopping at the first door he came to. He walked into the communications room and was greeted by the petty officer on duty.

"Good afternoon, Captain."

Halsted smiled. "Good afternoon. Could you get me Pearl Harbor on the line, please?"

The petty officer returned his smile. "Right away, Sir."

It took a minute, but Halsted found himself talking to his commanding officer. To his surprise, he found out the admiral already knew of the arrival of their guest.

"Andy, this is important," said the admiral. "They're implying the United States is in some way responsible for this disaster. I'm not sure what's behind the implication, but your new mission is to find out what they're up to. The officer on his way to you is the aide to the general in charge of their intelligence operation. His boss is on his way here. Either way, we'll find out shortly what the implications are. I understand this guy is pretty sharp, so don't let your people patronize him."

"Understood, Sir," responded Halsted. "How much access to the ship do I allow my guest, Sir?"

"Don't be impolite, Andy," replied his boss without hesitation, "but you will not compromise any of our operations. You're currently our on-scene commander."

"Aye, aye, Sir."

"Andy."

"Yes Sir?"

"Keep me informed. Hourly, if you feel it's necessary. I'll get back to you no matter what I'm involved in. If there's anything we need to do right now, it's getting to the bottom of this mystery here. Be tactful. The political waters we're currently navigating are treacherous. The Philippines is considered an ally and with the problems they're having in your current patrol area I'm sure you understand the point I'm trying to make."

"Yes, Sir. I do," Halsted replied. "We'll do what we have to, Sir."

"Good man, Andy."

"Thank you, Sir. I better go meet my guest."

"Good luck, Andy."

"Thank you, Sir."

As the connection went dead, a sailor came to the hatch of the communications center. Halsted set down the handset looking at the man.

"Captain?" said the sailor, "Captain Sanchez is in the Officers' Wardroom waiting for you, Sir. Mr. Smith sends his compliments and is awaiting further orders."

The captain smiled walking out of communications and into the hallway.

"Tell Mr. Smith to continue with his patrol and I'll be in the wardroom with our guest."

"Aye, aye, Sir!" replied the sailor.

Halsted went to the nearest ladder and down to the main deck where the Officers' Wardroom was located. An armed sailor stood watch at the hatch. As Halsted approached the sailor came to attention. Inside the wardroom he could see a Philippine Army officer looking at pictures on the bulkhead. He looked tired, but the uniform still looked sharp and fresh. He had the bearing of a man who was used to getting his way and looked to be intelligent and well educated. Halsted turned his attention back to the sailor by the hatch.

"As you were," the sailor relaxed. "No one is to be allowed in here without my permission."

"Understood, Sir."

The man stood looking at a painting of John Paul Jones. Halsted entered the room, and he came to attention.

"As you were, Captain," said Halsted trying to sound relaxed. "I'm Commander Andy Halsted, Captain of the *John Paul Jones*. What can I do for you today?"

"Captain Jorge Sanchez at your service, Captain," replied Sanchez. "I'm here on an inquiry from my commanding officer."

"Your commanding officer is in the intelligence business, I'm told."

Sanchez looked surprised. He replied cautiously. "Yes, Captain. General Mangoba is on his way to Pearl Harbor regarding this matter. I would like to talk to members of your crew about the sinking of the freighter the other night."

"A team from your government has already done that. You're covering ground already traveled, Captain. Is there another reason you want to talk to them?"

Sanchez saw he was going to have to be direct.

"Yes, there is, Captain. We have recovered an American mark 46 torpedo right where your people said we would find it. How come you didn't tell the investigators you knew the torpedo was American?"

Halsted looked Sanchez squarely in the eyes.

"Your people never asked, and we only suspected it was a Mark 46."

"Your people said nothing. Is that normal procedure?" asked Sanchez looking for a reaction.

"I did the same thing you and your boss would have done in the same situation," said Halsted smiling. "My people were told to answer the questions they were asked directly and not to volunteer any information. Your people never even asked if we suspected anything. Just direct questions which got direct answers. They also never were told that my sonar person feels the sub was a diesel. At least it made noises like one."

"I apologize, Captain, if I implied your people deliberately kept information from the investigators," said Sanchez rubbing his eyes. "You're correct. I would have done the same thing in your place."

Halsted smiled.

"Call me Andy. Say, you look tired, would you like some coffee or something?"

"That would be nice, Captain," said Sanchez, seeming to relax. "I've been going for so many hours without a rest that if I slow down, I might fall asleep."

"Then you can crash in the extra stateroom we have. Have you eaten at all?"

"Not in some time."

Halsted walked over to a phone hanging on the bulkhead picking up the handset. He pushed a button on the telephone and waited.

"Bridge, Lieutenant Smith," said the voice at the other end.

"Mr. Smith, Captain Sanchez will be with us at least overnight. He'll need quarters and we'll be using the wardroom to ask our people some more specific questions. Have the galley send up whatever food they might have and plenty of coffee. Both you and Chief Martinez have your people on call."

"Aye, aye Sir!"

Halsted turned to the Filipino officer. "Do you need any help with the torpedo? I have a couple resident experts on the mark 46 on board."

Sanchez looked surprised. "That would be nice, Captain. All of ours are out of Luzon and won't be here for some time."

"Mr. Smith," speaking back on the telephone, "contact *Doyle* and have her take our patrol position. When they verify, set course for the site where the Philippine Navy has found the torpedo. Also, get me a yeoman down here to help with the statements and make sure Captain Sanchez has someone assigned to him around the clock while he is on board."

"Aye, Sir. Right away."

Halsted hung up the handset and looked back at his guest. The officer looked at him in amazement. "I must be honest, Captain. I didn't expect this much cooperation."

Halsted smiled, "We have nothing to do but cooperate. My boss said to be polite and that I can do. Ask anything you want. I have the feeling you'll get all the cooperation you need and, hopefully, we can find out who's behind this. Now, let's look at who you need to talk to."

King Kamehameha Hilton
Honolulu, Hawaii
December 31, 1994
0930 Hours

Jon and Nancy brought the kids to the swimming pool early. They planned to spend part of the morning and early afternoon shopping and site seeing.

The kids were then going to the Gateway's where they would spend the night. They were going to a New Year's Eve party with Kevin and Kathy Gateway at Josh Ericson's restaurant. It was a formal gathering, so Jon would be wearing his dress whites, while Nancy needed to shop for something to wear. Fortunately, Kathy knew where to go shopping to get what Nancy needed. Today was just a quick run around Honolulu for the last time. They would be on the plane for home tomorrow.

The boys where in the pool for about twenty minutes. Jon went in for a few minutes, swimming to loosen up. He got out and was reading the newspaper and a book he was trying to finish up. He was wearing his swimsuit, a colorful shirt, and an oversized straw hat. Nancy laughed because he'd gone out of his way to look like a tourist. She sat in the lounge chair next to him trying to work on her tan. She was wearing a tasteful one-piece bathing suit. She was pleased that she was able to relax and work on her tan almost everyday since being here. She was even happier Jon's assignment in the islands ended early and he was able to help her take the kids around to all the sites. She was not sure who was worse around the grass skirts though, her husband or her oldest son.

Nancy lay on the lounge with her eyes closed and could hear the kids laughing in the pool. She could also hear people walking up and down the patio around the pool. She was enjoying this last day in the sun before returning to the cold and snow of western New York.

"Have I ever told you, Jaime my friend, about my high school classmate who married the prettiest girl in New York State?" said a familiar voice from Nancy's past. "She always did look good in a bathing suit."

Nancy opened her eyes to find an oriental man standing over her. He was looking down at her, a big, toothy smile on his face.

"I'll be a...," said Nancy jumping up hugging Mangoba. "What are you doing in Honolulu?"

"I'm here on business, unfortunately. Where's that pirate of a husband of yours?"

"Honey, quit flirting with every foreigner that comes by the pool, will you?' said Jon looking over his newspaper.

Robbie looked over to where Jon was sitting and started to laugh. He let go of Nancy and quickly moved over to his old friend. Both men threw their arms around each other and hugged.

"Still the master of disguise," said Mangoba. "If I hadn't recognized Nancy, I would have walked out of the hotel without thinking twice."

"You always were better at recognizing women," said Nancy with a smile.

Mangoba laughed and hugged the woman again. Standing nearby stood an older man looking uneasy. Summers took off his straw hat and walked over to the man holding out his hand.

"My name is Jon Summers," said Jon in perfect Filipino. "I apologize for my friend's bad manners in not introducing us."

The older man took Jon's outstretched hand. He looked genuinely surprised at how well Jon addressed him in his native tongue.

"I'm Jaime Franco," said the older man in excellent English. "I'm here with General Mangoba on business."

"Nancy," said Mangoba, "your husband's still a showoff."

"True," she said, "but that's why I married him."

"Jaime," said Mangoba, "Jon went to the same high school I did when I was an exchange student in the United States. Nancy was his sweetheart then and now has the misfortune to be his wife. Jon is also in their naval reserves, and from what I've heard isn't really popular with their regular navy right now. He just beat their best and brightest in a big war game."

Franco's eyes seemed to light up. "Ahhh, Mr. Summers, it seems you are the talk of the navy. They don't like to lose. I'm a policeman by trade and collecting information is also my job. In the short time I've been here, that defeat seems to be the talk of your navy, although they don't call you by your proper name."

"That's right," said a voice behind them. "I haven't heard Jon referred to by his proper name since just before Christmas. Then I guess that depends on whose perspective you're looking at it from."

Everyone turned to find Vice Admiral W.C. Putnam standing behind them. Admiral Putnam was CINCPAC's head of intelligence and considered one of the top people in the field. Putnam was dressed in whites and accompanied by a chief petty officer.

"Admiral," said Mangoba, "sorry to keep you waiting."

"No problem, General," said the admiral, "now that I know you're acquainted with Jon, I know better how to deal with you. How's your vacation, Jon?'

"Fine, sir," said Jon apprehensively.

"Mrs. Summers," said Putnam as he took her hand, "it's been a long time. You are looking as pretty as ever."

Nancy never liked the politics required for navy wives but managed to compromise with her husband in the past because she did enjoy the attention that came her way as Jon was promoted up the chain of command. Putnam was always one of the good guys in her mind. She liked the way he took time for the families of his subordinates.

"I'm doing quite well, Admiral," she responded blushing slightly. "Thank you for asking. You haven't caught us at our best though."

"The fact you know General Mangoba here tells me you could be right," laughed Putnam, "but other than that, you're on vacation. Far be it for me to tell your husband how to dress."

They all laughed.

"Nancy, I have to ask you a favor," said Putnam. "I would like to borrow your husband for a couple hours to help with an issue we're looking into."

Nancy's facial expression showed her disappointment.

"Nancy, I promise, I'll have him back here by noon," said Putnam almost pleading.

Nancy smiled at how uncomfortable Putnam looked. That was why she considered him one of the *good guys*. He cared about the families and what military life could do to them.

"Make it eleven thirty and you can have him. We have an appointment at noon."

"With whom?" asked Putnam. "I'll talk to them and make things right if you're a few minutes late."

Nancy pointed over her shoulder at the three boys swimming in the pool.

"Eleven thirty it is," said Putnam smiling, "even if I have to fly him back."

"Thank you, Admiral," said Nancy smiling. "The boys will appreciate that."

"Just good military strategy, Nancy," said Putnam chuckling. "Four against one aren't good odds."

Putnam and his driver pulled into the reserved parking space for him next to the building. Summers followed them in a second vehicle. Security gave them no trouble entering the base and the additional security check point to enter the lot was equally unchallenging. Jon guessed it was because of Putnam. Jon exited the rental car he was using. As they walked, Putnam explained why Robbie and the policeman were in Hawaii.

"So the torpedo is a Mark 46?" asked Jon.

"Yes," said Mangoba, "but I don't believe it came from an American vessel like some of my countrymen have alluded to. You have absolutely nothing to gain by sinking one of our merchant ships."

"And everything to lose," said Franco coming into the conversation for the first time.

"I don't mean to sound rude, Captain Franco," said Putnam ushering everyone past the front security desk, "but no one has told me why a Homicide detective from the Davao Police Department is accompanying the head of the Filipino intelligence service to follow up on a torpedo. It looks to be a military intelligence matter and not one for the police."

Mangoba opened his mouth as if to say something, but Franco put a hand on his shoulder stopping him.

"General Mangoba and I are working on the same thing. Someone is attacking and killing people in our country, and I believe they're all connected."

"Even this last incident?" asked Putnam.

"Yes," answered the policeman. "I don't understand how yet, but they're all connected in some way. I'm also not sure these attacks were done by separatists."

They entered the Admiral's office. Putnam motioned for everyone working there to carry on.

"So what you are saying, Jaime," Summers clarified, "is the Davao University attack, the attack on Princesa, the car bombing in Pagadian, all these ambushes and assassinations, and now this sinking of the freighter are connected?"

Everyone but Mangoba seemed surprised Summers knew of all the incidents. Franco looked with interest at the naval officer. Jon changed before coming. Jaime knew little of the American military but recognized the naval Special Warfare Trident the man wore over his pocket. Judging by the number of ribbons under the insignia, he did his job well.

"I'm interested in how well you know my country, Captain," said Franco. "No one else here seemed to know about most of those incidents."

Putnam flushed with embarrassment.

Summers looked Franco in the eyes. He saw no malice. It was just a simple question.

"I was stationed at Subic Bay for a while and worked with Robbie when we were both a lot younger. My father was also in the Philippines during World War II, so it's always held a special interest for me. Because of that and the fact my relationship with Robbie goes back to high school, I tend to zero in on any information coming to me about your country. I gather you're not putting much stock in this new separatist group operating on Mindanao?"

The smile came back to Putnam's face while he listened to the exchange between the two men.

"The MFA is well funded but came out of no where. It seems to be gaining a following, but the people we talk to say these people don't have the same political convictions the MNLF and other groups seem to have. I'm finding evidence they're more profit oriented than political."

"That would indicate some sort of outside funding?"

Franco nodded and started to say something when Putnam decided that it was time to regain control of the conversation.

"Gentlemen, let's get back to the matter at hand so I don't get in trouble with the captain's wife."

They all chuckled.

"You are all aware of the fact the torpedo that missed the freighter is an American Mark 46."

Everyone at the table agreed.

"Overnight, the torpedo was raised and based on information supplied by the General's people and the captain of the *John Paul Jones*, we've been able to determine this torpedo was sold to the Japanese government."

Both Mangoba and Franco looked at each other in surprise. Summers seemed to be deep in thought.

"This could have serious political repercussions. The Japanese have done much to repair their reputation since World War II, but there are many in my country who still don't trust them," said Mangoba.

"Sir," said Summers, "I'm going to guess the Japanese haven't been very cooperative, have they?"

"No, they haven't," said Putnam looking surprised. "After we gave them the serial number last night, they won't even return any of our calls. We know they were sent the torpedo. Damn, we can even tell you who in their navy signed for it. They've just stopped talking to us."

Summers turned to Mangoba.

"Robbie, I assume you agree with Jaime's assessment of the situation on Mindanao or the two of you wouldn't be here together?"

Mangoba cocked his head. "You're correct, my friend. Where are you headed with this?"

Summers waved his hand as if to put off his friend's question.

"I'm going to ask you this and I would like an answer even if you don't have the facts to substantiate it. Who do you think is financing this group?"

Mangoba gave his friend a hard look. He glanced at Franco, who was studying Summers's face.

"You still like to walk the line, my friend," said Mangoba. "This is an internal Philippine Government matter and you're asking me to tell you confidential secrets that even many of my own people don't know?"

Summers smiled.

"I can respect that, Robbie, so let's approach this in a different way. I'll tell you what I suspect, and you can either deny or keep silent about what I say."

Mangoba nodded his acceptance, never taking his eyes off his friend.

"You've talked to the MNLF and other known separatist groups, and they've denied having anything to do with these operations. If anything, they're being blamed for much of this by your government and their popularity is declining. From what I've been able to pick up, this new group is well trained and well equipped. I'm also going to guess the ones you've been able to capture or kill have some type of criminal past. That's not uncommon for someone to be involved in this type of business, but by your own admission you're not seeing the idealists normally drawn to this type of thing. In Princesa they killed without discretion. Not the way an army of liberation acts. You're dealing with someone who is looking for something you have on Mindanao. Natural resources would be my guess. Now we have a connection with Japan and you're looking to find out if the Japanese are invading again after fifty years. How'd I do?'

Mangoba and Franco looked at each other saying nothing. Putnam smiled, winking at Summers.

"You are very good, Captain," said Franco. "I am not sure what classified information the General has, but I'm trying to solve several murders. We've found we have the same goals and have come to the same conclusions. These are not your usual separatists. They are cruel, vicious, and sadistic. While the people in the MNLF are committed, they are not murderers as a rule. These people seem to thrive on it."

"Do you have any idea why the Japanese government is not contacting you, Admiral?" asked Mangoba.

Putnam did not answer immediately. He looked at a note Summers scribbled on a piece of paper. He looked at the Philippine general saying, "All of our people appear to agree as to why they don't respond. They lost a diesel submarine last year during maneuvers off their southern coast. There was never any wreckage found where the boat was supposed to have been operating. Vanished without a trace."

"And now the United States is asking about a torpedo found after the sinking of a freighter," said Mangoba thinking out loud. "I wouldn't respond back either."

Putnam chuckled at Mangoba's response. "The reason I wanted Jon to join us is I know he has different contacts in the Japanese intelligence community from the rest of our people. Hopefully, he'll have better luck."

They all turned to look at Summers who was deep in thought. He looked back at the admiral.

"I'm not even sure I can talk my contact into working with us. If this is what we think, the Japanese are going to be furious and will want to be part of any investigation that might help them find out what happened to the sub and its crew."

"I'm not sure my government will allow that," responded Mangoba.

"Robbie," Summers said quietly, "if you want to get the information we're looking for, you may have to ask your government to be flexible on this one. If my contact is willing to help, you'll find he will be willing to come to terms with your superiors. He'll want to be part of the investigation to get the answers they want."

Franco looked at the general. "My friend, right now all we have is a collection of puzzle pieces. None of them seem to come together even though we know they're all connected. If this is a way to connect more of those pieces, then we have to convince our people this is the path we need to go down."

Mangoba thought for a minute. He wasn't one to agonize over decisions but knew no matter what he did here today, he would come under fire. He knew he needed to look at all the possibilities and decide what would be the best for his country.

"I think I can sell that to Tobi," said Summers, holding his friend's gaze. "Now all I have to do is find him."

"Use the phone on my desk, Captain," said Putnam. "While Jon is calling whoever Tobi is, would you gentlemen like some coffee?"

While Summers made his call, Putnam moved to the door and asked the secretary to have coffee brought in. Summers was speaking Japanese to someone on the phone. Putnam sat down next to his guests shrugging his shoulders.

"I have no idea who he's talking to or what he's saying," Putnam said. "All I know is he has different contacts in Japan than my people do."

Summers raised his voice. He wasn't yelling, but it was obvious he was making a point.

"If things are normal in Japan, he's currently dealing with a self-important bureaucrat," commented Mangoba.

"What makes Japan any different than the Philippines?" asked Franco with a straight face.

"Or the United States," added Putnam without blinking.

All three men shared a looked and started to laugh. There was a knock at the door and a sailor entered pushing a cart with a coffee pot and some mugs on it. He left the cart next to the admiral leaving without a word. Smiling, the admiral poured the coffee and served his guests. Summers raised his voice again, still speaking Japanese.

"I don't think Jon needs any coffee," said Mangoba. "He sounds worked up enough, Admiral."

They laughed again. Summer's voice got softer, he now seemed to be talking to someone he knew. The conversation became more intense, as opposed to the superficial bluster of before. Suddenly there was silence. Summers got up, walking over to the table.

"My contact is on hold and he's willing to speak to us. The only condition is he goes by the code name I know him by. His identity is a secret, but I assure you, he speaks for the Japanese government. You also need to know they will be recording the conversation and expect that we will be doing the same."

The admiral quickly picked up the phone saying something quietly into it. He set the handset back in its cradle.

"Anyone have any questions?'" asked Summers.

There were none, so Summers pushed the button on a speaker phone.

"Tobi?" asked Summers. "Are you still there?"

"Yes, Jon, I am," said a voice in perfect English.

"Tobi, present with me are Admiral Putnam of the United States Navy, General Roberto Mangoba of the Philippine Army, and Captain Jaime Franco of the Davao Police Department."

"It is nice to meet all of you. Admiral Putnam, your reputation precedes you."

"Whatever Jon has told you is a lie," said Putnam.

There was laughter from the other end of the line.

"I don't think he did, sir. He said you had a sense of humor. I also know of General Mangoba. I don't envy the position you've been put in, sir. To make peace where there's none is a difficult task."

Mangoba looked at Franco as he answered. "I hope I'm up to the task, sir."

"My information is that you are. I wish you luck."

"Thank you," said Mangoba sincerely.

"Tobi," said Summers, "everyone knows you are recording this conversation and they'll only address you by the name we are currently using."

"Very good, Jon," replied Tobi. "Let me start by answering the inquiries Admiral Putnam's people made earlier. The serial number of the torpedo you asked about, Admiral, does match one of the Mark 46 torpedoes the United

States sold my country. As your people have correctly guessed, it was on the submarine we assumed was lost at sea. We're now reassessing that theory."

"Tobi, I'd like to ask a question?" asked Mangoba.

"Go ahead, General."

"First, I'd like to say we have the torpedo in our possession and would allow your inspection of it under controlled circumstances. If it'll give you any clues as to what happened to your vessel, we are more than happy to cooperate."

"That's more than gracious, General," said the voice. "My government would be extremely interested in doing that and will meet any conditions your government may wish to set. Our top priority is for us to determine what happened to our submarine and her crew."

"That's understandable," said Mangoba, "and under these circumstances, I believe cooperation will be mutually beneficial because someone is using your submarine to kill our people. Would the United States wish to be involved?"

Putnam took a couple seconds to think about his answer.

"Gentlemen, the United States is obviously interested in this for several reasons. We would be more than willing to offer our help to resolve this matter. This is an issue between your two countries, and we won't force our way into any solution. If you ask, we will be there for both of you. We obviously feel that there is now a safety issue with a possible renegade submarine sailing about. I would guess our naval presence in the area would increase to ensure safe passage of American flag vessels. Other than that, it would be up to your governments."

"That sounds like a reasonable response," said Mangoba, "Unless Tobi has an objection, I would like some technical experts made available."

"No objection on our part," said Tobi. "Technical assistance would be welcomed by us as well. I assume, Admiral, that will be from the United States Navy?"

Putnam finished taking a sip of coffee, "Or from the manufacturer, Tobi."

"More than acceptable," came the reply.

"General, my next question will be much more sensitive, and you may not be able to answer it immediately, but we obviously would like an opportunity to get our submarine back and find out what happened to her crew. I understand having my people running about asking questions would make your government nervous in the current situation. I am open to suggestions."

"You're correct about that," confirmed Mangoba. "I'm sure after conferring with my superiors, we'll be able to come to some agreement. My government would feel the same way if the situations were reversed, and our people were missing. You understand our current issues will dictate what they decide?"

"Yes, I do, General," said Tobi. "You're being more than gracious in the matter. I'll call you in two days at your office to see what progress you've made in this case. I don't expect it will be much, but it'll give us a chance to continue our dialog on the topic."

"Agreed."

"My curiosity is peaked, Captain Franco," said Tobi, "Why are you here with these spooks? An honest policeman such as yourself normally doesn't travel with the Roberto Mangoba's of your country."

Franco smiled. "That seems to be the most asked question of the day, sir, but has a simple answer. General Mangoba and I seek the same people for different reasons. We seem to be getting farther working together than we were separately."

"Not what I would call a match made in heaven, but I wouldn't want the two of you chasing me."

There was laughter from around the table.

"You are too kind, Sir," replied Franco.

This time, Tobi laughed. "Don't sell yourself short. My people just investigated your background, and you are an exceptionally successful detective. Combined with the good general, you two make a formidable team. You both have reputations for being relentless in your pursuit of your enemies. I'm sorry, that's a poor choice of words. I should say suspects. None the less, you're both extremely good at what you do and if the partnership is doing well, then I don't give the people you're after much of a chance."

"Thank you for taking the time to speak with us, Tobi," said Summers.

"It's I who should thank you, Jon," replied Tobi. "We would have sulked here until forced into action. Loss of face can do unhealthy things to people. You have offered us a productive way to regain that face."

"Tobi, you would have dealt with it the same way. Bureaucracy just seems to get in the way sometimes. Best to everyone."

"And to your family, my friend. Have a good New Year."

The telephone line went dead, and they all looked at each other.

"Well," said Putnam, "no major resolutions but I think we've given you some running room, General."

Mangoba nodded, "Thank you, Admiral, and thank you, Jon. We know several new facts I must report to my superiors. I would also like to get back to Mindanao as soon as possible, but I'm afraid that will have to wait until tomorrow. Is there somewhere I can make some calls? The line doesn't have to be secure."

Putnam smiled. "You can use my desk if you like. The line is secure, and you should have no problems getting through."

Summers stood up and faced Putnam. "Sir, if you're done with me, I'd like to be excused."

Putnam looked at the junior officer saying, "Jon, I can't tell you how much you've helped this morning. I might even get bonus points from Nancy because you're out of here on time, actually early,"

Putnam rose shaking Jon's hand. "I guessed it would be a matter of pushing the right button in Tokyo to get some resolution. I'm glad you were available."

"I was glad to help, Sir."

Mangoba and Franco rose from their chairs. Mangoba came around the table giving his friend a hug.

"Thank you, my friend," said the Filipino. "I can't tell you how much you've helped us. Would you and Nancy do me the honor of allowing us to take you to dinner tonight?"

Summers put his hand on Mangoba's shoulder. "Sorry, Robbie, but we have a previous engagement. Why don't you and Jaime come with us to the New Year's party we're going to. You know the host. I know Josh Ericson won't mind, as a matter of fact I know he would insist knowing you're in town."

Mangoba became serious. "The Master Chief was seriously injured the last time I saw him. Has he recovered?"

Both Summers and Putnam laughed. Franco looked puzzled, "I assume that indicates he did."

"No, Jaime," explained Mangoba, "he was paralyzed and confined to a bed the last time I saw him."

Putnam chuckled. "General, now I know you need to go with Captain Summers. About the only thing Josh Ericson won't beat you at is the dance contest, and then he'll give you a run for your money. He's still confined to a wheelchair, but he runs two of the nicest clubs on the island. There's even a rumor that' he'll venture into politics."

Mangoba stood looking at the two Americans.

"Rob," Summers said walking towards the door, "we'll call your room since we're at the same hotel and go together. Don't look so lost, you'll have a good time."

Franco thought it looked to be an interesting evening.

Ericson's Tropical Breezes Restaurant
Honolulu, Hawaii
December 31, 1994
2300 Hours

The evening progressed quickly, and everything seemed to be going well. Ericson was glad to hear Mangoba was in town and was all too happy to include him on the guest list for the evening. His restaurant was considered one of the finest in the islands and he always made a big deal about New Years. There were several large parties, all having a good time. He was even willing to tolerate Kingston and his party, but was pleased Summers decided to keep his distance. It was obvious from the moment Kingston saw Jon at Ericson's table he wasn't happy to be in the same room.

Kingston's party numbered about twenty. He was entertaining visiting businessmen for the navy. Josh made his way around to all the parties through the course of the evening expressing his thanks for their patronage. Kingston's party was the last to be visited. Kingston was polite, knowing of Ericson's connections in the navy and politically, but went no farther. Ericson knew this was because Summers was sitting at his table, along with other current and former team members. Ericson wheeled up to the table just as Jon and Nancy returned from the dance floor. Nancy was laughing and hanging onto her husband's arm. Ericson held her chair for her as she sat down between them. On the other side of Jon sat Kevin and Kathy Gateway. The Gateways were not only friends of the Summers but were also regular customers at the restaurant. Kevin took over the family publishing business from his uncle moving the family to Hawaii. While they weren't good friends, Ericson considered Kevin among his best and most loyal customers. Next to the Gateways sat several of the naval officers from the Teams stationed out of Pearl Harbor and their wives. This group included DeCook and his wife, Amy. Coming around the table sat Walt Samcevic and his date, as well as two other former SEALs and their wives. Next to Walt sat Mangoba and Franco. All were eating and talking.

"So how's the music skipper?" Ericson asked Summers.

"I just love the orchestra, Josh," replied Nancy. "We don't get out to do this enough with Jon being so busy."

Summers laughed looking at his friend. "Do you like how I threw my voice on that one?"

All of them laughed. Ericson was glad to see his former commanding officer was doing well since they last served together. There was a time shortly after they returned from their last mission, he thought Summers would allow himself to be consumed by the political mess that followed. He was happy to see Jon managed to put that behind him.

"You know," said Nancy, "I enjoyed that so much, I think I'd like to dance again."

"Sorry," said Jon holding up his hands in surrender. "I'm danced out, babe. You've got more energy than me."

Nancy laughed. "No stamina, Summers? Civilian life has made you soft. You used to be able to dance most of the night."

"That's true skipper," said Ericson. "You did used to be quite the party animal as I remember."

"Master Chief, you're supposed to support your commanding officer," said Summers sounding hurt.

"I bow to a greater authority," replied Ericson tipping his head to Nancy and waving his right arm in a gesture of respect one would show a monarch.

Nancy laughed and bowed her head in return. "Thank you, Mr. Ericson. You obviously are a gentleman and sensitive to the needs of a woman. Captain Summers I'm waiting. Shall we dance?"

The entire table laughed. Nancy rose from her chair, holding out her hand to her husband.

"I believe we call this mutiny in the navy. My former shipmates, respected officers of the service, and my friends all plotting against me," said Summers mockingly. "Where's the respect that was supposed to be accorded the rank."

DeCook said, "Correct about the mutiny, Sir. Mrs. Summers is prettier than you."

Nancy looked her husband with a big smile on her face and shrugged her shoulders.

"You might as well surrender sailor; you seem to be outnumbered."

Everyone laughed.

"You Americans," said Mangoba rising from his chair and walking around the table. "You really don't know how to dance with a woman. Mrs. Summers, would you do me the honor of dancing with me?"

When he asked, Mangoba bowed slightly from the waist and used the same arm gesture Ericson used. Everyone at the table roared with laughter. They laughed even harder when Nancy curtsied in return.

"Why thank you, General," she replied in her best southern drawl. "It would be an honor."

She turned to her husband sticking out her tongue. More laughter followed making them the loudest table in the restaurant. Summers noticed the disapproving look thrown their way by Kingston. He looked at Ericson and poked him, pointing to Kingston sitting on the other side of the room. The admiral turned away, seeing he was noticed. Both men laughed.

"Now, General, please be gentle," continued Nancy in her drawl, playing to the crowd. "I just couldn't bear it if you weren't gentle."

"As gentle as always, Miss Scarlet," replied Mangoba doing his best Rhett Butler.

As the two of them reached the dance floor the laughter subsided, and Jon turned to Ericson. "Josh, who are the civilians at the table with Kingston? I know the officers are from his staff, but I don't know the civilians."

Ericson turned to look at Kingston's table again.

"Every year one of the Admiral's gets the job of taking any of the contractors in the islands over New Years out to a party. I guess this year it's Kingston's turn."

"So, you're telling me they're contractors?" asked Summers.

"I guess. Why?"

"Because I know that Japanese gentleman sitting third from the end, by Kingston."

"From where?" asked Ericson looking more puzzled.

"It's a long story," said Summers as he got up from the table and started across the restaurant, "I'll tell you when I get back."

Josh tried to protest, but it fell on deaf ears. Summers crossed the restaurant quickly coming up behind the admiral, so he couldn't see him. Both Williams and Handcock saw him approach, stopping what they were doing. Williams looked more nervous than he usually did while Handcock smiled. The fact both of his aides were looking passed him caused Kingston to turn. He was smiling and laughing at a story that one of the contractors was telling. He continued to smile, but his eyes showed his hatred for the captain.

"Summers, welcome," said the admiral. "To what do we owe the pleasure of this visit?"

Summers smiled in return. He hoped his own displeasure at being so close to his old academy adversary didn't show as easily as Kingston's did.

"I stepped over to pay my respects, Sir, and to wish you and your party a Happy New Year. I also see an acquaintance among your guests I wanted to pay my respects."

Kingston raised an eyebrow, but before he could respond a voice from behind him said, in Japanese, "I am pleased to see you again Jon. You look well."

Summers bowed slightly responding in Japanese, "As do you, Toshio. I wished to pay my respects and see if this visit to my country is more pleasant than the last time we met."

Toshio laughed, "Much better. Thank you for asking. Your admiral doesn't seem happy to see you."

"We've had our differences."

"I can understand why," replied Toshio, smiling.

"We must still practice restraint, my friend. We may still have to serve together in the future."

Toshio laughed, turning to Kingston. He spoke to the admiral in English. "My apologies, Admiral Kingston. Captain Summers and I met in Washington a few months back when he saved me from being attacked by some drunken soldiers. I found out then he speaks excellent Japanese."

"Captain Summers seems to always be saving someone. Always the hero."

"It really was quite frightening," said Toshio ignoring Kingston's sarcasm. "They insulted me and then were about to beat me when Jon intervened. They then tried to attack him, but he was able to defend himself most bravely. The police arrested them all."

"I'm sure they did," responded Kingston coldly, still smiling.

"Anyway, Sir," said Summers evenly as he held the Admiral's gaze. "I wanted to pay my respect to both you and Mr. Akiyama. Have a good evening, Sir."

"Thank you, Captain," replied Kingston turning away.

Toshio got up from his chair and stepped over to Jon. He took Jon's hand and shook it while he moved the two of them away from the table.

"I would deal with the admiral with great care, my friend," said Toshio in Japanese. "I have the impression he would do you harm."

"Your impression would be correct," replied Summers. "We've had this relationship since we were at the naval academy together. Unfortunately, it only seems to get worse. I have to take some of the credit for that."

Toshio laughed. "I'm not sure you would ever be able to change the admiral's feelings on the matter. It was good to see you, my friend, please take care of yourself."

"I will and you have a profitable business trip and safe trip home."

They shook hands again going their separate ways. Something about Toshio didn't seem right. Jon felt this way since they'd first met. Summers couldn't put his finger on what was wrong. He was running the conversation through his mind again walking back to the table when someone grabbed his arm. He turned to find Lieutenant Handcock.

"Captain, you didn't hear me calling you?" she asked smiling.

Summers couldn't help but smile back. She was a beautiful woman, even with her glasses on and hair up. Her smile was intoxicating. He quickly reminded himself who she worked for, and she wanted something.

"I'm sorry, Lieutenant," said Summers regaining control. "I didn't mean to be rude. What can I do for you?"

"I believe this is our dance," she said dragging him onto the dance floor.

The orchestra was playing a slow number and the floor was crowded. Jon was able to see Nancy still dancing with Robbie on the other side of the floor. He managed to catch her eye. She said something to Robbie who looked around. He rolled his eyes, both seemed to laugh at him.

"So what do I owe the pleasure of this dance, Lieutenant?"

"I've never danced with a hero before," responded Handcock pressing close to Summers.

Summers could smell her perfume. For the first time, he noticed her pretty eyes. He looked hard to see what might be hidden behind them. It only took a second.

"I'm no hero, Lieutenant," he said. "Just a sailor who's done his job on more than one occasion."

Handcock held him closer as they moved across the dance floor. She began to stroke the back of his neck. Summers smiled but made no other indication he was affected by her advance. His blue eyes remained cool, and he remained relaxed as they danced.

"The Admiral speaks of you often. He seems to feel you've had some lucky breaks in your career." she said, discretely rubbing his back.

"Lieutenant, I'm sure the admiral has nothing good to say when he thinks of me. We've been at odds going all the way back to the academy. He's correct about the luck though. I've had my share."

"He did mention that you've had your differences. The exchange the other day showed me that. You certainly did push his buttons then. He doesn't like to lose."

"None of us do, Lieutenant," Summers said carefully. "Unfortunately, for the admiral, he was never meant to win this one. He was playing against a stacked deck from the start. Whoever drew that assignment would have been beat."

"You know," her voice grew softer, "you really are a hero. The way you stand up for the people who work for you. Look at what you did for Toshio. You fought off those marines in the hotel bar like you did. It was nice of you to come over to see him. He leaves for the Philippines tomorrow and you seemed to be the highlight of his trip. You really are a good man. It comes to you naturally. Look at the way you stood up to the admiral. You found his weakness and exploited it."

Summers found her last statement interesting but decided to follow up on the most obvious. "The truth be known, Lieutenant, until I saw Dick's reaction, I had no idea what his weakness was."

For the first time since they were dancing Handcock's body seemed to pull away from Summers. Her hands stopped rubbing his back and neck returning to where they should be. Her smile remained, but her eyes gave her away.

Summers continued, "I could care less what the man does on his free time as long as it doesn't affect how he performs his job. I'm not throwing rocks, Lieutenant. I don't care who you or he sleeps with. It's none of my business. If you get caught the navy will deal with it, not me. I just want to be able to do my job without having to have a firefight with the admiral every time we meet."

The song ended. Summers took Lieutenant Handcock by the hand and led her off the dance floor. Her eyes told him she wasn't happy she was no longer in control. Jon bent over slightly and kissed her on the cheek. She blushed backing away, bringing her hand up to where he touched her.

"Lieutenant," Summers said softly, "both you and the admiral can rest assured that all I want to do is my job without interference from him. I do have to say one thing though, you're a pretty lady, Lieutenant. You can do much better than an old sexist like Dick Kingston. Find yourself a nice young man and go on with your career."

Handcock's eyes softened. "You underestimate yourself, Captain. The admiral calls you a straight arrow, a boy scout. I hope you're always on my side. You're a nice guy, but you have the bad habit of not fighting fair. You call me next time you're in Pearl and you won't regret it."

Summers smiled at the last comment. "No offense, Lieutenant, but I probably would. Carry on, Lieutenant."

"Thank you, Sir," responded Hancock. She turned walking back towards the admiral's table.

Summers started to return to his table. He heard Nancy behind him, "You see how sailors get when they make captain, Robbie? They try to steal the admiral's aide right out from under him."

"Metaphorically speaking, of course," replied Summers, causing them all to laugh.

"You seemed to enjoy dancing with the Wicked Witch of the West," chuckled Nancy when they reached the table.

"Actually dear, she's more like the Spider Woman," said Jon seriously. "There's more here than you would suspect."

"Of course there is," giggled Nancy. "She's sleeping with the admiral and the two of them don't think anyone knows."

It was hard for Summers to keep a straight face when his wife was like this, but some how he managed, "No dear, the woman knows more than she should about something she should know nothing about."

Suddenly everyone was counting down to the New Year. Jon was standing behind her with his hands on her shoulders. When they reached the magic hour, the room erupted with *HAPPY NEW YEAR!* Confetti flew into the air. She hugged her husband, who picked her up and swung her around, kissing her.

"Happy New Year, Babe!" he whispered into her ear. Everyone around them was celebrating. He kissed her on the cheek. Jon happened to catch a look directed at them from the other side of the restaurant. He held their gaze until they looked away. He understood the look. He had just made himself a target.

Nancy leaned over and flicked her tongue in and out of her husband's ear. He shivered slightly turning to look at her. She smiled at him. "Say there sailor, ply me with alcohol and you just might get lucky."

He kissed her gently on the cheek and held her tight. It was going to be a good year.

Moro Gulf
Mindanao, Philippines
January 5, 1995
2000 Hours

The ferry was traveling from Landang to Malabang on opposite sides of the Gulf. She was carrying just over three hundred people, most of whom were military men and their dependents. This meant the vessel was overcrowded, but her captain didn't seem to be worried. The weather was good, the sea was calm, and sun was just starting to set. They were making good time. He expected they would arrive before midnight. There was a lot of commercial traffic in the area, and all were well lit to avoid collisions.

The captain looked out over his crowded vessel. He did this run twice a week. He prided himself on the fact they carried the most passengers across the Gulf. He lit up his pipe and drew in the smoke from the tobacco. Before he could exhale, there was a deafening explosion sending a fireball one hundred feet into the sky. The small ship broke in half. Both halves sank immediately taking with her most of her passengers and crew.

Three miles to the south a Japanese freighter saw the fireball and sent out the alarm. Two other ships nearby also saw the explosion sending out messages as well. Within minutes, three Philippine Navy patrol boats were heading to the scene at full speed along with several civilian ships. Four other patrol boats, accompanied by *Jones* and the *Doyle* set up a perimeter to the south, just after the Japanese freighter reported seeing what they thought was a periscope.

CHAPTER 11

RETRACING FOOTSTEPS

**Los Angeles International Airport
Los Angeles, California
March 13, 1995
1000 Hours**

The van pulled up into the unloading area of the airport, stopping near the skycap station. As the doors of the vehicle opened and the van's occupants got out, one of the skycaps stepped forward. Noticing it was a large party, the skycap called for one of his partners to give him a hand. They went to the back of the van where the driver helped them with the suitcases. Kevin walked to the back of the van, handing airline tickets to the first skycap. The man looked at the name on the first one.

"Mr. Gateway?" he asked politely.

"One of them," replied Kevin checking all the bags.

The skycap smiled at Kevin. "Welcome to Philippine Airways, Sir. You're allowed two pieces of checked luggage each and two carry-ons."

The skycap counted the tickets and then the bags. The second skycap was tagging each piece of luggage and handing the stubs to the first one.

"You can put all the stubs in any one of the tickets," said Kevin, now counting heads. The skycap nodded. Kevin handed the man a twenty-dollar bill.

"Thank you, Sir," said the skycap. "Your flight is on time this morning. Have a good day, Sir."

Kevin smiled at the man. "Thank you."

He returned to the rest of the family who were saying goodbye to Angie and her family. Standing off to the side he motioned to his father to move along. He felt silly doing this, but both Becky and his father appointed him the official trip timekeeper so they wouldn't be late. He understood they were making fun of him because of his phobia about being on time. He didn't mind being the brunt of their jokes.

He waved to Angie and her family pulling away in the van. His attention turned to his father throwing his arms around another man. A second man and a woman stood next to them. When he was done hugging the first man, his father hugged the second man.

"Be careful, Dad," said Kevin jokingly, "they'll come and take you away before you get on the plane."

Bill turned giving his son an annoyed look. Both his wife, Kathy, and his sister slapped Kevin on the arm. Kevin looked at both women, shrugging.

Bill smiled at his son.

"This is Sam Donavon, one of my platoon leaders during the Philippine campaign," Bill said putting his hand on the man's shoulder. "And this is Don Smith and his wife, Catherine. Don was my company clerk all through that campaign."

All three said hello as they were introduced.

"The impertinent young man there is my son, Kevin. He's really a good boy, but being the CEO of a big publishing firm, he forgets himself sometimes."

They all laughed, including Kevin.

"The lovely young lady next to him is my daughter-in-law, Kathy. How she puts up with her husband is beyond me, but I think she's an angel for doing so."

They all laughed again.

"And these two beautiful young ladies are my daughter, Rebecca, and granddaughter, Sarah."

They walked into the terminal, checking in at the ticket counter, and then headed to the security check point. They talked, joked, and laughed walking down the concourse getting to know one another. When they got to the gate they sat near the door. They didn't have to wait long before the airline started boarding passengers.

Becky was seated near Smith and his wife. While they waited for departure, they were getting to know one another. Becky knew Smith became a Methodist minister after the war but didn't realize he always wanted to go into ministry.

"If you always wanted to join the clergy, why did you go off to fight," asked Becky.

Smith chuckled, "Times were different then. The issues were clearer cut, or at least they seemed to be. There were the Hitler's of the world doing unspeakable things and then the surprise attack on Pearl Harbor. Emotions were running high, and everyone wanted to do their part to bring the war to a conclusion."

"But you could have served as a chaplain?"

"After four years of college, yes, I could. My friends were all being drafted and going off to fight. I wasn't afraid of being called a coward or anything like that. I guess I just wanted to do my part like everyone else."

"I can't imagine what it would be like. I've heard about some things you went through and I'm not sure I would have the courage."

The minister smiled and put his hand on Becky's. "Child, you're a doctor and every day you make life and death decisions for your patients. There's no real difference from that and what we did in the jungle. You would do fine, besides your father and mother taught you well."

Becky smiled, but before she could respond the pilot came over the PA and advised them, they were ready for departure.

Camp Freedom
Mindanao, Philippines
March 14, 1995
0700 Hours

Montoya stood stooped over a map when O'Keefe walked into the room. O'Keefe knew that the Filipino didn't trust him. But his employer expected him to help the man get this operation underway. O'Keefe carried two cups of strong coffee and looked around the room to make sure they were alone. Montoya looked up at the Irishman, then back at the map.

"Coffee, Montoya?" asked O'Keefe holding out one of the mugs.

Montoya looked up, this time holding his gaze. It was several seconds before he took the mug. Montoya made no secret of the fact he didn't trust anyone involved in the operation that wasn't Asian. He didn't say thank you.

"What are you looking at?" asked O'Keefe with genuine interest.

Montoya hesitated for a moment. "I'm not comfortable with the escape route from the hotel. There are too many places for us to be stopped by the police. We can't afford for that to happen. All would be lost."

"True," responded O'Keefe, looking at the map in front of them. "You know the area better than me. Do you see a different route?"

The sincere interest in his concerns about the operation took Montoya by surprise. He caught himself looking at the map with O'Keefe. He didn't trust the Irishman. He was a professional terrorist for hire, working for the highest bidder. O'Keefe never gave Montoya cause for the lack of trust, but that's how he felt.

"I've looked this over a dozen times and can't find a better route," said Montoya cautiously.

O'Keefe took the pointer finger of his right hand and rubbed it across the left side of his mouth. "Do you have extra people you can assign to escort the escape vehicle?"

Montoya gave the Irishman a blank stare.

O'Keefe smiled. "Let me explain. If you have enough bodies, you split them into five sections. The first section stays behind at the hotel and runs interference."

"Interference?" questioned Montoya.

"Yes," continued O'Keefe. "They stay behind and disrupt communication with the authorities and then separate and make their way to a prearranged meeting point. This will buy us a few minutes to get farther out passed their initial perimeters. Two of the sections can lead the escape vehicles and run interference as needed. While the other two follow behind to do the same thing. We get them all radios, so everyone talks to each other and away you go."

Montoya looked at O'Keefe, then at the map.

"That just might work. The escorts not only run interference but can scout alternative routes. I like it. Should take twenty people or less."

"Depending on your manpower you can even run some extra units to run interference and create diversions away from the operation site and escape route that will tie up responding police and military units."

Montoya suddenly glared at O'Keefe. "You're not in charge of this operation, yet you give out orders like you were."

O'Keefe's expression didn't change. "Excuse me?"

"You're nothing but a mercenary! A hired gun! You sleep with a Filipino whore, a murderess who is willing to sell her country for the price of trinkets and comfort you provide. You think you can tell me how to run this operation. Osaka put me in command because of his belief in a free and separate Muslim state on Mindanao. You are Catholic and can't be trusted. You walk in and tell me what I should do and expect me to cower at your presence. I am the leader of my people and will lead them to victory regardless of what you do."

The Irishman's reaction remained neutral. Montoya's eyes told O'Keefe he wasn't as confident as he was trying to sound.

"Montoya," said O'Keefe calmly, "you're right about me being a mercenary for hire. That's how I make my living. I don't go from bidder to bidder so to speak because Mr. Osaka pays me extremely well. I've also made commitments to him and have every intention to honor them. I may be a mercenary, but I do have a sense of honor when it comes to keeping those commitments. You're also right when you imply, I could care less about your Muslim state. I don't care, but not because I'm Catholic, so don't drag religion into this. This is strictly business for me. I've been asked to make sure this operation succeeds. I give you recommendations and nothing more. If you use them, you use them. If you don't, it's no skin off my nose."

O'Keefe's tone stayed even, showing little emotion. Montoya's response was one of shock. He expected O'Keefe to react to the insult, but instead got him agreeing with most of what he said. The expression on O'Keefe's face changed.

"Now my friend, regarding whom I choose to share my bed. That, Sir, is none of your business if I'm doing the job I'm being paid to do. Yes, the woman is Filipino, and I just might tell her what you called her. She really does enjoy killing people. She's discovered how easy it is and gets high on the excitement. I would walk very softly when it comes to that topic.

"I recommend," said O'Keefe, as his expression softened again, "you go on with your planning and I'll be checking the weapons, if you need me."

Montoya looked down at the table not making eye contact. The Irishman turned, walking out. Montoya continued to look at the map.

Osaka Pineapple Plantation
Mindanao, Philippines
March 14, 1995
0800 Hours

Osaka sat at his desk, going over information sent him from his key people. The plans looked solid, but he was still concerned about American involvement on behalf of the Manila government. He agreed with Toshio the United States would probably not commit troops, but if they did, he wanted to be ready. The reports coming from Boerst showed they were ready to handle anything the Philippine Army would throw at them. The reports from Holiday said the same thing. The government was still trying to find the mystery submarine attacking shipping on an irregular basis. Everything was going well.

The telephone rang. "Osaka."

"Mr. Osaka, you called me, Sir," said the voice with a thick Irish accent.

"Ah, Patrick," said Osaka a smile coming to his face. "I have good news. The people you wish to meet are on an airplane arriving in Davao later today. I thought you would like to know."

"Thank you, Sir," replied O'Keefe. "I can't wait to meet my father-in-law again."

"Patience, my friend," cautioned Osaka. "We all must have patience to get what we want. Toshio will be back about the same time. This information network he's set up is quite marvelous. We received a call as their plane was pulling away from the gate. He's done an exceptional job. How are the arrangements going?"

"They're going well. We'll be ready to jump off ahead of time if necessary. Boerst has thought of every contingency. We have only one problem."

"What's that?" asked Osaka with a hint of annoyance.

"Montoya's lack of trust for non-Asians. He got into it with me less than an hour ago. He feels none of us can be trusted and that will affect how he makes his decisions."

Osaka was silent as he contemplated his next move.

"Toshio anticipated this would happen, what are your recommendations?"

O'Keefe answered immediately. "He needs to be eliminated. He will be the wrench in this plan if he isn't dealt with. I can have it taken care of if you like?"

"No!" replied Osaka quickly. "I will make those arrangements. I agree it must be taken care of, but it must be discrete. It can't look like murder, or we'll have problems with the Filipinos."

"I was thinking more along the lines of *killed in action*," said O'Keefe. "That gives you a dead hero to promote to the people and he's out of our way. I would have a backup plan just in case we can't make that happen."

"I like that idea. Let me think on it and I'll let you know. How about our Filipino troops?"

"Most come from the private armies spread throughout the islands. Simply put, we pay more, and money will buy their allegiance. We have a few political types, but for the most part I'd say we have the edge. Not as well trained as our other troops, but equal to the task of going after the police and small garrisons spread throughout the island. The big stuff our guys will be able to deal with. I'm really impressed with Boerst."

"Good, Patrick, good," said Osaka. "We'll move as scheduled unless you hear otherwise from me. Toshio will meet you in Davao and give you any last-minute instructions."

"Understood!"

"Good luck. I'll call you when you get the prisoners back to the base camp."

"Thank you, Sir. I'm looking forward to it."

The telephone went dead. Osaka placed the handset back in its cradle and pushed a button on the telephone. Within seconds the office door opened, and Ishimoto walked into the room. The man said nothing. He simply bowed slightly when he reached the desk.

"Mr. Montoya has made himself expendable," said Osaka continuing to work without looking up. "He is willing to put the operation in jeopardy over petty prejudices. Patrick has recommended that he die in the fighting that will certainly ensue after this operation. I think that'd be most convenient. Would you make sure that takes place as soon as possible? Patrick has offered to help, but his methods are just a little too front door. Be discrete, but make sure it happens."

Ishimoto bowed again slightly, turning around, and walking out. As the door closed Osaka continued working as if the conversation never took place.

Grand Philippine Hotel
Mindanao, Philippines
March 14, 1995
1630 Hours

Bill and Sarah unpacked and went off to explore. This was their custom whenever they travelled together. Bill always thought his granddaughter inherited her curiosity from his wife, Mary. He loved spending time with his granddaughter and never passed up a chance to explore with her. They went down to the lobby where Bill ran into several people he knew from other military units. He talked briefly, then took Sarah out onto the street. They walked, looking at shops, and talking about the places Bill hoped they would visit. Sarah was having difficulty understanding not everywhere on the island would be safe for tourists. Her grandfather tried to give her the history of the islands and the separatist movement in the half an hour they were walking. She was still having difficulty understanding when they approached the hotel again.

Near the main entrance of the hotel, they came upon a street vendor selling flowers. He was a pleasant old man who asked Bill if he wanted to buy the young lady a flower in heavily accented English. Bill commented about how the city changed. The old man got caught up in the conversation giving Sarah a flower, putting it in her hair. Sarah's long, dark hair was complimented by the flower. She blushed when the old man said how pretty it made her look. Bill bought several more flowers for Sarah to carry and for Becky.

He was paying for the flowers when he caught a glimpse of a Caucasian standing by the corner of a building across the street. The face was familiar. He stopped what he was doing, trying to locate the face in the crowd again.

He looked up and down the street, but the man was gone. He thought his mind was playing tricks on him.

"Grandpa are you OK?" asked Sarah.

"Yeah," Bill hesitated, "yeah, I'm fine. Just thought I saw someone I used to know."

"You probably did, Grandpa. That's why you're here," said the young woman innocently arranging the flowers in her hand.

Gateway smiled, "Yeah, you're right. Say, let's find your mother and get some dinner."

"Sounds good to me," replied the young woman.

Gateway finished paying the old man for the flowers, saying goodbye. They turned, walking into the hotel lobby. There they ran into Becky and Sam who'd come downstairs looking for them. They gave Becky the flowers and Sam insisted on putting one of them in her hair.

"After all, this is the tropics young lady, and every pretty girl should have flowers in their hair."

Becky blushed when Sam put the flower on the right side by her ear.

"Say, Donavon," said Gateway "wasn't that you that bought all the flowers for those girls in the house in Zamboanga after we were pulled back?"

Donavon thought for a minute.

"No, that was Summers. That was the night he got the whole house for the company."

"I'm not sure Sarah and I want to hear this, gentlemen," said Becky.

"I want to hear, Mom. We're studying this stuff in school."

They were following Becky towards the restaurant.

"Give us a break, Rebecca. We'll keep it respectable."

Becky laughed. "Keep it anyway you want, Dad. You guys have been reduced to *stuff in school.*"

Gateway stopped for a second, then started to laugh. She was right about that. All they went through was reduced to words in a textbook and stories from old men. There was no way his children or grandchildren could begin to understand what they lived through. He smiled while they waited to be seated.

Their wait was less than five minutes, and they were seated near the window. As they viewed their menus Gateway found himself looking up and down the street.

"Are you looking for the person you saw earlier, Grandpa?" asked Sarah.

Gateway smiled. "As a matter of fact, I was. It wasn't someone I expected to see and was probably just someone who looked like him."

"Who did you think it was, Dad?" asked Becky.

"Oh, just someone I haven't seen in some time."

They finished looking at their menus and ordered dinner. They took their time eating and were finishing up when they noticed a pretty, dark haired woman making rounds of the tables. They ordered coffee and were just served when she reached their table.

"Hello," she said smiling. "I'm Suzanne Rolle. I'm one of the managers here. How are you this evening?"

Becky felt the woman looking directly at her. The smile didn't seem sincere. She didn't know what it was she didn't like about Miss Rolle, but it was instantaneous.

"We're quite well, young lady," said Sam. "You have quite a nice hotel here."

Rolle smiled at the four of them. "That's nice of you to say. Are you here for the reunion?"

"We sure are!" blurted out Sarah. "My Grandpa helped organize it. He was in the 41st Division."

Becky poked her daughter in the side, frowning. She felt Sarah gave too much information to strangers.

"That must make you Bill Gateway?" said Rolle to Gateway.

"Yes, Ma'am," he replied. "It's nice to meet you."

"I hope your stay with us is enjoyable. I look forward to seeing the reunion unfold," Rolle said. She walked by Becky. She looked down smiling, causing a shiver up and down the doctor's spine.

When she was out of earshot, Becky whispered, "She's spooky. I don't like her."

"She's just a pretty girl who's good at her job," said Sam.

"Too pretty." responded Becky.

Gateway looked at his daughter. "Women's intuition? Sam's right, she's good at her job. How many managers do you know walk around to see how their guests are doing? She stopped at every table in the room. It's the nature of the business, keep the customer happy or you lose their patronage."

"That's not it, Dad. I don't know how to explain it, but there's something dangerous about her. I can't explain it any better than that."

"The mysterious Orient," said Sam finishing his coffee, "happens all the time, look what happened to us on our last visit."

"Yeah," smiled Gateway, "there were thousands of Orientals trying to kill us."

"After getting to know you guys, who could blame them." said Becky.

They all laughed. The tension seemed to lift, and Sam said something about jet lag. They paid their bill and walked out. When they reached the lobby, Bill was stopped and asked to speak to a couple of television reporters from the United States. They interviewed him, taking only fifteen minutes and then left the hotel. The four visitors retired for the evening.

The man sitting in the lobby watched them for some time. He lowered the newspaper covering his face, watching the elevator close. O'Keefe put down the paper standing up. He walked out the front door knowing when he returned the next day, he planned a reunion of his own.

177 Pinecreek Drive
Rochester, New York
March 14, 1995
1840 Hours

Summers got out of work on time and was home for dinner for a change. On this evening, dinner with the family was Nancy and him. They decided to eat in the family room watching the news on the larger television. The news was uneventful, and Jon was thinking of turning it off when he heard the anchor say, "Over the last several years, we've been celebrating the fiftieth anniversary of World War Two. We have a report from Sandy Monroe about a reunion about to take place in the Philippines to commemorate that war and the men who fought it."

The television cut away from the New York studio and to black and white footage of the invasion of the Philippines. It showed landing craft ploughing through the surf and ships bombarding the beaches.

"They came by sea to land on a hostile shore," said the husky female voice. "They were kids who'd heard of the island of Mindanao and the Philippines only through books and school. They were to land on these islands and forcibly take them back from the Japanese in 1944 and 1945. It was a campaign that didn't receive a lot of publicity but was as hard fought a campaign as any other in the Pacific Theatre."

The screen returned to present day showing Monroe standing on a busy street filled with pedestrians, bicycles, and automobiles.

"Tomorrow, survivors from both sides will gathered here to honor their fallen comrades and relive times most of us can only imagine."

The scene switched to inside the hotel and showed Gateway and a few other men talking to Monroe. Standing behind Gateway were Becky and Sarah.

"This is a reunion pure and simple," said Gateway to the camera. "We're here to remember and honor the men who fought with us who didn't return, as well as renew old friendships. Another thing unique about this reunion is we have representatives of the Japanese units we fought against. It's not often former enemies can meet on the same battlefields and do so as friends. We're looking forward to having a good reunion and hopefully get a lot of history documented."

"Are you planning on visiting some of the battlefield sites?"

"Wherever that's possible, Sandy. We're standing on one of the sites right now. The division I was assigned to was involved in the liberation of the City of Davao. Many of the sites were in the jungle and, with the current issues the authorities are dealing with, will not be visited because the safety of our people could be at risk. We'll go wherever the Philippine government feels we can safely do so. Several of us have brought family members to show them the places that go with the stories they've heard over the years."

The television cut back to the street scene with Monroe.

"So, these old soldiers and their families have gathered here in the Philippines to remember a time when people gave their lives to free the world of tyranny. They remember a time when men from opposite sides of the world fought over the rights of countries to choose their own destiny. We'll be watching as these old foes meet in peace and see what enemies from half a century ago can teach us today. This is Sandy Monroe reporting from the City of Davao in the Philippines."

The television cut back to the New York studio and Jon hit the mute button on the remote control. Nancy looked at him as he cut the hot dog on his plate and put a piece of it in his mouth.

"Nice piece," she said. "Dad would be pleased."

Jon nodded as he chewed.

"Becky and Sarah looked nice, too, don't you think?" she added as she got up to take her empty plate into the kitchen. "I think the flowers in their hair were a nice touch."

"That would be Bill's idea," said Jon getting up to follow her. "As I recall that doesn't seem to be Becky's style. Sean will be pissed that he missed this. All he talks about is Sarah."

They looked at each other laughing. If things worked out the way they were headed, Gateway might get his wish and see the two families united by marriage. The kids were only sixteen, but they were communicating constantly since Hawaii.

Grand Philippine Hotel
Mindanao, Philippines
March 15, 1995
1200 Hours

Everyone gathered in the main banquet room for the opening of the reunion. It started as a luncheon, followed by the opening remarks. There was to be a formal banquet that evening, including Philippine officials. The trips to the more secure battle sites would start the next day. The Philippine Army brought in additional troops and the American military approved the additional security measures. Finally, in four days, everyone would gather back at the hotel for a farewell dinner.

Gateway and his party sat near the front of the hall. The tables were round, sitting ten people to a table. Two American Army officers filled the open seats at his table. The first was a lieutenant colonel and the second a captain. Both men were career officers and looked on this as little more than a public relations job. Their attitude seemed to change when they were placed at the table with Gateway. The colonel recognized him. A retired four star general suddenly made the assignment more important. Becky and Sam joked with each other, guessing this was no accident. The word was these officers were rude to one of the other organizers.

The lunch was excellent and was finishing up. One of the organizers stood, walking to the podium in front of the room.

"Ladies and gentlemen," he said, trying to quiet everyone. "Ladies and gentlemen, can I have your attention?"

The room quieted and the man continued. "I would like to thank you all for coming. I hope this reunion lives up to its billing. For those of you who don't know me, I'm Ernie Madison, chairman of the 24th Division's reunion committee."

There were cheers and howls from the far side of the room.

"Paratroopers," said Donavon to Smith, "landed too many times on their heads."

The two of them chuckled while the Army officers both gave them dirty looks.

"Now, I'm going to introduce a gentleman who served with us here in the Philippines as a captain in the 41st Infantry Division," continued Madison, "and after the war, he stayed in the Army, serving on General MacArthur's staff in Japan. He served in Korea and Vietnam before retiring as a four-star general. Ladies and gentlemen, I would like to introduce the chairman of the 41st Division's reunion committee, General William Gateway."

Everyone clapped as Bill stood walking to the podium. Madison took a step back, allowing Gateway to stand by the microphone. The clapping subsided.

"Thank you, ladies and gentlemen," started Gateway. "I would also like to thank all of you for showing your support for our fallen comrades by coming back to honor them after fifty years. It was my honor back then to lead a company of the bravest men I've ever had the privilege to know. The camaraderie from the time we spent here formed many friendships that have lasted for decades. I look forward to spending time with all of you over the next several days. There are one hundred and thirty-five of you here, so give yourselves a hand for making it this far."

The entire audience roared with applause. When the applause started to abate, Gateway continued. "I would also like to welcome members of the units of the Japanese military we met on the battlefield. We meet them today as allies and in peace. Please give them a warm welcome."

To Gateway's relief there was a good round of applause for the twenty-five representatives from the Japanese units. None of the people involved in the planning of the reunion were sure how the Japanese would be received. Based on what they saw thus far, they were pleased.

Gateway spoke again when the applause died down.

"Again, I would like to thank you all for coming. We'll see you at the banquet this evening and on the road tomorrow."

Everyone in the room stood, applauding Gateway. He shook a few hands moving back to his seat. When he reached the table, the applause subsided. Madison, back up to the podium, began going over the schedule for the next several days. As he spoke, Kevin looked at his watch.

"If you'll excuse me," he said, "I have to check in with the office."

He got up, walking to the rear of the banquet room. He didn't notice the waiters and waitresses were different from the ones who served them. The replacements were moving to strategic locations about the room. Some pushed small carts covered with tablecloths. Others carried trays covered by open napkins. They covered each exit and stationed people by the windows overlooking the courtyard.

Kevin opened the door to leave glancing at one of the men. He was shifting back and forth nervously from one foot to another. Kevin felt uncomfortable. The man was too nervous for a waiter. He left the room, heading for the lobby to complete his call and get back to the luncheon. He passed a Caucasian who looked familiar. He was walking with one of the managers, a pretty woman, and two other men dressed in hotel uniforms.

He reached the bank of telephone booths when he realized who he just saw. The man disappeared when Kevin was in grad school, but he remembered the family controversy about him. He now understood his uncomfortable feeling. He picked up the phone nearest him finding it dead. He picked up the next several, finding them in the same condition. He cautiously looked around spotting several people he guessed might be part of what was taking place. He found himself walking towards the stairs as calmly as he could. He made it to the lobby, again cautiously looking about. The people behind the desk were ones he hadn't seen before. He noticed several people about the lobby he suspected weren't supposed to be there. He quietly moved to the doors looking at his watch. He thought he might be rushing so forced himself to take an even pace. He hoped the people watching the lobby would think he was late for an appointment. Once outside, he realized his pulse was racing and his blood pressure was up. He needed to get to the authorities as quickly as he could.

O'Keefe passed the man in the hall thinking he looked familiar, but unable to place the face. He wasn't concerned about one potential hostage getting away when there were over one hundred and fifty still in the room. With him were Rolle, Montoya, and a guard recently assigned to Montoya.

They entered the banquet room. One of the Americans was speaking, giving a schedule of events for the next several days. O'Keefe grinned. He'd waited a long time for this day to come. Rolle stood next to him, a smile on her face. O'Keefe knew it was for a different reason.

Montoya took a step forward, raising a pistol over his head, firing it. There was silence in the room for a second. The screaming started when the men placed throughout the room began to pull out weapons. People began to rush about the room looking for ways to escape. The people at Gateway's table stood, then on his direction, climbed under the table. The colonel and the captain rushed the man nearest them. The man saw them coming and was able to strike the captain in the chin with the butt of his weapon. The captain fell unconscious while the colonel grabbed the waiter, struggling for control of the rifle. The weapon fired once, the bullet striking the top of Gateway's table and sending wood splinters into the air though the tablecloth.

Weapons were fired about the room. The first rounds struck the colonel who was killed instantly. Several more rounds struck Madison who lay bleeding to death near the door he was running for. Screams of pain could be heard around the room, but the shooting stopped. There was silence while the gunmen checked the crowd.

Becky threw herself on top of her daughter when her father shouted for them to get down. She could hear the cries from around the room and quickly raised herself off Sarah checking to make sure she was unhurt. She looked afraid but was otherwise fine. Next, she looked at Smith and his wife. Both appeared to have survived intact. She then looked over at her father and Donavon. They were unhurt. Both she and her father spotted Kathy at the same time.

She was lying on her side and didn't appear to be conscious. They crawled over to her. Becky checked her for a pulse, finding one. Examining her sister-in-law Becky determined she was hit just below the left shoulder. The bullet exited out the middle of the back. There was still a pulse, so it missed the heart. Becky couldn't tell what other damage the bullet might have done. She looked around and grabbing a linen napkin hanging off the table, placing it over the exit wound. Her father found another napkin, handing it to his daughter. She took his hand and the napkin placing it on the entry wound.

"Press here!" she directed her father. For the first time in her life, she saw fear in his eyes. She knew it was not because of the men with guns. He'd faced that fear before. Now his family was involved, it was hitting too close to home.

"How is she?" asked Gateway, his voice quivering.

"She's alive, Dad," said Becky again checking Kathy's pulse. "Other than that I wouldn't want to guess. She's hurt bad. The bullet went all the way through. It appears to have missed the heart, but I can't tell if there's any artery damage."

"She'll be okay though, right?" asked her father.

For the first time Becky heard her daughter crying behind her. She turned to find Sarah in the arms of Catherine Smith. She returned her attention back to the wounded woman. She was handed more linens which she placed on the exit wound as she rolled Kathy onto her back.

"I hope she'll be all right, Dad," she said pulling his hand away from the wound. "She's hurt bad and needs to get to the hospital before I can tell for sure."

Blood was soaked through the folded linen napkin. She removed it looking at the wound closely. The bleeding appeared to be slowing. She held her hand out. "Can I have more napkins, please?'

Several napkins were placed in her hands, which she placed on the wound.

"Thank you," she said simply.

"You're welcome," responded a familiar voice with a thick Irish accent.

Becky froze, not wanting to look up. She closed her eyes, took a deep breath, and opened them. She found herself face to face with her ex-husband. He stood over her smiling, handsome as ever. Standing next to him was the manager who stopped by their table the night before. She was carrying a sub-machine gun, a crazed look in her eyes.

"It's good to see you again, darlin'." said O'Keefe.

"I wish I could say the same thing, Patrick, but I'm a bit busy right now," she replied looking to her patient.

"I can take care of that." said Rolle, raising the weapon she was carrying, pointing it at Kathy.

Becky instinctively placed herself between the weapon and her sister-in-law. She could hear her father struggling. She saw he was being restrained by two men. When he started to object, O'Keefe wheeled around punching him in the stomach, causing him to double over, falling to his knees. Rolle pointed her weapon at Becky's head. O'Keefe's hand reached out touching the muzzle of the weapon, causing Rolle to lower it.

"Not here. Not now, darlin'," said O'Keefe to the woman next to him.

He looked back down at Becky, who'd already gone back to work trying to stop the bleeding. She took a second looking up, glaring at her ex-husband, and then going back to what she was doing. He laughed, "Rebecca, we have to go, leave her."

"No!" came the forceful response from the doctor. "She's hurt too bad to be left and besides, I stopped going anywhere with you years ago."

O'Keefe smiled. "It's nice to see you dedicated all that energy to something. I bet you're one hell of a doctor. You need to understand a couple of things here darlin'. First, this isn't a request. You come with me willingly now, or I allow Suzanne here to do what she wants with the good Mrs. Gateway. Second, you need to understand her coming with us will sentence her to death because there are no medical facilities where we're headed. Third, if you don't go, know there's a very nasty man on the other side of the room who'll probably have the whole lot of you killed just because he's not a nice person."

Becky glared at O'Keefe; her eyes filled with hatred.

"At least let me make her comfortable."

"You have one minute darlin'. Then the boss will order her killed," said O'Keefe checking Montoya's location in the room.

Becky worked quickly to bandage Kathy's wounds the best she could. She was trying to place something under Kathy's head when O'Keefe reached down and grabbed her by the arm, pulling her to her feet.

"We have to go now, darlin'," he said as he motioned for the others to be brought along as well. "We have to leave before the police and army show up to save all of you fine people."

Becky struggled slightly as O'Keefe dragged her toward the kitchen door. He finally pushed her ahead of him. He fell back to where Gateway was being escorted by two guards. The older man looked at the Irishman with disgust.

"There you go judging me again like you did sixteen years ago. You really shouldn't do that, you know General. I'm really an extremely sensitive fella."

"You're slime, O'Keefe," said Gateway moving forward. "I should have killed you years ago. You never brought my family anything but heartache."

O'Keefe laughed. "General, I always thought you were more civilized than that. Kill me, would you? What a way to talk to your son-in-law. Shame on you. I'll tell you this, I've waited a long time to settle this score. You separated me from my daughter, and probably lied to her about me as well. I swore my revenge years ago and now I'm going to have it."

Gateway shook his head as they entered the kitchen. "Revenge? You beat my daughter, nearly killing her. I react to that, and you talk to me of revenge? You really are a twisted personality, O'Keefe. You agreed to stay away, and we didn't turn you in. We let you get away from Federal authorities. Man, my career was on the line, and you want revenge? I just don't believe it. I should have called someone when I saw you on the street yesterday. I knew that was you."

"But you couldn't believe it, could you?" laughed O'Keefe as they headed down a stairway. "General, I tell you, I've spent a lot of time planning this day. And you threw in Sarah for a bonus. All the abuse I took from you. Always comparing me to that Summers kid, as well as every pimple faced boy your daughter ever dated. I'd bet you even asked your friends to turn Rebecca against me."

Gateway struggled to stay between his guards. When they reached the bottom of the stairway, it opened into a large, tiled storage area leading to a loading dock. Hostages were being loaded onto a tractor trailer marked frozen foods. Gateway was pushed inside and quickly found the rest of his family and friends. All around him, people were crying and moaning. There was still light from the open door, but Gateway knew that wouldn't last long, so he started getting people settled. While he did, his daughter made the rounds of the injured to see if there was anything she could do to help them.

O'Keefe watched as his prisoners settled in. One of his men came running down the stairs, excited.

"Mr. O'Keefe!" said the man gasping for breath. "It's Mr. Montoya. He's shooting the Japanese hostages!"

"What?" exclaimed O'Keefe.

"He's executing them one at a time. Shooting them in the head!"

O'Keefe bolted back up the stairs, rushing back into the banquet room just in time to see Montoya put his pistol to the head of one of the Japanese hostages and pull the trigger. The old man's head exploded sending blood and other debris all over his companions.

"Noooo!" shouted O'Keefe racing forward, knocking Montoya to the floor.

The men surrounding the group looked confused. Montoya was their commander and ordered the Japanese killed. Now O'Keefe, who represented Montoya's superior stopped them. They stood there, frozen, not knowing what to do. Montoya started getting up off the floor, raising his pistol. O'Keefe kicked it out of his hand. Rolle and two more men came up behind O'Keefe. She looked at the men near the Japanese hostages and ordered them to take their charges down to the truck. This seemed to snap them out of their stupor. They did as they were told.

"I'll have you killed for this, O'Keefe," Montoya stood up. "I'll be seeing Osaka about this!"

Strict orders were given not to use Osaka's name during the operation and Montoya spoke it in front of the gathered group.

"You're stupid, Montoya!" O'Keefe said. "You know better than to take time to do this when we should be getting away. You go ahead and tell whoever you want. Now, get everyone out of here."

The sound of gunfire erupted from the direction of the downstairs lobby.

"Do something useful and go check to make sure we still have time to escape," growled O'Keefe.

Montoya glared at the Irishman, then wheeled about and left. The man assigned as his bodyguard followed. O'Keefe looked at Rolle and the others remaining in the room. He motioned for them to follow him. They went through the kitchen and down to the waiting truck. O'Keefe saw the remaining hostages were loaded. He ordered the doors shut and the truck pulled away. Two smaller vehicles preceded it. O'Keefe, Rolle, and the others got in the remaining vehicles, following the truck.

Montoya moved quickly down the hallway. He was upset after the confrontation with O'Keefe. They entered the upstairs lobby finding two of his people firing their rifles down the stairs. He rushed over, looking downstairs. He could make out the uniforms of policemen behind furniture in the lobby. The police were returning fire both up the stairway and towards the front desk. He reached for his pistol, realizing too late it was on the floor of the banquet room.

Montoya didn't see his bodyguard nod to the others. The two men stepped forward firing several short bursts down the stairs, then jumped back under cover. When they did, the bodyguard pushed Montoya into the center of the stairway, just as the police returned fire. Bullets struck him in the chest and stomach, causing him to fall forward and down the stairs. He landed on the bottom with his arms and legs sprawled out. He was dead from the broken neck he received from his fall.

The firing stopped as suddenly as it started. The police slowly moved into the hotel to take control. Outside Kevin Gateway paced back and forth nervously, waiting to hear if his family was unhurt.

U.S.S. Nimitz
Pacific Ocean
March 15, 1995
1200 Hours

Kingston sat in his chair on the bridge watching the ongoing flight operations. They were doing shakedown exercises, testing equipment repaired after the exercise in late December. He was anxious for his first deployment in this chair. The flight operations were going as scheduled with no problems. He looked at the officers and men standing around him feeling secure in the fact this tour would get him another star.

Next to him stood his two aides. Williams looked bored. He'd served on a carrier and couldn't get excited over the day-to-day routine of the ship. Handcock on the other hand had never been to sea and was like a sponge soaking in every little detail.

A sailor walked over next to the Admiral, coming to attention. Kingston smiled. The young man looked squared away. The crew was starting to shape up.

"What is it, Petty Officer?" asked Williams, almost yawning.

The sailor glanced at the officer without moving his head. He held up a piece of paper.

"I have a flash message for the Admiral from CINCPAC, Sir."

Williams took the message saying, "Dismissed, Petty Officer."

"Yes, Sir!" replied the sailor and he smartly turned, leaving the bridge.

Williams handed the message to Kingston, who read it.

"Officer of the Deck!" Kingston said rising from his chair.

"Sir!"

"Notify Air Ops we are ceasing all operations and retrieve all aircraft immediately. Tell Captain Brothers and the CAG I would like to meet with them immediately in my cabin."

"Aye, Sir!" replied the officer.

Kingston left the bridge followed by his two aides. As they followed Kingston Handcock touched Williams on the shoulder asking, "What's going on?"

"Looks like terrorists in the Philippines are attacking in force. No details yet, but we're to join a couple of ships already on station off the southern Philippines."

"Admiral, you better notify Pearl Harbor you'll miss your appointment," said Handcock trying not to sound too excited.

Kingston entered his cabin, walking to his desk. He picked up a notebook, opening it. He tore out a page handing it to Williams.

"Go down to communications and send this message. Make sure they understand I want a confirmation the message was delivered."

"Aye, aye, Sir!"

Williams walked out to do as he was ordered. Kingston turned to Handcock, his face all business.

"Lieutenant, I want you to take notes on everything that takes place in this meeting."

"Aye, aye, Sir!"

There was a knock at the open hatch, and both turned to see Captain Brothers and the commander of the Nimitz's air group standing there. The meeting was about to start.

★ CHAPTER 12 ★
REACTION

Franco pulled up as close to the hotel as he could. He walked through the gathered crowd reaching the police line. The first thing he noticed was the glass was shot out of the large front windows. He could see bullet holes in two of the four police cars parked out front. It looked like the police came under immediate fire when they arrived at the scene.

Two young investigators walked out of the hotel to meet their captain. They both looked shaken.

"How bad is it?" Jaime asked.

"It's bad, Sir," said the taller of the two. "A quick count of at least seventeen friendly fatalities. Two of the terrorists were killed. We have at least ten wounded that we know of. We're still sweeping the building."

"Any of our people hurt?" asked their captain.

"One," answered the second investigator. "Minor leg wound as they entered the building. It appears they were firing wildly to keep our people busy while a larger group escaped."

"Escaped?" Franco questioned. "Do we have an idea what their purpose was here?"

Both men hesitated, looking at each other. Finally the taller one answered. "It appears, Captain they were here for a kidnapping."

Franco looked serious. "And?"

"And it appears they were successful," said the taller investigator. "We're missing over one hundred foreign nationals, mostly American. We won't know an exact number for an hour or more."

"How'd they escape without being seen with that many hostages?" asked their superior quietly.

"We're not sure at this point, Sir," replied the shorter investigator. "We have officers canvassing the neighborhoods looking for witnesses."

"Good."

Both investigators were surprised with his reaction.

"You," Franco motioned to the shorter of the two investigators, "call headquarters and get as many men as they can spare on this right away. Also, call this number and ask for General Mangoba. They'll put you off but tell whoever answers you're calling for me. Tell Mangoba or his aide what's going on and see what help they can send us. I want this block so secure, every time a bird lands it gets brought in for questioning. When that's completed you report back to me and no one else."

He scribbled down a number, ripping the piece of paper off the pad, handing it to the investigator. The young man looked at it, said nothing, and trotted off to do what he was directed. He looked at the remaining investigator.

"You show me the scene."

Franco followed the investigator. They quickly looked over the first floor. There was damage from gunfire all around them. Franco looked about but didn't ask any questions. He stopped at one point and looked at the uncovered body at the bottom of the stairs. He didn't bend down, just walked around the body to look at it from different angles.

"We don't have an identity on either of the dead terrorists yet. We expect to have an ID by morning," said the investigator.

"This one's name is Emil Montoya," said Franco knowingly, "but please go ahead with the formal identification. Where's his weapon, underneath his body?"

The shocked investigator didn't answer right away. He was impressed Franco was able to identify the man.

"We don't think so, Sir," said the investigator. "We also didn't find a weapon at the top of the stairs where he was initially hit."

"Maybe his comrades took his weapons with them?"

"Possible, Sir," said the investigator who hesitated a second, "but the officers thought the man might have been pushed out from cover. They responded by firing back at whoever was shooting at them, but several are insistent this man was suddenly there, off balance, and in the line of fire."

Franco stood in silence. He was lost in thought when the elevator door opened. Several medical people pushed a stretcher out with one of the wounded on it. A second elevator door opened and another stretcher with another wounded person was brought out. Franco and the investigator watched the two wounded being pushed out of the building. An excited police officer came up to them.

"Captain," he said, "we've found some additional bodies down the hall and upstairs. They appear to be employees. People from the front desk and kitchen area. All shot in the head at close range, just like the Japanese here for this reunion."

Franco seemed to come out of his trance, "Reunion? What reunion?"

The investigator answered, "We had many Americans and Japanese here for a reunion of their World War II military units. Ten of the dead are Japanese nationals that appear to have been executed, shot in the head at close range."

"And the Americans?" asked Franco.

"Two of the dead and six of the wounded are Americans. The rest were employees of the hotel."

"There's more, Sir," said the police officer. "We have information from some of the employees that one of the hotel managers was seen working with the terrorists. A woman, they said she was carrying a weapon and working with an Anglo."

Franco was absorbing what he was told when the elevator door opened again. Another stretcher was wheeled out. He immediately recognized the American walking next to the stretcher. He abruptly walked away from the two policemen.

"Kevin," said Franco approaching the man beside the gurney. "Kevin Gateway!"

Kevin looked up and almost didn't recognize Franco. Franco put his arm on his shoulder.

"They shot Kathy, Jaime," said the American, tears running down his cheeks. "I went out to call the office and check in and they shot her. It looked like Becky tried to help her, but they took her, Dad, and the rest."

"Kevin, I know this isn't the time, but do you know who was responsible for this?" asked Franco.

Kevin looked at the policeman. "I haven't seen him in years, but I recognized him."

"Who'd you recognize, Kevin?" asked Franco leading the American through the door after the stretcher.

"My sister's ex-husband. His name's Patrick O'Keefe. He was an IRA terrorist. I don't know why he's here, but I know he's involved in some way."

They reached the ambulance the paramedics were loading Kathy into. They were working to keep her stabilized. Franco looked at the one closest to him who returned his gaze. He nodded the woman would live and then motioned for the husband to get into the vehicle. Franco helped the American into the rear of the ambulance, closing the door.

He watched the ambulance pull away. The investigator handed him the picture of a woman.

"Who's this?"

"It's a picture of the manager the other employees say was involved in the kidnapping."

Franco raised an eyebrow looking at the picture again. A black sedan pulled up to the scene, stopping only a few feet away. The passenger door opened, and Mangoba stepped out. He looked about at the chaos surrounding him. He spotted Franco and walked over.

"Jaime," he said still looking around, "what's going on here? It looks like a war zone."

Franco looked up from the picture, "It is a war zone. We've had over one hundred foreign nationals kidnapped. Others were executed. Robbie, it's also gotten personal. Do you remember the Gateway's from Hawaii?"

Mangoba nodded.

"Kevin just took Kathy away in that ambulance," he continued, "She's been badly wounded."

"That's not all the bad news," said Mangoba in return. "We have reports of heavily armed forces moving on several remote outposts in central Mindanao. We estimate a regiment or more with helicopter and armor support. We're getting killed out there and there's nothing we can do about it. The worst part is we have no new information to follow up on. We're strictly on the defensive."

Franco held out the picture of the hotel manager to his friend. He didn't offer an explanation but watched his friend's expression change.

"You don't think…," Mangoba never finished his sentence.

Franco smiled. "Not only that. I have the name Patrick O'Keefe from a witness. A positive identification."

The soldier looked at the policeman. "I think it's time to visit our friend Benny again."

Town of Princesa
Mindanao, Philippines
March 15, 1995
1400 Hours

The line of refugees passing through the center of town seemed endless. They started shortly after the neighboring village was attacked. The word carried by the refugees was the enemy force was supported by tanks and armored personnel carriers. People about town were quickly packing to leave, further clogging the narrow streets.

The colonel was sent to the area with the first reports of fighting. The military headquarters in Davao was preparing to send troops to the affected areas of the island but was dragging its feet. He talked to many of the refugees himself and wasn't happy with what he was hearing. The army commander assigned to Princesa did an excellent job in preparing the defense of the town but couldn't anticipate the refugees. The colonel was concerned they couldn't mount a serious defense without endangering civilians. They wisely decided to evacuate and try to move the population down the road.

A company of soldiers was assigned to the town since it was attacked the previous year. It was by far the largest concentration of government troops in the area. They put out observation posts and check points on every approach to the town. The colonel was pleased, but now he was concerned support wouldn't arrive before they would have to test the defenses.

The colonel watched the unending stream of refugees when a captain came running up to him. The younger officer looked worried.

"Colonel," he said gasping for breath, "we've spotted infantry to our north disrupting the flow of refugees. They appear to be setting up a road-block. Many of the refugees are turning back towards Princesa."

The colonel was quiet for a second. "Do you have an estimate on their strength?"

"At least a company, Sir!"

"Captain," the colonel noticed the town was becoming more crowded, "contact all your OP's and let me know immediately what they report. It appears whoever this is has managed to either encircle us or there is more than one unit. Assume all communications are being monitored. I have a feeling we are on our own here."

"Do you have a plan, Sir?" asked the captain.

"I do," replied the colonel, "but I need that information, so hurry."

"Yes, Sir!' The captain rushed off.

The colonel looked at the two soldiers sitting with him in the jeep. Both were non-commissioned officers who served with him for some time. He looked at the radio and then at the man sitting next to it.

"I'm afraid to ask, Colonel," said the sergeant powering up the radio.

"I have a feeling before today is over, we'll have to resort to the strategies that have worked for our people for hundreds of years."

"We'll make it more portable, Sir," said the second sergeant getting out of the front seat and moving to help the other enlisted man.

Osaka Pineapple Plantation
Mindanao, Philippines
March 15, 1995
1430 Hours

Osaka paced back and forth while his aides' answered telephones and radio calls. Wilson was kept busy at the situation map updating the progress of the operation. They captured or destroyed many of the small installations the Philippine Army had throughout central Mindanao. They were now engaging the larger units sent to stop their offensive.

Wilson smiled at his boss. Osaka was not a man to be nervous, but this operation was nothing like he'd ever done before. He motioned Osaka over to the map. Osaka looked at the American.

"How do you remain so calm, Gerald? I'm about to be sick to my stomach."

The American smiled. "I'm just as nervous as you, Sir. It just comes out differently for each of us. I wanted to show you where we stand now."

Osaka stood next to the American looking down at the map. "How are we doing?"

"We have pretty much taken control of the whole of central Mindanao. We are currently moving on the town of Princesa. Boerst reports there's a company size force there, as well as a police unit, but they're meeting little resistance. The same thing is happening in other areas of the island. The Philippine Army seems to be collapsing, at least the smaller units of it."

"What exactly do we control?" asked Osaka still looking at the map.

Wilson used a pencil to point at the map as he answered, "We control the island from Surigao in the extreme north here, to Kling here on the Celebes Sea. The Philippine Army has set up a heavily defended perimeter on the eastern side of the island from just east of Kling all the way up here to Cateel on the western shore."

"It looks as if they intend to defend the Davao area," observed Osaka out loud.

"Correct, Sir," responded Wilson, "and they have also decided to set up defenses here at the start of the Zamboanga Peninsula between Kapatagan and Pagadian. Most of the additional troops they've brought onto the island seem to be concentrated in these two areas. The regional military commander apparently didn't see the need to put them into the countryside. That's made our job easier."

Osaka stood looking at the map. Wilson knew he was absorbed in what he was looking at.

"We look to be ahead of our schedule," observed Osaka.

"We are," replied the American. "But remember these areas are heavily defended, and we will have to consolidate our troops in order to fight."

"Our recruiters are still getting us more troops. Not these native troops, although that recruiting must continue. The word I have just received is we'll have a thousand fresh troops flown in by the end of the week. That won't solve the problem, but it's a start. Tokyo said they'll get you some aircraft as well. That should help."

"Within the week, we'll have the new political directives underway in the territory we now control. That should help in controlling the locals. When will you start negotiations with Manila?"

"Also within the week," said Osaka. "What do you think this regional military commander will do?"

Wilson took a breath before he answered. "He's already been replaced by Manila, Mr. Osaka. The new commander is the general from army intelligence."

"Mangoba?" asked Osaka.

"Yes, Sir," replied the American. "I have to say, he has a much more realistic view on how to run an army than his predecessor. He'll be tough to deal with. I would recommend we move our forces here and take the Zamboanga Peninsula. We don't have the men to take on the number of troops the Filipinos have concentrated near Davao. As it is our troops will be hard pressed to hold the territory we've taken already, they'll be spread too thin. The same thing could happen to us that just happened to the Filipinos.

"What does Colonel Boerst say about this?"

"These are his recommendations, Sir, and I concur with them. Until we get those extra troops here and in place, we're not capable of following through with the operation."

Osaka looked at his aide and then back at the map. He looked troubled. "I don't like this. On the one hand our little operation is so successful we're ahead of schedule. On the other hand, we can't capitalize on our success because we don't have the resources in place to do so. I'm not comfortable with the Filipinos changing their ground commander. Mangoba is good and won't be easily tricked like his predecessor. I'm worried he may plan a counter offensive before the week is out."

Wilson started to say something, but Osaka waved his hand stopping him.

"No matter," he continued, "anything he can field now will be destroyed before they can have any effect on the outcome. Gerald, please ask Colonel

Boerst to follow through with his plans to invade the Zamboanga Peninsula. I will put pressure on the Manila government through my contacts to negotiate a settlement."

Before Wilson could answer his employer, one of the men working in the room brought him a folded piece of paper. The American opened it up and read it.

"Good news," said the American, "O'Keefe has the hostages and will be at Camp Freedom within the hour. It also appears Mr. Montoya was killed during the kidnapping by the police."

Osaka looked at his aide.

"Tell Patrick well done when he checks in. Do we have a replacement for Mr. Montoya?"

"Yes, Sir, we do," responded Wilson. "He's not as well known to his people as Montoya was, but he's popular with the men he leads.

"Good, get him back to Camp Freedom so he can be brought up to speed with the operation. Tell him he's now the leader of his movement and great things are in store for him. Does that communication say anything else?"

"Yes, Sir, it does. I'm not sure of the importance of either of these items, but…"

"Come on, man, read them!" said Osaka impatiently.

"Well, Sir, the first thing is our people took the Town of Princesa without a fight. It seems the residents and the Philippine Army detachment there disappeared into the jungle. They decided not to fight."

Osaka thought about this in silence before asking, "And the second item?"

"It appears Mr. Montoya executed ten of the Japanese hostages before O'Keefe stopped him. Our man said he killed each of them himself, shot them in the head."

Osaka wasn't sure how the Japanese government would react to this but did know how his superiors in Tokyo would. He needed to contact them immediately to set the record straight to allow the operation to continue. He thanked Wilson for his update and retired to his private office to make the call.

White House
Washington, D.C.
March 15, 1995
0100 Hours

The secret service agent woke the President of the United Sates about fifteen minutes before the chairman of the joint chiefs and secretary of defense arrived. Initially there was no reaction from the White House in response to the Moro Separatist forces except to send the Nimitz and her battle group into the Celebes Sea. Unknown to the president and his staff, at the same time he was giving that order, Americans were being kidnapped in Davao. Both men entering the White House knew their boss wouldn't be happy. Just prior to retiring for the night, the secretary of defense assured the president Americans were safe in the Philippines. Now, just a few hours later, he needed to tell him over one hundred Americans had been taken hostage and were being held in an unknown location.

The two men were ushered into the oval office as soon as they entered the building, finding the president waiting for them. He was dressed in a pair of blue jeans and a Stanford University sweatshirt. He was pacing back and forth in front of his desk. Both men could tell he was upset. This wouldn't be a pleasant meeting.

"How could this happen?" asked the president before the door was closed.

"Mr. President," said the secretary of defense walking to where the president was pacing, "we had no way of knowing this group would be bold enough, or have the resources, to attempt something of this magnitude. They've staged much smaller operations to this point. Even Manila was taken by surprise. There have been small assaults or one on one attacks, but nothing to give warning about what's happening now."

"I assume you're referring to the full-scale war taking place on Mindanao?" said the president.

"Yes, Sir."

The president looked carefully at Norman Jeffers. He had selected this man to be his secretary of defense for several reasons. First and foremost because he knew he would be candid with him about military matters. Jeffers had served in the army while the president had never served. The president had taken some heat during the election for not being a veteran and found he could dispel some morale issues in the military ranks by appointing someone like Jeffers to head defense. Jeffers moved into government work immediately following his discharge. He was older than the president and enjoyed a reputation for being loyal and honest. He was a capable administrator and kept his house clean of scandal and corruption. This was the second reason why he picked Jeffers. The president had a credibility issue during the election because of some accusations about poor business dealings. He knew he couldn't afford more trouble if he wanted to be elected to a second term in office.

"Talk to me gentlemen," said the President, "I need to move on this immediately."

Jeffers looked to General Goodman, who spoke. "I can give you the facts as we have them, Sir. Currently, we know this group is holding over one hundred hostages. We'll have the exact count by 0600 for you. We're in the process of trying to figure out who's missing and who was out sightseeing from the group."

"General, were most of the hostages really with a veteran's group?" asked the president.

Goodman's expression answered the question. "Yes sir, they're members of various World War II veteran's associations and their families. That's where we're having the difficulty coming up with an exact number. They were in the Philippines for the fiftieth anniversary of our invasion of Mindanao and just started their welcome remarks when the terrorists hit. We know we have one American Army officer killed and at least one veteran. There were at least six more people gravely wounded that were left behind."

The president shook his head. "The VFW and the American Legion will have a field day with this. They're already pounding on me for a soft foreign policy when it comes to matters like this."

"Then you won't like the rest, sir. We know for sure they executed at least ten Japanese nationals that were there for the same reunion. Shot each of them in the head at close range. They also killed eleven Filipinos during their attack. The Davao Police said they killed one of the leaders, a man named Emil Montoya. Unofficially our Filipino friends think he was sacrificed because he was responsible for the executions. There was another American officer at the reunion, but he's among the missing. Also on the list of the wounded is the wife of publisher Kevin Gateway."

"Damn!" said the president. "Gateways an influential man in the media. Why was he there?"

"This is the bad part, sir," said Goodman. "Mr. Gateway's father is a retired general who was there for the reunion. He retired from the army in the early eighties. He's been taken hostage along with his daughter and granddaughter. Gateway's wife is in critical condition but is expected to survive. We'll take more heat about the father. He is extremely active in veterans' groups."

"What are our options?" the president asked the secretary of defense.

"We have a Marine amphibious unit about three days away and we could have rangers in place on board Nimitz within twelve hours on the outside. From there they can move to wherever we need them."

"We can make the troop movements, Mr. President," said Goodman. "But we have no idea where the hostages are being held. We'll need that information before we do anything beyond deploying troops."

The president looked at both men. He continued to pace but motioned for the other two men to sit. Neither took his offer, both remained standing. Off to the side of the room a television report caught the president's attention. The news was showing pictures of the Davao police moving to clear the streets around the hotel the hostages had been taken from. It showed police officers knocking on doors and questioning people. The president reached down onto his desk and picked up the remote, turning up the sound.

"...Police are making a concerted effort to find witnesses to the escape of the terrorists and their victims," said a female voice on the television. "There's no official count of how many people were taken hostage, but we have received information that the number could be as high as one hundred and forty people."

The scene changed to the countryside and column of trucks on a road. There was smoke and flames to the front of the column and soldiers were running for cover away from the vehicles. A caption saying *file footage* scrolled across the bottom of the screen.

"At the same time this attack took place in one of this island's largest cities," the reporter continued. "The countryside has erupted into open warfare. Reports have come in that separatist forces have defeated government troops in numerous skirmishes during the day and now control a substantial part of the countryside. The Manila government has been silent about this report, but the military here is mobilized and on the move."

The picture changed again showing Sandy Monroe standing next to a road busy with military traffic.

"The situation here on Mindanao will take several days to sort out according to local authorities. The government has made it clear they will prevail over this new threat, even though they seem to be on the receiving end of the current attacks. The bigger question here seems to be what the United States will do with an undetermined number of American citizens being held hostage. Americans who were here for a reunion to commemorate the liberation of this island from Japanese control in World War II. So far, the White House has been silent. This is Sandy Monroe from the City of Davao in the Philippines."

The president pushed a button on the remote control muting the sound.

"I've never cared for her," said the president flatly.

"Sir," said Goodman, "Manila has relieved their regional commander in the area and replaced him with General Roberto Mangoba. Mangoba has overseen their intelligence operations for several years and is a good friend of the United States. If we contact him and offer our help, we'll have a better chance of finding the hostages. He's a cautious man, but a realistic one. He may be able to give our people the right places to look."

The president continued to pace, but both men knew it was not because he was nervous or indecisive. He was the type of person that thought best on his feet.

"Gentlemen," he said stopping in front of his desk, "I want all our options in place as quickly as we can get them there. Start the marines and get them in the area as quickly as possible. Get the rangers in place and we'll use them as our first option when we locate where they have our people. Get hold of this General Mangoba and tell him anything he needs we'll supply as long as we get our people out of there. How bad is all this fighting on Mindanao?"

Jeffers and Goodman looked at each other. Jeffers answered, "It's bad enough, Sir."

"Then let's tell our people in the Philippines to evacuate all non-essential personnel from any facilities we may have on Mindanao. I'll meet with you two along with State at 6:30 so we can prepare a statement for the 8:00 a.m.

press briefing. Plan on meeting with the veteran organizations sometime in the afternoon. I want them to know we're not just playing cards around here."

Both men nodded.

"Now, I'm going back up to the residence and get into something more appropriate for work. It's going to be a long day."

Bachelor Officer Quarters
Fort Benning, Georgia
March 15, 1995
0145 Hours

The telephone rang waking Naylor from a sound sleep. He leaned up on one elbow as the telephone rang a second time.

"Naylor."

"Charlie!" said a gruff voice Naylor recognized as Ben Goodman's.

"Sir," responded Naylor, "to what do I owe the pleasure at this hour?"

"Listen carefully, Charlie," said Goodman. "The duty officer is also getting a call. This is the real thing. Pick your best and be on a plane within the hour for the Philippines to get some hostages back. You'll get your information in route. Take at least a company although you'll have to decide on the size of the actual rescue force when we get more information. Good luck!"

Naylor was still not fully awake but knew this was not a joke by the general's tone.

"Yes Sir. Thank you, Sir," replied the soldier.

"I'll talk to you when you're airborne."

"Yes Sir!"

The telephone went dead. Naylor absorbed the information he had been given. He pushed down on the receiver button to get a dial tone and dialed a number. The telephone rang once.

"Duty officer, Fort Bragg. Captain Winters speaking."

"Captain," said Naylor, "this is Lieutenant Colonel Naylor of the First Ranger Battalion. Would you please contact Captain Richard Klintworth of my Battalion and give him my compliments? Please have his company ready for deployment within the hour."

"Yes Sir!" replied the voice on the other end of the phone. "The general also gives you his compliments, Sir. He'll meet you on the flight line when you're ready to go."

"Thank you, Captain. I'll be at headquarters in about twenty minutes."

"Yes Sir," replied Winters. The phone went dead.

Naylor decided to take a quick shower, he wasn't sure when he would get another.

Zamboanga Peninsula
Mindanao, Philippines
March 15, 1995
1600 Hours

The artillery fired its first volley on the hour. The barrage lasted over five minutes with the shells landing all around the Philippine Army positions. The soldiers there took cover wherever they could. They'd been spending the last several hours preparing their defenses in anticipation of this attack. The barrage was intense, but short lived. Several trucks were hit exploding into flames. Soldiers along the line were thankful the civilian population from the area had been forced to evacuate hours earlier. Extra troops were rushed up the peninsula from Zamboanga immediately upon Mangoba taking command. There were no armor units, only infantry and their support units. Mangoba guessed this is where the enemy would attack to continue their quest for control of the island.

When there was no answer from government artillery, Boerst ordered his assault to start. Infantry units supported by tanks moved forward. They quickly covered the first half mile toward the government lines. Suddenly, they came under heavy small arms fire across the line. This was followed by well-directed artillery fire, damaging two of the approaching tanks. Boerst pressed the attack only to find the artillery fire intensify. When he started to take excessive losses in men, he ordered his troops to fall back and started to set up his own defensive perimeter.

The attack lasted fifteen minutes, but he sustained more losses than he wanted to. He took the cell phone he carried, calling Osaka.

"We're not able to break through their defenses without sustaining heavy casualties," said Boerst. "If I had the troops and air support, I would continue the attack, but we need these men elsewhere if we want our plan to succeed."

Osaka answered. "Agreed, Colonel. Well done. At least now we know our friend, Mangoba will be no push over. We'll make him sweat now."

"Understood, Sir," said the soldier. Boerst gave orders to his commanders to harass the government troops dug in across from them with hourly mortar and artillery barrages. They had plenty of ammunition.

Camp Freedom
Mindanao, Philippines
March 15, 1995
1710 Hours

The small convoy passed through the gates. The camp was heavily guarded and additional vehicles met them, joining the escort. The large tractor trailer moved slowly down the narrow dirt road leading up to the group of buildings in the center of the compound. It came to a stop in front of a fenced in area surrounding the largest of the buildings. Armed men and women swarmed around the back end of the trailer. O'Keefe exited the closest car walking through the crowd followed by Rolle. O'Keefe gave orders to open the gates of the fenced in area. He then ordered the doors of the trailer opened.

The people inside moved slowly. The bright sunlight made them squint slowing their progress. First one, then two jumped off the back end of the trailer. Progress was slow getting down because there were no steps. They helped each other, carrying the injured and wounded. When the last one was off the trailer, one of the guards signaled the driver and the large vehicle pulled away. They were herded into the fenced in holding area. Two armed men were assigned to guard Gateway who was being held separately. Becky and Don Smith helped organize a make-shift triage area, looking at the wounded and injured. About twenty of the group fell into this category. The rest of the hostages were moved inside the building, only a few were allowed to stay and help the doctor.

Gateway stood helplessly watching his daughter and his friend. His granddaughter was permitted to work with her mother. He didn't see O'Keefe quietly walk up next to him.

"She's a pretty girl, isn't she, General?" said the Irishman.

Gateway, taken by surprise, jumped when O'Keefe spoke. The terrorist smiled. "You know the two of us aren't much different. We're both soldiers for a cause each of us believes in."

Gateway didn't look at the man next to him. "The problem is Patrick, you've sold out."

"No, not really," replied O'Keefe. "I've just changed causes. I still believe in my original cause; I just couldn't find anyone else as committed as I was. At some point reality set in."

"It's selling out plain and simple. I didn't agree with your cause, but at least I could respect you for believing in it."

"You cost me everything, old man," seethed O'Keefe, the tone changing. "Now it's my time to get even."

Gateway turned to look at the man. There was no emotion in the eyes staring back at him. He looked back at his granddaughter.

"All you've ever done in your life is destroy things, Patrick. Now you want to destroy everything closest to you."

O'Keefe seemed uneasy looking at the old soldier. "You're the one who destroyed everything close to me. My wife was turned against me, and I was never allowed to see my daughter. That was all your doing, not mine. As far as causes go, I like this one. The people are committed, and I get a chance to see my family."

Gateway didn't look at his former son-in-law. "You beat and hurt my daughter so you can blame me for what you want, but there was no way I could let that happen."

O'Keefe stood staring at the older man. He didn't respond to Gateway but motioned for the men guarding him to follow as he led the way towards the injured. They came to where Sarah was helping Mrs. Smith with one of the wounded conventioneers. As they approached, she made eye contact with her grandfather standing up. Catherine looked up for a second, then went right back to work.

"So, this is who you saw yesterday, Grandpa?" asked Sarah smiling.

O'Keefe was taken by surprise when Gateway nodded. "Like I told you yesterday, I saw the face in the crowd and then it was gone."

Sarah turned her attention to her father. "I've always wanted to meet you. I'm not sure how I feel about this right now and all, but Mom and Grandpa have told me a lot about you."

"I'm sure they have," said O'Keefe with a sour tone, glaring at Gateway.

"No," responded Sarah in defense of her grandfather, "they told me mostly the good things. Grandpa told me you were very committed and his forcing you to leave Mom was probably the hardest thing you ever had to do. Mom told me about the good times you two had. She never dwelled on the negative and neither did Grandpa."

"But they did tell you the negatives they wanted you to know," replied O'Keefe.

"Yes, they did, and they both told me that at some point in my life I would be able to make the decision whether to find you and hear your side. They both insisted on that."

O'Keefe was again surprised, turning to look at Gateway.

"I never liked you, Patrick. That's no secret," said Gateway. "Sarah's a lot like her mother. If I were to dictate to her, she would still have to find out for herself. You're a passionate man. That's one of the things I admire about you. I'll even say I was jealous of you because of it. I would never knowingly turn a child against a parent. You seem to be doing that all by yourself."

The hate returned to O'Keefe's eyes. Before he could respond, screaming from the other end of the line of wounded caught everyone's attention. Rolle was pointing her sub-machine gun at Becky. Becky was screaming at Rolle not to shoot while she covered the man she'd been tending with her own body. Rolle in turn was screaming for Becky to move so she could kill the man. A strange smile crossed Rolle's face as she raised her weapon to fire. O'Keefe sprinted forward. The two men guarding Gateway held him where he stood while another terrorist, this one a woman, grabbed Sarah as she started to move to help her mother.

"Hold!" shouted O'Keefe moving between the two women. "We will not kill anyone just yet."

Rage filled Rolle's eyes, but she lowered her weapon.

"She's protecting the American officer. He should have been killed and left at the hotel," Rolle shouted.

"You're correct, Suzanne, my dear," said O'Keefe putting both his hands up in front of his chest motioning for her to back off. "But it didn't happen and now's not the time to correct that mistake."

Rolle's mood didn't calm, "You're forgetting what she did to you. She deserves to die. I'll kill her for you."

"Your choice in women has deteriorated since we divorced," said Becky.

Rolle raised her weapon to fire, but O'Keefe pushed the muzzle towards the sky. Rolle didn't pull the trigger.

"I told you, no!!" said O'Keefe, raising his voice. "There's a time for this down the road, but not here and now. Go somewhere and cool off while we get them all tucked away and checked in!"

Rolle looked at O'Keefe like it was the first time he'd raised his voice to her.

"Now!" added O'Keefe to emphasize he meant business. Rolle wheeled around storming off towards one of the other buildings. She took long strides carrying her weapon in her hands like she was trying to break it in half.

"Thank you," said a soft voice from behind him. He turned to see his daughter standing next to her mother. He smiled at her and then turned to the guard closest to him and motioned for him to get the wounded inside the enclosure.

As the man started to comply, O'Keefe grabbed him by the arm saying, "Get them all inside and squared away. Then make sure Doctor O'Keefe has any supplies she needs."

The man nodded compliance and then called out to the rest of the guards standing nearby. O'Keefe marched off to call Osaka and calm down Rolle.

Basilian Strait
Mindanao, Philippines
March 15, 1995
2015 Hours

Holiday was a very patient man. He was enjoying his present job because the intelligence he was receiving from Osaka's people was right on the money. They received word three large container ships were headed from Manila to Zamboanga. They were being escorted by four navy patrol craft. They had sonar but weren't equipped for anti-submarine warfare. He decided to risk attacking in shallow water because of the cargo the ships were carrying.

The sun was starting to set. They were taking a leisurely course taking them back and forth across the strait near the harbor. Holiday was pleased. The crew had performed better than expected to this point and morale was high. He expected an easy kill as the big ships were not very maneuverable. He was sipping a cup of tea when he saw his radar operator sit straight up in his chair.

"Sir," said the young sailor, "I have multiple contacts bearing 282. Range 20,000 yards. I count three heavy contacts and four smaller ones."

"Sir," chimed in the sonar operator, I have four active sonars."

"Very good, gentlemen," said Holiday finishing his tea and setting the cup down, "Helm, bring us in closer to the mouth of the harbor. Make your heading 290, ahead one third."

"Heading 290, ahead one third, Aye Sir," came the reply.

The submarine turned, moving closer to the mouth of the harbor. Holiday ordered the periscope to be raised and looked until he found the ships. They were staying in close to shore. They would have to go out into the strait to make the turn into the harbor and that is when he would make his move. The first of the large container ships started to change course and head out into the strait to make her turn. As she did, Holiday saw something. Inboard of her was another patrol boat, larger than the rest, one he knew to have ASW capabilities.

"Sir," said the sonar operator, "I have another contact."

"Yes, I know," replied Holiday, "inboard of the first container ship."

"No, Sir, coming out of the harbor," came the reply.

Holiday wheeled the scoped around and saw another fast-moving patrol boat coming out of the harbor. He could just make out the bow of another close astern to the first one. They were of the same class as the boat inboard of the container ship. He turned the scope back to where the container ship was. He could see the second ship was starting to make her turn. There was another patrol boat inboard of her as well. The odds were changing quickly.

"We're going to only have one shot, lads. We've now got eight patrol boats out there and four of them have ASW capabilities. I'm guessing there's a ninth boat behind that last container ship so..."

"Sir, all of their sonars are currently active."

"Have they seen us yet?"

"No, Sir!"

"Rig for silence!" Holiday ordered quietly. "Load tubes one and two."

"Aye, Sir!" replied one of the officers.

"Helm," said Holiday, "immediately after we fire, turn us to course 090 and give me flank speed. Sonar, you let me know when we have enough water under the boat to dive her more than one hundred feet without hitting something."

"Aye, Sir!" both men said simultaneously.

One of the two patrol boats coming out of the harbor turned towards the submarine. As the patrol boat made her turn the first container ship turned to enter the harbor. The submarine had a perfect shot at her, and Holiday gave the order to fire. Two torpedoes shot out of the front of the submarine and sped towards their target. Holiday watched intently through the periscope and wasn't surprised when he saw the patrol boat react by changing course. Expecting this, he gave the order to change course and head to deeper water to allow themselves more maneuvering room.

On the bridge of the patrol boat, the captain received word from his sonar operator there were two torpedoes approaching rapidly from the east. Without hesitation, he ordered his vessel to alter course and parallel the course of the container ship. As the patrol boat began to respond he ordered all non-essential personnel below deck topside. He knew what he needed to do to neutralize the threat before him.

As the submarine turned, Holiday continued to watch through the periscope. He couldn't believe the patrol boat wasn't trying to close the distance on the submarine, but instead was turning to a course to parallel the container ship. Realization of what the patrol boat captain was doing came too late. Suddenly, two more of the larger patrol boats came out from behind the first container ship at flank speed. He had to continue to run or risk losing the boat. He hoped the patrol boat captain would lose his gamble.

The patrol boat steadied her course with that of the container ship. Most of her crew came scrambling up ladders to her weather decks. One of the sailors on watch spotted the torpedoes about thirty seconds away. The captain gave the order for the rest of this crew to race topside, hoping he'd given them enough time to save themselves. It seemed like hours before the first torpedo struck the patrol boat amidships. The boat shook violently, knocking most of the crew off their feet. The second torpedo went astern of the patrol boat, but somehow missed all the other ships racing for the safety of the harbor. The captain of the patrol boat knew his vessel was fatally wounded, so gave the order for his crew to abandon ship. The patrol boat's engines were disabled by the torpedo. She was on fire and drifting towards shore. The crew began to leave the ship, the captain pleased that only a few of his crew were unaccounted for.

The other patrol boats raced passed their crippled sister in pursuit of the mysterious attacker. The sub was on sonar, and they were after her like hounds on a fox. One patrol boat moved next to the stricken craft to assist with the evacuation. Other patrol craft deployed to prevent the submarine from circling around behind the container ships scrambling for the safety of the harbor.

Holiday saw all of this through the periscope. The three container ships were now safely in the harbor. He cursed under his breath. The patrol boats were gaining on his boat, and he was worried they would get into torpedo range before the submarine would be able to dive into deeper water. In shallow water, they were too easy a target.

"Sir, we've reached the edge of the shelf. We have one hundred meters of water below us," said the sonar operator.

Holiday breathed a sigh of relief. "Helm, turn to course 180, all ahead flank. Take her down to sixty meters."

The helmsman repeated the commands as he complied. The submarine slowly turned and began to dive. Holiday was upset they missed their target. It should have been an easy kill. The Filipino tactics had become more aggressive. They were suddenly willing to sacrifice men and equipment to accomplish their mission.

Philippine Army Intelligence Headquarters
Mindanao, Philippines
March 15, 1995
2045 Hours

Franco passed through security on the base easily. He guessed they knew he was expected by Mangoba to update him on the hotel kidnapping. He entered the large community office. A non-commissioned officer met him at the door, escorting him to Mangoba's office. He sensed a shift in attitude. All military personnel in the room were carrying side arms. Soldiers covered up what they were working on as Jaime passed by.

Mangoba was dressed in a camouflage uniform and a pistol was sitting on his desk.

"I sense things have changed since yesterday," said Franco.

"Since we talked this morning, my friend," replied Mangoba. "I've been given the command of all military forces on Mindanao. My mission has changed just a bit."

Franco took a seat across from the general. "Interesting, I expect you don't have a lot of time to talk to me then. I can make this short."

Mangoba looked up. "Nonsense, Jaime, you now work for me. All military and police are now directed from this office. This kidnapping is critical to what is going on and is all I want you to work on. Manila also wants me to send Benny to them."

Franco sat up straight.

"Don't worry, my friend," continued Mangoba. "I expect you can lose him for a while. I know he has more information to share with us. My people will be too busy to continue the questioning so I thought you might like to have a crack at it."

Franco nodded. A colonel he met before came in with a handful of papers. The colonel looked at Franco. "I'm sorry, Sir. I didn't know you were busy. I'll come back."

"Nonsense, Colonel," said Mangoba. "What is it?"

The colonel looked at Franco and then back at the general. Mangoba raised an eyebrow.

"Colonel, please have a seat and share with us," said Mangoba, motioning to an empty chair. "There's nothing you can't say in front of Captain Franco.

He possesses sensitive information you haven't been privy to, so I think it's time we all know who the members of our team are."

The army officer flushed slightly.

Mangoba smiled saying, "I see I made my point. Now, Colonel, what is it?"

"This submarine the separatists have attacked the convoy in route to Zamboanga."

Franco watched his friend stiffen.

"The added escorts you sent seemed to catch the submarine by surprise. None of the transports were hit, but we did lose one of the escorts. The ship's captain ran interference taking a torpedo meant for one of the transports. He managed to save most of his crew. The tanks we needed on that side of the island are off loading as we speak."

Mangoba took a deep breath.

"You say the captain of the escort sacrificed his own ship?" asked Mangoba.

"Yes Sir," replied his subordinate, "he turned into the first torpedo and the second one missed. The escort ran aground before it could sink. Three sailors were killed and twelve were wounded. The other escorts pursued the sub, but she escaped into deep water."

Mangoba beamed. "Outstanding. Tell the captain he and his crew should be commended. They've given us the break we need to turn the tide here. Send a 'well done' to all the units involved and have the commander in Zamboanga get those tanks up to the lines around Pagadian by morning. We need to be ready to move in the next couple of days. Jaime, what's the count on the hostages? How's Kathy Gateway?"

The sudden shift in topics didn't take either of the men sitting across from the general by surprise.

"There are one hundred twenty-four American conventioneers and one American army officer unaccounted for," said Franco. "Mrs. Gateway is doing well, although her condition prohibits her being evacuated to Manila. Kevin is holding his own. We have also found out that there are fifteen Japanese conventioneers unaccounted for. They are presumed to be with the Americans. Two Americans were killed and eight were wounded during the attack. Ten Japanese nationals are also confirmed dead. Ten Filipinos are confirmed dead and eighteen wounded. The numbers have fluctuated some from the initial estimates because of the confusion at the crime scene after the attack. Two of the terrorists were killed and two policemen were wounded. The coroner has confirmed the one terrorist was Emil Montoya."

"Sir," said the colonel, "the Japanese government has filed a formal protest with Manila over the attack and kidnapping."

Mangoba looked perturbed the colonel brought up Manila. He looked at Franco.

"The Colonel's correct, General," replied the policeman. "Manila has also approved Tokyo's request to send an observer to monitor our investigation."

Mangoba looked as if he were pleading to move on to another topic. Franco grinned. "You've talked to the observer recently regarding some other issues."

Mangoba's attitude changed instantly. "Tobi?"

Mangoba thought for a second. "Colonel, along with your other duties, I'd like you and Captain Franco to keep in touch daily. The captain will be entertaining one of the top people in the Japanese Intelligence community. I'll need a daily update."

"Yes, Sir!" replied the Colonel writing information on a steno pad.

"Now, gentlemen," said Mangoba, "I have a conference call between Manila and Washington."

U.S.S. Nimitz
Pacific Ocean Southeast of Mindanao
March 15, 1995
2100 Hours

Kingston was sitting at the table in his quarters having dinner with his aides. It had been a quiet and uneventful trip. The task force was in a high state of readiness because of the submarine threat. They were passing between Mindanao and the Kepulauan Island group entering the Celebes Sea. Kingston thought they should have a quiet meal after such a long day.

Handcock sat to his right, Williams to his left. There was an empty chair where Captain Brothers was supposed to be sitting. This bothered him, but he knew there could be a good reason for the captain's absence. The stewards just began serving the salad when there was a knock at the door.

"Come!" said Kingston.

The door opened and Brothers entered. He smiled at the admiral, walking towards him. "Sorry I'm late, Sir. I was called to communications. We received a priority message."

Brothers handed a piece of paper to the admiral, then stepped back. Kingston motioned for Brothers to be seated. Brothers complied and the mess people served him his salad. Kingston looked up.

"And so it starts. How ready are we for receiving that many visitors?"

"I asked Captain Rice to investigate and report here with the answer. They'll probably leave some people here when they find out where the hostages are being held. A company will probably be too big a unit for the mission."

The admiral motioned for the mess people to come and remove the salad plates. Both Handcock and Williams sat in silence knowing they would eventually find out what was going on.

"Has there been anything from intel about a possible location?"

"No Sir," replied Brothers. "I think they're just getting our assets in place. They're also sending an Amphibious Ready Group into the area. They expect they should be close enough, if needed, within three days."

The stewards began to serve dinner. The main course was chicken served over rice. The room filled with the aroma of the food.

"What's the lead ship in that group?" asked Kingston.

Brothers looked over at Kingston, who was busy with is food. It was a natural question for him to ask because there was the possibility if the two groups merged, he, or the commander of the other group, would end up in command of both.

"The lead ship is the Tarawa, Sir," replied Brothers still watching his boss. "Skip Marienetti is in command."

"Skip's a good man," replied Kingston. "Make plans to merge both groups if necessary. I don't expect we'll have to, but we better be prepared."

Kingston's attitude appeared nonchalant, although Brothers knew it to be otherwise. Being in control was always the top priority in Kingston's life. That was the first thing his subordinates learned about him. Captain Skip Marienetti would pose no threat to that priority. As the four of them continued to eat dinner, there was a knock on the door.

"Come," said Kingston flatly.

Marine Captain Tiffany Rice entered the admiral's cabin. She closed the door behind her, stepping close to the table, and coming to attention. Rice was in her late twenties, with a pretty face and a nice smile. She had dark hair and dark eyes. Her hair was cut short falling just above her shoulders. Brothers found her to be an extremely efficient officer excelling at her job. He also thought she had a wonderful sense of humor. She was a good addition to the crew of the *Nimitz* as commander of the Marine security detachment.

Brothers knew this was the main reason Kingston didn't care for her. The admiral didn't keep his distaste for women on a ship of the line a secret. While he preached the party line, he made no attempt to hide his true feelings. Brothers was finding aside from some minor issues, the female personnel on board were doing an excellent job. Morale seemed higher. It was still a novelty. For the time being, though, he was more than satisfied with Rice's performance.

Kingston didn't say anything to Rice, letting her stand there at attention. He cut another piece of chicken, put it in his mouth and took his time chewing it. When he finished, he put his fork down looking up at her.

"As you were, Captain," he said allowing her to stand at ease. "What do you have to report?"

"Sir," she said, "I have located suitable quarters for the entire company of rangers when they arrive. There should be no problem in accommodating them if they stay on board for a period. We also have hanger space for any aircraft accompanying them for their mission."

"Thank you, Captain," said Kingston looking bored. "You may carry on. Report directly to Captain Brothers. That is all."

"Aye, aye, Sir."

Rice showed no emotion as she turned, leaving the room. Brothers wasn't happy with the way the admiral treated the marine officer but wasn't going to say anything to him in front of his aides. He would mention it when they were alone, although he suspected his concerns would fall on deaf ears. The fact both aides were smiling upset Brothers even more.

The Admiral looked at Handcock. "Lieutenant, after dinner, I have some radio traffic for you to take care of."

"Yes, Sir!"

177 Pinecreek Drive
Rochester, New York
March 15, 1995
0715 Hours

Nancy was headed through the kitchen on her way to the garage when the phone rang. She debated about not answering but decided it could be something important. She put her purse and school papers down on the counter as the phone rang for the second time.

"Hello?"

"Is Jon Summers there, please?" asked the tired sounding voice.

"No, he isn't," said Nancy cautiously, "May I take a message?"

There was a second of silence before the voice on the other end of the phone spoke again. "Could you tell me where I might contact him? It's an emergency."

Nancy's curiosity was peaked. "This is his wife. May I ask what this is about?"

"Nancy. Thank God," said the voice. "It's John Cummings. I need to speak to Jon right away. It's a matter of life or death."

Nancy smiled. "It always is, Admiral."

The comment took the man by surprise. Nancy's smile broadened. "I'm sorry, Admiral. That wasn't very polite."

"But true," chuckled Cummings.

"Look, Admiral," said Nancy. "He's already at school and probably up to his neck in bad little boys and girls. You can reach him at 555-1500 and then just follow the directions the automated switch board gives you. I'm sorry about giving you a hard time, Admiral. I didn't know who you were."

"It's my fault, Nancy. I should have identified myself. It's been a long night."

"Sounds serious," stated Nancy not thinking.

"You haven't heard?" came the surprised reply.

"No?"

There was a long silence before Cummings answered, "Nancy, turn on the news. Anything I can tell you; you can get from there. Look, I have to go. Thank you. I'll contact him at work. Have a good day."

"You, too, Admiral," replied Nancy, her interest peaked again. She hung up and reached for the small television they kept near the kitchen, turning it on. There was a news cast on showing the inside of a hotel lobby damaged by gunfire. Nancy looked in horror as the caption said *Davao, Philippines.*

"The terrorists struck as the opening remarks for the reunion were being made," said the female reporter. "They took hostages, the majority who appear to be American nationals. The total number remains undisclosed by the Manila government, but sources close to the investigation say the number could be as high as one hundred and forty people. There were several deaths during the attack, including two terrorists who were killed in a gun battle with responding police."

The picture changed from the damaged hotel to bodies covered by plastic. It then changed again to show medical teams rushing wounded people to ambulances.

"The number wounded has not been released, but it has been confirmed that the wife of publishing mogul, Kevin Gateway was among them. The..."

Nancy turned the set off picking up the phone again. She dialed a number and patiently waited. When the pleasant female voice answered, Nancy gave her name, grade level, and the school she worked at. She told the woman she needed the day for a family emergency. The woman verified the information thanking Nancy for calling. She then sat down turning the television back on, while tears started to run down her face.

Osaka Pineapple Plantation
Mindanao, Philippines
March 15, 1995
2130 Hours

Osaka was on the phone with Tokyo when the message was brought in. Wilson took it, reading it. He smiled and went back to what he was doing. His helicopters were being kept busy moving troops and supplies and it looked like they would be working well into the night. The speed with which they moved on the government troops surprised everyone. Many of the larger units disappeared into the jungle, not wanting to stand and fight.

Osaka was trying to negotiate the arrival of more troops so they could move on the two government strongholds left on the island.

Osaka finished, walking over to Wilson, who handed him the note. Osaka read it. He handed it back to Wilson looking down at the map.

"Our agent in Hawaii is worth their weight in gold. You read the message?"

"Yes, Sir, I did," replied Wilson. "Seems like a normal response for the United States. If the information keeps coming this quick, we'll be ready for any response the Americans make."

Osaka smiled, feeling everything was in place for their operation to be a success.

Lakeview High School
Rochester, New York
March 15, 1995
0830 Hours

It had already been a full day by school standards. Summers sat in his office reading over student referrals. He leaned back in his chair, sipping his second cup of coffee, reading the first referral. The phone rang causing him to jump, almost spilling his coffee.

"Jon Summers. May I help you?"

"Jon, its Susan," said the voice. "Are you going to be in your office for the next few minutes?"

"Yes, Ma'am," replied Jon. "I just sat down to deal with a few disciplinary issues."

"I'll be down in a minute," came the reply, "I have some people you need to meet."

"OK, boss," said Jon. "I'll be here."

Jon thought for a second, then got up walking into the outer office. He looked at his secretary.

"Mrs. Henderson, do you know if Mrs. Singleton was expecting any visitors today?"

Kathy stopped typing looking over her glasses at her boss. "Not that I'm aware of Mr. Summers. Why do you ask?"

"She's on her way down here with some visitors. I'll be in my office until they get here."

"Should I make extra coffee?" asked the secretary.

"I don't think so," replied Jon walking back into his office.

Henderson walked over to the coffee pot saying to herself, "What does he know? Men just don't get it."

Jon busied himself cleaning off the conference table. He wondered who Susan could be bringing down. Maybe it was a parent, that was their most common unannounced guest. Jon didn't think this was the case though. Susan took her job very seriously. If she had an upset parent in her office, she wouldn't sound so upbeat. She was good at giving her vice principals warning about that type of surprise so they could prepare.

Before he could finish cleaning there was a knock at the door. He turned to see Susan standing there. She was smiling and behind her were two men in suits. Behind them was a Marine Corps colonel Jon knew all too well. George Ellison was a handsome man with a wonderful sense of humor. They served together on several occasions, most recently during the Gulf War. Ellison immediately put out his hand.

"George," said Jon, sounding surprised, "what are you doing here?"

"It's been a very interesting morning, Jon," Susan said before the marine could answer. "It seems while you're here doing your job, dealing with our students and such, I'm busy on the telephone talking to the chairman of the joint chiefs."

Jon looked at his boss not understanding what she was talking about.

"Then, while I'm talking to him, who should get on the phone, but the President of the United States."

"I don't understand, Susan," said Jon looking puzzled.

"They were calling to talk to you, and somehow ended up with me. I believe it was because you were tied up with the planning meeting. They impressed upon me to allow you to be released for additional emergency military duty. Man, I tell you, the president is a charmer. Of course, I said *yes*. You never told me you ran in such high circles."

Jon looked at his boss raising an eyebrow. "I didn't know that either, Susan. I've never spoken to the president before. I also have no idea what's going on."

"Well, they won't tell me, all I get is that it's a military secret or something. The president said he knows it's unusual to request this type of a call up, but he wouldn't do it if it wasn't important. I didn't vote for the man, but I can see why a lot of people did. He can be quite sincere."

Jon looked at Ellison, who handed him an envelope. He continued looking at the man while he opened the envelope, taking out its contents. Jon read the memo on top, then looked up at the marine officer. Ellison smiled.

"It looks serious," Jon simply said.

"It gets worse," was the reply.

"What's serious?" asked Susan. "Sounds interesting whatever it is."

Ellison looked at the school principal smiling. "It's nothing to concern you, Ma'am. Just some issues that suits Mr. Summers many talents. Say, do you have some coffee?"

Susan smiled back at the colonel. "Why, yes, I believe I saw Mrs. Henderson making some as we came in."

"I'd love some coffee. Bad habit I picked up when I joined the Corps, Ma'am. Quit smoking three years ago, cut down on the alcohol I consume, but I still need my coffee."

Susan smiled at the officer knowing he was being very polite in trying to get rid of her. "Tell you what, Colonel. I'll go get us all a cup and leave you alone for a minute."

"Thank you very much, Ma'am," said the officer.

Susan left the group and went over to the coffee. The men didn't close the door but did lower their voices.

"I'd like to say it's good to see you, George, but under the circumstances, I think I should pass."

Ellison continued to smile. "It's the only kind of circumstances that allows us to see each other, Jonny."

Summers chuckled.

"As you can see," continued Ellison, "the brass is requesting your presence immediately in Washington to investigate this issue. They know your good friends with some of the hostages but want to talk to you before they react to this situation."

"And they didn't think I would come quietly so they sent you, with help," observed Jon motioning to the other two men.

Ellison blushed slightly. "Sorry guys, I get carried away sometimes and forget the basics. Jon Summers, I would like you to meet Mark Wells, special agent with NCIS, and Glenn Grey, special agent with the FBI."

Jon reached out shaking Well's hand. He was a slender man in his mid-thirties with a receding hair line. He wore a pair of wire rimmed glasses and a big toothy smile. Grey was a black man with short hair. He was about four inches taller than Wells.

"Gentlemen," said Jon, "it's nice to meet you. I have to say if you're keeping this reprobate company, your reputation will certainly suffer."

Ellison gave Jon a sour look while the other two men laughed.

"We're assigned to investigate how this incident took place and hopefully help in recovering the hostages," said Wells, looking serious.

"I'm sure the packet the colonel gave you will explain everything," said Grey. "We're leaving from D.C. late this afternoon to join the investigators already at the scene. We were hoping you would be coming with us."

Jon held up the envelope saying, "I may not have much of a choice."

The FBI man smiled back at Jon.

"Why is the Naval Criminal Investigation Service involved in the investigation of a terrorist act in the Philippines?" asked Jon.

Wells answered cautiously. "It seems that someone in Naval Intelligence has a theory that foreign industries are courting high ranking naval officers for more than the opportunities to sell their wares to the United States Navy. The CNO was disturbed by this initial report and asked us to follow-up. We were looking at several groups, including the one you identified in your reports. Now they show up linked to the attempted takeover of an Allied country and we get nervous."

"I gather this is not a routine investigation?" asked Jon flatly.

"Our main goal is to resolve this hostage situation, Jon," said Ellison. "Anything beyond that we get bonus points."

"You two don't need any more bonus points," said a voice from behind them.

All four men turned to find Nancy standing there holding a suitcase, duffel, and a clothes bag. Jon and Ellison both moved forward at the same time. Jon took the suitcase and the duffel from his wife, while George grabbed the clothes bag.

"It figures they sent you to round him up, George," said Nancy walking past the four men blocking the doorway to Jon's office.

"It's nice to see you, too, Nancy," replied Ellison. "Do you think I only show up to steal your husband to run off to some third world country and save the world?"

"Yes," replied Nancy getting up on her tip toes kissing Ellison on the cheek, "but I love you just the same."

Jon looked at his wife, "So does everyone know about this but me?"

"More than likely, Jon," answered his wife. "You left in such a hurry. Unless you caught a newscast, you wouldn't have had any idea. I wouldn't know if I hadn't taken the call from John Cummings."

Jon looked at his wife asking, "How bad?"

A tear was in his wife's eye, "Kathy Gateway's in the hospital in Davao according to the news. Kevin's OK, but I think the rest of the family is being held hostage. I'm really worried, Jon."

"Guys," Jon directed his next statement to the three men standing in the doorway, "give me five minutes to change and we can get out of here."

The three men backed out of the doorway, Ellison closing it behind him. Jon quickly opened the clothes bag and took out a blue uniform.

"I packed your blues and a set of whites," said Nancy, "not knowing what you're going to need. I packed khakis in the suitcase and some civvies as well. Your caps are in the clothes bag. Anything I forgot?"

"There was a package Dad had for Bill…"

"In your suitcase along with your .45 and your ammo."

Jon raised an eyebrow knowing how his wife felt about weapons.

"Daddy packed it for me."

Jon finished putting on his uniform except for his blue jacket. He was wearing highly polished black shoes, dark blue pants, and a white shirt with shoulder boards. On the table sat a white cap with gold braid on the black brim. Jon walked around the table to where his wife stood and put his arms around her and squeezed.

"I love you, honey. Thanks for being so understanding."

Tears were coming down Nancy's cheeks as she hugged her husband back. "I'm not being understanding, Jon. They've hurt people I care about. This is personal. You never think people you know, and love, will be part of something like this. This one just hit too close to home."

The door opened and Ellison poked his head in. "Jon, we better go. Principal Susan is asking too many questions and I think Wells is about to take her into custody."

Both Jon and Nancy laughed at the joke. Nancy put her hands on her husband's cheeks and kissed him hard on the mouth. When she was done, she rested her arms on his shoulders saying, "Kick their ass, sailor. It's personal and I want them to hurt."

She hugged her husband one last time before he left.

East of Kibawe
Mindanao, Philippines
March 15, 1995
2335 Hours

The colonel looked down at the map. He wasn't sure how they'd managed to do it, but they evacuated the population of Princesa into the jungles and mountains of Mindanao. He'd also found out many of the military units in the area did the same thing. He spent most of the day contacting many of those units, trying to organize formal resistance. He had been in touch with headquarters and found out he had a new commander. He was pleased with the orders he'd been given and was hoping to implement them in the next couple of days.

A noise from the cave entrance made him look up. An old man he recognized from Princesa. He walked up to the colonel and held out a cup.

"Coffee for you, Colonel," said the old man.

The colonel met the old man's eyes. They seemed to twinkle. The officer took the cup taking a sip.

"You've done this before?" asked the colonel.

"Yes, Sir," answered the old man. "Fifty years ago when I was a boy I hid in these mountains from the Japanese. I guided for the Americans when they landed."

The colonel waved at the map in front of him. The oil lamp he was using illuminated the map enough so the old man could see.

"Do you have any recommendations for other places we can hide people for a short period?"

The old man moved closer to the map. "I assume more of our people are doing what we did?"

The army officer looked at the map. "Call it an unplanned strategy, but yes, more than I expected. It looks like we have enough soldiers in hiding to create our own army."

"Don't forget the people," said the old man. "We're hiding, too, and want to go back to our homes. We'll fight as well, until help arrives."

The colonel smiled, nodding. There was another sound from the mouth of the cave and a boy appeared. He was carrying a plate of food which he handed to the old man. The old man in turn gave the plate to the soldier. The colonel looked at the food shaking his head.

"I can't take your food. There's so little to go around."

"Nonsense, Colonel," replied the old man. "There is nothing on this plate we didn't scavenge from the jungle. Eat well, and then get some rest. The one thing you'll be short of is sleep. Get some while you can."

The soldier looked at the old man and the boy. He smiled eating some of the food. He offered some back to his two companions. Both took some and began eating as well. The colonel was feeling optimistic.

Navy and Marine Corps Reserve Center
Rochester, New York
March 15, 1995
1030 Hours

The two automobiles pulled into the front parking lot of the center, taking the first two available spaces. The local FBI office was providing transportation and an air force jet was waiting for them on the commercial side of the airport. They would have gone straight to the aircraft, but Ellison wanted to check Summers out on a new handgun. They walked in the front door, the reservist sitting in the office by the entrance coming to attention when he saw the two officers.

"As you were, Marine," said Ellison to the man behind the desk. "I'm Colonel Ellison. I'm supposed to meet the range officer to qualify Captain Summers here on his new sidearm."

The corporal moved to the at ease position. "The Lieutenant and the Gunny are on the range, Sir. The rest of your people are waiting there for you, Sir."

"The rest of my people Corporal? I don't understand," said Ellison.

"The air force officer and the petty officer," answered the corporal.

There was a sign-in book on the counter near the corporal. Jon signed in while Ellison was speaking. He handed the pen to the other men with him, each signing in.

"I know the air force officer," continued Ellison, but I have no idea why there's a petty officer here."

"The petty officer would be here for me," said Summers.

Ellison shrugged his shoulders as he signed into the center.

"That clears that up. Where's the range, son?"

The corporal smiled for the first time since they'd entered the center.

"Captain Summers knows the way, Sir. Excuse me, Captain. Are you giving up on the forty-five, finally, Sir?"

Ellison smiled answering for Summers.

"Corporal, the Captain will probably carry that antique to the grave with him. I'm giving him an alternative weapon I think he just might use."

"I haven't seen anyone shoot like the captain with a 1911, Sir," said the marine. "I figured he would retire before using a different weapon."

"I just may, Corporal," said Summers flashing Ellison a dirty look. "The Colonel is a better shot than I am. I'm guessing he just is looking for a way to humiliate me."

"Don't believe a word he's saying, Corporal," said Ellison with a straight face. "He's just jealous. You know how SEALs get. The marines do the firearms instruction here, don't they?"

"Yes, Sir, they do," replied the corporal with pride.

"I rest my case," said Ellison. "Would you let the range officer know we're on our way down to him?"

"Yes, Sir!" said the corporal. "So you know, Sirs, one of the local police department SWAT teams is on the range, receiving automatic weapons training."

Ellison thanked the corporal following Summers down the hallway. They walked to the end of the hall. Summers opened a door, and you could hear the muffled sounds of gunfire. They walked into a large classroom with desks and a blackboard. Half of the back wall was glass, and you could see two Marines working with a dozen men dressed in black uniforms. Sitting at one of the desks was a female air force officer and a navy petty officer. The petty officer saw them enter and immediately stood, coming to attention. The officer followed suit. When Summers walked over the petty officer handed a large manila envelope to him.

"These came for you this morning, Sir," said McAvoy. "I was told to pack a bag, Sir, and to remain at your disposal."

"As you were," said Summers. "It'll be good to have you along, Petty Officer."

Summers turned to the officer. "Congratulations on your promotion, Captain"

"Thank you, Sir," said Judy Demmer. "It's good to see you again."

"What's your job on this mission?"

Demmer smiled. "Computer specialist."

The gunfire on the range stopped and Summers turned to see the black clad police officers turning around. He immediately recognized Ron Hapke. Hapke recognized Summers pointing him out to the officer who had been at the restaurant with him. The marine lieutenant came through the door, immediately coming to attention. This seemed to cause Hapke and his friends to laugh. The rest of the policemen looked disturbed by this, unconsciously stepping away from their comrades.

"Welcome to my range, Sirs," said the lieutenant. "What can I do for you, Colonel?"

"At ease, Lieutenant," responded Ellison. "I would like you to check out Captain Summers on a new weapon."

The younger marine laughed. "Giving up on the old forty-five, Captain?"

Ellison reached into his brief case pulling out a Glock handgun, placing it on the desk in front of him. He then reached in pulling out three magazines, each with thirteen rounds of .45 caliber ammunition.

"I see that you intend to move the captain up in the world, Sir," said the range officer.

"Correct, Lieutenant," replied Ellison with a smile. "We old soldiers can't get away from the heavy hitters. At least this will give him five more chances than the 1911."

"I've seen him shoot, Sir. He doesn't need the extra chances."

"You've never seen the Colonel shoot, Lieutenant," chimed in Summers. "He rates people by his standards."

There was laughter from the policemen huddled around Hapke. The lieutenant gave them a dirty look over his shoulder. "These gentlemen can take a break and we can do this right now, Sir, if you don't mind."

"That would be wonderful, Lieutenant," replied Ellison.

The younger officer opened the door and led the two men onto the range. When they entered the range, Hapke said something to the officers with him. They laughed, looking at the visitors. Summers and Ellison ignored the laughter, but it seemed to irritate the lieutenant. An older gunnery sergeant met them as they moved towards the range.

"Gunny," said the lieutenant, moving forward, "we're gonna take a quick break and recert the Captain on the Glock."

"Aye, aye, Sir," replied the sergeant. He glanced at Summers.

"You going to finally get away from the Colt, Sir?'

"Damn, Summers," laughed Hapke. "You gonna finally learn how to shoot after all these years? Ferland told me you were some sort of war hero or something. I guess he was wrong. I always figured you to be a pussy."

Summers ignored the comment and the laughter from the group. When Summers stepped up the line, Hapke moved forward a step.

"That night at the restaurant, you wouldn't fight. What's wrong? You a coward or what? You know your sister's good in bed. You cost me a good lay that night. I should just kick your ass now and get it over with."

Summers's face flushed, but he didn't respond to either Hapke's move forward or to the comment. The FBI agents in the classroom watched the men on the range. All of them started for the door, reaching for their weapons when Hapke jumped forward trying to push Summers from behind.

Summers exploded into the police sergeant, throwing him into the air, landing on his back with the naval officer on top of him. Summers had his left hand locked on the man's throat so he couldn't breathe, his knee on the man's chest causing added distress. Hapke was desperately trying to remove Summers's grip with his two hands. With his right hand, Summers managed to get Hapke's Beretta out of its holster. Hapke's friend from the restaurant tried moving forward to help his comrade only to find himself looking down the barrel of the pistol being held by Ellison. The man froze dead in his tracks, looking into the cold eyes of the angry marine. The other members of the group were quickly subdued by the lieutenant and the sergeant. The remaining members of the SWAT team decided not to get involved because the agents from the classroom came rushing into the range, covering them with their weapons.

Everyone froze when there was the sudden sound of gunfire. They turned to find Summers firing Hapke's weapon down range at one of the targets with his right hand, still holding the policeman's throat with his left. He fired until the pistol was empty, and the action remained open. He pressed the button on the side of the weapon, releasing the empty clip. He tossed the pistol as far down range as he could. He then let go of Hapke's throat, picked him up, and threw him face first into the window. One of the FBI agents grabbed Hapke's hands, placing them behind his head. The policeman was gasping for breath.

Marines, from elsewhere in the center, came rushing in. They were immediately ordered to disarm the entire SWAT team and move them to the classroom.

Wells looked at Summers asking, "What was the grab him by the throat thing?"

Summers took the Glock from Ellison as the marine moved his captive up against the glass wall. "Mr. Wells, they can't fight if they can't breathe."

"It's pretty basic stuff, Mr. Wells," added Ellison.

"Wait until I get you the next time we meet, old man," said the policemen. "Without that gun, you won't be shit. It could have misfired and killed someone."

Ellison leaned as close to the man's ear as he could. "Boy, I was killing better men than you in the jungle when you were five years old. The only thing I have that might misfire is between my legs. The very last thing that you want to do is make an issue out of this. You might not be as lucky as you were today."

"And besides, son," said Summers, as he pushed a full clip into the Glock, "the next time a man points a gun at you, make sure it's loaded and don't hesitate. It's the hesitation that'll get you killed. You should thank the colonel for the free lesson."

The policeman's mouth fell open realizing the weapon had been empty. Ellison smiled at the man.

Summers charged the weapon. "Lieutenant, which target would you like me to use?"

"Anyone that's free, Sir," came the reply.

Summers looked down range, brought his weapon up, aimed, and fired all thirteen rounds. When he completed, he lowered the weapon and took out the empty clip. The lieutenant pushed a button and the conveyer holding the target moved it to where they were standing. The target was a silhouette of a full-size man. All the hits on the target were clumped in a nice four-inch cluster in the center of the head area.

"I'd say that you qualify, Sir," said the lieutenant.

"What about the other target, Lieutenant?" asked Ellison.

The lieutenant pushed another button and that target moved to where they were standing. All the shots were in the torso area of the target, with a nine-inch group, and one lone shot about four inches above the others.

"You need more work Jon," said Ellison. "Maybe this guy will volunteer to let you choke him again."

"Boys," chimed Demmer from the range door, "we have a plane to catch if you're done playing."

"Go ahead, Sirs," said the lieutenant, "We'll take this from here. I'm sure their boss will be happy to hear how they disrupted my range. I know mine will be."

"The local FBI office will follow-up as well." Added the agent holding Hapke. He was still gasping for breath, pressed against the glass.

As they left, McAvoy was walking next to Demmer.

"You'll pardon me for saying, Ma'am, but these guys are certifiable."

Demmer looked at the young man, remembering a passage from her youth on the loss of innocence. She smiled as they walked out of the building.

U.S.S. Nimitz
Celebes Sea
March 16, 1995
0145 Hours

The rangers raced across the windy flight deck and into the cover of the superstructure of the ship. They were met by marines and sailors who led them to their quarters. Naylor was the last one in and was met by Rice.

"Colonel Naylor," said the young officer, "Captain Rice, Sir. I command the Marine security detachment on board *Nimitz*. Captain Brothers' compliments. He would like you to join him on the bridge."

The army officer smiled at his marine host. "Lead the way, Captain."

As they made their way through the superstructure, Rice explained to Naylor what accommodations had been made for his men. He listened quietly responding when needed. He was impressed at how organized the captain was. When they reached the bridge, the marine guard stationed at the entrance hatch came to attention. Brothers was standing with the officer of the deck discussing something when he saw his guest. He quickly finished, walking over to Naylor.

"Tom Brothers," said the ship's Captain.

Naylor took the man's offered hand. "Charlie Naylor, Sir, First Ranger Battalion. It's nice to meet you."

"Weren't you with the SEAL Team on that exercise in December?" asked Brothers.

"Yes, Sir, I was," said Naylor. "Had my ass handed to me royally, Sir."

Naylor noticed the hint of a smile on Rice's face.

"We all did, Colonel," replied Brothers. "If you'll remember, we all got caught with our pants down. This ship wasn't sunk according to the judges, but we took a hell of a beating."

"The admiral must have been incensed, Sir," said Naylor.

Brothers laughed. "You know the admiral, Colonel?"

"Let's just say we've had the opportunity to meet, Sir," replied Naylor. "He probably wouldn't remember the meeting."

Brothers smiled looking out the window of the bridge. "Don't ever underestimate him, Colonel. He can be a real bastard when you do that."

"Yes, Sir."

"We'll be receiving communications about three or four possible locations for the hostages. The new Philippine commander has been extremely cooperative in trying to locate where they're being held. Washington expects they'll be able to pinpoint the location in the next six hours."

"Very good, Sir," responded Naylor.

"The admiral expects you'll have breakfast with him at 0800. He would like to discuss strategy with you. Anything else you need, Colonel?"

"No Sir. I appreciate all the hospitality you're giving us."

"Anytime, have your people get some rest while they have a chance. See you in the morning."

"Yes, Sir."

Naylor turned to Rice. She turned leading the way off the bridge. When they reached the first ladder, Naylor asked, "I noticed you smiling when we were discussing the exercise in December, Captain. Why was that?"

She smiled again. "That exercise was right after I was assigned to *Nimitz*. I had a bet with some of the other officers about the outcome of the exercise and won. We were all sloppy in how we approached the exercise. OPFOR deserved to win."

Naylor returned her smile. He guessed Kingston must have had heart failure when this officer was assigned to his command.

White House
Washington, D.C.
March 15, 1995
1400 Hours

Summers and Ellison stood in the waiting room next to the Oval Office. It had already been a long day for the two intelligence officers. On the hour flight to Washington from Rochester, they went over information on the current situation in Mindanao. When they landed, they were rushed to the White House. No one in the group knew why the White House, but they were as ready as they could be for any briefing.

The White House staff brought them all coffee or tea. Summers and Ellison were trying to figure out why this little group was brought together. Demmer volunteered for her part, but even she didn't know what their mission was. The real mystery was why FBI and NCIS agents were included on a military mission. The most uncomfortable of the group appeared to be McAvoy. As he put it, he had been drafted.

Their thoughts were interrupted when one of the secretaries came into the room. "Captain Summers?"

"Right here, Ma'am?"

"Would you come with me, please," she said pleasantly. "Someone from Defense will be with the rest of you in a few minutes."

"Don't embarrass us, swabbie," said Ellison jokingly.

"That's why I'm going in and not you," replied Summers smiling.

Summers followed the woman out of the waiting room and into an outer office. There was a plain-clothes Secret Service man standing by a door they were walking towards. The agent looked at Summers, giving him the once over. He had been searched several times already and knew it was a possibility to be searched again. To his surprise the agent smiled and nodded. The secretary knocked on the door, opening it.

"Captain Summers is here, Mr. President," she announced.

Summers had butterflies in his stomach as he entered the room. He still wasn't sure why he'd been summoned to the White House. He should be on his way to the Philippines. Taking a quick look around the room he recognized General Goodman, Admiral Cummings, and the rest of the Joint Chiefs. There was also the Secretary of Defense, the White House Chief of Staff, and three civilians. All were sitting off to the side on chairs and couches. The president was sitting at the end closest to him. The president rose when Summers moved towards the group.

"Captain Summers," said the president extending his hand, "thank you for coming on such short notice."

"Any time, Sir."

The president motioned to an empty chair. As Jon moved to sit down, the president made some quick introductions. The three civilians were representatives from veterans' organizations. Frank Rizzo and Joe Franklin were from the American Legion and Paul Mott from Veterans of Foreign Wars. He immediately understood the purpose for this meeting.

"Gentlemen," said the president, "as I was saying earlier, getting our people back is our top priority. Our resources are in place to get them once we have an exact location. The President of the Philippines knows we plan to do this and has offered us any help he can to assist us."

"I wouldn't trust him, Mr. President," said Mott. "He's responsible for allowing these rebels to get out of control and take our people prisoner in the first place."

The president, Goodman, and Cummings all looked at Summers as if to cue him.

"If I may, Mr. President?" asked Summers.

The president nodded. "Please do, Captain."

Everyone's attention turned to Summers. Mott made eye contact with him, holding it. He was wearing a suit and looked fit. He had the look of a professional. Summers knew he needed to approach this gently.

"Sir," started Summers, "the Philippine government had no intelligence to indicate they would be dealing with something on this scale. The group that's taken responsibility for the kidnapping came out of nowhere. It's not a spinoff of any of the other separatist groups on the island but appears to be actively recruiting from them. They are better armed than any of the other groups, right down to armor and helicopters."

"What's your point, Captain?" asked the veteran.

"The money for this is coming from outside the Philippines. We haven't determined where yet, but the bulk of this army appears to be recruited from outside of the country as well. Mercenaries, if you will. The Philippine government got taken by surprise as did the rest of us. If there's a way, they will help us get our people back and rid themselves of these troops in the process. They'll give us all the help they can."

Rizzo leaned forward looking hard at Summers. He was dressed less formally than his colleague. Summers guessed him to be in his seventies.

"Young man," said Rizzo, "the ribbons on your coat certainly show you haven't been a wall flower during your career. But I must ask, Sir, how you can sit here assuring us all will be well when your stationed here in Washington while this unfolds on the other side of the world."

Before Summers could answer, the president spoke, "Mr. Rizzo, you've correctly assumed Captain Summers is with our intelligence community, but he isn't stationed here in Washington. He's with the naval reserves and has been for some time. He's here at my request because of something he's been working on for the Navy relating directly to this. We called him up from his job as a teacher just hours ago. The captain hasn't even received his final orders, but I can tell you he will be dealing directly with this incident in the Philippines. I want to know how and why this happened as much as you do, and that's what I'm sending the captain and a team to the Philippines to find out. I assure you we'll do everything possible to bring all those people home safely."

Rizzo had been looking at the president as he spoke. He was still leaning forward with his elbows on his knees. He turned back to Summers.

"I believe you, Mr. President," he said, "but I would still like to hear from Captain Summers. I'd like to know what makes him the expert."

Summers held the man's gaze. "Mr. Rizzo, I'm not sure what kind of answer you're looking for. I don't give guarantees to anyone in this type of situation. I know the regional commander for the Philippine Armed Forces and can tell you he'll move heaven and earth to resolve this. I can also tell you the Philippine people will do whatever they have to help get our hostages back. That's the type of people they are. I know that because I was stationed there and helped to train some of their military."

"You mean, their Navy?" corrected Rizzo.

"Frank, the Captain's a SEAL. He could have trained just about anyone in their military," said Joe Franklin quietly.

"Captain, is what Joe says true? You one of them commandos?" asked Rizzo.

"Yes, Sir."

"Then you served in Vietnam?" asked Mott.

"Yes, Sir," replied Summers, "in 1971."

"You were there in the end," added Mott, "not when the real fighting was going on."

Summers smiled. "I don't know about that, Sir. The bullets and shrapnel that wounded me were real enough."

There was silence amongst the little group for a second, so Jon decided to take advantage. "Mr. Rizzo, I understand your concerns, but let me re-assure you we will do everything we can to free General Gateway and the other hostages."

All three of the men sat straight up at the mention of Gateway's name. Summers pushed forward. "My father was one of Bill Gateway's platoon leaders during the Mindanao Campaign in 1945. They stayed close friends all through the years until my father's death this past winter. Kevin and Becky Gateway are friends of mine, as is Kevin's wife, Kathy. She's lying in a hospital bed in Davao. I don't mean to sound rude, but I do care and freeing them is my top priority if I have to go into the jungle to get them myself."

There was silence as Rizzo leaned forward resting his elbows on his knees again.

"That would make you Ray Summers's boy?" said the older man.

"Yes, Sir," replied Jon simply.

Rizzo nodded standing up. "Mr. President, I would like to thank you for taking the time to see us and to apologize if it sounds like we doubt you. This entire incident has upset our organizations greatly as you can well understand."

The president rose shaking Rizzo's hand. "I'll have someone from the White House keep you informed of our progress. We hope to resolve this terrible issue quickly and with no loss of life."

After shaking the president's hand, Rizzo walked over to Summers. "I'm sorry about your father, Captain. I met him once when he was with Bill. Do what you must, son. Bring them home."

"He's good at that, Frank," said Franklin from behind Rizzo. He walked past his fellow representative taking Summers's hand. "Rescuing people, that is. He helped me once back in the summer of 1978. Never had a chance to really thank you for that, Captain."

Summers smiled. "I thought you looked familiar, Sir. You look much better than when I last saw you."

"As do you, Captain."

"Thank you, Sir," replied Summers.

The three veterans' representatives were ushered out by the White House chief of staff.

When everyone settled back down, the president said, "That was well done, Captain."

"Sir?"

"The veterans' lobby is one of the toughest for this administration to deal with because I didn't serve my country in uniform. Thank you for handling that so well."

"Their concerns are the same as all of ours. They just needed to have it put into perspective, Sir."

"Most times that's easier said than done, Captain. Anyway, the reason I wanted to see you is because it seems you have been requested as the liaison between the Philippine military and our own because of your relationship with General Mangoba. The President of the Philippines wishes me to thank you for your assistance back in December. You made a positive impression."

"Thank you, Sir."

"You will take your team to Andrews and pick up your aircraft there. I made sure you have one of our command-and-control birds. Do what you must and get these people free, Summers. The rangers are in place and the marines should be within striking distance within the next sixty hours. If you need additional resources, contact General Goodman."

"Yes Sir."

"Now, about this issue you've reported where you suspect foreign business executives trying to influence high ranking officers, are you talking espionage?"

Summers looked at the entire Joint Chiefs before he answered. The expressions on their faces told him where he stood.

"Mr. President," Summers said cautiously, "I must say we don't have proof of anything, yet. This investigation started to look at possible influence peddling. Getting contracts for favors and that sort of thing. With the developments in the Philippines, I wouldn't want to venture where this may lead to. One of my prime suspects seems to be linked to the group responsible for the kidnapping."

The president raised an eyebrow. "And the officers?"

Summers looked at Cummings who nodded back in return.

"The one officer I currently suspect is, at this moment, in command of the *Nimitz* Battle Group."

There was stirring among the Joint Chiefs.

"I will be up front Mr. President. I have been reluctant to move on this without more proof," said Summers.

"Why is that Captain?" answered the president putting his hand to his chin.

"It's no secret, Sir, that there is no love lost between me and the admiral."

The president thought for a second. "Captain, you do what you feel you need to. Keep in mind the priority is freeing the hostages. Keep in touch with this office because you'll be representing me."

"Yes Sir!"

"Now, collect your team and get those people back."

"Yes Sir!"

The president rose from his chair shaking Jon's hand again. Summers was then ushered out of the oval office by both Goodman and Cummings. When they reached the outer office, Cummings asked, "Is there anything you need from us right now?"

"Yes, Sir, there is," said Summers reaching over to one of the desks borrowing a pad of paper and a pen. He started to write something.

"It was good you were honest about your relationship with Kingston. The president likes that." said Goodman while Summers continued to write.

Summers handed the paper to Cummings, who in turn held it so both he and Goodman could read it. Both men smiled.

"Any further orders, Sirs?" asked Summers.

"Kick ass!" replied Goodman.

Summers snapped to attention. "Aye, aye, Sir!"

He did an about face and marched out of the office.

CHAPTER 13

SHOT ON GOAL

Camp Freedom
Mindanao, Philippines
March 16, 1995
0530 Hours

The noise of a heavy vehicle moving past the compound woke Becky. She hadn't slept more than two hours. Once they'd been brought inside the prisoner compound, their priority was to make the wounded comfortable. There were enough pallets for about three quarters of the captives to sleep on. They set up an infirmary near a cooking fire in the center of the one room building. Their captors provided plenty of first aid supplies allowing Becky to treat the wounded. There was plenty of fresh water and they were provided tea and a stew. Once everyone ate, most fell asleep out of pure exhaustion.

Becky spent the rest of the night tending to her patients. The most seriously wounded was the army officer. While the wounds were bad, he would recover. She was more concerned for several of the older wounded. She was worried about one gentleman who had been shot in the leg. While there was no evidence of infection, she was worried because he was a diabetic. When she expressed her concerns, he smiled telling her it wasn't the first time he'd been wounded for his country. She cried and he'd comforted her.

The sun hadn't peaked over the hills surrounding the camp, so there was no light from outside. A few candles and oil lamps burned. She made out her father and several others huddled together near the fire. She guessed they were making plans. She was beginning to appreciate what these men went through so many years ago. She felt a gentle hand on her shoulder and turned finding Catherine kneeling next to her.

"Good morning, dear," she said. "I won't ask how you slept because I already know you got less sleep than I did. Your father would like us to join the little cluster of conspirators over there."

Becky smiled. "I'm moving just a little slow this morning. Sleeping on the floor has made me just a bit stiff."

Becky stretched and slowly got to her feet. She'd decided to sleep on the floor near the injured so she wouldn't have far to go if there was an emergency. She looked around for Sarah.

"She's over there," said Catherine, pointing to a location about halfway down the rows of pallets.

Becky looked and nodded. She walked past her patients to find they were all resting. Catherine followed her slowly, carefully watching which ones she lingered over. Catherine had been a nurse before becoming a minister's wife. She found the training quite useful over the years. It also allowed her to bring in a second income when she and Don started their life together.

Becky, satisfied all was well with her patients, turned towards the cooking fire.

"You're really very good," said Becky finding some hot water and tea.

"Pardon me?" asked the older woman.

"I mean as a nurse; you're exceptionally good. You keep your cool and keep the patients relaxed. It's a privilege to work with you."

Catherine blushed. "It's been so long; I'm just doing the basics. There've been so many changes over the years I'm afraid I wouldn't be able to cut it as a nurse in today's world."

Becky leaned over hugging the woman. "Nonsense, where we are today, requires someone who's good at the basics. All the fancy equipment and procedures mean nothing in a situation like this. Just keep on doing what you're doing, and we'll get through this."

Catherine hugged Becky back. They made their tea and walked over to the small group. One of the men stood by the window watching for guards or movement from the other buildings. They were sitting on the floor because there was no furniture. Gateway was sitting in the center of the group with Donavon to his right and Smith next to him.

"Welcome, ladies," said Gateway. "Please, have a seat."

Both women sat on the floor in a space made for them.

"We're not doing anything fancy here," said Gateway, "just making an inventory of where we stand and what resources we have. We need a plan, and we also need your input."

"You're not planning to try an escape, are you?" asked Becky, a sternness to her tone. "Most of the people here wouldn't make it."

Her father laughed. "No, nothing that dramatic, we just need to know what resources we have available to us. We want to make sure everyone here survives this nightmare. We also need to have a plan for when a rescue comes. Escape would be fatal. We're in the middle of the jungle and have no clue where to head if we were to get out of here."

Becky held her father's gaze. She thought to herself he really was good at this, the planning and organizing. She was proud of him. She nodded her acceptance.

"Now, what I need from you two is a rundown of the wounded and a general description of the overall shape of our little group here."

Becky smiled; she knew they were going to be a while.

U.S.S. Nimitz
Celebes Sea
March 16, 1995
0645 Hours

Naylor was up most of the night waiting for the communication regarding the possible detention sites. When it arrived at 0530, he'd managed about an hour's sleep. He was now in touch with Washington, trying to narrow down the site to the most probable. He felt, as did the Philippine military, the most likely site was a plantation in Central Mindanao. It was remote and surrounded by hills. The roads into the area were well traveled and maintained. It was also easily defended if a rescue force were to attempt to save the hostages. Naylor had enough men for the rescue but needed verification the hostages were there. He didn't need to land at the wrong location. It would only serve to warn the terrorists.

His primary target was about thirty-five miles inland from the coast. He would need an exit plan. Helicopters served best, but they were too easy for the enemy to spot and shoot down, if they were so inclined. Naylor knew their enemy was equipped to do so.

He spent his time in the ships Combat Information Center after the initial message arrived. Several of the *Nimitz's* crew were helping him piece the puzzle together. The officer of the watch in CIC came to him with some satellite photos. They were of the plantation he suspected.

"Sir," said the naval officer, "The other locations don't show any indications of activity. Washington feels this is the best target. They will be in contact shortly after they analyze the infrared and thermal scans from the satellite pass."

Naylor nodded. He motioned for the officer to come over and look at the pictures with him. Naylor pointed. "Look at this. It looks like a tractor trailer. Didn't the reports from the police say that some witnesses thought they saw a large truck leaving the rear of the hotel during the raid?"

One of the petty officers near him took a folder, opened it, and shuffled through some papers.

"Here it is, Sir," said the enlisted man, "says some of the witnesses thought they saw a truck pull out of the loading dock area behind the kitchen. They think that it was a refrigerated truck."

"Look, right there!" Naylor pointed. "Doesn't that look like the kind of generator attached to a tractor trailer when it transports frozen or refrigerated foods?"

"Yes, Sir, it does," replied the officer, "and look at this building here, Sir," the young man pointed to a large building in the center of the complex.

"Interesting," said Naylor, "a fenced in area around a building large enough to hold the hostages. Look there! Doesn't that look like a sentry?"

They were so excited they didn't hear Brothers enter the CIC behind them. He smiled watching them. His people were good at their jobs, and he was proud of the fact they would roll up their sleeves to help without having to be asked. One of the petty officers saw the captain and started to rise. Brothers motioned for them all to carry on.

"Sorry, Sir," said Naylor. "I didn't see you come in."

"Don't apologize for doing your job, Colonel," said Brothers. "It looks like you've narrowed down the target list some what?"

"Yes Sir, I think we've just about figured out where they are. Looks like we'll have to helo in and then walk into the location. They appear to be well defended by at least a company size force, maybe more."

"Sir," said a petty officer, "communications have a call for you. They're putting it over to that phone next to you."

"Thank you," said Naylor. The adrenalin high was beginning.

The phone next to him buzzed and he picked up the handset and put it to his ear, "Naylor!"

"Charlie," said Goodman, "you sound well."

"It's starting to get exciting on this end, Sir."

"I can imagine," came the reply. "How's Kingston doing with you and your men?"

"I haven't seen him yet, Sir. I have a breakfast date though."

There was silence on the other end. "Look, Charlie, we've been able to confirm that the plantation is the site. Don't ask me how, but apparently the Philippine Army has some ground assets still out there and they were able to eliminate the other sites as possibilities."

"Do they have anyone in the area of the plantation?" asked Naylor.

"I can't answer that. Intelligence was able to eliminate the other sites. This site is more remote than the others and I know they're trying to get more information on it. We feel the hostages are being held in the large building in the center of the compound. The thermal imaging from the last satellite pass shows the right number of bodies. We're sending you all the intel we have, and the president has given you a green light. Get your plan back to us and let us know when you're going to jump off."

"The plan is pretty much in place, Sir. The only thing that may change it is how many people I use if the Filipinos have any assets in the area."

"Good luck, son," said the general, "and keep your head down."

The line went dead. Naylor looked at Brothers.

"It's the place," said Naylor. "We have a green light."

East of Kidapawan
Mindanao, Philippines
March 16, 1995
0800 Hours

The four-wheel drive van moved down the road at thirty miles per hour. The vehicle contained Sandy Monroe and her news crew, plus a producer sent from Manila. They were trying to find the Philippine military front lines. Because of the kidnapping, the network sent several other reporters to the Philippines, all senior to Monroe. The producer decided what they needed was good video of the bigger situation. They passed a group of government soldiers about a mile back who waved their arms trying to stop them. They had been stopped at so many roadblocks the producer told the cameraman, who was driving, to go right past the soldiers.

The vehicle rushed down the road. He kept urging the cameraman to go faster, but the man kept his pace. They came around the corner, the driver slamming the brakes. In front of them, the road was blocked by two armored cars. Before the driver could put the van in reverse, they were surrounded by men pointing weapons at them. They motioned for the occupants of the van to get out. They were speaking Filipino and the only one who understood what they were saying was the Filipino sound man. They exited the van and were ushered to the front of their vehicle. The producer kept protesting.

"Hey, we're the press!" he raised his credentials to the soldier in charge. "You have no right to detain us. We're out here to do a story on all of you. You can't hold us!!"

"Quiet," said one Filipino. He pointed to the sound man saying something in Filipino. The sound man asked a question only to have a rifle pointed at him. There was a tense moment, no one moved. The two men stood staring at each other. The man finally lowered his weapon, turning to his comrades, and saying something, making them laugh.

The producer looked impatiently at the sound man, "So what's so funny. You'd think we're lost."

The sound man said quietly, "We are. These men are part of the rebel force. That roadblock you had us run about a mile back was the Philippine Army lines. This man is the sergeant in charge of this roadblock and says we're his prisoners. I would do wha…"

The producer started to move forward towards the sergeant. "Hey, you!! You can't hold us, we're fro…"

The sergeant quickly turned, raised the rifle, and fired. The bullet struck the producer squarely in the chest, killing him instantly. The impact picked him up off the ground carrying him into the rest of the news crew, knocking them all to the ground. The sergeant walked over to the three remaining members of the crew and raised his rifle again.

"Sergeant," said a voice with a French accent, "Lower your weapon."

The sergeant froze.

"Sergeant, did you hear me?" repeated the voice.

The man lowered his weapon stepping back. From behind him more soldiers appeared. Two were Caucasian, while the rest were Filipino. The sergeant lowered his head. "Sir, the American wouldn't cooperate. He came at me. I had to defend myself."

The Frenchman ignored the sergeant, walking over to where the news crew sat on the ground, dumbfounded at what had taken place. He looked at them, then turned to the other man with him. "Check the van to make sure they are who they say they are. Escort them to the holding area with the other prisoners."

U.S.S. Nimitz
Celebes Sea
March 16, 1995
0800 Hours

Naylor and Brothers worked on the assault plan since they'd confirmed the location earlier that morning. They were well into the plan when the admiral sent word it was time to have breakfast. They left what they were doing proceeding to the admiral's cabin. They knocked and Handcock let them in. Williams was with the admiral at his desk looking at dispatches.

"Colonel Naylor," said Kingston getting up, "how nice to see you again. I see you've moved onto a new command. I can understand how excited you must be."

Naylor took the hand he was offered. "Admiral Kingston. How nice of you to remember me, Sir. We met for such a brief time; I wasn't sure you would."

"One doesn't forget the meeting where one is assigned to command a battle group," commented Kingston. "Come let's eat some breakfast and you can tell me what you and the good captain have been planning."

Naylor was surprised the admiral knew he and Brothers were planning the assault. He smiled remembering Brothers' words about not underestimating the man. His thoughts were interrupted when breakfast was brought in. It started with fresh fruit and bagels. This was followed by eggs done to order, bacon, sausage, hash browns and plenty of juice and coffee. It was obvious to Naylor, Kingston felt breakfast was the most important meal of the day.

"It's an interesting plan you have, Colonel," said Kingston between bites. "You seem to be landing your strike force some distance from the target compound. Don't you think your chances of success would be better if you landed closer?"

"The troops guarding the compound will hear us coming from miles away if we land any closer," smiled Naylor. "It's a two-hour march from the landing site we've selected but we'll have the element of surprise on our side. As far as the intel we have, they have a re-enforced company guarding the compound. It's a large facility covering a lot of ground. That doesn't leave them many people for patrols. We should be fine with the number of people we're taking in."

There was a moment of silence.

"How many men are you taking?" asked the admiral.

"Two platoons, Sir," replied Naylor. "That gives me enough men to do what I have to and get everyone safely back. We have extra medics going with us to help with the hostages. The choppers can land in the compound and get us all out."

"Do you anticipate any trouble?" asked the Admiral.

"Insertions are always dangerous, but they don't know we're coming so I'm not too worried. I'd say most of our problems will come with trying to find a way into the compound. These guys appear to be high tech so I'm guessing they have motion and thermal sensors out there. Extraction will be from the compound, and we could be under fire at the time."

Kingston turned to Brothers. "Can we provide the Colonel and his people with air cover for their extraction?"

"I already have a plan to be submitted for your approval, Sir. I'll get it to you right after breakfast," replied Brothers.

Kingston smiled, turning back to Naylor. "It sounds like you and the captain have done well. Please forward a copy of your operational plan to one of my aides so if questioned by Pearl I can sound somewhat intelligent about what's happening."

"Yes Sir!" answered the army officer.

"Is there anything else we can do for you at the moment?"

"No Sir," replied Naylor, "except that I should get back to my people to get them ready."

Kingston smiled. "I understand how you feel, Colonel. Please be excused and let me know how your work progresses."

"Yes Sir!" said Naylor. "Thank you, Sir!"

He rose from the table, leaving the cabin.

U.S.S. Kamehameha
West of Samar
March 16, 1995
0800 Hours

Grant sat in his chair in the control room sipping his morning coffee. His boat was on maneuvers nearby until they received the flash message to proceed immediately to the Celebes Sea. The captain of the *Kamehameha* had been watching the situation on Mindanao with interest. He guessed before this conflict concluded more United States Navy ships would be committed to the area. *John Paul Jones* had, thus far, been leading the search for the mysterious submarine attacking shipping in the region. He knew there also was nine American subs either in Philippine waters or on the way to help neutralize the threat. He was pleased to be one of them. Each had orders to hunt certain areas independently, but not to engage the mystery sub. They wanted to try and capture it.

Grant was surprised they didn't want him to off load the SEALs on board before proceeding. They were to have been part of the exercise they'd been heading for but wouldn't be needed on the current mission. He continued to sip his coffee noticing his communications people suddenly busy.

"We have a flash message coming in, Sir," said the officer of the deck.

"Have it decoded immediately and brought here," said the captain calmly, setting down his coffee.

It was a few minutes before the message was decoded and handed to the captain. Grant read the message and then reread it. He turned to his communication people saying, "Call Pearl back and let them know we'll be proceeding to complete our mission."

"Aye, aye, Sir!" answered the radio operator.

"Officer of the Deck!" said Grant.

"Sir!"

"Maintain this course but increase speed to flank. Please have the XO and Mr. DeCook join me in the wardroom."

"Aye, Sir!"

Grant left the control room, grinning as he went down the ladder.

E-6 Tacamo
Over the Pacific
March 16, 1995
0800 Hours

The flight was long and uneventful. They'd boarded the converted Boeing 707 at Andrews Air Force Base stopping at Pearl Harbor along the way. When they landed there to refuel and give the crew a rest, Admiral Putnum met the plane talking to the entire team. The conversation was a lively one when Wells found out Summers had Josh Ericson and some former SEALs doing an informal surveillance on several locations in the Honolulu area. Even Grey seemed disturbed until Putnum showed the two men the evidence Ericson and his team gathered. Calls were made and Grey ordered around the clock surveillance including Ericson and his team. They already knew the schedules and terrain.

When the flight continued, the team went back to work, talking to their counterparts in Davao. The Davao Police had a new lead regarding the identity and possible location of the person behind this rebellion. While they worked to make this connection, Wells came to see Summers looking troubled.

"Jon, I think we need to have a talk," said the NCIS man.

Summers was sitting at a table with Ellison and Demmer. He motioned for Wells to take a seat at the table.

"No, I think I'd like this to be alone," said Wells.

"Mark, like it or not, we're all a team," said Summers. "If you're not happy with something I've done, everyone on the team needs to know. If you're not comfortable with that then we can find someplace on this aircraft for just the two of us."

Wells didn't look happy but sat down at the table.

"I'm not comfortable with the way you do business, and you're right when you say the rest of the team needs to know. Setting up your own surveillance could have jeopardized any case we might hope to get on these people. It might end up getting thrown out of court as it is."

Summers looked at the NCIS man. "You're right, Mark. Two hundred percent correct. I shouldn't have asked Josh and his people to watch those locations, but the navy didn't see fit to turn it over to your people or the FBI. I won't apologize or make excuses for what I did, but I will take full responsibility for the course of action taken. I'm trained to think and act like a commando and that means doing whatever it takes to get the job done. If you feel I've overstepped any laws or violated someone's rights, then you do what you must, and I'll take whatever punishment due me."

"I didn't mean to imply you crossed any lines here," said Wells, "I'm not personally comfortable with how this was done. You've admitted there is no love lost between you and Admiral Kingston, who you feel is the chief suspect on the navy end. I need to personally know where you stand and what you intend to do if we're able to prove anything?"

Summers looked at everyone else. Grey seemed to agree with Well's concerns while Ellison seemed to be irritated by the entire line of questioning. McAvoy was looking about with interest to see if anyone else would say anything. Demmer just looked at him smiling.

"Mark, you've raised an excellent question," said Summers returning his gaze to the NCIS man. "I guess the best way to answer it is to say you need to look at the evidence gathered. There's a connection between this organization and the United States Navy; you've all admitted that when we met with Admiral Putnum. From the start I felt NCIS, and the FBI should have been involved as you'll see in my initial report. Instead, we were told to monitor and keep the Pentagon informed if anything developed. I was assigned the duty to follow-up on what I had reported. I could only do that by putting out general inquiries and waiting for information to be returned to me. There were a few reports that panned out, but most proved to be dead ends."

"That investigative work should have been given to us to do. Having a Naval Intelligence officer doing it borders on being illegal," responded Grey.

"Under normal circumstances, I would agree," said Summers. "My superiors were adamant this stay in house because we knew the same thing you've figured out."

"And what would that be?" asked Grey.

"That the business conglomerate that's represented in this case is a front for Japanese Organized Crime."

Everyone was silent. Ellison turned to look at Grey. The FBI agent looked down at his shoes and then back at the marine colonel. Ellison looked at Wells. The NCIS agent showed nothing but shock.

"It's nice to see that I'm not the only one in the dark here," said Ellison.

"How long have you known this?" Wells asked Grey.

"Since you first showed me the report turned in by Captain Summers," replied Grey. "This is one of the organizations we watch on a regular basis."

"And we've linked them to the ongoing crisis in the Philippines?" asked Ellison. "Christ, this is a hell of a lot bigger than we thought it was."

Wells looked back at Summers. "What about Kingston?"

Summers calmly looked at the man sitting across from him. "I'm extremely bias on that point. You see, I'm convinced Admiral Kingston intentionally gave an order that got several members of my SEAL team killed or wounded when I was an Ensign. Josh Ericson was one of those men. Frankly, he feels the same way."

"Why would he do that?" asked Wells.

"Because his hatred of me is so intense he would do anything to destroy or discredit me," answered Summers.

"I can vouch for that," said Demmer. "I saw the Admiral's reaction firsthand."

Ellison said, "If he's linked to this Japanese group involved in the Philippines, that means this could involve..."

"Espionage," finished Summers. "That's for Mr. Grey and Mr. Wells to prove. My priority has to be the hostages. Now listen, this is what each of you will be responsible for on this mission..."

Summers and the team talked on about the mission at hand. All the cards were now on the table.

Camp Freedom
Mindanao, Philippines
March 16, 1995
1000 Hours

The guards allowed the hostages into the fenced in exercise yard outside. Becky asked for help moving the wounded into the sun for a time. Sarah was helping her when she noticed her ex-husband entering the yard with four guards. They walked slowly to where the two women were working, the guards on the outside of the fence carefully watching.

"Rebecca," said O'Keefe, "I would like to walk with Sarah for a bit. I would like to get to know her better."

Becky glanced at the man. She recognized this was a statement of what was about to take place rather than a request. Out of the corner of her eye she caught movement coming from the building. Her father, followed by a half a dozen men were approaching at a fast pace.

Gateway looked flushed. "O'Keefe, my granddaughter will no…"

He was cut short when his daughter raised her hand. She turned to her father. "It's okay Dad. I can deal with this."

She turned back to O'Keefe. "Patrick, no matter what I say, you're going to have your way."

"True enough, darlin'," grinned the Irishman.

"Then, I'd say the choice is Sarah's. Not mine," said Becky.

O'Keefe nodded his agreement.

"And I have your word you'll return her here to me?" asked Becky.

O'Keefe nodded again. "You have my word, Rebecca."

Becky turned, looking at her daughter. The young woman looked older. No, older wasn't the right word. More mature was the correct term. Sarah looked at both her mother and grandfather.

"Guys, I want to go," she said. "I have to go."

O'Keefe looked at both Becky and Gateway. "She'll be safe, trust me."

Becky nodded to both her ex-husband and daughter. Before she could think about what was taking place, O'Keefe took Sarah by the hand, leading her towards the gate. The guards who were with him backed slowly away, watching the gathering hostages. O'Keefe led Sarah out the gate and across the compound to a building looking like a house. It was surrounded by a porch having a table and chairs to the left of the main entrance. The table was set for tea and what looked to be a light breakfast. They walked up the steps and O'Keefe motioned for Sarah to sit down.

"I thought you might be a little hungry. I know there's plenty of food for the prisoners, but I want to make sure that you get enough."

"Is that what we are to you, prisoners?" asked Sarah.

O'Keefe smiled. "I have a job to do and, unfortunately, at the moment, that includes holding you, your mother and all the rest as hostages. If all goes well, you should be free in a couple of days, and I'll get you back to the United States."

"Then you're not going to kill us?"

O'Keefe smiled again. "Darlin', I don't know what you've been told, but I don't enjoy killin'. I've had to kill in the past, but that was either self-defense or business. It may not sound like much of a business, but I make excellent money at it. Would you like some tea?"

Sarah shook her head as she reached for one of the pastries. "No, thank you. Would you have a Coke or a Pepsi?"

O'Keefe called one of the guards over and whispered something into his ear. The guard went inside the house.

"Do you think of me as a monster, Sarah?" asked O'Keefe.

Sarah again shook her head. "No, I'm confused on what to think about you. I think both Mom and Grandpa have been good about trying to give me both sides about you. I know Grandpa doesn't like you much and Mom seems confused when it comes to you."

"That's encouraging to hear," remarked O'Keefe. "About your mother, that is. I'm not sure the general and I ever liked each other. Maybe we're too much alike."

"Only when it comes to doing your jobs. Other than that, I don't think you're anything alike."

O'Keefe was taken aback by the girl's comment. It must have shown on his face because she added, "I didn't mean that in a bad way. I mean, your personalities are different. Grandpa is so set in his ways, so rigid, but funny if you know what I mean. You're dashing and enthusiastic and so full of life. More like Uncle Ray than Grandpa."

O'Keefe's smile returned when he realized his daughter wasn't trying to insult him. "And how is dear Uncle Ray? The last time I saw him, he was forcing me out of town like one of your old western sheriffs. Never did know how to read him."

"Uncle Ray died just before Christmas, from cancer."

O'Keefe's face became solemn. "I'm sorry to hear that. I think the man stopped your grandfather from killin' me in one of my less impressive moments. Has your mother been seeing his son, Jon?"

Sarah's face seemed to brighten. O'Keefe felt his heart sink. "Daddy, she hasn't. I don't think she's seen him in quite some time. But I'm seeing his son, Sean, and he's really cool..."

O'Keefe breathed out a sigh of relief as his daughter rambled on. He wasn't sure why he felt the way he did because he knew he didn't have a chance at getting his wife back. The fact there seemed to be no one serious in her life now seemed to make him feel better. As Sarah talked, the guard returned with a Coke and handed it to the young woman. Sarah continued to talk for several minutes while O'Keefe just sat there enjoying his daughter's company. He always wondered how this would be, regretting it came about as it had. The scene was interrupted when Rolle came out of the house. The expression on her face told O'Keefe she hadn't yet forgiven him for stopping her the night before. She looked at Sarah, her demeanor becoming even colder.

"Suzanne," said O'Keefe pleasantly, "welcome. Please join us. You know my daughter, Sarah."

Sarah rose and put out her hand. Rolle immediately seemed to soften and took the outstretched hand. "I believe we met in the restaurant the night before last."

Rolle almost looked ashamed. O'Keefe couldn't help but smile. His daughter managed to reach one of the most cold-hearted people he'd ever met. Her mother and grandfather had done a good job. He would have to thank the two of them when he had a chance. Rolle sat down with the two producing a piece of paper from the pocket of the vest she was wearing. She handed it to O'Keefe to read.

"The United States is going to try a rescue attempt. As you can see, we can take them before they get here."

O'Keefe glared at Rolle. She realized she'd made a mistake. O'Keefe said nothing to the woman but turned to his daughter. "Darlin', somethin' has come up requiring my immediate attention. The guard will take you back to the compound and I'll try to get together with you later."

"That would be nice, Daddy. Meeting and getting to know you has been one of my dreams for as long as I can remember."

The young woman leaned across the table kissing her father on the cheek. The man blushed, feeling ashamed he was sending her back to prison. He knew for now she would be safer there. She got up and left.

He turned his attention to the woman sitting next to him. He'd learned to control his temper after being forced to leave Becky so many years before. He hadn't hit a woman since then, but right now he wanted to reach out and beat Suzanne until she learned to hold her tongue. He knew there was a better way to deal with this and in due time he would have to. Right now he had business to take care of.

Sarah almost ran to the holding area. The guards struggled to keep up. When she got to the gate, it was opened, and she rushed inside, being met by Donavon.

"Thank God, you're all right, child," said Donavon. "Your grandfather and your mother have been worried sick."

"I need to see Grandpa right away, Sam. Where is he?"

Donavon could see the girl had something important on her mind. He motioned for her to follow him and led her to the far side of the building. There, they found Gateway talking to the army captain. The man looked much better and was even able to move slowly with help. Sarah immediately told her grandfather what Rolle said to O'Keefe.

"Sounds like Patrick's still having woman problems after all these years," chuckled Gateway.

"Grandpa, he really tried to be nice to me," objected Sarah. "And I agree with Mom, this woman is evil."

"I'm sure your father would agree with you," replied Gateway seriously. "So they know there's going to be a rescue attempt. What do you think, Captain?"

The wounded soldier looked up at Gateway. "I would guess Special Forces of some type, most likely rangers, or delta. Anyway we can warn them?"

Gateway thought for a minute. "Probably found this place using satellite. The only way I can think of getting them a message is to make one they can see from up there."

"And one the goons won't recognize as a signal," added Donavon smiling. They had already nick-named the guards. Gateway blamed it on too much television.

Sarah looked around at the men saying, "I'll go tell mom to get ready for more wounded."

Gateway looked at his granddaughter. "That would be a good idea."

Davao International Airport
Mindanao, Philippines
March 16, 1995
1100 Hours

The plane landed and was instructed to taxi to a secure hanger reserved for military aircraft. When the plane stopped, the ramp was wheeled up, and the team started to disembark.

Grey was met by the senior FBI agent dispatched to the island when the kidnapping had taken place. There was a team of six agents working with the Davao Police. They arrived within hours of the incident. This was standard procedure and was being coordinated through the State Department. The Japanese had a similar mission currently in place as well.

The team was to proceed to meet with Mangoba at his office. They were to look at the site where the hostages were being held and get a briefing about the assets the Philippine government had in the area. Wells was in contact with the surveillance teams in Hawaii and was coordinating their activities with the team in the Philippines. Ellison and Summers were going to look at the plans for the rescue and see what support they could get from the Filipinos. Demmer's job was to make sure the team log was kept up to date on the lap top computer she carried. Her unofficial job was team computer hacker. McAvoy was carrying a small satellite communications system and was to keep in contact with the plane, Washington, and anyone else Summers decided to talk to.

The team was dressed in casual, civilian clothes not wanting to draw attention from the media. They were there strictly on a support role and Summers wanted to avoid any possible entanglements with the press. They were met at the bottom of the ramp by Sanchez. He, too, was dressed in civilian clothes.

"It's good to meet you, Captain," said Sanchez. "I've heard stories about you for years."

"The General speaks highly of you, as well, Captain," replied Summers. "Don't believe the stories."

"Regrettable with his new duties, he isn't available to meet with you. He's asked me to take you and your team to meet with Captain Franco. Based on the information you provided, they had the opportunity to arrest Toshio Akiyama. Apparently, there was some suspicious activity at the premises where he was located, and they arrested everyone there."

"Lead the way, Captain," said Summers. "I haven't seen Toshio since he was being entertained on New Year's by an old friend."

U.S.S. Nimitz
Celebes Sea
March 16, 1995
1100 Hours

Three Super Stallion helicopters sat on the flight deck, their large rotors spinning, ready to launch. Loaded with two platoons of rangers, they were waiting for Naylor who was receiving last minute instructions. He stood at the hatch leading out to the flight deck, speaking with Klintworth. He was leaving Klintworth in command of those being left behind. He was taking two platoon leaders and Carmichael with him on the mission. Klintworth was disappointed but knew why he was staying behind. Naylor didn't trust the navy to be gentle with the troops who were still the guests of the *Nimitz*. He guessed a strong officer would be enough to keep the navy at bay.

Rice came moving quickly down the nearest ladder. The army officer looked at his marine counterpart.

"Nothing new, Sir," said Rice. "You still have a green light."

Naylor nodded, extending his hand to Klintworth. The two men shook hands and then hugged one another.

"Bring 'em back, Sir," said Klintworth.

"Stay out of Kingston's way, Dick. He can be nasty if he has a mind."

"Yes Sir," answered the junior officer.

Naylor turned his attention to Rice. He extended his hand to her, and she reached out shaking it. "It's time to kick some ass, Rice. You stay out of the admiral's way, too."

"Who-ya Sir!" replied the young marine.

Naylor turned, running to the closest helicopter. The aircraft lifted off the flight deck, then the second launched, and finally the third. Once all three were in the air they circled the ship, banking to the north starting on their mission.

On the bridge of the *Nimitz* several officers watched as the helicopters started on their trip toward shore. Several F-18s, assigned to escort the helicopters, could be seen circling above the rotor driven aircraft. Kingston looked at Williams nodding. The aide excused himself, leaving the bridge. Kingston looked at Brothers shaking his head.

"I can't help but think this is a mistake, Brothers. They haven't even tried to negotiate for the hostages' release."

Brothers looked at his commanding officer. "You know the policy's not to negotiate, Sir."

"That's not what I meant," snapped Kingston back at the ship's captain. "They haven't given the Philippine Government a chance to try to talk to the terrorists."

Brothers decided not to be drawn into the conversation any further, so kept silent. Kingston noticed, turning to face the junior officer.

"I have a bad feeling about this mission. Mark my words, Brothers, something about this mission doesn't feel right."

With that, Kingston walked off the bridge followed by Handcock.

Davao Police Headquarters
Mindanao, Philippines
March 16, 1995
1135 Hours

The trip from the airport to the police station took thirty minutes because the streets were more crowded than normal. When they arrived, they were ushered to the fifth floor and to a squad room. They were met by Franco who quickly explained what was taking place.

"We had a tip from another prisoner about a safe house some members of this group had been known to use. The prisoner is one we've been working on for some time. He was captured in the Princesa raid, and we've managed to keep him under wraps. He's also the one who gave us the name of the man we think is behind this entire operation. Our Japanese friends have been extremely helpful in getting us information."

"What do you have on this guy you're questioning?" asked Grey.

"We were watching the safe house when we saw some known members of the group involved in the kidnapping enter the building. When we hit the building, we found the suspects and a room full of weapons. Mr. Akiyama happened to be in the same room."

"Have you gotten anything from him yet?" asked Wells.

"He insists he's a businessman out on a night on the town and went home with the wrong people. He's sticking to the story and I'm not sure I can break him. We know he's dirty and think he's the brains behind the intelligence operation for this group. He shows up in too many places."

"How long until you have to call the Japanese Consulate?" asked Grey.

Franco looked at Summers, then back at the FBI agent. Summers smiled. "Is Tobi here, Jaime?"

"Yes," grinned Jaime, "he's watching the interrogation at the moment."

"Tobi?" asked Grey. "Who's Tobi?"

Ellison laughed. "A representative of the Japanese government you don't want to meet if they think that you've been involved in a plot resulting in the disappearance of a Japanese submarine."

Wells shook his head. "Japanese Intelligence, the man doesn't stand a chance."

"Probably not," said Franco., "but he's well disciplined. The Japanese have even tried to question him, and he hasn't talked."

"Then we wouldn't be much help in the questioning," said Grey flatly.

"Unless we find something that really scares this guy," chimed in Wells. "Then we might have a chance to crack him."

"The Japanese have been most helpful in that respect," said Jaime, "but we've found nothing."

There was silence for several seconds.

"You know, Sir," said Demmer, "That night in the bar in Washington the guy was really scared shitless of those marines who wanted to beat him up."

Everyone looked at her. Demmer had been quiet throughout the trip. She took everyone by surprise with the comment.

"Captain Demmer," said Jon shaking his head, "I'm ashamed of myself for not thinking of it. He was absolutely terrified of the marines that night. He could barely speak in his defense when they were pushing him around."

Demmer was smiling.

"That's all well and good," said Franco, "but where am I going to get a squad of United States Marines in the next hour?"

Everyone on Summers team turned to look at Ellison. The man was not usually slow on the uptake, it took several seconds for him to realize he was now the center of attention.

"What?" he said loudly. "What'd I do?"

Ellison was looking around at everyone else. They were all looking at him, smiling. The only one who didn't understand was Franco.

"Hey look, guys," said Ellison, "I can get you a squad of marines here, but it'll take at least a couple hours."

Wells shook his head. "I think one really pissed off Marine Corps Colonel is better than a squad of marines any day."

Grey nodded his approval. "But he'll have to be in uniform. It won't work without the uniform."

"Hey guys," said Ellison as he shrugged his shoulders. "I must have missed something here."

"You know, George," said Wells, "the old 'good cop/bad cop' game."

"With you as the 'bad cop'," added Grey.

Ellison seemed to light up, "I've done this when I questioned prisoners before. I'm always the 'bad cop'. The part seems to suit me."

"I can't imagine why," snickered Wells.

"Who'll be the 'good cop'?"

"Having already talked to the gentleman at length I think that honor should go to Jon," said Franco. "I think Captain Demmer should go in with him. He'll look on her as being less threatening."

"But what about my uniform?" protested Ellison. "It's back on the plane."

McAvoy got up from where he was sitting and started for the door.

"Where are you going?" asked Summers.

"To get the Colonel's uniform, Sir," answered the petty officer.

"Why?"

McAvoy shrugged his shoulders. "Sir, last time I checked I'm the bottom of the food chain on this mission. It's not a problem. I'll be back before you miss me."

"McAvoy, get back here. Last I knew, you're the only one who knows how to use that fancy new radio you been lugging all over the place. Am I correct?'

"Yes, Sir. You are."

"Then son, you may be at the bottom of the food chain, but you don't leave my side. The colonel can get his own uniform."

Ellison was already moving toward the door with two of Franco's policemen. As he passed the sailor, he said, "Don't worry about it, son. The good captain does this to me all the time. It's a *pick on the guy in the green uniform thing* for him. Get that radio set up. We have guys going in after the hostages and we'll need to talk to them if we get anything."

Ellison turned, smiled, and winked at Summers. The naval officer smiled back nodding. Ellison was out the door, followed by the two policemen.

U.S.S. *John Paul Jones*
Celebes Sea
March 16, 1995
1135 Hours

John Paul Jones had been sailing slowly back and forth over the area where the submarine was last seen, searching for anything resembling a submerged contact. There had been no luck so far. *Doyle* was doing the same thing twenty miles to the east. Halsted sat in his chair on the bridge looking out over the calm mid-morning sea when the officer of the deck advised him communications was receiving a priority call for him. Halsted entered communications a minute later. His communications officer was talking on one of the handsets. Seeing his boss, he rose from his chair.

"It's the Admiral, Sir," he said. "Priority message."

Halsted nodded sitting down in the chair the man vacated. He picked up the handset. "Hello, Sir."

"Andy," said the admiral, "sorry for all the secrecy, using a scrambled channel and all, but this is important."

"Yes, Sir," replied Halsted, looking at both the communications officer and the petty officer on duty. Both men shrugged their shoulders indicating they didn't know what was going on.

"You're being assigned as the commander of a task force to find this submarine and either capture or destroy it. The Filipinos are busy with other issues currently and our presence in the area is going to increase greatly over the next several days. You'll have to cover the entire southern and east coasts of Mindanao."

"That'll be tough with only two ships," said Halsted.

"We figure the sub runs out of the southern coast somewhere. Your ship and Doyle will cover that. *Forester* will cover the east side."

"That still leaves us thin, Sir."

"Only in surface ships, Andy," said the admiral. "The *Los Angeles*, *LaJolla*, *Portsmouth*, *San Francisco*, *Buffalo*, *Helena*, and *Pogy* are either in the area or headed your way. *Hawkbill* and *Columbia* are both assigned to the *Nimitz* Battle Group and will be instructed to give you assistance. The *Kamehameha* is in the area on another mission and will be available to you when she's done with her assignment. I'm also flying you two SEAL platoons in case you get a shot at capturing the sub."

"Whew," said Halsted without thinking, "that's a lot of subs. This must be a priority."

"It is Andy. Use the subs to set up a picket line and get this guy. There are too many friendly ships moving into the area and I don't want them in harm's way because some renegade is loose out there. *Nevada* is also on the way and she's real quiet. *Milius*, *Callaghan*, and *Ingraham* will be there in a day or so and I'll see if I can steal them for you to augment your surface force before Dick Kingston does."

"That'll be a good trick, Sir, since Admiral Kingston gets most anything he wants."

There was a moment of silence. "Andy, Dick Kingston isn't to know anything of your operation or what your assets are. That's from the top, do you understand?"

"Yes Sir," said Halsted sounding puzzled. "I understand the order, but I guess I don't understand why he's not to know. He's the senior officer in the area and, by rights, should know what we're doing."

"I would agree, but the CNO himself called me and gave that order. If Admiral Kingston starts to give you a hard time, you contact me immediately," said the admiral.

"Aye, aye Sir."

"Andy, your full orders will start arriving soon. Get me a draft of your operational plan as quickly as you can so I can take it to CINCPAC. Also any questions or problems you have I need to know immediately."

"Understood, Sir," replied the ship's commander. "We won't let you down."

"I'm counting on that, Andy," said the admiral. "Good luck and good hunting."

The connection on the radio went dead and Halsted put the handset down. He looked at his communications officer and smiled faintly.

"We're about to get exceptionally busy, Lieutenant," he said to the young officer. "Put additional radio personnel on duty to handle the increased traffic. Also have all officers and chiefs not currently on duty meet me in the wardroom in five minutes."

"Aye, Sir."

"As soon as the admiral's operational order arrives, I want it in my hands before the ink dries."

"Aye, aye, Sir!" responded the officer again.

Halsted rose leaving the compartment. Before he was out the door the teletype began to punch out the order. The officer and the young petty officer looked at each other grinning. This is what they joined the navy for.

The hostages watched the guards open the gates and push three individuals into the holding area. There was no formal announcement of their arrival, suddenly they were being released into the compound. Becky noticed certain hostages had been assigned duties by her father. Donavon seemed to be the official gate greeter. Sam, along with several other hostages were assigned the duty of making sure they weren't surprised by the guards. She didn't initially understand the need for these assignments, but soon realized morale stayed higher if you were given some purpose for the common good.

Becky watched Sam gather up the small group before they could wander about the compound. She smiled when she saw another hostage take Sam's spot-on lookout. They didn't miss a thing. At times she thought these senior citizens were enjoying parts of this nightmare a bit too much. She could understand why, it brought them back to a time in their lives when they made a difference. She was proud of her father and all the rest of the veterans. She thought she was starting to understand the difference between their generations.

She moved to the infirmary area knowing Sam would bring the new prisoners there. Her father had been specific about procedures to be followed with new arrivals. They were about to test those procedures. Some of the wounded had been brought back inside because of the heat. Most of the hostages had been dressed casually at the time they were taken prisoner and weren't ready for the sun and the heat. Becky noticed there had been a female and two male prisoners led to the holding area. She wondered who they were while she readied the area where they would be examined. Out of the corner of her eye she could see Don Smith leading a group in prayer. Being the only cleric in the group, he found himself in great demand. Beyond the group she saw her father headed towards her.

Gateway arrived just as Donavon walked through the doorway with the new arrivals. Becky thought the woman looked familiar. Her father walked up shaking her hand.

"Miss Monroe," said Gateway, "are you alright?"

The reporter looked at him. "General Gateway, I guess I'm ok. They killed my producer. Shot him right in front of us."

Becky moved the two male prisoners over to where she could examine them. She now recognized these people as being one of the news crews from the hotel. The soundman was Filipino and spoke excellent English. The cameraman was American. Gateway moved the reporter over to where Becky could look at her. The entire time she was being checked she talked about their experience with the troops at the roadblock.

"I didn't think the rebels had that many troops they could cause this much trouble for the Philippine government," said Gateway.

"These aren't Moro Separatists," said the soundman. "They appear to be more mercenary than anything else. The officer who took us prisoner was French. The other Caucasian also appeared to be European. Many of the troops are Filipino, but not Moro."

Gateway looked at the man for a second, asking, "Can you prove this? We have information there's to be a rescue attempt and now you're saying that these people appear to be professional mercenaries."

"They couldn't be any match for our army," said Monroe "could they?"

Gateway looked at the young woman. "The American military probably trained half of these people. I hope they know this, or the operation will be a disaster."

Gateway turned his attention back to the Filipino. Monroe broke down in tears crying on Becky's shoulder. She was beginning to feel like the veteran.

Northeast of Cotabato
Mindanao, Philippines
March 16, 1995
1230 Hours

The helicopters moved in low just over the treetops after coming in from the coast. They moved fast because they would have to march to where the hostages were being held. That was expected to take at least two hours through the jungle, then another two hours to set up for the attack, the actual rescue, and extraction at dusk. Naylor was optimistic because he was sure they had planned for every possible contingency. He watched as the helicopters started to circle the large clearing designated to be their landing zone. The pilots were being cautious.

There was no fire coming from the tree line around the clearing, so the first helicopter slid in, landing in the three-foot grass. The ramp came down in the rear of the chopper and the first part of the strike force under the command of a platoon leader raced into the clearing, setting up a perimeter. The helicopter started to rise, moving off to the west, just missing the trees. The next two helicopters repeated the process, dropping off their cargo.

Naylor hunkered down next to his radio man at the edge of the clearing. He watched as the lead squad moved into the jungle and gave the word for the rest of the column to follow. Slowly, in twos and threes, the rangers slipped into the jungle until they all were moving along a path. They moved in about two hundred yards and the column came to a halt. Naylor planned for a quick meeting of all officers and sergeants to go over their final plans before moving to the detention site. He realized once they arrived at the site, they would need to move quickly to avoid detection from the terrorists. There would be no time for a meeting when they got there.

Carmichael was in the center of the column and his location was the designated meeting site. The platoon leader from the front of the column quickly moved back to where Carmichael was waiting on the path. Naylor was with the rear guard, so it took him a few minutes to move up to where they were. As he passed his men, he felt pride. He had picked this platoon because they had done the best in jungle training. Each soldier squatted, facing the jungle, each man facing the opposite way of the man in front of him. Each soldier looking intently at the jungle in front of them.

Naylor approached the site where Carmichael and a small group of officers and sergeants waited. There was a thumping sound followed by a high-pitched whistle. He couldn't believe it. Realizing what he heard was incoming mortar fire, he looked for cover. There was an explosion and flash of light. Naylor was knocked to the ground. He lay there for several seconds before feeling the sharp pain in both of his legs. His head was spinning wildly but he thought he could hear gunfire and other explosions. When he tried to get up, he lost consciousness, falling back to the ground.

All around him the ranger column was overwhelmed by a much larger force. The first explosion killed Carmichael, both platoon leaders, and most of the sergeants. Before the column could react, they were overrun and taken prisoner. Naylor's radio man managed a quick message out before being wounded. Their mission had failed.

Davao Police Headquarters
Mindanao, Philippines
March 16, 1995
1230 Hours

Toshio sat at the table in the interrogation room. He was listening to shouting down the hall and on at least two occasions heard his name mentioned. He wasn't comfortable being held here. Being a foreign national caught in a situation of a questionable nature he understood there was little his contacts could do to get him out. He also knew the Philippine authorities had little or no proof to hold him on anything except being in a location where an illegal activity was going on. The Philippine terrorists he was there to see only knew he came to deliver a package and could link him to nothing beyond that. The package was destined to be delivered to O'Keefe and contained coded orders on how to deal with the hostages. O'Keefe would know what to do when the package didn't arrive.

The door to the room opened causing Toshio to jump. He was surprised to see Summers walk in accompanied by a pretty woman with blond hair.

"Jon??" exclaimed Toshio. "What are you doing here?"

Summers smiled at the Japanese businessman. "I should ask the same of you, my friend. I'm here because of the kidnapping from the hotel yesterday."

Toshio looked surprised. "But you're in the navy reserves. Why would the United States send you?"

Summers sat down at the table across from Toshio. The man made his first mistake. He'd let Jon know he knew more about him than he should. Summers motioned for Demmer to sit down in the chair next to him.

"They called me up because I went to school with the Philippine commander in the area and they need a liaison during this crisis. This is Captain Judy Demmer of the United States Air Force. She's here to help me."

Toshio bowed slightly. "Nice to meet you."

"You haven't answered my question," continued Summers. "Why are you being detained?"

There was silence for a second before Toshio spoke, this time in Japanese. "She is a pretty girl. Have you slept with her?"

Summers's expression did not change. "You're avoiding my question, Toshio."

"She would bring a good price in Tokyo," said Toshio, looking at Demmer. "I would pay for her myself."

Summers caught Demmer shifting uncomfortably. He knew she didn't understand what was being said, but guessed she sensed she was the topic of conversation.

"Toshio," said Summers leaning across the table, "the police captain here is an acquaintance of mine and contacted me because he knew I spoke Japanese. He also has a very irate marine corps colonel down the hall who says you were with the people who are responsible for the killing of an officer who was a friend of his."

The color immediately drained from Toshio's face. Demmer stopped shifting, smiling at the man's discomfort.

"Now," continued Summers, "I can try to help you, or I can just walk out of here right now. It's your call my friend."

The screaming down the hall was getting louder.

There were a few seconds of hesitation, "I was in a house raided by the police. They say the men who were there were involved in the kidnapping. I was given a package to deliver to that address and was in the process of doing that when the police burst in."

"Who gave you the package?" asked Summers.

"I didn't know him. He was Filipino. I think Muslim. He paid for my cab and for a night's pleasure when I returned from the delivery."

The noise in the hallway became louder and Toshio was visibly more nervous.

"You'll have to give me something that'll prove your story in order to get you out of here."

"I can't..." Toshio started to say. He stopped because it sounded as if the commotion was right outside of the room. There were several loud thuds against the wall.

"Come on, Toshio, talk to me!" demanded Summers.

"I can't...." There were more thuds against the wall and the door rattled.

"Toshio damn it! Talk to me, now!" demanded Summers again, this time his voice raised.

"Captain!" said Demmer reaching out to touch his shoulder. "What's going on?"

Toshio looked back and forth between the two Americans. The female looked scared, while Summers looked upset. Toshio was confused and scared. He was alone and he didn't know what to do. He needed to call Osaka and warn him the man he feared could cause them problems was in Davao but had no way to do that. It sounded like a war was taking place right outside of the doorway and he knew it was the marine Summers had mentioned. He needed to do something to get out of this, but what? Suddenly the door burst open, and Sanchez fell through, landing on his back. Right behind him a uniformed policeman flew through the door, landing on the other side of the room.

Right behind him came a large American in the green uniform of the marine corps. There were several men hanging onto him as he walked through the door. Toshio got up out of fear, tripping over his chair trying to move away. He fell to the floor crawling towards the far wall. Summers went to meet the man and was struck in the jaw by the marine and knocked to the ground. When the marine tried to move forward Demmer and several policemen were on top of him. Sanchez and the policeman who was thrown through the door were both back into it with the marine.

In the corner of the room Toshio cowered, mumbling incoherently. Franco and a casually dressed Japanese man walked past the craziness by the door unnoticed. As the policemen dragged the crazed Marine from the room, the Japanese man spoke softly to the man on the floor. His voice was soothing. He started to calm Toshio down. His questions were deliberate, and the answers were recorded. Outside the room, the noise continued, although it was getting quieter. Demmer helped Summers up from the floor. He rubbed his jaw and looked at the young woman.

"The Colonel would probably say he owed it to you for something," said Demmer.

"He'd probably be right," said Summers still rubbing his jaw. "He did a good job of it anyway."

Summers listened to what was being said on the other side of the room. The answers to the questions seemed to be flowing freely from the business-man being helped to the chair by the two men with him. Toshio was visibly shaking. The questions were being asked in Japanese so he would understand through his fear. Summers listened to the exchange as Demmer helped him towards the door. When they reached the open doorway Summers stopped cold. He turned to look at the men at the table, finding the Japanese inter-rogator looking at him, as surprised by the last answer as Summers.

Summers broke away from Demmer and rushed into the outer office where Ellison was laughing with some of the policemen involved in the cha-rade. Ellison started to say something to his friend, but Summers rushed past him to where McAvoy sat with the radio. Summers said something to him, and the young sailor immediately started to contact someone on the satellite set. When there was a response Summers took the handset to the radio and began talking. The conversation was short. Summers gave the handset back to McAvoy. He then sat down in the chair next to the young man and put his head in his hands. The rest of the team looked at him wondering what had just taken place.

"Where you in time, Jon?" asked the Japanese man.

Summers looked up. There were tears in his eyes. He stood up looking at the rest of the team before answering. "No, Tobi, I wasn't. They had a message from the rescue column just a few minutes ago that they were under attack. Then the radio went dead. It doesn't look good."

"What's going on?" asked Wells who was standing with the rest of the team.

"Sounds like the rangers got ambushed right after they landed," re-sponded Ellison.

The team members looked at each other in disbelief. The silence was broken by Tobi. "He very clearly said someone in your military gave his people the information but wouldn't give the name. He knows it but is more afraid of his people than us."

Summers started to move forward when he was stopped by Grey. "Jon, do you think this is smart?"

"I think it's exactly what needs to be done," said Franco. "This man feared what some marines threatened to do to him, and Jon saved him. If he knows Jon is angry, then he might be more scared of him than whoever currently controls him."

"More than that," added Tobi, "he respects Jon and has lost face in front of him. He's a modern Japanese man, but old ways die hard in my country. I think it'll work."

Toshio sat by himself in the interrogation room. Things were starting to quiet down, and he was beginning to regain control. He knew what would happen if he told his captors more than he had. He was startled when the door to the room open. He fears subsided when he saw Jon walk in closing the door behind him.

"You're all right, my friend," said Toshio. "I was worried when I saw you hit by that soldier."

Jon sat across the table from the Japanese businessman looking him squarely in the eyes. Toshio shifted nervously but would not maintain eye contact. A strange smile crossed Jon's face, "You have every right to be worried, Toshio."

Toshio looked across the table at the American. He could suddenly feel his body start to shake again, the color draining from his face.

177 Pinecreek Drive
Rochester, New York
March 15, 1995
2330 Hours

The door opened and Howard Quinn carried in an arm load of suitcases. He was followed by Louise Summers, whose arms were full of presents for her grandchildren. Howard put the suitcases down turning to close the door behind them. Emily came out of the kitchen giving Louise a hug.

"How was the flight?" she asked.

"As good as could be expected under the circumstances," answered Louise. "I was hoping Jon was retiring completely from the navy this year. I go crazy every time he goes overseas like this. I guess misery loves company, so here I am."

Howard laughed and picked the luggage back up. "I'll put your things in the guest room, Louise."

When Emily guessed her husband was out of earshot she said, "Men think they're the only ones who suffer when they go off to war. Nancy's a basket case but won't admit it. I'm glad you're here. The boys think this whole thing is cool and the big kid who took your luggage doesn't help. I went nuts when he was away during the Second World War, and he stayed in the States."

Louise smiled.

Davao City Hospital
Mindanao, Philippines
March 16, 1995
2300 Hours

Summers talked to Kevin for some time in his wife's hospital room. Kevin was doing well, except for lack of sleep. He'd been lobbying both Philippine and American authorities to rush forward with the rescue of the hostages. With the news he'd received prior to Jon's arrival all hope of rescue seemed to be dashed. Kevin was speaking to Jon about his frustration when a voice from behind them startled him.

"You shouldn't be so negative, dear," said his wife softly from her bed. "You must remain objective. Remember, you're here to do a job too."

Both men stood. Kevin moved quickly to his wife's side. "You weren't supposed to hear that. I was just venting to Jon."

"Has anything changed?" asked Kathy.

"Nothing, yet" replied Kevin avoiding his wife's gaze.

Kathy looked from her husband to Jon. Jon held her gaze but showed no change in expression. It suddenly dawned on her Jon was a new arrival. She found it strange he was there dressed in civilian clothes. He smiled at her shaking his head.

"I need the truth, Jon, please," she said in a weak voice.

"The rescue attempt appears to have failed. There's been no contact with the rangers for almost twelve hours. I'm sorry I can't be more specific than that, Kathy."

The woman in the bed smiled faintly as her husband gave Summers a sour look. Kathy squeezed Kevin's hand. "Don't be upset with Jon. He knows what I need is the truth."

"He could have sugar coated it some," replied Kevin.

"Would you have wanted it that way?" asked his wife.

Kevin shook his head.

"You're here to make sure that they get out, aren't you?" asked Kathy.

"That's the priority," responded Summers still holding her gaze. "At the moment I don't feel really successful though."

There was a moment of silence in the hospital room as their gazes met. Jon said, "Look, I can promise you this. I'll do everything in my power to get them back. I've been out of the field operations end of this business for some time, but if I have to go into the jungle after them myself, I will."

Both men looked at Kathy, who had drifted back to sleep. The medication she was on kept her unconscious most of the time. Kevin looked at his friend. "Jon, you do what you must. Just get them back. I don't trust O'Keefe or what he might do to Dad. I don't think he'll hurt Becky or Sarah, but I just can't take that chance."

Kevin stopped when he heard the door open behind him. Both men turned to see Mangoba and Franco walk into the small room. Mangoba quietly put his arms around Kevin giving him a hug.

"I'm sorry it's taken so long to get up to visit my friend," said the General. "Things are hectic in my world right now. How's Kathy doing?"

Kevin kept his hands on the Filipino's shoulders. "She's doing as well as can be expected. There was a lot of tissue and artery damage. The doctors are keeping her medicated to keep her still. I should be able to travel with her in about a week."

While both Mangoba and Franco paid their respects Jon excused himself, walking into the hallway. He found a waiting area, sitting in one of the chairs. He put his head back closing his eyes. It had been some time since he had slept, so it seemed like an eternity when he heard someone approaching. He opened his eyes as Mangoba and Franco sat down next to him.

"It's sad," reflected the policeman, "the innocents suffer the most."

The other two men nodded in agreement.

"Jon, all of our assets are in place for this operation of yours," said Mangoba. "We'll have to move quickly, or we'll lose the element of surprise."

"Both Wells and Grey are in agreement you'll have to make the connection in order to make the arrest," added Franco. "That means forcing him to make contact again. That will be extremely risky and possibly tip your hand."

Summers turned and looked at the policeman. Franco smiled at the American saying, "I didn't say it was impossible, Jon. Just that it would be risky. Mr. Wells isn't a risk taker, and he is willing to go through with this."

Jon smiled at the policeman's comment turning to the general. "Would one of your men like to go along for the ride to make this little excursion legal?"

Mangoba laughed. "Captain Sanchez is already packed."

Camp Freedom
Mindanao, Philippines
March 16, 1995
2315 Hours

Naylor could hear voices but didn't recognize them. He kept telling himself to open his eyes. There was the smell of antiseptic biting at his nostrils. The voice most pronounced was female and kept asking him how he was doing. His eyes finally forced themselves open and he found himself staring at the rafters. He slowly moved his head and found himself looking at a pretty woman with light brown hair. She had a bandana in her hair to keep it up, smiling when she saw his eyes open.

"Good, you're awake," she said, then turning away. "Dad, the Colonel's awake."

She looked back at him. "Listen to me carefully, Colonel. You were wounded in both legs so stay still. I operated and removed what fragments I could, but I'm afraid there's still some in there. You lie still and get some rest. You're in good hands and we'll keep you comfortable."

An older man appeared next to the woman, "How is he?"

The woman looked irritated at the question. "He's still groggy but appears to be coherent enough to listen. Go ahead and talk to him. I'm not sure he's ready to answer, though."

The man leaned down, "Colonel Naylor, I'm Bill Gateway. You've been wounded and captured by the same terrorists who took us hostage. You're fine and in good hands. My daughter is an exceptional doctor and will make sure your wounds are tended to."

Naylor tried to speak finding his mouth dry. The woman produced a cup, raising his head, and allowing him to take several sips of lukewarm water. When his head was back down on the pallet he tried to talk again. His volume was low, but he managed to get the words out.

"How about my men? How many dead? Wounded?"

Gateway's facial expression told him everything.

"Fourteen men were killed, including all your officers and your doctor. Another twenty-three were wounded and the entire team was captured."

Naylor felt as if he'd been shot out of a cannon into a steel wall. The whole column was taken and now they were part of the problem. He guessed his career was over if he ever made it back.

"Colonel, look," said Gateway, "they knew you were coming. They were waiting for you. Get some rest and we'll talk in the morning. All your people are in good hands."

Naylor closed his eyes slipping into a deep sleep. His last thoughts were that he would wake up in the morning and discover he was having a nightmare.

White House
Washington, D.C.
March 16, 1995
1315 Hours

The president looked at the proposal on his desk. Norm Jeffers and General Goodman stood on the other side of the desk in silence. They knew the chief executive was not happy with the failed rescue attempt and the media circus that followed. He was not a man to be pushed around, but at the same time didn't like to act rashly or impulsively.

"Now let me get this straight," said the president, "you want my approval on this mission after the failure of the last one. Since these rebels announced they'd taken American troops prisoner the media's been pounding me constantly. They're calling it the worst military fiasco since the failed rescue of the hostages in Iran. Now, I have a dead news producer, a missing reporter, and film crew."

"Mr. President," said Jeffers, "we know why the rescue mission failed and know what we need to do to fix it. This is the only way to take care of both at the same time."

"Sir, Captain Summers is putting everything on the line for this one," added Goodman. "Even the more conservative members of his team are in agreement with the plan."

The president looked unhappy with the proposal, standing as he spoke, "I don't like this as an option. The risks outweigh the expected returns on this little gamble of yours. Gamble is the only word I can think of to even describe this. Every fiber in my body tells me to throw this thing away and not even look at it. I can't justify this to Congress or the American people after what took place this morning. If I allow this to go forward, we'll all be tendering our resignations by tomorrow morning. You must give me a better option to take to the hill."

Both men looked at their feet and were trying to think of a response to the president's displeasure.

"General," continued the president, "get me that other option to run up the flagpole and while you're putting it together, tell Summers to kick this guy's ass. I want him taken down and I want it done quickly. No one does this on my watch and gets away with it. I want those hostages and the captured rangers back and I don't care what he needs to do to get it done. I want it done, gentlemen!"

Both men looked at the president and then at each other in amazement. The president sat back down moving the operational plan off to one side of the desk. He looked back up finding both men still looking at each other in disbelief.

"Are you two still here?" asked the president. "I said now and that's what I meant!"

The president smiled watching the two men trip over each other leaving the office.

U.S.S. Nimitz
Celebes Sea
March 17, 1995
0130 Hours

Kingston stormed onto the bridge and up to Brothers. The captain held back an amused smile watching the admiral's two aides come to a halt behind him.

"What's the meaning of this message, Captain!!" demanded Kingston. "You have a messenger wake me at this hour to give me this?"

Brothers didn't look at the paper Kingston was waving. He smiled at his superior taking a deep breath, telling himself this was one of those times he would have to hold his temper.

"Sir," he said calmly, "all I know is a message came for you from CINCPAC. It was to be given to you immediately upon arrival. I have no idea what the contents are."

"This is just routine traffic! I'm to cooperate with some intelligence flunky coming to investigate what happened to the ranger mission! I am not to be disturbed again! Do you understand!?"

"Yes Sir" replied Brothers, the smile disappearing.

"Captain," interrupted the OOD, "that helo is inbound, Sir. Touch down in less than ten minutes."

Brothers nodded. "Thank you, Commander."

"What helo is this, Captain?" asked Kingston.

"I believe it's your investigator, Sir. We got a message to expect some intel people this morning."

"Have them report to me at 0900," snapped Kingston. "I want them out of here by 1200. Do you understand? I'm not going to have them disrupting routine on board while we're dealing with this crisis."

"Yes, Sir," replied Brothers again.

"I'm turning in, Captain, and I don't want to be disturbed for anything."

Before Brothers could answer, Kingston turned walking off the bridge, followed by his two aides. Brothers finally allowed himself to laugh quietly. He turned his attention to the inbound helicopter. He looked out into the darkness searching for anything that could be considered an aircraft. He finally made out the aircraft's landing lights as it slowly circled the ship.

The aircraft came in, landing softly on the deck. The pilot immediately shut down the engines and the doors opened on the side. Members of the ships' crew assisted the passengers out of the helicopter and towards the superstructure.

Brothers was glad the helicopter finally landed. It had been a long day. He heard footsteps on the deck behind him turning to find several men approaching. The first was wearing the uniform of a navy captain. The second was a Marine Corps colonel, who was followed by a female air force captain. There were four other men, a navy petty officer, a Philippine Army officer, and two civilians, who stayed at the entrance to the bridge. Brothers raised an eyebrow thinking this a strange mix for and investigative team.

"Captain Brothers, I'm Jon Summers," said the naval officer.

Brothers got out of his chair taking the man's offered hand. "Captain, it's nice to meet you. The orders I received said we were to cooperate with you to see what went wrong with the rescue mission. We should be able to do that and have you out of here in a few hours. The admiral would like to meet with you and your team at 0900."

A strange smile came over Summers's face as he handed Brothers an envelope. Brothers opened the flap, pulling out the papers inside. When he'd read halfway down the first sheet, he looked at Summers. "I don't like giving up command of my ship, Summers. You know I'm going to verify these orders."

Summers watched the expression on Brothers' face as he read through the next several pages. He could see how troubled the ships' commander was.

"Captain, I must pay my respects to Admiral Kingston then I'll meet you in your quarters. In the meantime, I believe Mr. Wells and Mr. Grey will be able to answer most of your questions."

Before Brothers could say anything, Summers turned and left the bridge followed by the marine officer. Brothers found himself looking at the air force officer.

"Captain Brothers," she said pleasantly, "I'm Captain Judy Demmer. Why don't we go to your cabin, and we can explain to you what's going on here?"

"Damn, you people sure have some brass to do this," said Brothers.

Demmer smiled following the ships' captain towards the hatch leading off the bridge. "Thank you, Sir. We'll take that as a compliment."

Summers and Ellison moved through the passageways of the ship until they reached the admiral's cabin. There was a marine corporal posted at the door. He came to attention when both officers stopped in front of the door.

"Captain Summers and Colonel Ellison to see the Admiral," said Ellison as he showed the sentry his ID card.

"I'm sorry, Sirs. The admiral has left specific orders not to be disturbed."

"I'm afraid we must insist, Corporal," said Ellison, feeling sorry for the young man. "We have orders that the admiral is to see us immediately upon our arrival."

The corporal jumped as the door opened behind him. Kingston stood there in a white t-shirt and his khaki uniform pants. He looked at the two officers and his face immediately flushed. He was further stunned when both officers pushed passed both the sentry and him. The admiral didn't close the door to his cabin taking a step towards the two officers.

"What is the meaning of this, Summers!?" said Kingston with a raised voice. "You still don't know how to follow orders. I want you off this ship immediately."

"It's good to see you, too, Admiral," responded Summers pleasantly, handing an envelope to Kingston. "I have orders from CINCPAC to hand to you personally upon my arrival."

Kingston opened the envelope reading the one sheet memo. He looked at Summers and then back at the paper. His face remained red realizing both Summers and Ellison were listening to the shower run in his personal bathroom. Summers looked at him smiling.

"This says I'm to get you to the landing zone the rangers used and provide an escort."

"Yes Sir," replied Summers still smiling.

Kingston walked over to his desk and picked up the telephone. He pushed two buttons. "Captain Brothers, get hold of Captain Rice and have her lead an escort for Mr. Summers leaving the ship within the hour. Include the Marine sentry at my door."

He hung up the telephone and walked back over to the two officers.

"I want you off my ship, Summers. Take the escort and be out of here before the hours up," said Kingston bluntly. He turned to Ellison. "Colonel, you report to me at 0900 and I'll tell you how this investigation is going to be run."

"Aye, aye, Sir," said Ellison coming to attention.

"You're both dismissed!' said Kingston turning his back on the two men, while again looking at the orders he'd been given.

The two officers turned and left immediately closing the door behind them. Kingston went to his closet pulling out the khaki shirt that went with the pants. As he was putting it on, he looked into the bathroom. The shower was still going, steam pouring out.

"Honey," said Kingston, "I have to step out for a minute to deal with something."

"Okay," answered Handcock. "I'll be here when you get back."

Kingston then went to his desk and wrote something down on a piece of paper. He folded the paper in half leaving the cabin. The marine sentry came to attention as the admiral left. He said nothing to the sentry, closing the door, and walking down the corridor. Kingston made his way through the ship to the communication room. When he entered all the personnel in the room stood, coming to attention. He walked over to the closest petty officer handing him the folded paper.

"Send this immediately, sailor," said Kingston. "I'll wait until you're done. This doesn't get entered into your log. It's a personal message."

"Aye, aye, Sir," replied the sailor who immediately sat down sending the message. When he completed his transmission, he waited for several seconds and got a reply the message was received and would be forwarded. The sailor stood back up facing the admiral.

"Message sent, Sir. Pearl has confirmed they've received it and will forward it immediately."

Kingston reached over picking up the folded paper, walking out of the radio room. When he was out of sight, Demmer appeared in the hatch.

"How did we do, Ma'am?" asked McAvoy.

"We got both good video and audio on it. Let's get it to the captain before he leaves," replied Demmer. She turned to the chief petty officer on duty. "Thank you, Chief, and remember, none of this leaves this room."

"Yes, Ma'am." replied the chief watching McAvoy retrieve a small video camera from behind the workstation he'd been sitting at.

CHAPTER 14

BACK INTO THE WOODS

U.S.S. Nimitz
Celebes Sea
March 17, 1995
0210 Hours

The team was watching the video when the door to the ready room flew open and Rice stormed in, followed by several marines.

"Who the hell's the asshole that pissed off the admiral and now he's sending one of my people into danger," said Rice pushing past McAvoy.

"That would be me, Captain," said Ellison from behind her.

Both Rice and her marines wheeled around, immediately coming to attention. Ellison was sitting with Grey looking over blueprints of the ship. He stood, walking over to the officer.

"You're Captain Rice?" asked Ellison cautiously.

"Yes, Sir! Captain Tiffany Rice," answered Rice, still at attention. "I apologize, Sir. I didn't know it was you, er, I mean someone of your rank, who was involved. I expected a more junior officer, Sir."

"Jonny, she's a woman?" Ellison said to Summers. Demmer walked behind Ellison and hit him lightly between the shoulder blades.

"The admiral did say *her*, George," replied Summers walking toward the marines. "Captain, I assume you haven't any combat experience?"

Rice looked at Summers out of the corner of her eye. The man was dressed completely in camouflage, with no rank insignia visible. The man was slightly shorter than the colonel. She guessed him to be a naval officer. She didn't think he had the look of a marine.

"Have you ever been in combat, Captain?" Summers asked again quietly.

"And you would be who, Sir?" Rice replied.

Summers smiled.

"Captain," said Ellison, "that's an impertinent response with me standing right here. All you need to know is the gentleman holds the same pay grade I do. Now answer the question."

Rice took a deep breath. "Aye, aye, Sir. I think the gentleman already knows the answer. I'm a female and therefore am not allowed in combat."

"Then why would you be assigned to escort someone into a combat zone?" asked Ellison.

The door opened again and Klintworth and Reardon entered. They said nothing seeing Rice was the focus of attention. She was starting to look nervous.

"Stand at ease, Captain," said Summers. "And please speak candidly. Anything said in this room remains here."

Rice relaxed turning to face Summers. "Thank you, Sir. To be candid, the admiral doesn't care for me much. I don't know why because my record is spotless."

"I know why, Captain," replied Summers. "You're a female with responsibility and they let you play with weapons, so you threaten him. I won't go into the psychological bull that accompanies that diagnosis because we don't have time, but don't' feel bad. You're in good company. The admiral has hated me for years and unfortunately that's why you're assigned to this mission."

"Yes Sir," replied Rice weakly.

"We're going into harm's way, Captain. Do you have any qualms accompanying me on this mission? If you do, I need to know now."

Rice looked stunned. "You still plan to take me, Sir?"

"I have orders from a higher authority to take you. The only reason I wouldn't at this point would be if you don't feel up to the challenge. The balls in your court, Captain."

Rice looked carefully at the man. He seemed sincere and didn't seem to have the time to play the political games routinely played in the service.

"Sir, I'm up for it if you'll have me," replied Rice. "How many of my people will you require?"

"Sixteen. You pick them and your corporal can volunteer not to go if he wishes," said Summers flatly. "Be ready to launch in forty-five minutes. Sergeant Reardon!"

The Ranger came to attention responding, "No qualms, Sir!"

"Same order to you, Sergeant," said Summers smiling. "Pick sixteen of your people, besides yourself, to accompany me on this mission. You and your people check with the captain and her men to make sure they're properly equipped for a walk in the woods."

"Sir," said Klintworth stepping forward, "request permission to replace Captain Rice and her men on this mission with myself and more of my people."

"Permission denied, Captain," said Summers. "I have another mission for you. More important than the mission I'm going on. You stay here and we'll explain it to you while the Captain and the Sergeant get ready. Ladies and gentlemen, we shove off in forty minutes."

U.S.S. Kamehameha
Moro Gulf
March 17, 1995
0225 Hours

The *Kamehameha* moved slowly through the shallow waters of the Gulf. They had completed their mission and were moving leisurely to take up the station assigned to them by *John Paul Jones*. Grant sat in his cabin catching up on the never-ending paperwork. He stopped writing for a minute to take a sip of coffee. He wasn't surprised when the telephone on the wall next to him buzzed. It had been too quiet over the last twelve hours, and he was catching up on his work.

"Captain."

"Skipper," said Krause, "we have a submerged contact moving 024."

Grant stopped writing, "Does it look like our boy?"

"It's not one of ours, Sir," replied Krause, "We haven't been able to determine if it's a diesel boat yet, but I'm guessing we've found the phantom sub."

"Do they know we're here?"

"Negative, Sir, we've maneuvered around so we're in her baffles. Currently, we're following her. She looks to be headed towards the coast."

Grant rubbed his eyes. "Are we able to send out a message, Bob?"

"Yes, Sir, we are," came the quick reply. "At the moment we're trying to monitor any traffic from the contact."

"Forget that. Her captain will have everything scrambled so we can't copy a thing. Contact the *Jones* and let Andy Halsted know what we've got. Keep the frequency open for a reply and keep the messages short because he's probably listening. Go to general quarters and rig the boat for silent running. I don't want this guy getting away from us like he has everyone else."

"Aye, Sir."

"Tell the sonar boys, *well done*," added Grant. "I'll be up to the control room in a few minutes."

Grant hung up the handset and got up. He walked over to a small sink on the far wall of his quarters and turned on the cold water. He quickly threw some on his face and turned off the water.

U.S.S. Nimitz
Celebes Sea
March 17, 1995
0250 Hours

The strike force gathered in the pilots' ready room to check their equipment. Rice had knots in her stomach. She'd trained for this and expected some anxiety. She was scared to death she would fail to do her job. She watched Summers, who was checking his equipment. He seemed so calm for a naval officer. She couldn't help but think there was more going on here than she was being told.

She jumped when she felt someone touch her shoulder. She turned to find Reardon standing there.

"Sorry I startled you, Ma'am," he said, "but I need to check your equipment."

Rice cocked her head looking carefully at the ranger standing in front of her. A smile came over his face and he blushed slightly under the camouflage paint.

"Sorry again, Ma'am," he said. "I know how that must sound like a come on and all. We're buddies on this mission so we need to make sure each of us has the right equipment."

Rice nodded. She realized Reardon was nervous, too. He didn't seem the type of man who would be embarrassed by this type of conversation with a woman, even an officer. He started going through her ruck sack as she said, "You said we're buddies?"

"Yes, Ma'am," he responded taking a sleeping bag off her ruck. "Swim buddies. We're using SEAL rules, Ma'am. We're all assigned to two-man teams."

"SEAL rules?" asked Rice. "Never heard of that, Sergeant."

Reardon smiled. "Sorry Ma'am. It's our own lingo for how they set themselves up. Two-man pairs, then a squad, then a platoon, and so on. We did some training with the SEALs recently and coined the term SEAL rules on our own."

Reardon moved to her weapon and was doing a thorough job of inspecting it.

"Why SEAL rules to take some intel guy into enemy territory?" asked Rice.

Reardon didn't look up. "Because this intel guy is a SEAL, Ma'am. He's seen more combat than either you or I and from what I've seen, he's good at it."

"You know him, Sergeant?" Rice sounded surprised.

"Yes, Ma'am. He bought me a beer once."

Rice was startled again looking up to find Summers and Ellison in front of her. The captain was dressed the same as the rest of the troops going on the mission. He carried a smaller version of her M-16, the CAR-15. He had a towel he carried around his neck and boonie cap he allowed to hang off his ruck sack for the time being.

"Are you ready, Captain?" asked Summers.

"Yes, Sir," answered Rice. "Nervous, but the sergeant here took care of that when he told me he was here to check out my equipment. I've never seen a ranger blush before, Sir. It's nice to know that I'm not the only one that's scared." Reardon blushed again. Both senior officers smiled.

"I wouldn't have anyone along on this mission that didn't admit to being scared, Tiffany," said Summers. "Besides, knowing Sergeant Reardon as I do, he's probably checked out your equipment long before this. If he's been on board ship more than four hours, I'd check your shower to make sure there's no closed-circuit cameras there."

Both Rice and Reardon laughed looking at each other.

"Whoya, Sergeant," said Rice.

"Whoya, Ma'am," answered the ranger.

Summers turned to Reardon. "How's she look, Sergeant?"

Reardon smiled, but Summers did not flinch. He was back to business.

"Not bad packing for a girl, Sir," replied the Sergeant. "Only a few non-essentials and the only make-up she packed was her camo paint."

"Outstanding," said Summers. "Looks like we're good to go."

Wells walked up to the group. "There's two transports in route with the extra personnel that Glenn and I requested along with an added bonus."

"Bonus?" asked Summers.

"Admiral Putnum," answered Wells. "I also have a message for you from CINCPAC."

A chief petty officer opened the door to the ready room and stuck his head in. "Helo's ready, Captain. Time to load the strike team."

"On our way, Chief," answered Summers.

The door closed and Summers turned to Ellison. "George, I'm going to check this message. Get these guys loaded."

Ellison nodded and put his arm around Rice's shoulders. "Come on, Captain. Let's get the troops on board."

Rice followed Ellison out into the passageway. They moved slowly towards the flight deck, sailors moving out of their way as they did. Rice couldn't help but feel the looks they were being given were reserved for those condemned in some way. She was starting to feel uneasy again. She looked over her shoulder and could see the nervous faces of the troops behind her.

"Don't let the looks get to you, Rice," said Ellison. "I've seen the looks before and you have to remember they don't know what you do. You're a marine and there's no one meaner in a fight. We're feared because of our ability to improvise on the battlefield. Being female, you also bring the aura of unpredictability to the situation. I wouldn't want to be the enemy."

"I can't stop feeling like we're the bait for something larger, Sir."

Ellison looked down at the junior officer. "You're also very astute, Captain. You are bait, but not in how you may think. You do your job, rely on your training, learn from Jon Summers and Sergeant Reardon, and your mission will be a success. You're going into battle, Rice. But you're going into one we control."

When they walked out onto the flight deck, Rice could no longer hear Ellison over the noise of the helicopter rotors. She boarded the CH-53 followed by the rest of the team. Ellison stood by the ramp, his dark hair blowing in the breeze created by the rotors. Summers came running out of the superstructure, carrying his rifle and boonie cap in his hand. He stopped by Ellison shaking the colonel's hand.

"See you in a day or two, George."

"Keep your head down, sailor," responded the marine. "Kingston would love to have you be a statistic on this one."

Summers smiled at the last comment slapping his friend on the shoulder. He ran up the ramp of the helicopter which slowly closed behind him. The next move in this chess match had been made.

U.S.S. Kamehameha
Moro Gulf
March 17, 1995
0300 Hours

Grant stood at the periscope watching while the enemy submarine docked. It amazed him how well his crew reacted to this twist. He never expected to be the boat to find the mystery submarine. The crew did their job by the book and now they had a chance at capturing the vessel instead of having to sink her. They followed her for half an hour before she surfaced, heading to shore. Grant followed her as far as he dared, then brought the *Kamehameha* to a full stop. Using the night vision capabilities of his scopes, he sat offshore and watched.

"XO," said Grant.

"Yes, Skipper," replied Krause.

"Take a look."

The executive officer slid in, looking out the periscope. A smile crossed his face. "Too bad they want this baby intact. We've got the perfect shot."

"That we do." said Grant in response. "Send a message to the *Jones* and give her our location. Tell them we're monitoring as requested."

Krause looked at his boss with a grin. "Too bad we can't use even one little torpedo."

**East of Camp Freedom
Mindanao, Philippines
March 17, 1995
0300 Hours**

The column of men snaked their way through the jungle, moving quickly. Most of the people in the column were Filipino, but there were a few foreign nationals. The officer in charge of the platoon size force was German and expected the column to be in place for their ambush within half an hour. He led the force that ambushed the rangers and expected to do the same thing to this smaller force. He was surprised at the accuracy of the intelligence information he was getting. He gave credit to the people he was working for; they had a good organization in place.

The column moved through the jungle. They were moving faster than he would normally, but they controlled this sector. The unit they were to ambush was small. He guessed its purpose was reconnaissance and not rescue. His unit was over twice the size and knew they could deal with the new threat.

He looked ahead to see where the point man was. They were in a straight stretch of the trail, and he was surprised he couldn't see him. An alarm went off in his head, too late.

All around him, there were explosions, followed by heavy small arms fire. Before he realized what happened, he found himself on the ground, in pain. He guessed he'd been hit at least twice. His mind raced trying to guess how they'd just ambushed his column. The small arms fire seemed to intensify, bullets hitting the ground near him.

As suddenly as the gunfire started, it stopped. He lifted himself up on one elbow. Camouflage clad men came walking out of the jungle all around him, moving cautiously, their weapons at the ready. Some were Philippine

Army troops, but there were others. He guessed them to be American Special Forces. Had they been given the wrong time for the landing? He had to warn the base camp they were on the ground and with a larger force. He looked around for his radio man but couldn't see him.

There was a sudden noise behind him, and he turned to find two men, both pointing their weapons at him. He looked the other way finding four more soldiers watching him. A tall soldier moved out from behind the four men, approaching him.

"What have we here, boys?" asked the soldier in English.

"Looks to be an officer," responded one of the men from behind him.

The German watched as another man, a Filipino, walked up next to the tall soldier. For the first time, he noticed the large number of government troops. He guessed between fifty and sixty men. This was equal to the size force he commanded. He watched while the troops went about their business. They moved like well disciplined, first line troops.

"Thank you for the lesson, Lieutenant," said the Filipino to the tall American. "The ambush we could set, but the placement of the explosives made everything so much easier."

"Any time, Colonel," nodded the American who then motioned to the man on the ground. "I think we have their commanding officer here, Sir. Doesn't look to be much of a rebel."

The Filipino officer smiled. "What nationality do you think?"

"I'm not sure, Sir. Chief, care to make a guess?"

The man on the ground was grabbed from behind. While one of the soldiers held him, the other searched him. His pistol and knife were taken, and his hands were bound. The bigger of the two men searching the prisoner found a letter and picture in one of his shirt pockets.

"Looks to be German, Sir," said the soldier. "I'd guess East German by the contents. It appears to be a wife or girlfriend."

The Philippine Army officer watched as the wounded man shifted nervously. He wondered what was going through the man's mind. A foreign national, a mercenary, captured by government troops and one of his captors speaks his language fluently enough to read a personal letter. He knew the man had to be frightened beyond comprehension. He also knew he had to take advantage of the situation.

"Lieutenant," asked the colonel, "do you think you can spare Chief Wiedenkeller to help with the interrogation of the prisoners? He appears to have a grasp of the man's native language that would be helpful."

The American officer nodded.

"I'm not sure that'll be necessary, Sir," said Wiedenkeller. "I've been watching this guy and he appears to understand everything we're saying. My guess is he speaks English."

The American officer smiled. "Then the job should be that much easier, Sir. The Commander ordered us to help you with the ambush while he met the helicopter. There appears to be about a dozen survivors, so we'll help you take them back and get ready for the next phase of the operation."

"Very good, Lieutenant," replied the colonel.

He looked pleased with the cooperation between his soldiers and the American's so far. The last day had been exciting. As the American officer moved off to check the rest of the ambush site, the colonel moved closer to Wiedenkeller and the prisoner. The American was now tending to the man's wounds.

"Since the Chief believes you understand English, you should know we're taking you somewhere to be questioned," the colonel said to the prisoner. "Since you're not a Philippine national, you'll eventually be imprisoned. This will, unfortunately, be very unpleasant as our prisons have the reputation of being less than hospitable. I'll ask you to think about this while we travel."

He looked at Wiedenkeller who began speaking to the man in German. At one point while the American was speaking, the prisoner's head jerked around to look at Wiedenkeller and then shifted to the colonel. Then, he looked down at the ground. When the American finished, the colonel looked at him.

"Repeated what you told him, in German, Sir, and then told him he should think hard about what you said, Sir, because the Moros currently fighting with us would be real interested in spending some time with him for what they've been blamed for."

The colonel smiled at Wiedenkeller's improvisation. "You are quite right, Chief. They would sell their mothers to spend five minutes with him."

The colonel watched the prisoner's reaction and was pleased with what he saw.

"Do you think he knows who you are?"

"Yes, Sir, he knows," replied Wiedenkeller, "and by now he knows we're not the people he was sent to kill."

The prisoner watched as the Americans and the Filipinos dragged the bodies of his soldiers into the jungle. He watched as each man was stripped of weapons and ammunition. He looked around, noticing Philippine civilians helping in the clean-up. His superiors didn't know they were about to lose a war.

U.S.S. Nimitz
Celebes Sea
March 17, 1995
0305 Hours

Putnum exited the aircraft stepping onto the deck of the ship. He hated flying in these small transports out to a carrier. The ride was usually bumpy, and someone always got sick. He hadn't been disappointed. Several NCIS and FBI agents were sick all over themselves. Putnum was glad to be out of the plane and able to breathe the fresh sea air, even with the smell of aviation fuel mixed in. He was met by Brothers and Ellison, both escorting him into the superstructure. Once inside, it was quiet enough to talk.

"Admiral, I have an empty cabin at your disposal, Sir," said Brothers. "I'll have you escorted there to freshen up."

"Thank you, Captain," responded Putnum. "I need to throw some water on my face and get the smell of puke out of my nostrils. Damn, I didn't think people could get so sick."

Putnum noticed Ellison smile.

"Colonel Ellison, when they leave this ship, I'll make sure that you're on the same plane they are."

Ellison tried to hide the smile. "Yes Sir."

"Where are you set up, Colonel?" asked Putnum.

"We've taken over one of the ready rooms, Sir."

"When do you expect to go?"

"Within the hour, Sir," responded the marine. "As soon as we hear from Summers."

"And if we don't hear from him?"

"Then we'll know there was an ambush, and plan B didn't work, Sir."

Putnum shook his head. "It's a dirty business, gentlemen. I appreciate all your help in resolving it. Colonel, did Captain Summers receive a message before he left from CINCPAC?"

"Yes, Sir, he did, but I'm not aware of the contents of the message."

"It was a relayed message from the president giving him an unofficial green light. The politics of this type of thing say that if the mission fails, Jon will take the fall. The president felt he needed to know that. More importantly, he wanted Jon to know the mission couldn't fail and he had the president's full support."

"Unofficially, of course," said Ellison. Brothers flinched, looking uncomfortable with the marine's last comments.

Putnum looked at Ellison. "Colonel, you've been around the block more than once yourself and know the politics being played here."

"Yes, Sir, I do," Ellison replied calmly. "That doesn't mean I have to like it, Sir. I also understand the president didn't have to send the message at all. The fact that he did speaks highly of him. I meant no disrespect. I was only stating a fact, Sir."

Putnum smiled.

"The fact you're not afraid to speak your mind, Colonel, has always held a special place in my admiration for you," said Putnum. "You've paid the price more than once for being honest. I'm glad they assigned you to this detail."

"Thank you, Sir," responded Ellison.

"Now, get those agents cleaned up and ready to do their job. We move within the hour, hopefully."

Putnum turned, walking away.

U.S.S. Kamehameha
Moro Gulf
March 17, 1995
0345 Hours

Grant was surprised at how fast he received help. *Buffalo* arrived on scene several minutes previous. She was taking up a position to the east of the *Kamehameha* and according to her captain was ready to rock and roll. Grant knew *LaJolla*, another *Los Angeles* class submarine, and *Doyle* were due to arrive within the next two hours. He hoped they would be ready.

"Sir, have you seen the number of ships in the area for this operation?" asked Krause. "It's like we're mounting an invasion."

Grant took the paper his executive officer was holding. "The invasions already started, Bob,"

"I'm surprised Admiral Kingston hasn't sent out any orders in regard to what we're doing," said the XO.

Grant looked at his second in command. "Bob, I don't think Kingston knows we're here."

The executive officer gave a puzzled look.

"Think about it," said Grant, "since we've been assigned to this mission, the only orders we've received have been through Pearl Harbor or Andy Halsted on the *Jones*. Not one word from Kingston, who would have half our boats assigned to his little task force and circle them around his carrier."

"What you're saying Skipper, is there's two chains of command here?"

"That's exactly what I'm saying. Someone high up in both chains is deliberately keeping this operation away from Kingston. Mind you, I'm not complaining. What are the orders for the rest of the boats assigned to this mission?"

Krause looked at the paper in front of him. "They're to maintain their patrol areas for the time being. The same thing goes for the surface vessels. Looks like they're worried this might expand a bit."

Grant took a sip of coffee. "Good possibility. You have an army trying to take over a country allied to the United Sates. A strong naval presence in the area seems like a logical response."

"I would agree, Sir, since they've just added five more ships to the Nimitz Battle Group for a total of thirteen. The Tarawa Ready Group has eight ships plus close to 2,500 Marines. With the ships on our mission, that's a total of thirty-nine American naval vessels. Yep, I think we're serious about this."

Grant laughed. "You know; you need to exercise more or something."

East of Cotabato
Mindanao, Philippines
March 17, 1995
0357 Hours

The helicopter came in low dropping into the clearing in a matter of seconds. The rear ramp dropped, and thirty-nine passengers rushed into the darkness, taking cover by the tree line. The CH-53 launched into the air, racing for the safety of the carrier. They hugged close to the ground listening for a few minutes before heading to the side of the clearing where the path they needed was located. They spotted a dim red light flashing to their north. This was repeated several times before Rice answered with her flashlight.

Summers gave the word to move and one of the rangers led off. After several minutes, they stopped, and Rice again signaled with her flashlight. Her signal was answered, and they moved forward again. They reached the path and were challenged by a faint voice in the dark. Summers answered the challenge and half a dozen men materialized out of the darkness.

"Good to see you again, Captain," said DeCook.

"You, too, Commander," replied Summers. "Let's get under cover and I'll make introductions."

"Follow me, Sir," said the man. They followed in a single file line, moving quietly, listening for any noise that didn't belong. They traveled down the trail about five hundred yards, where they stopped and clustered together.

"Commander DeCook of SEAL Team Five, I'd like you to meet Captain Sanchez of the Philippine Army. You know Sergeant Reardon, and this is Captain Rice of the United States Marine Corps," said Summers.

DeCook looked at Sanchez shaking his hand. "Nice to have you along, Captain. So far, I'm impressed with how your people have been able to function in this type of warfare."

"Thank you, Commander," said Sanchez, "but this type of warfare is part of our heritage."

"I'll say this much," responded DeCook smiling, "the odds of this mission succeeding increased about two hundred percent when Colonel Lacson and his small army showed up."

"About how many men?" asked Sanchez.

"Four hundred give or take."

A smile crossed Sanchez's face.

"As well as about twice as many civilians," added DeCook. "That number increases by the hour."

The smile disappeared.

"Sergeant Reardon," said DeCook turning his attention to the ranger, "how nice of you to join us."

"It's good to be here, Sir." came the simple reply.

"Captain Rice," said DeCook extending his hand, "what did you do to be sent out here."

Rice took DeCook's hand shaking it, "I work for Admiral Kingston. My guess is he's not expecting me to return."

DeCook looked at Summers, "A responsible female who gets to play with a man's toys?"

Summers nodded. "Where do we stand, Commander?'

DeCook got down to business. "You were right, Sir. They sent a platoon size force to ambush you. Chief Wiedenkeller and Colonel Lacson took care of them. We think they were part of the same group from yesterday's ambush."

"Prisoners?" asked Summers.

"Yes Sir. About a baker's dozen according to the radio report, including two foreign nationals. Mercs. Looks like we'll be dealing with some professionals."

Summers looked at Sanchez who nodded in return. DeCook noticed the exchange between the two men.

"Where do we stand with the rest of the mission?" said Summers turning his attention back to DeCook.

"Colonel Lacson and I have put together a plan we think will do well. We've been discreetly scouting the site over the last day and think we've found enough weaknesses to exploit. We'll need to get going so we can hit the base before everyone wakes up."

"Right after I make a phone call," said Summers. "Where's your radio?"

U.S.S. Nimitz
Celebes Sea
March 17, 1995
0425 Hours

The ready room was filled with people. Putnum looked around noticing sailors, marines, soldiers, and civilian law enforcement agents all working together. They were checking weapons, floor plans and just talking. He was upset about the reason for all of this but was proud of their cooperation.

"Sir?"

Putnum turned to find Summers' young radio operator.

"McAvoy, right?"

"Yes, Sir."

"What can I do for you, Petty Officer?" asked Putnum.

McAvoy shifted nervously. "Sir, I have a message from Captain Summers."

McAvoy stood waiting for a response. Putnum looked at the young sailor. "Petty Officer, I think you had better give me the message. Everyone in the room appears to be waiting on you."

For the first time, McAvoy noticed all activity stopped and everyone was focusing on him. The sailor blushed. "The message said, *Pathfinder is back in the woods, surprise party canceled.*"

Ellison moved up next to McAvoy.

"Sounds to me like Jon was right, Sir," said the marine.

"About a lot more than you think, George. Mr. Grey!"

The FBI agent moved forward, followed by Wells. "Yes, Admiral."

"This is now a criminal case. A case of espionage. You are in command of the operation. Notify all your people and shut this thing down now."

When Putnum finished, he left the room. Ellison knew he had to contact some people including CINCPAC and the president. He wondered what the admiral meant with his last comment. Ellison guessed he would never know and focused on the work at hand.

Grey was giving last minute orders to the three teams ready to deploy. Wells and Ellison were to lead the team hitting the admiral's cabin. Two other teams would hit the quarters of his aides at the same time. Based on information provided by Ellison, they expected to find Handcock's cabin empty. Each assault team was assigned several FBI and NCIS agents and was backed up by a fire team of rangers and marines.

"I don't want you shooting anyone," Wells said to Ellison.

Ellison put on his best pout. "Mr. Wells, you take all the fun out of life. Do you know that?"

Wells smiled, "I say that because I know how much you enjoy your work."

Ellison grinned from ear to ear. "Mr. Wells, you have no idea."

FBI Stake-out Site
Honolulu, Hawaii
March 16, 1995
2230 Hours

Ericson sat in his wheelchair next to the van that brought him. He watched as the FBI SWAT team moved into position, backed by a small army of FBI agents, NCIS agents, and local police. Curious neighbors had been quietly moved away and the perimeter was secure. The FBI agent in charge of the operation had given Ericson a radio so he could monitor the progress of the operation. He knew they were about ready to hit the house. They were just waiting for word from a higher authority.

Suddenly he heard the words 'green light' several times over the radio, and everyone moved at once. Tear gas canisters broke through windows, immediately followed by the sound of breaking wood as all three entrances to the one-story home were breached at the same time. Men dressed in black fatigue style uniforms, Kevlar helmets, and carrying Heckler and Koch MP-5 submachine guns poured into the house, quickly taking all four occupants into custody. The prisoners were immediately handcuffed and brought out on the front lawn where they were searched. They were then placed in four unmarked government cars and spirited from the scene. The entire operation was completed in five minutes. The clean-up and investigation would take days.

Ericson heard footsteps coming up behind him but didn't turn. Out of the corner of his eye he saw someone in a white uniform stop next to him to watch what was taking place.

"Good evening, Master Chief," said CINCPAC. "Pleasant evening, don't you think?"

"It is now, Admiral," responded Ericson.

Both men watched as the FBI agent in charge of the scene trotted up to them. He was wearing a baseball cap with FBI embroidered above the brim and his navy-blue windbreaker had the same letters stenciled across the back.

"Mr. Ericson, Admiral," said the agent.

"Thank you for letting me observe," said Ericson handing the man back the radio.

The agent smiled. "I should be thanking you, Sir. You did such a thorough job of scouting this site out it made our job easy. Seriously, Mr. Ericson, have you ever thought about teaching tactics? We can use good instructors for this type of thing."

Ericson smiled at the man shaking his head. "I don't think so, but thanks just the same. Tell you what though, call me and we'll set up a party for you and your people, on me."

The agent nodded. "I'll do that Mr. Ericson. You take care of yourself. Admiral, I'll be in touch once we have a chance to talk to these guys."

"Call me directly," replied CINCPAC. "I'll be in my office all night."

"Yes, Sir," answered the FBI man.

"Does Jon Summers know it's over, Sir?' asked Ericson.

The admiral did not answer right away.

"It's not over yet, Master Chief. Captain Summers went back into the jungle to draw Dick Kingston out. That's why we were able to hit this house so soon."

"The ass will get himself killed doing shit like that. I thought I trained him better," was Ericson's immediate reaction.

The admiral smiled. "You trained him well enough, Master Chief. My guess is that Jon will walk out of the jungle with the hostages. He planned this one well and used all his assets, including you."

"How big was this operation, if I may ask, Sir?"

"Various agencies in several countries hit sites in Los Angeles, San Francisco, San Diego, Washington, Manila, Davao, and in Japan. Once they knew the trap Captain Summers set was sprung, everyone moved at once."

"Trap? What trap?"

"They planned to ambush the captain and his party when they landed in the bush."

"I'm afraid to ask, Sir."

"You trained Pathfinder, Master Chief," chuckled the admiral. "You tell me what he did."

"I haven't heard that call sign in years. I thought it was retired for good."

"A lot of people did," said CINCPAC. "He must have thought it appropriate to bring it out of retirement. Master Chief, why don't you come with me, and we'll monitor the rest of the mission together."

"I'd like that very much, Sir. Thank you," answered Ericson.

The admiral turned to one of several younger officers standing nearby. "Lieutenant, would you please drive Master Chief Ericson to my office."

"Aye, aye, Sir!" snapped the young officer as his boss walked past him.

The young officer walked up to Ericson, "May I help you into your van, Mr. Ericson."

The officer didn't see his admiral stop, turning to observe the reaction from the man in the wheelchair.

Ericson grinned at the young man. "You may not, Lieutenant. You ride in the passenger seat. No one drives my van. By the way, Lieutenant, my business associates call me Mr. Ericson and my friends call me Josh."

"Yes, Sir," said the young officer showing a weak smile.

"You can call me, Master Chief," said Ericson, the van's lift started upward. "Come on, Lieutenant, get a move on. You don't keep an admiral waiting."

CINCPAC smiled watching the young officer scramble to get in the passenger door of the van.

"Commander," said the admiral to another aide.

"Yes, Sir."

"If the Master Chief's van isn't at the office before we are, send out a search party to bring the lieutenant home."

U.S.S. Nimitz
Celebes Sea
March 17, 1995
0435 Hours

The three teams stood outside in the passageway, ready to move on orders from Grey. When he knew each team was prepared, he gave the word. They burst into the compartments. The first team found Handcock's quarters empty as expected, but they set to work going through her belongings. The second team surprised Williams sleeping. The third team burst into the admiral's cabin. Within seconds, they were at the bed containing both Kingston and Handcock. Handcock started to scream, rolling out of the bed and onto the deck. While she continued to scream, Kingston reached for a nightstand drawer next to him. He stopped, realizing he was looking down the barrel of a handgun being held by Ellison. The screaming stopped when Demmer covered Handcock with a sheet, removing her from the compartment with the help of NCIS.

Kingston looked at the man on the other side of the gun. "You don't have the balls to shoot me, Colonel."

Ellison said nothing. A smile slowly came over his face. His eyes told Kingston he had misjudged the marine.

"Is your weapon loaded this time, George?" said Wells hoping to break the tension. "I certainly hope so because I'd hate to shoot the admiral myself if he goes for that weapon in the nightstand."

Kingston shifted his eyes from the marine to the NCIS agent. When he did, he withdrew his hand slowly. This prompted Ellison to lower his weapon slightly. Two NCIS agents immediately moved in, handcuffing the admiral. Once done, they helped him into a pair of shorts and then pants. When they went to move him out of the compartment, he shoved one of the agents with his shoulder, knocking him onto the bed. Kingston turned, finding himself face to face with Ellison. The marine gently kicked the prisoner's feet out from under him, causing him to fall to the deck. Kingston was brought to his feet by the NCIS agents and restrained.

"You'll pay for this with your career, Colonel," screamed Kingston.

Ellison smiled looking at Wells. "Isn't that what Jon said he would say?"

"Seems to have a limited vocabulary," chuckled Wells motioning for his people to move the prisoner out of the compartment.

"This is mutiny," shouted Kingston. "You'll all hang for this!"

"They won't, but you just might," said a voice from the back of the compartment.

The color drained from Kingston when he recognized Putnum. He stood motionless, staring at the Pacific Fleet's Intelligence chief. Putnum moved closer.

"I can think of a dozen charges to file against you right now, including murder for the men killed in the rescue attempt."

Kingston stood motionless, stunned over what was happening.

"The person I really feel sorry for is your wife. Fortunately, I'm don't have to explain to her you're out here screwing one of your aides while the FBI is raiding her home."

Kingston's head dropped.

"Mr. Wells," said Putnum.

"Yes Sir!" Wells led the prisoner out.

Putnum turned to Ellison. Klintworth was standing next to him.

"Colonel," said Putnum, "don't you have someplace to go right now?"

"Yes Sir!"

"Then get there and take Captain Klintworth with you!"

"Aye, aye, Sir!" said the marine with a grin. Both men left the compartment.

Camp Freedom
Mindanao, Philippines
March 17, 1995
0500 Hours

The guards entered the compound moving quickly. They woke all the prisoners up, making them stand where they had been sleeping. Once everyone was standing, Rolle walked slowly into the building. She walked up and down the rows of people for several minutes saying nothing. She finally stopped where the wounded were being forced to stand. She stood directly across from Becky and Sarah staring at them. Sarah looked away. Becky didn't.

"The American government sent a second rescue attempt. Unlike the first, it's been wiped out. Our sentries reported hearing the gunfire early this morning. Because of this arrogance on the part of your government, we'll have to make an example of one of you to show them we're serious."

There was silence around the large room.

Gateway stepped forward, standing in front of Rolle. "Young lady, we both know this will accomplish nothing."

"Ah," said Rolle, "the brave general expects us to cower before him. I think not. My orders are to make an example of you for what you've done to Patrick."

"I would expect nothing less from him," responded Gateway.

"Take this one and the other two," said Rolle turning to leave the building. Guards grabbed Gateway starting towards the door. Others did the same with Becky and Sarah.

**177 Pinecreek Drive
Rochester, New York
March 16, 1995
1700 Hours**

The door opened and Nancy walked in from the garage followed by Julie. They were met by Howard, who was headed the other way.

"Welcome home, honey. How was your day?" Howard asked kissing his daughter on the cheek.

"Hi there, Dad," answered Nancy. "Couldn't keep my mind on a thing with Jon overseas."

"Hello, Julie," said Howard kissing her on the cheek as well. "Know just what you mean, dear. Can't keep my mind on my job either with him gone."

"And just what is your job, Howard?" asked Julie kissing him back.

"Retirement, dear," answered the older man, stepping into the garage. "Can't seem to get around to it with Jon gone. *Howard, can you fix this? Can you get that?* It's like being married to four women."

"Dad, where are you going?" shouted Nancy after her father.

"Out to the local pub," he replied smiling, "the only place left in this world to find peace and quiet from women and kids, and they're trying to move in there, too."

He got into his car closing the door.

"He's actually going out to the grocery store, dear," said Emily.

Nancy nodded not wanting to say she already knew the obvious.

"Any word from Jon, yet, dear?" asked Emily.

"None," answered Nancy. "I was hoping you guys heard something."

Her mother shrugged shaking her head. Louise walked in and the two younger women hugged her. Julie put her arm around her mother.

"How are you holding up, Mom?" asked her daughter.

"Okay," answered Louise. "I'm more worried about Nancy."

Nancy shook her head. "Between us girls, I'm a wreck. I don't' know where he is or what he's doing. Close friends are being held prisoner on the other side of the world and I'm convinced he's in the middle of this mess. I can't concentrate on a thing."

"I had a call from an old friend of Hector's today," said Julie. "He's a sergeant on the city SWAT team. He said they were told a couple of the Lakeview cops got into it with some military types and some feds at the Naval Reserve Center while they were training."

Nancy grimaced.

"One of the Lakeview cops was Ron Hapke," continued Julie. "He called because of my former relationship with Ron, but more importantly because of whom he suspected one of the military people was."

"I'm afraid to ask," said Louise.

"From what I was told, Ron Hapke went after one of the military officers on the range and was taken down by the throat."

"That would be Jon," said Nancy lowering her head and covering her eyes.

"And while he had him down," continued Julie, "he took Ron's pistol away and fired at the target, hitting a bulls-eye every time."

"Oh, my God," said Nancy shaking her head. Louise just smiled.

"That's not all. I guess the other military type drew down on Ron's friend from the restaurant with an empty gun. Made him believe he was about to die. They say he had an accident in his pants. The marines at the Reserve center took four of the Lakeview officers into custody at the request of the feds at the scene. They're in big trouble from what the city cops hear."

Nancy was still shaking her head. Emily chuckled and Louise joined in. It broke out into open laughter. Nancy gave them the most severe look she could muster.

"The other officer would have been Colonel George Ellison, United States Marine Corps, *king of the mind games.* He probably thought it was just as funny as you two do."

Julie was also laughing. "Come on Nancy, Ron deserved it. He's been trying to provoke Jon forever. That night at the restaurant proved that."

"I'd laugh, Julie, but if this is as serious as I think it is, your friend Ron is lucky. Jon gets a mind set when he's doing a mission like this that's scary. I saw it in his face when he was with the teams, and I saw it again yesterday before he left. I used to call it his war face. No, Ron Hapke and his friend messed with him at the wrong time and my guess is God was smiling on them. I wish I knew what he was involved in."

Louise came over putting her arms around her daughter-in-law as she started to cry.

White House Situation Room
Washington, D.C.
March 16, 1995
1700 Hours

When the President of the United States entered the room, everyone rose to their feet. He motioned for them all to be seated, but none did until he sat at the end of the table. He looked tired and worn out. Norm Jeffers and Ben Goodman didn't look much better. The only one of the Joint Chiefs not at the table was John Cummings, who was in the communications room next door.

"Where do we stand?" asked the president.

"Mr. President," said one of his advisors, "I think this second attempt to rescue the hostages is ill-advised. The force is too small to deal with the garrison at this Moro stronghold. I recommend you recall the entire unit and extract them before there's a repeat of the earlier disaster. I have a message sent by Admiral Kingston saying just that. He's the senior commander in the area and has an impeccable record."

The president stiffened at the mention of Kingston's name. He didn't verbally respond but held up his hand to stop the man from talking. He looked at Jeffers.

"Gentlemen," Jeffers started, "I first apologize for keeping you in the dark, but there has been a major security breach on this operation and, we now assume, on others in the past as well."

Jeffers smiled watching everyone in the room shift nervously.

"Admiral Kingston was passing information to the enemy force on Mindanao and has been taken into custody. Admiral Putnum, the chief intelligence officer for the Pacific Fleet is now on *Nimitz* and in full command of the operation. So you know, the force we landed linked up with a larger force of SEALs inserted at the same time the rangers landed. Both forces have linked up with a larger force of Philippine soldiers who went into the hills rather than surrender to what we all believed were separatist forces. This is an attempt to wrestle control of Mindanao away from the Philippine government using an army trained and supported by mercenaries."

"Who's behind all this then?" asked one of the advisors.

"That's not the important issue at the moment," interrupted the president. "You'll all be fully briefed on the entire operation before you leave here. The focus here will be to get our people out of there."

Cummings walked out of the communication room. The president looked at him.

"They're set to go, Mr. President. Our last units are moving into position now and the operation will start within the hour. There are several problems which you should know about."

The president nodded.

"Extraction by helicopter would be suicide. They've found too many SAM sites in the area, too many for them to neutralize and expect the safe return of all hostages. They've selected a site for an extraction by sea. It's all here in the report."

Cummings handed the two-page report to the president and continued while he looked it over.

"The second problem is that while the enemy doesn't know we're there, every Filipino within a hundred miles does and is coming in to help or be rescued. The size of the Philippine military force grows by about ten men every hour, while the size of the civilian population grows by about one hundred times that in the same period."

"Admiral," said the president, "tell all our assets they have a *green light*. I may regret this entire thing, but I want those people back and I want them back now."

"Yes Sir!" replied Cummings wheeling around and going back into the communications room.

The president looked at everyone at the table for a moment before he spoke. Not one word was spoken during that time.

"Ladies and gentlemen, I've just committed a sizable military force to foreign soil to win the release of captive Americans. I may be looking for a new job tomorrow if this doesn't work, and maybe even if it does. Your job right now is to help me sell this to the leaders of Congress who I meet within an hour and a half and then to the American people. This espionage thing hurt our effectiveness, and we can't let that become the focal point because it's been going on for years. Long before this administration came into office. We have an hour to come up with a workable plan. Let's get to work folks."

U.S.S. John Paul Jones
Moro Gulf
March 17, 1995
0500 Hours

Halsted sat in his chair on the bridge. He was just brought a flash message from CINCPAC to all commands currently operating around the Philippines. It had been a long day already since the *Kamehameha* spotted the sub moving towards shore. He expected these were his orders to commence his operation to capture the mystery submarine. He opened it:

> *TO: ALL COMMANDS PHILIPPINES AREA OF*
> *   OPERATIONS*
> *FROM: CINCPAC*
>
> *EFFECTIVE IMMEDIATELY, REAR ADMIRAL RICH-*
> *ARD KINGSTON IS RELIEVED OF COMMAND OF THE*

NIMITZ BATTLE GROUP AND ALL RELATED OPER-
ATIONS. VICE-ADMIRAL W.C. PUTNUM WILL IMME-
DIATELY ASSUME COMMAND OF ALL OPERATIONS
IN THE AREA. ALL UNIT COMMANDERS WILL CON-
SULT WITH ADM. PUTNUM BEFORE DEPLOYING
THEIR COMMANDS.

Halsted was just starting to realize what he read when Lieutenant Smith
brought a second message.

TO: CMDR. JOHN PAUL JONES
FROM: ADM. W. C. PUTNUM

COMMENCE YOUR OPERATION AGAINST ENEMY
VESSEL AT 0545 HOURS TO COORDINATE WITH
OTHER OPERATIONS STARTING AT SAME TIME.
CONTACT IMMEDIATELY IF TARGET ATTEMPTS
TO MOVE.

PUTNUM

Halsted looked at the second message a second time before he reacted.
He had just been given the 'green light' to commence his operation.
"Mr. Smith!"
"Sir!" responded the young officer.
"Pass the word to all vessels in the command. General quarters at 0515.
All operations commence at 0545."
"Aye, aye Sir!"
The word was passed and everyone in the command came awake.

Camp Freedom
Mindanao, Philippines
March 17, 1995
0500 Hours

They had been passing units of the Philippine Army for the past twenty minutes. It was obvious there was a large force ready to move on the installation in the valley below. Spread out amongst the Filipinos were small units of SEALs who hailed their party when they passed. They came to a halt. Men were moving out in different directions, causing Summers to look at his watch. It was time for many of the smaller units to take up their positions for the upcoming attack.

"Commander," said Colonel Lacson, approaching them, "all the units are starting to move out to their jump off points. We should look over the plan one last time."

DeCook nodded and started to introduce Summers but was interrupted by Lacson.

"So you are the one they've sent to command this operation?"

Lacson looked the American over carefully, not all that impressed. The American held out his hand.

"I apologize if you've been led to believe I've been sent to command this operation," said Summers in Filipino.

Lacson was taken by surprise. Summers continued.

"I would never presume to command Philippine troops in their own country. I am only here to get some friends out of trouble and take them home. If, in the process of doing that, I'm able to help you with your operation, so be it. Colonel, may I introduce Jorge Sanchez of General Mangoba's staff."

"Colonel," said Sanchez, shaking the man's hand, "we're all proud of what you've managed to do here. You've managed to put together quite a resistance."

The colonel nodded but didn't take his eyes off Summers. Summers, in return, held his gaze.

"Your name must be Summers," said Lacson. "I've heard about you."

Summers looked puzzled. "I wasn't aware that I had a reputation."

Lacson's smiled, motioning for the American to follow him. They walked over to a group of soldiers getting ready to move out. Helping them pack their gear were a few civilians. Among this group were the old man and the boy who had been helping the colonel since they'd moved into the hills. The boy looked up and made eye contact with the two men, smiling at them both. The old man looked up for a second and then continued with his packing. He stopped what he was doing looking back at the American and froze. This was so out of character for the old man. A tear was running down his cheek.

"Hello, Fidel," said Summers. "I see after all these years you're still guiding young men through your hills safely."

The old man ran over to the American throwing his arms around him. DeCook, Rice, Reardon and the rest of the Americans looked at each other in amazement. The rest of the Filipinos stood up doing much the same thing.

"Jonny," said the old man in English choking back tears, "I knew you would come to help us free our country, just like your father."

There was a buzz amongst the Philippine troops.

Summers put his free arm around the old man. He looked down smiling.

"I'm here to take back some hostages from the people who are trying to take over your island. Do you remember Captain Gateway, who served with my father?"

The old man let go of Summers taking a step back. He wiped tears out of his eyes saying, "I remember him. He was a good man."

Summers put a hand on the old man's shoulder. "Fidel, both he and his family have been taken prisoner and are being held in the camp below. The job of the American's here is to get them back and take them home. We plan to do just that."

The old man puffed out his chest. "Then I will guide you safely through the hills to where you need to get to. I would like you to meet someone, Jonny."

The old man led Summers over to the boy. The young man stood up straight smiling at Summers.

"Jonny," said Fidel, "this is Ramon Franco. His father is a policeman in my town and his grandfather is an important policeman in Davao. Could you take him and his family to safety with you when you go?"

Summers knelt.

"Ramon," said Summers in Filipino, "I know your grandfather and I know he's proud of you for what you did during the attack on Princesa. You keep your family close to Fidel and we'll get all of you out of here."

When Summers stood back up, he turned to the old man. "Get your people ready to move Fidel. When we leave, we'll be going fast. Everyone will have to go with us."

"Then you're not leaving by helicopter?" asked Lacson.

"No," replied Summers, "too many SAM sites. We wouldn't get far. Why don't Captain Sanchez and I brief you on what's about to take place while Captain Rice phones home to let Captain Franco know his family is, okay?"

"Aye, aye, Sir," responded Rice smiling.

While Summers walked off with DeCook, Sanchez, and Lacson, the marine officer radioed in the message. When she completed the job, she looked at Reardon and sighed.

"Rough day, Ma'am?"

"Does everyone know this guy, or have I missed something?"

Reardon smiled. "Whoya, Ma'am."

Camp Freedom
Mindanao, Philippines
March 17, 1995
0515 Hours

The three of them were walked out of the gate and taken to a different building. They were now in a small building adjacent to the one where Sarah met with her father. Inside they found only one room. Gateway guessed by the way it was furnished, it was used for interrogation. There were four heavy chairs in the center of the room. On each were heavy nylon straps fastened on both the arms and the legs. There were some lighter weight chairs near a table on the other side of the room.

The four chairs were set up so that they were facing each other, but far enough apart so an interrogator could easily move around. All three of the captives were strapped into one of the chairs while Rolle watched, smiling.

"Why don't you take them back to the prisoner compound," said Gateway testing the straps. "I'm the one O'Keefe wants to kill!"

Rolle pulled a large combat knife out of its sheath on her belt, walking over to Sarah, and putting the blade next to her face. Tears streamed down Sarah's cheeks.

"Momma," she whimpered, "make her stop, please. She's going to hurt me."

Both Gateway and Becky struggled against their restraints, they were screaming at the woman. Rolle looked at Becky, grinning.

"If I choose her, it'll hollow you out," she said almost chuckling.

"You're doing this to get at me because of Patrick. You're more stupid than I thought. You're nothing more than a fucking, ignorant whore he uses to fill his bed," said Becky trying to bait the woman away from her daughter.

The bait worked. Before anyone could react, Rolle closed the distance between Becky and herself. She struck Becky several times in the face with her closed fist and then lashed out with the other hand, ripping Becky's blouse with the knife. Rolle ripped what was left of the piece of clothing from Becky. Sarah screamed and Gateway shouted with rage. The door of the building flew open, and O'Keefe charged in with another man on his heels. Becky's eyes met her ex-husband's. She was unhurt except for blood coming from her mouth from being hit and a cut on her shoulder from the knife.

An enraged O'Keefe turned to face Rolle.

White House
Washington, D.C.
March 16, 1995
1730 Hours

The president walked back into the situation room, having just left a meeting with the leaders of Congress. They were still upstairs so they could be briefed on the progress of the mission.

"Where do we stand?" asked the president taking his seat.

"All the units are in place and ready to move," said Jeffers, "but there was some recent movement of three of the hostages. They just took them into another building away from the main holding facility. They're verifying their location before they go."

"How long?"

"Just minutes, Mr. President." responded the secretary of defense.

"Pale Horse to Pathfinder," came a voice over the speaker in the center of the conference table. "Your target appears to be about fifty yards to the southeast of the structure with the veranda all around it. Three hostages escorted by four hostiles. Two more hostiles just entered the structure. Three friendlies and six targets inside."

"Pathfinder copies that, Pale Horse," came the reply. The president recognized Summers's voice.

"Pathfinder to all Horsemen, you are cleared to fire. We go on your command."

"Pale Horse copied."

"Roger that on Black Horse."

"Red Horse is good to go."

"White Horse is ready."

The president looked across the table to Goodman and Cummings, who were huddled together.

"SEAL sniper teams, Mr. President," said Cummings to the unasked question.

The president shook his head.

"Either I'm more tired than I thought, or Mr. Summers has too much time on his hands for reading. James Fennimore Cooper and Revelations, what a combination."

Camp Freedom
Mindanao, Philippines
March 17, 1995
0532 Hours

The guard tower closest to the main gate was the first target of the Pale Horse team. Each team was assigned several of these towers. Each tower was manned by two soldiers and was checked routinely by the officer of the guard. They had been watching the routine in the towers ever since they arrived the day before. It never varied. The man behind the .50 caliber sniper's rifle knew he had seconds to take out both men in the tower before one would raise the alarm.

The closest man turned away from his partner in the tower. Within seconds, the second man was lifted off his feet and thrown into the wood beam behind him. His chest exploded with blood where the heavy round struck him. When the closer man turned to see what happened, he was knocked to the floor when a round struck him squarely in the chest.

This tower being neutralized, the team moved on to their next target. This was silently repeated all around Camp Freedom as the four sniper teams went about their deadly work.

"Pale Horse is clear," said the spotter for the first sniper into the headset.

Each sniper team repeated the same message as they completed their assignments. While they waited, they began to identify additional targets.

"Pathfinder to all Horsemen, go to secondary targets. Fire at will. Pathfinder to all units, commence your assault."

Camp Freedom
Mindanao, Philippines
March 17, 1995
0535 Hours

They moved to within one hundred meters of the main gate. Reardon was on point, calling a halt so the sentries outside the gate wouldn't see them. Because of the early hour, the four men posted there were far too relaxed. They didn't see the two SEALs crawl up to within a few meters of them. Without warning, the SEALs rose shooting the men where they stood.

Before the last body hit the ground, the column was ordered forward by Reardon. When they reached the gate, Rice placed a small charge on the lock waving everyone clear. Seconds later, there was a pop and the gates swung open. Teams of American and Philippine soldiers moved off in predetermined directions. It wasn't long before the first bodies were found, enemy soldiers who had become prey to the four Horsemen whose guns were still firing on targets of opportunity. Summers was moving towards the main building with a small team of SEALs going after the three hostages separated from the rest of the group. DeCook and another team of SEALs supported by Philippine soldiers were moving toward the main prisoner compound. Rice's team moved towards barracks facilities for the troops manning the installation. Lacson and a larger force remained near the gate, ready to move in any direction for support as needed.

Rice and her team approached the buildings used to house the mercenary troops. The door to one of the wood frame buildings opened and a man stepped outside, raising a rifle. Before the weapon was in place, the man dropped to the ground, blood splattered on the wood behind him. Two more men appeared in the doorway and were immediately thrown back inside when one .50 caliber projectile passed through the first man and into the second. Small arms fire began to break out throughout the compound as small units of defenders began to engage the attackers. As the enemy resisted, the snipers neutralized the targets, sending remaining defenders running for cover.

The guards at the entrance to the prisoner compound shifted nervously hearing the gunfire inside the compound. Additional guards rushed to help their comrades defend the prison, when DeCook and his men attacked, catching most of the guard force in the open. In a short, but heated firefight, most of the guards were killed or wounded. Guards assigned inside the prisoner compound moved to eliminate the hostages but were cut down by the deadly accurate fire from the hills above. There was a small explosion as the rescuers blew the lock off the gate. This was followed by a rush of armed men racing through the gate.

Summers and his team reached their target just as Rice and her group engaged the first of the defenders. They could hear yelling from inside. Summers glanced inside quickly, seeing the three captives bound in the chairs. He recognized O'Keefe as the man arguing with a female terrorist standing near the captives. The other four soldiers were standing near the table on the far side of the room, their weapons down. O'Keefe was screaming at the female for putting his daughter in danger. The female was becoming more agitated with O'Keefe. Summers could see by her body language she wouldn't take much more from the man.

Summers used hand signals, telling the team they were going to breech. Two members of the team moved to the other side of the building to cover the windows. Summers and three others would go through the door, while the remaining members would provide external security.

Inside, Rolle was incensed O'Keefe was going to stop her. O'Keefe managed to get between her and the three captives. He was pointing his finger at her and ordering her to put the knife away.

"You will not hurt anyone without my specific orders. I know what Osaka's orders were and who they were meant for. You are out of control and need to get your ass out of here before I have to do something I'll regret!!" shouted O'Keefe.

Rolle didn't say anything in return but understood she crossed the line for the final time. He was about to end their relationship. There was the sudden sound of gunfire close by. The four guards in the back of the room turned their heads for a split second and Rolle drew the pistol she carried. As she raised it at Becky, O'Keefe jumped in front of his ex-wife. At the same time, the door crashed open and four camouflage clad men burst in. The guards in the back of the room all started to raise their weapons and were met by a hail of bullets from two of the four intruders and from those hidden on the other side of the windows. Rolle fired twice hitting O'Keefe in the chest both times. As he dropped to the floor, she turned to meet the threat coming through the door. Summers fired twice, the first round hitting her in the head and the second in the chest. She flew backwards, hitting the wall, sliding to the floor.

The attack only took seconds but was so intense the silence that followed was deafening. The only sound for the first twenty seconds after the attack was Sarah sobbing. Summers looked around the room quickly making sure all his people were accounted for. He was the first to say, *clear*, and was quickly followed by the rest of the team. The only man who didn't respond was the man standing next to him. Summers looked at him closely. He was standing there looking at the crumpled heap against the far wall.

"You okay, sailor?" asked Summers.

"That was a woman, Sir!" said the young man still half in a trance. "You shot a woman."

The man behind him put his hand on the young man's shoulder. "Snap out of it, Smith. Check the body."

The young man seemed to come back to reality. "Right away, Chief. Sorry."

The sailor moved forward.

"Sorry about that, Sir. This is only his second mission."

Summers glanced at the SEAL standing next to him. "Don't apologize, Chief. Just remember what it was like your first time."

The man smiled. "You have a point, Sir. Say, not bad shootin' for an old guy."

Summers glanced from the bodies to the hostages. "Chief, get a couple of corpsmen in here right away."

Aye, aye, Sir," replied the chief.

It was only seconds, and two SEAL corpsmen were next to the three restrained captives. While the two medical corpsmen looked to their charges the young sailor bent over to look at O'Keefe. He jumped back away from the body when he found the man breathing.

"Chief," said the young man, his voice raised a few octaves, "this guy's still alive."

Moro Gulf
Mindanao, Philippines
March 17, 1995
0545 Hours

The word from Putnum to commence with all operations came almost to the second. Halsted immediately gave the word to move, and the coastal patrol boats *Hurricane* and *Zephyr* went to full speed, beginning to move on the docked submarine. The *Doyle* moved in as close to shore as she could to support the two smaller craft. *Hurricane* moved in with surprising speed. Before the sentries on the pier could see the threat, they were neutralized by sharpshooters from the deck of the fast-moving ship. The guards fell silently at their posts, never knowing where the attack was coming from.

Hurricane came to a sudden stop within feet of the submarine and twenty men went over her side and onto the deck of the sub. They immediately spread out, moving to secure the deck of the sub and the pier area. At the same time *Hurricane* sped off, *Zephyr* came in next to the sub repeating the operation. Another twenty SEALs went over the side joining the men already there. They began to move up the stairway leading to the plantation above and a team entered the sub. *Zephyr* held her station, while members of the crew tied a tow line to the sub. The crew of the submarine was being led out of the boat by the SEALs. They were told to lie down on the pier, face down, and put their hands over their heads. Within minutes the entire crew of the submarine was evacuated and being searched for weapons. Another squad of SEALs searched the sub for booby traps.

The squad working its way up the stairs on the cliff came under fire from a sentry at the top of the cliff. The sentry was joined by another, and they were able to pin down the approaching SEALs. *Hurricane* circled around and was close into shore. Her Mark 19 automatic grenade launchers fired several rounds impacting around the sentries. This eliminated the threat to the SEALs. Suddenly, a flight of twelve Philippine Army helicopters flew past the American ships, beginning to circle the compound at the top of the cliffs. Machine guns on the helicopters began to fire in bursts, trying to clear a landing zone. Two of the helicopters swooped down offloading their cargo of Philippine Marines. This was followed by each helicopter in succession, until all completed their mission.

The Marines quickly secured most of the compound but were taking sporadic fire from hidden rebel soldiers. Intense fire suddenly came from the direction of the main house on the plantation. A group of about twenty men were running for the stairway that led down the cliffs. The Marines returned the fire, quickly eliminating most of the resistance. As the groups of retreating rebels approached the upper landing of the stairway, they were met by the squad of SEALs. The man in the lead, Ishimoto, immediately raised his rifle to fire and was cut down. The rest of the group dropped their weapons and raised their hands in the air.

Osaka looked from his dead bodyguard to the rest of his men, who were surrendering. He reached into his coat for something and was knocked to the ground from behind. He looked up to find himself facing two rifles. One belonged to a very nasty looking Philippine Marine, the other to a serious looking SEAL.

"I would pull your hand out slowly," said a voice in Japanese from behind the two men.

When Osaka did, the SEAL backed away, allowing the marine to reach under the coat, pulling out a revolver. The marine backed off as well. Two men came into Osaka's line of vision. One wore the uniform of the Davao Police Department and the other the uniform of the Japanese Army.

"I think you're in serious trouble," said the man in the Japanese Army uniform. "This is Captain Franco representing the Philippine government. He's here to take you into custody for attempting to overthrow the rightful authority here on Mindanao. As a representative of the Japanese government, I'm here to represent you because you're a Japanese national. Unfortunately for you, we would like to question you as well regarding why you're in possession of a submarine belonging to us."

Osaka's eyes were wide open.

"You know, Tobi," said Franco, "I think we can come to some arrangement on this, but we should move out of here before some more of his troops decide to come and rescue him."

Tobi smiled, turning to the SEAL, "Ensign, do you think we might trouble you for a ride?"

A smile came from behind the blackened face paint. "No problem, Sir. The sub and her crew are secure and ready for your inspection."

Tobi looked at Franco, who in turn nodded to a marine officer. The officer gave orders for his men to destroy the plantation.

White House
Washington, D. C.
March 16, 1995
1805 Hours

"Damn!" said the president pleased with what he had just heard. "Thirty-five minutes and the hostages are liberated, and the subs captured. Not bad ladies and gentlemen. Not bad at all."

He looked across the table and saw long faces on his military people.

"What's wrong?" asked the chief executive.

"We may have freed them, Sir, but they're not out of there yet," said Goodman. "We've shot the enemy in the heart, but the brain doesn't know it's dead yet."

"I don't understand?" asked the president.

"Happens, Sir," answered Cummings. "The military branch of their operation doesn't know we've taken the heart out of their little rebellion. They may even get nastier when they find out there's no payday at the end of this."

The president's jubilation disappeared.

"How long until they're clear?

"Eight to twelve hours, Sir," answered Goodman. "They must get to the beach, but more importantly, we have to get our ships there. Admiral Putnum has things in hand, but the Tarawa Battle Group is still several hours out."

"Mr. President," said one of the aides, "we'll have to make a statement. We'll never be able to keep this under wraps."

The president sat up straight looking around the table.

Mindanao, Philippines
March 17, 1995
0615 Hours

Rebel forces reeled back from the heavy attack by government forces on all fronts. The artillery barrages were devastating, hitting targets with unusual accuracy. Tanks appeared where they hadn't been several days earlier, leading the advancing government troops. They were taking their toll. Mercenary forces tended to band together to find some way to avoid capture, while domestic forces were either killed in the ensuing battle or ran into the jungle. Boerst tried in vain to reach Osaka to ask for both direction and help but was met by static. When he received word additional government forces landed on the north end of the island, he put the word out to all his troops to withdraw and rally at Camp Freedom. They would pick up supplies and fight their way out.

When he tried to call O'Keefe to warn him about what was taking place, an American answered the radio telling him O'Keefe wasn't available. Fearing the worst he ordered his troops to move immediately.

Camp Freedom
Mindanao, Philippines
March 17, 1995
0630 Hours

The installation was secure for the time being. All the hostages were outside the compound and medics were working with Becky to make sure they were comfortable and ready to move when required. Becky's own injury had been tended to and one of the medics had given her a camouflage shirt to replace the blouse that had been destroyed. To the pleasure of both Lacson and Summers, there were no friendly casualties. Both men knew this would change if they didn't get on the road quickly.

The senior officers were huddled for a quick conference to discuss their options.

"Sir," said Rice, "this base not only seems to be their base of operations, but also their major supply depot. We've found food, guns, ammunition, medical supplies, spare parts, and a ton of trucks. We've also found two working tanks and some armored cars."

"My people are getting the trucks ready to transport as many as we can to the evacuation site. Last count shows over one hundred transport vehicles," said Lacson, "we won't be able to transport all of the civilians, but some have indicated they would rather go into the hills and fight."

"Judging from the reports they won't have long to wait," said DeCook. "We've intercepted a message indicating the first of the enemy units should show up here about 0700."

There was silence for a moment while Summers thought.

"How long until those transports can be ready to move?"

"Less than fifteen minutes," smiled Lacson.

"Then let's get them ready to move out no later than 0645. Distribute the food and medical supplies to anyone who needs them. Let's take any of the weapons and ammo you feel we may need in the next twenty-four hours. Destroy the rest."

"Consider it done, Captain," said the Colonel, "I'll also make sure that the enemy is delayed. I have some units volunteering to set up ambushes and the Moro rebels are interested in revenge. As you American's say, *it's payback time.*"

"Enemies fighting together against a common enemy," chuckled Summers. "What's this world coming to? Captain Rice!"

"Sir,"

"Make sure that all of the freed rangers able to fight are armed and good to go."

"Aye, aye, Sir."

"Also make sure all the hostages are loaded on vehicles and ready to move. Disperse your people as needed to make sure they're protected."

"Aye, aye, Sir!"

"Mr. DeCook."

"Sir!"

"Tim, I want anything they might be able to use in flames when they get here. No booby traps, too many civilians around to walk into them once we leave. Nothing left. No supplies. No buildings. Nothing."

"Aye, Sir!" said DeCook with a grin.

"Let's move guys. We don't have much time!"

Everyone but Lacson immediately disbursed. He was still smiling.

"You seem very happy this morning, Colonel," said Summers.

"I have to be," replied the Filipino. "I expected a long campaign in the jungle and now it looks as if I might get to see my family sooner than expected. You're very efficient, Captain, and it is an honor serving with you."

Summers looked at the Filipino and started to answer, but the officer put his hand up to stop him.

"You care for the people under your command and are sensitive to those who are not. My previous contacts with American commanders haven't been as good. I sincerely mean what I said. You should know Captain Sanchez has asked permission to leave all the prisoners except for the foreign nationals. I will arrange for the others to be picked up by the units we are leaving behind."

Summers nodded his acceptance of Lacson's decision and knew it was the only one he could make. He held out his hand to the Philippine officer shaking in friendship.

"Colonel, the honor has been all mine. The main mission is to get as many of these people to safety as we can, and I think we just may do it."

The Philippine officer laughed slapping Summers on the back. "Of course we will."

Lacson moved off to check his people, who were already lining up vehicles and loading civilians. Summers was optimistic walking to where the hostages where gathered. Rice managed to feed them and was in the process of arming the rangers. Morale was high as Summers approached. When he entered the group many of the rangers snapped to attention recognizing him from Hawaii. Summers motioned for them to continue with what they had been doing.

Gateway noticed the man talking to the rangers guessing he was in command of the rescue. He decided to introduce himself, so walked over to where the man was talking to one of the wounded rangers. As he approached, the officer looked up at him smiling.

"It's good to see that you've survived, General," said Summers.

Gateway was surprised the officer knew who he was and thought there was something familiar about him. He returned the man's smile stopping next to him. The officer said something quietly to the wounded man and stood up. Gateway watched a ranger sergeant run up, stopping next to them.

"Sir," said the sergeant without skipping a beat, "the two tanks are Abrams M-1's, Sir. Looks like we have a bit of a punch now. I've sent a couple of the guys to tune them up, Sir, and get them moving."

"Good job, Reardon," said Summers. "How long until they're ready to move?"

"They were made ready, Sir. Just give the word and we'll take the point."

"Sergeant Reardon, I'd like you to meet General William Gateway."

Reardon snapped to attention, saluting. "Sir, a pleasure to make your acquaintance."

Gateway smiled at the sergeant nodding as the man winked at Summers and ran off.

"General would you like to accompany me as I meet the hostages?" said Summers.

Gateway, taken by surprise, said he would be delighted, and they spent several minutes wandering through the World War II veterans. When they would come across any of the active-duty service men they were treated with a great deal of respect. Gateway saw the pride the men had when this officer talked to them. When they approached where Becky was getting some of the wounded ready to be loaded onto trucks, they ran into an old Filipino man who the officer introduced as Fidel. Fidel looked familiar to Gateway as well, but he chalked his bad memory up to his age. As they approached Becky, Fidel followed Gateway like a puppy.

"How's the patient, Doc?" asked Summers looking down at Becky and Naylor.

Naylor looked up covering his eyes. "It's you! I heard they sent you in but didn't believe it."

Summers knelt next to the doctor smiling at the wounded officer.

"Never better, buddy. Never better. I guess my careers about fried, but other than that I'll live," Naylor answered Summers's question of Becky.

Summers put his hand on the man's shoulder. "You were set up, Charlie. We got the bastard, but not until after he got your command. I'll give you the details over a beer when we get back."

"You make this sound so nonchalant," said Becky adjusting a bandage. "I have a friend who has the same attitude and at times it's scary. All this death and destruction around you and it's like it doesn't affect you."

Summers looked at her.

"You're the one who shot that Suzanne woman aren't you?" continued Becky, her father looking perturbed.

"Yes, Ma'am, I am," came the reply.

"I want to thank you for protecting my family. I've never wanted to kill anyone myself until I met her. I'm not sure whether I'm comfortable with those feelings or not, but I have them just the same. I had a good friend tell me once that killing is easy. With her I could have proved him right."

"It's been a pretty rough time for a flower child like yourself. Be proud. You've done well," said Summers smiling at the doctor. "Most times not killing is harder to do than killing. That's true for sure in this business. The young lady this morning was infected with that madness. It leaves you no choice but to shoot. Again, Doc, you did well. You can ship with me anytime."

Becky looked at the man kneeling next to her. Something in the words he said made her think she knew him. Underneath the boonie cap and camouflage face paint she could see a gentleness in the blue eyes looking at her from behind the dark rimmed military issue glasses. Gateway was also taking a closer look at the man, trying to remember where he knew him from.

"Doc, you better get your patients ready. We leave in ten minutes," said the officer standing up. He moved over to where the wounded O'Keefe lay. He was being tended by a Navy medic and was holding his daughter's hand. The terrorist looked up at him and acknowledged his presence. Summers nodded in return. The young woman didn't look up. Summers knelt next to her.

"How are you holding up, Sarah?" he asked.

The girl looked at him finally; her eyes glazed over saying nothing. Nothing needed to be said. Summers looked at the medic.

"He can travel, Sir, but he still has two bullets in him and will need surgery. If all goes well, he'll make it."

Summers smiled at the young sailor asking, "How are you holding up?"

The sailor returned the officer's smile. "This is a little bigger than what I'm used to, but I'm doing just fine, Sir."

"Good for you. Carry on, sailor."

"Aye, Sir."

Summers started to rise; he was grabbed by O'Keefe. The wounded man motioned for Summers to lean down closer. When Summers did, the wounded man spoke in a weak voice, "I know who you are."

Summers looked down at the man but didn't respond.

"Thank you for saving my family," continued O'Keefe struggling for breath. "The old man was right about you. I should have let you win."

Summers continued to hold the man's hand. "Well, he was wrong about you, and I think you about him. We'll talk about that when you're feeling better. By the way, there was never any contest."

O'Keefe smiled weakly at Summers letting go of the man's hand. Summers turned, walking towards Gateway.

"Who was that, Daddy?" asked Sarah watching Summers.

"Stay close to him, Darlin'," responded her father, "He's the man getting all of us out of here."

The SEAL acting as Summers's radioman seemed to be busy with some traffic over the satellite set. Gateway was next to him when the SEAL held out the handset to Summers.

"The commander of Liberty flight from the *Nimitz* is approaching the area."

Summers took the handset. "Pathfinder to Liberty flight. Over."

"Liberty One to Pathfinder, copy you five by five. We're just in the area and thought we'd check in to see if you need an assist."

"Appreciate the thought Liberty One, but you're in unfriendly skies, if you understand my meaning."

"Nonsense, Pathfinder," came the response in an irrepressible Texas drawl. "We don't fly anywhere but in friendly skies, if you understand my meaning."

Summers chuckled. "Copy that Liberty One. We're expecting company from the east within the next thirty mics, could you recon and advise."

"Copied that Pathfinder and remember we're only a phone call away."

"Roger that, Liberty One. Thanks for the assist. Pathfinder out."

Summers handed the handset back to the young SEAL who continued with his business.

"What's going on here?" Gateway asked Summers. "I think I should know; in case my people have any questions."

Summers smiled at the older man. "It's called control of the battlefield, General. We are now in the process of evacuating both American citizens and refugees to safety. This column will not be taken by surprise and your lives put in jeopardy if there is anything humanly possible, we can do about it. Let's get your people loaded onto the trucks before Colonel Lacson has a fit."

He nodded his compliance to the last statement and followed the officer back to where Becky was starting to load the wounded onto the trucks. All up and down the line, hostages and refugees were climbing into the large military trucks. Philippine and American service men hustled around the vehicles making sure they were ready. As they were loading one of the wounded onto a truck, Smith came up to Gateway and Summers.

"Anything I can do?" he asked.

Summers answered without hesitation. "You can help keep an eye on the wounded on this truck, Reverend."

Smith and Gateway looked at each other and then back at the officer they were standing with.

"Do I know you, Sir?" asked Smith.

"No, Sir, we've never met."

"Then how did you know he was a minister?" asked Gateway.

Summers smiled at the two men as he answered. "The same way I knew you're a general. It's my job. Like you, I like to think I'm good at it."

Gateway was feeling foolish and decided not to ask if he knew the officer from somewhere.

Smith was joined by his wife and the officer acknowledged her presence.

"Ma'am, can I help you on the truck?" said Summers with a smile.

As he helped Catherine onto the truck, her husband said, "I've spent all this time praying with people and my bible is back in the hotel room. This is embarrassing. I'm out here without the basic tools of my trade."

"Don't worry about it, Don," replied Gateway, helping him onto the truck. "The circumstances are just a bit out of the ordinary."

"But, still, Bill," said the minister, "you would think I would have had the foresight to have a pocket Bible with me."

"I think he understands, Reverend," said Summers looking up. He was reaching into a pocket in his ALICE pack and came out with a small book with a zipped cover. Its cover looked old and worn. He tossed it up to the minister who caught it. "It's only the New Testament, and its King James. Not one of the new revised versions, but it's better than nothing."

The minister looked at the small book he held in his hands smiling down at the officer.

"As you may recall from the last time you were in this country, Reverend, you don't' need the book to pray. My guess is you've done fine so far."

Smith held the book up. "It's well used."

Summers laughed, "Yes, Sir, but more by my father than me. He gave it to me."

Smith turned to help his wife settle the wounded and make them more comfortable. Summers and Gateway moved onto the next vehicle where they were loading Naylor onto the rear bed. He managed a weak smile and waved at Summers. Right behind Naylor they were bringing a stretcher carrying O'Keefe.

"I don't want him on the truck," said Gateway sharply, taking his granddaughter by surprise. Tears were starting down the girl's cheeks again. The two servicemen loading the stretcher looked past Gateway to Summers for direction.

Summers put his hand on Gateway's shoulder. "Don't have time for family squabbles, General. You ride on this truck and so does he. He took two bullets meant for your daughter. The least you can do is allow him the best medical attention available, and that would be the Doc. Gentlemen, load Mr. O'Keefe on the truck."

"Aye, aye, Sir!" said the corpsman. Gateway stood looking at the man standing next to him. His expression was a mixture of anger and shock.

Behind them, Becky smiled. Her father wasn't used to taking orders and was just put in his place by a professional.

"General," said a female voice from behind them, "I've found our van and it's intact. Do you think they'll let us take it with us?"

The two men turned to see Monroe and her news crew walking up behind them. Before Gateway could answer Summers said, "Miss Monroe, it's good to see that you're safe."

"Sir," interrupted the SEAL acting as Summers's radio man, "it's Eagle and he's asking why we're not moving yet."

Monroe looked from the SEAL to Summers.

"Miss Monroe," asked Summers as he nodded to the SEAL, "does your equipment work?"

Monroe turned to look at her cameraman and soundman. They both nodded affirmative and then the cameraman said, "It'll take about thirty minutes to get it ready though."

Summers looked at the two men. "You have five minutes and I want it right here by this truck. How many refugees can you carry?"

"None," said Monroe, "the equipment is too valuable. I don…"

"Then I'll destroy the equipment to make room for people."

"Five or six," said the Filipino soundman quickly.

"Thank you," said Summers in Filipino. "Would you make sure it's taken care of for me, please?"

"Yes, Sir," replied the soundman in English.

Summers turned to face the truck again. Two Philippine soldiers were helping Sarah onto the vehicle. Gateway looked at the officer. "What do you think our chances are?"

Summers smiled back at him. "You did this considerably longer than I. You tell me."

Gateway smiled shaking his head. He turned following Donavon onto the back of the truck. The SEAL next to Summers said, "Sir, Liberty One has the point elements of the enemy units ten minutes out."

Summers took the handset. "Pathfinder to Liberty One, it's time to see exactly how friendly those skies are. I need you to buy me some time, son.

"Roger that, Pathfinder. Consider it done," was the response.

Summers looked up at Gateway who nodded his understanding of what was meant. Summers gave the handset back to the SEAL and winked. The man smiled in return, shaking his head. Summers turned to see the last of the wounded was loaded on a nearby truck and Becky was collecting some supplies with one of the corpsmen.

"Doc!" shouted Summers. "Come over here and get on this vehicle."

Becky not only had a camouflage shirt on, but had come into possession of a camouflage boonie cap. She trotted over to where Summers was.

"What is it?" asked the doctor indignantly. "I need to get supplies for the wounded."

Summers shook his head. "No, Doc, we're not in your hospital now. Get on this truck and we'll get supplies to each truck. My people are good at their jobs and know what they're doing."

Suddenly two F-18's streaked over and fired missiles at a target some distance away. Other jets were seen nearby also firing missiles. The sound of distant explosions was heard. Becky looked nervously about.

"They're our Navy F-18's firing on an enemy column on its way here and on some SAM sites nearby."

Becky looked at the man, not feeling at ease knowing the same people who had taken her family prisoner were close by.

"Be a good girl for once, Flower Child, and do what you're told."

The statement caught her by surprise, and she wasn't prepared when he grabbed her about the waist and lifted her into the truck. She didn't take her eyes off him as he turned away shouting, "Captain Rice!"

The marine officer came running down the column of vehicles stopping next to Summers. Explosions inside the compound could be heard close by and black smoke began to spiral into the morning sky. Rice turned to look and smiled.

"Rice, make sure that each vehicle has food and medical supplies if needed," said Summers. "Also make sure we have soldiers in each vehicle to provide protection. You take personal charge of this vehicle with the general and his party."

"Aye, aye, Sir," replied the marine officer.

Another series of explosions erupted as more F-18's flew over. Rice turned smiling at Summers. "Looks like Commander DeCook is busy, Sir."

Summers returned the smile. She was no longer wearing her helmet, having attached it to her pack. She now had on her head a basic marine issue fatigue cap. There was no mistaking the fact she was a marine.

"It's nice you like your job, Captain," responded Summers. "Carry on."

"Aye, aye, Sir," said the marine going about her duties.

Summers turned to see the reporter and her crew found their van and moved it to where he requested. They also enlisted the help of eight Filipinos, who undoubtedly would be transported by the vehicle when they left. He walked over and began talking to the reporter. His radioman followed him.

Smith settled next to his wife on the truck. The wounded were as comfortable as they could be made. All the vehicles were starting their engines, which meant it was almost time to move out. He reached into his pocket and pulled out the well-worn Bible the officer had given him. The brown cover was such that you could no longer read the printing on it, but the zipper worked well. As he unzipped it, he noticed the pages were indeed well worn. The inside cover indicated that it was a King James version of the New Testament. Smith guessed it to be from the 1940's or 1950's. When he opened the cover to the first page, he glanced at the inscription someone had written years before. He rubbed his eyes and read it a second time.

Catherine noticed the sudden change in her husband's demeanor and was about to ask him what was wrong when he jumped up from where he was sitting and wildly began to look around. Gateway and Donavon were standing in the truck behind Smith's and saw their friend looking distressed. They waved to get his attention. Smith was trying to yell something to them, but they couldn't hear him over the noise from the big diesel engines. More jets flew over at low altitudes, followed by explosions close by.

Smith finally found who he was looking for. The officer who gave him the Bible was standing near the news crew, talking on the radio. His CAR-15 slung over his shoulder with the barrel facing downward. The officer saw the minister standing nodding to him. Smith collapsed back down next to his wife.

"What is it, dear?" she asked anxiously. "What's the problem?"

Smith handed her the Bible and she opened it and read the inscription.

To my Grandson
Lt. Raymond Summers
From your loving Grandmother
Anna Mae Summers
September 1944

★ CHAPTER 15 ★
EXTRACTION

The president waved his hand for the aide to turn off the television. He just saw live pictures from Camp Freedom and couldn't believe the number of refugees there looking for help. Summers freed the captive news crew and used them to set up the live video connection to show them what he was dealing with. The president still couldn't believe the magnitude of what they saw. Summers laid out the evacuation plan and the president approved it. The White House had the network president on hold waiting to hear if they could break the story. He looked at all his military advisors. They, too, had not anticipated the volume of refugees walking out of the jungle. They were pleased with the response from the troops on the scene. Everything was under control and the American and Philippine forces were working well together.

His advisors were mixed as to whether a statement should be made regarding the situation on Mindanao, but after seeing the video, he had made up his mind. He picked up the telephone nearest him and then pushed the button that was blinking.

"This is the President. I appreciate your waiting."

"No problem, Mr. President," said the man on the other end. "I know you don't want us to run with this story, but I'd like to get your permission to take some video since we have a camera crew on scene."

"Mr. Meisenthal," said the president, "I will be addressing the nation in less than five minutes about this situation and all I will ask is that you and your people be discrete and not jeopardize the ongoing operation."

"Sir?" said the surprised newsman.

"I have to rush off," continued the president. "Again, I appreciate your patience with us. Have a good night."

The president hung up the telephone leaving the room with a smile on his face.

The Road to Camp Freedom
Mindanao, Philippines
March 17, 1995
0655 Hours

The F-18s had been harassing their advance for the last fifteen minutes. Boerst called for SAM fire to scare off the aircraft, but all that seemed to do is bring in more. Every time a SAM radar was turned on, the radar unit and all the missile batteries attached to it, were immediately destroyed by other aircraft. The lead element of his column was now within two miles of the main gate to Camp Freedom. He expected they would be inside the camp in fifteen minutes, even with the American aircraft. As the first vehicle of the column came to a bend in the road, there were explosions on both sides. For one hundred yards on either side, trees and splinters of wood were blown into the column blocking the road. This was immediately followed by heavy small arms fire pinning down the forward elements of the column. Boerst moved up reinforcements, only to have them hit by accurate mortar and rocket fire. Several of their armored vehicles were damaged and two trucks were destroyed. The small arms fire increased and then stopped altogether.

Fires sent columns of black smoke into the air. When the small arms fire ceased, the troops started to come out from cover, only to find the American and Philippine Air Force planes were back to pound the column. More vehicles were destroyed and their attempt to retake Camp Freedom was postponed again.

177 Pinecreek Drive
Rochester, New York
March 16, 1995
1900 Hours

The entire family was eating late because of schedules. Sean had been after school for swimming and Justin and Stephen had karate lessons. The adults were all in the same frame of mind spending most of their time trying to get some news on the situation in the Philippines. All agreed they thought Jon was there. They were all sitting in front of the large television in the family room watching the nightly news. When the news ended, the anchor stated the President of the United States would be addressing the nation following the news.

The news ended and the president was introduced. He was not in the press room, but behind his desk in the Oval Office. He looked tired and his expression was serious.

"My fellow Americans, I address you tonight about an issue that has consumed our energy here at the White House for most of the past two days. Several days ago, people that we presumed to be with the Moro Separatist movement on the island of Mindanao took over one hundred American and Japanese citizen's hostage. Many of you have heard the news of our failed rescue attempt yesterday. I am here tonight to address both issues, and let you know that at this moment, the hostages have been freed by American and Philippine military forces.

"First, I would like to say the intelligence communities in the United States, the Philippines, Japan, and several other allies have determined beyond a shadow of a doubt this was an independent operation aimed at overthrowing the existing power structure of the island of Mindanao. They have tried to accomplish this by employing an army consisting of locals trained and backed by mercenaries. This is the current threat still facing the island, as the political and financial end of the operation has been eliminated. There are still large units of this mercenary army in control of sections of the island.

"Second, I would like to say there was a rescue attempt yesterday that was unsuccessful because of a breach in security. How serious the damage to that operation is currently being assessed and I cannot comment on the investigation. After identifying and dealing with the breach, a joint operation conducted by American and Philippine forces commenced at 4:30 a.m. Philippine time and as of 6:30 p.m., Eastern Standard Time, all hostages being held by enemy forces have been freed. The operation to extract them from Mindanao is ongoing and I commend all the brave men and women of both the American and Philippine armed forces who are involved. The troops involved in the operation now face the difficult task of maintaining the safety of not only the freed hostages, but of thousands of refugees gravitating to their presence on the island.

"For that reason, I have decided to commit the additional troops necessary to ensure the safe extraction of all foreign nationals in the combat zone, as well as ensure the safety of all refugees within the areas we control. I ask you all to remember this is a mercenary army the Philippine government is fighting and our presence there is only for the protection of our own people and other helpless civilians.

"At this time, I would ask that Americans pray for the safe return of the freed hostages and our brave service men and women who have made this possible. Thank you and good night."

The television held on the president for several seconds before cutting away.

"Now I'm more convinced than ever Jon's over there," said Nancy picking up some empty plates.

"At least we know he's safe," said Emily helping her daughter.

The television cut back to the New York studio.

"As you may have heard, the president just stated the United States will be committing more troops to the situation on Mindanao. To expand on this story, we now have several reports. The first is from Sandy Monroe, who was recently freed with the hostages. Sandy, what exactly is the situation there?"

When the network cut to Monroe's location you could see the chaos taking place. Monroe's usual neat appearance was missing; the clothes she was wearing were rumpled and dirt stained. You could also see the exhaustion in her face. Behind her were trucks being loaded with refugees. Soldiers in uniform were helping the refugees onto trucks.

"The scene behind me is actually much more organized than it looks, Peter," said Monroe. "American Special Forces and Philippine Army personnel are loading as many of the refugees as possible onto anything that will carry them to a safe extraction point. The mercenary military presence behind the current difficulties here is well funded and well-armed. American military personnel have refused to evacuate the freed hostages by air for fear of the high number of casualties that could occur because of surface to air missile sites located nearby. As you may be able to hear this strike force is being supported by American Navy planes and the Philippine Air Force. The current rush is to get as many people as possible out of here because of approaching mercenary forces."

Stephen, who was sitting on Louise's lap, pointed to a man loading a child onto the truck behind Monroe.

"Look Grandma," he said innocently, "there's Daddy."

There was complete silence in the room as everyone focused on the man in the background. As the boy was placed in the rear of the truck the man turned and was handed the handset of a radio by another soldier. Nancy dropped the dishes that she was holding starting to feel weak in the knees. Howard rushed over, grabbing her before she fell, as did Julie. They both moved her to the sofa and helped her lay down.

"I watched the news every night that boy was in Vietnam, and never once did I see him," said Louise in disbelief. "Now when I least expect it, there he is. Son of a bitch!"

Stephen gave his grandmother an irritated look, "Grandma!!"

The telephone rang and Howard answered.

He handed the telephone to his daughter who looked up in disgust.

"You need to take this, dear," was all her father said.

"Hello?" said Nancy weakly.

"Nancy, its Josh. We need to talk."

Camp Freedom
Mindanao, Philippines
March 17, 1995
0700 Hours

Summers looked at his watch shaking his head. It had taken longer than expected to load the trucks and the enemy units, while currently pinned down, would be here shortly. The radio being carried by the SEAL next to him came to life and the sailor spoke softly into the handset.

"Sir," said the SEAL, "Colonel Lacson says they're ready to move."

Summers looked at a ranger sergeant sitting on top of an armored car nearby. The soldier was watching him for some sign. Summers raised his hand in the air, made several circles with it over his head, and then pointed it towards the main gate. The sergeant yelled something down to the driver and the vehicle sprang forward. The armored car was followed by two more of the same type vehicles and then by a tank. The first two trucks following the tank were filled with Philippine troops. The next truck was the first with refugees in it. As the trucks moved out, they went by where Summers was standing. When they passed, the refugees would wave, and shout thank you in English. The soldiers assigned to each truck looked confident and would nod or salute.

While Summers watched the procession go by, one of the SEAL squad leaders pulled up behind him in a jeep. Summers RTO got into the vehicle, joining Captain Sanchez in the back. When the truck carrying Gateway and his family passed the retired general looked down at the officer and saluted. Becky looked over the side of the truck as they passed watching the man standing there. She thought she saw him wink at her. He was deliberately trying to irritate her, but she couldn't figure out why. When the truck carrying the Smith's passed the reverend shouted a thank you to Summers, calling him by name. Summers smiled back at the man and waved.

Behind them there was a series of explosions close by. This was immediately followed by secondary explosions shaking the ground around them. Summers got into the jeep.

The squad leader looked at him asking, "Where to, Sir?"

"I think it's a good day to go to the beach, Mister."

The younger officer smiled. "As you wish, Sir."

The jeep pulled away leaving the compound.

U.S.S. Nimitz
Moro Gulf
March 17, 1995
0705 Hours

Putnum stood next to Brothers on the bridge listening to the radio traffic from the ongoing operations. The statistics were impressive thus far, considering they were supporting a ground operation. *Nimitz* pilots had confirmed the destruction of an even dozen SAM sites and twice as many enemy vehicles. The pursuit of the refugee column would be costly if they had anything to do with it. F-14 Tomcat fighters fitted with special camera pods had over flown the area and were returning with pictures of the entire situation.

Putnum saw the video broadcast to Washington by the news crew and was worried the refugee column wouldn't clear the area before they were engaged by the mercenaries. Even with the Philippine military moving in on all fronts he was worried about the ability of the mercenaries to inflict heavy casualties on the column. He was impressed with Brothers and his people. They managed to merge two battle groups into one while carrying on combat flight operations without missing a beat. Brothers and Captain Skip Marienetti of the Tarawa Battle Group didn't let egos get in the way of getting the job done.

"Sir," said the OOD to Putnum, "Liberty One reports the column is on the move."

Putnum nodded as he listened to an exchange on the radio.

"Liberty One to Pathfinder. Bad guys are still pinned down, but they won't stay long."

"Copy that, Liberty One. Appreciate the assist. Just keep them down for a few more minutes and that will buy us the time we need."

"No problem, Pathfinder, but we'll be turning you over to Outlaw flight. We have to go back to reload and gas up."

"Outlaw One to Pathfinder. We'll keep them down. You guys just hustle along."

"Pathfinder copies, thanks again."

"Outlaw Four to One. Get a load of the damage the Liberty guys did to that installation down there."

"Six to Four, catch that fireball down there. Man that's beautiful. What do you think it is?"

"Its aviation fuel, you asshole," came the response from the other end of the radio. "Pay attention to your job or one of those SAMs will kick you in the ass. We're not coming back in to get you if you fly stupid. Pay attention to your job!"

The two senior officers looked at each other and began to laugh. Brothers managed to say, "That might be the first time I ever agreed with a SEAL."

Refugee Column
Mindanao, Philippines
March 17, 1995
0710 Hours

The column was moving forward at a good clip. There were four of the more seriously wounded in the truck besides Naylor and O'Keefe. Besides Gateway, his daughter and granddaughter, there were five other freed hostages. The soldiers had managed to squeeze in about ten refugees, most from the same family. This included Fidel, the old man. The vehicle load was rounded out by Rice, Reardon, and another ranger. The old man sat near Gateway clutching a bag he seemed to be guarding with his life. Gateway could no longer resist and decided to talk to the old man.

"I used to know a man named Fidel," started Gateway. "He scouted for one of my platoon leaders fifty years ago."

The old man gave Gateway a big smile revealing several missing teeth.

"He was one hell of a guide," Gateway got his daughter's attention. "Your Uncle Ray used to swear this guy was the best guide on five continents."

The old man chuckled. "Not true, Sir, only here on Mindanao. Lieutenant Summers was always too kind to me. I was sorry to hear of his passing."

Becky, Gateway, and Donavon all looked carefully at the old man. Donavon moved forward to get a better look.

"I'll be damned!" he said quietly.

"Hello, Lieutenant Donavon," said the old man still smiling, "it's good to see you again."

Donavon threw his arms around the old man, tears running down his face in a show of emotion.

"Damn, Fidel, it really is you," said Donavon wiping the tears away. "I'm glad you're here. If the worst happens at least, I know we'll get out through the hills. Man, it's good to see you again."

Gateway held out his hand shaking the old man's.

"Of all the people I expected to run into coming back here I have to admit you weren't one. Sam's right, it's great to see you. You look well."

"I'm well." answered Fidel. "It's nice to see all of you. I'm sorry I didn't see you before all this took place."

Gateway shook his head. "Nonsense, Fidel. I'm sorry it had to be now. You said you knew Ray passed away. How'd you know?"

The old man bowed his head. "Sadly, I only recently found out. His family has kept in touch off and on throughout the years."

"How do you know the American officer in charge of this mission?" asked Becky. "He seems irritating to be around."

Both Gateway and Fidel smiled at the comment.

"You think the same thing about Jon Summers most of the time," said Gateway grinning at his daughter, "but last night you said you wished he was here."

The father and daughter looked at each other. Becky's face blushed. The comment was made the night before during a moment of weakness, and she hadn't wanted it shared. Fidel smiled at both.

"He's a great warrior, missy," said the old man. "I met him after your war in the Vietnams. He trained here and I got to know him well. He became one of us. He learned our language and customs and became our protector. My people have great respect for him, and I know he'll get us all to safety."

"How can you know for sure?" questioned Becky. She was startled when Naylor reached over and touched her hand.

"The old man's right, Doc," said the wounded ranger. "Trust this guy. He has everyone working together and that's no easy task. He has control of the battlefield and that's tough when you're on the defensive like we are. I don't know why they sent him here, and frankly I don't' care because I know him by reputation and there's no one better for this than him."

"How would you know that Colonel?" asked Gateway.

"Because he's done this before," answered the ranger, "and he always brings everyone back."

There was silence while everyone on the truck thought about the comment. Rice, who was sitting by the tailgate had been silent. "He came to flush out a traitor, Colonel."

Everyone turned to look at her. "He told me before we left. He was the bait. His job has been to find out who set your unit up, Colonel, and my guess is he was successful. The person he was after sent both of us out here to die, and yet, here we are. We're on our way out and the entire United States Navy is offshore to ensure we make it. He's a scary guy. One minute you think you understand him and the next minute he's off the wall crazy."

"If what you say is true, Captain, then you should realize, no matter who ordered you to go on this mission it was still his choice to bring you along," said Naylor. "You need to know he could have ordered Brothers to hide you on board ship until everything was squared away."

Rice looked at the ranger lying on the stretcher thinking about what he said.

"You're right, Sir, I guess he could have…"

"Hey, why are we slowing down?" interrupted Donavon.

Rice looked out towards the jungle. "Sniper team coming in. Make room on board."

Seconds later, two camouflage clad men climbed on board and the truck resumed its speed. One of the men carried a heavy McMillian .50 caliber sniper rifle in his hands and a CAR-15 slung over his shoulder. The second man carried an M-16 fitted with an M-203 grenade launcher.

"Reardon," said the second man smiling, "it's about time you got here. I thought we were going to have to do this without you."

The ranger returned the man's smile, "They sent me in to make sure you guys got it right Wiedenkeller."

The SEAL had a radio head set around his neck. He raised the mic in front of his mouth, "Gray Horse, to Pathfinder. On board, all teams accounted for."

"Roger that, Gray Horse, welcome back."

Wiedenkeller looked down at Naylor, "Good to see you again, Sir. How're you doing?"

Naylor smiled back. "As well as can be expected, chief. It's certainly good to see you. Good shooting."

"It's not me, Sir. It's Barbaro here."

They turned to look at the young man standing next to Wiedenkeller. He had a large grin.

"Barbaro," snapped Wiedenkeller jokingly, "get that .50 set up on top of the cab. Now, Barbaro, now!"

The young sailor seemed to chuckle, "Right away, Chief."

He immediately crawled over everyone in the truck and climbed onto the cab where he set up his weapon. As he did this, Wiedenkeller turned his attention back to Naylor.

"Is that really him on the other end of my radio, Sir?'

Naylor nodded in return.

"Do you know the Captain, Chief?" asked Rice from behind him.

Wiedenkeller turned taking a second look at the marine officer. His eyes squinted in the sunlight as he looked at her. He then offered his hand to her. She took it.

"I apologize for my rudeness Ma'am. I thought you were just another marine officer."

"To be ignored, chief?"

"That would be correct, Ma'am."

"Easy, Al. She's OK," said Reardon.

Rice glared at the sergeant for a second and then back at the SEAL.

"Ma'am, if the sergeant has high praise for you, then I'll follow you anywhere."

"That was high praise?" questioned Becky.

The chief reached into the side pouch of his pack and produced a flask. He unscrewed the cap and offered it to Rice.

"No hard feelings, Ma'am."

Rice took the flask and took a swig, never taking her eyes off the SEAL. When she finished, she handed the flask back to the Chief, who took a swig himself. When he finished, he screwed the top back on, putting it back in his pack.

"Hey!" said Reardon. "What about me? Am I invisible or what?"

Wiedenkeller looked at Rice and winked, "You been holding out on me, man."

Rice blushed underneath the camouflage face paint.

"Whoya, Ma'am," said Wiedenkeller.

"Whoya, Chief," answered Rice.

"Whoya," echoed Reardon with a grin.

Gateway smiled.

U.S.S. Nimitz
Moro Gulf
March 17, 1995
0800 Hours

The three prisoners had been housed in the ship's brig since they were taken into custody. NCIS and FBI agents took the place of the marine guards in the brig area. Each prisoner was provided council from the legal department on board ship and the questioning had begun. The agents involved were being very cautious with how they proceeded because they didn't want anything thrown out of court later. The JAG officers on board were in contact with Washington to make sure every precaution was being taken in the defense of the three suspects. Grey, who was heading up the investigation, also kept an open line to his office in Washington.

The most uncooperative of the three was Kingston. He kept saying he refused the JAG officers legal advice and wanted his own civilian attorney to represent him. This effectively shut down any further questioning of him by the agents on board. The other two suspects accepted council from the JAG officers on board and were in the process of giving statements. Grey, frustrated by Kingston's arrogance, agreed to try a questionable tact Wells came up with. The admiral was moved under guard to one of the wardrooms set aside for their use with two JAG representatives present. Wells sat across from Kingston while Grey and Demmer observed from another table.

"Good morning, Admiral," started Wells. "I'm Agent Mark Wells. How are you this morning?"

Kingston leaned across the table towards Wells. As he did the two agents assigned to guard him, moved forward. Wells held up his hand to stop them.

"I'm not answering any questions to the FBI until I talk to my personal attorney in San Diego," said Kingston with a raised voice. "These people will not represent me. I want a real attorney, not someone who'll railroad me, so the Navy looks good."

One of the JAG representatives, looking very perturbed with Kingston's last comment, said, "Mr. Wells, I thought you agreed that there would be no further questioning of the admiral."

Wells did not look at the attorney but held Kingston's gaze. "I didn't think asking Mr. Kingston how he was feeling today would be included in that. I apologize, councilor and retract the question."

The JAG officer sat back in his chair looking equally perturbed with Wells. Grey turned his head so the JAG officers couldn't see him smile. Demmer didn't try to hide her delight. Wells smiled at both the JAG officers and Kingston knowing the reaction he would get.

"Mr. Kingston," said Wells leaning back in his chair, "my name is Wells, and I'm not with the FBI. I'm an agent with the Naval Criminal Investigative Service. My purpose here is not to question you, but to advise you of the charges being filed against you. This conversation is being recorded so we can give an accurate accounting of this meeting to your attorney of record, whoever that may be. I have asked the JAG representatives on board ship be present so there is no question this meeting was conducted in a proper manner. I would like to ask all of those present in the room to state their name, rank and purpose for being here."

For the first time, Kingston noticed the tape recorder on the table in front of him. He went beet red with anger looking at it and then at Wells. Each person in the compartment stated the information requested and then they all waited for Wells to continue.

"Now, Mr. Kingston," continued Wells, "as I said..."

"It's Admiral Kingston."

"Huh?" said Wells looking puzzled.

"It's Admiral Kingston," repeated the suspect. "I've earned the rank and I expect it to be used."

Wells leaned back in his chair again. "Right, as I was saying earlier, I'm going to read to you what the current charges are being levied against you. Do you understand that?"

Kingston just looked away from the man across the table from him.

"I'll take your silence as consent," said Wells looking at the two JAG officers. Both men answered in the affirmative.

Wells started to read the charges off a sheet of paper he had in front of him. While he read charges, Kingston looked about the room trying to ignore what was going on. When he completed reading the list in front of him, Wells again asked the Admiral if he understood.

"You'll never prove any of it," said Kingston. "You have no proof at all."

"On the contrary," said Wells. "I believe we have quite a bit of proof. Statements from both of your aides as to your activities, statements from Captain Summers and Captain Demmer as to an ongoing investigation they've been conducting for several months."

"It's hearsay," snapped Kingston. "They'll do anything to save themselves. Their careers are over and they're trying to take me with them. And as for Summers, it's no secret we've been at odds since we were at the academy together. I don't know Demmer, but he's lying, too."

"Then there's the videotape of you ordering Petty Officer McAvoy to send a message to Pearl Harbor. We have statements this message was subsequently delivered to agents there and then a message was transmitted to the mercenary forces on Mindanao, ordering the ambush of Captain Summers' unit after they were inserted."

"Nonsense!" said Kingston angrily. "You're making this up as you go."

Kingston's face was bright red with anger. Wells looked at the two JAG officers to see if they were going to caution the suspect before he went any further. Neither man made a move.

"Unfortunately, I'm not, Mr. Kingston," said Wells smiling, seeing Kingston was near the breaking point. "I'm going to be providing your attorney with a copy of that video as well as statements from McAvoy and Captain Demmer to…"

"Demmer?" shouted Kingston. "Who the hell is this Demmer?!?"

Wells pointed to Judy Demmer behind him. "That, Sir, is Captain Judy Demmer of the United States Air Force."

"You're the whore with Summers in the bar the night Toshio was attacked by those Marines," blurted out Kingston.

The two JAG officers immediately objected and stated they wanted the meeting concluded instantly. For the first time, Kingston noticed two video cameras on either side of the room. He launched himself out of his chair and in the direction of Wells. The two agents who were there as security, grabbed Kingston before he was halfway across the table. They brought him down hard on top of the table, cutting open his lip in the process. Two more agents, who were standing outside the hatch rushed in.

"You can't do this to me!" shouted Kingston.

Wells never lost his composure. He'd jumped back when the suspect lunged for him, but now leaned close enough to smell the sweat on the man's brow.

"For your information, the lady was General Michalowski's aide at the time and was delivering a message to Captain Summers from the General. I will also remind you this is being recorded and, on advice from acting council, this meeting is over."

"Summers should have died in Vietnam when he went to get those POW's that were left behind. That order should have killed him, but he keeps coming back!"

"What order?" demanded Wells without thinking.

"Don't answer that, Admiral!" interjected one of the JAG officers moving in next to his client. Kingston was weeping in the arms of the agents who were restraining him.

"Back in 1978," sobbed Kingston, "when they went in to get those POW's. I stopped the extraction, but he came back anyway. He always comes back. He's a devil."

No one in the room moved. Wells turned to look at Grey, who looked back at him. The only noise in the room was the sobbing coming from the suspect.

"Glenn," said Demmer, "everyone in this room is to be isolated until they can be debriefed."

Grey turned to look at the young woman standing next to him.

"You knew about this? Is it true?"

Demmer looked back at the FBI agent. The only reply from her was a nod.

Outlaw Flight
Mindanao, Philippines
March 17, 1995
0917 Hours

The jets were patrolling over the convoy. The trucks were moving along at a fast pace but were still two hours from their extraction point. The flight was low on fuel and about to be relieved by the next group. They managed to knock out four more SAM sites and several more vehicles before flying combat air patrol over the refugee column.

"Outlaw Two to Outlaw One," the voice woke everyone up.

"Go ahead, Two."

"Boss, I have some incoming bogies at the extreme edge of our radar. I count eight, maybe more aircraft coming along the treetops bearing 085."

"Boss, this is six, I confirm that. I count ten, repeat ten bogies."

"One to all Outlaws, hang tough boys while I phone home," said the flight leader, "Outlaw one to Eagle."

There was silence for a second before there was a response.

"Outlaw One this is Eagle. We've been monitoring your transmissions and are checking with Davao to see if the Philippine military has anything in the area."

"Copy that, Eagle. They are 084 from our location and their low and slow. Looks like choppers. The current count is twelve."

There was another second pause before hearing from *Nimitz* again.

"Outlaw One, this is Eagle. Davao has nothing in the area. Say again, no friendly aircraft in the area. Bogies should be considered hostile. Advise as to their present course."

There was silence as the flight leader checked his targeting radar.

"Skipper this is Four. Looks to me like they're going to fly right into the refugee column."

"I concur, Four. Eagle this is Outlaw One. Bandits will over fly Pathfinder in five minutes."

"Copy that, Outlaw One. You're clear to engage."

Road to Point Bravo
Mindanao, Philippines
March 17, 1995
0919 Hours

They hadn't slowed down in over an hour. The ride was almost pleasant enough to make you forget why you were making it. Wiedenkeller had disconnected the headset so they could all monitor the progress of the column. They were able to pick up the chatter between Summers and the aircraft overhead, as well as the radio traffic between all the ground units. The wounded were dozing, and Becky sat with her head back and eyes closed. Rice watched the jungle. It seemed so peaceful.

"Outlaw One to Pathfinder, over," squawked the radio, waking everyone up.

"Go ahead, Outlaw One, you must be ready to head back for lunch."

"Negative Pathfinder, we're tracking twelve bandits headed straight for you. Looks like enemy choppers. We're going to engage. Wild Card flight is coming in to cover you."

"Pathfinder copies, good luck Outlaws."

Almost immediately the flight of F-18's screamed overhead on their way to intercept the threat.

Mindanao, Philippines
March 17, 1995
0920 Hours

Wilson kept his eyes on the horizon, watching for Philippine aircraft. They were predictable in how they approached their targets. He knew he would see them before they got too close. He noticed a large pillar of smoke to the south, in the direction of Camp Freedom. He managed to catch intermittent transmissions from Boerst's column and knew the Philippine Air Force was giving him a hard time. He smiled, knowing the German was giving back as good as he got.

Suddenly something streaked by his helicopter. One of the other aircraft in the flight exploded into a fireball. This was followed by a second and a third. Before they had a chance, eight of the helicopters in the flight were falling into the jungle in flames. Wilson wildly looked about for the aircraft firing on them. He was panicked, these were not the tactics used by the Filipinos. Suddenly one of the jets streaked past his aircraft. It was an American F-18. They had closed in to finish the remaining helicopters with their guns.

Wilson turned his gunship sharply to the right and dove, so he was flying as close to the trees as he dared. As he dove, he could see two more of his helicopters falling to earth. He increased his air speed as much as he could, knowing he couldn't outrun the fighters. His aircraft shook violently and lost altitude suddenly. Seconds before they plowed into the trees below, he knew his tail rotor had been destroyed. He was the last aircraft in his flight to go down.

U.S.S. Nimitz
Moro Gulf
March 17, 1995
0955 Hours

Putnum listened to the chatter as the Navy pilots engaged the flight of helicopters. The entire confrontation lasted no more than five minutes. Several of the helicopters crashed reasonably intact so he ordered the Philippine military notified in case they had troops in the area.

Putnum looked at his watch. They were racing against time, and he was worried they wouldn't get to the extraction point before a large enemy force did. The extraction point was currently secure, and Summers and his people would only enhance that. What he was worried about were the reports from Mangoba's people that large groups of mercenaries were moving about the countryside. The current worry was these groups would try to retake the hostages or move on the refugees.

Brothers looked at Putnum and could see the worry.

"Don't worry, Sir," said the ship's captain, "Summers and his people have done their job. We'll do ours. Skip says his Marines are ready, it's just a matter of getting them close enough."

Putnum didn't answer because Grey walked onto the bridge. He carried a manila folder, looking serious. Brothers noticed the admiral's shift in attention. Grey looked like a policeman. While he did not care for why the man was on his ship, he hadn't bothered the smooth operation of the vessel during a combat operation.

"Admiral, I have something we think you should see immediately," said Grey offering the folder to the flag officer.

Putnum took the folder, opened it, and started to read the top page. After a moment, he looked up at Grey and asked, "Is this accurate, Mr. Grey?"

"Yes Sir. Completely," answered the FBI agent. "Captain Demmer has knowledge of this and stopped the interview the second this information was revealed. She's on the horn to Washington to see how much she can brief us on."

"I hate secrets," said Putnum to himself. "They always seem to come out at the worst times. Captain, I'll be below. Call me immediately if there is any change of status."

Brothers was confused about what was going on but knew better than to ask questions. "Aye, aye, Sir."

Refugee Column
Mindanao, Philippines
March 17, 1995
1030 Hours

The column hadn't slowed since they picked up Wiedenkeller. The wounded in the truck were resting comfortably, and all were sleeping except Naylor. He insisted on staying alert. He was propped into a sitting position near the cab, a young Filipino named Ramon tending to his every need. O'Keefe slept, the entire time holding Sarah's hand. Gateway watched in silence while his granddaughter tended to her father. Becky kept busy going between the wounded, constantly checking their condition. She seemed to grow concerned about her ex-husband.

"What's wrong, Ma'am?" asked Wiedenkeller.

She looked at the SEAL, surprised he'd noticed. "This man is dehydrating. I need to get some fluids into him, or we'll lose him."

Gateway started to say something but cut himself short when his daughter looked up. The expression on her face told him it was better to stay silent.

Rice, hearing the conversation, motioned for a ranger to cover the tailgate. When he was in position, she moved forward next to Reardon.

"We have some water, Ma'am if that'll help," answered the SEAL.

"It will, but it won't solve the problem," snapped the doctor, "I should have been allowed to finish collecting those supplies. I need an IV for thi…"

Rice put her hand on Becky's arm.

"Doc, take it easy," said the marine officer. "We'll get what you need."

Rice then looked at Wiedenkeller, who nodded and then made a call over the radio. Rice and Reardon raised the Irishman's head and, using canteens, tried to induce small amounts of water down his throat. Most of it went down the side of the man's face. There was traffic on Wiedenkeller's radio, and the chief answered quietly. Becky looked at the SEAL with a questioning look.

Wiedenkeller smiled at the doctor, "The IVs are on the way, Ma'am. They'll be here in a few minutes."

The roads became smoother and easier to ride on since they reached the paved highway. The roads were also wider allowing for the smaller jeeps to move up alongside the larger vehicles. It was less than a minute when one of the jeeps pulled up alongside their truck. There were four camouflaged clad men in the vehicle all looking very warm in the midmorning sun. The one in the passenger seat appeared to be carrying a pouch of some kind. The jeep maneuvered within a meter of the truck and the passenger stood in his seat. Wiedenkeller made himself ready to receive the pouch, but to his surprise the man came over with it. He jumped from the seat, grabbing the side of the truck. He found a foothold on a rung along the side. He pulled himself up and straddled the sidewall of the bed.

Summers returned the smile, shaking Wiedenkeller's extended hand. "Good to see you, Chief. Tell your people good shooting."

Wiedenkeller looked at the man on top of the cab. "Barbaro, the boss says you need to work on your marksmanship."

You could hear the man on top of the cab chuckle, "Aye, aye, Chief."

Summers looked around the bed of the truck until he found Becky. She was sitting next to Rice and Reardon who were working on getting the unconscious terrorist to keep fluids down. The camouflage shirt she had been given was unbuttoned because of the heat so you could see inside it. The boonie cap was pulled down over her eyes to keep the bright sun out of them. She was watching the unconscious man as she took his pulse. Summers smiled noticing Naylor looking at the same thing he was. Naylor responded by grinning and shrugging his shoulders. They both laughed. The laughter caused Becky to look up catching Summers looking at her. She knew she was blushing but did not know why.

"I believe this is what you wanted?" said Summers handing her the pouch. She took it. Inside were three IV's ready to go. She pulled one out and started to set it up.

"I'll need someone to hold this up," she said looking around the truck.

Before anyone could volunteer, Summers said, "General, why don't you help the Doc with that."

Gateway's face reddened, but he immediately moved over to where he could do as requested. He sat down and Becky handed him the bag with the clear liquid in it. She then kissed him on the cheek.

"Thanks, Dad," she said.

"Only because he's Sarah's father," was his reply.

Becky looked at the man. He smiled back at her and nodded towards her daughter. Sarah was sitting next to her grandfather, still holding her father's hand. She wrapped her arm around her grandfather's leg and rested her head on his knee. Becky smiled in return.

"I think that's the exact point the man's making, Dad," said Becky as she kissed her father on the cheek again.

While the doctor attached the IV, Summers motioned Rice over, whispering something in her ear. The marine was silent for a second, then giggled. She moved off towards the back of the truck, again changing positions with the ranger. As he did this Summers said something in Filipino. Several women in the truck responded by rummaging through the bags. Summers looked at Wiedenkeller winking. The chief just shook his head.

"Sorry to spoil the show, Chief," said Summers.

"All good things must come to an end, Sir," replied the SEAL.

With that, Summers jumped back to the jeep, and it raced off towards the front of the column. Becky looked up to thank the man for bringing the supplies she needed, only to find him gone.

"Doc!" said Rice motioning the doctor to the rear of the truck.

Becky slowly moved to the rear of the vehicle and knelt next to the marine. Rice reached into her ruck and pulled out a folded green tee shirt. Becky looked at the female officer in astonishment.

"What's this for?" asked Becky.

Rice took her right pointer finger and opened the shirt Becky was wearing just enough for her to understand without explanation. "I know it's getting hot, Ma'am. This will help."

"But no one's noticed."

"Ma'am," answered Rice, patiently, "every man on this vehicle has noticed. It's a distraction we don't need now."

"He put you up to this, didn't he?"

Rice smiled.

"What did he say?" demanded the doctor.

"He said he's waited years to see that Ma'am, and he wasn't disappointed, but he couldn't have his people watching you instead of the jungle," said Rice with a grin.

"The man's a pervert!" said Becky loud enough for all to hear.

The statement was met by laughter, including from Gateway.

"Hell, Ma'am," said Rice, "we're simply happy to find out the man's human."

This was met with more laughter.

Becky held up the shirt and started to say something when several of the Filipino women suddenly moved over to her and surrounded her with blankets to give her privacy to change.

"See, Doc," said Wiedenkeller, "The Skipper thinks of everything."

There was even more laughter. It was less than a minute and Becky was out from behind the blankets and moving back to where the wounded were. She was wearing the green tee shirt and had the camouflage shirt tied around her waist. As she reached her father, he smiled saying, "You were right. He is irritating, but I wish I could remember where I know him from."

Becky returned her father's smile. "He does seem familiar, doesn't he?"

"I'll give him this," said Gateway, "he knows his job."

The column continued to move swiftly forward.

177 Pinecreek Drive
Rochester, New York
March 16, 1995
2245 Hours

Two police cars remained outside the house, while a third patrolled the neighborhood. Jon's appearance on TV had prompted this precaution to keep the curious away. None of the media showed up, although several local television stations called, trying to get information about Jon Summers, vice principal at Lakeview High School, currently serving in the navy reserves in the Philippines. The video also was the reason Debbie and Peggy came over to check on the family. The telephone calls were endless, most fielded by Peggy, Debbie, and Howard. The neighbors were supportive, they kept the policemen on duty in coffee and food. Some gathered in small groups on the sidewalks in front of their homes on the cool spring night. While nothing was officially said, everyone knew it was Jon on television right after the president's address. There was talk of how he was a good neighbor and upstanding member of the community. Most didn't know he was in the navy.

The entire family sat in front of the television set in the living room, watching for additional news most of the night. Stephen and Jason fell asleep curled up on the laps of their relatives. They were carried to their beds by Nancy and Louise. Sean decided to follow his brothers up to bed because of an early morning. Howard, Julie, Debbie, and Peggy were all that remained in front of the television. Emily was in the kitchen making tea. While they quietly watched the late-night news, they heard a car pulling into the driveway. Howard looked out the window, seeing a dark colored sedan. The driver of the vehicle was talking to one of the policemen.

"Who is it?" asked Julie from the couch.

"Looks like an unmarked car of some kind, although my guess is it's not the local gendarmes. Maybe the FBI or some federal agency. Hey, they're getting out of the car."

The three ladies joined Howard at the window and watched as three men and one woman exited the car. The policeman talked to them for several seconds and then shook the hand of one of the men.

"I know who that is!" exclaimed Debbie.

The other two ladies looked at her in disbelief.

"General Samuel Michalowski," said Howard without thinking.

"I give up," said Peggy looking somewhat puzzled. "Who is General Macwhoever?"

"I'll get Mom and Nancy," said Julie quietly. She looked pale.

Howard took her gently by the arm saying, "Honey, he looks pretty upbeat out there, so don't think the worst until we know for sure. He could be bringing good news. They do that on occasion."

Julie looked at Howard and managed a smile. She put her arms around the older man hugging him tightly.

"Thanks, Howard," she said softly, "you're the best."

There was a knock at the door. All four of them looked at each other and then moved to the front door. Just before they opened the door, Peggy asked again, "So, who is this guy? No one ever answered my question."

Howard opened the door to find Michalowski standing on the other side.

"Mr. Quinn?" asked the retired general.

"Yes Sir," answered Howard. "You're General Michalowski. Please come in."

Michalowski returned the smile taking Howard's extended hand, shaking it.

"I'm here on an errand that'll hopefully explain a lot of things. Is your daughter at home?"

"Jon's, OK? He's not hurt or anything?" asked Julie anxiously.

Howard put his arm around the young woman, "General, this is Jon's sister, Julie."

Michalowski's smile was infectious, Julie smiled in return. He extended his hand to her, and she took it.

"General," said Howard, "this is Peggy Edgerton and Debbie Bush. They're friends of Julie's and co-workers of Jon's."

Michalowski followed suit with the other two young ladies and introduced the members of his party. One of the males and the female were FBI agents who had picked him up at the airport and the other male was his assistant. Howard led them into the living room where they all found a seat. Emily came into the room carrying a tray with tea on it. She was introduced to everyone and immediately excused herself to make more tea and coffee. Peggy excused herself to help. The group talked about the day's events and was surprised Michalowski seemed to have information he was willing to share.

Michalowski suddenly stood up and everyone turned to see Nancy and Louise standing in the entrance to the living room. The general walked over to the two ladies and introduced himself. He then escorted them into the room and found a place on the couch for both. Emily and Peggy suddenly returned with more coffee and tea. Once everyone was settled, Michalowski leaned his elbows on his knees and started to speak.

"I'll start off by saying that I'm not here to bring bad news. I'm here to tell you what's going on and then my own personal story of thank you."

"You'll pardon me if I sound skeptical, General," responded Nancy. "I've seen what the military can do to a person and have to say I'm glad Jon made the decisions he did."

Michalowski smiled. "Actually, I'm glad he made those decisions, too."

Nancy looked puzzled and the General continued.

"Look, Mrs. Summers," said Michalowski, "there's someone who wanted to speak to you after the television showed Jon and that's part of why I'm here."

"So that really was Jon?" asked Nancy simply.

Michalowski didn't respond to the question. Instead, he was handed a cell phone by his assistant and began dialing a number. There was a delay of several seconds before Michalowski said, "Yes, it's Sam Michalowski for the President."

There was silence in the room while the General waited.

"Hello, Mr. President."

Michalowski looked at Nancy and smiled.

"Yes, Sir, she's here with me."

Michalowski handed Nancy the telephone.

Refugee Column
Mindanao, Philippines
March 17, 1995
1105 Hours

The column was slowing down. They weren't sure if it was because they were reaching their destination or the large number of refugees walking on both sides of the road. Becky noticed the military people on the truck looking about nervously. They seemed to be scanning the jungle on both sides of the road. Wiedenkeller's radio suddenly came to life. They all tried to listen, but none of them could understand what was being said.

"Chief," asked Rice, "did you catch that?"

"Something about being at the extraction point and traffic cops Ma'am," answered the SEAL. "I didn't catch the entire message."

"Sounded like Charley Brown's teacher on the cartoons," said Becky looking at Naylor's bandages. "Blah, blah, blah."

Everyone laughed and seemed to relax some. They were slowing even more and the refugees on either side of the column were shouting and cheering.

"Roadblock ahead!" shouted Barbaro suddenly from his position on the top of the cab of the truck.

Wiedenkeller climbed up with the sailor and looked for himself. When he came back down, he said, "Looks like Philippine Army troops combined with marines and rangers. We must be heading for a beach location for extraction."

"That would make sense. Looks like the captain has thought of everything," said Naylor.

The truck slowed almost to a stop while it made a turn. Suddenly four camouflaged clad soldiers climbed on board the truck. One went to Naylor's side.

"Good to see you, Sir."

Naylor smiled, "Good to see you, too, Klintworth. How long have you been here?"

"They had us choppered in right after they arrested Kingston."

"What!?" exclaimed Rice and Naylor at the same time.

Everyone on the truck was now listening to Klintworth.

"All I know is Kingston's in the brig with his two aides and a three-star named Putnum is now in command."

"W. C. Putnum is Naval Intelligence out of Pearl Harbor. Why would he come out here and take command?" asked Rice.

The truck was bouncing about enough that their attention turned to the wounded and keeping them comfortable. It was obvious they were off the main road. Trees were close by on both sides. Barbaro came off the top of the cab. Suddenly the jungle around them opened and they were on a plain of tall grass and sand. Ahead of them were some gentle hills of sand rising from the beach on the other side. Small groves of palm trees were scattered about the grass. You could smell the salt air from the Moro Gulf on the other side of the dunes. The trucks ahead of them were pulling off to the side and into what appeared to be a staging area. Their truck was waved ahead to one of the small groves of trees where there were several tents set up. When the truck came to stop near the tents, sailors came running out, immediately dropping the tailgate. Rice was the first one off, followed by

Klintworth, Reardon, and other rangers. The sailors began to help the hostages and the refugees off the truck. Once they'd been removed and hustled off to the side, the wounded on stretchers were taken off and lined up by the tents. Becky was there explaining to the corpsmen the current situation with each of them. The corpsmen wrote information on a tag attaching it to each stretcher. A naval officer in his khaki uniform stood behind Becky while she explained the situation with O'Keefe to the corpsmen. He listened intently to the diagnosis. He finally knelt next to her, she looked over at him. They nodded at each other; Becky continued to talk. When she stopped the corpsman continued to write on the tag. When he finished writing, he tied the tag onto the stretcher moving away.

"Doctor O'Keefe," said the officer, "I'm Doctor Johnson from *Nimitz*. I'm in command of this aid station and have to say I'm impressed with the way you handled yourself considering what you've been through."

Becky managed to smile pushing the brim of the boonie cap up away from her eyes. "Under other circumstances Doctor, I might take offense to that comment, but I'm just too damned tired to fight right now."

"This patient appears to be the worst of the lot. We're set up to operate. We can take him in right now and be done by the time the evac comes."

"What about blood? Supplies?" asked Becky. "This isn't the place for this type of operation."

"We have plenty of supplies and I brought the best of my staff expecting to have to do this type of thing. I'm not bragging Ma'am, but this is our job and we're damned good."

"Good!" said Becky sounding more confident than she had a few minutes before. "I'll operate and you can assist."

"No!" said a calm voice from behind them.

They turned to see Summers standing there. Both stood up, but Becky moved forward to within inches of the man's face.

"You have no right to tell me my business," said Becky raising her voice. "He's my patient and I'll decide who operates on him!"

There was a second of silence before the officer spoke.

"Doc, look at yourself. When was the last time you ate or slept? You've been going non-stop since you were taken hostage, haven't you?"

The silence told Summers he was right.

"Doc," continued the officer, "you're too close to this one. As tired as you are, if you made a mistake, you'd never forgive yourself."

There was another few seconds of silence as the doctor stood there looking at the officer. The anger in her eyes started to soften, but she still didn't give any ground.

"Honey," said Gateway coming up behind his daughter, "remember what you said to me on the truck. The same goes for you now. Sarah deserves the best chance to get to know her father. You're one of the best doctors I've ever known, and that's not just because you're my little girl. Let Doctor Johnson take care of the operation. If nothing else the navy has first class medical care."

There were chuckles from Klintworth and Reardon. Rice and Wiedenkeller gave the retired Army officer a dirty look closing in around Summers. Becky put her arms around her father.

"You're right Dad," she said. "You're both right. I'm exhausted and would probably kill him on the table, and I don't want that."

She looked at the officer standing across from them. He still seemed very familiar, and it bothered her. Standing next to her father, she watched the corpsmen taking O'Keefe towards the tent where surgery was located. Doctor Johnson walked up to her and put his hand on hers.

"Doctor," he said softly, "he'll be fine. My people are the best. You rest out here and if I need any help I'll call. The important job of keeping him stable during the journey here was the critical part. The surgery looks straight forward."

Becky nodded. Johnson turned and followed his patient into the tent. Becky sat down, exhausted, joined by her father and daughter. Donavon and the Smith's walked over, joining them. Smith held a small book in his hand. He smiled at the officer.

"Reverend," said Summers, "I hope the book has been helpful?"

Smith chuckled. "It's been very revealing Captain. Thanks again for the loan."

Gateway looked up at his friend and then at the officer.

DeCook came running up to the group joining Rice and Klintworth.

"Sir," he said, "Colonel Lacson's compliments. He's placing his men in position to protect the outer perimeter. He'll be at the roadblock on the highway to make sure that all the refugees get into the area safely."

"Very good, Commander," said Summers in acknowledgement. "You take your SEALs and cover the left flank of the encampment. Captain Rice, you will take position to protect the center. Captain Klintworth, you, and your rangers cover the right flank. Make no mistake ladies and gentlemen; we're not out of the woods yet. Our air cover has seen large groups of mercenaries still roaming the countryside. With the word out that every refugee on the island is on their way here because the American's are here to protect them you can count on a visit."

"Orders, Sir?" asked DeCook.

"Protect everyone in the encampment, Commander," replied Summers. "Do what you have to do to keep them safe."

"Aye, aye, Sir!" responded DeCook.

"Sir, I'm feeling just a tad defenseless." said Naylor sitting up in his stretcher. "You wouldn't have a spare weapon about?"

Summers smiled at the army officer, pulling the Glock pistol out of his holster. He took out the clip and cleared the action before he gave it to the soldier. He also took three spare clips of ammunition out of his web belt and handed all of it to the wounded man.

"Don't you think you'll need this, Sir?" asked Naylor.

"No, Colonel," said Summers as he pulled an old Colt model 1911 from his pack along with several spare clips. "I'll use old reliable."

Summers looked up at the three officers in front of him. "Don't you people have something you should be doing?"

U.S.S. Nimitz
Moro Gulf
March 17, 1995
1235 Hours

Ellison was upset the admiral wouldn't let him go with the rangers and marines who were sent to secure the extraction point. He understood why he needed to stay but was unhappy with his orders just the same. He stood on the bridge next to the admiral helping to interpret intelligence briefs as they came in. The big concern was they would have to deal with a large, rogue mercenary force before the battle group could land reinforcements.

The fighters flying air cover saw several such groups while flying over their patrol areas.

"Sir," said Captain Brothers, "air has two large forces converging on the evac area. Estimating about a thousand troops."

Putnum's face remained unchanged watching the sea ahead of them. Outside, you could hear the flight operations continuing. The admiral turned looking at Ellison.

"George, do you think they'll attack the troops at the site?"

"Yes, Sir, I do," said Ellison. "They're financial backing and the escape routes are gone, and they'll be looking for anything that'll pay the bills or get them off the island. Recapturing the hostages, as well as taking the refugees would give them leverage to bargain with both us and the Filipinos. It might also recoup some of their losses if they thought they could get some ransom."

Putnam continued to watch the sea in front of them. He was silent for several moments and then spoke with confidence. "CINCPAC agrees with your assessment, Colonel. Because of that, we are to proceed into harm's way to make sure that doesn't happen. Tom, contact Skip Marienetti. We start landing Marines at the earliest possible moment. Let him know we'll support them with everything we have."

"Aye, aye, Sir!" said the ship's captain moving off to pass on the message.

"Colonel," continued Putnum, "you let General Mangoba know what's going on. I know his troops are busy along all their fronts, but maybe he has some ideas about how to handle the situation. It's his country. He at least deserves the courtesy of a call."

"Aye, Sir," answered the marine.

"Also make sure that Grey and Wells have a suicide watch on that son-of-a-bitch below. The only way he's going to get out of this voyage is if we lose any more kids on this mission. I'll have him spread eagled over one of his precious jet engines and test fire it myself. You take personal charge of him. Do you understand, Colonel? I don't want him having an accident."

"Understood, Sir," answered Ellison. The marine officer left the bridge to follow his orders. He passed Brothers, who was returning from the comm room. Brothers winked and smiled, happy to be part of the mission. Ellison just wanted to be on the beach with the rest of the marines.

**Refugee Encampment
Mindanao, Philippines
March 17, 1995
1445 Hours**

The early afternoon was quiet. All the hostages gathered near the medical tents to be checked over by the corpsmen. They were fed and provided with fresh water and sanitary items. The American servicemen hastily set up latrines, not knowing how long until their relief would arrive. The navy dropped enough supplies to take care of a small army. The former hostages were soon sharing with the thousands of refugees crowding the beach head. As the early afternoon sun began to get hotter, the activity about the camp diminished. People found shade wherever they could and seemed to be resting for the first time in days.

Gateway sat under a tree with his granddaughter leaning against him. Donavon sat next to him, as well as the Smiths. Donavon sat with his head back, holding a half full bottle of water in his hand. Catherine, her head on her husband's shoulder was dozing while he read from the small bible. Around them groups of former hostages were doing much the same thing.

"You know what, General?" asked Donavon.

"What's that, Sam?" answered Gateway, looking at his friend. The man still had his head back and his eyes closed.

"I was just thinking about the last time we were on a beach here in the Philippines."

There were a few moments of silence. "We'd been pulled back out of combat and the war had ended. It was just as peaceful as now."

"Seems like only yesterday," said Donavan. "I can still see all the faces and hear the voices of the men who were there with us. Makes you wonder why we were the ones able to return."

"That was fifty years ago, people grow old. Look at us. Back then we would be the ones running around in uniform getting ready to repel an enemy attack. Man, we were good though, weren't we?"

"Seems like there was more honor in it then. We had a purpose, rid the world of a great evil. Something like that anyway."

"Don't kid yourself, Sam," said Gateway, "There's just as much honor and pride in it for these kids as there was for us. That evil's still there, the battlefields have just changed. These are our grandchildren an..."

"And children," added Smith from the other side of the tree.

Gateway gave an irritated look, "...and children, and they're forced to defend their country in a completely different way than we did. We're now the big guy on the block and everyone is looking at us as a protector or an enemy. These kids not only have to keep in mind who the enemy is, they also must make sure that we don't become the enemy ourselves. In a lot of ways, it's a lot tougher than we had it. There're more rules and the conflicts are on a smaller scale. Police actions, we're now the world's policemen, and you know how people feel about cops. Either they like us, or they hate us. Not much in between."

"War's now a bad word, Sam," said Smith moving around to their side of the tree. "It brings on visions of total annihilation, stuff like that."

"Like I said," chuckled Donavon. "It seems like it was much simpler in our day. Pure, if you will. The good guys versus the bad guys."

"That depends on which side you were on," smiled Gateway.

"Well, we certainly can't call them the good ol' days because...," said Smith until he was interrupted by the sound of small arms fire to the northeast. "I rest my case."

Around them American and Filipino servicemen snapped into action. They all ran to their defensive positions. Becky came running up to where her family was standing now, looking in the direction of the gunfire.

"My God!" she screamed. "You were in the United States Army how many years and you're standing out here like a rubber-necker at a crash on the freeway. Get my daughter undercover."

Before any of them could move, Sandy Monroe and her news crew came running up. They had been doing pieces on the individual hostages, as well as the refugees finding their way to the beach.

"What's going on?" asked the reporter. Becky exchanged nervous glances with her.

Before anyone could think of an answer Summers came running by, his weapon at the ready. Right behind him was his RTO. They both slowed when the officer saw the group huddled near the tree.

"Doctor, General, get your people up near the aid station and keep them there," said Summers. "Miss Monroe, I would like your news crew there, too."

"But it'll be safe there!" said the reporter without thinking.

"This is non-negotiable, Miss Monroe. I won't have you jeopardizing my people's lives for the sake of a story. You'll get all the story you need to from the aid station. Who knows, maybe it'll be like a real war, and they'll attack the aid station as one of their primary targets."

"You think they might?" the reporter almost seemed delighted. Gateway gave Monroe a disgusted look. Her cameraman and soundman grabbed her at the same time.

Summers ran off towards the sound of the small arms fire. He reached Rice's position settling into her command post. Both his RTO and Rice's were picking up radio traffic from the unit Colonel Lacson stationed on the highway. They were under heavy attack and had been calling in mortar fire until the fighting had become hand to hand. The reports were sporadic as the sounds of the fighting became more intense. Summers' asked for his RTO to check with the other positions.

"Sir," said the young sailor, "Colonel Lacson left Captain Sanchez in command of the outer perimeter while he reinforced the unit on the highway. The only action seems to be there. Both Mr. DeCook and Mr. Klintworth report no contact."

"Get me Eagle," ordered Summers thinking about his next move. The young RTO switched channels on his radio, immediately calling the *Nimitz*. When the sailor got an answer, he handed the handset to the officer.

"Eagle this is Pathfinder. We have contact with an enemy force on the highway. Check air strikes in that area, too many friendlies."

There was the sound of someone talking on the other end of the handset, but no one in the bunker could make it out.

"Roger that, Eagle," said Summers, "we can buy you that time. Make sure you're on the money, or you'll be the one buying the drinks when we get out of Dodge. Pathfinder out."

Summers handed the handset back to the sailor and looked at Rice. She glanced at him with a quizzical expression.

"Colonel Ellison," answered Summers to the unasked question, "if he doesn't keep his promise, he'll have to buy us all a beer."

Rice smiled. "I'm not a big beer drinker, Sir, but I could sure use one right now."

Summers looked at his RTO, they could only hear occasional fire now.

"Nothing from Colonel Lacson, Sir," responded the young man.

Summers looked over the top of the bunker. He seemed to be watching something in the perimeter line about two hundred yards in front of them. The outer perimeter was a series of bunkers and foxholes quickly put together. Both soldiers and civilians worked to get them completed in the short time they had. The perimeter's makeup consisted of the various infantry units of the Philippine Army. They put claymore mines and explosive charges in front of their positions, as well as a few large obstacles to slow down any armor the mercenaries may have. The inner perimeter consisted of a similar series of bunkers and foxholes. The difference was this is where they placed the tanks, armored cars and other heavy weapons taken from Camp Freedom. They also placed the mortars and anti-tank rockets in this perimeter.

Summers continued to watch what was going on along the line of troops in front of him.

"Captain Rice!" he said "every other man in your unit forms on me. The rest hold their position and wait for further orders."

With that Summers and his RTO went up over the top of the bunker. She passed on her orders watching the two men race across the open space between the two perimeters. She could hear the chatter on the radio as Summers informed the rest of the command of his last orders. Suddenly, she and half of her command went over the top following him to the positions being held by the Philippine Army. When she got to the perimeter, she found Summers and Sanchez interviewing the men who had fallen back from the highway.

"Where is Colonel Lacson?" asked Sanchez in English.

"He went down, Sir," answered one of the men shaking uncontrollably. "I saw him go down at the roadblock."

"Was he killed?" asked Summers grabbing both arms gently. The man stopped shaking.

"I...I don't know, Sir," answered the man looking back at Summers.

"Then we go back to see if he's alive. We don't leave our wounded to the enemy, son. Will you show me the way?"

Sanchez turned, looking at the American with surprise. Rice moved forward so Summers could see she and her marines were there. Summers turned to Sanchez and gave some orders in Filipino. Sanchez took the handset from his RTO and began talking into the radio in Filipino. Along the line of soldiers, every other man took out their bayonet fixing it to the end of their rifle. Sanchez gave his RTO back the handset and looked at the American officer.

"Ready to go, Sir!" said the Filipino.

Before Rice could ask, Summers looked at Sanchez saying, "OK, Captain, let's bring them back."

The Filipino soldiers who had made it back from the firefight on the highway led the way, followed by Summers and his RTO. The Philippine soldiers who fixed their bayonets left their positions and began moving forward. Rice looked at the men moving towards the highway and then back at the line of marines next to her. They all looked back. She looked at her RTO.

"Did he say for us to stay here?" she asked him not quite believing what was going on.

The young marine shook his head, "No, Ma'am, he just left."

Rice looked down the line of Marines again. They were still looking at her. She hesitated for a second, then pulled her bayonet out of its sheath and mounted it on her M-16. The rest of her people did the same thing and then followed her over the top after the others. When they cleared the positions, the remaining troops began pulling back the claymores and explosives.

The assault force moved in silently. They could still hear quite a bit of noise from the roadblock. Summers and the soldiers leading the way were out in front. The advance suddenly stopped when Summers ordered a halt. Rice watched Summers talking to Sanchez. When he finished, Sanchez picked about a dozen men, disappearing into the jungle to their north. Summers took several soldiers forward placing them in positions where they had an open line of fire into the roadblock. Summers guessed there to be about a hundred troops, a few trucks, and an Abrams tank. He could see several armored cars burning nearby. They had taken the roadblock, but at a heavy cost. Summers looked at the tank closely. The crew was outside, and the hatches were wide open.

Summers gave the order for the rest of the troops to move up and into position. He observed several foreign officers questioning prisoners at the front of the column. He immediately became angered. It appeared they had executed several prisoners in front of Lacson, who was bound to the barbed wire obstacle from the roadblock. There were five more prisoners lined up in front of the colonel, all on their knees and with their hands bound. Lacson himself looked to be wounded. The man doing the questioning was Caucasian and speaking to Lacson and the prisoners in English.

Summers began to move the remaining troops forward slowly and quietly. Sanchez and his group had been gone a little over a half an hour when the RTOs picked a short one-word message in Filipino. Rice watched as Summers took a squad and began to move dangerously close to the roadblock by the front of the enemy column. The security was tight on both sides of the highway, although attitudes seemed lax. Summers ordered a halt in some rocks about twenty yards to the south of the roadblock and about thirty yards from the tank. Rice noticed the tank crew was outside and the hatches were open. She now understood the gamble Summers was taking. She motioned for her people to get ready.

Boerst stood in front of the wounded Filipino and was losing his patience. He had already shot three of the officer's men and was now convinced he would have to kill them all, including the officer, before he proceeded onto the beach and the refugees. He guessed American Special Forces, along with the Filipinos, were responsible for the attack on Camp Freedom and the release of the hostages. His main concern was to find a way off the island before being caught by the government. He expected he wouldn't be dealt with kindly by a government he tried to overthrow. He guessed his best bet was to retake the hostages and bargain his way out. He knew he had the advantage in numbers with over twelve hundred men at his disposal. Most were Filipino, and expendable.

"One last time, Colonel," said the German looking at the gravely wounded officer. He had been shot in one leg and in the side. The barbed wire on the obstacle also cut him up badly. Boerst continued, "All you have to do is tell me the troop strength on the beach and their placement and you and your people will be given medical attention and set free. There's no need for any more of you to die."

Boerst nodded to the tank commander looking up at the .50 calibre machine gun mounted on the top of the turret. The soldier nodded starting to climb to his post. There was the deafening sound of gunfire from both sides of the highway. The tank commander was hit and fell into the open hatch, blocking it from being closed.

The attack was so sudden and ferocious many of the mercenaries froze; giving the attacking troops the time they needed to take the advantage. When they came out of the jungle with fixed bayonets and the rebels saw American marines fighting alongside government troops some of them dropped their weapons and ran into the jungle. The firefight was one sided until the tank began to move. At that point, the Filipinos and the Americans began to hesitate. Suddenly, two of the Filipinos who moved forward with Summers were on top of the tank and each man threw a grenade into the open top hatch. They jumped off. Other hatches started opening, the crew trying to escape the impending explosion. That came seconds later. The tank came to a stop, thick, black smoke pouring out of the open hatches.

Boerst rallied some of his people, moving forward to kill the prisoners. They arrived to find the prisoners were gone. He could see the last of them being led into the jungle. By the obstacle there were several men trying to free the Filipino officer. Boerst raised his pistol to fire at one of the men. He was taller than the rest and obviously American. By his dress, he guessed he wasn't a marine like the other Americans involved in the attack. He was Special Forces and probably responsible for this ambush. He started to pull the trigger when gunfire increased from the other side of the road. A small force of Filipinos was moving out of the jungle to join in the attack on his column. He turned to look at the new threat, firing at the American. He saw him go down to one knee, reaching for his side. He smiled, quickly checking the attacking soldiers to his left. There appeared to be about a dozen. Suddenly, the two men next to him fell. He glanced quickly seeing they both were dead. He turned, finding the American he thought he'd shot attacking with more Filipino soldiers. Two more men in the squad surrounding him fell to bullets from the American. He ordered the rest of his people to fall back, planning an immediate counterattack.

Rice saw the mercenaries were falling back but guessed their reinforcements were only minutes away. Summers came around the side of the destroyed tank with two Filipino soldiers. He looked at Rice saying, "Captain, get on the radio and tell them we're falling back with the enemy close behind. Any casualties?"

"None here, Sir," said Rice. She noticed Summers's weapon was still smoking from recently being fired. She gave her RTO the message to send then started to rally both her Marines and the Philippine soldiers in the area. She noticed Summers's RTO was limping off with the soldiers carrying Lacson. Sanchez came running up to Rice. "I had two wounded, what about you?"

"All okay," responded Rice motioning in the direction of the young sailor who was hobbling into the jungle.

"That makes three, not bad considering we've counted twenty-three enemy KIA plus the tank."

The sound of heavy engines made them turn. They were down the road, but the noise meant the counterattack was on its way. Summers jogged up.

"Come on, you two, there's no time for chit chat," said Summers. "Let's get your people back to the inner perimeter on the double."

"The inner perimeter, Sir?" questioned Rice.

"You heard the order, Captain. I'm not in the habit of repeating myself."

He moved into the jungle followed by the two Filipino soldiers who appeared to have adopted him. Both Rice and Sanchez immediately started moving their troops back into the jungle. They were both the last of their units to fall back. They looked back at the destruction they were leaving behind and then at each other. It was the first time either had been in combat and they were feeling mixed emotions.

The soldiers were moving quickly towards the outer perimeter defensive line. Wounded were being carried so the withdrawal was being done as fast as possible. Summers and the two Filipino soldiers came across his RTO, who was limping more slowly than the rest of the troops. As the officer came up to the radioman, the sailor handed him the headset.

"Pathfinder to Mohawk Six," said Summers into the radio.

"Mohawk Six on," came the reply from DeCook.

"Six, we're returning hot. Get ready for a heavy reception."

"Roger that, Pathfinder. We're ready on this end."

Summers handed the handset back to his RTO and started to walk off. The RTO limped behind them unable to keep up. Summers stopped turning to look at the young sailor.

"What's the problem?" he asked the SEAL.

"I'm not sure, Sir," answered the sailor, "but I think I caught part of a bullet in my leg on a ricochet in the rocks. It's hard to walk on."

Summers trotted back to the SEAL, followed by the two Filipinos. The young man limped to a stop.

"Sorry Sir," said the sailor. "I can make it back. Go ahead and I'll catch up."

"Don't be stupid," said Summers. "You won't make it halfway across the field before they get you and then we have to do this all again. Give me the radio."

The sailor looked hurt taking the radio off his back. He handed the radio to Summers, who, in turn, handed it to one of the Filipinos. As this was taking place, Rice, Sanchez, and their people were moving through. They looked at this little scene with amusement. Summers took the SEAL's weapon and handed it to the other soldier. He then picked the young serviceman up in a fireman's carry and began walking towards the outer perimeter.

Rice and Sanchez stopped laughing when Summers carried the wounded man towards safety. They immediately were reminded how dangerous their chosen profession was and started to move their people along at a faster clip. Rice watched as Summers carried the wounded man past the outer perimeter positions and continued towards the inner perimeter. She didn't realize the outer perimeter was unguarded until she stood inside one of the bunkers finding it empty. She was confused and looked to Sanchez, who gave the order to continue to move towards the inner perimeter. Rice motioned for her people to follow suit and they moved quickly across the open field. It took about fifteen minutes to get everyone from the vacated outer perimeter to the safety of the inner perimeter. It was crowded, but it was well defended.

Summers reached the inner perimeter and set his passenger down in the command bunker. The SEAL limped out of the way and found a place to sit where no one would bother him. The two soldiers carrying his radio and his weapon returned the items to him, leaving the bunker for their positions. The young sailor seemed happy to have his equipment back and immediately set up shop. Medical people were moved up to the perimeter to help receive and process the wounded being brought back from the highway. Becky came forward with the corpsmen to help. She helped triage the wounded having them sent back to the aide station. After most of the wounded were being moved, Becky turned her attention to the wounded SEAL who continued to broadcast.

Becky ripped open the sailor's camouflage pant leg to expose the wound and make it easier to work on. It was a small entrance wound with the projectile still embedded in the SEAL's calf.

"You'll need this operated on soon, but you're better off than a good number of the others," said Becky. "Let's get you back to the aid station and we can do a better job of bandaging that leg."

The RTO stopped talking on the radio for a second looking at the doctor. "Ma'am, I appreciate your takin' care of my leg an' all, but right now my place is here."

Becky didn't react. She continued to bandage the man's leg. "Not a problem, my guess is you're just as safe here as you are back at the aid station."

Several marines standing nearby laughed. The sailor gave them a dirty look. Becky finished bandaging the leg. She also gave the marines an irritated glance.

"Let's look at the arm," continued Becky turning her attention back to the sailor.

"Arm, Ma'am?" asked the puzzled SEAL. "I wasn't hit in the arm."

"Right there," said Becky as she pointed at a stain on the man's shirt sleeve.

The sailor looked where the doctor was pointing. He undid the buttons on the cuff and rolled up the sleeve. There was no wound or injury that would have caused the stain.

"I don't understand it, Ma'am," said the sailor. "I wasn't hurt, and I don't remember being that close to anyone that was wounded."

"How'd you get back here?" asked the doctor.

The sailor pointed to Summers. "The Skipper carried me across the field. Ran most of the way."

Becky turned to look at the officer. He was busy talking to Rice and Sanchez, as well as using Rice's radio to talk to other positions. She watched him quietly for almost a minute before she saw the stains on his uniform on the right side. The sailor saw them as well.

"Well, I'll be damned," said the sailor looking at his commanding officer. Becky got up and walked over to Summers. The officer continued talking on the radio turning to look at the doctor.

"Doctor now is not a good time. We're about to be attacked."

"You're wounded," said the doctor bluntly as she pointed to his side. "It could be serious. You should have it looked at."

Rice and Sanchez both looked to where the doctor had indicated. This close, they could see there was quite a bit of fresh blood on the senior officer's uniform.

"Sir, she's right," said Rice without thinking. "Maybe you should have it looked at."

Summers flashed Rice an angry look and then looked back at the doctor. "Right now is not a good time."

As if on cue, there was the sound of incoming mortar fire and the explosions that followed. Even though the rounds impacted on the far side of the outer perimeter, Becky hunched down for cover. When she got back up Summers smiled and motioned to Sanchez. "Captain, have two of your men escort the doctor to the aid station. If you must assign them there to make sure both she and Miss Monroe stay there during the attack, please do so."

Sanchez called to the two closest soldiers and gave them their orders. The two soldiers picked up the equipment the doctor had brought with her and waited for a second while Becky stood looking at the officer. She turned, walking away. "I'll be back to look at that if you live through the day."

Summers looked at the other two officers standing with him. "I look forward to that, Doctor."

Summers turned his attention back to the attack.

Mercenary Positions
Mindanao, Philippines
March 17, 1995
1500 Hours

Boerst moved his men out of the jungle and towards the outer perimeter line. He was on the radio to his armor, a column of six armored cars and ten armored personnel carriers moving down the same jungle trail the trucks carrying the refugees used. He had two tanks and some other transport vehicles he kept on the road to hold that position. He was using the big guns on the tanks as artillery. The outer perimeter defenses were taking a pounding as the mortar and tank fire zeroed in on the larger bunkers. After ten minutes of this, he ordered his infantry forward, supported by the armor.

The first wave of infantry reached the perimeter line unopposed and moved on through. The second line of infantry and the armor had reached the line just as Boerst realized he committed a mistake. There was a sudden series of explosions along the perimeter line when Summers ordered the detonation of the claymores and explosives. Several vehicles were destroyed, and the infantry took heavy casualties from the shrapnel from the claymores. Summers immediately ordered the mortars and tanks to open fire on the approaching vehicles. The fire from the two Abrams tanks was so deadly it only took five minutes of constant fire to destroy six more of Boerst's vehicles. Without being told the infantry units began to fall back. They'd taken heavy losses and Boerst decided that he needed to try a different tact.

Boerst stood on top of the armored car he was using as a command vehicle. Watching his troops withdraw, he was pleased with the discipline they showed. He realized, at this point, there was no way he and his army could win the war, but they needed a break allowing them to safely escape. He suddenly heard a noise bringing fear from the depths his soul. He looked to the skies but couldn't see them. He knew they were up there, on their way to harass his troops.

The first wave of F-18s streaked in from the sea dropping bombs on the retreating troops. The explosions created by the bombs, along with the noise created by the jets, ended all discipline in the retreat. The ground shook from the explosions, those that hadn't been killed or wounded took cover or ran. A second wave of Hornets came down the highway bombing the vehicles holding positions there. Three vehicles, including one of the tanks, were destroyed. The troops there raced for cover, as well. Yet another wave of aircraft came in from the ocean and began to strafe the mercenaries running for cover.

Boerst was knocked to the ground from his perch but hadn't been wounded. Once in the safety of the trees, he began to assess the damage and rally those troops still able and willing to fight. He still had more troops than the Philippine Army and the Americans on the beach. He knew a frontal assault wouldn't work. American air cover would prohibit any large-scale operations. He gave orders he hoped would give him the advantage he needed.

Refugee Camp
Mindanao, Philippines
17 March 1995
1530 Hours

With the mercenaries falling back and the smoke on the battlefield clearing, it was obvious they managed to beat a numerically superior force again. There were no casualties among the defenders, although, if they attacked again, Summers guessed they would be heavy. The mercenaries fell into their trap and taken the casualties this time. They wouldn't fall for it a second time.

Summers was busy talking to the units covering their flanks. He didn't expect the enemy to come at them from across the field again, but rather try and infiltrate the flanks along the beach. That's what he would do. He looked at his RTO still seated in the corner of the bunker. He was talking to the aircraft flying overhead. They were no longer attacking targets, but rather supplying the troops on the ground with information of any movement they saw.

Summers turned to move and almost doubled over in pain. In the excitement of the attack he forgot he'd been shot. Rice moved to grab him, but he put his hand out to stop her. He moved his hand away from his side to find it covered with fresh blood. He looked at the marine officer shaking his head.

"Captain," he said quietly, "I'll be on the beach getting some air. Send me a corpsman."

Rice looked at him and didn't know what to say. She nodded as the senior officer turned, walking out of the bunker. When he walked past his RTO the sailor tried to get to his feet. Summers put his hand on the man's shoulder.

"Stay put, son," said Summers. "Keep off the leg like the doctor said. I'm only going over to the beach. Just make sure that the good Captain gets me a corpsman."

The sailor looked up. "Aye, aye, Sir, and thanks for getting me back."

"That's what we're supposed to do, son," said Summers walking out of the bunker, "bring each other back."

Summers walked past groups of refugees and hostages. They called out to him, and he would answer. None asked what happened. They mostly shouted a hello or congratulations for pushing back the attack. Summers began to move away from the crowded area and went up and over the dunes.

He reached a second set of dunes and sat down where he could see the Moro Gulf. The waves were coming in, creating a rhythm he found soothing. The breeze was gentle, and he breathed in the fresh sea air. He already felt better. He knew the wound wasn't a serious one, but he needed to stop the bleeding, or he'd be in trouble. He put his right hand over his eyes to block the hot afternoon sun and smiled. He looked up and down the horizon and then put his hand down on his knees, followed by his head. He took a deep breath and put his head back up. His eyes were closed, and he took another deep breath. He was tired and knew he wouldn't get to sleep for a while yet. At least he was relaxed.

He sat there with his head back and eyes closed. He could hear them coming. There were two groups. One from directly behind him, the same route he had taken, and the other from off to his right. He stayed in his position with his eyes closed as both groups approached. His left hand held onto his rifle sitting next to him. The group to his right was closest, in the small gully between the two sets of dunes. Both groups could see him. He had a decision to make. He also knew he'd made a mistake by coming alone.

Gateway decided to go with his daughter when they went to find the wounded officer. They were accompanied by one of the Navy corpsmen and two Filipino soldiers. Becky was complaining about the stubbornness of the officer for not allowing her to treat him earlier. He agreed with her publicly, but privately understood the reason for the man's decision. You had to deal with the business at hand. As they topped the first row of sand dunes, they could see the officer about fifty yards away on top of the next set of dunes. He was sitting up and appeared to be relaxing. Gateway understood the need to be alone. He suddenly remembered a time fifty years before when he had approached a friend on the beach on the other side of the Moro Gulf. He found it funny and started to smile picturing Ray in his mind.

While Gateway was daydreaming, the officer suddenly exploded into action rolling to his right. Before anyone could react, he brought his rifle up to his shoulder aiming into the gully below. They were in a position where they couldn't see what was down there, and the reaction of the two soldiers and the corpsman was to drop down taking cover near the crest of the dune. Just as the officer began to fire into the gully, Gateway pushed his daughter down into the sand following her there. Initially he was the only one firing followed by screaming below them. The four men in the party crawled to look over the crest of the ridge. They found a squad of mercenaries, numbering about fifteen, had made their way through the perimeter and were using the gully as cover to make their way closer to the refugees and former hostages. Summers's fire took them by surprise and three of the soldiers were in the process of falling. The remaining soldiers were returning fire. Summers started down into the gully, firing as he did. He hit one more mercenary. They fired back. Bullets hit the sand around him as he moved forward. Suddenly, he lost his footing and he fell into the sand rolling down the hill.

Several of the mercenaries noticed the men on the other side of the dunes shifting their field of fire when the two Filipino soldiers fired on the men in the gully. Several more of the enemy fell, causing the rest to hesitate. Gateway watched as Summers fell down the hill and ended up coming up on his left knee. He lost his rifle in the fall, so he drew his pistol. He fired at the man closest to him, hitting him in the torso. As that man fell, he fired at the next man, also hitting him. Within seconds, two of the mercenaries were within feet of him. Both were raising their weapons to fire. Summers fired wildly at one as he physically jumped at the other.

The first man fell away, having been struck by the bullet. Summers hit the second man so hard he lost his pistol in the struggle. As the two fell to the ground, there was a sudden explosion of small arms fire from above the gully on both sides. There were screams from other members of the mercenary unit as the hail of gunfire came down around them. Summers ignored the gunfire as he struggled with the man on the ground. They were fighting for possession of the man's rifle. The soldier let go of the stock of the rifle and hit Summers in the head as hard as he could with his fist. The force of the blow knocked Summers off balance, but he weighed more than the man he was fighting, so it didn't make much of a difference. Summers was on the soldier pressing down on the trigger area of the rifle with his left hand and arm. This pinned the man to the ground who continued to hit the American. With his right hand, Summers began to hit his opponent in the face repeatedly. After about the fifth time the man stopped struggling. Suddenly he found his arm restrained noticing other people in the gully for the first time.

"I think he's down for the count, Sir," said Wiedenkeller letting Summers's arm go. "You, okay?"

Summers rolled off the soldier and began to do an assessment of himself.

"Hit in the side and in the leg, Chief," said Summers without thinking while he sat in the sand.

"Corpsman! Over here!" shouted Wiedenkeller kneeling next to Summers. "Now I understand how you won the medal in Nam, Sir. You're fucking crazy. Glad to have you on board, Skipper."

Summers looked at the man kneeling next to him and could make out the smile from underneath the camouflage paint. A corpsman and Becky came running up. The corpsman began to look at his leg wound. Summers started to notice other things in the gully. Wiedenkeller was talking to a Filipino sergeant who was commanding the Philippine troops responding to the firefight. It appeared the mercenaries were caught in the crossfire between a squad of Philippine soldiers and a squad of SEALs. There looked to be four prisoners not wounded and five more that were. Gateway approached him grinning.

"The last time I saw moves like that was fifty years ago," said the veteran. "I had a platoon leader, natural soldier he was, that could do that. I was never able to move like that, but Ray was good."

Summers was about to say something when he was pushed to the ground. The next thing he knew Becky and the corpsman had moved him onto his left side and were looking at the wound on his right side.

"You're lucky you're alive," scolded Becky working at cleaning the wound. "Running all over this island, bleeding on everyone. Now you have a leg wound so I'm taking you out of circulation for a while. You're lucky though, both bullets passed right through without hitting anything vital. You could have been killed doing something like that. Running into fifteen soldiers by yourself."

"Nonsense," interrupted Gateway. "It was a brave thing to do. He saved us and who knows how many others by doing that. It allowed our troops time to react."

"It's not time for heroics, Dad. The man's hurt bad and from the scars, it's not the first time," said Becky looking at his back.

Summers grimaced with the pain. "You're right there, Doc, I'm not a virgin, but it doesn't make it hurt any less. General, hindsight being what it is, I have to say I agree with your daughter. It was a damned stupid thing to do."

Two soldiers brought a stretcher over to where he was lying on the ground. They were joined by the sergeant and two more of their comrades.

They gently placed Summers on the stretcher and waited for the word to move him back to the aide station. The sergeant bent down and picked up a Colt from the sand looking at it. He walked over to Summers kneeling next to him.

"This is yours, Sir. I saw you drop it in the battle," said the sergeant. "It seems to have brought you luck. It would be a shame to lose it now. It's a weapon of a different era judging by the markings."

Summers smiled. "Thank you."

Other soldiers were coming, and the wounded mercenaries were being tended to. Wiedenkeller gave the word, and the four soldiers lifted the stretcher carrying Summers towards the aid station.

Refugee Encampment
Mindanao, Philippines
March 17, 1995
1615 Hours

The sound came to them first. The soldiers and sailors guarding the encampment began to look to the skies. The first wave to come over were jets from *Nimitz*. They came in low dropping large ordinance on the jungle in front of their positions. The second wave of aircraft did the same. The third wave of aircraft were Harriers, and they fired their missiles into the same area of the jungle. The marines cheered because they knew the Harriers weren't from *Nimitz*. Harriers were used by the marines for close air support on marine amphibious operations, which meant *Tarawa* was within striking distance.

Boerst found his people starting to run as the air strike intensified. When he saw the Harriers fly over, he knew what was coming next. They needed to disappear into the jungle and do their best to escape. He guessed about two thousand United States Marines were about to land and that would tip the scales against them. Now was the time to escape.

His people began moving out of the jungle and onto the road. Another wave of aircraft flew over strafing the troops. Boerst and several members of his staff jumped into a jeep and left the area as fast as the vehicle could carry them. Several more vehicles full of mercenary troops followed them. They raced down the road coming to a sharp turn having to slow down to negotiate it. When they came around the bend, they found the road blocked by several trees. When the vehicles came to a stop Boerst ordered the men with him to clear the trees. When they began to dismount their vehicles, they came under heavy small arms and rocket fire. Boerst was hit, falling out of the jeep. All around him men were cut down while they tried to find cover. One of the trucks carrying troops exploded when it was hit by an anti-tank rocket.

The small arms fire stopped and those responsible began to walk out of the jungle on both sides of the road. Boerst was trying to crawl away until he found himself looking at a set of boots. He looked up finding the eyes of a determined looking Filipino.

"Please, please don't shoot me," begged the mercenary.

The man looked disgusted watching Boerst try to beg for his life. He raised his rifle and fired three rounds into the man at his feet. Boerst collapsed lifeless.

On the beach the first wave of helicopters was coming in. They were preceded by Marine Cobra attack helicopters that peppered the tree line with rocket and cannon fire. What was left of the tree line took another beating as the gunners on the CH-53 helicopters fired in that direction while dropping the first wave of marines. The landing zone was the open field between the two perimeters. The wind from the rotors of the helicopters kicked sand into the air as they dropped their cargo and increased power to take off again. As the first wave of helicopters left, the next came in repeating the procedure.

Summers had been taken to the aid station but hadn't stayed confined to the stretcher he was brought in on. His RTO was moved from the command bunker and brought to his location where they began to set up a new command post. Rice and her marines were moved back to protect the encampment area. She and her RTO set up shop with Summers and between the two radios they were keeping track of the entire operation. Fidel found Summers a crutch and he managed to get around his new command area quite well.

"What are you doing up!" demanded Becky when she saw him moving around. "You need to be still, or you'll start those wounds bleeding again."

Summers turned to see the doctor standing near the entrance to the tent where they were doing surgery. He smiled at the woman. "Doc, get over with the rest of the foreign nationals and get ready to be evacuated. You go out on the next flight of choppers."

Becky looked like she was about to argue the point. She looked around at the wounded and started to object when a marine officer came jogging up to Summers. He was followed by a small entourage of marines.

"Sir," said the marine introducing himself, "I'm Colonel Montgomery. I'm in command of the Marine Expeditionary Force. Looks like you've had your hands full. Colonel Ellison sends his regards and regrets. Apparently, the admiral won't let him out of his sight."

Summers laughed. "Nice to make your acquaintance, Colonel. My guess is W. C. has George chained to the wheelhouse."

Montgomery laughed. "From what I hear the last time you two were together on a mission, the admiral had reason to worry. So did the enemy."

Montgomery turned his attention to Becky who was still standing impatiently by the tent.

"Ma'am," said the marine officer, "I apologize for the interruption."

"That's okay, Colonel," responded Becky. "I was just chastising this irresponsible, obnoxious ..."

Summers chuckled interrupting. "Flower Child, it's time to catch your flight."

Becky flushed with anger asking, "Why do you keep calling me that?"

Summers held her gaze shouting, "Captain Rice!"

Rice rushed over to where Summers and the Colonel stood. When she saw Montgomery, she snapped to attention. Montgomery looked surprised to find a female officer in battle dress and carrying a weapon. He looked at Summers who winked in return.

"Captain, would you escort Doctor O'Keefe to her ride and make sure she doesn't miss it."

"Aye, Sir!" answered Rice quickly. She immediately rushed over to Becky and took her by the arm. "Come on, Doc. They'll be leaving any second."

As the two women moved off, Montgomery looked at Summers. "I'd heard Kingston was upset with a marine officer and sent them out here with you, Sir, but they didn't say it was a female officer. How'd she do?"

"She's a marine," chuckled Summers. "She did the corps proud."

Montgomery stood a little taller grinning.

**Special Report
Morning News
March 17, 1995
0705 Hours**

The scene behind Sandy Monroe showed a busy beachhead after an invasion. Marine Corps armored cars and tanks moved passed the camera as the reporter spoke. Marines and Philippine Army troops could be seen distributing food and other supplies to the needy refugees. Monroe's face was clean, and her hair looked like it had been washed and tended to, but she was still wearing the same clothes she was in the last several days. Everywhere people looked to be happy.

"… and with the arrival of the marines, the tense situation that could have led to a blood bath and affected thousands has been averted. On a personal note, the actions I've had the privilege to witness over the past several days helped me to redefine a word many of us take for granted.

"From the hostages, who returned here to honor the memory of those who fell in the cause of freedom, I learned this attribute doesn't have an age limit attached to it. These amazing people refused to quit when most of us would have thrown in the towel. They resisted and refused to cooperate with those who held them prisoner. In many cases they suffered because of it. Their spirit wasn't dampened, and they always looked to the future with hope and faith. Through my entire time with them during this ordeal, I heard not one of them complain, if only as an example for the rest of us.

"From the Philippine people I learned life is a daily struggle you have to face with conviction and dignity. No matter how much pain and adversity there is, you must have faith there is a bigger purpose for what's happening. In the middle of this tragedy, I found the people most affected by what was going on to be polite, outgoing, and gracious. We can all learn something from a people such as this.

"Finally from the members of the American and Philippine military who came to our rescue, I learned the meaning of sacrifice. This wasn't one of those bloodless rescues that we all would like to see happen. These anonymous individuals showed me no matter what the odds are, you stay with the job until it's done. They repeatedly put themselves in harm's way without regard for themselves. Their only mission, to get those of us being detained against our will home safely.

"To all of these people I say thank you for showing the meaning of the word courage."

The camera cut back to the studio in New York.

U.S.S. Nimitz
Moro Gulf
March 17, 1995
1915 Hours

The former hostages were transported to *Nimitz* and *Tarawa* by helicopter. Gateway, his family, the Smiths, and Donavon were transported to *Nimitz* together. They were given clean clothes in the form of uniforms. Most of them were in officer khaki, but a few, such as Sarah, were in enlisted blues. They were now in the process of getting something to eat in the officer's mess. Gateway brought a small pack Fidel gave him when they boarded the helicopter. The old man said it was from a friend and he was to wait until they were safe to open it. He wasn't especially hungry and decided to look at what was inside. Putnum joined them, introducing himself. He was talking to the rest as Bill opened the pack. Inside he found two envelopes. The first was a large manila envelope with something thick inside. The second was a standard white envelope having *Open me first* typed on it. Also inside the pack was a World War II issue web belt and several canteens.

Gateway took out the envelopes, opening the first one. Smith, who was sitting next to him, seemed to be the only one paying attention. When he pulled out the piece of paper from inside, a second, smaller piece of paper fell out. Gateway picked it up and froze. The paper falling out of the envelope caught everyone else's attention. Gateway looked pale.

"What is it?" asked Sarah.

"It's half of one-peso note given to your grandfather on the day he left the company in 1945 by the new company commander," said Donavon.

"Who was that?" asked the young woman.

Smith's eye didn't leave his friend, "Ray Summers."

"But Uncle Ray passed away. How did Fidel get the envelopes?"

No one answered Sarah while her grandfather opened the folded piece of paper. Putnum looked up from his coffee smiling.

Gateway read the letter to himself.

Thanksgiving Day 1994

Dear Bill,

I hate to say it, but if you're reading this letter at the reunion instead of talking to me in person it means I've lost my battle with cancer. Here is the other half of the note that hangs in your study. I'm keeping a promise we made to each other so many years ago and welcoming you back into the company. They are all good men, the best I've ever known or had the privilege to know. In the second envelope you will find the sketch book I kept during our time in the Philippines. Please distribute them as you see fit. They really belong to all of you guys.

I have asked Jon to make the trip to the Philippines for me to make sure you get these items. Please understand this trip will not be easy for him for several reasons. The first one is obvious, but having served in combat, he understands the bond that exists between those of us who served together. I'm not sure what the second reason is. Only that something terrible happened to him when he was stationed there. He has agreed to deliver these and at my request has done it unannounced. Please don't be upset with him. He was only following my wishes.

Well, I could write to you guys forever, but it is time to go. Know that I'm confident we'll meet again in a better place. I also know the bonds we forged on the battlefields of World War II are strong enough to last forever, no matter where we are. Take care of yourself and that wonderful family.

Your friend and comrade,

Ray

P.S. No matter what you thought, I really did make a better teacher than a soldier. The canteens contain thirty-year-old scotch. I expect you to drink to that.

Gateway handed the letter to Smith, who began to read it.

"You all right, Dad?" asked Becky.

"Yeah, I'm fine," answered her father. "Ray just managed to sneak one in from the grave. And I didn't even know he was there."

Smith pushed the small Bible he had been carrying over to Gateway. "Read the inscription."

Gateway did as he was instructed and then looked up at his friend.

"I'd like to know who that man was who was in charge out there. He kept calling me Flower Child," said Becky. "There's only one person I'll let call me that and..."

She was interrupted by laughter from her father and Smith. Putnum got up from the table smiling at Becky. "Doctor O'Keefe, the man you're referring to doesn't exist."

"But he..."

"He doesn't exist, Doctor. He was never there. It must have been your imagination."

Becky sat there not knowing what to say. When Putnum walked past Gateway and Smith, he winked. Both men smiled.

Davao International Airport
Mindanao, Philippines
March 17, 1995
2100 Hours

The three prisoners were helped off the small transport. They were in a secured area of the airport where two jets waited. Along with the prisoners were the NCIS and FBI agents who had been on board *Nimitz*, as well as Ellison, Demmer, and McAvoy. It'd taken several of the small aircraft to transport all of them. The three prisoners were headed to Pearl Harbor as the investigation continued. The other three were to wait for Summers to return from his mission and then proceed on to Washington. As they walked towards the waiting aircraft, they saw a line of soldiers heading towards them.

Ellison looked at the approaching soldiers smiling. He looked at Demmer with pride, "Marines. I love it."

Demmer laughed, shaking her head. McAvoy just shook his head. As the marines got closer, Ellison recognized the officer walking next to the column. So did Kingston who immediately looked down at his feet.

"How was it, Captain?" asked Ellison.

"No casualties, Sir!" answered Rice as she snapped Ellison a crisp salute.

"Whorah, Captain," said Ellison as he returned her salute.

"Semper fi, Sir!" said Rice as she marched her people towards the waiting aircraft for their return to the Nimitz.

As they walked by, Kingston said, "Bitch."

The last three rows of men stopped dead, causing the agents escorting the three prisoners a great deal of concern. The marines were looking angry, and the agents didn't want an incident at this point.

"As you were, marines!" said a voice cutting through the tension. The marines snapped to attention and agents backed away. Summers hobbled forward on his crutch, standing between the marines and the prisoners. He was still dressed in his camouflage battle dress. He looked at the people on both sides and then faced the marines.

"Gentlemen, your loyalty for your commanding officer is commendable, but you would dishonor her and the Marine Corps if you acted on impulse. Keep in mind what you've accomplished and go back to your command with your heads held high. Gentlemen, he's not worth it."

The marines looked at each other and then back at Summers. The closest one, a corporal, spoke for them all. "Sorry, Sir. We got upset with him calling the captain a name."

Summers smiled, "Captain Rice."

"Sir?" answered Rice immediately.

"Captain, you have marines to tend to. Get to it."

"Aye, aye, Sir," said Rice saluting Summers. The marines all fell in, and she led them off towards the waiting aircraft.

Summers turned to Kingston and his two aides. Wells and Grey both looked at him. He looked like hell. They nodded and told the agents guarding the three to allow Summers through. Summers limped over to the three, stopping in front of Kingston. Williams and Handcock wouldn't look at him. Kingston looked broken, but still had enough contempt for Summers, staring at his old rival.

"Hello, Dick," said Summers.

"It's Admiral."

Summers smiled. "You gave that privilege up from me when you tried to kill me, asshole. You need to know the case against you should get you convicted. If it doesn't, start looking over your shoulder because there is a growing group of people who would like to see you dead."

"You're threatening me."

"No," said Summers with a smile, "just the fact the truth is finally out, and you're ruined is enough for me. The families of the men who didn't come back from your treachery might have something to say about it, though. You've added a whole group to that list with your last little escapade. I wouldn't want to be the one to have a bunch of upset rangers after me. I know some SEAL families from years ago that aren't going to be so happy with you, either. Face it, Dick, you fucked up. Pray you get convicted. It'll be a whole lot healthier."

As Summers began to turn away, Handcock started to sob. He continued walking, while the agents escorted their charges to the aircraft. Ellison, Demmer, and McAvoy walked up to Summers.

"So," said Ellison with a grin, "how ya feeling sport?"

Summers looked at his friend and said, "Like shit, asshole. Where were you when I was being shot at?"

"Practicing for what I'm going to be doing when Nancy gets her hands on you. You made national TV, son. The real battle hasn't taken place yet."

The three of them laughed as Summers threw his hands up in the air. They helped him onto the aircraft and headed for home.

★ E P I L O G U E ★

CELEBRATION

Gateway Compound
Oahu, Hawaii
November 24, 1999
1200 Hours

The wedding went off without a hitch and Becky felt like getting drunk. Her daughter was married to a fine young man, and they were starting a new life together. She managed to get through the ceremony without shedding too many tears and was feeling very much like a left-out mother. Because the groom was in the navy, there were uniforms everywhere. The fact she and her father had invited as many of the people involved in the Mindanao rescue from years before helped to multiply that fact. Charlie Naylor, now a full colonel, was here with his new wife, Connie. Dick Klintworth and his wife were present. He had been promoted to major. George Reardon was a sergeant major and ready to retire in a couple months. He kept following Tiffany Rice around, who'd also been promoted to major. Tim DeCook was now a full commander and he and Al Wiedenkeller were still with the teams. Becky found it puzzling all the SEALs and rangers at the reception were on their best behavior. She was briefed on what to expect before inviting them. The party bordered on being boring.

Even her father put on his old uniform to walk Sarah down the aisle. The groom's father had been promoted to Rear Admiral two years prior, so it was pretty much a military wedding. Sean was in the last year of a three-year enlistment. He and Sarah knew the life as a young couple in the navy would be difficult, but they had a plan. He was currently serving on carriers out of San Diego and expected to reenlist for another three years. Sarah would continue to live at home and would finish going to school to become a doctor. They would have times together, but Sarah could make good use of the extended times Sean was deployed overseas.

Becky was most upset she and Jon hadn't had a chance to spend some time together. Both Nancy and Louise assured her Jon was not avoiding her, but they never seemed to find the time. Her brother, Kevin, managed to monopolize most of Jon's time. The two of them were always off working on some project regarding a video. She was taken aback when she saw him in uniform at the ceremony. She hadn't heard he had been promoted to admiral until they arrived in Hawaii and was required to pay his respects to the Commander of the Pacific Fleet. Her father accompanied him and came back quite pleased with himself. When Jon smiled at her during the ceremony, she felt a strange kinship to him she hadn't felt before.

The ceremony and the reception were outside at Kevin's house. It was decided to have the wedding in Hawaii because of Sean's carrier being based in Pearl Harbor. The weather cooperated, and the breezes were gentle, making the first part of the day perfect. Tents were set up on the lawn and Josh insisted on his restaurants being allowed to cater the affair as his gift to the couple. A dance floor had been laid down on the lawn and patio, and a live band brought in. Becky was a little embarrassed by the amount of money being spent on the occasion, but her father had been insistent. For one of the few times in their life, her brother sided with their father about the size of the wedding. Neither of the kids seemed to mind, or care, because they were too much in love.

Becky found a table near the bar with a few familiar faces. Nancy, Louise, and Julie were sitting with her sister-in-law, Kathy. Also at the table were Matt Summers' wife, Karen, Tiffany Rice, and a woman in an Air Force uniform. She found a free chair and carried it over to the table.

"Ladies," said Becky as she sat down, "none of you are dancing?"

"As usual all the men are at the bar. The only one who has the sense to be on the dance floor is Howard," said Louise as she pointed to Howard and Emily Quinn who were dancing.

"That's because Dad and Mom enjoy dancing," said Nancy, "and there're no ships around here for him to crawl around."

They laughed.

"Becky, I don't believe you know Judy Demmer," said Nancy in introduction. "She works with Jon in one way or another. You know all that secret intel stuff."

Demmer smiled politely. "Doctor O'Keefe, it's nice to finally meet you."

"Call me Becky. We're all friends here, Judy. That is, unless you've listened to the stories Jon tells."

"Knowing the admiral, he got whatever he deserved in any of those stories," said Demmer.

Becky gave the air force officer a serious look. Demmer noticed and continued. "He can be an impossible person to deal with. I can't imagine growing up with him."

Nancy laughed and a smile crossed Becky's face. Judy returned the doctor's smile.

"You'll have to pardon Judy," said Julie. "She's only known Jon professionally and hasn't seen his other side. This wedding has been a real eye opener for her. Every time they've been together, he's been kicking someone's butt. She didn't know how boring he really is."

"He's much quieter today than the first time I met him," said Rice.

"I didn't know you ever met Jon, Tiffany," said Becky.

Rice looked at Becky and was silent for a moment. The whole table was silent until Rice replied.

"He's the one who recommended me for my Bronze Star and promotion to major."

"For the action on Mindanao?" asked Becky.

Rice nodded her reply.

"Wouldn't he have had to be your commanding officer there to do that?"

The table was silent as they watched Becky's reaction to her own question. Rice didn't have to answer.

"That son-of-a-bit..." Becky cut herself short.

There were smiles around the table and Becky even managed one after a few seconds. She looked around the table at the other women there. They all appeared to know.

"I was pissed this guy kept calling me flower child because I only let Jon call me that. That..."

"I know, dear," said Louise putting her hand on Becky's arm. "We've all felt that way about him at some point. The only reason all of us know is because he was on the news."

Becky looked immediately to Nancy. "You must have gone crazy."

Nancy nodded. "He paid for it though."

"Boy, did he?" added Julie with a chuckle.

"That son-of-a-bitch," said Becky, this time completing the phrase.

A very distinguished looking man in a foreign military uniform appeared at the table.

"Excuse me, ladies," said Robbie Mangoba, "but I'm on a mission."

"Ahh," said Louise, "a gentleman at last."

"I saw all of you over here and you all look so lonely. I have made it my mission to dance with each of you at least once before this party has ended."

"Then you can start with me," said Louise standing up. "By the way Rob, where is that good for nothing son of mine?"

"That would be Jon?' asked Mangoba with a smile. "He would be at the bar with all the other gentlemen discussing world politics or some other boring topic. They have no appreciation for the finer things in life."

Louise leaned down between Nancy and Becky saying, "Ladies, you're on your own, but I would drag them out before this party's a bust."

They laughed watching Louise go out onto the dance floor with Mangoba.

Nancy leaned over to Becky, "You go get Jon and give him hell for not telling you. I already had my revenge."

"But don't you want to..."

Nancy pushed Becky up. "I'm gonna go dance with someone of a higher rank than he is. You go get even."

Becky looked at Nancy, not sure what to do. Nancy hugged the woman next to her whispering in her ear. "Go girl. If you're not sure about how he feels about the friendship, there's only one way to find out. I think you'll be surprised."

Becky looked at the woman as she was dragged along. Nancy held Becky by the hand and was heading towards the bar and the men. When they passed Louise and Robbie on the dance floor the older woman nodded her approval. Mangoba smiled and whispered something into his dance partner's ear. She laughed watching the two younger women approach the bar.

There were two groups at the bar. On one side stood the senior officers and older enlisted men. With them were most of the civilians including Matt and Kevin. On the other side were the younger enlisted men who served with Sean. With the carrier in port for some needed repairs, there were a good number of the crew present. Nancy pushed her way to the center of the crowd where Jon was. With him were Gateway, Putnum, Michalowski, Brothers, Ellison, Ericson, DeCook, Wiedenkeller, and others.

"Ladies," said Kevin. "How are we enjoying ourselves?"

"We're about to turn up the party, Kevin," answered Nancy. "This is a celebration, not a political discussion."

"Why, Mrs. Summers that sounds mysteriously like an ultimatum to me" said Putnum smiling at the woman.

"W.C. it sure as hell is," answered Nancy with a grin. "How would you like to dance?"

Nancy put Becky's hand in Jon's and then took Putnum's offered arm. Before they walked off to the dance floor, Nancy turned back to Jon. "Before you take that young lady on to the dance floor, Admiral, do something about the swabbies on the other side of the bar. They look a bit overwhelmed. That's an order."

Jon returned his wife's smile saying, "Aye, aye, Ma'am."

"Pushy ol' broad," said Ellison grinning at his friend's wife.

"You're next, marine," said Nancy pointing at the man.

"Say your prayers, Colonel," said Putnum smiling. "I think we've just determined who's really in command."

While Putnum escorted Nancy onto the dance floor Jon smiled at Becky, "Master Chief Wiedenkeller!"

"Sir!" answered Wiedenkeller as he followed Summers and the doctor to the group of young, enlisted personnel. When Summers approached, they all instinctively came to attention. This included Seaman Justin Summers, who was fresh out of boot camp and managed to be at the wedding as his brother's best man.

"As you were," said Summers, stopping in the middle of the group. "Ladies, and gentlemen, it's been brought to my attention some of you may be self-conscious about enjoying yourself because of the amount of brass present."

There was no verbal answer, but he saw a few heads nod, including one from his son.

"Well then, I guess we need to resolve this problem. Doctor, do you have a recommendation?"

Becky smiled at Summers squeezing his hand. "Well Admiral, I think we ought to order them to have a good time. You can do that, can't you?"

A few the enlisted personnel shifted nervously. Behind them Wiedenkeller cleared his throat.

"Master Chief," asked Summers, "do you have something to say?"

"Sir, and Ma'am," said Wiedenkeller sounding very serious, "please don't give that order. It goes against all tradition."

There was laughter from the officers and older enlisted men behind them.

"And what tradition would that be, Master Chief?' asked Summers.

Wiedenkeller was silent for a moment and then said, "Sir, it has to be against some tradition to order these sailors to have a good time at a party. Respectfully, Sir."

There was more laughter from behind them.

"Chief," interjected Becky, "this comes directly from the Admiral's wife and me, the mothers of the bride and groom. You will have a good time! Since the two of us out rank all the brass here, you know what that means."

Wiedenkeller smiled and signaled for the members of the Team at the wedding to step forward. They all moved forward and mixed in with the other enlisted personnel.

"As long as you put it that way, Ma'am, I feel much better we have the brass out ranked an all. Being a good, enlisted man, I will obey all orders given me by a higher authority. Whoya, Ma'am."

"Whoya, Master Chief," answered Becky.

"I'm sure that really worried you, Al," chuckled Summers.

Wiedenkeller smiled back and went about his task with his usual zeal. "All right people belly up to the bar and order a beverage of your choice. We're going to toast Petty Officer Third Class and Mrs. Sean Summers."

There was a cheer as the enlisted people all pushed their way to the bar. It was several minutes before they all had something to drink. Wiedenkeller sent Barbaro with a glass of champagne for both Summers and Becky. Once everyone had a drink the toast was made, and everyone began to loosen up. Summers was glad to see many the officers joined in the toast. Justin smiled his approval to Becky and his father as he was dragged to the bar by Wiedenkeller.

Summers pulled Becky away from the crowd and onto the dance floor. The song was a waltz, and they moved gracefully about the floor. Jon noticed Putnum was now dancing with his own wife and Nancy, true to her threat, was now dancing with Ellison.

"You're a real fucking asshole for a war hero. You do know that don't you?" said Becky.

Jon did not look shocked returning her gaze. "When did you figure this out?"

Becky looked about the dance floor to see who was near them before she answered. "Everyone knew, but me apparently. You had me so upset by running all over Mindanao shooting and blowing things up while you were bleeding all over everyone it never clicked. I should have figured it out when you kept calling me flower child. Even Patrick knew, didn't he?"

Jon nodded.

"The Bible Don Smith had was yours?"

"It was Dad's. He gave it to me when I went to Vietnam."

"Don knew on Mindanao," asked Becky, "didn't he?"

Jon nodded again.

"Then Dad figured it out on the *Nimitz*. I'll get him for not telling me. Apparently, everyone else saw you on television."

Jon looked at his dancing partner and smiled.

"You bastard!" said Becky as she gently hit him on the shoulder. "What'd they give you for all of the pain and suffering, another medal?"

Jon chuckled, "Three actually, and the opportunity to torment an old friend while we took a ride through the jungle."

Becky flushed looking back at Jon. The song ended and the band began to play a slower one. Becky pulled herself close to Jon and placed her head on his shoulder.

"How are the wounds?" she asked.

"All healed completely," he answered. "I had an exceptional doctor or so they told me at Bethesda."

Becky blushed.

"Look," she started, "I want to apologize for how I treated you when you went to Vietnam. I was a basket case when you were almost killed. I felt responsible."

"For what, Becky?" said Jon looking into her eyes. "Speaking your beliefs? That's why I was fighting. To make sure you could keep doing that. I didn't even notice. I was focused on one thing and that was my job. As I remember, I treated you pretty rudely myself. That argument certainly wasn't one sided. You've always been the best friend anyone could ask for. That's what I remember when I think of you."

Becky kissed him gently on the cheek. "You're not such a bad friend yourself."

"Why thanks, Flower Child."

"I think you and Patrick would have gotten along famously under different circumstances."

Jon laughed.

"What's so funny about that?" asked Becky.

"How would you like to take a trip with me the day after tomorrow to the Philippines?" asked Jon.

Becky gave him a puzzled look. "Why?"

Jon grinned as he answered. "I have to go back with Robbie on some DOD business and thought you would like to come."

"Patrick?"

Jon nodded. "He testified against Osaka and the rest of the conspirators. Based on his testimony, Osaka, Akiyama, the American pilot who survived, and the British sub captain were all convicted. He'll be in prison most of the remainder of his life, but at least they're not going to execute him like they are the rest."

"You see him pretty regular, don't you?"

Jon nodded again. "And you're right, we do get along well. I thought you might want to take the video of the wedding and some pictures to him."

A tear came to Becky's eye as she listened to Jon. She hugged him as they danced. She wiped her eyes with her hand and looked at Jon.

"You know for someone who doesn't exist, you're a pretty good dancer."

They both laughed.